P9-EMQ-994

PEOPLE *of the* WEEPING EYE

W. MICHAEL GEAR
AND KATHLEEN O'NEAL GEAR

TOR®

A TOM DOHERTY ASSOCIATES BOOK
NEW YORK

This is a work of fiction. All the characters, organizations, and events portrayed in this novel are either products of the authors' imagination or are used fictitiously.

PEOPLE OF THE WEEPING EYE

Maps and illustrations by Ellisa Mitchell

A Tor Book
Published by Tom Doherty Associates, LLC
175 Fifth Avenue
New York, NY 10010

www.tor-forge.com

Tor® is a registered trademark of Tom Doherty Associates, LLC.

ISBN-13: 978-0-7653-5293-4
ISBN-10: 0-7653-5293-1

First Edition: April 2008
First Mass Market Edition: December 2008

Printed in the United States of America

0 9 8 7 6 5 4 3 2 1

To Kent Havermann,
for his enthusiasm for books and bookselling and for
his respect for and promotion of authors

Acknowledgments

We would like to acknowledge John Blitz, Matt Gage, and Katherine Michelson of the University of Alabama for their kind assistance during our visits at the Moundville archaeological site. Mary T. Newman was kind enough to share her in-depth knowledge of Southeastern ceramic manufacture. Our special appreciation is extended to Dan and Vicki Townsend for their love of shell carving, and for keeping the tradition alive.

Bob Pickering, Ph.D., longtime Midwestern archaeologist and current curator of collections at the Buffalo Bill Historical Center, kindly read the manuscript and provided salient and perceptive comments. We are most grateful for all of your input, Bob.

Once again, Traci, B.J., and the rest of the staff at the Hot Springs County Library performed their magic by obtaining rare and out-of-print archaeological source material, including Frank G. Speck's *Ethnology of the Yuchi Indians*. Their help was instrumental in the writing of this novel.

Gerald and JoAnn Gerber, of the Storyteller Bookstore in Thermopolis, Wyoming, also worked diligently to obtain out-of-print source material, including the Bureau of American Ethnology's Volume 42 on the Creek Indians, and the BAE's 44th annual report on the Chickasaw. Should you ever be in Thermopolis, drop in for a cup of their wonderful coffee, fine hospitality, and good cheer.

As always, the Thermopolis Holiday Inn of the Waters provided us with a place to decompress, warm Guinness, fine buffalo burgers, and a soul-filling view of the Bighorn River. We offer a special thanks to Jim, Tuck, Mary, Chris, Jake, Dawn, Jimmie, Kenny, Dusty, Karla, Pete, and the rest of the staff.

A Note to the Reader

Writing *People of the Weeping Eye* has been a labor of years. Depicting the rich variability of Mississippian archaeology in all of its complexity was a daunting challenge. As the epic of Trader, Old White, and Morning Dew played out, the manuscript grew ever larger. As a result the publisher made the decision to break the story into two books: *People of the Weeping Eye* and *People of the Thunder.*

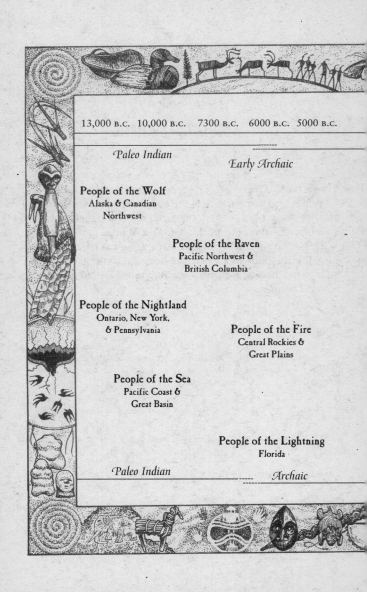

13,000 B.C. 10,000 B.C.   7300 B.C.   6000 B.C. 5000 B.C.

Paleo Indian

Early Archaic

People of the Wolf
Alaska & Canadian
Northwest

People of the Raven
Pacific Northwest &
British Columbia

People of the Nightland
Ontario, New York,
& Pennsylvania

People of the Fire
Central Rockies &
Great Plains

People of the Sea
Pacific Coast &
Great Basin

People of the Lightning
Florida

Paleo Indian

Archaic

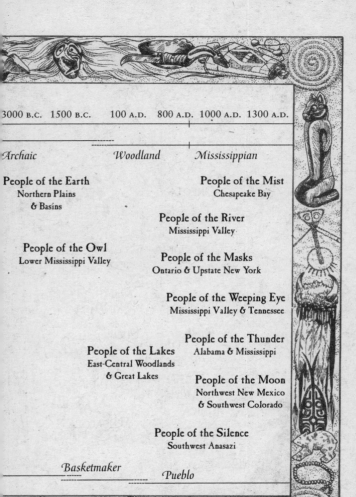

3000 B.C.	1500 B.C.	100 A.D.	800 A.D.	1000 A.D.	1300 A.D.

Archaic   Woodland   Mississippian

People of the Earth
Northern Plains
& Basins

People of the Mist
Chesapeake Bay

People of the River
Mississippi Valley

People of the Owl
Lower Mississippi Valley

People of the Masks
Ontario & Upstate New York

People of the Weeping Eye
Mississippi Valley & Tennessee

People of the Thunder
Alabama & Mississippi

People of the Lakes
East-Central Woodlands
& Great Lakes

People of the Moon
Northwest New Mexico
& Southwest Colorado

People of the Silence
Southwest Anasazi

Basketmaker   Pueblo

YUCHI ↑

Bowl Town

Wind Town

Fast Legs held here ×

Burned Wood Town

Lightning Town

Thunder Town

Sandstone × Quarries

High Water Town

Clay Bank Crossing

Green Town

High Town

Great Corn Town

Bird Town

Split Sky City

NORTH

CHAHTA ←

White Town

km

Black Warrior River

Red Reed Town

Alligator Town

PENSACOLA ↓

Preface

People of the Weeping Eye and its sequel, *People of the Thunder*, are largely based on Alabama's Moundville archaeological site. Today it is an open park dominated by grassy mounds and tree-shaded ravines above the Black Warrior River. The site has a small museum and interpretive center, the University of Alabama archaeological laboratory, picnic facilities, a conference center, and campground. A visitor coming from busy Tuscaloosa or Birmingham is struck by the expanse of grass, open space, and charming vista. He sees quiet countryside, but for the passing of an occasional train. Moundville deceives.

Archaeologists tend to be a politically correct lot, and they don't like to use the word *imperial*—but that's what early Mississippian culture is beginning to look like. From the huge urban center at Cahokia, just across from St. Louis on the Illinois shore, expeditions were sent up and down the rivers, including the Tennessee. We see the spread of Mississippian culture, their square earthen mounds, pottery, trench-wall houses, and artistic styles. Cahokia's influence spread north into Minnesota, westward up the Missouri, as far as Oklahoma in the southwest, and to Florida in the southeast. Descendants of its hegemony would speak Siouan, Muskogean, Iroquoian, and Caddoan languages.

Readers of our novel *People of the River* are familiar with Cahokia. After its decline around A.D. 1150, a political vacuum formed. Settlements vied for influence and control, warring with their neighbors. Muskogean peoples migrated eastward across the Mississippi to fill the Southeast. In the end, several centers—including Moundville, Ocmulgee, Spiro, and the Lower Mississippi Valley sites like Emerald Mound—flourished until the 1400s, then faded. Of them all, Moundville was the most spectacular.

In archaeological terms, the huge earthworks .of Moundville went up in an incredibly short period of time, as did a twenty-foot-tall perimeter wall with platform-topped bastions for archers. Such fortifications indicate that all was not peaceful in the Mississippian Southeast. Over the next 150 years, the walls would be replaced several times and finally abandoned as Moundville's military and political leaders pacified the Alabama, Black Warrior, and Tombigbee River basins. The city's population moved out into the fertile bottomlands, building towns around smaller mound centers up and down the Black Warrior Valley.

In writing *People of the Weeping Eye* we have drawn heavily on Chickasaw, Alabama, Choctaw, and Yuchi ethnography. The Chickasaw—the most likely descendants of Moundville—are Muskogean speakers. Both Koasati and Alabama are the probable descendants of the West Jefferson culture. Alabama language, though structurally different, contains a great many Chickasaw words—expected if they had been in physical contact, but separated by strict social divisions. Despite extended contact the Alabama remained a separate and distinct culture until their absorption into the Creek Confederacy.

Between A.D. 1200 and 1380, Moundville was the largest urban center in North America. What today is quiet countryside was the capital for thousands of people who inhabited central Alabama and western Mississippi.

Think not of Moundville as quiet and dead, but alive with multitudes dressed in their best, faces painted in bright colors. Hear thousands of voices, shrieking children, barking dogs, and the distant sound of drums and flutes. Smell the musky wood smoke, the scent of cooking corn, fish, and venison.

Only then will Moundville live.

Prologue

The second week of October was always special for Mary Wet Bear. In her little frame house outside Tishumingo City, in Oklahoma, she began making pottery in midsummer. She did it in the old way, digging her own clay, washing it, and screening it through fabric. She formed the bowls with paddle and anvil. Then she incised the outside with a pointed piece of turkey bone, or a bit of copper wire.

She fired them in her yard, using hardwood to create the bed of coals, and poplar to finish the process. Lastly, she dropped a dried corncob inside to burn hot and seal the clay. These vessels she carefully stored away, wrapping them in newspaper and setting them to the side on the floorboards of her creaky wooden porch. As each one was finished, she would look out at the apple tree, and watch the ripening fruit. When the fall colors came, and the apples had either fallen or been collected for preserves and pies, she would load her wrapped pots, one by one, onto the floor of her old Ford van. Inside, she would already have stowed her bedroll, Coleman stove, and lantern. The folded white canvas vendor's tent fit neatly under the wooden bed her cousin had built into the van's rear. She left the big blue plastic cooler by the side door to be filled at a Safeway in Tuscaloosa.

Then she would start the engine and pull out of her narrow dirt driveway. The Ford van would nose its way down the drive, its sides caressed by thick stands of lilac.

Peering through the cracked windshield, she would follow the back roads east.

I-20 would have been faster, but the narrow county lanes winding from Oklahoma through Arkansas and Louisiana suited her just fine. She liked this route, far from the main thoroughfares. It reminded her of the old days, and left her marveling at the path her ancestors had taken on their journey west from the ancestral homelands.

In Mississippi, she would stare at her worn road atlas and pick the least-traveled path toward Tupelo. In one of the state parks outside the city, she would camp for a night, sitting on her cooler, listening to the Spirits of the Old Ones. At times, if she was quiet, and drove thoughts of Washington, television shows, and the radio news from her souls, she would see them.

The spirits of the Chickasaw still lingered in the deep forests and the swamps; their dark forms would flit between the oaks, shagbark hickory, and pines. The city of Tupelo, Mississippi, itself had been placed near a spot labeled Chickasaw Old Fields on the ancient maps.

Sometimes she would Sing to the ephemeral ghosts, sensing their curiosity and delight as they crept closer to her van. She still knew some of the old Songs—had learned them at her grandmother's knee on long-vanished nights in the Oklahoma summer. And when she packed to continue her journey, she left offerings of cornmeal and tobacco from cigarettes she had peeled free of paper.

Crossing the divide east of the Tombigbee, she wound through the forested hills to Tuscaloosa, and the final leg. Through her window she would watch the trees, stare out into the white man's fields, and wave at the stolid-faced blacks who watched her pass.

Even these newcomers had grown old in a land without time.

She had first come to Tuscaloosa in the early fifties to study history. At the university, she had stumbled across a book, a big thing, written by a white man. The title had sounded exotic: *Certain Aboriginal Remains of the Black Warrior River*. The author had been a rich northern adventurer named Clarence B. Moore. She had stared at the drawings of decorated pottery, the fine stone axes, and the copper ax heads.

A voice had whispered to her souls, familiar, haunting.

The next day, she had driven south to Moundville: the little town beside the great mound complex.

It was while walking through the grass-covered earthen mounds that she had heard the Singing. Only when she walked down to the river, along the slumped bluff, did she see the swirling water.

"Are you there?" she had called.

As the river's surface smoothed, the Song had slowly faded away.

Later, while she was asking among the historians and elders of her people, no one could tell her anything of the place, or of the people who once lived there. Not even the archaeologists who periodically took their students to dig and sift the soil could be certain. But she knew. She had heard the Song.

Then had come marriage, children, and finally retirement to her little house outside Tishumingo City.

A magazine ad had finally brought her back. It boasted "The Moundville Native American Festival."

So she had come. The Moundville Archaeological Park now had a campground, and vendors: other people like her, who heard the call of the Spirits.

With her cooler full, Mary Wet Bear paid her fees, drove to the campground, and chose her usual spot. That night, in the company of her fellow artisans, she sat in the light of her Coleman lantern and ate peaches from her cooler, then cooked a catfish she'd bought frozen. They told the old stories, exhibited the fine shell carvings, stickball racquets, and atlatls they had brought to hawk to tourists and students.

On the third day of the festival, she woke to a cloudless

sky, the breeze blowing up from the gulf. She had had two good days, selling enough of her traditional brownware pottery to at least pay her gas back home.

That morning, she had dressed in a gay red skirt with flying serpents embroidered in black patterns. She chose her ruffled white blouse, braided her long gray hair, and pinned a beadwork barrette in the back. In the truck mirror she fastened on the silver serpent earrings a friend had made for her, copied from a design in one of Mary's Moundville books.

Moundville lives during the festival. She spent the morning with flute music drifting in from the stage behind the museum. Children were playing stickball, and the smell of fry bread and roasting corn hung on the air. Most of her time was spent ensuring that the hordes of schoolchildren didn't break her pottery. Trade was slow.

"Watch my stuff, huh?" she called across to Dan and Vicki Townsend. "I'm going for a walk."

The shell carver gave her the high sign, and she settled a sheet over her goods.

She walked slowly, taking her time, smelling wood smoke from Mary Newman's pottery exhibit as it mixed with the odors that food vendors depended on to tempt an empty belly. Cheap flutes were for sale to the children; and—much to her distress—too many had bought them. Toots and shrill tweets could only be endured for so long.

Passing the flint knappers, she stopped for a moment, listening to the snap and glassy ring of their work. They plied their trade in a midst of shattered stone, tapping away with batons, pressing flakes, and grinding edges.

She ended up behind the conference center, overlooking the river. Stone riprap had been dropped here to keep the current from chewing relentlessly away at the high bluff.

The water rolled sluggishly, softly lapping at the sandy beach below. How many years had it been since she heard the Song rising from those depths? Time, so much time. She'd been a young woman then, rich with life and brimming with promise.

"Are you an Indian?"

The boy was ten, maybe eleven, dressed in a red T-shirt that advertised SWAMP RAT in big blocky letters. His baggy jeans dropped in folds around expensive running shoes that sparkled with little lights each time he took a step. What his parents had paid for those would have covered her rural Oklahoma bills for two months.

"I'm Chickasaw," she told him.

"How come you look like everybody else?"

"Many of my ancestors are white."

"Then, you're not a real Indian."

"Is that a fact? What makes an Indian?"

"The way they look."

"Oh? I'm glad it finally got so simple."

She turned her eyes back to the river.

"Why are you here?"

"My people come from here."

"How do you know that?"

"I know."

"My teacher is Mr. Roberts. He says that no one knows who lived here."

"I do. And the archaeologists are pretty sure."

"He says that archaeologists can make up anything they want. That all they have is little pieces of pottery and broken stones."

"Perhaps Mr. Roberts doesn't know as much about archaeology as he thinks he does."

"Are you saying he's dumb?"

She considered that. "Not dumb. Ignorant, most likely. Archaeologists work under very strict guidelines. They have a booth set up over by Mound B. You should go ask them. What they can tell you might be surprising."

He shrugged. "Too many people there."

She shot him a sidelong glance. "Shouldn't you be with your class?"

The boy glanced around nervously. "The bus doesn't

leave until two." He showed her his watch—a gaudy thing made of bright yellow plastic. Then he looked back toward the site. "Who'd want to live here?"

"Myself, I wonder who'd want to live in New York. People make the kinds of homes that suit them. But here, all you see is the foundations. The palaces, temples, houses, and grain bins are gone. This was a big city once. Everything you see out there beyond the river was cornfields. People came from all over the United States to trade at Moundville. Even from as far away as Wisconsin."

"How? They didn't have roads."

"They had rivers. They still do. Some things never change." She pointed to where a barge, pushed by a tug, had just rounded the far bend of the river. "See. We still move goods the same way the Indians did."

"But we've got cities. They just had tents."

"Look," she told him. "We don't do a very good job of reconstructing Indian cities. You go someplace like Williamsburg, and you'll see a Colonial town, just like it was. Old forts and Western towns are rebuilt as tourist attractions. Americans don't celebrate our Indian heritage."

"They've got those little huts with statues in them." He pointed over toward one of the exhibits.

"My people didn't live quite like that. When people show ancient Indians, they make everything brown and dirty." She frowned. "Did you see the sandstone paint palette up at the museum?"

"The one with the eye in the hand?"

"That's it. It was a paint palette for mixing colors. My people had superbly carved and painted wooden statues of Spirit animals and mythical heroes. They raised them before their houses and temples. They wore beautifully dyed cloth, and painted bright designs on hides. They lived in a world of color." She turned him, pointing. "Up there, on top of that hump of dirt, would have been a tall building with a huge steep roof that shot up into the sky.

And over there, that's where the stone workers cut and carved stone."

"And you know all this?"

"I do."

"Why don't they show it that way?"

"Because most people have no idea that we have a rich cultural past before Columbus. They would rather dream of the Mayans, or the Egyptians, as if truly great cultures flourished everywhere but here. Like your teacher, they walk ignorantly over the land, thinking it was nothing but wilderness. This river behind me, the banks were filled with towns. Your Mr. Roberts would be shocked." She looked out at the river, watching the barge pass accompanied by the roar of diesels.

He looked skeptically up at her. "Then, where did they all go?"

"Most of them became people like me." She gestured out at the land. "But back then the people living here were the Alabama, Chickasaw, and Choctaw. You've heard of them?"

He nodded.

"Well, there you go."

"In school, Mr. Roberts said that when the white people came, all the Indians died."

"Many did, but a lot of us survived. And if you really think about it, we did pretty good. It's been five hundred years . . . and we're still here. Even after the diseases, the wars, and every other thing."

"Do you live here?"

"Oklahoma. But I come for the festival every year."

"Why?"

"For the trade," she said. "Because there is Power in it."

"Power? You get rich?"

"No, I put my souls in order."

"You mean your soul."

"No, souls. Like the Ancestors, I have two. Some, like the Yuchi, thought they had as many as four."

"People only have one. I learned that in church."

"Then answer me this: Why do people make those little shrines along the roads where someone dies; and then they place more flowers on the grave, and keep a dead person's possessions? Can the soul be in all those places at once? You know, hanging around the side of the road, at the grave, and in Grandma's old music box?"

"The soul goes to God," he said with authority.

"Then why are people driven to place memorials in so many places? If it's not for the different souls of the dead, who's it for?"

He screwed his face up, trying to find an answer.

"Look, uh . . . What's your name?"

"Joshua."

"Look, Joshua, you've got to learn to think on your own. That's a gift Breath Giver has imparted to each one of us. All of your life, people like Mr. Roberts are going to be telling you things. Some are true, and some aren't." She paused. "I first came here fifty years ago, and I heard something, felt something, and it changed my life. Maybe that's why you came today."

"I came because it's field day."

She lifted an eyebrow. "Maybe. Or perhaps it was Spirit Power that brought you here. Maybe you were sent here today, to meet me, to hear these things because somehow, in spite of all the noise from the radio, movies, and video games, you will remember. Sometime in the future, you'll say, 'That old Indian woman taught me to see the world differently.' And all along, it was Power moving you. Don't ever underestimate Power."

"What's Power if it isn't money?"

"It's the breath that God breathed into this entire marvelous Creation."

She reached into her purse, removing a clay gorget on a string. She made these by the hundreds, pressing a blob of clay into a mold; then she fired the pieces and strung them on fishing line. This one was a simple cross contained in a circle.

He took it, frowning at the design.

"The circle is emblematic of the world. The cross portrays the four directions: east, south, west, and north. At the center burns the sacred fire that was given to us by God. You keep that. And years from now, when you hold it, you will remember this day. And, if you're lucky, how it changed your life."

He looked up at her as he ran his fingers over the clay relief. "Do you think this place changed a lot of lives?"

"Oh, yes. And when you start back to find your teacher, you look around at the mounds, at the open spaces. When you do, look back through time. If you can free your imagination, you'll see those places full of people, with great buildings, and tall granaries. People *lived* here in all of the ways humans do. They loved, and fought, and died, and laughed, and cried."

She looked at the boy, feeling a shift in time, her souls having the briefest glimpse of the past.

"Joshua, this was the home of my ancestors." She spread her arms. "They did marvelous things! Terrible things, filled with blood and pain, and suffering. They took this land, and built a city while living in the fading shadow of Cahokia. If you close your eyes and smell, you can catch the odor of fire and smoke. Treachery occurred here, and undying love. Heroes and cowards walked this very soil. It was a center for *people*. Living, breathing human beings like you and me. Can you feel it? The blood and spirit, the chaos and beauty? Magic happened." She pointed. "Just out there, in that river before you."

"But it's gone."

"No, it lives. Only your city senses are closed to it."

She hesitated, hearing the faint Song from the river. "And, Joshua, if you can empty your mind—cease listening like a white man—you will find that quiet place inside. When you do, you will hear their voices. Even today."

He mumbled his thanks and walked away, his eyes fixed on the sacred-fire gorget she'd given him.

She turned back to the river. The current seemed to swell and shift, eddying sideways and around.

"Did he understand? Or is he lost like so many of these kids today? In the battle for his soul, will the video games win, or will he taste the elixir of Spirit Power? Will he ever take the time to find himself?"

The Song grew louder, and she squinted down at the water.

Something moved in the river, slipping along below the surface. Sunlight glittered on the shifting current, and she swore she saw rainbow colors sliding in the depths. Was that a sparkle of sunlight, or a great crystalline eye watching her?

"Is that your Song, Grandfather?"

The water swirled, sucked, and smoothed.

"Oh, what a story you could tell."

The Singing grew fainter, and the thing was gone.

Makatok

Makatok." *In the Mos'kogee language it means, "It was said long ago." Makatok is the word that starts all of our stories of Power, of prophecy, and legend. When a story is begun with Makatok, the audience knows that they must listen intently, that what is being told to them is not frivolous, but contains great lessons, truths, and portents for the conduct of their lives.*

Makatok is not a word that is used casually. It implies obligations from both the orator and the listener. You must understand: A story is more than just words; it has an existence of its own—a soul and presence that must be experienced and felt. A story lives, breathes, and has its own heartbeat. This must be respected.

When an orator begins his story with Makatok he places his audience on notice that what they are about to hear must be carefully considered, for it concerns the way they live, how they perceive their world and relate to the people, places, and things in it. It tells them that what they are about to hear has implications from the past, value for the present, and ramifications for the future.

Ah, I see the look of confusion in your eyes. Have you never considered that time is alive? Do you think the past dead? Is the present only the breath in your lungs? Are the rhythms of the future but fantasy to you?

Extend your senses; see through the eyes of the spiral. Time is relationships. The past spinning itself into the present, weaving events that will form and color the textile of our future.

What? You need an example? Very well. In the eye of your souls, visualize an arrow in flight. Imagine it, shining in the sun, the keen point slicing the air. Hear the feathers hissing in the wind.

Can you imagine it? Good. Now, what does it mean, this arrow arcing through the sky?

To know, you must relive the intent of the archer who nocked this fletched shaft in a taut bowstring. You must sense the urgency in his heart when he drew the nock back to his ear. Were his souls possessed with fear of an untimely death? Anger at betrayal? Hatred for a despised enemy . . . or perhaps just the desperation of an empty belly? Only when you understand the archer can you either admire or fear the arrow's flight. In this moment you can anticipate or rue its eventual impact as it finds or misses its intended target.

Ah, now you begin to see. The present began in the past. Everything, from the patterns of clouds in the sky, the path of a beetle across the dirt, the love in a father's eyes, to the wails of a dying captive, was spun from decisions made in the past. Each will extend beyond this moment to the future where they will be played out. Close your eyes; sense the movement of time around you. It is inexorable, flowing like a great river through and around us. Can you not comprehend the majesty of it? Is it not one of the miracles of creation?

Nevertheless most of us muddle along, mired only in the present, involved with our mundane tasks. With each step we stare at the clinging mud beneath our feet instead of the glorious path ahead.

For that reason, the great stories begin with Makatok. *The word tells you to open your souls and pay attention, to realize the marvel of what you are about to hear. Drop your preoccupations of the moment. Expand your understanding of the universe around you.*

The momentous surrounds us. Stop and listen, learn, think, and see how decisions in the past fill the present and will forever change your future.

Such is the story I will now tell.

Makatok. . . .

Moon of the Angry Winds

A harsh winter wind blew out of a midnight sky. It roared out of the frigid north and thrashed the brooding forest. The force of it bent trees, whipping their bare branches like angry lashes. Shrieking across the river, it drove a stiff chop against the shore. Curling waves sawed at the sandy beach, and spray whisked in gleaming droplets to soak the long dugout canoes pulled up on the bank. Racing up the bluff, the wind crested the heights and savaged the city.

Gust after gust worried thatch roofing, shook the corn cribs and drying racks, and hammered relentlessly at the intricately carved clan poles. Fingers of wind rolled baskets, whirled away matting, and flung streamers of ash and bits of detritus into the air. The high palisade with its square bastions and archers' platforms trembled under the gale; bits of clay cracked and fell from the weft of dried vines woven between the vertical logs.

Perched atop its dominating mound, the high minko's palace bore the worst of the storm's brunt. Wind pulled at the tall building and ripped angrily at the tightly bundled thatch roof. It whistled against the ornate wooden statues of Eagle, Woodpecker, and Falcon that protruded from the peaked ridgepole.

Despite being built of deeply set logs, the great building shook and creaked. Gusts slipped through gaps and doorways. Eddies and currents ghosted along dark hallways and danced around cane-mat walls. The draft teased fabric door hangings and shivered the sacred masks hanging from their strings. It touched bare flesh with a chill kiss.

The boys' room opened off a central hallway. Embers cast a faint red glow from the puddled clay hearth. As the draft fluctuated, patterns shifted among the coals, gleaming and fading—like eyes staring from the Underworld.

The twins huddled on their pole-frame bed, arms around each other, eyes on the capricious patterns traced in the hearth. For the moment the mighty wind was forgotten. Father's angry shout carried down the hallway.

Mother's piteous "No" was followed by the meaty sound of a slap.

The boys flinched, eyes widening as they glanced fearfully at the doorway. In the reflected hearth light they watched the dark door hanging. The fabric swayed ever so slightly, teased by the icy breeze.

"Will *he* come?" one whispered.

"Hush, Acorn," the other barely mouthed. "Don't even think about him. Your thoughts might touch one of his souls. Might bring him here."

Their twin faces made reddish disks in the dim light, eyes wide, dark, and liquid. Button noses over soft lips gave their expressions an impish quality added to by the tousled mats of their unkempt black hair. The blanket that hid their small bodies was intricately woven, covered with images of artistically rendered ducks and turtles. The bare poles beneath their bed frame gleamed like freshly skinned bone. Two toy bows, small quivers of arrows, and piles of rumpled clothing had been laid by the foot of the bed. On the wall behind them hung a magnificent wooden carving of Eagle Man. Each feather radiating from his wide-spread arms was intricately rendered. His nose became a curved beak, and twin rattlesnakes coiled in his hands. The gorget pendant on his breast was copper, as was the bilobed hairpiece with its distinctive arrow. The image wore a chief's kilt, the long tail of it falling suggestively between his braced legs.

"Foul camp bitch!" The words carried down the hallway. "I'll make you spread your legs for me!"

The boys cowered deeper into their blanket, Acorn closing his eyes as Mother screamed in response to a slapping blow.

"Please, Breath Maker, make him stop," Acorn pleaded, a tear escaping the corner of his eye.

"Shhh!" Grape hissed. "If he comes, close your eyes. Play asleep."

Acorn swallowed hard, hearing faint weeping from the room down the hall. "Where's Hickory?"

"Sneaked out of here if he knows what's good for him." Grape tightened his arm around his brother. "Last time Father beat him half to death."

"I thought Uncle was going to kill Father."

"Uncle's a coward," Grape said hollowly.

"Is not."

"Is."

"Is not."

"If he wasn't a coward, he'd have driven Father off by now."

Acorn didn't respond as Mother's half-choked scream was overwhelmed by a roaring gust of winter wind. After it passed, the twins could hear the familiar grunting as Father coupled with Mother. When it happened this way, her face would be bruised in the morning. Often she walked with an awkward, wide-legged gait, and they could see finger marks on her neck that she tried to hide with strings of beads. A brittleness would lie behind her eyes, like an old potsherd: fragile and easy to snap.

"I *won't* share you with a dead man! Move for me, bitch!" Father cried angrily. "I said, *move*!"

Then, as if the world held its breath, the night went silent.

"Enough!" The voice wasn't Mother's, but higher, a squeal strained with rage, terror, and disbelief. Acorn could barely recognize Hickory's voice. Was his older brother mad to challenge Father when he was in this kind of mood?

"You little whelp!" Father bellowed. "Don't you dare to—"

A snapping impact carried on the chill air.

Father screamed: the sound of it bloodcurdling.

Then the winter wind hammered the building with renewed fury.

For long moments the boys waited, arms about each other.

The hanging swayed as a dark form eased into the room. Grape gasped, clamping his eyes closed, his breathing too fast for a boy feigning sleep.

Help me, Breath Maker! The silent prayer repeated in Acorn's frightened souls.

The dark apparition stepped forward, short, slight of build, something heavy hanging from its right hand.

"Are you awake?" came the hesitant call.

"Hickory?" Acorn almost cried with relief. "What's happened?"

Hickory stepped up to the bed, his form silhouetted by the glow from the firepit. He looked like a gangly bird, thin of limbs, his hair mussed. "I want you to run to Kosi Fighting Hawk's. Go now. Hurry."

"What about Father?"

"That's why you've got to go now."

"But if we—"

"Go *now*!" Hickory ordered in a voice strained beyond violence. They flung the blanket aside, feet slapping the packed clay floor of their room.

"Go!" Hickory cried. *"Here he comes!"*

Acorn led the way, bolting into the hallway, turning left, and running across the fabric rugs underfoot. He jetted into the main room, barely aware of the intricate copper-covered reliefs of Horned Serpent, Cougar, and Woodpecker gleaming on the walls. The great stool where Father held sway was draped in cougar hides. Lines of human skulls hung in the rear, where a war shield looked ruddy in the firelight. The central fire leaped and bent with the breeze that filtered through the plank door.

Acorn hit the door, throwing his weight against it. Grape was smart enough to reach up and throw the thong off its hook. They crashed through, flinging the door wide and charging out into the windswept night.

Powered by fear like he'd never known, Acorn raced to the gate in the high palisade and struggled with the heavy wooden gate. With Grape's help, he managed to pull it aside far enough that he could wiggle through, Grape on his heels.

At the edge of the high stairs he paused to throw a look over his shoulder. A fierce gust of wind blew the gate wide. Through the portal, Acorn could see Hickory standing in the doorway, his shape outlined by the flickering fire. The object he held pulled his shoulder down with its weight.

"Hurry!" Grape cried, and began descending the wooden steps. Below them, Split Sky City was hidden in the night.

Acorn fixed the image of Hickory between his souls, identifying the thing that hung so heavily from his right hand. Then, Hickory turned, disappearing back inside. Acorn fixed his attention on the steps. The way down the high earthen mound was long and steep. In the darkness, battered by the chill wind, it was even more ominous.

Grape beat him to the plaza, and together they ran, bare feet hammering the trampled winter grass. Several bow shots to the east, Kosi Fighting Hawk's palace stood like a shadow. Its earthen mound rose from the ground like a small mountain. Acorn made a face against the chill wind that shot ice into his naked body. He ran around the head of the steep ravine, breath tearing in his throat, straining his young legs. Grape's body was a lighter blur in the darkness. Grape was always faster.

Acorn was winded; tears spurred by worry and fear

trickled down his cheeks. He rounded the square base of the earthen temple and staggered past the guardian posts—sculpted figures of Falcon, Hawk, and Turkey—that stood beside the stairs.

"Wait!" Acorn cried. "I've got to rest."

Grape turned on the steps, his breath coming in gasps. "What if Father's right behind us?"

"He's not."

"Where's Hickory?"

Acorn jerked a nod back the way they'd come, forcing his trembling legs upward as he began the climb. "Hickory didn't follow us," he managed between breaths. "I saw him go back inside."

"Father's really . . . going to hurt us," Grape managed. "He's going to be so mad."

"Hickory stayed behind."

"Breath Maker save him . . . and us."

"Please."

"Father won't forget we ran away."

"I know." Gods, could Kosi Fighting Hawk really protect them?

Acorn burst into tears as images played across his imagination. He could see the expression on Father's face: implacable rage behind his dark eyes; cold fury in the set of his mouth; the way his jaw muscles would bunch under his tattooed cheeks as he used cane slats to whip them.

"Stop it!" Grape pleaded, as if the same visions were blazing in his little souls. He, too, was sobbing as they clambered slowly up the worn wooden steps. Shivering from cold, scared like they'd never been, the boys finally reached the wooden gate in the palisade that surrounded the flat top of the Raccoon Clan's high mound. To their surprise, the wind had pushed the heavy door ajar, leaving a gap wide enough for two skinny little boys to wriggle through.

Grape led the way past tall guardian posts to the dark building. The door was latched from the inside. Acorn first stumbled over a wooden mallet laid to one side, then used it to pound on the door.

"Coming!" a faint voice could be heard over the wind.

Moments later the door slid back to reveal Kosi Fighting Hawk, a breechcloth hastily wrapped around his thick waist. It took him a moment of searching the darkness before he looked down far enough to spot the boys.

"Acorn? Grape? What's the matter?"

"I don't know," Grape muttered, suddenly abashed.

"It's Father," Acorn whispered under his breath. "Hickory . . ."

"He stayed behind," Grape added. "I'm scared. Our sister is with cousin Blue Shell tonight."

"Come in. Come in," Kosi said wearily, reaching down to grasp Acorn by the shoulder. "You are both like ice." He pushed the heavy door closed behind them and led the way to the fire, now a series of coals that peeked from under layers of ash.

Fighting Hawk bent, used a stick to fish out the largest coals, and added kindling. He blew with the practiced ease of a man who had made many fires in his life. Within moments the flames were casting a strengthening yellow light across the room. From the walls, masks stared down, their empty black eyes surrounded by shell and copper. They were painted, carved with intricate detail to represent Birdman, Long-Nosed God, Horned Serpents, Man-Eating Bird, Tie Snakes, and Water Cougar. Between them—hung from hooks—were gorgeous feather cloaks, colorfully dyed and embroidered fabric capes, shirts, and blankets that winked with a wealth of copper, shell, and mica sequins.

The tishu minko's stool stood just behind the fire, its form covered with a blanket made of white heron feathers. Behind it, on the wall, hung a giant carving of the human hand, and within its palm, a single wide staring eye: the Seeing Hand. Guardian of the Sky Road to the Land of the Dead. The insignia of their people.

"He's going to kill him," Grape whispered miserably.

"Kill who?" Kosi Fighting Hawk asked. The fire lit his round face, tattooed as it was with the forked-eye design; a red bar across his cheekbones delineated his status as a chief. Kosi was the tishu minko, head chief of the Raccoon Clan who had married Mother's sister, Warm Fern. As such, Fighting Hawk wasn't their true uncle, or *mosi,* but rather they referred to him by the term *kosi,* which included any man married into their mother's lineage.

"Hickory." Acorn gulped and shivered from the cold. "He told us to run. He stayed behind. He . . . he had Father's ax."

"The ceremonial one?"

Acorn jerked a nod, aware of his uncle's growing unease.

Fighting Hawk rubbed his face. Then he looked absently up at the masks, murmuring, "If he catches Hickory so much as touching that ax, he'll whip the boy to within a hair of his very life." He paused. "At least your sister is away."

"Kosi?" Grape asked, "Can't you do something?"

Fighting Hawk smiled wearily. "Was he beating your mother?"

Both boys nodded in unison.

"Why she puts up with him defies any sense of logic or reason. It goes back to losing the war medicine. Power was broken when the Yuchi took it . . . and Hickory's father." With that he clapped his hands on his knees and stood up. "Here, let me find you a blanket. Warm up by the fire. I'll go see to Hickory. See if there's anything I can do short of getting myself killed."

"Are you a coward?" Acorn blurted, then clapped a hand to his mouth in horror.

Kosi Fighting Hawk turned. Not finding a blanket, he took down one of the feathered capes and fingered the warm garment thoughtfully. "A coward? No. It's just that this thing with your father . . . it's complicated. Partly political, partly your mother's curious guilt. She blames herself for the death of Hickory's father . . . for the loss of the war medicine."

He walked over, settling the warm cloak over the boys' shoulders. "As much as we need your father's talent in war, your clansmen would have killed him but for your mother's pleas." Uncle bent down to look into their eyes. "Remember this: No matter how tough and dangerous a man might be, there are always ways to eliminate him."

"Is Father wrong?" Acorn asked.

"Wrong in the head, wrong in the souls. As wrong as a man can get." Their uncle rose and walked to the far wall, where he picked up a slender war ax. It was beautiful thing, the supple handle carved in the shape of a rattlesnake. The war head consisted of a double-bitted billet of beaten copper sharpened to a fine edge.

Fighting Hawk paused at the door, adding, "His souls are out of harmony, filled with chaos, pain, and rage." His eyes narrowed. "He's a dark man." Then he stepped out into the wind-ravaged night.

Acorn stared at the fire and pressed closer to his brother. Grape's shudders were as violent as his.

"Chaos!" They heard their uncle's faint call.

Grape met Acorn's eyes. In one motion they flung off the feathered cape and raced out the door. A yellow gleam could be seen over the top of the palisade, but they ran to where Kosi Fighting Hawk's thick body was outlined in the portal. Crowding around his legs, they stared in disbelief at the sight.

Atop the high minko's mound from which they had just fled, the great palace burned like a monstrous torch. Wind-blown flames fed on the roof thatch; tongues of yellow ate at the heavy log framework that supported the building. Across the distance, Acorn could hear jars of hickory and bear oil exploding and adding to the inferno. Even as he watched the raging fire consume his only home, he could imagine his bow and arrows, all of his clothes, everything he had ever known, devoured by the intense heat.

The fire's gaudy yellow light illuminated the whole of Split Sky City; shadows leaped and wavered behind the mounds and buildings. They could see across the plaza—the chunkey and stickball grounds flat and barren. The tchkofa, the great Council House, looked like an odd, two-headed turtle behind its palisade. Houses, like little wedges, were scattered in a haphazard fashion under the far palisade. Distant people were already stepping out, braced against the wind, watching with horror.

And Mother and Father? Were they still in there?

Hickory? What of Hickory?

As he watched, he longed desperately to see his older brother fleeing the flames, even if he had to roll down the sides of the high mound like a chunkey stone.

Another violent gust of wind ripped away part of the thatch roof. The flaming mass spiraled through the air to fall near the base of the tchkofa's oval-shaped mound. At that instant the remaining roof with its sculpted guardians dropped into the interior. A vomit of sparks and flame jetted up to twirl out over the city, dance, and die.

"May the Sky Beings save us," Kosi whispered.

Another gust of wind hurled his words away as if they'd never been.

One

Time and the seasons had left the old woman's face a ruin.

Much like my own. The man called Old White reached up, running the tip of his finger along the wrinkles that ate into his brown skin. He traced them where they deepened around his mouth, followed their patterns as they mimicked the uncounted ghosts of smiles and frowns long past. His forehead was a mass of ripples, his cheeks loose like flaps. A lifetime of blazing suns and scorching heat alternating with periods of frost-dimmed and aching cold had left its mark on his skin.

"What are you doing?" The old woman was watching him as he fingered his wattled chin. They sat in her thatch-roofed dwelling, high atop a long-abandoned earthen mound. Beyond the cane walls, he could hear the south wind in the trees as it blew up from the gulf. A fox squirrel chattered in one of the oaks.

He shot the old woman a sidelong glance. "Comparing my face to yours."

"You always were a silly goose." She sat across the fire from him, her bony butt on a tightly woven cattail mat. A worn fabric dress hung from her sunken shoulders. From a leather thong a pale shell gorget dangled below her withered neck. Long white hair was drawn into a bun behind her skull. Expressionless, she watched him with pensive eyes like polished pebbles; they seemed to read his souls. "There are no answers there, you know. A face is nothing more than a flawed mask. Ungovernable, it often hides what you wish given away, and betrays that which you most wish to conceal."

"I was thinking of how beautiful you were the first time I ever saw you." As clearly as if it were yesterday, he remembered the moment he'd laid eyes on her. She had been naked, bathing in a small pool in the creek that lay a short distance north of her house. He'd been fleeing down a forest trail, his pack on his back. At first glimpse of her, he had stopped in surprise, his form masked by a tangle of honeysuckle. He could still smell the flowers, hear the whizzing chirr of the insects, and sense the faint rustle of wind in the gum and hickory leaves.

She had looked up, meeting his stare. To his surprise there had been no fear, no startled widening of the eyes. Instead she'd raised an eyebrow, demanding, "Are you going to stand there and gape, or will you come down and scrub my back?"

Awkwardly he had stumbled down the leaf-matted slope, thick black soil clinging to his moccasins. Somehow he'd managed to help her bathe, wondering at the perfect form of her lithe body, painfully aware of the full swell of her pointed breasts and moonlike buttocks. It was later he'd finally remarked, "It was as if you knew I was coming."

She'd narrowed her eyes, voice softening. "Oh, yes. I'd heard your souls whimpering from quite some distance."

He had stayed, and she had partially healed him. Hand in hand they had explored the old earthworks, line after line of curving ridges. Forest had reclaimed what had once been a great city, but in the backdirt of squirrel caches, and in places where the leaf mat was disturbed, old cooking clays, bits of pottery, and chipped stone tools caught the light.

"What was this place?" he had asked in awe.

"The ghosts," she said softly, "they tell me this place was called Sun Town. They say it was the center of the world. All manner of men and Spirits came here to marvel. That is, if you can believe the ghosts."

"Can you?"

She had shrugged. "Even ghosts lie."

He had studied the layout of the place, so different from that of the peoples he knew. He had sketched it out in the black loam, and thought it in the shape of a bird. It was while digging for greenbriar root that he noticed the little red jasper owl lying among the old cooking clays.

Her eyes had shone, pensive and intrigued when he'd given it to her.

"Masked Owl," she'd told him. "He comes to my Dreams sometimes and tells me stories about the past. Tales of murder, intrigue, and poison."

"Then your Dreams are as haunted as my own." And he had looked sidelong at his heavy pack where it lay beside her door.

Several hands' journey to the south, the Serpent Bird band of the Natchez had built a town around several temples atop tall mounds. Despite being so close, they shunned the quiet ruins of Sun Town, left it to the ghosts and the solitary woman who lived atop the tree-studded mound. But on occasion some individual, driven to desperation, would brave his or her fear and follow the trails north, seeking the Forest Witch for some cure or other.

That long-ago summer had been blissful for him. He'd been alone, with only her knowing eyes and her soft touch for company. She had heard his story, and salved his souls in the house she'd built atop the ancient tree-studded mound.

"You are lost in the past," the old woman said, breaking into his thoughts. "What brought you back to me after all of these years?"

He took a deep breath and looked around the walls of her little house. Cane posts had been planted upright in a square trench, soil piled around the bases, and the uprights tied together like an oversize mat to make the walls. Overhead, batches of moldy thatch had turned gray, most covered with soot. Her few possessions consisted of cooking pots and net bags that held her herbs,

dried corn, and Spirit Plants. Two plucked ducks he'd
brought with him slowly roasted in the ash of the firepit.
Tantalizing odors rose to his nostrils as fat sizzled and
spit. The skin had begun to brown just right.

"The *Katsinas,* out west at Oraibi Town, told me to go
home," he told her. "Then, when I reached the western
Caddo, I had a Dream. It has plagued me. Over and over,
I see her."

"Her?"

He nodded. "A young woman. Maybe a girl. I don't
know. She watches me. Sees through me. When I really
look at her, I see fire reflected in her eyes. Not just a
cooking fire, but a conflagration. A huge roaring fire. It
spins out from her fingers, and where it touches me, my
skin freezes. Then she laughs and turns off to the south,
pointing. But when I turn to look, I can't see any way
but north. Upriver."

The old woman watched him thoughtfully. "Still the
Seeker, aren't you?" A bitter pout lined her mouth.
"What I would have given to have kept you all those
summers long ago."

"I had to go. The Dreams . . ."

"I know." A wistfulness lay behind her faded eyes.
"Only a fool loves the Seeker."

"Or a witch."

She nodded. "You were the only fool in my life,
Seeker."

He cocked his head. "But I heard you had a son."

She gave him a flat stare. "He was born six moons after
you left."

A cold understanding flowed through his gut. "Why
didn't you say something?"

"It wasn't the time . . . or place." The ghost of a smile
on her lips conveyed no humor. "Power had other plans
for you."

"And my son?"

"What boy wants to live in a forest with a witch? My
sister took him after several years. He likes living in the

society of men. He comes through every couple of summers. Lives down on the coast. He's married. His wife has children. For all I know, the children have children."

"I would like to know him."

"He doesn't know about you."

He stiffened in response to her serene expression.

"Stop it," she said softly. "Would you have given up your quest? Hmm? Ceased to punish yourself, or—pray the gods—actually have forgiven yourself?" A pause. "That's what it takes to be a father. And, perhaps, even a husband. No, old lover, don't look at me like that. You made your choices. All of them, knowing full well the consequences. It's too late now to change them."

"I would know what he—"

"You didn't come here to find a son you didn't know existed. You came to find a girl."

He opened his hand, staring down at the callused palm. Old scars had faded into the lines. Her words echoed between his souls. "I have lost so much, in so many places."

In a gentle voice, she asked, "Did you find the ends of the world?"

He shook his head. "It's not like the stories the Priests tell. The gods alone know how big the world really is. I can't tell you the things I've seen. You wouldn't believe the different peoples, the forests, the deserts, the lands of ice and snow, the endless seas. I've seen an eternity of grass that ripples like waves in the wind, buffalo herds . . . like black cloud patterns as far as the eye can see. Mountains, thrusting spires of naked rock into the heavens so high that you would believe the very sky was pierced. Rivers of ice that flow down valleys like . . ." But he could see that he'd lost her. He lowered his head. Even she, who knew everything, couldn't conceive the reality behind his pitiful words.

"That was the Trade you made," she told him. "The manner in which you insisted on punishing yourself."

"Why did I come back here?"

She laid a hand on his shoulder. "So that I could tell you it was time. The circles of Power are closing."

As she spoke he could see the Dream girl's face. She was young, barely a woman. Her long black hair gleamed in the light, waving as if teased by wind or waves. Reflections filled her large dark eyes. The images seemed to shift and beckon, mocking in their mannerisms. Smooth brown skin, unmarred by wrinkles or scars, molded to her bones; and her smile was a darting and tempting thing.

"Go to her," the old woman said. "I can see her in your eyes. Powerful, this one. So very Powerful."

"She has called me from across half a world. Will she kill me?" he wondered. "Is that why I Dream the fire in her eyes? Will she burn me to restore the balance?"

The old woman lifted her shoulder in a careless shrug. How characteristic of her. The Forest Witch had never hidden the truth or played games with him, never smoothed the rough edges of life. Not even back then, when he'd been frightened, lonely, and horrified. Now, as he looked at her age-ravaged face, sadness filled his breast.

"What are you thinking?" she asked.

"That I would make you beautiful again. That I would go back to that morning I found you by the stream, and we would live it all over again."

"And that you would never leave?"

He nodded.

"I thought you had ceased to delude yourself with foolishness. Wasn't it doing 'what had to be done' that got you into this in the first place?"

He stared at her over the roasting ducks.

"Of course it was," she answered for him. "We're both beings of Power, you and I, so let's stop wishing for what never could have been and eat these ducks. Then, tomorrow, fool-who-loved-me, you can be on your way north."

"North? Upriver? But she points south in the Dream."

"You say that she touches you with fire, but it freezes your flesh?"

He nodded.

"She points south, but you can only see north? Upriver?"

"Confusing, isn't it?"

"Contraries generally are."

He shot a quizzical glance her way, then felt the certainty of it. "I should have known."

"Oh, I think you did. Coming here was a way of admitting what you already knew. You're bringing the circle full. What was begun must be ended." She paused. "Wait, I have something for you." She pulled at the grease-black leather thong around her neck. From inside her dress came a small hide bag closed with a drawstring. This she opened, fishing out a little red stone object.

He looked down after she placed it in his hand. The small potbellied owl with its cocked head and masked eyes rested warmly against his skin. The circle come fully closed. Beginning and ending.

"Perhaps, when this is done . . ." He couldn't finish.

She extended her withered arm across the hearth to place a finger on his lips. "A lie is as venomous when told to yourself as it is when told to others. Tomorrow, go. And never come back here, my vanished love."

"Is that all that is left to us?"

"The only reason you ever came to me was to leave." She smiled wearily as she used a stick to turn the ducks where they roasted among the embers. "Go, find this woman of fire who freezes in your Dreams. I have given you all that I can. With the return of that little owl, we owe nothing more to each other."

The Copper Lands lay along the rocky western shores of the great lakes. Some called them the Freshwater

Seas. For generations local peoples had mined sacred copper from the green-crusted rocks. Copper was Traded the length and breadth of the great rivers. Beaten flat, sculpted into images of gods, heroes, and sacred shapes, it was prized by the great lords of the south for its polished beauty. Shaped into ax heads, maces, and jewelry, the mere possession of it demonstrated a man's authority, wealth, and status. Ownership of copper was the province of chiefs and chieftesses, of Priests, Dreamers, and great warriors. The mighty and influential adorned their bodies and buildings with it, and the lucky few carried it with them to their graves.

A small nugget of copper was worth a man's life. Empires had risen and fallen over its control. While occasional small nuggets had been found in the southeastern mountains, the finest copper came from around the great freshwater lakes. Mostly the locals mined it, hammered it into shape, and Traded it downriver. But on occasion, a willing individual with more than his fair share of ambition dickered with the local tribes for the right to mine his own.

The man known as Trader wiped a gritty sleeve across his sweat-streaked face and looked up at the gray scudding clouds. They came in low over the choppy waters of the great lake, driven by a wet and pregnant north wind. Trader could smell the moisture, cool, promising rain and dreary skies.

For three days he had worked in this hole. Spoil dirt from generations of previous excavators had trickled down the steep slope. From the lip of the hole, Trader had a good view of the river valley below, where Snow Otter's village—a cluster of bark-sided lodges—stood on a knoll above the sandy beach. Canoes, looking like dark sticks from this distance, were pulled up on the bank. Smoke puffed from the lodges in blue wreaths.

The surrounding hills were covered with thick growths of pine, hemlock, silver fir, birch, maple, and cedars. To the north, he could see the endless horizon of the great lake. He had never felt comfortable in these far northern lands. Born in the warm hickory woodlands of the south, he'd never adjusted to the chill that stalked the blue shadows beneath the conifers and birch. He could sense it, waiting, knowing that the days need but shorten before it would creep out and smother the trees, soil, and stone.

Trader swiped at the cloud of mosquitoes humming around his head. He was handsome, with a finely formed face, strong jaw, and high forehead. Not particularly tall, he was wide shouldered and well muscled from years of plying a paddle against the current. His face bore only outlines of tattoos, as if they had been interrupted before being finished. His eyes were surrounded by forked-eye designs; and a bar ran from ear to ear high across his cheeks and over his broad nose. When he laughed, his teeth were white and straight, his lips mobile and full. Women smiled when they met his gaze, a quickening sparkle in their eyes.

He turned his attention to the depths of the hole. An oversize wolf might have worried such a lair out of the earth's bones. The walls were irregular where stones and soil had been pried away. Trader shuffled his feet on the broken rock and squatted, a stone maul in one hand, a hardwood stake in the other. Bending, he picked a crack in the greenish stone and began driving the ashwood stake into it.

"You work like a beaver," an accented voice called from above. The man spoke in the pidgin common to the rivers, a mixture of Mos'kogee, Siouan, and Algonquin tongues that had adapted itself to the Trade over the generations. Like Trade itself, "Trade Tongue" was sacred. Those who spoke it did so with a sense of respect and awe. It was said that the gods listened in. Rumor had it that nowadays even some chieftains spoke in Trade Tongue when finalizing the most solemn of agreements, wanting the imprimatur of its Power.

Others insisted it was yet another trick that rulers had

taken to, one they used when intent on fully duping their subjects.

Trader didn't look up from his labor as he hammered the splintering stake into a widening gap in the rock. "I paid you a great deal to come and sweat myself to death in your hole. Don't distract me. I want to enjoy every moment of my suffering."

Trader didn't look up as Snow Otter laughed, then said, "In a very short time you're going to be wet to the bone. Rain's coming. I can smell it."

"So can I, but you don't have to stay here. Go keep dry and warm. I'll be down to the village by nightfall." Trader glanced up, seeing Snow Otter where he crouched at the edge of the excavation. The man was fingering a white shell gorget that hung from a string around his neck. Yes, paid well, indeed. The southern chiefs would have killed him on the spot if they'd known he'd Trade a sacred artifact like that to a northern barbarian. The concave surface of the gorget bore an image of the three-tiered cosmos with a spiraled pole rising from the sacred fire cross in the center. The Four Winds were depicted by woodpecker heads on each side. The Mos'kogee believed the image to have Power. Not the sort of thing to be bartered off to a nonbeliever like Snow Otter.

Trader smiled at the depths to which he had fallen. Who would have thought?

"I have copper," Snow Otter insisted. "Lots of it. Enough that you don't have to labor like some southern war slave. Come away from here. Let's go down to the village. My wife's roasted whitefish wrapped in goose-foot leaves. She'll lay it on a steaming bed of wild rice. I've got some of that raspberry drink left."

"I thought you said we drank the last of it last night."

A pause. "I might have miscounted the pots in my cache."

"Just like you'd miscount those pieces of copper you want to Trade me."

"You wrong me!"

"A man who knows you as well as I do would never wrong you by making a simple statement of the truth." Trader reached for another wooden stake and glanced up at Snow Otter. The man looked as if he'd just suffered a terrible affront. "Oh, stop that. How many years have I been making the trip up here?"

"Five, perhaps six."

"Yes, my friend, and in that time I have come to know you inside and out. You'll do anything to come out ahead. I think you'd sell your souls if it meant gaining an advantage."

"And you wouldn't?"

If you only knew how foolish I've been. Trader chuckled, hearing the satisfying smack as he used the stone-headed maul to drive the stake into the crack, widening it further. "I just Trade to Trade."

Silence was broken only by the snapping impact of the stone hammer on the hardwood stake.

Finally Snow Otter asked, "So what do you want? I'd really like to know. Season after season, you travel the length of the rivers, make the portages, and carry your goods from one end of the land to the other. In all that time, never have I heard you talk of home. You speak fondly of no people. I don't even know your nation. Not one single woman seems to linger in your thoughts, yet you watch any attractive female with a wistful longing in your eyes. It's as if you are cast loose, like the wild birds . . . a thing that migrates and has no will to stop."

Trader looked up, rubbing a grimy hand across his forehead. "Maybe that's what I am, nothing more than a bird."

"What's your name? Seriously. You just go by Trader. It's as if you're not even a full person. You have to have a name."

"Trader is enough." He lowered his eyes to the stake where it wedged into the rock. "A name is nothing. A word. Once it passes from the lips it might never have existed. Like the breath behind it, it's gone. And so shall I be. And soon, Snow Otter. Very soon."

"That's all you want from living? Just to pass like a word?"

Trader managed a bitter smile. "Maybe all I want is wealth. Something that will take a high chief's breath away. Something so precious I can Trade it for a whole fleet of canoes. Yes, that's it. I want something so precious that the very sight of it will make people swoon and gasp with awe. I want to see their eyes fill with envy!"

"For what purpose? Just to have it? To hoard this great wealth like a packrat over a gleaming white shell? Bah! You'd rot on the inside trying to keep it."

"Maybe I'd Trade it for something."

"Ah, now that makes sense. Would you buy yourself a farm, slaves to work your fields, and compliant women? Is that it? You'd lie around, get fat, and sire children?"

Trader shook his head. "What? And send my harvest off to the high minko of whatever land I ended up in? No, I've seen that and want no part of it."

"So I'm back to my original question. What do you want?"

Trader hammered absently at the stake. "Great wealth."

"Just wealth?"

"That's right."

"Just to have it?"

"That's why I'm down here digging," Trader muttered. "I can feel it."

"What did you say?"

"I said, I can feel the copper. It's here."

"Of course it's there," Snow Otter agreed. "I've pulled a lot of copper out of that pit, but it's all been small nuggets. Small nuggets aren't that bad. You can take a lot of little pieces of copper and beat them into one sheet."

"The color's not consistent."

The first drop of rain spattered on Trader's neck. He grunted at the cold trickle that ran down into his collar.

As the rain increased he resumed his hammering, letting the cold impacts on his back goad him to further effort. Sand caked his damp hands, grating on the wooden handle of the maul. Snow Otter's questions left him irritated and touched at the old wound deep between his souls. He had been stripped of all the essentials that made a man: family, status, place, and possessions. A man with nothing wanted everything. One day, he would obtain some item so valuable and rare it would be the envy of all: chief, Priest, warrior, farmer, and slave. Then, by blood and pus, he'd show them.

"You're a fool!" Snow Otter called from the rim of the hole. He was holding a section of tanned deer hide over his head. Rain battered at them.

"So are you . . . for staying here."

"My conscience won't allow me to leave an idiot to his fate."

"And you're curious," Trader muttered under his breath as he straightened his back against the strain and selected another of the hardwood stakes. Through the pelting rain he could see another crack opening to the side of the rock he worked on. Bending at the hips, he began hammering another of the pointed stakes into the faint gap.

"You're a lunatic!" Snow Otter called from above.

The rain fell in relentless sheets, turning the hole into a mucky mess. Trader slopped about on soaked moccasins. He could feel sand between his toes. His long black hair had matted to his head, and cold droplets were tracing paths down his cheeks. The stone mallet head now slipped when he pounded it against the mushrooming wood.

"That hammer's going to fall apart," Snow Otter observed from above. "The head is only held on by shrunken rawhide. Once it's wet . . ."

"I know." Trader whacked the stake with growing frustration.

Cold fingers of water trickled down his ribs. Was it

worth it? Snow Otter's wife would have a smoky but warm fire going down in the village. He could imagine that baked whitefish melting on his tongue. This was crazy. What had prompted him to think he could dig his own copper anyway?

"I'm leaving," Snow Otter said pointedly.

"Smart man," Trader muttered, whacking the stake one last time.

The rock shifted enough to allow him to slip his fingers into the crack. Trader lifted, feeling stone slide on stone. He rolled the angular fragment to one side, staring at the backside of the rock as rain spattered it. The stone looked as if it were veined with fungus. Lines of green seemed to dive into the rock's heart. Green. But not metallic.

You're nothing. Just some bird. You lost it all, and you'll never have anything again. Not a friend. Not a wife. Only a canoe, and whatever trinkets you can barter.

A memory flashed from deep down between Trader's souls. He saw his brother Rattle's eyes, the cunning and deceit turning to fear as Trader's club whistled. He felt the anger surge within, a hot red Power, as he put his weight behind the blow. He remembered Rattle throwing himself backward in the vain attempt to save himself. Trader relived the instant that sharp stone ax had smashed into his brother's head. He could still feel the blow that crushed Rattle's skull, as if the memory was embedded in the bones and muscles of his arm.

I killed him. Became the man I swore I never would.

Trader blinked it away. He was once again standing head-deep in a mucky hole, wet, cold, and hopeless. Frustration made him lift the hammer high. The blow struck the center of the mottled green stone, the crack like thunder as the hammer head disintegrated into shards that spattered around the inside of the hole.

"Hey!" Snow Otter cried. "That's my best mallet!"

Trader stared at the ruined maul, then at the cracked

stone. With one hand he pulled a spalled section away and blinked. The color was unmistakable.

"You're going to have to replace that!" Snow Owl insisted from above. "Good hammers like that are hard to come by. I spent days making sure that one was just right. It cradled in my hand like a fine woman. It had a special balance."

Trader used a fragment of broken rock to crack off more waste stone.

"Why don't I ever learn?" Snow Otter was saying to the falling rain. "Other people never treat your tools with the respect they should. What is it about these foreign Traders? Why do they flock to me with their destructive lunacy?"

Trader cradled his find as he looked up into the rain. "I get to keep it, right?"

"The broken hammer? It's yours . . . as long as you find me one as good to replace it."

"No, the copper," Trader said. "The deal was that I got to keep all the copper that I dug up."

"That was the deal *before* you ruined my hammer," Snow Otter growled. "That's why I brought you up here to this old hole. We've never dug anything but small . . ." He was squinting through the downpour. "What have you got there?" The metallic sheen from beneath couldn't be anything but metal.

"Copper," Trader said reverently. "And from the weight of this rock, a lot of it."

Snow Owl forgot his deerhide cover and scrambled down into the narrow pit. He cocked his head, fingers running across the rain-spattered copper. His eyes widened with disbelief, words catching in his throat. "That's worth a fortune!"

Trader stared at the gleaming metal, the cold rain forgotten. "Yes, I know."

Two

The trail Old White followed up from the river wound through the trees, skirting ropy masses of vines that hung from the oak, beechnut, and maples. Overhead the branches intertwined to create a lacework of gray between him and the cloud-banked sky. Squirrels, those few that had avoided the stew pot, watched from heights beyond the range of a boy's arrow. Fresh leaf mat carpeted the forest floor in light brown, draping logs too rotten for firewood. Every other stick of wood had been scrounged over the last couple of years for village fires.

Old White cocked his head and listened. The sounds of war were unmistakable. He'd heard them often enough through the years. He grunted under his breath and resumed his pace along the narrow forest path. He grimaced as a loud shriek carried on the north wind. Humans could be such noisy beasts. Only the herons on their migrations, and the geese passing overhead, made such a racket.

He had seen at least fifty-some winters pass. But, truth to tell, he'd lost count some years back. It didn't seem to matter much, given the places he had been, the things he had seen. A man could have too many memories. Fact was, he had accumulated more than any man he had ever known. So many trails had passed beneath his feet during his wanderings. And with his death, the sights, sounds, faces, and places would vanish.

And perhaps this cockeyed venture would, too.

Trouble was, ever since his days with the desert

shamans, he'd taken his Dreams seriously. Now he felt his heart quicken. Though the path he followed was unfamiliar, a curious tugging on his souls led him forward. Downriver, he had heard tell of a woman possessed of the Spirits. Rumors hinted that even her family had begun to fear her. Was this the place? Images of the girl had filled his restless sleep. In the Dream, she'd been prancing and pirouetting around a lightning-riven tree. One that had looked hauntingly like the storm-scarred oak above the canoe landing where he had just left his long Trade canoe.

But then, he had chased will-o'-the-wisps before, only to meet blank stares at lonesome villages when he tried to explain his quest. But for the Trader's staff he carried, many of those backward farmers would have been just as happy to drive him off with firebrands.

The river landing, below the blasted tree, had been packed with pulled-up canoes: a clear indication that a settlement was close. But so many canoes? The sound of battle clarified the potential ownership of many of those craft.

An ululating scream carried on the fall air and sent a chill through Old White's bones. He'd heard that same scream before. It had come trailing out of the Dream like the smoking wraith of a ghost. He had felt pain that he supposed was hers, and that she was desperate.

Two Petals. That's the name they had called her by. In the Dream, her eyes had sharpened at that name.

He stepped out of the trees and stopped short. Sunlight gleamed on his white-streaked hair, now pulled tightly into a braid that hung down over his left shoulder. Countless seasons of sun, wind, and storm had creased his face and darkened it to the color of a burnished brown pot. He wore a serviceable brown hunting shirt, belted at the waist with wraps of rope to support the heavy fabric pouch at his waist.

The seasoned Trader's staff he held in one callused hand was as tall as he; made of hickory, its top had been carved into the shape of an ivory-billed woodpecker. Just below the bird's head long white feathers flipped and tossed in the breeze: the universally recognized sign of Trade. Intertwined rattlesnakes had been carved along the shaft; shapes, representative of the portals between the worlds, decorated the serpents' sides. Each of the writhing snakes sprouted wings a third of the way down its length. Once painted, the colors had faded: One was barely discernible as red; the other still sported patches of faint white.

Old White wore a cape that had seen better days. Cut from a buffalo cow's hump, the hair had been scuffed off in patches, the leather polished black from grease and charcoal stains. Beneath the cape, and bulging like a misshapen hump, a square wooden pack rode the middle of his back, its weight borne by two wide leather straps that crossed his shoulders. A second pack, this one of fabric, hung looped from his left shoulder. The large pouch at his belt was tied with a drawstring. His feet were clad in travel-worn moccasins, the soles cut from the thick skin on a bull buffalo's forehead.

His sharp brown gaze fixed on the sight before him. A wooden palisade surrounded a village that lay just beyond a series of recently harvested cornfields. Here and there gray-black columns of smoke rose just high enough for the wind to bend them into the far fringe of trees. The fight was nearing its final stages. Lines of warriors ran forward, shooting arrows at defenders who ducked back from the gaps in their palisade. A pile of brush had been laid against the defenders' walls and set afire. It now ate at the wood, weakening the deep-set posts.

Gods, I am living the Dream. He could see the events about to unfold.

Old White started forward, not even bothering to wince as another shriek carried on the air. Men made that sound when an arrow sliced deeply into their guts. Partly it was pain, but mostly it was the disbelieving knowledge that a slow and agonizing death was inevitable. He had often treated the dying as pus and gut juices slowly ate a man's insides.

He had crossed all but the last of the cornfields before one of the attacking warriors caught sight of him. The young man turned, calling out and pointing as he nocked another arrow in his bow. Several of his companions whirled, each fitting an arrow as they began to charge in Old White's direction.

He stopped, raised his staff, and let them see the gleaming white feathers fluttering below the wood-pecker head. The warriors slowed, glanced uneasily at each other, and muttered before one split off, racing for a knot of men standing just beyond arrow range of the besieged village.

"I am no threat," Old White called out as he approached the warriors. "I would speak to your war chief." If the vision had been correct, his use of the A'khota language should mollify them for the moment.

"Your accent is terrible," one of the warriors answered in Trade Tongue, an arrow still riding his bow. He was wary, eyes shifting back and forth in search of other enemies.

"My apologies," Old White countered, inclining his head. "I learned a little of your tongue, but it has been, let's see . . . ten winters? No, perhaps more like twenty."

A tall man broke from the knot of warriors, trotting his way. The fellow was young, muscular, a round-headed war club gripped tightly in his fist. His expression communicated a grimness of purpose that didn't bode well.

"Greetings," Old White called in A'khota. "I have come in peace."

"Talk in Trade Tongue," the war chief growled. "You sound like you've got rocks in your mouth. What is your purpose here, Trader?"

Old White drew himself up, both hands on his staff. "I have come for a young woman."

The war chief grinned sourly and gestured at the village. "It won't be long and you can take your pick." A shrug. "Assuming you have something to Trade for her."

"While I have seen her in Dreams, I have also heard tell of her. Young, perhaps sixteen or seventeen summers," Old White said softly. "It is said that she can charm the birds. I have also heard that she talks with the Dead. Others say the Spirits speak through her."

The smug assurance faded from the war chief's face. "Two Petals."

"That is the name I heard downriver." Old White nodded amiably.

"What is your purpose with her, old man?" His tone turned hostile as he backed a step, raising his war club.

Old White tilted his head. "Have you seen the Crow Mound?"

"Of course. I am Fast Palm, war chief of Black Sand Town. My people are the A'khota. The mounds carry our messages to the Spirit World, act as portals between their world and ours. Do not toy with me."

"Oh, quite the contrary, I assure you." Old White raised a calming hand. "Now, imagine the Crow Mound with only one wing. Incomplete, out of balance, not a thing of Power at all, only a misshapen lump of earth."

"I don't understand." Fast Palm was fingering his war club, shifting from foot to foot, clearly contemplating whether to smack the old man—and take risk offending the Power of Trade—or just order him away.

"The Crow Mound is but one of many your people have fashioned for the gods and spirits. My quest is but one of many that holy people, Dreamers, and Healers have. However, for me, it is most important. Two Petals—like one wing of your mound—completes the picture."

"She is a *witch*!"

"She has been touched by Power."

"She is *murdering* our chief! She spoke an incantation when he visited here, jabbering to demons and malicious spirits. She said she wanted him; then she threw up all over him when he touched her. Her bile took possession of his body and is killing his souls. He coughs up blood. His flesh is melting from his bones. She must die."

"The fate of your chief doesn't concern me, Fast Palm. My vision does. You will cease your attack and allow me to take Two Petals from here."

The war chief narrowed an eye. "Assuming I agree to this silly idea, what makes you think Spring Rock Village will give her to you?"

"Like you, they won't dare to cross me."

Fast Palm tested the balance of his war club, pensive eyes on the wooden ball at its end. The orb was scarred, nicked, and dented from previous impacts. "If you value your life, old man, leave now."

Old White reached into the fabric sack hanging from his belt, his right hand rummaging through the various bags, boxes, and containers within. "I ask you once more to surrender her to me."

"I don't even know you. You speak like a barbarian. Your dress is unfamiliar to me. What is your name?"

"I am called Old White."

Fast Palm's eyes widened. "Him? The one they call the Seeker?"

"Him."

"He is a legend." A wary smile crossed the war chief's face. "But you . . . I think you are no legend. Just some silly old fool. The Old White of legend would simply sweep me and my men aside, walk through a wall of fire, split the Spring Rock palisade, sprout wings, and bear Two Petals off. You're not him."

"Stories are like penises. They tend to swell with the telling. In this world, I have never sprouted wings." Old White arched an eyebrow. "Fire is another thing. What if I told you I could breathe a fire into your eyes that would burn without flame?"

Fast Palm glanced at his warriors, chuckled, and thrust

out his chest. "I'd call you a liar." He didn't seem to notice, but the attack on Spring Rock Village had slackened, his warriors backing away to watch the curious meeting. Many were slowly inching closer, heads cocked to hear the exchange.

· Old White withdrew his hand from the bag, extending it, fist closed. "Look closely. You have never seen fire held in a man's hand like this."

The war chief did as he was bid, bending down, a disbelieving frown on his wary face.

Old White opened his hand to display a red powder on his open palm.

Fast Palm sneered. "That's not fire! Just some—"

Old White blew, jetting the powder into the war chief's face.

Fast Palm darted back, taking a deep breath. "You old *fool*! You are about to find out just what my wrath—" He coughed, then sneezed, reaching up to rub his eyes. The coughing and sneezing intensified. When he could catch his breath, he wailed, shrieking, dropping his war club to paw at his eyes. Tears were streaming down his face. "Gods! It burns! *It burns!*"

Old White raised his staff as the warriors pressed forward, eyes wide, mouths open. "Leave him be. I have done no permanent harm, only taught him a painful lesson in respecting unknown elders. And, I hope, given him a dose of humility."

War Chief Fast Palm sank to the ground, weeping, moaning, tears rubbed wetly over his cheeks as he pawed at his eyes, kicked, and coughed out of control. "Gods, it hurts! Stop it! *Stop it!*"

"Will you give me the woman?" Old White asked. He stared sidelong at a warrior who had half drawn an arrow that rested on his bow. Extending his staff, he added, "You're next." The warrior slackened his pull, swallowed hard, and stepped back slowly. The others watched their war chief's misery through horror-widened eyes.

"Stop it!" Fast Palm cried, trying to blink his swollen

red eyes. He'd smeared snot across his cheeks, but the coughing had weakened. "In the name of the gods, *stop this*!"

"I want the woman called Two Petals."

"Yes! Yes! *Anything!*"

"And you will not try to retaliate, or I shall call the fire to burn forever in your lungs. It has had a taste of your souls now. I can send it back, even from a great distance, should you give me reason."

"I agree!" Fast Palm whimpered.

Old White motioned to the warriors. "Bring water. Use a damp cloth and carefully wash his face. I have sent the fire away, but like flames smothered in a hearth, the heat will have to slowly dissipate." He hesitated, leveling a hard finger on the warriors. "Do not make the mistake of thinking your war chief weak because of what happened here. A lesser man's face would have melted and dripped from the bone like heated fat. He is strong, this one."

Old White walked with the assurance of a Cahokian lord as he strode up to the palisade. Using the reprieve, the defenders had managed to slosh water on the burning brush that had been gnawing at the base of their palisade. He could see wary faces peering out from between slits in the log walls.

"I am Old White. I have stopped the attack. I have come for Two Petals."

From behind the posts a voice asked, "Old White? The one they call the Seeker?"

"I am he."

"You're supposed to be a legend."

"Then the legend has come for Two Petals."

"How do we know this isn't just one of Fast Palm's tricks?"

"As soon as he stops crying, you can ask him." He cocked his head. "I am only here for the girl."

"What do you want with her?" an older, more suspicious voice called from within.

"I need her help on a journey."

"And if we refuse?" the first asked.

Old White chuckled. "I will burn down your palisade and hand you over to your enemies. Perhaps War Chief Fast Palm will be more forgiving than I."

"A moment, please," the older man called back.

Old White could hear voices muttering back and forth. Within moments an old man emerged from behind the double-walled entry. He looked haggard, as if someone had cored a hole into his heart and let its contents leak out. His face sagged with a weary resignation. A fine beaverhide cape hung from his shoulders, and a medicine bag made from a raccoon hide was suspended on the knotted cord belt at his waist. His finely woven hunting shirt dropped to below his knees. Flower patterns made from small colored wooden beads had been sewn onto his sleeves, the breast, and the hem of the garment.

The old man glanced suspiciously at the hostile warriors who clustered around Fast Palm. Many of them glared menacingly in their direction. "How did you stop them?"

"With a breath across my palm. He'll be all right . . . provided he doesn't irritate me again."

The old man narrowed his eyes, studying Old White. "Are you truly the Seeker?"

"I am called that."

"I am Skaup, of the Wide Thistle Clan. I sit on the Council here, and am a respected elder among my people. If you are who you say you are, I am honored to meet you." The old man reached up and rubbed his chin, the action pulling his wrinkles back and forth. "But what would a man like you want with my crazy daughter?"

Old White studied him thoughtfully. "*Your* daughter? Has she always troubled you?"

"As a little girl she was precious, a delightful darling of a child. She was smart, happy, with laughter like a bubbling brook. No child ever brought a father more joy." His smile failed. "The voices began whispering to her just before her first woman's moon. Soon after that, her mother was killed in a raid. Since then, she's grown progressively worse." He sighed, and half turned to face the menacing A'khota warriors. "There has been talk among my own people that I should just walk up behind her . . . put her out of her misery." A pause. "But I still see my little girl."

"A family must take responsibility for its own."

"I know. But I am weak when it comes to her." The old man shot Old White a sidelong glance. "When Fast Palm came here, demanding that I turn her over, I thought perhaps, just maybe, he would turn around and leave when I refused."

"Apparently he is motivated." Old White indicated the smoldering section of palisade off to his left. The wood had been considerably weakened.

Hopelessness and fatigue dulled the old man's eyes. "My people have been blaming me and my daughter for this attack. It's my fault. Two Petals brought this down on us." He made a face before adding, "Fast Palm's chief must really be witched. I'm afraid she did it to him. She thought he was an arrogant mallard when he came through here. He thought her simple. Sought to lay with her. When he tried to force her, she threw up all over him. Afterward she said some things. It sounded like nonsense. Things about his belly slowly filling with pleasure, about how he would swallow most gleefully. Last I heard, the man's gut was a burning agony, and he was throwing up all the time."

"Do you really not understand what she is saying?"

He made a puzzled face. "Something is turned around in her souls. She just can't get anything right. I know she's not stupid. Tell her to enter and she goes away. Tell her to leave and she sits right down on the spot. It's a soul possession of some sort. You wouldn't believe the things I've tried: burning her with sticks until she screams; beating her with clubs; piercing her flesh with thorns; anything to drive the demons from her souls."

Gods, could she really be a Contrary? "I need her help."

"I don't understand. How could my spirit-haunted daughter be of help to you, of all people?"

"I have crossed half of our world to find her, Skaup. Power has led me to her. I wish to ask her to accompany me."

The old man made a face. "She is like a black oak in a lightning storm. She'll draw trouble to you. And whatever your mission here, people will be skeptical of you as long as she's with you. I can't make sense of her anymore. No one can. Ask her if she's hungry after a day of fasting, and she'll lie and tell you her belly's so full it's about to burst. Do you want to subject yourself to that?"

"I will take my chances. Besides, what choice do you have? If she doesn't go with me, Fast Palm will take her, and kill a great many of your people in the process. If you manage to fight off the A'khota, your own people will demand that you deal with her in a way that will permanently wound your souls. I, however, give you my word: I shall do my best to ensure that no harm comes to her."

Skaup focused his unsure gaze on Fast Palm. The war chief was on his knees, and his warriors were sponging his face with water. "So much pain, she causes. And the constant lies . . ." His expression tightened. "She is my daughter, don't you understand? She's all that I have left. I can't just turn her away."

"May I at least ask her?"

A voice from inside the palisade shouted, "If you don't give her to him, we will!"

"By the Morning Star, that's rotted right!" another called angrily.

"Get rid of her, Skaup! We've had more than we bargained for already!"

A chorus of shouts rose from behind the defenses. The A'khota immediately reacted to the angry voices, fingering their weapons, ready for a counterassault.

Old White added softly, "I offer you an option, Elder Skaup. In my custody, she will be safe. Perhaps I can help her come to grips with the Spirits. My abilities as a *Hopaye* are considerable."

"A what?"

"A *Hopaye,* a Healer. I have been many places, talked with a great many shamans, shared the secrets of the plants and cures. If I can cure her, and if she desires to return, you may yet see her fulfill her destiny."

"I could come along, help you with—"

"No."

The gruff voice behind the palisade insisted, "Get rid of her, Skaup. Or we will!"

"Sometimes," Old White soothed, "the only way to help someone is to let them go."

Skaup stared miserably into Old White's eyes, the last of his hope snuffed like a spark beneath the weight of a war moccasin. He turned, calling, "Bring my daughter to this man."

Old White leaned on his Trader's staff, hands grasping the snakes carved in the wood as if to crush them. His heart began to pound, excitement pulsing with each jet of blood through his veins. *Is this the one? Is she the girl in my Dreams?*

Bodies moved behind the gaps in the palisade. Sounds—like those made by a wounded bobcat—could be heard.

A middle-aged man emerged, followed by several anxious-looking young men. They carried her trussed body, swinging from a pole like the carcass of a slain deer. Her hair was an unkempt mass of raven black, the expression on her young face that of a barely controlled rage. The muffled squealing would have been ear-piercing shrieks but for the wad of cloth jammed between her jaws. They had wound rope around her arms and ankles before knotting it firmly to the pole. Another rope snaked about her waist and bit deeply into the dirt-smudged fabric of her coarsely woven dress.

Old White experienced a surge, like the electric crackle of rubbed fox fur, when her wide shining eyes met his. For a long moment he couldn't breathe. He shook himself, smiling, his souls warmed by the raw emotion that seemed to glow around her struggling body. She flopped like a fish, straining the arms of the nervous young men who bore her beyond the narrow entry.

They weren't kind as they dropped her onto the beaten earth. Old White saw pain in the father's eyes as he bent down and said, "This man says he is Old White, the Seeker. He has offered to take you away, to keep you safe. I . . . I have agreed." He gave her a weak smile. "Is that your wish?"

She glanced from her father to Old White, and again he felt the prickle run along his spine. Power shot like a thing alive from her frantic eyes as she looked from face to face. A desperation filled with love, fear, and resignation reflected from her panicked expression. She swallowed hard, mumbling against the cloth shoved into her mouth.

When the old man reached down and pulled it free, she spit, worked her lips, and declared, "I wish you would all twist and burn. Foul people, I detest you all. Go with him? Put up with his torture? Never. Stake me to the ground here. Bind me tight to this soil. No, never bear this body beyond the palisades of Spring Rock! Spill my blood and spit here, you foul whelps!"

The old man winced, pained, and in a quick move, thrust the rag into her mouth again as she drew another breath. Had he not noticed that the men surrounding her had been fixed on her as surely as a snake homed in on a bird? Did he not see the effect she had? Was he deaf to the love and desperation struggling behind her words?

"My little girl," old Skaup said wearily. "Who would have thought?" He looked up at Old White. "We know your reputation. You, who have traveled the whole world, can you help her?"

"As much as she will help me," Old White replied with a sense of relief. He could feel Power swelling, shifting around him. High above, an eagle screamed, and he raised his eyes, seeing the white head and tail as the sky hunter tucked, then rocketed away toward the south. Yes, this was right. A part of the puzzle. But what part? The vision hadn't been clear.

That was more apparent as Two Petals flopped, and wailed against the gag. Her terrified eyes had fixed on her father, tears streaking down the sides of her smudged face.

So what is she? A true Contrary? Or just plain insane?

Aloud Old White said, "If you would bear her to my canoe, I would be most appreciative. The A'khota will no longer bother you."

Turning, he raised his staff, walking straight away from Spring Rock Village, not even bothering to see if they followed his orders.

They would. They always did.

Three

Snow Otter had dozed. He hadn't meant to, but the rain pattering against the bark-sided lodge had lulled him. Then, too, it was warmer than usual inside due to the large fires he had ordered stoked in celebration. Worse, he had eaten too much; a full stomach always predisposed a person to slumber. The soft robes sewn of martin, beaver, and otter on which he had lain hadn't helped matters. Nor had a playful bout of coupling with his wife. Despite the fact it was an act to encourage the Trader, he'd nevertheless exhausted his loins. That sort of thing, too, drained a man's ability to remain alert. Thus, he was grateful when an owl hooted in the night, bringing him awake and indicating that the worst of the rain had passed.

He blinked, lifting his head to stare about. The far wall was faintly visible in the glow cast by the two fire pits, one at each end of the lodge. He could just make out the lighter framework of supple poles that had been sunk into the earth and bent over before being lashed together to make the loaf-shaped roof overhead. Crosspieces had been tied to the uprights to provide stability, and overlapping sections of bark had been lashed on to cover the whole of it. In the bluish haze that drifted up toward the smoke holes, he could see bags of corn, goosefoot, marsh elder, and cattail root hanging in their net bags. Along the walls, sleeping benches, like the one he lay on, were covered with hides. Below them, decorated bark boxes held all manner of awls, stone tools, clothing, and the other accoutrements of a successful household. Round-bottomed pots lay canted in a row, ready for use.

Snow Otter ran his tongue over his teeth, feeling the furry covering left from the roasted acorns he had fed to Trader as an addition to the fish cakes. So, too, had he broken open not just one, but two of his prized jugs of berry juice.

Worry over what he was about to do came rolling back like some dark wave to wash over his thoughts. Trade was spiritual—a thing of Power. It wasn't just that the gods and Spirits had given men a sacred trust allowing them to cross nations, cultures, tribes, and customs, but it served to fulfill spiritual and physical needs.

He fingered the shell pendant Trader had given him for the right to dig for copper. Among his people, the shell gorget engraved with woodpeckers and the sacred pole was worth an entire winter's food supply. At the time—when Trader had offered it—it had seemed an incredible coup! Imagine: the whelk-shell gorget in return for the privilege of digging around in an old exhausted hole in the ground, one that had only produced small nuggets of copper? Ludicrous!

Who'd have thought the foreigner would discover a deposit of huge wealth, worth many times the value of the white shell gorget?

Snow Otter made a face at the darkness. Power, the whole thing reeked of it. A Trade: one large value in exchange for an even greater one.

He closed his eyes, remembering the thick slab of copper. It ran through the rock in a sheet as thick as a man's meaty palm. The metal had gleamed wickedly in the firelight. Snow Otter could feel it calling to him from across the lodge. Such wealth! The likes of which he had never seen in all his life—and he, a copper Trader of no small means. Possessing that sheet of copper would make him the wealthiest man among his people. Travelers would come from all over, providing him with gifts and offerings just to see it. And eventually word would spread down the rivers and still more Traders would come from as far away as the distant gulf, each bearing unimaginable wealth. Each would offer something, competing, fed by lust for that thick slab of copper. In their frenzy, they would pile goods before Snow Otter the likes of which no chief of his people had ever seen, let alone a clan leader such as himself.

So much to gain. So much to lose.

He glanced over at the robes where Trader lay sound asleep next to Snow Otter's daughter. Power permeated Trade. He could feel it in the air, almost a tangible thing. The shell gorget on his chest seemed to weigh heavier than his thoughts. His palms were damp and sweaty. He would have to be most careful. Both his wife and daughter could be trusted to keep their tongues. Compliance, if not complete understanding, had been in their eyes when he'd ordered a feast, plying their guest with food and drink. His daughter had swallowed reluctantly but nodded assent when he'd whispered in her ear that her best interest would be served by offering herself to the Trader.

"And not just once," he had insisted, waving his finger before her face. "Do you understand? He's a young man. Use your hands, your mouth, whatever. He should have three or four vigorous couplings in that strong body of his."

The fact that she'd complied had pleased him; that she had erupted in moans and sighs three different times had shocked him. A father shouldn't know such things about his daughter.

He swallowed hard. If the thing was to be done, it was better done now. The Trader should be in deep sleep, his belly full, his manhood depleted, his souls lulled by a sense of satisfaction.

You are defiling the Power of Trade! The thought rolled around in his head as he carefully lifted his blanket and eased out from beside his wife's warm body.

Reaching under the bed, he found the long copper

knife. The corded handle felt solid and firm in his sweaty grip. Heart pounding, he tiptoed across the lodge to his daughter's bed. This would have to be done just so. He needed to slip the blade straight and true, driving it up under the sternum to pierce the heart. Pressing the man down into the bedding, he could keep the bleeding to a minimum. With one hand on the man's throat, the cries could be smothered. Then, he need only drag the corpse outside, down to the canoe landing, and a short paddle later, he could drop the stone-laden Trader over the side to sink in the night-black waters of the lake.

Power will find a way to punish you for this!

He stilled the voice in his head. Rot it all, he'd find a way to make it right with Power. As a rich man, he could assuage the gods. Far more worrisome would be if other people found out. Such a thing could ruin the Trade. Cause his people to be boycotted, avoided for years, should word leak out. In defense, his own people might murder him, sending word down the rivers that the vile Snow Otter had been punished for his misdeeds.

So do it right!

He filled his lungs as he stopped before his daughter's bedding, and carefully reached for the blanket with his free hand. The miracle was that no one seemed to hear his pounding heart. Fear ran electrically down his nerves and muscles. His mouth had gone so dry that his tongue stuck to the roof.

As if lifting the cover from a serpent's lair, he eased the blanket away from the still form. Even as he did, he knew something was wrong. The shape wasn't right.

In the dim glow of the fire, he could make out his daughter's slight form. She was curled on her side, dark hair a tangle on the bedding. Her breathing indicated that she was sleeping most soundly. Where the Trader should have been lay two familiar and bulky fabric bags—the ones his wife used to store hickory nuts beneath the sleeping bench.

Trader was gone.

Origins

Where did the People come from, you ask? We Albaamaha know the truth. Watch me as I reach down. See
this black earth that I claw from the ground? See how
moist it is? Smell it; is it not rich? We are of this land,
unlike these silly and pretentious Chikosi. Let them babble away in their Mos'kogee tongue about being born of
distant mountains. We, the Albaamaha, come from here.
From this soil! This earth I hold even now in my hand.

"Down south, just over there, across the hills, flows
the Albaamaha River. Back in the first times, just after
the earth had been raised from the waters, a great tree
grew. The World Tree that the Chikosi perverted into
their Tree of Life. The World Tree's roots wound deeply
into the ground, sucking nourishment from the Below
Worlds. Its branches reached high into the sky, caressing the winds, clouds, and Abba Mikko: He-Who-Sits-
Above-and-Never-Dies.

"Our people lived in a great cave way down inside
the earth. They had been molded and formed of clay,
made into the shape of people. It was down there, deep
in the earth, that they found the roots of the great World
Tree growing along their cave walls. In the Council
House they talked about the roots and wondered what
they portended. After many days it was decided that they
should investigate.

"It took those first People a long time to find pine-
knot torches. As you can imagine, such torches are
rather rare deep in the Below Worlds. But when they had

enough, they lit them, and began climbing up along the roots. The journey wasn't easy. Climbing, as you know, is strenuous. Nor was the way without risk. The ·Below Worlds are filled with terrible monsters. Tie snakes would dart out of the shadows and drag people back into the darkness. Witches left poisoned food, and when some people ate it, they became paralyzed and had to be left behind. No one knows what the witches did with them. At least four different water panthers preyed upon the people.

"Four times they made camp, lighting fires in the shape of a spiral to ward off evil beasts and malevolent little people. In the light of the fire they could see Cannibal Giants in the gloom, but the flames kept them away.

"Finally, after the fourth camp, they climbed out into this world. Some, the Albaamaha, emerged from one side of a huge root. The others, who would become the Koasati, climbed out on the other side, which is why to this day we are so similar in all but the pronunciation of a few words. It was coming out on either side of that root that separated us.

"And then the first Albaamaha looked up. What they saw amazed them. The great trunk of the World Tree towered above the mouth of their cave, its base so huge it took days to walk all the way around it. Then they saw the branches stretching out in all directions. Finally there was the sky with all of the thousands of Star People. Sister Moon glowed down from the west, almost full. They had never seen such bright light.

"Ah, I can see your expression. You can guess, can't you? Yes, they emerged at night, first felt the wind on their faces, and sucked the cool smells of the forest, river, and rain into their nostrils. Here, they thought, was paradise.

"The people Danced and celebrated. They clapped their hands, Singing their thanks for the new world they had found. They were so loud that Owl looked down, saw them, and cried, Hoo Hoo Hoooo Hoo.

"What did you ask? Of course panic broke out. People

screamed, fearing this new beast that hooted from the high branches. Some froze in fear; others scattered, running this way and that. But many of them ran back into the cave. So great was their fear that they charged heads and heels back down the way they had come, never to return again. . . .

"Hmm? Oh, sorry. I lose my thoughts sometimes. Thinking, you know . . . thinking about all those Albaamaha who fled back down into the Below Worlds. What do you think happened to them all? Do they still remember us? Do they tell stories down there in the deep earth, remembering those of us who stayed in this world?

"I agree; it's an unsettling thought. We look down at the ground, and somewhere, four days' journey into the earth under our feet, someone is looking up with equal curiosity. I tell you, what a difference that owl made. In frightening so many people into fleeing back down the cave, those of us who remained—us and the Koasati— are so few as a result.

"Hmm? Pardon? Of course things would be different today. These Mos'kogee would never have been allowed to settle in our lands. Instead of scattered farming villages, they would have found a strong and thriving population capable of resisting their incursions. Rather than coming here, they would have looked elsewhere for a place to settle. This land—from which we sprang in the beginning—would have remained ours, and ours alone!

"You see, it all goes back to that owl. Even today the owl's haunting night call still raises the chill-flesh on our skin. It's a portent. A sign that somewhere, someplace, ill is befalling someone. No matter what, should you ever hear an owl hoot in the night, be sure to touch your most sacred objects. You never know when it might be hooting for you."

Four

The old man—an Albaamaha elder known among his friends as Paunch—rested on a log and stared thoughtfully at the brown and somber day. The ridgetop where he sat high in the rolling hills west of the Black Warrior River bottoms was obscured by a thick forest that carpeted the uplands. Winter colors daubed the land in a mixture of browns, grays, and occasional greens where evergreens could be seen through the maze of trees. A somnolent breeze blew down from the north, its path marked by a faint whisper through naked branches and interlaced vines. Here and there worn gray sandstone outcrops peeked furtively from beneath a thick blanket of new-fallen leaves. They carpeted the uneven hilltop and made a resilient mat underfoot. Faintly spiced, the scent of wood, mold, and moisture carried heavily on the air.

The old decayed log beneath Paunch's butt had been long softened by rot and was spotted with moss. It had been a huge black oak once, a virtual forest giant, and its fall had opened a small clearing in the trees that thrust up from the ridgetop. His single companion was a slender young woman who stood at the clearing's edge, vacant eyes fixed on something far down the slope. He straightened his back and made a face as if in pain.

White hair had been pulled up into a bun atop the old man's head. Star-patterned tattoos had faded, barely recognizable on his sunken cheeks. He clasped a furry bear robe around his shoulders, hair catching what gray light managed to filter through such a cloud-packed sky. Beside his gnarly feet, two ceramic bowls rested on the leaf mat. The first was blacker than a cave's heart; its polished slip had a deep luster, the finish so perfect that it reflected a dark mirror image of the world. Water covered the bottom of the luminous ebony pot, making the bowl's dark recesses oddly bottomless. On the leaves beside it, its mate consisted of a simple burnished brown bowl, its sides decorated with the effigy of Tailed Man, prancing, his arms raised. The brown bowl contained a gray-white paste: a concoction of ground plant material and grease. The paste's surface betrayed where two fingers had dipped lightly into the contents.

Paunch gave the slender girl a worried glance, then tilted his head back to stare upward. Skeletal trees seemed to finger the dull winter sky with their thin branches. Squirrel nests, mistletoe, and vines had captured clots of the fallen brown leaves. Grape and green-briar wound up around the tree trunks like futile ropes. The effect was as if they were seeking to restrain the forest giants that reached so diligently for the sky.

The girl stood like a slim pole, her back to the old man. Her breasts were young and full; the rounded curve of her hips narrowed to long legs. The cape she clasped around her thin brown shoulders had been festooned with chevron patterns of yellow, blue, green, and red feathers. Belted around her waist, a white hemp-fiber skirt was decorated with a pattern of alternating ducks woven into the fabric. A rope belt clung to her waist; its intricately tied knot hung down the front to indicate her status as an unmarried virgin. Her feet were covered with fawnskin moccasins topped by dark beads crafted from freshwater clamshells.

She slowly lifted her eyes to the southeastern sky. There, through the pattern of branches, a plume of black smoke hung like a worm that inched off to the south. The thick winter forest combined with the curve of the hill to hide the source of the blaze.

"Alligator Town," the old man said thoughtfully.

"Can you feel the flames?" She raised a hand, palm outward, as if to savor the sensation.

"No. But then, Whippoorwill, my powers were never like yours." He glanced down at the two bowls resting by his feet. "You saw the fighting in your vision. The smoke comes from the right place."

Whippoorwill's long black hair shone as she nodded. "Surprise was complete. Many are dead. The Auntie People chiefs may succeed in feeding the survivors at Alligator Village, but bellies will be pinched this winter."

"Only among *our* people," the old man muttered sourly. "If there's starvation, the Chikosi won't feel it."

Whippoorwill turned to study him. Her delicate and triangular face made her eyes look large. They glistened, dark and liquid, like midnight pools. Smudges of gray could be seen on her temples where bits of paste had flaked. She pursed her full lips. "What are you willing to sacrifice, Grandfather?"

"To be rid of them?" Paunch ran callused hands down his thin shins. "Anything."

"How many would you starve?"

"Of my own people? None! I'd take it out of those filthy Chikosi mouths. I want to see their bellies gaunted up, their ribs sticking out like basket staves."

"In order to win, our people must lose." Whippoorwill's gaze wavered as if unable to find its focus. She seemed to look through him, to see something beyond his world. "How long has it been, Grandfather? Are you sure that our people even care to be freed of the invader?"

Paunch narrowed his eyes as he struggled to see through the haze of branches to the distant smoke's source. "They came in the time of my grandfather's grandfather. The Albaamaha were spread up and down the Black Warrior River bottoms, living in villages, hunting, fishing, farming. Clans feuded with clans. Sometimes Pensacola raiders would come up the river and steal away women or children . . . take them off to the gulf and make slaves of them. But villages protected their own."

She listened intently, as if hearing the thoughts hidden behind his words.

"Their warriors came first," he continued. "A large band of twenty canoes, they traveled down from the portage, down past the fall line. Two hundred warriors armed with shields, powerful bows, and deadly arrows—our people just watched them pass. No one would dare to challenge such a force. Especially unsophisticated hunter-farmers like we were."

Paunch rubbed his lined forehead. "They knew where they were headed, of course. Their Traders had been through this country from top to bottom. They knew everything about us. We had sheltered them in our villages, told them of our petty squabbles, and shown them our best land. Among their Traders were farmers, men who knew corn and soil. They had picked out the bluffs a long time before those canoes came down the river."

"I've seen these things." Her expanded pupils made black pools. "The memories of my Ancestors cry within me. My eyes look through theirs. I feel their hearts beating within my own."

"If they are showing you these things, then you know how the Chikosi established a camp on the heights that would become Split Sky City. You've seen how they erected their first fortifications and sent out parties of warriors to meet with our headmen. They promised us protection from raiders—an end to our petty feuds, and food for all in return for obedience. Many of our chiefs agreed and asked the bristling Mos'kogee warriors to intimidate their enemies and rivals. Those who refused stood no chance against such trained and disciplined fighters. Their farmsteads were burned, and the lucky ones were killed outright and left to rot in their fields. The unlucky were taken back to the bluffs. The tendons in their heels were severed so they couldn't run away, and they were put to work raising the high mounds even as more parties of Chikosi came traveling down the river."

"Some of our people revolted," she said in a breath-heavy voice.

Paunch shook his head. "We were like children shrieking at adults. They crushed any opposition. Those who obeyed without complaint were made headmen, given gifts and lands, and allowed to live in the shadow of Split Sky City."

"Split Sky," she said listlessly. "Even the name reeks of their arrogance."

Old Paunch picked up the beautiful black pot at his feet and cradled it in his bony hands. He could see the curved image of trees and sky reflected in the polished mirror-black exterior. Water filled a third of it; his reflection mirrored in the dark depths of the bowl. His eyes appeared to be holes in his face, and he could feel tendrils of Power, as though the reflected image was from another world. "It is said that these Well Pots are doorways."

"Oh, yes, Grandfather."

"Does Sister Datura Dance in your blood now?" He shifted his gaze to the gray paste still visible on Whippoorwill's temples. He had watched uneasily as she had scooped the mixture of ground datura seeds and bear grease from the brown pot and rubbed the concoction onto her temples. Sister Datura was a dangerous Spirit, one whose very touch could kill. Nevertheless, among those who courted Power, she granted the most awesome of visions.

"We are clinging to each other and swaying in time." The girl's eyes enlarged, as if to take in the entire world. She wrapped her arms tightly over her breasts, her hips moving slowly side to side. The virgin's knot began to gyrate in a sensual manner.

"Take the Well Pot," he coaxed gently, offering the bowl.

"Are you sure you wish me to do this? Seeing into the

worlds of Power is fraught with danger. The very act of looking can unleash terrible consequences. The balance between order and chaos will be shifted, changed. Once I have looked, there is no going back."

"I must know."

When Whippoorwill finally nodded, her face had gone pale, her eyes glassy with fear. Her arms trembled as he placed the bowl in her hands. He would remember how her long thin fingers embraced the smooth sides of the gleaming black pot. She seemed unbelievably fragile as she sank gracefully to her knees and gently laid the Well Pot on the cushioning mat of leaves. A low Song began deep in her throat, and she leaned over the bowl, looking down into its depths.

She froze, as if locked in place, her wide eyes staring down into the black water.

For long moments Paunch waited, his anxiety growing. Whippoorwill didn't seem to breathe. Her hair swayed with the breeze, but even the pulse in her neck had ceased.

"Child?" he asked tentatively, only to reach for her in concern.

"Leave me!"

He drew back with a start, sure that the snapping voice had barked from beside him. He glanced back at the girl, fully aware that her lips had not moved. *Who called? From where?* But he and the girl were alone in the clearing.

Slowly, carefully, he retracted his hand and reseated himself on the rotted log to wait.

Hands of time passed. Daylight had begun to drain away. Still the old man waited. As many winters as he had lived, he knew how to conjure patience. Whippoorwill might have been a pretty statue, so motionlessly did she stare into the Well Pot.

The old man snapped his head around, catching the faintest of whispers by his right ear. Nothing. He reached out, fingering the empty air. Moments later he heard a woman laughing, but when he turned only the lonely clearing met his eyes. Nervous, he began rubbing his hands together.

A disembodied scream curdled his blood. He bolted to his feet to peer this way and that. It had been so loud, so close.

"Where are you?" he whispered frantically.

Silence filled the forest as late-afternoon light filtered through the trees.

Close by a baby bawled in frustration and fear. He stiffened, back arched as he gaped. *Close, so very close. I should be able to reach out and touch the child.* No squalling infant lay on the flat leaf mat. He shook his head and clamped hands over his ears.

Someone laughed at him, the sound coming from down in the trees below. The sound pierced his flesh and echoed inside his skull. He turned, craning his neck as he peered through the trees.

"Where are you?" He lowered his head, cocking it to hear better.

"Right here, Grandfather," Whippoorwill said behind him.

He whirled, seeing Whippoorwill, straight as a rod before the Well Pot, her eyes like shining lakes in the soft brown of her delicate face. The sounds stopped as if cut off, the world grown oddly silent.

"What . . . what have you seen?" His throat had gone oddly dry.

She fixed him with her eerie eyes. "The circle is coming full. Dreams are about to be shattered. I have seen murder and death. In the end, despite the blood, rape, and treachery, our schemes shall all come to naught. My sister is the key. She will Dance with Power and draw the monster into the coiled grasp of the Horned Serpent."

Sister? She has no sister. What monster? And how is the Horned Serpent involved? Paunch stared down into the gleaming Well Pot, trying to see into its depths.

From his angle, only a crescent of tree-furred sky reflected from the surface. "Then the Albaamaha shall be free?"

"We've always been free, Grandfather. That's the divine joke." She paused, pointing down the hill. "There, can't you see them laughing?"

The old man turned, half-afraid he'd finally discover the source of the whispers and cries. Far down the slope, winding through the trees, he could make out a line of warriors trotting past in single file. They had painted their bodies in red and black, the colors of war. The sides of their heads were shaved, the tops roached high, forelocks beaded. Gleaming copper ear spools caught the light. All carried bows, but their quivers were mostly depleted of arrows. Wooden and wicker shields hung from their backs. They hurried along, some sporting bloodsoaked bindings on their arms, heads, and legs, obviously wounded.

A string of captives followed, outlying guards prodding them with clubs and spears. The prisoners were bloodied, men looking downcast and afraid, women staring about in doe-eyed disbelief. All had been stripped naked, and looking close, Paunch could see that each of the men had been scalped of his forelock, the exposed section of skull blackened with dried blood. Lines of it had trickled down their faces.

"Will they see us up here?" Paunch asked.

She stepped up beside him, emptiness in her eyes. "They see nothing but their victory."

At the end ran a final warrior. He was young, strong-limbed, and agile. A bulky wooden box was strapped to his back like an awkward pack. An ornate thing, its sides had been intricately carved and inlaid with white shell; exposed wood had been brightly painted, and the bas-relief images it sported were clad in beaten sheets of polished copper.

"He carries the war medicine box, Whippoorwill," old

Paunch noted. "A great deal of responsibility for one so young. Is he their leader?"

The girl narrowed her eyes as she watched the young warrior pass and vanish into the trees. "It is well that we can only see as far as our Dreams, Grandfather. That young man drowns in visions of glory, status, and honors. In the eye of his souls, he is already standing atop the Chief Mound in White Arrow Town. His bed is filled by a warm and willing woman, and all bow before him. In his Dream he is aging, surrounded by his many children. Chiefs from all over seek his audience and advice. He wears a wealth of shell, copper, and fine white fabric adorned with feathers of every color. His enemies tremble."

The old man glanced back at the black smoke plume hanging over Alligator Town. "But that is not to be?"

"There is no more tragic a fool than the one who lives only in his Dreams." She had fixed her depthless eyes on him. "The Dream becomes obsession, doesn't it? It Dances behind our eyelids at odd moments, and swirls like a current . . . only to carry us to certain doom."

"So the young man is a fool?"

She smiled, flashing strong white teeth. "He is the single stick in the beaver's dam. Remove him, and the whole structure will disintegrate into a flood of brown water that will wash everything before it." She arched an eyebrow. "Can you swim, Grandfather?"

"Then, you see the end?"

Her eyes grew distant. "The fool has made his play. His blood will run hot and red across the ceremonial sword and stain his lover's fingers. Power is stirring. Old blood cries out for revenge. Forgotten passions simmer. Brothers must be crossed before all will be made anew." She glanced off to the north. "My sister brings the father of my child."

He shook his head. Whipporwill's mother was long dead. There would be no sister. "The father of your child?"

"He thinks he can outrun destiny. But the net is closing as Power draws the lines tight."

"And then we will be free?"

Her only answer was a bitter peal of laughter.

Five

Old White considered Two Petals as he paddled out into the Father Water's lazy current. Her clansmen had literally tossed the bound woman into the bottom of his canoe. She looked like a war captive: dirty, wild-eyed, and disheveled. Was this bound and gagged creature really the woman he had been looking for? The Dream had only come in fragments: Often the images had been so ambiguous. What if she wasn't the Contrary that the Forest Witch had spoken of so many moons ago? Indecision ate at him.

He used his paddle to correct his course, aware of the slanting of the western sun. This late in the year, the great river ran smoothly, its surface placid for the most part. The current had a green clarity. When the sun was high, he could see the bottom, much of it thick with moss and water plants. On occasion he'd spot a great paddlefish or sturgeon gliding along the bottom.

As Old White followed his bow downstream, he cast mild glances at the willows that lined the shore. It was possible that one of Fast Palm's warriors might have followed, heart set on taking a parting shot by launching an arrow in his direction.

He took another swipe with his pointed paddle and turned his attention on the still-trussed female. She reminded him of some huge fish, a trophy landed and dropped amidst the various packs, robes, and baskets that lay in the bottom of his dugout canoe. Wrapped in her rope, the gag in her mouth, she looked pathetic. Her eyes fixed on his; passion and fire, like gleaming dark coals, burned behind her thin face.

"Would you like that gag removed?" he asked.

She shook her head violently, mouth working as if she was trying to spit out the dirty cloth.

Old White leaned forward, grasped the cloth, and pulled it free.

She rocked her jaw back and forth, made a face, smacked her tongue, and spit dryly to one side. "Delightful. Wonderful taste. Like cooking goosefoot bread on a greased stone." Her gaze returned to his. "Worthless bastard of a crawfish hunter. You're a pus dripper for sure."

He cocked his head as the canoe rocked in time with her attempts to find a more comfortable position. His vessel was made of bald cypress from the southern swamps. The hull was wider than the girl's shoulders, so she'd sunk down between the gunwales.

"When did the Spirits come to you?" He took another cut with his paddle, just enough to follow the current's line as it bore them toward a cottonwood-screened bend.

Her eyes slipped sideways. "I've never seen Spirits. Not even that one over there. I can't see Deer Man out there standing on the water. It's impossible." She frowned, perplexed. "Why doesn't he sink? He has hooves for feet."

"Deer Man?" Old White knew the Spirit. He'd seen him drawn in shell art, depicted on hides and cave walls. "Is he the only one, or are there more?"

"They don't exist," she whispered. "Not like my husband. Golden . . . shining. Wings of feathered fire. Diamond scales, gleaming quartz on his back and thighs. Shhhh! Shhhh! The rattle shook. Thunderous in its silence. He smiled at me. Like this." She grinned widely, exposing her strong white teeth in a caricature. "His eyes, oh sunshine, what worlds they were. Fire and snow, turning and twisting like rope from his very gaze. It wound around me. Tied me up. Like this rope." She bent her wrists so that her fingers could claw impotently at the rope.

"He was old? Young?"

"Young." Her head bobbed in a frantic nod. "Very young." The saucy grin returned. "Spiked me with his rod, I tell you. Shot his warm seed like liquid fire into my sheath. When I looked down, I could see it. You know, inside. It glowed like copper in the sunlight, spreading through my hips, warming my bones."

Old White tilted his head as he studied the girl. "His face, was it human with a nose and mouth, or birdlike with a beak?"

"Human." She nodded assertively. "Most definitely human. Did I tell you that he smiled? Like this." She repeated the wide rictus that displayed her teeth.

"So you said." He took another stroke with the paddle. "What did he tell you?"

The grin faded. "That I would follow the backward birds. Like those." She jerked her chin upward. Old White followed the direction of her gaze, seeing a high-flying line of ducks winging south for the winter.

"Ah, yes, south." Old White nodded sagaciously. "And what will you find there?"

She turned serious eyes on his. "Ashes. That's what's usually left after a fire burns itself out. Nothing but ashes . . . gray . . . cold . . . and fluffy." She puffed out her cheeks, blowing hard, as though at a long-abandoned fire pit.

Old White swallowed hard, nodding. "The world is full of ashes, isn't it?"

"And rot, too," she added. "Lots of rot. It's because we're food for Mother Earth, you know. Without the dead to eat, she'd starve to death, grow ever thinner and thinner and thinner, and finally the serpents and water panthers and turtles and worms would wiggle around inside her like maggots inside an old acorn. The ground would be all hollow. You could pound your foot on it and it would boom like a great drum."

"Did you really witch that chief?"

"He wanted nothing to do with me. There wasn't even a shadow of lust in his souls . . . had no desire to slide his shaft into my sheath, I tell you. Blackness Danced ever so brightly on his heart. Thought me way too smart and clever to let him drive his spear into my loins. But I'm ugly, and I know it. Be sure you'll catch me wiggling on some man's shaft just because he fancies me too quick!" She rocked her head from side to side. "Power shifts, good and evil. I told him he'd enjoy his meal. May he digest in peace."

Old White tilted his head back, sniffing through his nostrils, taking in the scent of the river, of the fall-yellowed willows and leaf mats beyond the shore. "You really disliked him, didn't you?"

"Loved the man, actually," she snorted. "I hope you decide to slip yourself into me. I'd look forward to that."

"Have you had trouble with that?"

"I'm too ugly. Too skinny. Men never stare at my chest or hips. Not when I'm clean. No appeal here."

He arched an eyebrow. Beneath the smudges, baggy clothing, and layers of rope, she seemed to have a delightfully proportioned body. Were her hair washed and combed to a shine, and her face sponged of the filth that encrusted it, he had no doubt that any man worth his spit would glance more than once in her direction. Even the way her very round hips were wiggling against the ropes had an effect. If she could stir him, old as he was, think what she'd do to a young man still full of his juices.

"I've no interest in your body, Two Petals. Power sent me to you." Old White stroked with his paddle and used the blade to steer. "Were I to untie you, would you try and leap out of the boat?"

She turned her shining eyes on him. Her voice dropped, as if straining from the effort to focus. Her face contorted as if with great effort. "What do you want, old man? Why did you come for me?"

"I'm headed south," he replied wearily. "I have

something to do before I die. Somehow, I think it's time to see to the ashes."

She nodded, eyes losing their focus, a frown dancing lightly across her forehead. "Turn me loose, I'll be over the side in a heartbeat. Treat me kindly, and I'll be gone like a shot arrow. Give me pain, and I'll stick by you until you begin to think we're joined in one body. I promise none of these things."

Old White pursed his lips, lowering his chin onto his chest. "I have no idea what Power wants with the two of us. For all these years, my travels have been alone. Why I should need you is beyond me."

"That's all right, little boy, I know everything!" she chirped excitedly; then her expression dropped to one of confusion, the frown in her forehead deepening. "No. That's not right. I *know* I know everything."

"You're sure you won't run away first chance you get?"

"First chance? On my word, I'll run like a deer."

He chuckled under his breath, and balancing, leaned forward, untying the knots that bound her so tightly. "Just don't capsize us when you wiggle free. The water's cold, and I don't swim so well these days."

"I'll do my best to tip us over, for sure," she agreed solicitously as she began tossing off the binding ropes. "And if I went over the side, I'd flounder and sink like a rock."

A faint smile bent his old lips. "We'll make quite a pair, you and me."

"Just us, just us," she chortled, making a face as circulation began to pain parts of her limbs. "Boring, boring, boring. He'll never find us now."

He'll never find us? "Who? Who is he?"

She cried out as she rubbed the blood back into her arms. "That feels so good! Like the caress of a lover!"

"Who will never find us?" he demanded in frustration.

"No one," she answered simply, as if it were all forgotten. She had shifted, gasping as she bent her legs and arms. With a deep sigh, she flipped over onto her stomach atop his packs, and hung her head over the gunwale. "Look, I can see through the air!"

Old White lifted his eyes to the heavens, where yet another V could be seen high in the sky. This time the faint tooting sounds told him the migrants were blue herons headed south. "Why me?" he wondered.

"Because of the future," Two Petals whispered. "It's completely forgotten about you."

It was said that in the beginning times only water and sky existed. Crawfish brought mud up from the depths to establish the first land. A great buzzard had flown over the muddy mass, its huge wings beating down the valleys and raising the mountains with each stroke. And then the great serpents emerged from the Underworld.

Snakes were water beings. They called the rains and clustered around springs, passing between the worlds. Like all waterways, the Horned Serpent River had been created when giant serpents crawled down from the heights, their bellies dredging the channels. To this day, the water flowed, its movements mimicking the motions of those great serpents. One need but watch the river to see the coiling of its muscular currents and catch the shimmering of waves that caught the sunlight like scales.

Over the years, the Horned Serpent's channel had cut its southerly path through rolling hills covered with pine and hardwoods. Its tributaries flowed past broken beds of sandstone and limestone that grayed and weathered in the sun. Below the forested ridges and hills, terraces protruded into the river's course, forming flat promontories around which sluggish swamp waters had to pass. It was to these farmlands overlooking the floodplain's rich soils that the ancestors of the Chahta People had come.

Like all Mos'kogee people, the Chahta divided themselves into moieties: the White Arrow and Red Arrow. In their movement east from the Father Water, they had established holdings along the Pearl River before moving into the Horned River Valley. The hills and valleys of the Horned Serpent were occupied by scattered groups of hunters and farmers. These loosely related villagers called themselves the Biloxi.

Working feverishly, the Chahta had ringed the old-growth forest trees, allowing them to die. During the dry days of fall they set fire to the dead trees. The following spring they labored amidst the blackened stumps, hoeing, tilling the ash-rich soil, and planting fields of corn, beans, and squash. In smaller gardens they grew tobacco, mandrake, ground potatoes, datura, and rattlesnake master.

At first the local Biloxi people offered little resistance; their lives consisted of mostly hunting with some farming. By the time they realized the growing threat, it was too late. The Chahta were firmly entrenched, their disciplined professional warriors invincible when matched against loosely organized hunters. Dispossessed, all but a few of the Biloxi retreated south, leaving their ancestral lands behind rather than confront the sharp blade of Chahta warfare.

Over time the Red and White Arrow moieties built six major towns that controlled the most productive farmlands in the valley. White Arrow Town was the strongest and most influential of these. The town's location was high enough above the river to be safe from the periodic spring and summer floods that swept the floodplain, yet still close enough that slaves could easily retrieve water for the town's needs.

White Arrow Town rose above a flat-topped ridge that jutted out from the western bank of the Horned Serpent River like some oversize thumb. Below its steep bluff, the sluggish brown waters swirled and eddied. At the root of the thumb a tall palisade—six hundred paces in length and offset by archers' platforms atop bastions—guarded the land approaches. Behind its secure heights, square houses had been built in haphazard clusters. Additional ramadas, elevated granaries, and charnel houses filled the open spaces. Elite houses and a platform mound that supported a tall chieftain's palace with its peaked roof of thatch dominated the center of the town. A tchkofa, or council house, stood to one side of the square plaza, as did the warriors' lodge and several of the Priest's temples. The Women's House had been built across the plaza from the warriors' lodge. There the adult females of the White Arrow Chief Clan retired to spend their menses in seclusion, away from men and isolated from artifacts and places of Power.

Inside the structure, firelight flickered on mudplastered walls. It gleamed on the peeled wooden posts that supported a heavy roof. The room measured ten by ten paces, with a puddled clay hearth in the center of the floor. Sleeping benches lined the walls, each belonging to a specific lineage or clan. The walls had been painted red, the color of a woman's cyclical bleeding. Looms, pottery molds, and half-finished textiles, along with containers of partially crafted shell beads, offered entertainment to the occupants while they spent their three or four days of solitude.

On this night, two women occupied the room. One old and self-possessed, the other young, with the energy of a caged lark. The elder, called Old Woman Fox, studied her granddaughter curiously as the young woman added another length of wood to the fire.

When young Morning Dew looked up, she could see the latticework of poles in the ceiling and make out the cord that bound thick shocks of thatch together. All was covered with a fine coating of soot that softened the lines. Here and there, bundles hung from cords. Some were net bags filled with herbs; others held bone tubes for sucking cures. Leather sacks contained different pigments to be mixed with grease to create paints. The colors were used ceremonially to adorn bodies, carvings, and woodwork.

Benches had been built along the walls to a midthigh height above the floor. People thought that no flea could jump that high, and thus the sleepers were safe from vermin. Morning Dew, however, knew that to be false. Most women spent their days squatting or kneeling on the floor mats. There they had ample exposure to fleas. Once they took them to bed, the little beasts infiltrated both hides and corn-shuck bedding to bedevil everyone.

"It's a fib," her mother, Matron Sweet Smoke, had once confided. "Actually, the sleeping benches are built to be under smoke level. High enough for easy breathing, but low enough that the smoke keeps mosquitoes at bay. And in winter, that's where heat from the winter fires keeps a person at just the right temperature."

Morning Dew had always wondered why some nonsensical explanations supplanted the perfectly reasonable.

Below the sleeping benches lay wooden boxes with intricately carved sides that depicted flowers, bees, and spiders. Others were decorated with geometric and spiral designs and painted in gay yellows, reds, blues, and greens. Here and there incised ceramic jars, water bottles, and beautiful baskets stored foodstuffs, grease, tools, and personal effects. Each container was the inviolate property of its owner.

"Is it time to change your padding?" Old Woman Fox asked from where she knelt across the fire. She was spinning myrtle fibers into cordage, holding one end and rolling the fibers against her thigh.

Morning Dew made a face and reached under her short skirt to retrieve the pad of hanging moss from between her legs. She tossed the sticky bundle into the fire and said, "Sacred Fire, make my red into white."

"And what does that signify?" Old Woman Fox asked.

"The burning of my blood. Red is the color of chaos.

White is purity and order. When it burns in the fire, blood is turned into white smoke."

"Very good. Now, replace your pad and wash."

Morning Dew took another pad—a bundle of hanging moss tightly wrapped with cord—and pressed it between her legs. Finally she dipped the fingertips she'd used to touch the pad into a bowl of water to her left. She then flicked the droplets into the fire.

"Grandmother, I still don't understand." Morning Dew watched the flames consume her pad. "It doesn't seem so dangerous. You'd think if anyone went crazy from menstrual blood, it would be women. After all, we're the ones who bleed. But we're to believe the mere thought of it can make a strong man weak?"

Old Woman Fox laughed. "Blood is Power, girl. We bleed with the moon; but not from a wound, and mostly we do it without pain. It comes from inside us, flows through our sheaths. Nothing fascinates a man as much as a woman's sheath. He Dreams of it, desires it, and fears it."

"Fears it?"

"Of course, girl. It is a mystery to him—a source of obsession, desire, and incredible pleasure. He will cry out in delight as his seed jets inside you. Then it will grow, and nine moons later an infant will pass through that same pink opening. Your loins, girl, are a miracle—and at the same time, a place of terrible pollution."

"Pollution?" Morning Dew glanced down, trying to imagine how such terrible things could be hidden between her hips.

"You bleed once a moon," Old Woman Fox said sagely. "Yet you do not die." She gestured around at the Women's House. "That is why we come here. Because if we touch a man with our sheath's blood, it will ruin him, pollute his purity, and make him susceptible to illness, bad luck, and sickness of the souls."

Morning Dew chewed her lip as she considered. Like any young girl, she'd anticipated the day that her first menses would bring her to the Women's House. Passage into womanhood had preoccupied her for years. She and her friends had waited anxiously for this moment to come. Now she found that it was a nonending session of lecture after lecture. Things she already knew: Women sat with their knees together. Only men could sit cross-legged. Women did not touch a man's weapons under pain of a severe beating. Women dared not set foot in the Busk Ground until the fourth day of the green corn ceremonies. And on and on. Each of the rules of proper conduct had been repeated over and over. Do this. Don't do that. You're a Chief Clan daughter. One day you will be the matron. You have more responsibilities than other women.

"You were thinking something?" Old Woman Fox turned keen eyes on Morning Dew.

"I was thinking about responsibility. It's been hammered into my head with a pestle all of my life. Be responsible. You are different from other women. Responsible, responsible, responsible." She looked up. "Sometimes I think I'm just a responsible womb walking around on two legs."

Old Woman Fox nodded. "Do you understand why it's so important for you?"

"Because I'm Chief Clan by birth." She turned her hands palm up in supplication. "Because one day I will be the matron of White Arrow Moiety. My son will become high minko."

"And what do you think of this Screaming Falcon Mankiller you are betrothed to?"

"His new name sounds strange on my lips. It will take a while to stop thinking of him as Amber Stone." She smiled secretly. "I've been in love with him forever."

"Yet you complain about your fate?"

Morning Dew shook her head. "No, Grandmother. . . . I mean yes. I do and I don't. I know how lucky I am. I've watched him from the time I was a little girl. He has a sparkle in his eyes, a smile that melts my heart. And he's always looked at me in a special way, with a promise in his eyes. I watched from the trees when he was given his warrior's mantle last year and took his war name. No young man has ever become such a praised war leader at so young an age. He has dealt the Sky Hand People a terrible blow, burned the corn in Alligator Village, and taken the chief there captive along with his family. In a couple of years, Amber . . . Screaming Falcon Mankiller will topple their mighty walls onto their filthy heads." She snorted derisively. "And we will deal with the Chikosi's hand-licking Albaamaha slaves, too."

Old Woman Fox gave her a sober look. "I wouldn't underrate the Sky Hand People."

"Oh?"

"We are all Mos'kogee. It hasn't been that long since their Ancestors and ours lived under the mantle of Cahokia. Like us, they, too, came to this country, subjected the people they found, and built a nation. Screaming Falcon Mankiller's great raid will bring a response. And it will come soon," Old Woman Fox said softly. "Like us, they do not forget the ghosts of their slain. They know that the dead will never rest until their blood has been avenged."

Morning Dew arched a disbelieving eyebrow. "My man will repulse them. They'll run back east to their walled city, wailing and crying through the forest-covered hills. And then they'll quake in fear, knowing that Screaming Falcon will be coming after them." She paused. "Especially that putrid worm Smoke Shield. Remember how he watched me? He couldn't keep the drool from running down his ugly chin."

Old Woman Fox pursed her thin brown lips, the lines in her face deepening.

"What?" Morning Dew asked. "Put in words the disapproval I see in your face."

"First you complain of being nothing more than a walking womb. Then you spout silly nonsense. You are smarter than that, Morning Dew. But if you're not, well, at least you have that wonderful sheath. Let us hope that Screaming Falcon Mankiller's seed fills it with many children so that our clan is at least replenished."

"You don't think Screaming Falcon will be great?"

Old Woman Fox pulled at her grizzled white hair, speculative gaze boring into Morning Dew's eyes. "I think he will unleash the winds, girl. But I am not sure he can deflect them. If the winds blow us away, what then? If it falls to you, how will you save our people?"

"It won't come to that," Morning Dew replied saucily. "Seriously, Grandmother, could the Sky Hand People have anyone who could compare in war with Screaming Falcon and our White Arrow warriors? Surely not that scar-faced Smoke Shield, with all his superior strutting."

Old Woman Fox continued to watch her for several heartbeats. "Humor me. How would you save our people?"

Morning Dew snorted, giving her grandmother a condescending stare.

In a toneless voice, Old Woman Fox said, "That's what I thought."

Morning Dew glowered. "You'll see, Grandmother. A new day is coming to our people. My man is going to make sure of it. And if he doesn't, I will."

"Ah." Her eyes narrowed. "So you will accept responsibility for your people, no matter what?"

"On my blood." Morning Dew crossed her arms, absolutely justified in taking her people's most binding oath.

A cynical disbelief formed behind Old Woman Fox's eyes.

His full name was Flying Hawk Who Calls the Morning Mankiller, but his title was simply high minko, or hereditary ruler of the Sky Hand Mos'kogee. Age had settled into his skin, bones, and muscles, leaving its legacy in wrinkles, aching joints, and sapped abilities. His mind, however, remained keen behind a knowing brown gaze. As a young man he had been tattooed with forked eyes that mimicked a peregrine falcon's, and a wide red bar across his nose and cheeks indicated his clan status. Tattoos, he had discovered, never looked as striking in sagging old age as they did on fresh young skin. In contrast he made sure that the copper ear spools that filled his enlarged earlobes were polished until they shone. The feathers bound to his arms were bright red, blue, and yellow. He wore colorful fabrics dyed in bright colors, and the copper hairpiece that proclaimed his status as high minko had been polished until it shone like the light of the sun.

He sat in the middle of the great war canoe, paddles rising and falling as muscular young men drove them forward amidst a V of smaller craft. The waters of the Black Warrior River had a clear green translucence common to the late season. Gone was the muddy opacity of the summer caused by constant rains and floods. Down in the depths, he could make out the moss, clusters of mussels, and the occasional large fish.

Normally he wouldn't have been traveling this late in the season, but the attack on Alligator Town belied any sense of normality. War parties were a thing of summer, not the late fall, when straight-thinking men should be out hunting deer, their wives collecting nuts from the forest floor. No, this was unexpected, like a sudden slap from a longtime lover. It had kindled a slow-burning anger, one he would be happy to feed until it burned brightly among his people.

On the left bank trees thinned to a clearing. At its base a canoe landing could be seen. Beached craft, like driftwood logs haphazardly laid out, rested on the dark sandy bank. Through the trees he could make out a pall of white smoke.

Alligator Town had been built on an older Albaamaha village site. The place had been occupied off and on, but finally abandoned because of its location so far downstream. Then, during the rulership of his cousin, Fire Sky, a party had come downriver, and with Albaamaha labor, they had built a town here. As was demonstrated on this day, a location so far from Split Sky City was difficult.

Flying Hawk considered the problem as his canoes closed. The town had been built on a low rise, above flood stage, with fertile soils close by. The place had good access to the western uplands, while cypress and tupelo swamps were located just upstream. The resources could support a larger population, a stronger military presence, but it was difficult to force people to live so far from their relatives and clan holdings. It would be worse after this. Rot and curses, he wanted this place as a southern bastion of Sky Hand authority.

"Be ready," his nephew Smoke Shield called. A different tension ran through the warriors. Their eyes sharpened as scouts appeared on the bank, waving the all-clear.

"Take us in," Flying Hawk said evenly.

At his order, the canoes lanced across the roiling river, the first of them driving onto the beach as the warriors piled out. As if demonstrating their proficiency before their high minko, the warriors deployed in a perfect skirmish line, two of their fellows pulling the lightened canoe higher onto the bank. Canoe by canoe, his warriors landed and swarmed up the bank, shields held at the ready, bows and war clubs in their hands.

He felt his heavy war canoe grate as it slid onto the canoe landing. As quickly, the warriors leaped over the gunwales to pull the craft onto the beach. Paddles clattered as they dropped them for bows, shields, war clubs, and lances.

Smoke Shield was standing, hands on hips as he looked up the canoe landing toward Alligator Town. Apparently satisfied with the distribution of warriors approaching the town, he turned toward Flying Hawk and strode through the beached canoes. The man moved like an agile cat, strength coiled in his smooth muscles. A fiery anger betrayed the calculating passion that burned behind his gleaming black eyes.

I see trouble brewing there, Nephew. Pray that this time you unleash it on our enemy.

Flying Hawk rose from his seat and took his war chief's hand. His young nephew steadied him as he stepped out onto the shore. Smoke Shield Mankiller, Flying Hawk's sister's son, was next in line to follow him as high minko. The war chief had just passed his twenty-sixth winter, and—but for the hideous scar that marked his crushed cheek—would have been a most handsome young man. On this day he wore a spread of red, white, and black feathers in the high roach atop his head. A single warrior's forelock hung down almost to the bridge of his nose. Three pristine white beads were knotted along its length. The forked-eye design had been tattooed around his eyes; but the red bar across his cheeks had been mangled by the deep scar that left the side of his face misshapen. For the purposes of this day Smoke Shield had painted half of his face red, gathering the color's Power for war; the other half was black, symbolic of mourning for the dead.

Flying Hawk's warriors had stopped in a defensive formation, feet braced on the packed sand of the landing. Their keen eyes studied the brush lines on either side, weapons and shields up in case of attack from the ruined village just beyond the terrace. Flying Hawk could see the partially charred walls of the palisade.

"Your litter, High Minko," Smoke Shield said as porters came forward with his covered seat. Six brawny Albaamaha men lowered the litter to the ground, stepping back so that Flying Hawk could seat himself. He checked his hairpiece to make sure it hadn't shifted. The ornament was made of thinly beaten copper the length and width of his forearm; a rendering of an arrow splitting a cloud in two. The base was inserted into the hair bun he'd twisted tightly against the back of his head.

A bright cloak made from flamingo feathers Traded up from the south covered his shoulders, and a large shell gorget decorated with the symbol of his people—a human eye staring out of the palm of an extended hand—hung on his chest. About his waist was a warrior's triangular-shaped scalp apron, the point of which hung down between his knees. The spotless fabric was bleached to a startling white and contrasted to the stylistic black hawk embroidered on the flap.

Smoke Shield handed him his mace. Chipped from fine chert and nearly as long as his arm, it flared at the top in the shape of a turkey tail, a symbol of his people's victory over one of the monsters in the Beginning Times, before the current world came into being.

"Let us go and see to the damage," Flying Hawk said as he settled himself cross-legged in the litter. His men barely tilted the litter as they lifted it to their shoulders and started up the terrace from the canoe landing.

Generations of native Albaamaha had denuded most of the immediate forest, using the wood for fires, buildings, and other constructions. In an effort to both control and protect this far-flung settlement, Hawk's predecessor, High Minko Fire Sky, had sent additional warriors and Albaamaha to construct fortifications, add another level to the mound, and maintain local control. The outposts's existence had always been tenuous.

Alligator Town lay two long days' travel downriver from Split Sky City. The location was vulnerable to raiders coming upriver, and from those traveling cross-country through the forests. Mostly the latter consisted of White Arrow warriors from the Horned Serpent River. Only on occasion did the Pensacola from Bottle Town downriver, or Koasati—relatives of the Albaamaha, who lived several days' journey to the east—dare to strike into Sky Hand territory. They had come to appreciate the consequences of doing so.

As his litter crested the terrace edge, Flying Hawk was greeted by charred devastation. They passed part of the palisade that had fallen outward. Fire had scored portions of the wall that still remained standing. Within, only a few skeletal house walls remained, their sides blackened, roofs incinerated. Corpses, dead dogs, broken basketry, smashed pots, and overturned racks littered the ground. Here and there, broken arrows, scattered shields, abandoned war clubs, and other detritus of war could be seen.

The Alligator Town chief—a member of Flying Hawk's Chief Clan—had constructed his Chief's House atop a low mound, little more than waist high. Charred wall timbers, like diseased black bones, were sticking up from the smoking ash. The three-legged stool—from whence the chief had ruled his charges—still stood in the gray ash of the fallen roof. Smoke curled from the check-patterned char.

In the village proper, corn cribs—once cylindrical cane-walled structures set on high poles—were nothing but smoking wreckage. Blackened corncobs were all that remained of the near-record harvest. Even the plaza center pole, the symbolic unification of the worlds, had been burned, though the alternating stripes of red and white could still be seen at the top.

"They were very thorough," Flying Hawk noted dryly as he was borne into the center of the small plaza. The scattered corpses caught his eye. Partially clad in rumpled and torn fabric, most had been scalped; the round domes of their skulls were now black with dried blood. Others were missing hands or forearms. One sprawled body lacked a head; fragments of the spine protruded from the hacked stump of his neck.

From behind the ash-coated wreckage of houses, solitary people began to converge. They might have been wraiths, visions of lost souls seeking the Westward path toward the afterlife. All were smudged with soot, making them colorless and gray. Their faces betrayed shock and dazed disbelief. Some approached with children clutching at their legs. Terror lived behind their eyes.

"What happened here?" Flying Hawk demanded.

One warrior, a haggard-looking young man, stepped forward. His face was streaked with blackened blood, and his left arm hung limp, as if broken. With his right he pointed toward the portion of collapsed palisade. "They came in there. Just after dark they began digging out the soft dirt. They worked silently, their efforts covered by the rain that fell that night. It looks like they used ropes to pull the posts outward until the very weight of it pulled the binding vines apart and it fell. Our people were awakened by the thump. They were among us before we knew what was happening."

"What of my chief here?" The man's name was Stuffed Weasel. In accordance with the appellation, he'd been a short-tempered and perhaps unjust man, but he'd been effective: the sort who balanced determination with pragmatism. Flying Hawk had thought the man perfect for so delicate a job as binding his southern border to Split Sky City. From the look of the corpses lying about, none belonged to Stuffed Weasel.

"They took him, High Minko," one of the Albaamaha cried in poorly pronounced Mos'kogee. "He was wounded. They tied him and the others together and marched them out." The man pointed toward the forested hills to the west.

"It's been four days," Smoke Shield noted. His eyes were narrowed to slits, as though seeing past the hills to the sinuous Horned Serpent Valley beyond. There, to the west-northwest, lay White Arrow Town, fortified on its terrace overlooking the river.

At this very moment Stuffed Weasel was no doubt hanging spread-eagled from a wooden square where the White Arrow people would heap insult and abuse upon him. Beyond the humiliation, Flying Hawk could well imagine what awaited Stuffed Weasel and the rest of the captives. His tormentors would revel in the torture they inflicted, delighted in the notion that their Power was greater than Split Sky City's. They would sear the man's flesh, amputate his fingers, genitals, and ears. Bit by bit they would slice Stuffed Weasel's skin so that his blood leaked away drop by drop.

"We must retaliate," Flying Hawk said wearily, as if he could feel the shifting of Power. The balance had been changed by the ferocity of the attack. He could feel the gods watching him, asking, *"What are you going to do about this?"*

"It is late fall, Uncle," Smoke Shield said, his gaze turning to the southern sky, where the sun was even now low in the horizon. "Most of our men are in hunting camps in the highlands. Our people are dispersed. No one expected a raid this late in the year. Not of this scope."

"I heard his name," one of the Albaamaha called out as he pushed past some of the outlying warriors. "He was young, this war chief. Little more than a youth. He wore a medicine box on his back. They called him Screaming Falcon."

Smoke Shield glanced curiously at the man. "He wore the medicine box? You're sure of this? It wasn't just wooden armor tied to his body for protection against arrows?"

The man stepped closer. He might have passed forty winters, his hair going gray; the few remaining teeth in his mouth stuck up as brown stubs. A terrible wound had left a deep scar across his forehead, as if it had stopped an ax sometime in the past. As he came close he dropped to one knee, palms up in the supplicant's pose. "Great War Chief, I know a shield when I see one. I also know a medicine box. These White Arrow People would not send a mere youth out with such a thing unless they set great store in his Power. I watched, War Chief. His warriors—many of them much older— never hesitated when he gave orders. He might have been young, but he commanded and received their immediate obedience."

Smoke Shield shot Flying Hawk a thoughtful glance. *Yes, he's thinking the same thing I am. Screaming Falcon is no doubt a newly taken man's name. Who would this young war chief be?* There had been talk about a young man of uncommon promise. He was a friend of Biloxi Mankiller, the White Arrows' young high minko. Flying Hawk tried to remember the boy. It had been years since he had seen him. Bow Mankiller, of the Badger Clan, had been the lad's uncle, as well as the acclaimed tishu minko at White Arrow Town. The boy's mother had been Red Hair, an intelligent and attractive woman. But the boy . . . All Flying Hawk could remember was a scruffy-looking little urchin. Brown face, large eyes, skinny arms. Little boys all pretty much looked the same.

"Rise, good man." Flying Hawk made a gesture with his hand. The Albaamo man did, unease in his movement. Not many of his people liked being the subject of such close scrutiny by a high minko of the Sky Hand. "Do not fear," Flying Hawk added, his voice loud so that all could hear. "More than anything, we need the truth. If we do not know how this was done, we can't stop it from happening again."

"They will be saying that even their children can beat us at war," Smoke Shield groused, his jaw muscles flexing and jumping as his hot gaze cataloged the ruins.

"Screaming Falcon?" Flying Hawk repeated the name. "A very young man, recently named, which is why we have never heard of him. The White Arrows were grooming a boy for the chieftainship. Amber Stone? Was that his name?"

"That's it," Smoke Shield agreed. "From one of the White Arrow Moiety clans, as I recall. I remember him from when I was there last summer. The White Arrow brag about the sort of war chief he will be. It is said that this Amber Stone will marry the Chief Clan girl, Morning Dew, when she finally comes of age. Morning Dew is Matron Sweet Smoke's daughter." A thoughtful look cloaked his eyes. "The engagement has existed for some years."

One of the Albaamaha called out, "They bragged, High Minko! I heard them cry out that this was a wedding gift! That they would kill the last of their captives in celebration of Screaming Falcon's marriage!"

Smoke Shield stiffened, thunder behind his eyes. The tightening of his jaw made the scar on the side of his head twist into a terrible shape.

Flying Hawk said, "Sweet Smoke's son, Biloxi Mankiller, was made high minko last year, wasn't he?"

Smoke Shield appeared to get hold of himself. "I was there for his confirmation last summer. Remember? I thought him young, fat, and stupid. To get a man's name, it is said that he killed an old Biloxi slave. He reminds me of a dead fish."

"How's that?"

"Bloated with hot and stinky gas."

"It appears that he may have blown some of it our way." Flying Hawk pursed his lips as he considered the implications. He hadn't been paying as close attention as he should have been during these last moons. Instead his time had been taken up with the always-treacherous politics of the Albaamaha–Sky Hand alliance. It was a quagmire of factionalism, gamesmanship, and strategy that could easily consume a man.

Flying Hawk added, "You went with the delegation we sent to White Arrow Town when he was made high minko. You personally presented young Biloxi with our gifts. Did you think at the time he would be a threat, no matter how filled he was with himself?"

Smoke Shield frowned. "I thought Biloxi was a fool. It's partly Sweet Smoke's fault. She fawns too much over the boy. Kept him home instead of sending him out. She couldn't bear the thought that something might happen to him. He's never been out of the Horned Serpent Valley."

"So he judges the world by what he's been told." Dangerous. Most dangerous. "Did you spend time with him? Get a feel for how he thinks?"

"Sadly, no." Smoke Shield smiled sourly.

"Ah, yes, I remember the stories. You were more interested in the sister, this Morning Dew."

Smoke Shield gave an absent shrug, fixing his eyes on a smoldering pile of corn where a granary had collapsed.

Flying Hawk considered his nephew. "Liked her, did you?"

"She wanted nothing to do with me." Smoke Shield couldn't hide the narrowing of his eyes, or the sting of rejection that thinned his lips.

Ah, the stories were true. He was infatuated with the girl. Rumors were that Smoke Shield had been even more moody since his return from White Arrow Town. It was whispered that he'd come home preoccupied, some said obsessed.

"She only had eyes for Amber Stone." The scar that marred Smoke Shield's cheek seemed to writhe.

Smoke Shield had always been a plotter, enough so that it often occupied Flying Hawk's attention to the detriment of other pursuits. But, perhaps this time, if properly directed . . . "I have always worried about your passions, Nephew. Rage and anger can be of great value in life . . . provided they are channeled and balanced. If I give you this woman, this Morning Dew, can you find that balance?"

A faint smile curled Smoke Shield's lips, his calculating souls twisting like serpents behind his gleaming eyes. "We have been attacked, Uncle. Blood has been shed. Our kinsman, Stuffed Weasel, is being tortured to death even as we speak. We are obliged to strike back, to return the balance. The dead must be appeased. It is how Breath Maker created the world. If we leave this out of balance our souls will sicken. Power will drift away from us, focus itself on other peoples."

"Dare not to lecture me on the different ways Power is balanced in the world." He extended the heavy stone mace, resting the turkey-tail shaped head on Smoke Shield's shoulder. "How many warriors will you need to take White Arrow Town? How much time will it take to plan? When you strike, I want it to be swift, sure, and complete, not some botched raid where surprise is lost, our warriors are killed, and after a futile demonstration outside their walls, you just come home and declare victory."

Smoke Shield's gaze had fixed on one of the sprawled corpses; late-season flies were feeding greedily on the man's bare skull. "I can take them within the moon, Uncle. Provided that the Council will allow me to do this thing my way." A pause. "And if they will trust me with our people's war medicine."

Flying Hawk sucked pensively at his lower lip, his sidelong glance fixed on his nephew. *If he fails, if he loses the medicine, it will be a symbol to the Albaamaha, to the Chahta, the Yuchi, the Pensacola, and every other enemy we have that we are weak. The entire world will consider us broken, and pounce on us as if we were wounded rabbits.*

Smoke Shield reached up and touched the scar on the side of his head. "You talk of passion, Uncle? When it came upon me, at least I was smart enough not to murder my brother."

You tread on dangerous ground, Nephew. "Very well. If the Council allows, you will have your raid." His voice went hoarse. "And the medicine to accompany it."

Smoke Shield smiled in satisfaction.

Flying Hawk added, "You know what failure will mean to the people?"

Smoke Shield stepped over to the closest corpse and dropped to his knees. He ran his callused fingers over the blood-clotted skull. "We will all end up like this. Food for maggots and beetles." He looked up. "I am no war chief like the long-dead Makes War, to be captured and lose the war medicine. No, Uncle, as you shall see, I am very different."

From somewhere in the past, Flying Hawk could hear his murdered brother's eerie laughter.

Six

Trader faced a dilemma. He considered it as he sat on the bow of his beached canoe and watched sunset shine its last light on Red Wing Town. Wealth was a blessing, the thing of Dreams and ambition. At the same time, it was a terrible curse.

Red Wing Town was a large urban center that served some five thousand souls both within the town walls and from the outlying villages and farmsteads. It stood on a rise just back from the eastern bank of the Father Water. Surrounded by villages and cornfields, its high clay-coated palisade protected several platform mounds topped with grand buildings. There the High Oneota chiefs held sway, seeing to the comings and goings of the seasons, governing their subjects, attending to their wars, Trade, and ceremonials. Generations past, they had traveled north from Cahokia—refugees fleeing the Great Sun after losing a particularly bitter civil war. Rather than face eventual capture, humiliation, and death, they had paddled upriver, outrun the Great Sun's pursuit, and established themselves in the rich bottomlands.

As exiles, they had lived quietly at first, battling the local A'khota peoples and hacking a chiefdom out of what was essentially wilderness. They had built their great city above flood stage at the confluence of the Wild Rice River with the Father Water. Two mounds supported large palaces in which the rulers lived. Charnel houses, temples, and multiroomed society houses

choked the space between the plaza and the high walls
that surrounded the city.

Trader thoughtfully studied those distant walls as the
last rays of sunset bathed them in a mellow golden light
that contrasted with the purpling of the eastern sky. His
canoe was pulled up on the packed landing below the
city. Around him, tens of other canoes rested on the
stained sand. Most belonged to the Red Wing People,
and had been inverted atop sections of driftwood so that
rain wouldn't pool inside the hulls. Other boats, like his,
belonged to Traders and visiting A'khota who had come
to Trade, deliver tribute, seek redress for injustices, or
barter goods among the locals.

Trader used a long stick to prod at the small fire he'd
kindled. He fed it from a stack of driftwood he'd picked
up from the riverbank during his travels earlier that day.
Being familiar with Red Wing Town, he'd known that
wood was scarce for a distance in any direction from the
big city.

But what did he do about his dilemma? Here he was
comfortably seated, smoking a bowl of red willow bark
mixed with tobacco, his warm feather cloak about his
shoulders and a cheery fire at his feet. He shared the
company of Fox Down, a Trader from the Ockmulgee,
way off to the southeast. They had just finished a dinner
of fire-roasted fish and corn cakes. That was fine, but
just up the bank was Red Wing Town. He was a Trader,
hang it all, and that town up there was just bulging with
goods to inspect.

"You wish to go up there? Go," Fox Down said amiably. "I'll keep an eye on your packs." He was a thickset
man with bulging shoulders from years of paddling up
and down the great rivers. Tattoos covered his wide
face; the designs included starbursts, geometric lines,
and two shapes that looked like faded wings on his
cheeks. A buffalo robe hung over his shoulders and he
smoked a tubular stone pipe, its sides stained from years
of use. On his chest hung a gleaming pendant; a highly

stylized rattlesnake had been carved on the polished whelk shell.

Trader smiled. "I'm in a hurry. I just thought I'd spend the night here. That's all."

"You want to go up there. I can see it in your eyes," Fox Down said gently. "You're a Trader. Of course you want to go." He gestured with his pipe. "What have you got in that canoe, anyway? You've spent the summer up north? From the look of your packs, I'd say you've got bales of fine furs, maybe some spruce needles, copper if you're lucky, tool stone, and some other odds and ends."

Trader nodded, a prickling of worry gnawing at his spine. He tried to look unconcerned as he puffed at his pipe. "As a guesser, you're pretty good. Have you thought about spending your life as a Trader? I'd say you have a natural aptitude for this sort of thing."

Fox Down threw his head back and laughed. "For thirty-five winters I have been a Trader. I rotted well should have some idea how this works." The smile faded. "The gods alone know what I'd do if I couldn't do this. I can think of no fate more terrible than being stuck in one town, one valley, one river for the rest of my life."

"You're headed back now?" Trader was happy to change the subject. He pointedly avoided looking up at the town gates, though his souls ached to know what was happening up there. He could imagine the locals bartering colorful fabrics, finely wrought stone hoes, perhaps some great bargain like an Osage wood bow or a remarkably decorated buffalo hide. The desire to see was like an itch stuck between his souls.

"I'll keep an eye on your stuff," Fox Down reminded lightly. "I hate to see a man torturing himself so."

"I thought we were talking about whether you were headed back to the Ockmulgee lands."

Fox Down puffed at his pipe and grunted. Inspecting the bowl, he knocked the dottle out, fished in his belt pouch, and tamped a pinch of shredded narrow-leaf to-bacco into the bowl.

"Here." Trader left his stick in the flames long enough to catch it afire, then handed it across. Fox Down took a couple of draws and puffed out a blue wreath before handing the stick back.

"Thanks, Trader." He pulled at his pipe again and leaned his head back to blow a smoke ring toward the column of mosquitoes that had begun to form in the cool air. "Yes, I'll be headed back. I've been upriver for two winters now. Most of my load consists of furs. Winter hides Traded down from above the Freshwater Seas. The packs are pressed, tied tightly. If I can get them home without them getting wet and molding, it'll be worth a fortune."

"How will you go? Downriver to the Mother Water?"

"And then down the Tenasee to the Yuchi towns. Depending, of course, on whether I might Trade a bale of furs for a warm woman and a bed until the cold passes. Then I've only got two portages and a float downstream to the Ockmulgee country." He smiled as he saw it unfold in his souls' eye.

After a pause, Fox Down asked, "You?"

Trader poked at the fire with one hand and puffed at his pipe with the other, exhaled, and said, "I don't know. Maybe the Natchez Towns . . . maybe the Tunica. The Caddo nations would be ripe for northern goods. Especially some of the medicine plants."

And that was just the problem. He was sitting on a lifetime's wealth of copper—enough to ransom a chiefdom. So much wealth that people wouldn't think twice about murdering him for it. That fool Snow Otter couldn't have been blunter, offering food, his daughter, and every other excess in an effort to lull Trader off his guard. The shocked look Snow Otter's wife had given the man had been a dead giveaway.

So just where am I going to take this copper? Who am I going to Trade it to, and for what?

"Split Sky," Fox Down said softly, his knowing eyes on Trader.

"Split Sky?" The statement caught Trader by surprise.

"That's your accent, isn't it? How long since you've been back?"

Trader arched an eyebrow. How long had it been? "A lot of winters."

"You still have family there? Or did you slip your shaft into the high minko's daughter and have to leave in a hurry?"

Trader chuckled dryly. "Oh, I left in a hurry all right. Family? Yes." He pointed with his pipe stem. "And I swear on my blood and bile, I never laid a finger on the high minko's daughter. That was all a filthy lie meant to discredit me. Though I've heard she still searches for me, much to her husband's and clan's displeasure."

"Gods help us. If you're ever around my daughters, I'm sending them off to some old woman shaman in the forest."

Trader stared speculatively at his pipe. "I'm hurt. Cut to the bone."

"You're a lying, deceiving, overinflated raccoon, Trader." His grin faded. "Does it bother you, never being able to return?"

"What makes you think I can't return? That's not the only place I've driven women mad. Did I ever tell you about the time—"

"Something in your voice, Trader. But, if you ever need to get a message to anyone—say a brother, sister, your clan kin—I'd be happy to see to it. Sometimes it's good to know that old friends and family are still healthy and think about you."

"That's a kind offer." He stifled a yearning, ignoring the pain he'd borne for so many winters. "But actually, I can go back any time," he lied.

Fox Down grunted neutrally and glanced at the town walls—as purple now as the night. "You sure you don't want to just walk up there, see what's available?"

"No. Not tonight. I think I'll turn in, shove off with

first dawn, and make time headed south. Who knows how long the weather will hold. If I hurry, I can be fishing on the gulf shores by winter solstice."

Saying good night, he relieved himself at the river's edge and retired to his canoe. He was used to sleeping on his packs, and rolled himself in a buffalo robe, all the while listening to the hum of mosquitoes. A grease-based paste concocted of crushed larkspur, gumweed, and spruce needles kept the little beasts at bay.

If only the human bloodsuckers could be discouraged as easily. He fingered the war club that he now slept with. Taking a deep breath, he considered his strategy. No one with a huge amount of wealth—oh, a thick sheet of copper, let's say—would land his canoe at a major town like Red Wing. And if he did, no furtive Trader in possession of such a prize would just hang around the canoe landing, smoking, chatting with fellow Traders, and acting nonchalant.

Would he?

Trader made a face. He was nose to nose with the eternal human problem. Searching for wealth was always difficult. While finding it was hard enough, keeping it was even more perilous.

He shifted uneasily, remembering the kind twinkle in Fox Down's eyes. He'd known countless men like him during his years on the river, all taken with the Power of Trade, with the adventure of traveling the rivers. But for the copper, Trader wouldn't have thought twice about leaving his canoe under Fox Down's watchful eye while he walked up to inspect the goods available in Red Wing Town. Traders watched out for each other. It was part of the Power of Trade.

Or so he'd thought up until he'd seen that obsessive gleam fill Snow Otter's eyes.

So many years. Have I learned nothing about the twists and turns of men's souls?

With his free hand he reached up under the buffalo robe and patted the thick lump of stone-encrusted metal.

He'd wrapped it in layers of an old Caddo blanket and now used it for a pillow.

Images slipped through his souls: Treasures waited just inside the walls of Red Wing Town. Pretty young women were offering him gorgeously painted buffalo robes, ceramic jars full of Healing herbs, wooden statuary of Morning Star, Birdman, and Long-Nosed God. Strings of pearls were laid out on colorful blankets, and wonderful cloaks of soft beaver hide, muskrat, and wolverine literally begged him to Trade.

Yet there he lay, by himself, captive of a fortune in copper.

Gods, I'm the loneliest man alive.

The island Old White had chosen was little more than a lens of sand tossed up by the current. Along its length, willows had managed to catch a toehold. In their wake, cottonwoods had sprung up: young trees, little more than twice a man's height. Thick grass had carpeted the narrow strip, and now sagged, waiting for the frost to brown and dry it. A few straggling leaves still fluttered yellow on the cottonwood branches.

Old White had landed on a sandy beach halfway down the island, and had been grateful for Two Petals' help dragging the heavy canoe partway up the bank. Every muscle in her body ached, and she'd rubbed the rope burns as they had scavenged driftwood for the fire. Now, as night deepened and stars began to spot the sky, a cheerful blaze crackled.

Two Petals crouched by the fire, curious. What was Old White's purpose with her? Images spun between her souls. Fragments of Dreams and visions crowded her thoughts. Sometimes the voices that spoke to her out of the air left phrases that stuck. *"You have a destiny. Dance with the brothers, and make the world right."*

She cocked her head, staring off to the side. Just a moment ago, a huge black wolf had been standing there, watching her with glowing yellow eyes. When she finally blinked, it had vanished. From old experience, she knew that were she to go look, no tracks would be imprinted in the damp sand.

Old White extended his hands to the flames, sighing as if thankful for the heat. He sat with his back to a rotting log: an oak that some long-forgotten flood had deposited crossways on the sandy spit. He had his legs folded, back bent. The ornately carved wooden box he carried lay by his side. When he had placed the heavy fabric sack atop it, the wood had clunked, as if the bag's contents were stone. That was puzzle enough, but what could such a beautiful box contain? She stared at the carvings visible in the firelight. Some were winged snakes with horned heads, others panthers with circles adorning their bodies and legs. Pearls had been inlaid for eyes, and now they gleamed maliciously in the firelight.

Having warmed his knobby fingers Old White reached into his belt pouch. Squinting in the dancing yellow light, he used a chert flake to carve at a round section of whelk shell about the size of his palm.

Two Petals hunched beside the fire, checking the brownware pot that rested beside the flames. She kept peering in at the contents: cornmeal, sunflower seeds, bits of dried pumpkin, and meat from a small turtle who had lingered too late in the season before diving to the depths.

"Fast Palm was a poor war chief. No way he could have taken our town. Surely you didn't drive him off. Not an old man like you. Tell me you didn't use a weapon. Did you?" she asked.

Old White smiled. "An herb. Comes from the far southwest. I came to appreciate it when I lived with the Azteca."

"Oh, them. Lots of Azteca around, yes?" He used so many names she'd never heard before.

"A people way down in the south." He paused, looking up from his carving, an expression of amazement on his face. "You wouldn't believe. They make temples out of stone. Pyramids taller than the highest of our mounds. Well, maybe not Cahokia, but stunning nevertheless. I went there, ventured into their lands in the company of the Pochteca."

"My father had Pochteca. Two of them in his pack."

"Traders."

She was suddenly confused, seeing little people in her father's pack. "How did they fit inside there?"

"They don't come here." He smiled. "We have nothing they want."

She made a scoffing noise. "Everyone wants something that someone else has. Like the way you bested Fast Palm."

"It's a powder called chili. In the southwest it is used as a food. It's hot. Like beeweed, only hotter. I blew a pinch of it into Fast Palm's face."

"Not Power?"

"Of a sort, I suppose."

She caught him studying her from under his brows. "What?"

"You're speaking more plainly. Can you control it? Or does it just come upon you?"

"It comes and goes. Goes and comes. Dancing like butterflies wiggling through the mud. Charms glitter in the sunlight," she answered softly, using a stick to stir the contents of the pot. "Sometimes I'm riding a log over a waterfall. I just hang on and hope that when I finally hit the bottom, the foam will be soft."

She waited for that look of irritation and disbelief. He only nodded, intent once again on his carving. He fascinated her. Since the night when Power first came to her, she'd trusted no one. This man, however, hadn't looked at her with revulsion, fear, or disgust. Not once. Even when she turned, talking back to one of the voices, or staring at the sudden apparitions that formed out of midair. When the Power was flowing through her like a spring current, he listened, and even seemed to understand.

"These Azteca, did you see them?"

"I did."

She hesitated. "Were they real? Did they leave prints in the dirt?"

"Yes."

"They didn't vanish?"

"No. They are real people. I went to see them."

"Why?"

"To see if the stories were true."

"Were they?"

He looked up. "Until you have seen, you would never believe."

"I believe everything. It helps."

"I'm sure it does."

"Where else have you been?"

"Everywhere." The word carried the weight of the world.

"Why?"

In the firelight, she could see sadness cross his face. "I was looking for the end of the world."

"Did you find it?"

"Yes." A pause. "No."

After a longer silence, he said, "It depends on the direction you go. In the east, the ocean washes the land. Those who have tried to sail out on it say it goes on forever. Few who have sailed out beyond the horizon have ever returned. But there are rumors. Among the Chumash, on the western ocean, they tell of Traders who venture in from across the sea. The Chumash say they learned to build their plank canoes from these people. And up among the Pequot, I have personally seen a man, his skin white, like the best tanned leather, and hair all over his face. He was the only survivor of a huge wooden canoe. I have seen some of the pieces of wood the Pequot kept. Supposedly there is a land far across the eastern ocean. I have never gone that far."

"And to think people tell me I am full of wild tales." At his disapproving glance she asked, "Well, these Azteca, are they at the end of the earth?"

"They told me of still more peoples, and more peoples beyond them. In the north, I learned of distant peoples clear up to the eternal ice."

"You really went all those places?"

He nodded.

She desperately wanted to ask why, but countered with, "I thought the earth had ends."

"So did I. Once." He shifted, turning his piece of shell toward the firelight. She could barely see the etching he was making.

"Do you know what that's going to be?"

"A gorget."

"And the drawing?"

"A rendition of our world. The outer circle is the Sky World; the pole in the center is the Tree of Life. The lower circle is the Below World."

Her curiosity was piqued. "And you've been to these places?"

He shook his head slowly. "Only in my Dreams."

That she understood. The things that popped up in her Dreams—sleeping and awake—were startling enough. She wrapped her long black hair in a nervous twist. "Then why are you drawing it?"

"Because it's the world my people have always believed in. Sometimes illusions are comforting. They are familiar in the way an old blanket is. You find comfort from it because your parents did before you. You think it will always keep you warm, even though the threads are frayed and it's full of holes. Still, you pull it around you in the blackness of the coming storm, assuring yourself it will keep you safe—and all the while the first sprinkles of freezing rain are stinging your skin with the certainty that it is no longer the protection you once thought it was."

She used a doubled fold of cloth to move the pot back from the flames. "You're a strange man."

"Perhaps that's why I was drawn to you."

Power shifted, surged. It seemed to rise from the ground, to pulse in the air around her. It leaped with the firelight, and Sang with the breeze in the cottonwoods. Her heart skipped, then stopped dead in her breast. Breath caught in her throat. No, not now. Please. Not right at this moment. She closed her eyes, knotting her fists. Breath by breath, she made herself breathe deeply and calmly. Only when she was sure it was past did she open her eyes.

Old White was giving her an evaluative stare.

"I'm all right," she said warily. "It comes and goes. Mostly I can't control it."

"The greater the gift, the more hideous the curse," he said in answer.

"What was your curse?"

"A mixture of love and justice."

Though a thousand questions crowded her tongue, his tone of voice left her mute. Pain and regret seemed to ride his shoulders like a too-heavy blanket. The lines in his face, the lack of any tattoos or ear spools, all bespoke a life interrupted.

Who is this man? And why did he come for me?

"All in due time," he whispered softly.

Seven

Transporting furs was always problematic. Moisture was the enemy. When brain-tanned furs grew damp, circles of fungus would creep into the leather. Hair slipped and fell out by the handfuls. Any strength and resilience the hides might have had vanished. Smoking during the tanning process helped, but a thorough and comprehensive smoking took as much as a moon. Few of the northern tanners bothered with that. After all, why invest that kind of time when another pine marten was as close as the next forest.

Trader, however, was taking his two packs of expensive furs south. He scowled up at the misty rain that trickled down from the gray skies and low clouds. It came in spiraling stringers of mist, curling downward to chill and soak the river. It landed on the leaf-bare trees, collecting to drip on the soft forest floor. Patterns of it fell on the smooth roiling waters, only to be whisked away as the current eddied and sucked.

The world seemed to hunker down. The thick forest lining both sides of the river looked sodden and miserable. Even sound had disappeared, damped and heavy, gone to earth with the cascading droplets of water. The few birds Trader saw were perched on limbs, feathers ruffled, heads tucked low on their shoulders. This was the kind of day that even fish stayed undercover.

Trader glanced at his two packs of furs. He had fashioned a birch-bark cover for both, beneath which was a waxed leather sack that would divert any leaks. The furs had been pressed using leverage from a log that pivoted on a fulcrum, then had been tightly bound into a square bundle with double-knotted basswood rope. The packs rested on two aspen branches laid side by side on the canoe bottom to keep them out of shallow water and allow air to circulate. It had been raining for hours. A pool had collected in the canoe bottom.

Trader used his finger to measure the depth of the water. It reached up to his first knuckle.

Shipping his paddle, he bent and used a ceramic jar to scoop and bail until it was no longer worth the effort.

"Hope this breaks," he muttered as he took up the paddle and corrected his course for the center of the current. He had been making good time, but then traveling downriver seemed like flying after the hard paddle upstream.

As he rounded one of the endless bends in the river, the forest gave way to a clearing on the eastern shore; several small farmsteads dotted the now-brown fields. Blue wreaths curled from the smoke holes, seeming to flatten against the endless drizzle. Four canoes had been pulled up on a landing where the bank had collapsed on the downstream end of the clearing. They looked disconsolate, crudely made from hollowed logs, unlike his sleek birch-bark vessel. No one was about— not that he'd have expected them to be given the conditions. It was only fit weather for idiotic Traders traveling late in the season. As quickly, the farmstead fell behind.

Trader sighed, imagining the friendly fires, and how warm and dry the interiors of those lodges were. A pot of deer or perhaps turkey stew would have been boiling, sending a warm aroma to combat the chill air.

His thoughts were thusly occupied when a shout from shore caught him by surprise.

"Greetings, Trader!"

He turned, seeing two men, each dressed in a wolfhide cloak with a bark rain hat on his head. They carried bows, fletched arrows filling the quivers on their backs. Their thick trail moccasins and leggings looked soaked.

"Greetings yourself," Trader called back in pidgin. He backed water, sending his canoe toward their bank. He stopped several body lengths from shore. Traders were protected, guarded by the Power of the Trade, but one still didn't take any chances.

"Have you seen a dog?" one of the men asked.

"In my travels, I have seen many. But I suppose you are asking about a particular dog?"

"We chased him into the river," the second man said. "He dove underwater."

"He's a demon dog," the first asserted. "Since he showed up three days ago, hanging around our village, we've had nothing but misfortune. His feet turn into hands at night. Nothing else could explain how he can open our corn granary. He was seen in the night, stalking through one of our houses. The following morning, Old Root was found dead, eyes wide open, and crossed."

"Any dog that dives underwater can't be normal," the second man insisted.

"No, I'd say not," Trader agreed.

"We thought to warn you, lest the demon dog leap out of the water and attack you. No one expects to have his throat ripped out by some water-borne mongrel."

Trader considered the stories of tie snakes and Horned Serpents he'd first heard in his youth. Few people doubted the existence of water cougars, either. Deep water was the home of numerous monsters. "Personally, I've never been troubled by the things that live underwater. But I shall be careful." He hesitated. "How shall I know this demon dog?"

"Black, with some brown, a white face and chest. Long hair, long pointy nose like a fox. You'll see a glow in his eyes, like red embers in a fire."

Trader nodded. "I shall be on my guard."

"Where to, Trader?" the first asked.

"Far south. Perhaps all the way to the salt water."

"You've several moons of travel ahead of you yet. And it's not that far to solstice."

"I know. Peace and health to you."

"Beware the demon dog!" the second man warned. "He'll steal your packs."

Trader allowed himself to chuckle when he'd drifted out of the hunters' sight. Demon dogs? What next?

He glanced at the somber waters around him. The current seemed to flex, sending his canoe headlong down the channel. After his years on the rivers, reading the current was almost second nature. Today, the water was dark green, like a fine translucent chert. It fooled the eye with the illusion that one could see through it, but stole detail when a person peered into its depths.

Surely there was no dog down there. He took another look into the dark green, half expecting the shadow figure of a dog to be stalking him down there in the depths.

"You're being silly as a stone-struck loon." He shook his head, returning his attention to the river ahead. He kept an easy rhythm, stroking along, dragging the paddle blade for a rudder. He always sought to move faster than the current, keeping steerage, making time as fast or faster than most men could run. But for the oxbows, bends, and twists, he could have made the gulf in less than a moon. As it was, the river wound back on itself in a serpentine path.

As he rounded one of the interminable bends, he spotted a twirling raft of driftwood in the current. While such hazards to navigation were thick during spring flood, they were rare this late in the season. He closed on it, figuring to pass well clear to the left.

That's when he saw a streak of white at the edge of the thicket of floating branches. It flowed up from the dog's chest, bordered in damp brown and wet black. A button point of a nose tipped the long muzzle. Pricked triangular ears were laid back. Soft brown eyes met his with an unmistakable supplication. Adding to the unhappy illusion, the dog shivered so hard droplets flew from his ears.

The demon dog?

"You look anything but demonic," Trader called as he backed water, slowing to the floating driftwood's speed.

Barely audible in the sodden air, a soft whine carried to him. Trader raised his paddle, figuring to bypass the whole affair, but when he did, the dog let out a yelp and pushed away from the driftwood float. He began swimming madly downstream, using the current to make as much distance as possible from the canoe.

Trader followed as closely as he dared, watching the long black hair on the dog's back flow back and forth like midnight moss. The animal was panting, shivering, and clearly running out of strength.

"They said your paws turned into hands," Trader remarked neutrally. "That true?"

The panicked dog paddled harder.

Trader frowned. This was scarcely the sort of beast that would leap out of the river and rip his throat out. Was that his imagination, or was the dog's head lower in the water?

The animal went under, pulled down by a sucking whirlpool that spun off to the side. When the nose broke surface, the dog tried to sneeze and cough, only to flounder again. Then he thrashed in panic, choking and coughing as he was sucked down.

Impulse overcame reservation. Trader reached out, grabbed a handful of fur behind the animal's neck, and lifted. The dog wasn't that big, but his thick fur was logged with water. The canoe rocked as Trader found the right balance and dragged the dripping beast over the gunwale.

With one hand he reached for his war club, a wicked copper-bitted thing more handy for close quarters. Rather than try and smack the dog with the long paddle, Trader could easily brain him with a short stroke of the war club if he lunged at him. The dog staggered to his feet, sneezing, coughing, and shivering out of control. He gave

Trader one terrified glance through glazed eyes, arched his back, and threw up.

Trader glanced at the shivering cur, then at the pitiful bits of leather, splinters of charred bone, moldy pumpkin husk, and yellow bile.

The dog licked his pointy nose, looked up, and cowered back in horror.

"That's all you've got in your stomach?"

The dog continued to shiver, staring up with terrified eyes.

Dangerous? Still, one could never tell. A demon dog, drowning in the middle of the river, wouldn't want to come across as an immediate threat. No, he'd want to lure an unsuspecting Trader into a false sense of security before he leaped up to sink fangs in a man's throat.

The canoe was drifting sideways, spinning lazily out of the current. Trader lowered his war club, extending his paddle to right his course. The dog cowered in anticipation of a blow.

Trader considered as he stroked his way back to the center of the current. "If you're truly a demon dog, you can understand human speech. So you should know, you're not acting like a good demon dog should. Or is it that you're a really poor specimen of a terrible demon? Is that why you've only got old garbage—and not much of it at that—in your stomach?"

The dog's head lowered, ears pinned back. The soft brown eyes reminded him of worried wet pebbles.

Trader satisfied himself with his course, and reached down with the ceramic cup. The dog scrambled backward, trying to make himself small and invisible against the closest pack. Trader scooped up as much of the dog's goo as he could. He washed the cup out over the side and scooped up some more of the spreading stain. Fortunately water drained out of the dog's thick fur fast enough to help keep the mess in place. With each movement, the dog cringed as if trying to sink through the canoe bottom.

Trader replaced his bailing cup and cocked his head. Out of the water, his coat soaked, the thing looked like a collection of walking bones. Ribs, hips, and spine stuck out, while the belly made a hollow behind the ribs.

"I have to say, for a tricky demon, you haven't been eating well."

The dog blinked frightened eyes.

"Oh, blood and piss," Trader exclaimed, the dog cowering back at the tone.

Trader reached into a leather sack beside him and drew forth a slab of dried venison. "Here." He bit off a piece and spit it onto the canoe bottom in front of the dog.

The pointed nose quivered, ears slowly rising. A fit of shivering barely distracted the animal, and a thin filament of drool appeared at the corner of his mouth. Still the wary eyes remained fixed on Trader.

"It's all right," he said gently. "I think you're starving."

Hunger overcame the dog's good sense. With deliberate care, he reached out and plucked up the morsel. The jerky vanished in a wolfish gulp. To Trader's surprise, the tail thumped twice.

For the next hand of time, Trader alternately chewed on his jerky and shared it with the shivering dog. The thing was ravenous. Nor did he ever snap, growl, or show so much as a whit of the glowing eyes the two hunters had described.

"What do I call you? Everything has to have a name," Trader told the dog. The shivers had stopped as the dog's stomach filled. The continuing drizzle ensured that his coat wasn't going to dry out anytime soon.

"I don't think calling you Demon Dog would go over well." He imagined them pulling up at the Four Lance Town landing. "Greetings, I am called Trader. And this is Demon Dog." He could see the suddenly grim faces, then *Thwok! Smack!* He could hear the sounds as a worried local drove an ax through the dog's skull. Trader would probably feel more than hear the crack of his own head, unaware that another frightened individual had sneaked up behind him while he was talking.

People took things like demons much too seriously.

"Just like at that village back there." He paused, trying to fit the pathetic beast crouched in his canoe with the story told by the hunters. "Let's say that you showed up just as they had a little bad luck. Sometimes that happens. Traders are particularly wary of it. We always find an excuse and leave if someone comes down sick." He took another sweep with the paddle. "Of course, we're protected by the Power of Trade. People know that in return for protection while inside their borders, we won't witch them. And if we ever learn of anyone using the Trade as a means of covering witchcraft, we'll kill them outright."

He glanced down at the dog. "Which means, if you really are a demon dog, I won't put up with any wickedness on your part."

The dog watched him, ears up, head slightly cocked.

"So, how did you get to that village back there?" He watched the trees break to expose another farmstead. It consisted of three bark-sided, round-roofed houses in a cultivated clearing on the high bank. This settlement, too, seemed to huddle beneath a haze of blue smoke, its people inside to avoid the cold and wet.

"You don't look like a wild dog. And if you'd been from any of the surrounding villages, someone would have noticed you. You don't see many dogs around with your colors. Most are some combination of brown and white. Black is rare."

He tossed another piece of jerky to the dog.

"Which brings us back to a name." He ran a series of them past his souls. He-Who-Escapes-Underwater? No. It would get shortened to Under. Besides who ever named a dog Underwater? People would think he was a fish. Escaper? Maybe. Rotted Lucky? Now there was a fitting name. But for the dog's rotted luck, he'd have been sucked under and drowned. No, he'd known too many Traders' dogs called Lucky. And looking at the soggy and cold cur, he sure hadn't been living up to any kind of luck recently.

"Swimmer." It just seemed to pop out of his head. "Yes, you were sure a swimmer. Even if you were almost at the end of your string, you got away from those two superstitious farmers. Now, me, I'd bet when you jumped in the river, one of those little whirlpools that form around the bank sucked you under. Just like that last moment before I fished you out."

Swimmer was listening closely, ears pricked.

"Who knows, maybe you even pulled that raft of driftwood loose from the bank somewhere while trying to get out." He emphasized it with the paddle. Swimmer flinched. "As long as you didn't get too cold, that raft would have put you ashore sooner or later. I've known Traders who capsized their canoes who just hung onto the gunwales until the current dropped them close to shore."

He gestured toward the towering trees crowding the riverbank. The river here was little more than a long bow shot across. "The channel is relatively narrow. It doesn't seem like it, but wait until you get downriver. At times all you can see is water. Now, down there in the south, getting cast loose in the current becomes a bit more dicey. Why, I wouldn't doubt but that this old Father Water might sweep you right out into the gulf."

He grinned down. "Am I talking too much?"

Swimmer didn't answer, his brown eyes pools of worry.

"I suppose I am." Trader sighed. "I haven't had anyone to talk to for a long time. Well, but for the Trade. The point I'm making is that there's no one to talk to while I'm on the river. There's myself, of course, but somehow I always win the arguments. Oh, I know. I could have done something about it. Fact is, I had a dog once for almost three moons." He shook his head. "There was just something about Rascal. I'd swear he had stone for a brain. Some dogs just don't learn. Have you noticed that?"

Apparently Swimmer hadn't, because his expression didn't change.

"Village dogs got him and tore him up down at Winter Town on the lower river. I warned old Rascal, told him not to leave the canoe." Trader made a throwing-away motion with one hand. "Never could break him of the habit of chewing on the packs, either."

Trader glanced up at the graying skies. "Well, night is coming. What do you say that we put in? We'll make us a camp with a fire and cook up something. I've got corn cakes dry in a pack somewhere. Then we'll see if you're still around in the morning."

Swimmer's tail slapped the wet hull twice.

"And if you try to witch me, or do any demon things, you'll get the sharp edge of my club."

Swimmer dropped his nose onto his paws.

"Demon dog," Trader muttered. "Just my luck."

Eight

Smoke Shield closed his eyes as Thin Branch applied the last dabs of brilliant red color. Smoke Shield enjoyed the soothing sensations of Thin Branch's fingers carefully smoothing the paint over his forehead. He took a deep breath, letting the tension seep from his tight muscles, and tried to ignore the ramifications of the coming Council.

"Feel better?" Thin Branch asked in his accented tongue. He was Koasati by birth. As a child he had been captured in a retaliatory raid down on the Albaamaha River. Smoke Shield had passed but eight winters when Uncle Flying Hawk presented Thin Branch to him as a gift. They had been together since.

"Yes. Gods, I could just lie back and sleep."

"Liar."

Smoke Shield smiled. "How do I look?"

"Marvelous. Power rides with you. Your mixture of the colors was extraordinary."

Smoke Shield opened his eyes, glanced at Thin Branch to read satisfaction in his expression, then climbed to his feet. They had been seated on one of the double-knotted rush mats in the palace great room. The high stool with its cougarhide covers stood before the back wall. Behind it, a huge copper relief of Eagle Man hung from the wall. So, too, did old shields—war trophies from Flying Hawk's colorful exploits in combat. Mixed with them were assorted masks, some carved from wood, others from whelk shell, and a few from gourd husks. Each had been painted to accent the features of the Spirits, gods, and sacred beings they represented: Old Woman, Long-Nosed God, Horned Serpent, Eagle Man, Morning Star, and lesser beings.

Thin Branch handed him his palette—a round sandstone disk, its border scalloped and bounded by three thin lines that represented the worlds of Creation. A man's palette was one of his most precious possessions. Creating colors was a sacred process, akin to the Creation of the worlds. Colors were not only an affirmation of life, but by their very nature attracted and concentrated different types of Power. White symbolized order, goodness, reflection, and peace. War, chaos, creativity, and struggle lived in the color red. Blue and purple were the sky colors, symbolic of air and the Above World, domain of birds, thunder, and the cloud beings. Yellow was that of healing and growth, while brown became death, corruption, and the Underworld with its creatures. Black was the color of mourning—of nighttime and the creatures that prowled it.

With the application of colors, a man's souls could attract the essences of those Powers to him, incorporate them, share them for whatever task was at hand. In this case, Smoke Shield was preparing for a war council. He had chosen red for his forehead, lower cheeks, and chin. The tattooed bar across his upper cheeks and the bridge of his nose was rendered in black, the forked-eye tattoos around his eyes were in a pale gray, while a single blue line ran down from his lower lip to his chin, homage to the justice of his cause in instigating war, and the risks that such behavior entailed. Three large white beads cut from the columella—or center swirl of a whelk shell—hung from his forelock.

"I think it is time," Thin Branch said, hearing Flying Hawk's brisk steps from down the hallway that led to the back.

Smoke Shield swung his arms to loosen them, slipped his palette into its wooden box, and slung his triangular white apron around his hips. He tied it securely, and checked to make sure the long point of it hung down straight between his knees. Finally, he reached into a cedar-wood box and removed three small white arrows. He admired them for a moment. Each had been bestowed as a token of honor for his exploits as a warrior. Among the Sky Hand People, no greater honor could be granted to a warrior. Smoke Shield was slipping the last one into his hair as Flying Hawk strode into the room.

"Ready?" his uncle asked, giving him a thorough scrutiny. Flying Hawk had dressed himself in a similar white apron, the center of it decorated with an elaborate eye-in-hand motif. His face had been carefully painted: The black bar tattooed across his cheeks had been darkened with charcoal; bright hematite-red covered the rest of his face with the exception of a thin black line running straight down his forehead, nose, mouth, and chin—a symbol of the grief he expressed for those so ruthlessly slain at Alligator Village. He wore his heavy copper hairpiece: an arrow splitting a cloud. No less than eight of the small white arrows had been laced into his greased hair.

"Ready." Smoke Shield reached for a copper-headed war club and gestured for Flying Hawk to precede him.

As they left the room, Thin Branch began replacing Smoke Shield's paints in their small wooden case. As he did, he gently Sang the ritual song of thanks for the Powers imparted by the colors.

"Have you given thought to your words?" Flying Hawk asked as they walked out into the morning. Golden sunlight spilled out of the southern sky and cast a lattice of shadows from the high palisade that surrounded the mound top upon which they walked. To either side of the palace entrance, two guardian posts had been carved into the shape of watching eagles, beaks painted yellow, their eyes black and shining. The outline of intricately feathered wings had been carved in the sides, as if they draped possessively around the poles.

Two steep stairways descended from the gated heights: the Star Stairs to the north, and the Sun Stairs to the east. Hawk led them to the latter, passing through the heavy oak gate and descending the worn wooden steps. Split Sky City spread around them. It thrived as its people went about their daily lives, some walking or packing loads, others pounding corn in hollow mortars. The sound of shrieking children mingled with flute music. Wreaths of blue smoke bent off to the south, borne by the fall breeze. Hundreds of houses lined the plaza, their gray roofs stippling the ground beneath the city's high wooden walls. The slanted morning light gave them a slightly hazy look as it passed through the moist air.

Two bow shots to the east, the tishu minko's tall palace gleamed in the sunlight atop its steeply pitched earthen mound. The thatched roof, replaced but a half moon ago, still reflected a golden hue as it pointed skyward. High atop the ridgepole the wooden guardians—shaped in the form of raccoons and rattlesnakes, freshly painted—glared out at the world.

At the bottom of the Sun Stairs, Smoke Shield and Flying Hawk turned right to cross the beaten clay of the chunkey ground. As they neared the tall center pole with its red and white spirals, both men knelt, inclining their heads in recognition of the Tree of Life that speared up from the Underworld, through this world, and into the sky.

Straightening, they pursued their path past the Tree of Life toward the elongated oblong of the tchkofa. The structure topped a rectangular mound oriented toward the lunar maximum where it rose on the northeastern horizon every eighteen and a half winters. A wide wooden stairway led up a ramp to the palisaded summit. Behind the log walls, the tchkofa's three rounded roofs could be seen; the taller middle roof reminded Smoke Shield of a squatting turtle behind a line of reeds. The smaller humps were the attached moiety houses.

He and Flying Hawk bowed to the effigy poles planted

in the earth on either side of the stairway; both had been carved into falcons, the heads painted gray, beaks yellow, and eye bars black. Their eyes, made of polished shell, seemed to glare malevolently.

"See into our souls, Grandfathers," Flying Hawk greeted the totems. "Should you carry our words to the Above World, know that we speak only the truth."

Smoke Shield took a breath as he placed his foot on the first step and began the ascent. At the top of the stairs stood two warriors, human versions of the falcon guards right down to the designs painted on their faces and the falcon-feather capes around their shoulders. They nodded and tugged on their warrior's forelocks, a token of respect for their high minko.

Flying Hawk nodded in return, and Smoke Shield followed as he led the way through the portal. The small courtyard sprouted additional totems, heads carved from the tops of the upright logs. Here the turkey-tail mace represented the Chief Clan, while Raccoon, Panther, and Crawfish Clans filled out the Hickory Moiety on the east. The carved effigies on the west were occupied by Skunk, Hawk, Fish, and Deer totems, each perfectly carved and painted, their expressions vigilant.

The path between them led to the narrow doorway that opened into the great structure.

The tchkofa consisted of a great round dome, with smaller earth lodges attached at each end by means of a short covered hallway. The smaller rooms were used when moiety business needed to be discussed in private. Hickory Moiety's chamber lay to the north, Old Camp's to the south.

"This is it," Smoke Shield said under his breath.

"You'll do fine," Flying Hawk told him with a smile, reaching out to pat his shoulder before ducking into the cavelike passage.

Smoke Shield placed a hand to his breast in an effort to still his pounding heart; then he followed behind his uncle.

After the pure sunshine, the effect was like entering a pit. A low babble of voices went silent as Flying Hawk walked through the gloom to a stout wooden stool covered with cougar hides. It stood in the northern curve of the big earth-covered building. Smoke Shield fought the urge to squint and followed from long practice, trusting Uncle not to trip over something, or someone.

The place smelled smoky, perfumed with red cedar wood. As he passed one of the thick pine roof supports, his fingers traced the polished wood. How many fingers like his had caressed that same post, seeking reassurance in their passage? Without embarrassing himself he took his position behind Uncle's right shoulder.

Thick logs supported the heavy roof. Stout cane poles had been laid for walls, the whole then covered with earth. Clay had been used to plaster the interior, and then painted in red and white pigments, the colors of chaos and order. To the north—just before the entrance to the Hickory Moiety hall—a clay altar, two paces long, and hip high, had been built. Upon this rested a large red cedar box made of perfectly joined wood. The outside was carved with the hand-eye symbol of the people, the eye rendered in copper with a large section of whelk shell for the pupil. In relief to either side, S-shaped images of Winged Serpent seemed to guard the seeing hand.

The sacred fire burned brightly in the tchkofa's open center. Smoke Shield focused on it as his eyes began to adjust. The clay hearth contained four logs laid out north to south, east to west, their joined ends afire. He touched the shell gorget on his chest. Engraved in its concave surface was an image of Spider. The cross carved in the middle of its back represented the Sacred Fire taken from Father Sun. According to the story, no other animal had been able to bring fire back to a dark and unfriendly earth. Opossum had tried to carry it in his furry tail, but it caught fire; which was why to this day, his tail was hairless. When Vulture flew up to the Sky World, he placed fire on his head; and to this day his failure was marked by red, blistered-looking skin. Many-colored Crow made the next attempt, but the fire had scorched his feathers, which left crows eternally black. It was Spider who spun a web, and thus was able to tow fire back to earth. For that reason, Spider continued to build its web in the shape of sunlight.

The sacred fire burned constantly, fed day and night by careful hands. Each summer, with the ripening of the green corn, the most important ceremony in the Sky Hand world was held. After four days of purification, all fires were extinguished throughout the land. Then, one by one, they were relit throughout Split Sky City and the Sky Hand territory. Each blaze was rekindled using fire carried directly from the tchkofa's sacred fire.

The only time in memory when the fire had gone out had been in his grandmother's time. The disaster occurred the same night as a destructive fire that had razed the high minko's palace. Since then, the sacred fire had been burning, a supply of wood constantly at hand. Smoke Shield glanced at Flying Hawk. It was said that someone had extinguished the Sacred Fire that terrible night when the high minko's palace burned. It was also said that from that night, trouble had continued to brew, that it had led to Flying Hawk killing his twin brother.

Smoke Shield couldn't stop himself from fingering the scar on the side of his head, remembering, wondering if the events of the past continued to spiral down through the present.

Before the fire, atop a small altar, stood the Eagle Pipe with its long stem. Carved from pink granite, the pipe depicted Eagle Man, a combined image of human, eagle, and snake. He crouched, wings to the side, his hair pulled into a tight round bun atop his head. His mouth was open, eyes staring out from inside their forked design. The center of the image's back had been hollowed for the bowl; a stem as long as a man's leg protruded from behind.

As his vision improved, Smoke Shield could see most

of the tchkofa's occupants were staring pensively at Flying Hawk and him. Others were talking to their neighbors in low voices. The leaders of the Sky Hand clans had been called here by a crier dispatched by the tishu minko, and had each come with his own deputy, generally a brother or favored nephew in the line of descent for rulership.

Five men and one woman, they had arrived prior to their high minko's entrance, as was respectful and polite. Two Albaamaha, both moiety elders, had also been summoned. They had taken places beyond the circle, and stood as was custom, their hands clasped before them. Their faces might have been carved from wood, for all the emotion they displayed.

But they shall have their day. They have grown too arrogant over the winters.

Immediately to Smoke Shield's left sat the tishu minko: Seven Dead Mankiller. His younger brother, Blood Skull Mankiller, knelt just behind his right shoulder. Leaders of the Raccoon Clan, their voices would be critical to the coming discussions. Once the Raccoon and Chief Clans had been close, often marrying to solidify their ties, but that had changed when Flying Hawk had been a boy. That rift, too, was said to have started the night of the fire.

Seven Dead Mankiller had seen nearly thirty winters, and he carried himself with the demeanor that an often-bloodied warrior should. His dark eyes gleamed in the firelight, gravity in his straight posture. Blood Skull, his younger brother, was known to oppose Flying Hawk. He was wedded to the betterment of his clan, and he'd always been suspicious of Smoke Shield's motives. More than once Smoke Shield had seen Blood Skull sneaking around, and once the man had almost caught Smoke Shield in the arms of a married woman—which would have brought disaster and disgrace.

Someday, old enemy, when I am confirmed high minko, you will rue the day you crossed me.

Panther Clan had the only female representation. Night Star was remarkable, not only for her sex, but for her size. Despite having passed more than fifty winters, her head barely reached as high as a normal man's belt. Being a dwarf imbued a person with great Power, but in Night Star's case, her shrewd head had only added to her prestige and authority. She had never taken a husband, fearing what might ensue should she become pregnant. Her reputation for celibacy had given her an advantage in the world of clan politics. She wore her gray hair in a tight bun, more a male fashion than female.

Beside her, Pale Cat had his eyes fixed on the fire. He was her nephew, a thin man with Dreamy eyes, and the most Powerful *Hopaye* in Hickory Moiety. In addition to being a Priest, he was Smoke Shield's first wife's brother. They had never thought much of each other— Pale Cat having opposed Smoke Shield's marriage to Heron Wing. Because Smoke Shield spent as little time as possible with Heron Wing—especially after the birth of her son—avoiding each other's company was relatively easy.

Pale Cat wore a gauzy white robe decorated with images of tie snakes, Horned Serpent, and the hand-eye design. A single thin green snake was wrapped around his right hand. It was said that the little serpent whispered the secrets of magical cures to him, and often traveled with Pale Cat when he sent his souls flying through portals into the other worlds.

The man called Wooden Cougar was the head of Crawfish Clan, known as the finest weavers within Split Sky City. While for the most part a congenial sort, Wooden Cougar could on occasion become obstinate and surly. For reasons of his own, he'd take an uncompromising stand over the silliest of causes. A weak leader, perhaps he just needed to dig his feet in on occasion to prove his mettle.

Beyond his sometimes obstinate nature, no one understood Trade better than Wooden Cougar, unless it was his nephew, Cleft Skull. Cleft Skull, too, deceived. As a child he had been struck in the head with a thrown rock that had left a dent in the left side of his head. While he sometimes stuttered, and had trouble finding words, his skill at keeping track of goods was unexcelled. When it came to calculating the benefits of war, Cleft Skull would be one to win over.

Old Camp Moiety was seated to Smoke Shield's right. First came Vinegarroon. Named for the dark creature that lived under logs, he was as ugly as his namesake. Nearly as wide as he was tall, with a pockmarked face, broad froglike mouth, and protruding eyes, he wore an alligator cape over his shoulders, the skinned head sewn on backward to hang down over his spine. He said the Spirit of the slain beast told him when anyone tried to slip up unannounced behind him. Long scars ran up and down his right leg, received in a battle with the bull gator whose hide he now wore.

But as formidable as Vinegarroon looked, he liked to spend his time with children and elders. His laughter could shake trees when he heard a bawdy joke, and his appetite was the thing of legend. It was said he once ate an entire deer during a solstice feast, and the doing of it took him but a single night. Some thought he stored extra food in his oversize genitals. Perhaps that was the secret of his large brood. His five wives had borne him twenty-four children so far, and three more were on the way.

His brother, Fire Wing, had been sired by a different father after Vinegarroon's was drowned in an accident. While he shared some of Vinegarroon's features, he was a great deal easier on the eye. With a high forehead, his hair slicked with grease, and sporting an eagle-tail hairpiece, he had deep-set but unfocused eyes. His sharp cheekbones gave his face a triangular effect that emphasized his pursed mouth. He was the quiet one, slow but methodical in his approach to problems.

Hawk Clan sat in the next position, and Black Tail, the *Hopaye,* was an old man, white haired and frail looking. His eyes had gone gray and milky, but his mind remained sharp. No one, it was said, knew so many of the rituals. From the time he was a boy, he had studied the arts of Healing. Even Pale Cat deferred to the Old Camp Moiety's *Hopaye*. On this day he wore a simple tunic woven from undyed hemp. His right hand had developed a wobble over the years, and Smoke Shield had never seen it still.

More an attendant than anything else, Pearl Hand acted as the old *Hopaye*'s guide, eyes, and assistant. Pearl Hand was young, having not quite passed twenty winters, but he had taken on the duties and trappings of Black Tail's authority. Everyone believed that after the old man's passing, the clan would confirm Pearl Hand's status as their new leader. He was a quiet but firm man, not taken to boasting or to misusing his authority or position.

The final seat belonged to Deer Clan. There, Two Poisons watched Smoke Shield and Flying Hawk with probing eyes. He was nearing fifty now, and his reputation as a speaker and leader was justly earned. His voice in Council carried more weight than his low clan should have merited. For this meeting, he had painted his face in alternate lines of red and white, signifying that he would require a potent argument to switch from one side to the other.

His sister's son, Smells-His-Death, sat beside him, chewing on his lower lip. He was new to the Council, having replaced his older brother when the man died from an infected leg. Of them all, he was at once the newest and the most unknown.

Finally, in the back stood the two Albaamaha elders, Amber Bead and Red Awl. While they had no actual voice in the Council, prudence had often necessitated hearing their opinions, especially when policy might affect relations with the Albaamaha. They might be a subject people, but not even the blindly foolish would chance igniting their passions.

Amber Bead's old face sported star tattoos on his sunken cheeks. He had his white hair pulled back into a ponytail and wore a simple light blue tunic. Most thought him a mouthpiece for Sky Hand policies. The old Albaamo wasn't prone to disagree with anything. Smoke Shield dismissed him as nothing more than a hand-licking lackey.

Red Awl, however, was another matter. He was younger, his hair thick and black. Noted for calm judgment, he had come from a small farmstead upriver near the fall line. His wise council had not only kept the peace among his own people, but had led him to moderate several serious differences of opinion with the Sky Hand conquerors.

Smoke Shield studied the man. If trouble was coming, it would be at this man's hands. He was too new, his motives undetermined. People looked up to him as a rising leader. This was the kind of man who could be dangerous, the sort the Albaamaha would rally around. Red Awl and his wife, Lotus Root, were too good to be true. Smoke Shield needed little imagination to see him and his gorgeous spouse conspiring to discredit the Sky Hand.

What are you plotting, Red Awl? How close are you to treason?

Flying Hawk stepped forward from the tripod and walked to the Eagle Pipe where it rested on its small altar. With great ceremony, he poured chopped tobacco from a painted gourd, then used a small wooden pestle to pack the bowl. Seven Dead, the tishu minko, stepped forward and lit a twig in the sacred fire. This he held to the bowl as Flying Hawk pulled on the long stem.

Turning, Flying Hawk exhaled the blue smoke and raised his hands. "Hear me, gods of the Sky, Earth, and Underworld! I am Flying Hawk Calls the Morning Mankiller, high minko of the Chief Clan of the Sky Hand People. I have come here to speak and hear the truth! Know that my words come from the heart, without deceit or falsehood. Carry these words to all beings and know that they are just."

He stepped back as each of the Council members in turn of their rank came forward to take a pull from the pipe, exhale the smoke toward the high roof, and repeat the dedication.

When they finished and returned to their places, Flying Hawk took the floor. He let his gaze take in each of the seated chiefs.

His voice rose firm and clear. "In the beginning, all was Power. Breath Giver breathed this Power in and out. When the Sky was separated from the waters, before Crawfish brought the first land from the depths, Breath Giver's Power was divided in two. Then, when the land was formed, it was split into three. Order was separated from Chaos, and what was one, was many, but equal. Each of the worlds—Sky, Earth, and Underworld—had its own kind of Power, and it was harmonious and in balance.

"The People have tried to live with this harmony. They have tried to keep Power in balance. When we use one kind of Power for some worthy purpose, we attempt to restore the balance that Breath Giver intended. We are not gods, or Spirit beasts. We are not arrogant in the belief that we know better than Breath Giver's wisdom. We are only men, seeking to do what is right. What is in harmony."

Again the Council uttered a soft assent and nodded their heads.

Flying Hawk clenched his fists. "But now the balance is shifted. Alligator Town has been attacked. Blood has been spilled. Fire has scorched the lives of the survivors. The dead cry for justice. Chaos is loosed on our land. Our harmony is disrupted. Can you feel it? Does it shake your realms as it does ours?"

Growls of anger went from lip to lip.

"In the beginning times, when Eagle Man slew the monsters," Flying Hawk continued, "he gave us the knowledge of how Power had to be restored when it is out of balance. He taught us that it is up to men to struggle to keep the harmony. The burden of that struggle has been placed squarely on our shoulders."

Flying Hawk lowered his gaze to the Council, then fixed it on Pale Cat. "*Hopaye,* what happens when Power is out of harmony?"

Pale Cat stood, the folds of his robe falling straight. "Soul sickness, High Minko. We are weakened; illness comes upon us. The ghosts of the dead congregate around the living, pawing at them, demanding that their murdered Spirits be freed to follow the path westward, there to pass through the Eye Hand into the Sky World."

Flying Hawk nodded slowly. "We all know the route to the afterlife. Just as we all know how we'll end up if we do not restore balance to our lives and souls. The *Hopaye* has told us we will sicken. And we will. But rotting from within isn't the only danger. If we do not respond, the Chahta, Yuchi, Pensacola, Charokee, and others will think us weak. They will believe that Power has abandoned us. Mark me, they will come, war parties bristling, eagerly anticipating the joy of picking our bones clean before their rivals have a chance to do so."

Two Poisons stood, head tilted skeptically. "I do not question that something must be done, High Minko, but is now the time? We are late into fall. Most of the young men are up hunting, laying in meat for the winter while their families collect hickory and beech nuts. The berries are ripe, and people are spread all over the country." He gestured at the Albaamo, Amber Bead, who stood behind him. "We must have all the food laid in that we can get. If not, how can we feed those hungry mouths robbed of their harvests when the White Arrow Chahta burned it?"

Amber Bead nodded his agreement, shooting a curious glance at Flying Hawk.

"We do not recall our warriors," Flying Hawk said firmly. "We don't have time."

"Then will you draw warriors in the dirt?" Night Star asked. "And perhaps have the *Hopaye* breathe life into them? Is our Power that great?"

"Do not mock me, Chieftess. You know better than that."

At the tishu minko's nod, Blood Skull stood, crossing his arms. "Ah, but that seems to be the problem, doesn't it? The Chahta attacked when they shouldn't have. Knowing full well that we do not have the forces to respond." He gestured around the Council. "We understand the grievance, High Minko. And well do we know the danger of chaos when out of balance with order. The question is: What do we do to maintain ourselves until we can accumulate enough warriors to attack White Arrow Town?" He smiled grimly. "That is, outside of blowing Spirit into warriors you've drawn in the dirt."

Flying Hawk deliberately turned his head to Smoke Shield.

Smoke Shield took a deep breath, stilling his nerves. "I think I know a way. But we must act now, while they think we are weak, and before we can recall any of our warriors." He began outlining his plan, but as he spoke, only images of Morning Dew filled his mind.

Nine

Amber Bead threaded his way through the clutter of houses, corn cribs, and ramadas that lay between the plaza and the south gate. Split Sky City buzzed like the summer insects. People clustered around cooking fires, their talk centered on the just-concluded Council in the tchkofa. Children—unconcerned with the politics of the day—ran back and forth, laughing, playing tag, or tossing deerhide balls with small stickball racquets. If only Amber Bead could be so free of worry. But the children's time would come when they, too, adopted the mantles and cares of adulthood.

The fragrance of wood smoke, grilling meat, fish, and fowl favored the nostrils with an incense that tickled Amber Bead's empty stomach. He stilled his hunger, mind on the plan that Smoke Shield had just outlined. The idea was daring, and so fraught with risk.

But what does it mean for my people?

As he observed the faces of the adults around their cook fires, he realized their expressions mirrored his own: concerned. The Sky Hand people took the balance of Power seriously. They believed with all of their hearts that unless the White Arrow Chahta were successfully punished, and the balance between life and death, order and chaos was put back in harmony, they would suffer for it in the end.

He could hear Singing, accompanied by the clacking of rhythm sticks and the hollow melody of flutes in the night. Like the concept of universal balance, the lilting melody mitigated the worried conversations with hope of redress in the grander Spiritual world.

He stepped around a broken basket that lay in the path and glanced up at the evening sky. High overhead, against the day's last light, a V of geese winged southward, their honks barely audible over the sounds of the city.

"Mikko?" someone called from a nearby fire. "What news from the Council? You were there, weren't you?"

Amber Bead raised a hand, ducking his head as was required of an Albaamo when addressing a Chikosi. "A decision is made," he said carefully, recognizing the speaker, a middle-aged man of the Deer Clan. "My apologies, respected sir, but I am forbidden to speak of it. Your chief, Two Poisons, is the one to ask. Again, my apologies."

He hurried on before the man could rise from his fire and pursue more. Gods, the wrath of the world would fall upon his aging shoulders if he disclosed any of the Council's decisions. After so many years, and endless accusations by his own people that he was nothing more than a Chikosi lap dog, he should have grown used to such burdens.

Perhaps that will change. And a faint flicker of hope was kindled in his old breast.

He rounded one of the last granaries. Six paces across, the granary had been built on peeled posts so that the floor was head high, the upper walls made of woven cane and saplings. The thatched roof extended so the drip line was well out from the walls, the whole structure designed so that air circulated around the cached corn to keep it from molding. The posts, too, were greased so that wily raccoons, opossums, and rodents couldn't climb up the slippery wood to the bounty stored within.

He nodded respectfully to the warriors standing at the gate and walked through the narrow gap and into the night beyond Split Sky City. A soft sigh of relief passed his lips. He always felt trapped within the city. Once again he was nominally in Albaamaha territory, though the many camps, houses, and granaries clustered just as thick outside the gates. Here, too, people crouched around their evening fires. The place smelled of humanity, smoke, urine, and dung. He nearly tripped over a broken piece of pottery and stepped around a wad of discarded cloth too worn for any function but to foul a man's feet in the deepening dusk.

"Mikko?" came calls in his own language as people recognized him.

"I can say nothing," he told the crowd that seemed to materialize out of the gloom. "The chiefs will make an announcement when the time comes."

An old woman stepped out to block his path. "My daughter and her family were murdered at Alligator Town," she cried harshly. "They will get blood, won't they?" she asked, referring to the Chikosi.

He could see several Traders in the crowd. One could never trust the Traders. The only master they served was themselves and the Power of their Trade. "I can only say that the Sky Hand People take the outrage at Alligator Town very seriously."

"Most of the dead were *our* people," the old woman cried, raising a chorus of muttering assent.

"It's the Chikosi," another growled. "Always the Chikosi."

"Hush," someone rejoined. "Do you want them to hear? You'll end up a slave, cleaning their chamber pots."

"Someday," another added ominously, "we'll have our chance."

"Enough," Amber Bead said gently. "Leave this to the Sky Hand. Let them deal with it."

"Figures we'd hear that from you," a young man in the back replied. In the gloom Amber Bead couldn't make out the speaker's identity.

"Ah." Amber Bead kept his voice reasonable. "Then perhaps you should walk through those gates, climb the

Sun Stairs, and tell the high minko how to run his affairs. I'm sure he's pacing the floor up there, waiting for some green Albaamo youth to come whisper wise counsel into his ear." He got the laughter he wanted, then added, "When the time is right, you shall hear what decision has been made. Until then, I am tired, hungry, and wish to eat." He paused just long enough before adding, "Alone!"

The crowd gave way as he walked boldly through.

"It had better be justice for our dead," the old woman cried in a parting shot. "If not, there are others among us who will act."

Amber Bead turned on his heel. "I know. Tensions are high. But do *not* start down a path that will lead us all to disaster!" He did his best to stare them down in the darkness, and received silence instead.

After a moment, he continued on his way, passing the last of the camps. Stepping off the trail, he skirted his small garden, the squash, pumpkin, and corn stalks brown and shriveled. His house, as benefited his position, was larger than most. Like two humped beehives joined at the hip, it was made of individual saplings sunk into the ground, then bent over and tied at the top. Green vines had been woven through the saplings to strengthen the walls, and thatch was tied over the whole.

Amber Bead ducked through the low doorway and straightened. No fire gleamed from his hearth. The boxes, matting, and sleeping bench made darker shadows. A faint reddish glow came from the doorway into his second room.

The savory smell of roasting catfish filled his house and brought the juices of anticipation to his mouth. Three people sat on the matting around the central fire: Old Paunch, Whippoorwill, and young Crabapple looked up as he entered.

"It is done?" Paunch asked by way of greeting.

"It is done, Paunch."

Paunch looked at the youth. "Crabapple, go outside.

Make sure that no one sneaks out of the dark to place his ear next to the wall. We need to talk without worry."

"Yes, Uncle." The youth jumped lithely to his feet, nodded respectfully to Amber Bead, and ducked out the doorway.

The girl, Whippoorwill, stood. She took Amber Bead's elbow and helped him down as he took his seat on the rush matting. His bones cracked in the process, and he gasped with relief as he relaxed.

Behind him, his bed was a confused tangle of blankets on a waist-high pole bed built against the wall. Several cloth bags hung from the walls, and brownware ceramics made a disorderly collection under his bed. The catfish, wrapped in large basswood leaves, sizzled on a green willow rack, just high enough off the coals to keep from charring.

Whippoorwill reseated herself, her virgin's skirt swaying. As was proper, she sat with her knees together while the men sat cross-legged. She had laid a muskrathide cape to one side. The red light bathed her face and skin, touching her full breasts ever so softly and casting shadows in the hollows behind her collarbone. She would have been a most attractive girl but for her large haunted eyes. Something in their depths sent a shiver down his spine. She seemed aloof, as if this world was but an illusion and her souls resided elsewhere.

"What have they decided?" Paunch asked.

"Smoke Shield will attack White Arrow Town. He has gone straight from the Council to the Men's House to begin fasting and purifying himself for battle. He and what warriors remain will leave four days hence, and secretly travel to White Arrow Town."

Paunch frowned at the fire. His white hair looked rosy in the glow of the embers. Despite his name, he was a thin man, hollowed out with age. His face betrayed too many seasons of sun, rain, and weather. Deeply etched lines camouflaged the faded tattoos of his youth. Now he fingered the skin sagging from his chin, and nodded slightly. A ratty brown hunting shirt hung from his shoulders and was belted at his waist with a double wrap of rope.

"He will have what? Perhaps thirty warriors? Forty? Is that enough to take a defended town?"

"Smoke Shield said that there will be a wedding. That Chahta from all over have been invited to the celebratory feast. Hundreds are expected to come from all the Chahta clans. People will be everywhere."

Paunch blinked. "It will be like a hornet's nest, filled with warriors from every Chahta town. Does Smoke Shield—arrogant as he is—think he will live long enough to even reach the outer wall?"

"Dreams," Whippoorwill said absently. "He lives in Dreams. They are no more than mist in the forest."

Amber Bead snorted. "Smoke Shield doesn't strike me as the Dreamy kind. Unless, of course, they are visions of blood and agony."

Whippoorwill fixed him with her uncanny eyes, and Amber Bead squirmed.

"Not Smoke Shield," she insisted as if Amber Bead were a silly child. "Screaming Falcon Dreams his future. He sees his prestige and greatness in the eyes of his worshipping people. It is well that he Dreams these things." Her eyes lost focus. "It is so much better to live in one's Dreams. Don't you think?"

"Dreams do little for our people," Amber Bead muttered in return. Happily, he turned his attention to Paunch, who seemed particularly unsettled by Whippoorwill's words. "Our people are worried about this. No one expected the Chahta attack. It came out of nowhere, at the wrong time of year. War is better conducted in the summer. The entire harvest at Alligator Town was destroyed. Our people down there will have to disperse, make their living out in the forest, beyond the protection of Sky Hand warriors. In little groups of families, they will be vulnerable to Yuchi and Pensacola raiders, let alone the White Arrow, should they come hunting for more slaves and scalps."

"The Sky Hand have made too many enemies of the surrounding peoples," Paunch agreed. "Some of them will take this as an opportunity to avenge themselves, and it won't be the Sky Hand who take the brunt of it, but our people."

"The high minko says he will provide whatever food is necessary." Amber Bead watched Whippoorwill reach out with tongs made of hickory sticks. She used them to carefully lift the catfish from the fire and place it in a wooden bowl crafted from a slab of walnut. The bowl had a duck's head carved on either end.

"And where will he get it?" Paunch asked, eyes on the steaming fish.

"From the Albaamaha granaries up and down the river," Amber Bead answered. "Thank the gods we've had a better harvest than usual, but to feed that many people? Bellies will be rubbing backbones by spring."

Whippoorwill used the tongs to pull back the basswood leaf wrappings. White flaky catfish steamed in the dim light. Amber Bead's belly growled loud enough that both of his guests glanced his way.

"You had best eat," Paunch added. "If predictions are right, we'll be hearing enough of that sound come spring."

"The combination of empty bellies and the prospect of Smoke Shield succeeding Flying Hawk could lead to a simmering discontent among our people. Even the Chikosi dread the day Smoke Shield becomes high minko."

"What if an envoy were to travel to White Arrow Town?" Paunch asked as Whippoorwill used the duck-head handles to place the plate before Amber Bead. "What if someone were to whisper in Screaming Falcon's ear that an attack was coming? What if Smoke Shield's war party was destroyed?"

Amber Bead raised the plate and blew to cool the

fish. "There will be chaos like we have not seen since the day the Chikosi lost their war medicine to the Yuchi, and the high minko named Makes War was captured and tortured to death in a Yuchi square."

"You call that chaos?" Paunch asked. "The Chikosi replaced Makes War with Bear Tooth, and you'll recall the sort of monster he was. It was a blessing when he burned to death that night. Things were better when Fire Sky was made high minko in the aftermath. What could the Chikosi have been thinking to confirm that murdering Flying Hawk in his place?"

"Smoke Shield carries the war medicine." Amber Bead circumvented the tirade.

Paunch stared at him in incredulous silence as Amber Bead plopped a piece of fish into his mouth.

Finally Paunch said, "That's insane! The war medicine is their heart! Lose it, and it will be like driving a burning stake through their bodies. They'll be terrified that Power has turned against them! This could be the moment we've waited for!"

It would take but a single runner, someone who could pass into White Arrow Town and spill the whole thing like a stew at Screaming Falcon's feet. An excitement like he'd never known began to burn in Amber Bead's breast, the fish forgotten in his mouth.

"Yes, Grandfather," Whippoorwill cooed. "Do this. Watch our people Dance with fire. You will see Chikosi become Chahta, and the scalps of our people will be buried in a sack in the forest. A Councilor will die, and a new leader will rise in his place."

"What do you mean?" Pauch turned worriedly to his granddaughter.

Her eyes, however, had fixed Amber Bead in their bottomless stare.

A Councilor will die? "Then, the Chikosi will blame me?"

"Fear not, Mikko, you shall die an old man. But you balance on a thin rope. Below you, monsters snap in the boiling brown water. Choose this path, and freedom might come for our people. Oh, yes. But at what price?"

"What are you talking about?" Paunch demanded, clearly unsettled.

Amber Bead stared into the girl's eyes, like looking into an endless void. He felt himself falling, and reached out to brace himself, letting the plate of fish fall from his lap, where it spilled on the floor. An unbidden image of ruined villages, scattered corpses, and broken houses formed. He could see dogs, foxes, and crows feeding on the half-rotten bodies.

"Gods," he whispered. He blinked, breaking her spell, and then rubbed his eyes. "What was that?"

"Life after the fall of the Chikosi." Her voice sounded distant and muddled, as if he'd heard it through a hollow log.

"I don't understand."

Her eyes seemed to swell again. "Until my sister arrives, the fate of our people lies in your hands, Mikko. How do you choose?"

Someone turned the earth upside down. The air had to move somewhere else to make room," Two Petals declared as she stared up at the great mound jutting into the sky atop the Cahokia bluff. The slanting sides of earth rose to a dizzying height, the building high atop the great mound looking small, the palisade like fuzz along the mound's lip. "Did you bring me here to see all those ghosts?"

"No. I brought you to see a woman." Old White reached down into the canoe, pulling his wooden pack from inside the hull. He struggled with the weight, happy to have Two Petals help him slip his arms through the straps and settle it onto his back. A cold wind blew dark clouds out of the northwest and sent ripples of murky water to pat the sandy canoe landing. No less than twenty canoes had been pulled up on the beach, two of them belonging to Traders who had called greetings as they stowed loads prior to pushing off.

Old White patted his belt pouch, sure that it was snug at his waist. He looked at the trail zigzagging up the steep bluff. His aching bones didn't relish the climb. Trees had started on the slope, a circumstance that once would have been intolerable. The sand here was black, filled with the ash of a thousand long-gone campfires. Broken pieces of fire-cracked rock, bits of pottery, and other trash were scattered about. The place reeked of old urine and feces.

"So this is the great Cahokia?" Two Petals asked.

"What's left of it." Old White reached for his staff and started forward, the white feathers fluttering in the gusty wind. He shivered as the cold ate through his hunting shirt. "It's almost time for buffalo robes."

"Too warm," Two Petals replied, her eyes fixed on the stupendous mound rising above the bluff. Atop it, a wooden palisade barely masked the great building that rose three stories into the sky. "Could men really build such a thing? Did they Dance as they raised Mother Earth to Father Sky? It would have taken wings, beating in the sunlight. They would have blackened the sky, slipped sideways in the wind. Can you hear their voices, shish, shish, shish? Over and over."

"I would have liked to have seen it when the lords of Cahokia were at their greatest," Old White told her. He gestured with his staff. "The palace was once five stories tall. And the palisade, that was plastered with painted clay that caught the sunlight and shone like polished shell. Once this place ruled most of the world."

She walked beside him, head cocked, listening to something he couldn't hear. "Because of that, you became great. That has to be worth something."

Old White shot her a sidelong glance. "Who are you talking to?"

"Her name is Lichen. She lives here."

"Who?"

"Lichen," she told him crossly. "This woman walking along with us."

Old White followed her pointing finger, seeing nothing but trampled grass beside the trail.

Two Petals had gone back to listening, saying, "Yes, I'll be careful."

"Careful of what?" Old White asked.

"Black Tooth."

He grunted. Everyone was careful of Black Tooth. Word must have traveled as far north as her village. "What else does this Lichen tell you?"

"Oh, about when evil Tharon lived here."

"You've heard of him?" He shot her a glance, happy that she was having a good day. He had been worried that she'd float away to wherever her Contrary soul went. For the moment, her imaginary friend and the giant building atop its brown grass-clad mound filled her world.

"They burned him as a witch. Lichen says that he broke Cahokia's power. That after that, in the reign of Petaga, a great war broke out."

"There has always been war," he grumbled. "It runs in our veins like fire. It is the heat that warms our flesh."

She said nothing as they started up the winding trail from Cahokia Creek landing. Old White dedicated himself to the climb. He made the first switchback and stopped, puffing to catch his breath. "The first time I came here, I trotted up this like a yearling deer. Age is an inevitable curse."

"Curses are never inevitable," she murmured. Her hands were moving in a sort of fluttering agitation that he'd grown accustomed to. Sometimes she'd tap her fingers in a perfect synchrony.

He turned his attention to the city. Gods, even in his lifetime he had watched Cahokia deteriorate. How many times had armies sacked this place since the days of Tharon and Petaga? How many peoples had conquered the once capital, thinking that they would restore the Power here?

"Once Power is gone," Two Petals said, "it flies like the birds. North and south, settling here and there. You'd think there would be droppings under the branches."

"Do you hear my thoughts?"

"Never."

He gave her a worried glance and attacked the last of the trail. Stopping at the top, he stared. Old sections of palisade had fallen, the wood rotting. On the flat before him, grass waved in the wind where it hadn't been beaten flat. Small copses of trees had sprung up between the tall square mounds. Had he not been here before, he would have thought the landscape hilly, but each hillock had once supported a grand building. Only a few temples remained standing; most mounds were topped with low piles of debris, their fallen structures looted of logs for building materials or firewood. Occasional patches of brown corn stalks rattled in the wind, but even they looked ratty, many having been taken for fuel.

"It's huge," Two Petals announced. "See the people! Hear the Singing?" Then she pirouetted around in a circle, her arms spread wide. "So many people. All Singing. The world is alive with Song."

He shook his head, seeing the vacancy that now filled her eyes. A shiver prickled along his skin, more than just the cold wind with its threat of rain. The change came on her so quickly.

"Look at this," she chimed, clambering over the rotting logs of the fallen palisade. "It's all green and alive." They were passing between the great mound and a line of four smaller mounds capped with saplings that grew out of the debris. "Who is playing chunkey over there?" She pointed at a forlorn cornfield. "Look how he's dressed. Have you ever seen such colorful feathers? He could be made of living copper."

If a chunkey court had once existed there, it was long gone. "You're seeing ghosts, Two Petals."

"They glow," she said, rapt in wonder. "I think they're made of sunlight."

He glanced up at the skulking clouds. A little sunlight would be nice. He led the way forward, glancing down to see a partial human skeleton eroding out of a hole where a badger had disturbed the soil. The brown bones were flaking away, the skull crushed, dark orbits flattened, yellowed teeth like sordid pearls in the broken jaws.

Had the great lords ever dreamed their grand city would come to this? He looked up at the sparse palisade surrounding the temple atop the great mound. Black Tooth, the chief who lived there, belonged to one of the Dehegihan tribes, but most of his people were farther to the west now, living on the prairie edge of the Great Plains. The man was reputed to be something of a madman, but he still organized a Trade fair here every summer solstice, as if living on the legends of the past. Most of his energies went into maintaining the tall building atop the mound, as if that grandeur alone could maintain the Power of Cahokia.

The path ran past sunken storage pits and the rubble of long-decayed houses. Potsherds gleamed in the bottom of the path along with flakes of stone and bits of charred bone and corncobs. Cahokia was a place of trash.

They passed the base of the great mound, entering the grand plaza. To the right was a square mound topped with a thatch-roofed farmer's dwelling much smaller than the splendid temple that had once graced its heights.

"Are we going up?" Two Petals pointed at the ramped stairway leading to the tiered heights of the great mound.

"Our destination lies there." He pointed across the plaza to the south, past two low mounds. There a conical mound stood west of a larger square mound topped by a thatched structure. It was to the latter that Old White was headed.

"Charming place, I'm sure."

"She has her ways," Old White replied.

Two Petals' gaze sharpened, and he could see her struggling. "Why did we come here?"

Old White smiled to himself. "To finish something started long ago. To say good-bye. To close a circle." He paused. "And to see if she can help you."

"Circles, circles," she chided, slipping away again. Her eyes had taken on that vacant look. "Round and round. Like the world. Nothing straight."

Old White glanced back at the great mound, seeing a lone figure high atop the stairway watching them. "No, nothing straight." He led the way out onto the plaza, the grass at the side of the trail rustling as if trying to grab his legs.

The wind battered at them, almost knocking him sideways. *Not as spry as I used to be.* The pack seemed to weigh a ton. His cloth pack swung back and forth; it might have been maliciously trying to counter his balance. Did he feel the smooth stone within humming in time to the wind? How many years had he carried it, the weight forever reminding him of the past?

Should have left it behind years ago. But the stone had become part of him, his burden and curse.

"Only the young walk with a sprightly step," she said in a singsong voice.

"If only you knew."

"I know everything."

"Must be comforting."

"Like a leaf in the wind."

They followed the path in silence to the foot of the mound. Though dwarfed by the great mound, it was still huge. But being close, he could see slumping along the east side where a patch of earth had slid down to leave a scar. Virgin levels of clay and colored soil could be seen in the exposed profile.

Old White led the way to a stairway consisting of logs laid into the steep side of the mound. Some had been recently replaced, as evidenced by their color, and disturbed earth marked where one had been dug out. He was winded by the time he made it to the top.

As he stopped to catch his breath, Two Petals climbed up beside him, looking back across the grand plaza with its abandoned mounds. The vista only emphasized the great mound with its three-story palace to the north.

"The ghosts yawn," Two Petals said wearily. Her gaze had fixed on the palace. "He's watching us."

"I saw. Probably the guard. Our business isn't with the chief."

"No, not him. The old man with white hair. He's worried about spiders."

Old White shot her a sidelong glance. "What old man?"

"He's there." She pointed at the palace. "Just like he's always been."

A scratchy voice behind him said, "I see him often."

Old White turned. The crone stood in the doorway of the two-room house. The dwelling fit the woman. Its thatch had weathered beyond gray to a dirty white, as had her hair. Reminiscent of the woman's skin, chunks of plaster sagged or had fallen from the walls to expose the poles beneath. Once-bright paintings of birds, people, and deer had faded into faint patterns on the remaining plaster. The old woman, too, had been beautiful. Her skin was tattooed with a series of dots that ran down from her chin. She wore a long dress of threadbare fabric, and a ragged blue-feathered shawl hung from her shoulders. Now the wind tugged at the feathers, threatening to tear them away.

"It's been a long time, Silver Loon." Old White stepped forward.

She squinted. "A great many winters have passed since I have gone by that name. Do I know you?"

"Perhaps. But that was long ago. I was a different man then, and went by another name."

She watched him approach, curiosity in her dark gaze. "Refresh my memory."

"You took me in, called my wounded souls back to my body. You called me your 'broken pot.' Not the most flattering of the names I've had over the years."

"Runner," she said flatly, eyes narrowing. "After all these years. Should I throw my arms around you, or poison you the first chance I get?"

"If you decide on the poison, please, use something other than water hemlock. I'm not sure I have the energy for the thrashing and convulsions. The twisted facial expressions, along with the bugging eyeballs and foaming at the mouth, would be unseemly for a man of my age."

She watched him in silence, her expression pinched, then looked past him to Two Petals. "And who is this?"

"A companion."

A bitter smile died on her lips. "You always had a way of attracting beautiful women." She hesitated. "A bit young for you, isn't she?"

"Way too young," he agreed.

She gave a slight shrug of the shoulders. "Come inside. This wind is drilling through me like sharp chert. I don't take the cold the way I did once."

"None of us do."

She turned, ducking through the low doorway.

Old White glanced at Two Petals, only to find her frozen in place, her eyes like gleaming lakes. Her lips had parted, an expression of indecision on her young face. Wind whipped loose strands of her black hair this way and that.

"Are you coming?"

She stood mutely, and he reached out, taking her by the arm and dragging her forward. Her legs worked woodenly, and she shot him a frightened glance. "Not here," she whispered. "Brittle bones. Flying ash. It's all about."

"What?"

"Like sleeping in the air," came her disjointed response.

"Worried about poison?"

"Don't eat. Bad squash."

Old White managed to drag Two Petals through the doorway. He blinked once inside, his eyes slowly adjusting to the dim light. Silver Loon was adding wood to the central fire. She had quite a stack piled by the doorway, and he could be pretty sure that she hadn't packed it in.

Reading his interest, she shrugged. "The locals bring it. For the most part they take care of me. Fix the roof, patch the plaster, bring food. In return I cure their ills, deliver their babies, and provide charms for lovers, hunters, and anyone else who needs a little help believing in himself."

"You've quite a reputation."

The crackling fire shot yellow fingers through the wood, illuminating the interior. The place was crowded with large ceramic jars, decorative baskets, ornate wooden boxes, and sacks of this and that stowed along the walls. Net bags filled with leaves, dried roots, and various plants and animal parts hung from pegs. A large clay statue of Corn Mother sat in one corner and portrayed her hoeing industriously as corn looped about her body. In the other corner, a waist-high statue of a pregnant woman stared at him with shell eyes that gleamed in the firelight. The statue's pointed breasts and round belly had been polished to a glossy sheen.

In the rear, a beautiful fabric hung over a doorway. The weaver had woven intricate patterns that depicted herons, deer, raccoons, and panthers into the fine material. From the ceiling, human and animal skulls, long bones, and other fetishes hung. All had a fine patina of soot coating them.

Silver Loon reached to one side, then settled a pot beside the fire. "It's squash seasoned with mint, raspberry, and grape. It will take awhile to cook." No humor filled her eyes as she said, "Don't worry. I won't poison you until after I hear your story."

"Not true," Two Petals whispered as she wrung her hands and stared wide-eyed at the statues, bones, and pots. "She'll never do as she says."

Silver Loon cocked her head, eyes narrowing as she studied Two Petals. The old woman rose stiffly, and Old White was gratified to hear the crackle of her bones. Silver Loon inspected Two Petals with wary eyes, taking one careful step at a time. She seemed to take in the girl's posture, the way her eyes slipped this way and that. The oddly fluttering hands caught her attention.

"Do you hear the voices?" Silver Loon asked gently. "Are they speaking to you?"

"Silence," Two Petals insisted frantically. "Deafening silence. Can't . . . hear . . . a thing."

For the first time, Silver Loon's expression eased. "Relax, girl. Listen. Listen harder. Once they know you can hear, they'll stop shouting at you. Your fear has them worried. Tell them you won't hurt them. They're just afraid, that's all."

"Afraid of what?" Old White asked.

"Of her Power, old fool." Silver Loon shot him a glance. "Where did you find her?"

"I think she found me."

"Of course she did." Silver Loon shook her head as if to rid herself of something uncomfortable before retreating to the fire. "Gods, you haven't changed. You turned my life upside down the first time I saw you. Now, here you are, with all the grace of a buffalo in a cornfield, turning everything upside down again."

"I seem to have that gift."

She squatted by the fire, pressing her reed-thin hands to her ears, as if blocking out the noise that only Two Petals seemed to hear. "Power has always crackled around you like lighting on a summer night. What are you calling yourself these days?"

"Old White."

She lifted a suspicious eyebrow. "The Seeker?"

"Some have called me that."

For the first time, a faint smile bent her lips. "I should have kept you. Together, you and I would have remade the world."

"As I recall, it was my decision to leave."

She grunted under her breath. "You have no idea how well I recall that morning. I woke up to find you missing from my bed. I had no idea what you'd done. Not until later that morning when I found the goose you'd drawn in the dirt outside my door." She closed her eyes, expression pained. "I *loved* you. Loved you as no man I have ever known." She swallowed hard. "And you didn't even have the guts to tell me you were leaving."

"I was younger then. Once, long ago, I set fire to my souls. It was consuming them, burning me from the inside out."

"Is that what drove you from my bed? A fire in your souls?"

"It would seem that it has driven me to the ends of the earth."

"And what did you find, Seeker, that I could not have given you?"

He frowned, meeting her hot glare. "The telling of it would take a lifetime."

"And are you still burning?"

"For a while yet, yes."

She snorted derisively, jerking her head toward Two Petals, who seemed frozen, her head tilted, eyes squinted as if against pain. "And what of her? Do you expect her to douse your flames?"

"I do not yet understand the role that she will play. I suspect, however, that it will be most interesting."

Silver Loon took a deep breath. "Well, come. Sit here and share the fire while the meal cooks. If I couldn't understand you as a young man, why should I expect to now, after all these years?"

He turned, placing a hand on Two Petals' shoulder.

"Come, girl. You're chilled to the bone. Warm yourself. Then, later, you can tell Silver Loon about the voices you hear."

He pressed her down, and she sank like a green plant whose stems resisted bending. Old White then shrugged out of his cedar-wood pack and lowered his stone-weighted bag to the floor.

Silver Loon indicated the latter. "I see that you still carry that. I would have thought by now you'd have Traded it off, or buried it somewhere."

"I am bound to it by blood."

"You carry more burdens than most, Lost Man."

He extended his hands to the warmth. "It has been a long time since I've gone by that name."

"Then perhaps we aren't so different, you and I."

Ten

With the coming of the storm, Trader fought the current to nose his canoe into a small creek that fed the Father Water. Swimmer perched at the bow, sniffing and switching his tail in lazy expectation. The narrow stream was deeply incised, exposing yellow silt, the trees almost touching overhead. At a trail crossing, he paused long enough to land, walk into the trees, and bury his copper. Thus reassured, he and Swimmer had paddled another half-hand's journey up the creek to a village euphemistically called Sun Pearl. Though, in all of his previous stays, he had never understood what could have fostered such an optimistic title for such a pitiful bunch of thatch and bark houses behind a flimsy palisade.

What Sun Pearl Village did have, however, was a hot fire, a dry bed, and a warm woman by the name of Fox Squirrel. For a trinket, she would take a lonely Trader in for the night, feed him a cooked meal of pumpkin, boiled sunflower seeds, corn cakes, and whatever sweets she had on hand.

While the villagers were Dehegiha—allegedly descended from one of the towns north of Cahokia Creek—they now lived as mere shadows of the high chiefs who had sat at the Great Sun's court high atop Cahokia.

Fox Squirrel, however, came from a different background. She called herself Dené, and claimed to be from a people in the far northwest. Stolen as a child, she had passed from people to people, working her way down the western rivers to end up here. Rumor had it that more than one Trader had offered to take her away, but for reasons of her own, she stayed in Sun Pearl Village. There, over the years, she had amassed quite a bit of wealth, everything from pots of yaupon, sharks' teeth, conch and whelk shell, strings of beads, jars full of olivella shells, flats of copper, and a luxurious supply of finely tanned furs.

For the moment, Trader was thoroughly enjoying one of those selfsame furs—in this instance, a softly tanned cougar hide on which he lay, naked, while cracking hazelnuts between a stone pestle and mortar. Every other one, he shared with Fox Squirrel, who lay just as naked, her warm skin pressed against his.

She lay on her belly, propped up on her elbows, the nipples of her pointed breasts hard as they rubbed the soft cougar fur. Her long black hair fell around her shoulders in a tangle and spilled down her back almost to the twin moons of her buttocks. She kept raising one sleek calf before letting it fall rhythmically back to the bedding.

A fire crackled and spit, occasional sparks rising toward the soot-blackened roof. Outside the rain had turned to sleet.

Swimmer lay at the door, occasional drafts of cold air ruffling his long black fur. Beside him, safe and warm as Trader himself, the packs were stacked.

"You say he's supposed to be a demon dog?" Fox Squirrel asked in her thickly accented voice. Over the years she'd become quite fluent in Trade Tongue, but the accent would always be there.

Trader laughed. "You know how some of these backwoods farmers are."

"Dumb like Traders. Huh, don't I know?"

"I think he's just a dog. Smart, too. I just have to tell him things once. I think he'd do anything, so long as I keep his belly full."

She glanced sidelong at him. "You, Trader, are demon, too."

He cracked another nut, handed her the meat, and tossed the collection of shells into the fire. "How is that?"

"I know you for what? Four summers? You young. Always travel alone. Always have that look in your eyes."

"What look is that?"

"Haunted."

He snorted derisively.

"True," she insisted. "You always apart. Even when around other Traders. Everyone talks of home. Of wives and children. Of where they grow up. But not you. Always it is about Trade, about where you go, where you been. Never about home." She gave him a sidelong look with knowing brown eyes. "So, tell me about home."

"It's long gone. Far away from here." He reached another nut from the sack. "It doesn't exist anymore."

"People talk about you."

"I'm sure."

"One of stories is that you did something terrible. Maybe pee on sacred fire?"

He gave an amused smile. "I never had that urge."

"Some say you stole something from the temple."

"Believe me, if I wanted something from the temple, someone would have given it to me. No, I've never been a thief."

"Some say it was woman."

He gritted his teeth, then muttered, "I don't want to talk about it."

"Another say it was forbidden love. A mother-in-law."

"No."

"A sister."

His laughter was like a harsh bark. "I never had a sister."

"What then?"

He shook his head. "That life doesn't exist."

She reached out. "What about in here? You keep memories, no?"

As her finger touched the side of his head, he recalled

the smells of hominy cooking in the morning. He could hear the ritual singing as the *Hopaye* greeted the morning, calling on the gods and Spirits to bless the day. He could feel the soft red leather of his long-gone quiver, its outside decorated with white shell beads.

As quickly, the memory changed to the tight grip on his war club, the anger that broke loose inside him as he stepped into the Men's House doorway. The charge in his muscles had been like lightning broken loose in his body as he drew back with his war club. He could remember the club's impact; it had run from the handle, through his hands, up his arms, and shocked his very souls.

"What?" she asked.

"Nothing." He shook his head. "The most terrible nightmares are the ones you lived before they came to stalk you in the night."

"So why you run away from home?"

"What about you? Are you ever going back to your people?"

Straight white teeth backlit her smile. "Why should I? Leave this?" She indicated the piles of wealth surrounding her. "And go back to blowing snow and drafty tent? Just to feel back pain as I flesh hide after hide? Why would I want to lay with smelly hunter who wears same parka all winter? Then pack meat, and pop one child after another from my sheath?" She shook her head.

"Some Traders are smelly, too."

"But I can say no. Or tell them to take bath." She shrugged. "Tell me, does my sheath care if it takes the same man's shaft over and over, or different shafts each time? What happens in the end is always pretty much same, no?"

"But what if someone plants a child in you?"

"Here, I have ways. Medicines. Back home, no way."

"I see."

She gave him an impish smile. "Now, enough eating

nuts. Talking of sheaths makes me want to use mine." She pulled him on top of her as she rolled over and wrapped her brown legs around his thighs. "Time to make this shaft hard. Not take long."

It didn't. She sighed as he slid into her and she tightened around him. He closed his eyes, imagining another woman, how it might have been. Long, long ago . . .

A loud shriek brought Two Petals awake. She sat up in the darkness, peering around anxiously. Through the panic, she realized she was in a dark room. The hard patter of rain on thatch and the cadence of water dripping onto hard ground alternated with gusts of wind. A reddish glow reminded her of the place: Silver Loon's house.

She trembled as whispers of assent came from the boxes, jars, and bones. She could feel the Spirits backing away.

"Heard that, did you?" a calm voice asked.

Two Petals peered across the fire, seeing the old woman where she sat braced against a willow backrest. Images from her Dreams began to fragment, slipping from her souls. "I heard a scream. I thought, well . . ."

"That it was in the room." The old woman nodded. She pointed with a ghostly arm to the skulls hanging above. "It was Takes-His-Head. As unhappy as he was in life, his Spirit is just as miserable in death."

Two Petals raised her gaze to the dark ceiling, now a maze of black shadow. "Why don't you make him go away?"

"Make him? Hah, I've driven him out more than once. He keeps coming back. He tortured himself when he was alive. I thought he'd get over it when he died. Some people are odd that way. I finally came to the conclusion that when rage and misery are all they have, they're afraid that if they let it go, they'll have nothing at all. So they cling, too frightened of the alternatives."

Two Petals swallowed hard, working her hands, struggling to keep from falling over the precipice. "I know." It was so hard to hang onto herself, to this world. Now she wasn't sure if the voices she heard belonged to Silver Loon's Spirits, or her own.

"Why do you fight it?"

"Fight what?"

"Power has touched you, girl."

"My father said I was crazy. He thought some malevolent Spirit had taken control of my souls. He tried to beat it out of me."

"And what do you think?"

"If some Spirit did take me, I can't feel it. Not like something wrong inside me."

"Ignorant farmers."

"I don't understand."

"No, I don't suppose you do." The old woman hesitated. "It's hard work to hang onto this world, isn't it?"

Two Petals nodded, dropping her chin to her knees. "It makes more sense if the world is backward. But no one can see it but me."

"Let go, Two Petals. Become one with the Power. Dance with it."

"I'm afraid."

"Of course you are. You have no training. You must not fight Power, but accept it."

"But if I do . . . I don't want to . . ."

"What? Lose yourself?"

She jerked her head in quick nods.

"Surrender yourself, Two Petals."

"If I do I'll never be right. Never be like everyone else."

Silver Loon's soft voice told her, "It's too late, girl. Far too late."

Two Petals blinked at the tears welling hot in her eyes.

A warm wind blew up from the gulf. Fluffy white clouds marched northward in patterns across the light blue sky. Solstice lay but a scant moon away.

Morning Dew checked the large brown pot and used a stick to stir the hominy. Its pungent tang filled her nostrils. She worked under a ramada, warmed by the rays of low sunlight that found their way through the clouds. Around her White Arrow Town seemed to pulse with life and excitement. The people were still swollen with excitement at the success of the raid on Alligator Town.

And well they should be. We are on a new path now. Gone are the days of deferring to the wishes of the Sky Hand People.

"Thinking of something?"

Morning Dew turned to see her mother, Sweet Smoke, where she had emerged from their house. As befitted her rank of Chief Clan matron among the White Arrow Chahta, the dwelling was imposing, containing no less than four rooms. With a high roof and carved woodpecker heads rising above the center pole, it rivaled the palace atop its platform mound a stone's toss to the north. The walls were plastered with white clay overlaying the posts set in the trench foundation. Two carefully carved and painted ivory-billed woodpeckers topped poles that stood on either side of the door. Mother looked regal as she stood between them, dressed in a short black-and-yellow fabric skirt; an otterhide cape hung over her shoulders.

In her youth, Mother had been tattooed with a series of dots that circled her mouth, curled around her cheeks, and then joined under her chin. She wore her long black hair pulled up and pinned with a copper skewer that caught the light. She remained a handsome woman, her breasts still firm, though her hips had widened from the bearing of four children. Only Morning Dew and her brother, Biloxi Mankiller, had made it to adulthood.

"I was thinking of the future," Morning Dew replied happily. Like water running downhill, her eyes were drawn to the Men's House, barely visible beyond the palace mound. She could also see the plaza. There, before the stair-clad ramp that led to the mound top, several wooden squares had been erected side by side. Within each hung one of the miserable bodies of the rulers of Alligator Town. They might have been dead the way their heads lolled over their chests. They had been tied with wrists and ankles bound to the four corners of the square. Though none of the captives moved, she knew they still clung to life. Several townsfolk stood, inspecting them and talking.

Behind them, in the plaza, the tall pole representing the World Tree with its red and white spirals seemed to shine in the sunlight.

"Ah," Sweet Smoke added, following her gaze. "Screaming Falcon. He still has four days left."

"Why does purification take so long?"

"Because war is pollution."

Morning Dew was used to her mother's sharp tone.

"You still don't think the attack on Alligator Town was right?"

Sweet Smoke gave a wistful shrug. "That was the decision of the Council. Your brother is high minko now. He and the rest of the men were persuaded by Screaming Falcon's plan." A pause. "Who knows? Perhaps they are right. Perhaps Power has abandoned the Sky Hand People."

Morning Dew turned her attention to the captives. A band of little boys had charged into view; laughing and calling, each carried a stick. As if in a game, they ran past the captives, slashing at them with their flails. Their attack elicited a response as the captives writhed under the blows. The adults who had been watching joined in the laughter.

"Do you see, Mother? That's what's become of the Chikosi rulers. One day, Smoke Shield will hang there, and I will take just as much pleasure whipping his defeated body."

Her mother kept her own counsel, but returned her attention to her daughter. "How is the hominy coming?"

"The kernels are swelling and cracking. I added some water."

"Good." She stepped closer. "And what about you? Are you getting ready for the big day?"

Morning Dew laughed. "Of course. This morning I studied the route I will run. I think I'll take a path from the Sun Stairs around the House of the Dead, then head straight for the palisade. If I run between the big storehouses, he won't know if I'm turning right or left when I reach the palisade. He can't cut the corner and catch me. He'll have no choice but to follow."

"Screaming Falcon is fast on his feet. We'll give you enough of a head start so that he won't be close by the time you reach the storehouses." Sweet Smoke smiled wryly. "As much as you might want to be caught, you've got to make it look good. His friends will be following. They'll tell him which way you've turned."

"And my friends will be ready," she countered. "I'm going to tell them to look to the right once I'm hidden by the storehouses. It might be enough of a hint that he cuts to the right of the storehouses."

"And you'll turn to the left."

Morning Dew laughed. "Pretty smart, don't you think?"

The bridal chase had a long history, going back to the beginning times, just after the Chahta had emerged from their ancestral earth: a great mountain far to the west. For generations, they had traveled the world, each night making camp and erecting the World Tree pole that they carried with them. The next morning, they would awaken to find the pole leaning in the direction they were to travel that day. Finally, one day they had camped in the Horned Serpent Valley, and when the Ancestors awakened that next morning, the pole had been straight, indicating that here, at last, they had reached their home.

The bridal chase had started, it was said, when a young woman wished to know if the handsome man she wanted to marry was lazy, or if he would be ambitious, hardworking, and a dedicated hunter. To find out, she had waited until the moment before they were married, and broken away, leading him on a merry chase. Since that day, it had become custom; if a young woman could outrun her man, the marriage was off. It was also said that the longer and harder the chase, the greater their love and commitment would be to each other after a successful capture had been made. Morning Dew planned to make Screaming Falcon's chase the thing of legends.

"People have already begun to arrive. Two camps were set up last night outside of town. Rumor has it that some are coming from as far away as the Natchez lands to the west." She sighed. "News of Screaming Falcon's victory over Alligator Town has traveled like the wind. As much as people wish to see this union, they are just as interested in Screaming Falcon, and what his plans are for the future."

Morning Dew's heart warmed. "I've heard some talk, too."

"Children carry their parents' gossip where prudent adults wouldn't think to speak. What have you heard?"

"That many hope Screaming Falcon will finally break the Sky Hand People's Power. The hope here, and among the other clans upriver, is that what the Sky Hand now possess will become ours. That our chiefs will sit inside the Chikosi palaces, and we shall control all the lands between the Natchez and the Ockmulgee."

"That is a most ambitious future."

"You don't think we can do it?" Morning Dew stirred

the hominy. Why did Mother always see the least instead of the most?

"Daughter, do you also understand the terrible risks involved? You have never seen the strength of the Sky Hand People. You don't know what they—"

"Their high minko *killed* his brother! The same thing almost happened again. But for a poorly aimed blow, Smoke Shield would be a long-rotted corpse by now. How can Power support a people whose rulers keep murdering their kin? The Chief Clan of the Sky Hand is tainted by blood and chaos."

Sweet Smoke chuckled to herself. "Perhaps you are right. By Breath Giver's shining light, I hope it is so."

Morning Dew emphasized her point with the stir stick. "People are coming from all over for my marriage. They are going to see, Mother. This is more than just a joining between Screaming Falcon and me. We will use this as an opportunity for others to decide that we can lead them."

"You've discussed this with your brother?"

"Biloxi understands completely. He has sent for hunters to bring in extra game. He has already talked to the warriors, and they will be at their best. He intends to hold ballgames after the wedding."

"I heard. I didn't think it wise. And he didn't tell me that the games were to showcase our strength. What if we lose? Hmm? Think of that?"

"Mother, you have to believe in us. In our Power." She grinned up. "Besides, you know that no one can whip us in stickball. You're the best woman player among our people. And you taught me everything you know."

Sweet Smoke's expression hardened. "I am still matron, head of our clan. I wish he would have discussed this with me."

Morning Dew shot a glance back toward the Men's House, seeing Biloxi Mankiller, resplendent in a feathered headdress, his white apron immaculate, as he strode toward them at the head of a procession of warriors.

"Well, here he comes. And dressed as if for some ceremonial occasion. What do you think this means?"

Sweet Smoke turned, standing straight and tall as the procession passed the Sun Stairs leading up to the palace. Most of the warriors laughed, making mocking gestures of obeisance to the suffering captives. Behind them, Morning Dew caught sight of two naked women, heads bowed as they shuffled along.

Biloxi Mankiller was indeed resplendent. Upon closer examination the headdress was a gaudy thing, filled with bristling white heron feathers intermixed with blue, green, and red that shimmered in the light. Splays of turkey feathers had been tied to each shoulder, and strings of polished copper beads gleamed around his neck. A large white whelk shell pendant depicting Spider bringing the sacred fire down from Breath Giver hung on his chest.

Beside Biloxi came Screaming Falcon's old uncle, the tishu minko, Bow Mankiller. He was a stately man, tall, with gray hair bound up in a warrior's bun. He carried only a chunkey stone, the one he used in ritual games, in his right hand. His white apron sported a falcon—its wings spread, beak open—woven into the fabric. Feather plumes from an osprey were tied like sunbursts to his shoulders.

"Greetings, Matron," Bow Mankiller called formally as the party came to a stop.

The warriors spread out to either side, the disheveled captives standing with wrists bound before them. The women never looked up. Bruises could be seen, mottled black, green, and yellow on their dirty skin.

"A good day to you, Tishu Minko." Sweet Smoke had adopted a serene look, though Morning Dew knew that she, too, was burning with curiosity.

Biloxi stepped over, taking his place slightly to the right and ahead of his mother. He had his chin up, as if expectant. Morning Dew could read the barely suppressed excitement behind his eyes.

Drawing himself up, Bow Mankiller cradled the round disk of his chunkey stone. "From the beginning times, it has been our custom to provide the bride's clan with gifts as a demonstration of our goodwill. In view of the upcoming marriage which will once again join our clan with yours, I have come to offer a small token of our appreciation. We offer these slaves, taken in our recent attack, as but the first of our gifts. We hope that they serve you well."

The two warriors flanking the captives reached over and pushed the women forward. "Kneel," one ordered.

Both women dropped to their knees before Biloxi Mankiller. Neither raised her head.

"They will serve you well," Bow Mankiller said evenly. "If you have any trouble with them, and decline to discipline them for whatever reason, I personally will be happy to remind them of their status."

"I think we can handle them," Biloxi replied.

"And if they should run"—Bow Mankiller grinned meaningfully—"we will take it as a personal affront." Bending down, he said loudly to the women, "My kinsmen would run them down like dogs in the forest."

"Your gift is kindly received," Biloxi answered. "Perhaps you might tell my mother who these women are?"

Bow pointed a finger at the older woman on the left. "This one is of the Sky Hand Raccoon Clan. She was once the wife of the minko at Alligator Town." He glanced back at the hanging captives in their squares. "It is believed that she no longer has use for that husband.

"This one"—Bow Mankiller indicated the younger— "is her daughter. Both are from the lineage of which the man called Seven Dead Mankiller is head."

"The tishu minko of Split Sky City, I believe." Biloxi almost chortled.

"That is correct. These women are cousins." Bow Mankiller bowed slightly, enjoying the theater.

Biloxi, as was his right as high minko, spoke for his clan. "We thank you, good friend. Your gift comes at the perfect time. Our hunters have brought in many deer in preparation for the marriage feast." He glanced skeptically at the captives. "They don't look like they have much practice fleshing hides. I have heard that Seven Dead's kin are accustomed to much softer labor."

Laughter broke out among the warriors.

Morning Dew full well knew what that implied. Since returning from the raid, half the men on the war party had been between the captives' legs.

"We thank you for your gift," Sweet Smoke said politely, but Morning Dew could see the worry behind her eyes. "They shall be a great asset to this household."

"We are humbled by your thanks." Bow Mankiller nodded again. "Oh, and Matron, a certain young man sends his fondest regards. From the looks of things, after his final purification, and immediate marriage, he will be unable to address you with his respect and appreciation."

Bow Mankiller referred to the strict rules of avoidance that the Chahta practiced between mother-in-law and son-in-law. It would be a terrible breach of manners, protocol, and custom if they so much as spoke to each other after the marriage. The origins of the behavior went back to the Creation, when Eagle Man's mother-in-law, growing infatuated with him after he married her daughter, seduced him to her bed. The offspring from that union had been a wicked young man who did much evil before Eagle Man was finally able to kill him.

Morning Dew flushed with pride. The gift of two slaves—let alone such high-ranking ones—was a most auspicious wedding offering. The news of it would be on every tongue by evening. She had to use all of her control to keep from bouncing on her toes.

"A most pleasant day, Matron," Bow Mankiller said, and nodded. "And to you, High Minko." With that, he signaled his warriors, turned on his heel, and headed back the way he had come.

"Slaves!" Morning Dew cried as soon as they were out of earshot.

"Well," Sweet Smoke said with resignation, "there are hides to flesh." To her son, she added, "Make sure you get enough work out of them to justify the food they eat."

"Get to work, slaves," Biloxi ordered.

For the first time, the older woman looked up.

The woman's expression startled Morning Dew. Her face was slack, and emptiness lay behind her eyes, as if her center had been cored out, and her souls gone hollow.

A shiver ran down Morning Dew's spine. *No matter what, I shall never be such an abject thing. This I swear!*

Eleven

The sweat lodge consisted of a circle of saplings set into the ground, bent over, and tied to their opposites to create a low dome. Other saplings had been woven between the bows, then thatched and the whole of it sealed with clay. Snow had covered it with a white mantle when they arrived to kindle a fire in the low pit outside.

Old White sat naked in the pitch darkness, his bony butt on a doubled blanket. To his right, Two Petals clasped her knees to her breasts. He could sense the girl's fear, a tangible presence in the heat that poured off the stones. They had been cooked to a red glow in a roaring fire outside and carefully carried into the lodge perched on smoking sticks.

Silver Loon sat to the left. He could hear her shuffling as she prepared the last of her things: a pot of water, a branch of sage, tobacco, and the cup of tea she had brewed earlier. Before entering the lodge, they had disrobed in the cold air while flakes of white snow melted on their skin. They had offered prayers to the four directions, to Father Sky, and finally to Mother Earth. Silver Loon had blessed the water, sage, and tea. Then, one by one, they had placed the stones on the hard earth at the center of the lodge and seated themselves, shivering and puffing white breath. The last one to enter, Old White had reached over and draped the covering across the low doorway to seal them in blackness.

"Water is life," Silver Loon said softly as she reached into the water pot and sprinkled it on the glowing rocks.

Steam hissed, exploding from the stones and rising. The first faint touches began to caress Old White's aged hide.

"Fire is life." Silver Loon sprinkled the stones again.

"In it we are cleansed," Old White added. "Let our souls wash clean."

"Purify our bodies."

Steam hissed angrily as Silver Loon added more water.

Old White could feel prickles of heat eating at his skin. He drew a deep breath of the hot wet air. How long had it been since his last ritual bath? Too many moons. A man needed this to cleanse his souls, purge his body, and reorder his universe.

While the idea of a sweat had appealed to him, the purpose behind it had left him uneasy. He remembered the certainty in Silver Loon's eyes as she had said, "She is fighting the Power. Until she gives herself to it, she will be tortured, unpredictable, and dangerous."

"Dangerous?" he had asked incredulously. "She's just a girl."

"Didn't you tell me you took her out of a battle? Didn't you say she witched an A'khota chief?"

"I think he was sick from something else."

"All these years, and you still delude yourself."

"I'm not—"

"She called you from halfway across the world, and you still doubt her Power?"

"She kept appearing in my Dreams."

"Do not let her fill your nightmares."

He had paused, meeting her knowing gaze.

Silver Loon finally asked, "What is this all about?"

"I'm not sure. I was in Oraibi. A mesa-top city far to the southwest. It happened in a kiva. During a Dance, a *Katsina* appeared to me."

"A what?"

"An explanation would make no sense to you. All that

matters is that the *Katsina* told me to go home. That the way would be long. I started four days later. I've crossed half the world since."

"Called by this girl."

"That came later, while I was with the Caddo."

She had nodded. "It all goes back to the past, doesn't it?"

"What happened back then . . ." He shook his head. "It just doesn't make sense."

"What doesn't?"

"Why Power would take such steps to set things right. There's no need to involve Two Petals—no need for such extremes."

"And just what did you think would restore the balance?"

"It's simple, really. All I needed to do was die."

She had studied him thoughtfully. "Whatever it was that you did was but the beginning. This is about more than just your actions. It has grown, spiraling, like a raging inferno spun from a carelessly tossed ember." Her eyes went vacant. "You are at the center of a struggle that was begun long ago. Darkness and light. Chaos and order. Red and white. It always goes back to the passions between the brothers."

At her words, a cold chill ran through his souls. "And I suppose murder is at the heart of it?"

She had nodded, eyes like dark moons. "Oh, yes. You see, in the beginning, Wolf Dreamer killed his brother."

I'm scared," Two Petals said softly, her chin quivering. Her bare skin prickled and burned from the relentless steam. She could feel it, like little needles burrowing into her hide. A trickle of sweat ran down her forehead to burn salty in her right eye. She rubbed at her face, now slick and wet. Each breath was like a hot knife in her throat. Breathing through her nose was like drawing in stilettos of fire.

"Don't be afraid," Silver Loon soothed. "Relax. Breathe. Feel the tension drain from your limbs."

She heard Old White run his hands over his arms and legs, slicking the beading sweat over his skin. As more steam hissed up from the stones, Two Petals tried to curl into a tight ball.

"It's hot," Two Petals protested.

"You will grow used to it," Silver Loon told her. "If your souls slip from your body, we will catch them."

"You can do this," Old White reassured. "I brought you to Silver Loon for a reason. She can help you."

"She can make this go away?"

Silver Loon's calming voice said, "I can help you to find the way. You must trust me."

Anything, just get this over with. "I—I'm ready."

She heard Silver Loon shift, then say, "Two Petals, I am handing you a cup of tea. Find my hand. That's it. Now, as you take the cup, be careful not to spill anything. You must drink it all. After that, you will feel better. Do not fight; just let your souls float."

Two Petals placed the thin rim to her lips. The liquid was cool, flavored with mint to cover a bitter taste. She gulped it frantically, feeling the chill rush through her hot gut.

"There, I'm done."

"Good," Silver Loon told her. "Now, you only need endure for a while and Sister Datura will come and Dance with your souls."

"Sister Datura?"

"She will show you the way."

Two Petals scooted imperceptibly back so her spine touched the uncomfortable wicker of the lodge wall. She was panting, taking shallow gasps of the hot air. The voices—stilled for the moment—began whispering just beyond her ear. She felt the pull, could feel herself slipping. No, not now.

She clenched her teeth and blinked at the stinging sweat that trickled into her eyes. Gods, couldn't this just be over? It would be so easy. She just needed to turn, rip the cover away, and she'd fling herself out into the soothing chill of the day.

She swallowed hard, already seeing the disapproving expression that would mar Old White's face, but she was going to do it. She couldn't take another instant of this burning heat.

When she reached out, her arm seemed rubbery.

"Not yet," a voice told her.

She jerked her head around, searching the darkness for the voice that had spoken so close to her ear. Sweat tickled as it ran down her chest. She gasped frantically. The world seemed to spin.

"Not long now. Come, take my hands. Come Dance with me."

"Who, who are you?"

"I am your sister."

"I don't have a—"

"Shhh! Of course you do. We are all sisters. You, me, Old Heron, Nightshade, and so many, many others. Lichen came to you earlier. She, too, is my sister."

From a great distance, Two Petals heard Silver Loon warn Old White, "Don't. She's falling into the Dance."

Dance? A flash of light—golden, purple, and orange— flickered in the darkness.

Two Petals drew rapid breaths; her skin seemed to crawl loosely over her muscles and bones. A distant flute could be heard, its notes mellow and rising on the darkness. She could feel the blanket beneath her rising and shifting, as if the earth had gone fluid.

"What's happening?"

"We are going to Dance the future. I want you to see the shape of things to come. Only then can you look

*back and see the path to your husband. Power calls, and
you shall Dance with it."*

"I am afraid!"

"Reach out. Take my hands. Let me lift you."

Two Petals extended her hands toward a magical
glow that shimmered in all the colors of the rainbow.
She felt herself rise, her souls being pulled inexorably
into the light. . . .

The fire crackled and spit futile sparks toward the high
ceiling of Silver Loon's house. Old White stared at the
bags, boxes, jars, and bones. He sat on a pole bed along
one wall and sponged Two Petals' forehead with a damp
cloth. The girl remained as still as the dead, the only
signs of life the occasional gasped breath and the sometimes frantic movements of her eyes beneath closed
lids. Despite the warm house, her flesh might have been
cold clay.

"You were sure of the dose?" he asked again.

"One can never be sure," Silver Loon replied from her
backrest by the fire. She occupied herself sewing small
white shell beads onto a fine blue dress she had taken
from one of the boxes. "You have been around long
enough to know the dangers of Dancing with Power.
Sometimes, if the soul is found weak or cowardly, the
beasts of the other worlds snap it up."

"That was the story the great Lichen told, wasn't it?"

"And, according to legend, after Birdman ate her, she
came back alive, more Powerful than ever. She was the
ruler behind Petaga's throne." She glanced in the direction of the great mound. "In those days, Cahokia reached
its greatest Power. People came here from all over the
world. And from here, they went back, filled with the
Dream of Cahokia."

"And now it is but the stuff of legends."

"Polluted," she said. "By that barbaric beast, Black Tooth, who lives in his pitiful temple." She shook her head. "After Tharon's taint had been burned away, Petaga built a five-story palace atop the great mound. Can you imagine?"

Old White nodded. "I've seen such things."

"Where?"

"Among the Azteca, and at the ruins of Teotihuacan. And in the southwest, I've walked the crumbling walls of Talon Town. Heard the late-night wailing of murdered matrons. Like Sun Town, with its little red owls, this, too, will fade. Cities, like men, are born, grow, and then age and die."

"You sound saddened by that."

He shrugged. "It is the way of things. That's all. In spite of all my travels, I have learned that only the sun, sky, water, and earth are eternal. What is made must crack and collapse."

"What else have you learned, Runner? You have seen more than any man alive, talked to peoples beyond number. Of all those places and peoples, what great truth have you discovered?"

He grunted. "I found no great truth . . . only an endless number of small ones. And people"—he raised a finger—"are just people. Great or small, mighty or meek, no matter their delusions of greatness and influence, at root they are the same beast as a woodcutter, farmer, or weaver."

"And for that you had to travel the world?"

"I did." He smiled to himself as he carefully rearranged Two Petals' long hair on the bedding. To carry the girl back, Silver Loon had asked some of the local village men for help. Despite their combined efforts, she and Old White wouldn't have been able to negotiate the steep stairway to the house atop its mound.

He fixed his gaze on Silver Loon. "But you would not believe the things I've seen. War, hunger, blinding blowing snow, sunset on the gulf, a bearded white man. The midnight lights that twinkle, beam, and glow in the far north . . . So many things that can be described, but never understood. I have seen cactuses the height of trees. A canyon that splits the world. Mountains that spew fire and smoke above the clouds. Can you believe herds of buffalo that blacken the landscape for as far as the eye can see? Or fish out on the gulf that jump from the water and fly off on clear shining wings?"

She arched a suspicious eyebrow. "I've heard of the buffalo, and even seen the night lights. But these other things?" She shook her head. "No."

"They are as real as I am."

She glanced at him. "Did you ever find love?"

He lowered his eyes. "Several times. Once with you."

"Then why did you leave? Do not tell me it was over this crime you committed in the south. I would have taken you no matter how polluted and guilty you were."

He sighed. "I suppose I left because I was deeply, truly, content with you. I was in love, and loved back. You lifted the darkness from my souls, and I loved living again."

"Was that such a burden?"

He glanced at the fabric pack resting atop the cedar one beside the door. "No, it was an injustice."

She had followed his gaze to the pack. "You could have just thrown it into the river, perhaps smashed it to pieces and tossed it into a busk pit somewhere as an offering of appeasement to the gods. You didn't have to continue punishing yourself."

"You don't know what I did."

"I know more than you think."

"Really?"

She shrugged, going back to her beadwork. "I looked in the sack once while you slept."

He swallowed hard. "And what did you see?"

"Your rotted conscience."

"Well, it is of no matter. I am going back. What was done shall be made right."

"I suppose that will allow your souls to travel to the Sky World without regret. And once there, will you be received by your Ancestors with open arms?"

He glanced up at the soot-thick bones. "I don't know what to believe about the afterlife. Among the Azteca, I saw people sacrificed to their rain god."

"That happens here. Prisoners are killed before the palaces and thrown down the mound."

"One or two, yes. But not thousands. For four days, from the first light of dawn to the last rays of sunset a solid line of captives was marched up the high pyramid. They were bent backward over a stone, their beating hearts cut from their bodies. Then the corpses were tossed bleeding down the steep stairs. As fast as they fell, slaves hauled them off to the fields for fertilizer." He saw her shock. "They painted their tall stone mound with blood. It shone crimson in the sunlight." A pause. "And the rains didn't come. So seven days later, they started the whole ugly process again."

"You joke."

He sadly shook his head. "How can one believe in the gods after seeing something like that?"

"But you still believe in Power. You followed your Dreams to this girl."

"In Power, yes. I've touched it, Danced with it. I've felt it rush through me like a hot wind. It's gods that I no longer believe in." He looked down at Two Petals' slack face. "But then, you always thought I was a fool."

You could stay with me for a while." Fox Squirrel's words echoed between Trader's souls as he used a broken branch to dig his copper out of its cache. The snow had ceased, the air crisp. Around him the forest dripped, and occasional bits of icy snow clattered as they fell from the branches. At the trail crossing, brown water swirled around his canoe. The forest was quiet, as if waiting, the Dreams of the trees hidden down in the roots beneath the frosty leaves.

"What do you think?" Trader asked Swimmer as the dog lifted a leg to pee on a sapling. "If I left the copper, no one would find it. For half the packs we're carrying, Fox Squirrel would keep us for the winter."

Swimmer cocked his head, probably the same way he would if listening to a lunatic.

"It's a warm place to stay. And she liked you. Scratched your ears and belly like it was you giving her gifts instead of me."

Swimmer turned his attention to sniffing a zigzag pattern down the trail. He seemed particularly interested in a set of turkey tracks that were fading in the melting snow.

Trader pulled the last of the dirt free and reached down for his pack. "Of course, the weather will break. These fall storms, they drop a couple of days of snow, then the air warms right up. Won't be true cold for another moon."

Swimmer came trotting back, his furry tail wagging. He stopped to pee on the same sapling, then switched sides and peed on it again.

"Just making sure, huh?"

Trader lugged the heavy copper down to the canoe and settled it. "Come, Swimmer. If I'm being an idiot, I'd best be about it."

The dog jumped nimbly to the canoe, clambered onto the packs, and settled into his place on a fold of fabric Trader had placed for him. Trader pushed off, raising his paddle and driving the canoe into the current.

"Oh, I guess it's not the last foolish mistake I'll make in my life." He nosed the canoe past the creek mouth and into the main channel. "Still, there's something about her. Our dear Fox Squirrel has a certain spirit. And it's not just the coupling. The thing is, she really likes men."

He glanced at the dog. "Not all women like men. But I guess you wouldn't know about that. I think it has to do with the people. Different people have different ways about how men and women deal with each other. Now, among my people, women are . . . well, they care for the house. That's their duty. That and raising the children. Men make the decisions. I guess you'd say there's a wall. A difference that's bred into us. Men and women have to be so very careful not to get too close."

Swimmer stared at him from under lifted eyebrows.

"No, I'm serious. Coupling is all right. As long as you're married. And to each other. And it's not too close to some sacred time. And you're not trying to purify yourself to keep some lightning-blasted Power in balance with some other crazy Power. Rules, rules, rules. That's what we have."

He pondered that, swinging his paddle in a steady rhythm, reading the current.

"Makes you wonder how that all got started." He nodded back toward the shore. "Fox Squirrel and I, we had fun. We coupled and talked, laughed, and talked some more, then we coupled." He paused. "The thing is, I really enjoy spending time with her."

Swimmer shuffled on his fabric and dropped his muzzle on his paws.

"Among my people, a man who spends too much time with a woman is considered weak. They believe that he picks up a woman's ways, and his heart turns watery. Then you spend time in an A'khota village and they have women warriors. Not many, but women who go on battle walks, shoot arrows, and swing war clubs. Mention that among my people and they'll think your head's gone softer than your heart."

Swimmer tapped his tail a couple of times.

"So," Trader mused, "we'll go to the lower river. Down past the Natchez and Caddo. I know of a band of Tunica down there where the women are as much fun as Fox Squirrel. Not as attractive, mind you, but willing."

He frowned. "Of course, they don't speak much Trader Tongue. You can get the point across: These furs for a night with you." A pause. "Trouble is, after Fox Squirrel, lying with a woman who can't talk to you just isn't the same."

From Swimmer's expression, he wasn't sure the dog believed him.

"What?"

Swimmer perked his ears.

"Oh, that." Trader cleared his throat. "All right. There was a woman once. I was madly in love with her. She filled my Dreams, day and night. I watched her, and she watched me. It wasn't that she was forbidden, as Fox Squirrel would have had you believe. She wasn't a relative. Fact is, she was in a proper clan. My clan representatives had spoken to hers; a marriage was already arranged. I knew that. We knew that," he corrected.

"I might have been young, but I gave my heart to her, Swimmer. And you know what, she still fills my Dreams. Even after all these years." He nodded at the dog. "That's what happened while I was coupling with Fox Squirrel."

He watched the endless trees crowding the bank. "Why do I tell you things I wouldn't even admit to myself? What is it about you? Are you really the demon dog those silly farmers thought you were?"

Swimmer thumped his tail again.

"That's what I thought." Trader smiled. "Yes, that's why I left. That's why I always leave. I meet a woman, like Fox Squirrel, then at just the wrong time, *her* image seems to bloom like some exotic flower between my souls."

Trader paddled for a while, an empty feeling inside.

"I'll bet you're wondering why I don't go back and get her?"

He bit his lip, wondering if he could say this, even to Swimmer.

"Because I killed a man over her. By now, she's long been married. It's bad enough what my people would do to me. They don't take kindly to murder . . . especially over a woman. But the worst thing is, I couldn't stand the look she'd give me. Maybe it would be hatred, or worse, loathing. And what would I do if her expression proved she despised me? Hatred? Loathing? I guess that's all right. But being despised, now that's like a knife in the heart."

When he looked down, Swimmer was asleep.

But then, being ignored was better than being despised.

Twelve

Power, like air, permeated the world. It could flow like a subtle breeze through a man's life, or blow like a gale, flatten his house, and send him tumbling to ruin. Unlike air, Power could be managed. To channel it toward a given purpose took specific rituals, and the greatest of respect and preparation. Like fire it could burn just as easily as heat. Do not believe for a moment that humans can ever control Power. The foolish might try, but in the end, they would be consumed by the very force they sought to master. Rather, like a river, it could be used, diverted to a specific end, but eventually its water must return to the river.

For war, the red Power bestowed its wielder with prowess, courage, skill, and endurance. To call Power to his aid, Smoke Shield followed the prescribed ritual: He had painted his body red, with black on his lower face. Then he had dressed in his war shirt, collected his bow and arrows, and his shield. He had slipped his three small white arrows through his hair and picked up his war ax. Three times he had circled the tchkofa mound, calling out for warriors. People had gathered, watching solemnly. Among them, his wives, Heron Wing and Violet Bead. On his last round, he had seen both women retreat through the crowd, each headed to her house where she would clean the place, sweeping any trash to a pile in the corner.

Since both had just recently emerged from the Women's House, neither could taint any of his possessions. A woman during her moon could pollute a man, cause Power to shun him. After cleaning the house, they would prepare a feast, using care to follow the rituals, never touching the food with their bare hands.

After finishing his three circles of the tchkofa, Smoke Shield had led the way to the Men's House. For three days the thirty-two men who had joined him had secluded themselves. They had assiduously avoided any contact with females, fasted, bathed in the sweat lodge, and drunk a broth made of button snakeroot.

On the third day, High Minko Flying Hawk entered the Men's House. He had painted his face red with black bars running parallel across the cheeks. The heavy copper headpiece had been polished to a sheen, and his eight small white arrows—symbols of war honors—had been poked through his hair. He carried a hafted stone ceremonial knife; chipped from fine chert imported from the Charokee lands, it was as long as his arm, and used to ritually execute prisoners. Flying Hawk had worn his best white apron, the tip of it hanging down between his knees.

Smoke Shield watched as the high minko looked at the expectant warriors who sat on the benches. A low fire— its embers carefully carried from the tchkofa fire— smoldered in the central hearth. On the walls hung shields, skulls, and weapons taken from long-vanquished enemies. In the east, on a clay altar covered with a blanket festooned with ivory-billed woodpecker feathers and strips of cougar hide, sat the red cedar box that held the war medicine.

It was said that within the ornately carved box were scales and bits of horn taken from the Horned Serpent by a great *Hopaye*. There, too, lay an arrowhead from the beginning times that had once tipped one of Eagle Man's shafts. With it, he slew Cannibal Turkey. Sprigs of red cedar, shining pieces of galena, and the scalps from dead enemy chiefs added to the war medicine's great Power. So, too, did a piece of copper sculpted into the shape of Morning Star. Some said the red color of the wood had resulted when a great war chief sustained many wounds, the box soaking up his blood and giving him strength to continue and win his battle.

Below it, on a wooden stand, rested the war pipe, a heavy thing made of stone and carved into the shape of Morning Star as he knelt over a dead enemy and severed the man's head. Into its back a large hole had been bored for the bowl. The long wooden stem, carved into interwoven serpents with pearls for eyes, sat just below on a raccoon skin.

Flying Hawk turned to the men. "Is there any man among you who is not ready for war?"

Smoke Shield replied first. "I am pure of heart, and am prepared."

One by one, the others repeated his words.

Flying Hawk nodded, then walked to the altar, kneeling. "Bless us, great Spirits of war. What has been wronged must be set right. Hear the cries of our dead, calling for justice. The White Arrow Chahta have attacked our relatives and spilled their blood upon the dirt. They have broken the harmony of Power. Chaos— you who have been let loose—aid us now. Flow through us. Strengthen our hearts."

From a box beside the altar, he shook out tobacco and carefully tamped it into the great pipe's bowl, using a wooden pestle so as not to touch the sacred leaf. Lifting the heavy stone bowl, he placed it on the hard-packed red clay floor and carefully inserted the long stem. Then, he nodded to Smoke Shield.

With great solemnity, Smoke Shield rose from the bench and stepped to the pipe stem. Taking it in his mouth, he watched Flying Hawk light a twig in the fire and hold it over the bowl.

As Smoke Shield puffed, Flying Hawk stood, raising his hands to the warriors. "You are about to attempt a most daring thing. We have been unjustly attacked. Our people are at risk. There is no time to call additional warriors from the hunt. Everything rests on you. Do you understand?"

Smoke Shield grunted assent as he exhaled blue smoke and watched it rise toward the high ceiling. As he stepped aside, Blood Skull, who would be his second, took the pipe stem and sucked. At the same time, Smoke Shield stepped over, touching his medicine pouch to the war medicine box. "Bless me with courage and skill. Grant me cunning and the ability to outwit my enemies." Then he hung the small bundle around his neck.

He stepped aside as Blood Skull touched his medicine pouch to the war medicine and asked for its blessing.

As the warriors, one by one, smoked from the war pipe and touched their medicine to the cedar box, Flying Hawk told them, "In all of our history, none of our Ancestors has been called upon to attempt so daring an attack. The White Arrow do not expect you. They will be comfortable, happy, and lax in their vigilance. Their thoughts are only centered on this marriage, not on our attack. But you must be wary. You must sneak through the forest as silently as cougars on the hunt. You must be as keen-eyed as a hawk, and see before you are seen. Like wolves, you must not sleep, but be eternally vigilant. I warn you, do not be too eager. Do not take a single scalp just because you find some solitary Chahta along the trail, but avoid him. Remember the greater purpose of your attack. It is up to you to pass unnoticed."

He glanced at Smoke Shield. "My nephew, cunning as the raccoon, has told you his plan. You will not travel as warriors, but as hunters. You will not wear your finery, but simple hunting shirts. Your shields will be cased in fabric sacks to look like burdens of food. When you walk, it will not be as warriors, but as simple hunters, returning with a bounty for the wedding feast.

"You will approach from the north, acting and talking like some Chahta from distant places. Avoid conversations. Say only that you are in a hurry to bear your catch to White Arrow Town.

"You will time your arrival until just after dark. In the darkness, you will enter White Arrow Town and find a house close to their palace. Inside, you will quietly kill the occupants, and only then will you uncase your shields, war clubs, and don your warrior's clothes. But I warn you, do not take time with vanity. The Chahta will not care that your faces are not perfectly painted."

Nervous laughter erupted from the warriors.

Flying Hawk used his hands to still them. "I know it will be hard. But subdue your passions until that moment when you burst from the house and climb the steps to the palace, and then you may let your furies loose. At that moment, scream like a thousand demons. Your job is to frighten the enemy, run through them like red wolves among quail. Instill fear and panic, and they will flee, thinking themselves overrun by overwhelming numbers. In the darkness, they will not know. Do you understand?"

"Hay-haw," they all answered.

Smoke Shield took their measure, seeing the gleam in their eyes. *Yes, they are keen now, but will they be as committed when we are sneaking through a dark and hostile forest?*

"When you have taken their high minko and this Screaming Falcon, make your way to the canoe landing. Steal whatever craft you need, and set the rest adrift. The White Arrow will have no trail to follow when they finally gather their wits. Before they are organized, you will be downriver, and most of the way home."

Each of the men was nodding.

Flying Hawk touched his breast. "I know that sometimes, late at night, you will hesitate, wondering if you made the right decision. No one lives forever, and should anyone die, he *will* have his souls avenged. You need not return to Split Sky City to know this. You will hear the screams of the captives from far beyond the walls."

Sobered, the men nodded, glancing at each other in reassurance.

"The Sky Hand People have never been as proud of our warriors as we are of you at this moment." Flying Hawk bent down, taking the last puff from the war pipe. Exhaling the smoke through his mouth and nostrils, he said, "Let us go now. A great feast has been prepared. Let our people adore you, and as you feast, look into their eyes, see their gratitude, and keep that memory next to your hearts as you do this great thing."

Smoke Shield clapped each of his men on the back as they stepped out into the fresh air. He could hear the cries of joy as his people met their heroes.

"You made a good speech," Smoke Shield said as he lifted the war medicine and ran his arms through the straps.

"You just make a good raid," Flying Hawk replied, worry in his eyes.

Heron Wing clapped her hands, raising her voice along with others as the warriors trotted grandly out of the plaza; through the maze of houses, granaries, and workshops; and down to the canoe landing northwest of the Skunk Clan grounds. There, among the multitude, she watched Smoke Shield and his warriors clamber into their canoes. They pushed off and began paddling downriver, heads up, looking for all the world as if they had already won.

"Will he come back?" Violet Bead asked from beside her.

Heron Wing grunted. "Would we care if he didn't?"

"I'm not looking forward to having my hair cut, howling in the night, and acting like a widow."

Heron Wing shrugged. "But for the cut hair and howling, what would be the difference?"

"Not much." Violet Bead turned; she was a tall woman, attractive, with long glistening hair. Her two children, girls of three and four, stood beside her. Having seen twenty-one summers, Violet Bead was five years younger than Heron Wing. Smoke Shield had been smitten with the woman's beauty the first time he'd seen her, and had pressed Flying Hawk to arrange a hasty marriage. Violet Bead's people were weavers, their lineage of little status and less authority among the Crawfish Clan. But then, what Smoke Shield wanted, he always got. In the case of Violet Bead it had taken several years before he tired of her.

She did better than I at holding his interest. The thought came unbidden. What did she care? She glanced back at her son, now eight. He was playing in the dirt, drawing in the soot-stained soil among bits of shell left by the shell carvers. He liked to draw, but as Pale Cat's nephew, he would be directed toward the arts of a Healer. She had already had talks with her brother about what to do if Healing didn't mesh well with the boy's creative spirit. At least he was nothing like his father.

She absently reached up, fingers tracing the faint scar on her cheek. Smoke Shield had given her that after a particularly bitter argument. In truth, she didn't mind him bedding the slave women and frolicking with the prostitutes, but he didn't have to be so rotted blatant about it. As far as she was concerned, if he was driving himself into the slaves, prostitutes, and several other men's wives, he wasn't crawling into her bed. It was bad enough on those rare occasions when he felt compelled to. People had begun to talk about how for eight years he hadn't planted his seed in her sheath.

There are advantages to having a Hopaye *for a brother.* Pale Cat gave her the necessary herbs and had instructed her on how to irrigate her sheath to avoid pregnancy. She had told him it was for one of her friends on whose behalf she'd asked; nevertheless, he probably suspected. Pale Cat, however, held no great fondness for Smoke Shield, either.

"Have you thought about asking him to divorce you?" Violet Bead asked dryly.

"Is it that obvious?"

Like most co-wives, they had never been particularly close, but they tolerated each other better than most.

Violet Bead glanced around to be sure they couldn't be overheard. "I've been thinking about it myself. The father of my children was almost caught the other day. He was slipping himself inside some Fish Clan woman. Her husband went looking for her when his supper wasn't cooked. He even looked in the granary where they were coupling. Fortunately, she'd been wise enough to pile the corn so he didn't see them."

"It will happen eventually. It always does." The Sky Hand People vigorously punished loose behavior among married people. Men were merely humiliated until they outlived it; but women were disfigured, often outcast, and sometimes killed for infidelity. Heron Wing studied Violet Bead from the corner of her eye. The woman liked the trappings of wealth and status that came from being Smoke Shield's wife, and having a house so close to the great mound. She also liked the affection and attention of men. More than once Heron Wing had observed shadowy male figures slipping into Violet Bead's house late at night. Assuming she survived discovery, and could induce Smoke Shield to divorce her, what would she do? Heron Wing had little doubt that she would join the professional caste of women who freely sold their services. Even in their chaste society, such females enjoyed a certain stylish status, if not respect.

Violet Bead shot her a knowing look.

Heron Wing said softly, "One of the curses of being raised with everything is that you never understand that not everything can be yours."

"Are you speaking of yourself, or him?"

Heron Wing ignored the slight, attempting to mislead Violet Bead's thoughts. "Young and beautiful as you are, it wouldn't be long before someone was talking to your mother about another marriage."

"So, why haven't you pressed him to divorce you?"

Because I am a trophy more than a wife. "There are benefits for my clan," she lied.

"I hate politics."

"Unfortunately it crawls into your bed along with your husband when you marry the man who will be high minko."

Violet Bead asked, "Are you sure it's just the prestige that keeps you together?"

"Meaning what?"

"Nothing." Violet Bead was staring at the river, her beautiful face expressionless as a dance mask. "I have to get back. There are dishes to clean."

Heron Wing watched the woman turn and head back through the crowd.

Divorce. The word sounded so alien, so impossible.

Why had she ever married Smoke Shield? Ah, the foolish decisions of youth. When Green Snake left, she should have severed all ties with the Chief Clan. Better that Breath Giver had never blessed the young with passion. It led them to wrong choices.

Heron Wing bent down and collected Stone's hand. Her son's fingers were grimy with the black soil. Despite her reluctant hopes, the past continued to cling to her like old spiderwebs.

In the Dream, Old White stood before a burning building, flames racing into the sky. The fire roared, searing his face and hands. Step by step he backed away, turning to run into the night. At the sight that greeted his eyes, he stopped short, seeing the high Azteca temple. The firelight cast the great pyramid's stone sides in a crimson light. Only as he looked closer could he tell that the stones seemed to be moving, writhing and swaying in time to the leaping flames.

Not stone. Bodies. The whole thing was made of blood-smeared bodies. Each had a gaping chest that opened and closed like a bloody mouth. They turned horrified faces toward him and fixed agonized gazes on his.

Behind him the fire seemed to eat into his flesh, pushing him ever closer to the hideous temple. One by one, the bodies began to reach out, blood-caked fingers like claws in the night.

"No," he whispered.

He tried to raise his hands, only to find them weighted. He gasped at the sight of his right hand. The war club it held was heavy stone, gleaming wetly with blood. Desperately he sought to loosen his grip, but the blood seemed to have welded it to him like glue.

He started to raise his left hand, to use it to pry the other free, and stared in horror at the beating heart it held.

"Gods!" He jerked awake, feeling the heat at his back. Scrambling away, he discovered that in his sleep he'd rolled next to Silver Loon's fire. His blanket was smoldering.

Cursing, he flung it off, rose to his feet, and stomped the smoking fabric into submission.

"What's all this?" Silver Loon asked, sitting up in her bed and blinking.

"Bad Dream."

"Nothing new for you. In the old days, I actually stooped to drugging you when I wanted a full night's sleep. A little crushed nightshade in your tea."

Old White muttered and stared at his blackened blanket. Rays of light were streaming through gaps in the thatch. Morning had come.

"Well, I should thank my lucky stones that you didn't bear a grudge. Who knows what sort of—" He stopped short. Two Petals' bed was empty, the blankets rumpled. "Two Petals?" he called out, stepping to the rear and staring into the back room. Only more jars, boxes, and piled hides met his gaze. "Where is she?"

"Perhaps she awakened and stepped outside to relieve herself. It's been two days. Her insides had to be full."

He hurried to the door and looked out at the snow. No more than a finger of it covered the ground. Outside was a maze of tracks: his, the locals', Silver Loon's. He walked out to the edge of the mound, staring down the steep stairs. At the bottom, the tracks went this way and that. Two Petals was nowhere to be seen on the flat mound top.

"There she is," Silver Loon said, pointing as she stepped out the doorway.

Old White followed her finger across the plaza to the distant figure climbing the stairs on the great mound.

"Rot and pus," Old White muttered. "What does she think she's doing? The last thing she needs is to set that Black Tooth off."

He ran for his coat, grabbing up his packs and shrugging them on. He plucked his Trader's staff from where it rested against the wall. Silver Loon pulled on tall moccasins, then wrapped a wolf hide around her shoulders. "This is not good," she muttered as she followed Old White out. "Watch your step! The stairs are icy. We'll do the girl no good if you fall and break your foolish old head!"

Despite several near missteps, Old White made it to the bottom. He took Silver Loon's hand, helping her down the last steps and over an icy patch.

Halfway across the plaza, he was breathless. "Not as young as I used to be."

"None of us are," she panted. "Did you really once chase me for miles through the woods?"

"Caught you, too. And some race it was. Never knew a woman who could run like you."

She jabbed at him. "I'm glad you remember."

"It was a memorable event."

"Thought you'd be too winded for anything else. Surprised me, you did."

"That was the time you scratched my back into shreds."

"It was a passionate night."

He forced the image of moonlight gleaming on her naked body from his souls, and put his energy into running, or whatever it was his flaccid muscles and creaking bones were doing. From a distance it would have looked more like a hobbling skip. With each step his stone-weighted fabric pack bounced painfully against his upper thigh.

They gasped and wheezed up to the foot of the great mound stairway.

"Gods, is that really that high?" he asked.

"Higher. Wait until you're halfway up," she managed, and started up the ice-clad steps. "Be extra careful. You slip on these, you'll be dead pulp by the time you hit the bottom."

He couldn't help it. He had to stop and catch his breath. Not once, but time after time. His legs throbbed and ached; his lungs burned. Feeling light-headed, he had to steady himself just to get his balance back.

Two steps higher, they found the moccasin. "It's Two Petals'," Old White said, picking it up. "But I don't understand. It's been untied."

"Perhaps Sister Datura still Dances with her."

As he looked up, worry spurred him on. He'd met Black Tooth once, when the Dehegiha had been a young man, blustery and devoted to warfare and raiding. Back then, he'd been a mountain of muscle, scarred from battles, with more of a reputation as a thief and raider than as a war chief.

"Why is he up here?" Old White asked as they stopped for air. "How come . . . no one's . . . driven him . . . off?"

"Mostly," she puffed, "no one cares."

The lords of Cahokia must have been stewing in the Afterworld. But when he looked around from the heights,

Old White could understand. A handful of small farm-steads stood here and there, and one small village was nestled among the abandoned earthworks. Was this all that was left of Cahokia's greatness? The thin fuzz of tree patches that had sprung up like mold was proof that the forest had begun the process of reclaiming the land.

The next moccasin lay abandoned five steps up.

"What's she doing?" Silver Loon asked. "Her feet will freeze."

Old White plucked up the second moccasin, running his fingers over the soft leather.

Worry burned bright inside him when he found the blue dress Silver Loon had been making for Two Petals. Cold sunlight sparkled on the patterns of shells sewn into the fabric where it draped over three of the stairs.

"This is madness!"

"So her father believed." Silver Loon lifted the gar-ment from the trampled snow on the stairs.

"A young naked woman, walking into Black Tooth's lair? Gods, we've got to hurry."

Reaching the top, they found the gate unguarded. The palisade itself, imposing from so far below, was a rick-ety thing, braced by slanting poles where the bases of the walls had rotted out. The miracle was that the last storm hadn't toppled it.

He might have been sick with worry, but he still mar-veled at the expanse of the high plaza before the brood-ing building. Old White hobbled desperately across the lower plaza, climbed the last set of steps, and entered the gate surrounding the three-story palace. This, too, was abandoned.

Gods, any sentries were probably waiting their turns at poor Two Petals. Somehow he managed to goad him-self onward, approaching the palace itself. The build-ing, despite dilapidation, was nevertheless impressive. Plaster had cracked off here and there, and he could see daylight through the upper-story logs. In places old cloth had been pressed into cracks to stop the draft.

The door was a thick wooden thing made of parallel poles. He muscled it to one side and led the way into the gloomy interior. No one seemed to notice. All attention was fixed on Two Petals as she stood before whatever kind of man Black Tooth had become. A roar of laughter broke from the men and women who crowded around. For her part, Two Petals seemed completely at ease. Her long hair hung down her slim back, reaching to her rounded bottom.

Old White took a quick glance around the room. Worn hides covered a floor where matting once would have lain. He could see more daylight through cracks in the walls. The hearth that should have held a grand fire cupped what would have served to cook a meager meal.

Black Tooth appeared fascinated. He sat jauntily on a three-legged stool like a high minko. The tripod, according to Cahokian legend, represented the three worlds— Sky, Earth, and Underground—all acting in support of the lord. The stool was draped with a silky black bear hide. The one that hung over Black Tooth's shoulders was an equally prime specimen.

The man had aged, but his thick body still intimidated, and the red war shirt he wore did little to hide packed muscle. Scars crisscrossed the man's wide face. Sometime in the past, a wicked blow had smashed his nose flat and crooked. For the moment, his head was back, laughter rolling up and out of his gut. Legs, corded with muscle, were as thick as logs. He held a stone mace chipped in the shape of a turkey tail clutched in his scarred hands. Two of his fingers were missing on the left.

"And what," Black Tooth asked in a booming voice, "would possess me to do that?"

"The long life that stretches before you," Two Petals said with an eerie certainty.

Again Black Tooth roared with delight, eliciting peals from the crowd. He said, "I will let you and the old man go? Just like that? Without paying tribute for passage through my lands? What do you think I am? Some petty chief awed by the Seeker's reputation?"

"No," Two Petals replied, a tone of great wonder in her voice. "You are the greatest lord of Cahokia that has ever existed. A thousand years from now, your name will be on every tongue."

This time he didn't laugh, but cocked his head. "Ah yes, we will rebuild Cahokia." He lifted the mace, symbol of rulership since the time Morning Star first cut the tail from Cannibal Turkey and placed it on his staff. "Once more, the great temples shall rise, and again, the rulers of all lands will flock here."

"You have made such great strides already." Two Petals raised her hands. "Look at the magnificence that surrounds you!" And with that, she turned on her feet, eyes gleaming as she inspected the exposed logs, and sooty spiderwebs hanging from the ceiling.

Old White gaped, watching her. She seemed oblivious of the decay, as if lost in a vision that only her shining eyes could see. He blinked, looking again at the cracked plaster, the spilled pottery, and dusty wooden boxes scattered around the room.

Everyone else, it seemed, was staring at her young body. Her high breasts were pointed, the nipples taut. Her slim belly, navel, and the dark triangle at her pubis would have drawn any man's attention.

Old White started forward, gripping his Trader's staff as if it were a war club. Her next words brought him up short. "All in time, Elder. Wait. Dance with me."

Silver Loon placed a restraining hand on his shoulder, whispering, "This is a thing of Power. Do not interfere."

"Dance with you?" Black Tooth demanded. "Oh, you and I shall Dance, all right. Here's how I do it. I put you on my staff, and you wiggle. You'll like it. I swear!"

Again the room broke out in laughter.

She had tilted her head. "Can you hear them Singing? Their voices are so beautiful."

"Singing? Who?" Black Tooth cocked his head. "I

hear only the wind, and your silly prattle. You're crazy, girl. Lost your souls."

"Gone, gone, gone," Two Petals agreed. "Flown like birds, right up to the sun. How right you are."

"Well, no matter. You won't need souls for what we're going to do next." He lifted his maimed left hand, beckoning. "Come here, little bird. Let me have a taste of that sweet body of yours."

At his order she began to back away.

"Ah, running at last? Maybe your souls aren't as gone as I think." He chuckled. "Go ahead, run away. It'll be sport."

Instead, she started toward him.

Old White would have rushed forward but for the tightening of Silver Loon's hand on his shoulder, and her whispered, "Watch. And learn."

"That's more like it." Black Tooth fixed gleaming eyes on Two Petals.

"I can see through your skin," she said. "Meat and bones. The blood races backward through your veins. I see deer meat spitting unchewed from your mouth. Backward, you're all backward."

"Enough of this," one of the men said. "Take her, and let us watch the sport of it. I'll wager a prime fox hide that you can't make her moan with pleasure."

"She hasn't the wits for that," another chimed in.

"Wits, wits," Two Petals said, closing the distance to Black Tooth. "No, I've no wits at all. Watching this from tomorrow, seeing, feeling the Power." She hesitated. "I see Seeker and me leaving. I see us climbing into his canoe. There are so many packs, all filled with wealth. And your people are hiding, fearful of Power loose upon the land."

Black Tooth threw his head back, breaking out in peals of amusement.

"You see this, do you?"

"Oh, yes. And many other things. Like what you wish most."

He stared greedily at the tuft of her pubic hair and licked his lips before adding, "I'm sure you know what I want now."

Raucous laughter burst out among the watchers.

"Then I will give you what you wish most," Two Petals said.

Black Tooth, grinning in anticipation, laid his mace to one side. He hitched his war shirt up, exposing his rising manhood, and reached out for Two Petals. She took his hands.

Old White broke free of Silver Loon's grip and charged forward. He was filling his lungs to scream, "No!" when Two Petals drew a deep breath and blew into Black Tooth's face.

The big man started, blinked, and froze. For a moment, the room was still. Then his arms pulled loose from Two Petals' and fell to his sides. The look of amazement remained fixed, his eyes like stones popped out from his skull. Imperceptibly at first, he began to lean, gaining momentum as he crashed to the floor, upsetting the tripod. It fell with a muffled clatter, the bear hide settling around it.

"That's what it's like to live forever," Two Petals said simply.

The loud man stepped forward, bent, and touched one of Black Tooth's staring eyes. No reaction followed as the man placed his hand over Black Tooth's open mouth. He looked up. "He's dead!"

Old White stared in disbelief. "What happened here?"

Silver Loon's voice carried in the chill air. "She blew the souls out of his body. Poor fool had no idea what was happening." In a lower voice, she added, "I think she saved your life, Runner. See that you use what's left of it wisely."

People backed away, mutterings of "witch" on the air.

"She is no witch," Silver Loon called, stepping forward. "Two Petals, don't come near me."

The young woman turned, eyes gleaming, and walked calmly to Silver Loon, who handed her the blue dress. "Do not wear this."

Two Petals blinked, seemed to focus, and took the dress, slipping it over her head. Around the room, people were backing away.

Silver Loon turned her attention to the room. "Tell me what happened here." At the silence she added, "You know me. Tell me, or it shall go ill with you next time any of you need my help."

One of the women, gray haired and wearing a smudged brown dress, stepped forward. "One of the guards saw them arrive before the storm. Black . . . That dead man." She pointed to Black Tooth, afraid to say his name and draw his ghost to her. "He wanted to know who had come. What they wanted with you. When two of the young men from Duck Foot Village carried the girl to your house, they learned it was the Seeker, with a young woman. Black . . . That dead man wanted the wooden pack the Seeker carries. He thought it would be filled with Powerful . . . things."

Old White narrowed an eye. "I am a Trader. Protected by the Power of Trade."

The woman swallowed hard. "That dead man didn't believe in the Power of Trade. He . . . He thought he was the new lord of Cahokia."

"*The* lord of Cahokia," Two Petals asserted. "Lord forever."

"We are leaving now," Silver Loon told them. "Do not interfere with us." She pointed at Two Petals. "The Contrary will know."

Old White was still staring back and forth from Black Tooth to Two Petals. The young woman suddenly smiled, the effect like sunlight bursting through clouds. "I'm so full I could burst. Can't eat another bite. Whatever you do, don't offer me another morsel of food. I won't take it."

"I wouldn't think of it," Silver Loon said. "I have

freshly baked acorn cakes in my house." She hesitated, smiled, and added, "But you're the last person on earth I'd offer any to."

"Then let's just stay here." And with that, Two Petals turned, heading for the door. "I'm sure glad I have these warm shoes on."

Old White stared at the moccasins he'd stuffed in his belt. "But . . ."

"Later," Silver Loon told him as she grabbed his sleeve and propelled him toward the door.

The sun stood at its midpoint by the time Old White, Two Petals, and Silver Loon loaded the canoe with packs. Silver Loon, for reasons of her own, had loaded them with provisions; then she had added additional packs filled with a wealth of worked shell, galena beads, copper gorgets, carved mica, tool stone, and finely flaked hoes from the quarries downriver.

The day had warmed, snow melting beneath the morning sun. A break in the weather was definitely welcomed.

"You could come with us," Old White suggested for the final time.

"Once, long ago, old lover, I would have." She looked back at the bluff, dominated by the great mound and the tall structure on its heights. "But that was then. My place is here, now. The people will need me with Black Tooth gone."

"We have lots of time," Two Petals agreed. Her eyes were fixed on the northern horizon, somewhere far beyond the bushy cottonwoods that had sprung up on the opposite bank.

"No," Silver Loon whispered. "We don't."

"Then we should be getting started," Old White said,

and bent to push the canoe into the murky water of Cahokia Creek.

"Do not forget, the Illinois are at war with each other at the confluence of the rivers. Be careful making your passage. Make sure they see your Trader's staff." Silver Loon gave Two Petals an uneasy glance, then fixed on Old White. "I think you're going to be in for a most interesting time."

When he looked back, Silver Loon was still standing on the abandoned canoe landing, watching him as he left her behind for the last time.

Thirteen

When it came to forest hunters, only the panther stalked with more stealth and cunning than the Sky Hand. Smoke Shield firmly believed that as he watched his warriors filtering through the trees. Beneath their feet, the leaf mat betrayed no sound.

Smoke Shield cocked his head, unable to hear the slightest rasp of clothing against the hanging grape and greenbriar vines. No stick snapped under a moccasined foot; no acorn or pinecone rattled when kicked by a careless foot. Instead his men might have been smoke, so silently did they pass through the uncharted maze of tall trees.

The day was cool, a breeze whispering in the high lacery of winter-dead branches. Here and there a squirrel chattered, and sometimes birdsong trilled, but Smoke Shield and his grim warriors had been born of the forest. It was here, more than in Split Sky City, that they were at one with their surroundings.

So far, all had gone as he had prayed it would. Power favored them. They had made their way across the uplands dividing the Black Warrior from the Horned Serpent River, trotting single file past the leaf-blanketed sandstone atop the ridges. Like a disjointed snake they had descended down one of the many drainages that led to the banks of the Horned Serpent. At the river they had paused, tying their weapons and provisions inside watertight hides. In a line they had swum the river, pushing their bobbing packs ahead of them.

On the far shore, they had followed the plan, leaving their weapons, shields, war clubs, and war shirts inside the packs and donning simple hunting shirts, some spattered with deer blood to signify successful hunters.

As a measure of their dedication, his warriors had followed the rituals of the war trail perfectly. No warrior sat during the daylight hours, no matter how weary he might be. At night, they rested on a stump, rock, or log, but never upon the ground. It was forbidden for a warrior to lean against a tree for any purpose. If a man had a persistent itch, he would use a stick to scratch. When urinating, or defecating, it was done in a manner to be least offensive to the Earth Mother, generally on a piece of bark or pile of leaves. No warrior would look directly at a crow or squirrel, lest it run to warn the enemy. No morsel of food was consumed unless given to a warrior by Blood Skull's hand.

Smoke Shield should have been keeping his own souls pure, but Morning Dew's supple young body kept slipping into his thoughts. How well he remembered the disdainful expression she'd given him when he'd tossed a pebble at her feet to attract her attention. He'd smiled, an offer of his affection, and then she'd looked at him the way she would green fuzzy mold on good corn.

In his souls' eye, he worked it all out. She would be bound, wrists before her, her head down. But he didn't want her as some dirty captive. No, he would have Thin Branch bathe her, wash her hair, and comb it to a glossy black sheen. She would be dressed in a fine white dress, one that was tied at the shoulders. Flower petals would be rubbed on her skin to sweeten her scent.

First, he would stand over her, taking his time, admiring her as she waited. All the while, she would know what was coming, have plenty of time to dwell on it. Then, when she first began to entertain hopes that he might just walk away, he'd reach down and sever her bound wrists. Perhaps she would resist, or she might rise, expecting that she was to be set free. That's when he would smile, reach out, and untie the laces at her shoulders. The dress would slip free, falling down her perfect body.

At that moment she would know beyond any doubt. He could see the knowledge behind her dark eyes as he undressed and pointed at the sleeping bench.

His hands were smoothing her skin, feeling her shudder. Her expression would almost be as much reward as mounting her. There, lying atop her, he would take his time, let her savor his hard rod against her smooth thighs. Then slowly, carefully, he would pry her legs apart.

Throw her from your mind! He'd almost stepped full on a stick. Cursing under his breath, he shook himself. *Fool! She could destroy you, and never even know it!*

Angrily, he forced himself back to the forest, to the task at hand.

But she will be mine.

With each step, Smoke Shield's heartbeat quickened. Closer, ever closer. He had to focus, sharpen his senses on now, and let the future care for itself.

This was enemy territory, and they avoided the main trails. Instead, he depended upon the keen eyes of his warriors to spot any threat first. If possible, they would seek to avoid any discovery, but, if not, they would approach casually, as though having nothing to hide, and hope to dispose of the opponent before an alarm could be given.

Two days, he thought. *Two risings and settings of the sun, and we will be in place.*

That last would be the most dangerous time of all, as they made their final approach to White Arrow Town. Fortunately, he knew the country, had hunted there as a guest of the White Arrow. And swimming the Horned Serpent had given him an idea: one that would significantly cut their risk of discovery. He knew of a trail, a path used by slaves on their way to fill jars at the riverbank.

He glanced at the warriors filtering through the forest. *Will they have the courage to do this thing?*

If they didn't, if even one man failed . . . *No, don't think it.*

In the event of disaster, it would be he who hung from a wooden square while the White Arrow women used sharp chert stones to slice his flesh from his body.

A chilly wind blew down from the north as Trader fed another section of wood into the crackling fire. He had put in at an overgrown canoe landing after following a small creek for several bow shots. The ruins of the abandoned village on its low rise made the perfect place for a man who wanted to camp alone and unnoticed. Willows had started up downstream, and where once the sand would have been beaten down, rushes now covered the landing and hid his canoe. He had cleaned out the mess and placed his camp inside the corner of two walls that remained standing in an abandoned house. There, protected from the wind, his fire was screened from the high bluff rising immediately to the east.

According to local legend, the village had been called Sunflower, for the major crop grown there. The people had been like so many others: descendants of the once-mighty populations of Cahokia. They had even built a low platform for their chief's house, and their dead rested in a conical mound just to the west. Then a terrible witch had come and cursed them all. After their souls were witched, the population had been decimated, until the few survivors fled. Since that day, none of the locals would come close to the place.

It was a good location. Over the years the creek had deposited enough high ground to leave the village above the spring flood. Immediately to the east, a narrow valley cut through the high bluffs, exposing sandstone that had weathered into a dark gray. From the heights, one had a good view of the river and woodlands to the west. For a man who didn't believe in the Power of local witches, it was the perfect place to stop. Trader and Swimmer would have no unwelcome visitors come snooping in the middle of the night.

For fuel, Trader used the roof fall, breaking it up into lengths. Now he enjoyed the reflected heat, extending his hands to the cheery warmth. Swimmer lay curled next to the packs, his nose on his paws as he watched Trader through curious brown eyes.

Evening had deepened into night, the sky partially obscured by high clouds. In the open patches stars blinked and shimmered. The land was only slightly illuminated by the sliver of moon to the east. Trader had a duck spitted over the flames, and the skin was just beginning to brown. Swimmer watched it, dividing his interest between the bird and Trader's preoccupation with the copper.

"If I can peel off more of this stone," Trader told him, "it will make this a lot easier to lug around."

He propped the heavy slab against his left leg and studied the stone. Rot it all, he wasn't an expert on working copper. On the other hand, he'd spent enough time in the copper lands to know the procedure. They used granite mallets to crumble the softer rock around the metal. It was time consuming, and one didn't want to hammer the stone into the malleable copper.

Trader began tapping away with a river cobble he'd picked up in the north. He had to be careful. The only rock along the river was sandstone, limestone, or shale; none of it durable enough for his purposes.

"There," Trader cried as a piece chipped away. "See? Another couple of moons, and we'll have a clean slab of copper worth a high minko's palace."

Swimmer gave him a skeptical look.

Trader had just repositioned the stone when Swimmer

leaped to his feet, staring down toward the creek. A low growl grew in his throat.

"What is it?" Trader let the slab fall and reached for his bow and arrows where they lay to one side.

Swimmer's growls grew louder.

"Shhh!" Trader gestured for silence, but Swimmer, for once, didn't seem inclined to obey.

"To the right!" came a voice from down the creek.

Trader dropped to his knees and clamped a hand around Swimmer's muzzle. The dog squirmed in his arms.

"This is madness," a man's voice announced. "We should have stopped in the daylight."

"Don't want to camp here." The voice was a girl's.

"That's what I was afraid of. I can't see a thing."

"To the left."

"Now we're grounded," the old man complained from beyond the willows.

"I said left. Left, left, left," the girl chortled.

"All right, to the right it is." A pause. "At least we're moving again."

"Now right." The voice came from the darkness just beyond where Trader had pulled his canoe up in the rushes.

"But that's the bank."

"Don't want to land here. Not the right place for us."

"If you say so."

Water sloshed. The man's voice declared, "I'm probably going to step into quicksand and sink out of sight."

"Drown here, you will," the girl insisted.

"Huh, footing's good enough. But why I let you talk me into splashing around in the darkness is beyond me. We could have sunk ourselves fooling around like this. And who knows what kind of trouble we're getting into."

"The worst," the girl assured.

Trader could hear the rushes bending and rasping on clothing. Swimmer might have had eight legs as he wiggled in ten directions at once. Trader managed to keep the worst of his growls and woofs muffled.

"There's a canoe here!" the man called, surprised. "Birch bark from up north. Just a moment. Bottom's wet. It's been in the water recently."

"No one here that we want to see," the girl added firmly.

"Now why doesn't that reassure me?"

Trader sighed, letting Swimmer go. The dog barked anxiously, bounding down toward the commotion in the rushes. Trader hesitated. Did he go after Swimmer in hopes he could keep the dog from a swinging war club, or try to hide his copper?

"Who's there?" the man's voice called.

Trader made a face, glancing back at the flickering glow of his fire. No, too late. "I'm called Trader. Don't hurt my dog."

"As long as he doesn't hurt us," the man answered. "We're friendly. I travel under a Trader's staff."

Another Trader—the situation was growing worse. He'd recognize the copper immediately, and he'd know its value.

I could kill them.

He nocked an arrow, calling, "Come on in." At least he'd see what he was up against.

The rushes parted, Swimmer backing away, his tail wagging as he barked and bounced around. In the half-light of his fire Trader made them out: An old man, white haired, holding a Trader's staff, was followed by a slender young woman.

"I am called Old White. Some know me as the Seeker. The young woman is Two Petals." He seemed to choke on the words. "A Contrary."

A Contrary? Trader squinted at the girl. Most Contraries had the reputation of being older individuals who dedicated their lives to the service of Power. And the Seeker? He'd heard of him: the stuff of legends related around fires, a man who traveled the ends of the earth just to see what was there. Trader had never thought him real. But maybe this was a trick? Had Snow Otter told someone of the fabulous copper? Even now were tens of pursuers fanning out on the river searching for him?

"How do I know you're the Seeker?"

The old man spread his arms, white feathers on his staff fluttering in the cold wind. "Could any other man alive have my kind of luck?"

Somehow, the resignation in the man's weary voice did more to reassure Trader than anything.

"He has no luck," the young woman declared. "None at all. He died of starvation when he was a boy. Have you ever seen such a poor wandering corpse?"

"Corpse?" The Seeker cast a nervous glance at the woman. Two Petals, is that what the old man called her?

"You might want to know," Trader said warily, "according to legend, this place was cursed by a witch. That's why it's abandoned. If you value your health, you might want to leave now."

"Bad curse," Two Petals agreed. "That's why you're here. Evil's flying all around you."

Despite himself, Trader couldn't help but cast uncertain glances at the surrounding darkness.

"She's a Contrary," the old man reminded. "If there was danger anywhere about, she'd know."

"Why are you here?" Trader demanded. The thought of that copper, gleaming in its coating of rock, ate like cactus juice in his souls.

"Not my fault," the young woman insisted.

"Yes, it is," the Seeker growled irritably.

"What do you want?" Trader insisted.

"Don't want to camp here," the Contrary said as she walked forward, bent down, and began petting Swimmer. "Not a good place at all. Roast duck! Can't stand it. Wouldn't eat it if it was the last food on earth."

The Seeker lifted his staff helplessly. "We mean you no harm. By the Power of Trade, I swear that."

Memories of Snow Otter lingered in Trader's souls. "I have recently discovered that sometimes, that's not enough."

"He wouldn't have killed you," Two Petals said. Was she talking to Swimmer or him?

"We will be happy to add to your meal," the Seeker offered.

Trader began, "If you wouldn't mind, I'd prefer—"

"The copper is worried," Two Petals stated.

"What copper?" Trader and the Seeker said simultaneously.

"The copper that Trader wants us to see."

Trader and the Seeker gaped at Two Petals.

"How do you know this?" the Seeker asked.

"Not from any vision I've ever had." Two Petals giggled as Swimmer licked her face.

The Seeker came forward, his staff lowered. "It's a long story, I'm afraid."

Trader swallowed hard. "You've heard about the copper?" He should kill them now. Drive an arrow into the old man, then the girl. Then keep shooting until his quiver was empty.

"I've heard of no copper." The Seeker was peering at him in the darkness. "But whatever you possess, I am bound by the Trade. Besides, I have no use for copper."

"That would make you a rare man, indeed."

"Among the rarest." The old man looked back at the rushes. "Go tend your fire. I'll get my packs." Then he turned back into the darkness.

Trader stood, his bow half drawn. Two Petals seemed oblivious, having found the place on Swimmer's belly that he loved having scratched.

Was this really the Seeker? He searched his memory for the stories. Supposedly the man of legend carried two packs, one of wood, the other something heavy in a cloth bag. But anyone trying to imitate him would know that. Or this could be some elaborate ruse, the girl playing the role of a Contrary to deceive him.

"Demon dog," Two Petals told Swimmer. "I've never seen such an evil one."

Fox Squirrel! He hadn't told the story to anyone else. She must have heard of the copper and sent these two after him.

"It won't work," he said, drawing his bow. "You can leave now."

"Going as fast as we can," Two Petals answered. "Hurry, hurry, run, run."

"If you're going to shoot her," the old man said, emerging from the rushes, "it would be a relief if you did it quickly. Traveling with a Contrary isn't as soothing as you would think. Of course, I'm not sure what Power would do to a man who murdered a defenseless Contrary. Might take his copper away from him." As the old man walked past, he added, "On the other hand, it removes a burdensome complication from my life."

Indecision weighed on Trader like a great stone. Frozen, he tried to comprehend what was happening. Adding to his confusion, Two Petals stood and pointed between her breasts. "Right here, that's where you'll shoot me." Then she walked calmly past him, Swimmer bouncing at her heels, tail wagging.

Trader shook his head as if to dislodge a swarm of insects and realized he was standing in the darkness, his bow at full draw, pointed at nothing.

He sighed, allowing the arrow to slowly slide between his fingers. When he stepped around the house wall, it was to find the Seeker inspecting his precious copper. Two Petals and Swimmer were just as engrossed with his roasting duck.

"No wonder you were wary," the Seeker said, looking up in amazement. "You could buy an entire town with that."

"Where . . . Where did you come from?" was all he could ask.

"I never had a mother," Two Petals replied. "This duck is little more than charred ash."

He glanced at the duck, still only lightly browned. The inside would still be raw.

"It's not even warm inside."

"I know," the Seeker said. "You get used it." A pause. "I think."

Trader still had wits enough to note the wooden pack that the Seeker had lowered to the floor. Atop it lay a cloth bag, something heavy inside. The other pack that the old man had placed on the ground lay partially open, a stack of something that looked like acorn bread inside.

"This is a Dream," Trader told himself.

"We should be so lucky," the Seeker muttered, straightening from the copper.

"Why are you here?" he insisted. "How did you find this place?"

"Ask her." The Seeker jutted a thumb in Two Petals' direction. "Had it been up to me, I'd have made camp upriver just before dark." He glanced around. "But not as nice a one as this."

"That's right," Two Petals insisted as she turned the duck on its spit. "No secrets between us. All is as clear as the night sky."

Trader looked up, seeing that clouds had covered the last of the stars.

"Yes." The Seeker turned speculative eyes on Trader. "That's the question, isn't it? Why would Two Petals lead me up some obscure stream in the darkness to a young Trader with a fortune in copper?"

"I have no idea," Two Petals insisted. Her tongue protruded from the side of her mouth, a dedicated expression fixed on the cooking duck. "The notion would never have lodged in my souls, that's for sure."

"Are you both crazier than head-struck geese?" Trader demanded.

"After two days in a canoe with her," the Seeker noted, "it might be a relief to find out I was."

"Acorn cakes would be terrible with this duck," Two Petals insisted. "I'd rather eat mud."

"Tomorrow, I say we all go our separate ways," Trader insisted, knowing full well he wasn't going to get a wink of sleep that night. His war club was going to be ready in his hands. At the first hostile move, he'd spring to his feet and brain them both.

"Separate ways," Two Petals agreed. "Three is too many. Never make it to Split Sky City that way."

"Split Sky City?" A cold shiver ran down Trader's back. "What do you know about Split Sky City?"

"Been there a lot," she said. "And I never saw you try to kill any man there."

The old man was watching Trader the way an osprey might a sunning fish. "You look like you've just seen a ghost, Trader."

Fourteen

In all of her life, Morning Dew had seen nothing to match the day of her marriage. The night before, she had stood at the high gate atop the palace mound. Despite the light rain that fell, she could see a sea of campfires out beyond the palisade. That entire day had been a confusion of introductions. She had met the chiefs from this village and that, the clan leaders, two chiefs, and no less than five subchiefs of the Natchez. All of the Chahta lineages had sent either their leaders or distinguished representatives.

Through it all, she had sat beside her mother just to the right of Biloxi's panther-hide-covered tripod in the great hall. Behind her had been the huge wooden carving of Falcon, his wings spread, talons wide as if to grasp prey. The great bird's mouth gaped, its tongue protruding the way it would in a terrifying scream.

She had been dressed in her finery, as befitted the daughter of Sweet Smoke, matron of the Chief Clan, and the sister of Biloxi Mankiller, high minko of the Chahta. Through it all, she had acted with the modesty and decorum expected of so exalted a woman. She had seen approval in Old Woman Fox's dignified nods.

Yes, this is fulfilling my destiny, she had thought.

That night she had been sleepless, her souls playing the events of the coming day over and over. Her friends and kin had been briefed on the route she would run. They knew what to do. The only worry had been the drizzling rain.

The first thing she checked after relieving herself in the brownware bowl she reserved for such things was the sky. To her relief, the clouds were breaking, scudding off to the northeast. To the south, the horizon was a pale blue. The cool damp air would be perfect for her run.

She had gobbled breakfast the way a starving woman would. She even ignored Grandmother's heckling. Of course she wouldn't eat this way in front of Screaming Falcon. In the eye of her souls, she was already in the house newly constructed for her beside the tishu minko's. She could see the fire, casting its warm yellow light onto the freshly plastered walls.

Screaming Falcon's steady hands were removing the cape from her shoulders, his smile betraying his anticipation. She could feel her skirt sliding down her hips. Then her nimble fingers would pluck the knot free on his apron, letting it fall away to expose him, stiff and ready for her. A warm tingle spread through her hips, causing her to sigh.

"There will be time enough for that later," Old Woman Fox growled, reading her expression. "I swear, I've never seen a woman as taken with a man as you are."

If any cloud blotted her day, it was the death of two of the captives hanging from the squares before the palace. They had apparently succumbed in the chill rain.

She passed the interminable hands of time in the company of her friends, trying to laugh at their gossip, half-heartedly hearing the crowd as they chopped apart the bodies of the dead captives. The whole process bored her. The last thing on her mind was the disposition of war trophies. This night, she would take a trophy of her own.

Will his seed catch? she wondered. The timing might be right, even if she was only a week out of her second visit to the Women's House.

The sun had dragged its way through the sky. Not even a young woman's impatience could stop it entirely.

Sweet Smoke entered the house, a knowing smile on

her face. "The people are assembling." She looked at the expectant girls surrounding Morning Dew. "You will all make it a race to remember?"

A chorus of cheers came in return.

Morning Dew's heart began to pound. "Is *he* ready?"

"As anxious as you, my daughter." A look brimming with love and wistfulness filled her mother's face. "Look at me. I've waited for this day, but now I hesitate. How did this happen so quickly?"

"Thank you, Mother." Morning Dew stood, flexing her fists, nervous energy pumping in her muscles. She had chosen a short skirt that wouldn't inhibit the run. It was white, made of light fabric, the pattern of a falcon woven into the front to impart swiftness to her bare feet.

"You have a blanket, Daughter?" Old Woman Fox asked Sweet Smoke, "You know, for the presents?"

"I do," Sweet Smoke said, but she didn't take her eyes from Morning Dew's face. From the intense scrutiny, she might have been memorizing every line of her daughter. To Morning Dew, she asked, "Are you ready?"

"Too ready."

"The rest of you girls, outside."

Like chattering quail, they ducked past Sweet Smoke and into the sunlight.

Morning Dew's mouth had gone dry. She gulped deep breaths, trying to still the anticipation. Mother leaned out the door, looking toward the tishu minko's. She gave a slight nod, then beckoned. "Be fast, Daughter."

For a moment, Morning Dew hesitated. Now that the time had come, it took all of her will to step to the door.

"Well . . . go!" her mother prompted.

Morning Dew ducked out, turned, and picked her path. She ran with all of her might, heading for the gap between the storehouses. She barely noticed her friends, gathered along the way. A great shout rose as she charged across the plaza. The cheers of her friends and kin were mixed with glimpses of them, all jumping, gesturing with their arms. She dared not glance back; a greater shout told her Screaming Falcon had begun his pursuit.

It's too far! In a moment of panic, she feared that Screaming Falcon's hand would fall on her shoulder at any moment. Redoubling her efforts, she sprinted full-out for the storehouses. She was still ahead as she flew between the buildings, only to find a basket in the way. It hadn't been there last night.

She jumped it, almost stumbled, and careened around the storehouse. Turning to the left, she took off along the palisade wall.

"Right! Right!" the crowd shouted on cue.

Gods, it was working, wasn't it? She desperately hoped Screaming Falcon had taken the ruse. She pounded past the palisade gate. Fifty paces beyond it, a large granary blocked the view from behind. She cut left again, heading for the base of the palace.

Screams and laughter carried on the air. Perhaps Screaming Falcon was having a harder time of it than she was? A lighthearted giggle vied with her heaving lungs. Weaving in and out, she passed ramadas, kicked at a barking dog that raced along beside, nipping at her, and raced past her mother's house. At the corner of the mound, she glanced back long enough to see Screaming Falcon pounding behind her. Rounding the mound, she leaped a storage pit and wound through the houses. When a young man stepped into the gap she was running through, she only had time to extend her arms, knocking him flat on his butt.

She staggered, caught her balance, and ran on. Behind her a wild shout went up from the crowd. Reaching the storehouses again, she cut right, figuring he'd never guess at the turn.

Gods, her legs were on fire, her lungs burning for breath. Her feet felt like blocks of wood. A glance behind her showed Screaming Falcon, no more than twenty paces back. For a moment their eyes held. A wide smile broke his lips.

She struggled to find more, to charge her legs.

She could hear him now, his hard bare feet slapping the damp ground.

"Almost got you!" he shouted behind her.

Entering the plaza, she shot another glance to find him a step behind her. Again he smiled, then, for no apparent reason, seemed to trip.

She almost stopped, but heard the crowd cry, "Run!" Doggedly, she continued on her way, lungs heaving, throat dry. Despite the cool air, sweat dampened her skin and ran down between her bouncing breasts. She could feel her muscles trembling and exhausted as she rounded the palace mound again.

She was flagging, down to a dogtrot.

"One more time around the palace," Screaming Falcon called softly from behind. "Let's give them a show like they've never seen."

Step by step, she made herself continue. Her chest felt like it would explode. She kept tripping, almost staggering. She rounded the palace mound, heading for the densest part of the crowd. Finally, when she could go no farther, his hand clamped on her shoulder. He steadied her as she came to a stop, kept her from falling as she wobbled on her spent legs.

A giant shout, fit to rend the very air, rose from the packed plaza.

"A run that will never . . . be forgotten," he gasped, white shining teeth behind his smile.

"I love you," she managed between heaving gasps.

"Here they come," he said, looking at the surging crowd.

"The bride!" they sang. "We want the bride!"

"Can't have her," Screaming Falcon declared. "Caught her. Fair and proper."

"The bride! We want the bride!"

For long moments, Screaming Falcon denied them, only to have them surge forward. Grasping hands tore them apart, and Morning Dew felt herself lifted. They bore her like a slain deer to the blanket on the ground before her mother's.

"Presents! Presents!" they chanted.

Morning Dew, laughing, panting for breath, was placed on the blanket. A sea of people pressed forward. Some laid hides upon her, others baskets of food. Someone placed a wooden carving on her lap. Another laid a fine Nodena bowl down. The pile grew around and on top of her. She couldn't stop laughing as the gifts continued to come, some draped over her head, others pressing in from all sides until she was buried. The weight continued to grow, pressing her down so that she tucked her arms in, hunched under the pile.

Gods, were they laying half the village on top of her?

From beyond the darkness of robes, fabrics, pottery, carved boxes, and baskets of food, she heard Mother's voice. "Is there any more?"

Someone cried, "Any more and we'll kill her!"

Had she ever heard such laughter and shouting?

"If you think the groom's covered, you ought to see the bride!"

Morning Dew wondered if her back would ever be straight.

Mother's voice rang out, "Take it away! My daughter will be crushed!"

Screams of delight broke out, and Morning Dew suffered under the melee as grasping hands pulled away the gifts, some women shouting, "Mine! Mine!"

Daylight pierced the gloom as the weight diminished. Morning Dew couldn't stop the laughter as she watched the scrambling women grabbing up the gifts. Someone stepped on the Nodena pot, crushing it.

In the end, battered and exhausted, the last of it was plucked up and Morning Dew was surrounded by a ring of smiling women, each clutching whatever booty they had snatched from the pile.

Morning Dew coughed. "I could have used all that!"

"You're rich enough already," Old Woman Fox told her, leaning forward with Mother to pull her to her feet.

"What a run!" one of the women cried as she clutched a finely woven basket.

"What a pile of gifts," Mother added. "I thought you'd be crushed."

"I was," Morning Dew replied wearily. "I'm dead."

"Then I guess I'll spend the night with that handsome young Screaming Falcon," Old Woman Fox said thoughtfully. "I can teach him a lot more than some virgin girl can."

"A dried husk just ruins a firm cob," another added wryly.

"Come," Mother said, shooting a disapproving glance at Old Woman Fox. "Let's go meet your husband."

Mother held her hand as they led the procession to meet Screaming Falcon. He looked as disheveled as she, his hair mussed, his apron askew. But his grin was the stuff of sunlight on a morning meadow. He laughed as he stepped forward, took her hand from Mother's, and raised it high for the crowd.

The shouts and cheers were deafening. It went on and on, people screaming, stamping their feet, Dancing, and jumping. Through it all, Morning Dew, still out of breath, could only smile, glance at Screaming Falcon, and wish she could sit down.

As the noise dimmed, Screaming Falcon called, "Is anyone hungry?"

Gods, where do they get the energy to shout and jump like that? Morning Dew wondered as the crowd whooped and yelled.

Through the afternoon, they sat side by side, eating, drinking, receiving the endless line of well-wishers.

"Never seen a run like that."

"If ever there was a perfect marriage, it's yours."

"Seeing this, well, it presages great things for our people."

"Seeing you two I know why the Sky Hand's days are limited."

"Never seen a pile of gifts that high. People will talk about it for summers to come."

By the time they got a break, Screaming Falcon asked, "Still hungry?"

"I'll burst like an overripe gourd."

"Me, too." He glanced around. "Think anyone would notice if we slipped away to our house?"

"Yes."

"Do you care if they do?"

"No."

"Good."

He stood up, offering his hand.

She rose on stiff legs, letting his hold steady her. "I thought Biloxi wanted you there when he burned the prisoners."

He glanced at the crowd surrounding the two remaining captives on squares. "I've taken my share of glory."

People watched and jabbed each other playfully as they made their way across the plaza to the new house. She could hardly care.

"Sore?" he asked.

"I'm going to feel it in the morning."

They ducked into the house, and cheering erupted behind them.

"I guess they know what we're going to be doing." She glanced at the door as he placed the hanging over it.

"Let them."

She stood in the dim light, watching him.

"We gave them quite a run."

"Did you really trip in the plaza?"

"I wanted to see how far you could go."

Then his hands removed the cape from her shoulders.

Trader sat across the fire from Old White. They'd stretched a hide over the house corner, piled the packs beneath it, and waited while a drizzling rain fell from the morning sky.

Still perplexed, Trader fingered his war club and listened to the old man's story.

"I had made my way as far as Morning Star City, down in the Caddo lands," Old White said. "That's the first time she called to my Dreams. The Caddo Healers were as puzzled as I was."

"So you came straight north?" Trader asked, staring across at Two Petals. Swimmer was sprawled across her lap, his sides rising and falling, his nose mashed against the ground in a most uncomfortable-looking manner. Dogs were funny. They could sleep in peculiar positions.

"I went to the Forest Witch. She lives at the edge of Natchez territory."

"I've heard of her. Dangerous, isn't she?"

"I'm an old friend."

From the way the old man said it, he was more than that. "It seems like a long way to come for a Dream."

"It is at that." Old White cast a knowing gaze at Two Petals. "But, no matter what you might think about Dreams, I found her. Now, I've been many places, seen a Contrary or two in my day, but never one so young."

"That's when you took her to Silver Loon?"

"It seemed the thing to do."

"Like the Forest Witch, people fear her."

Old White smiled wistfully.

"Let me guess," Trader said. "Another old friend?"

"You're quick for someone so young."

"And, it seems to me, you've survived a lot of frightening women for a man of your age."

"Must be my charm."

"Or you're just as Powerful a witch as they are." Was that it? Was the Seeker a witch, too? Trader tightened his grip on his war club. He could well imagine what a witch might want with a wealth of copper.

"A witch?" The old man shook his head. "No, but I've been rightly called a sorcerer. I have some knowledge of magic and plants. I've learned sleight of hand, and how to make things like hides move and jump. I'm a fair Healer, but through medicines, not Spirit Power. Though, I have to tell you, with the help of the plants, I've sent my souls to the Spirit World. Scary place, that."

Trader fought a shiver.

"How did she know of Split Sky City?" Trader nodded toward Two Petals.

Old White rubbed his chin thoughtfully. "She knows I'm headed there." He glanced at Trader. "That, you, too, are from there is something entirely unexpected. She struck you square last night when she mentioned it."

Trader looked down at his war club. "I killed a man there."

"And you fled."

Trader ground his jaws.

"Interesting," Old White said absently.

"What? That I killed a man?" Trader said hotly.

"No. Only that coincidence has amazed me more often than not in my life." His expression sharpened. "But this, I suppose, is more than coincidence."

"Meaning?"

"That you are destined to go with us."

"My path lies south. To the Natchez . . . perhaps to the gulf itself."

"Where you will Trade your copper? For what?"

"I don't know. Some favor from a chief." He glanced at the copper. "For that, I can spend a delightful and lazy winter. Eat all I want of delicacies, have a warm and compliant companion in my bed every night, and fill my canoe with the best the south has to offer for my next trip north."

"You could buy a town with that. More, a chieftainship. Do you plan to be a chief, and rule over several towns?"

Trader shot him a scowl. "What would *I* do with a chieftainship? Especially one full of strangers. And who's to say any clan would sell such a thing?"

"For such wealth," Old White mused, "believe me, they would."

"So there I'd be. Stuck with all the inconsequential troubles of clan politics, petty jealousies, and all the interminable little squabbles that people insist on occupying their time with."

"Not to mention your neighbors. You'd have to defend your boundaries, plan raids in retaliation for theirs. You would never be bored."

Old White watched the expression on Trader's face, reading his thoughts as clearly as if he'd spoken. "What?" the old man asked. "Doesn't appeal?"

"I'll stick with my original plan." Trader had become aware that Two Petals had finally turned her penetrating stare from the dog to him.

Old White slapped his knees. "So, there it is. You'd squander a fortune that would have humbled a lord of Cahokia for a winter's worth of pleasure, just to paddle back up the river with a pittance—extravagant though it might be—and do what? Fritter it away for a few skins here, a couple of medicine plants there, a couple of carved shells, some fancy fabrics?"

"It's what I do."

"And what if you capsize? Snags and sunken trees, floating rafts of tangled driftwood washed loose in the spring floods—all these things make a Trader's life hazardous." He lifted an eyebrow. "Not to mention the petty chieftains that have sprung up in the dead shadow of Cahokia. As it is, the Michigamea may take it all."

"The Power of the Trade will protect me."

"Will it?" Old White wondered. "Last night you were ready to kill us both. Great wealth, as you have discovered, tempts men to ignore the laws of Power."

"Chiefs who disregard the rules of Trade get bypassed by other Traders."

"Somehow, I fear those days are passing." He nodded. "There will be more like Black Tooth."

"I *don't* have to pass through Cahokia."

"No, but his kind are gaining prestige and authority. Not that Black Tooth will be a problem any longer." Old White pointed a finger. "If you are determined to head south to the Natchez, my advice is that you buy a chieftainship."

"I told you, I'm not interested in being a chief."

"After all," Two Petals said pointedly, "you weren't born to it."

Old White started, fixing his keen gaze on Trader. "Really?"

Trader tried to wave it away. "My past is dead."

Two Petals laughed, her eyes almost glowing as she studied Trader. "Just like the present. Dead and rotten. Bones. The future is turned to bones."

"No matter who you've killed," Old White said softly, "that piece of copper will buy you forgiveness."

Trader swallowed hard, remembering the sounds and smells of his home.

"No, you don't want to go back," Two Petals told him. "Not Trader. He's happy traveling alone, with no name, and no place to call home."

"Stop it!" he cried, leaping to his feet. He stood at the edge of the stretched hide, watching the rainwater drip onto the wreckage of the collapsed walls. The surrounding trees were wet and dark against the cloudy sky. Rain had stained the exposed rocks on the bluff to the east. His breath puffed coldly in the chill air.

Two Petals' voice, though low, sent a shiver through his guts. "She never thinks of you. You are gone from her memory. The wistful smiles she has in the quiet moments are for someone else."

Trader didn't look back; he stumbled over the fallen wall, walking fast as he passed through the desolate houses. The knot in his throat threatened to choke him. In his panic, even the copper was forgotten.

Fifteen

The smell of wood smoke told Amber Bead he was on the right path as he followed a trail down from the Albaamaha cornfields. Walking through the countryside always irritated him. On the trek, he passed field after field, each worked by a family. Even now, with the corn, beans, and squash harvested and packed to granaries inside the city walls, the extent of his people's labor was manifest. The stripped cornstalks rattled in the breeze, brown leaves waffling in the wind. Below the dead stalks, rows of bean plants lay hard and withered. The squash vines that laced between the mounded soil beneath the cornstalks had been picked clean of all but the most immature of fruits. Those pitiful remnants had shriveled, blackened, and waited for the spring.

Throughout the long summer months his people spent from daylight to dark tending these fields, sweating in the blazing sun. They broke their backs hoeing, planting, and, when the rains failed, carrying water up from the river. When the rains did come, they spent their time pulling weeds, picking worms and bugs from the plants, and pollinating the squash blossoms. In late summer, they even worked through the night, chasing away raccoons, crows, and other pests.

Then when fall came, they harvested the ears of corn, picked the beans, and snapped squash from the prickly stems. But for a couple of baskets—and what they harvested from their own gardens, cared for between working the fields—it was packed on their backs to Split Sky

City. Pack after pack, on aching legs, with pains shooting up their spines, they hobbled into the city. There, they climbed ladders to the high granaries, and dumped their packs. Only to go back for more until the entire yield of the land was locked away, property of one of the Chikosi clans.

Down between his souls, the resentment festered.

This was their land, the one they inherited after emerging from the World Tree's roots. Here, the Ancestors of their Ancestors had walked. Then had come the Chikosi, and they'd taken it all.

Now, for the first time, Amber Bead had a glimmer of hope. If the Chikosi were shocked, shaken down to their souls, their grip would begin to slip. If they could be lured away, into wars with the Chahta, and perhaps weakened, the Yuchi in the north, the Ockmulgee to the east, and the Pensacola down south would be tempted to strike.

The secret is to keep the enemies of the Chikosi informed of their weakness. Bleed away enough of their strength, and we can either drive them out, or crush them ourselves.

The coming months would tell. Not since Makes War had lost both his life and the war medicine to the Yuchi had the Chikosi suffered such a stunning blow as that inflicted by the Chahta on Alligator Town. It had shaken the Council to rashness. Only the desperate would have dispatched a party of thirty warriors to attack a congregation of Chahta at White Arrow Town. He could only pray that the defeat of Smoke Shield's party, and the loss of the war medicine, would rattle the Chikosi down to their bones.

Amber Bead had no love for Smoke Shield. The man couldn't keep his hands off women. How many Albaamaha daughters, sisters, and wives had fallen prey to the man's rutting lust? While the rumors said he occasionally dallied with a Chikosi man's wife, he was free to do as he pleased with an Albaamaha woman. Of course there would be nasty consequences if he was caught with a married Sky Hand woman, but no Albaamaha female could deny him. And if she did, Smoke Shield would take what he wanted anyway. If the family protested, they would be given a trinket, a string of beads, or a bit of pottery in compensation.

How happy I would be to hear that he is hanging in a square in front of the White Arrow palace! If only the other mikkos didn't object!

He crossed the last of the fields and entered the trees. Here the bank above the Black Warrior wasn't as high as at Split Sky City. He followed the trail down where it cut through the brush and into the forest. Through the trees, vines, and deadfall, he could see glimpses of the river.

The smell of smoke led him the rest of the way down the gentle slope. On a flat just above the shore, a crackling fire had been built. There, Whippoorwill used a stick to prop burning wood over the bowls she was firing.

Paunch sat on a fallen log to one side. He wore a fabric cape, worn and frayed about the edges. His coarsely woven shirt hung from his bony frame. The man turned a fish trap in his hands. The thing looked like a long, pointed basket. He turned it slowly as he wove a pliant willow stem through the lattice.

"Greetings!" Amber Bead called. "I heard that you would be here."

"Hello, Mikko," Paunch greeted, but without the enthusiasm Amber Bead had expected.

Whippoorwill looked up from her fire. Two stacks of wood lay to one side. The first—mostly oak and hickory—were used to make a hot fire that burned down to a bed of coals. The second stack, consisting of poplar, burned cooler. A sack of corncobs lay beside Whippoorwill's feet.

"Your pots are among the finest made by the people," Amber Bead told the young woman as he stopped and peered at the vessels nestled in the white ash. "Got your corncobs, I see."

"I'm just ready to drop them in." She bent, picking one of the cobs from the sack. She pulled her hair back with one hand and deftly reached out with the other, neatly dropping the cob into one of the bowls. Then, using her stick, she teased some of the burning brands up into a tripod over the bowl. The corncob smoldered, blackened, and burst into flame.

"Quite a trick, that," he murmured.

Whippoorwill stepped back from the heat, letting her long hair fall naturally. "Nothing burns as hot as corncobs," she told him. "It will seal the interior of the pot, Mikko. I wouldn't want you grinding grit between your teeth if you should end up with one."

"I've never had grit between my teeth when eating from one of your pots." Amber Bead had noticed that Paunch seemed unusually interested in his fish trap. "What word from you, old friend?"

"No word," Paunch said wearily, laying the fish trap to the side and looking up. Something lay behind his eyes, a deep reluctance.

"Did you send the runner to the Chahta?"

Paunch sighed, looked out at the river. "I did."

"Tell me you really didn't." Amber Bead closed his eyes, a hollow feeling growing in his heart. "You were supposed to wait for my word."

"But Crabapple was ready to go. Time is of the essence." Paunch cocked his head, seeing the dismay in Amber Bead's expression. "But . . . is something wrong?"

"I fear so. Is there any way to recall him?"

"Of course not! He's in the forest." Paunch was looking at him as though appraising a lunatic. "Explain this to me."

Amber Bead raised his hands unhappily. "I sent runners to the other mikkos telling them of our plan. Some sent runners back to me. For the most part I was given emphatic orders not to do this thing."

"But, surely you explained the opportunities to them!"

"I did." Amber Bead looked up from under raised brows. "The consensus was not to act at this time."

"In Abba Mikko's name, why not?" Paunch stared in disbelief, a hand going to his stomach as though easing a sudden pain.

"They say yes, there's a chance that Smoke Shield's raid will weaken the Chikosi. They understand that if we send a messenger, the Chahta will destroy the war party and capture the war medicine. On the other hand, the mikkos believe that will probably happen without intervention. If it does, we have achieved the same result. The Chikosi will be weakened."

"Then why would they object to making sure?"

"Because the mikkos don't want to take the chance that somehow, some way, the story will get back to the Council. The thought is that if the Chikosi find out, they will take out their wrath on us."

"Gods!" Paunch stomped back and forth. "We *outnumber* them!"

"But we are not warriors. The mikkos know this."

"We can learn! We have weapons. When the time comes—"

"The elders think it will." Amber Bead tried to assume a reasonable expression. "But they think the time to act is after the Chikosi have been fighting their enemies." He clasped his hands together. "This has to be done very carefully. Think this through."

"I *have*."

"Then you know their other concerns?" Whippoorwill said behind him.

Amber Bead spun on his heel. "Yes, girl, and what other concerns would the mikkos have?"

She didn't flinch but stared at him with unnerving eyes that seemed to dim his souls. Expressionless, she said, "Who will come after the Chikosi?"

"We will. We will retake what is ours!"

She cocked her head, thin lines forming on her brow.

"Do you believe a strengthened Chahta will leave us be? Or, if the Chahta and Chikosi bleed themselves dry in a war, that the Yuchi or the Pensacolas won't come in force and take this land for their own?"

"In short," Paunch asked, "what's to keep someone else from doing the same thing to us that the Chikosi did?"

"So, you've given up?"

"Not at all." Paunch sighed, reseated himself, and picked up his fish trap. He glanced apologetically at Whippoorwill. "I sent my cousin, Crabapple, to White Arrow Town. I did it in spite of all the arguments to the contrary."

"And we hope that you haven't killed us all," Whippoorwill said, her eyes fixed on some distant place.

"You were supposed to wait for my word," Amber Bead stated bluntly, aware that Paunch was still avoiding his eyes. "If so many, including Whippoorwill, told you not to, why did you?"

"Because I believe in you, Amber Bead. You are our ears in the Council. The Chikosi trust you. If it goes wrong, if they should find out, you will protect me." He finally looked up, his eyes swimming with hope.

Amber Bead nodded, lying with as much sincerity as he could. "Of course." He was aware of Whippoorwill's eerie stare eating into his back. Crabapple was halfway to the Chahta by now. Gods, this could turn into a disaster. Or a brilliant opportunity.

Paunch fumbled anxiously with his fish trap. "I have to believe in you. After Smoke Shield is destroyed, and the Chikosi have been bled for a while, the mikkos will rethink this. By then they will know the extent of Smoke Shield's defeat. That is when you must act."

"Act how?" Amber Bead narrowed a skeptical eye.

"The mikkos have to be convinced. They have to understand that when the Chikosi are weakest, we must strike, and when we do, it must be in a fashion that sends a clear message to the other chieftains. Something so terrible that no Yuchi, Charokee, or Chahta will ever consider invading our valley."

"So, we must plan on murdering them all," Amber Bead said softly.

"You can make them understand, Amber Bead. You'll have to. I've bet my life and my family on it."

"Yes," Whippoorwill said absently. "Isn't it refreshing to Dance so closely to Death?"

Amber Bead watched as another of Whippoorwill's corncobs burst into flame, searing its pot.

The first birdcalls woke Morning Dew. She lifted her head, seeing the faintest light around the gaps in the doorway. She lay on their pole bed, knees against the house wall, cushioned by a warm buffalo robe. Screaming Falcon's body pressed against her naked back. His arm lay across the small of her waist, his legs spooned into hers.

Had she ever been so happy? For two days now, when they weren't Dancing, feasting, or attending to visiting dignitaries, they had escaped here, to this wondrous sanctuary. When they did it was to frantically tear their clothing off before falling onto the bed, locked in each other's embrace.

Like last night. They had taken their time, and she'd closed her eyes, savoring the sensations of his movements, her legs locked tightly behind his knees. Like a falcon, she had hovered on the edge of that moment of freefall, only to have him tense, drive deep, and then gasp and stiffen. His seed jetting inside caused her loins to burst with a pleasure that rolled up her spine and shot lightning down her legs. The pulsing waves had left her limp, panting.

He had laughed, his body lax on hers as the sensations faded.

"What?" she'd gasped.

"After that, I think the whole town knows."

"You shouldn't grunt like that."

"Me? The way you yipped I thought someone stepped on a puppy."

Gods, who'd have thought? She'd heard the stories the women told. Nothing had prepared her for this. A smile bent her lips, and she hugged herself. She hadn't known that love could be such a blessing. Not just the coupling, but the warmth in his gaze, the way he laughed at her jokes. When they looked into each other's eyes, a golden ray of light reached out from their souls, touching, sharing.

Someday, of course, he would take another wife. As his authority and prestige grew, he would take even more. To do so was inevitable and necessary. For the moment, however, she could have him all to herself. And in the coming seasons, she would ensure that this special bond strengthened. Together, they would work as a team, building the greatness of White Arrow Town.

Yesterday they had discussed the possibilities of an alliance with the Natchez. With their combined warriors, they would whittle away at the Sky Hand.

"One day soon," Screaming Falcon said, "Biloxi will place his cousin atop the palace in Split Sky City."

She had mused, "It won't be right, him ruling a larger town than White Arrow."

"So," he said, "we build a bigger city here."

She gave him a taunting grin. "Just where will you find the labor? Surely you don't expect our people to dig and pack all that dirt. And you're going to kill off most of the Chikosi."

"The Albaamaha will have to do something. Besides, the Sky Hand have already broken them to labor. They can serve us just as well."

Considering that, they had spent more than a hand of time planning how much food would be necessary, where to set up a camp for the workers.

In Morning Dew's mind, White Arrow Town grew, covered with huge earthworks supporting great palaces and temples. She saw herself carried to Split Sky City on a great litter, and all the way, people bowed, touching their foreheads, saying, "There goes the great matron of the Chahta."

With those images spinning between her souls, she snuggled against Screaming Falcon, and was almost asleep when a guttural voice outside their door called softly, "War Chief? Can I see you?"

She blinked herself back to wakefulness and prodded Screaming Falcon. "Someone is outside."

"What time is it?" Screaming Falcon said muzzily.

"Early."

"War Chief?" the accented voice called again.

"Coming."

Screaming Falcon slipped from the robes, his body a shadow in the dark room as he wrapped his apron around his waist. "What's this about?"

"Message from the Natchez."

Screaming Falcon grunted assent, then staggered to the door. He was yawning like a panther as he ducked out. Through the door hanging, Morning Dew saw the barest of gray light. Gods, whoever it was must have been running all night to get here. What could be so—

It sounded like a loud slap. Then a huffing sound was accompanied by a hollow thud.

What?

Morning Dew scuttled out of the bedding, fumbled for a dress, and dragged it over her head. She was blinking, confused, as she ducked through the door. In the gray gloom she could see Screaming Falcon lying on the hard clay. Muddled by sleep, she instinctively ran to him, crouching.

As she did, arms like hardened wood clamped around her. When she opened her mouth to scream, a dark form jammed a wad of cloth between her jaws, almost gagging her. Her screams made muffled moaning sounds through her nose. She thrashed, trying to spit the thing out, but a cord was slipped around her head and knotted, tying the gag in place. Two strong men bound her arms behind her, oblivious to her desperate attempts to break free. Pushing her to the ground, they pinned her, quickly lashing her legs together.

As she jerked on the cold clay, one of the dark figures ducked into her door, hissing, "All clear."

"Good," her captor whispered back. "Set fire to it, then help me."

The attacker, a burly man, had bent over Screaming Falcon, using rope pulled from a bag to tightly bind him. Her husband only groaned, making no effort to resist.

Her nose flared as she sucked great gasps of air, her heart hammering at her chest. Though she fought the thick cord binding her, she couldn't break free.

From the corner of her eye, she saw the first flicker of fire, leaping yellow in the predawn gloom. It came from the palace, not a bow shot away. Tongues of yellow licked up from a lower corner of the thatch. She watched, terrified, as dark figures emerged from the great doorway, several of them carrying burdens as they made their way down the stairs.

She heard a jar break inside her house. A heartbeat later, the intruder ducked through the doorway. "Hickory oil," he said. "Broke it on the bed after I piled the firewood there. Used a bowl to scoop embers from the fire. It's going to burn hot."

"Good, let's go."

The two men bent; together they heaved Screaming Falcon's limp body over the shoulders of the burly man. As he started off across the plaza, the second man easily hoisted Morning Dew over his shoulders. Squirm as she would, the effect was the same as if she were a sack of squash.

Later, Morning Dew would remember glimpses: fires leaping up from roofs, running figures. The first scream engraved itself on her souls. Then someone shouted, "*Run!*" War whoops broke out in the still air, hideous bellows of rage, torn from human throats. Then the screams grew louder.

The image of a warrior, crouching, his naked body wet and muddy, was caught in the gaudy light of the burning palace. He had his bow pulled back. She saw the release, caught the moment when the barbed shaft drove itself into a fleeing man's back.

As her captor pounded past her mother's house, Morning Dew gaped at the flames crackling through the roof. Then her eyes fixed on her mother's sprawled body. She lay with her arms akimbo, her long hair spread across the ground. A dark stain had spread from the base of her skull. The firelight glinted from her wide fixed eyes.

It's not true. A Dream. Just a Dream.

Chaos, it was all chaos. From her bouncing perch, vision upside down, it could be only a malignant and vicious Dream. She lived an impossible nightmare as she was carried down the path to the canoe landing. There, she was dumped like a log onto the ground. The impact drove the breath from her body, but didn't loosen the tight cords.

"Guard them," came a harsh order. "Check the ropes, over and over. If one escapes, it will be on your head."

Sky Hand! The accent was Sky Hand! A cry knotted itself in her throat. She twisted, seeing Screaming Falcon's limp body. And then others. All bound, gagged, and under the scrutiny of two men who carried war clubs in the twilight.

The roar that had been building finally caught her attention. It even drowned the pitiful screams of the dying, and overwhelmed the whoops of the attackers. She bent her neck, staring from the corner of her eyes as an eruption of fire streaked into the sky, belching thick black smoke. The palace. Her palace.

Gods, where was Biloxi? Where was Mother? Not

that dead corpse she'd seen. No! Impossible! Tears of anger, fear, and disbelief shimmered in her eyes, then ran hot across her nose, and down her cheeks.

How could this have happened?

Waking early, sleeping little, just came with advanced age. Old Woman Fox had accepted that fact gracefully. In truth, however, it surprised her that she snapped wide awake that morning. For four days previously, she had been working, cooking, entertaining guests, gossiping, and generally behaving as an ex-matron should. Most people still called her "matron," even if she had given over the duties to Sweet Smoke.

With the household stores depleted from days of feasting, she had pulled her old dress on, lifted a basket, and trudged through the predawn darkness to the granary. There, she had raised the ladder, grumbled at her creaky bones, and climbed to unlatch the door. After filling the basket, she reversed the process, and hitched her load to her shoulders.

When the first screams broke out, she was halfway home. Stunned, she had stopped and watched the growing panic as warriors slipped between buildings, shooting arrows at anything that moved.

Knowing she was old and slow, and that she'd have no chance to flee, Old Woman Fox dropped her corn and scurried to an emptied storage pit. There, she huddled in the shadows and watched in horror. Though the sky grew brighter, the terrible scene was illuminated by burning buildings—great thatch-and-log torches that would have rivaled the sun.

"Run! Run!" The cries mingled with the whoops of the attacking warriors.

"To the forest!" The shout came from a nearby warrior. "To the forest! Hurry! Save yourselves!"

A little girl broke from one of the houses, squealing terror. The warrior turned, shifted his bow to his left hand, and grabbed a war club from his belt. In three paces, he caught the girl, barely breaking stride as he split her skull. He was still shouting, "Run!" as he disappeared around one of the houses.

In his wake, the little girl's corpse twitched, jerked, then went still.

Old Woman Fox gaped in disbelief. The man seemed to be instilling fear, not seeking a fight. And she placed that accent: Sky Hand, as sure as rain fell.

"Oh, dear gods, do not let this happen." She knotted her bony old fingers, wringing them. "Come on, rally! Where are my warriors?"

Then she saw Raven Mankiller pound past her hiding place, his naked body gleaming in the firelight. One of the Badger Clan's greatest warriors, he fled like a deer before a drive. Swiveling her head, she looked back at the great fire that consumed the palace and its surrounding houses.

That's what it was: a drive. But just the opposite of the ones her hunters used to surround deer. The tactic was to find a large meadow, generally one grown full of brush, hazelnut, and scrub. The hunters would ring it, setting fires that burned ever closer to the center. The fire, and the shouts of the hunters, would drive the deer into the ever-decreasing circle. Frantic, the animals would mill in a small knot. There, the hunters would shoot arrow after arrow into their dense ranks. Few ever escaped.

"Cunning," Old Woman Fox said. "This time the drive is the other way. And we are the deer."

Another warrior appeared, this one entering one of the houses, only to emerge moments later carrying a split cane torch. This he used to set fire to the roof. Peeking over the rim of her hole, Old Woman Fox watched him set fire to house after house.

She remained in her hole, listening to the roaring of the fires, while the morning light strengthened. The

shouts were distant now, coming from beyond the palisade gate. For a brief time, there was silence. Smoke
rolled past in waves, borne by the morning breeze; ash,
like bits of polluted snow, settled from the sky. A finger
of wind flicked ash into a whirlwind, dancing it around.
Then it went over to tease the little girl's hair before it
skipped away.

How could the Chikosi have done this? Every trail
and waterway was crawling with travelers headed home
from the marriage. Someone should have seen a war
party of this size. But what better time—assuming you
could avoid detection? White Arrow Town was reeling
from four days of festivities, Dances, feasts, and games.
Everyone was exhausted. With so many people everywhere, they'd believed themselves safe. The thought of
an attack wouldn't have crossed her mind.

A roof crashed as it fell into a gutted house and shot a
vomit of sparks into the choking sky.

Moments later, a conch horn sounded from behind.
Its mellow note rose on the dirty morning, hanging,
somehow mocking. Almost instantly the warriors reap-
peared, passing like gray ghosts through the smoke
haze. They glanced this way and that, bows at the ready,
arrows nocked. And then, like mythical beasts, they
were gone.

Only silence, the billowing smoke and ash, and the little dead girl's body remained. How long did Old Woman
Fox hide there? When it was over, she could only judge
time by the sun: a brown orb piercing the smoke, no
more than a hand's height above the horizon.

Old Woman Fox climbed out when two men appeared,
White Arrow warriors, advancing with drawn bows.

"Here!" she called, coughing from the ache in her
throat. "Don't shoot."

"Matron?" one of the men called. "Are there others?"

"Just me."

"Go to the gate. It's safe there."

She hurried past, coughing against the smoke-tickle

in her lungs. Here and there a house had avoided the flames. Corpses and the dying lay scattered amidst the trash that had been left from the feasting in Screaming Falcon's honor. No one had had time to clean up. The granaries were roaring infernos. Twice the burning granaries made her backtrack. She had to walk wide, shielding herself from the searing heat with her hand.

As she made her way through the bodies—many of them crudely scalped—it began to dawn on her: mostly children, women, and the elderly. The ones who couldn't run fast. With few exceptions, they had been shot in the back or clubbed from behind. Some still lived, writhing and groaning, the barbed shafts protruding from guts, chests, or thighs. The lucky ones had been hit in the heart or lungs, or subsequently had their heads caved in with a war club.

At the palisade gate, she found a nightmare. This had been the goal of the drive. Here people had crowded together before spilling out the gate, and the enemy archers had closed the circle. From the look of it, they couldn't miss. A pile of dead, three deep in places, lay in a ring, many bristling with three or four arrows. Some still writhed and moaned; the sight of the moving dead numbed her souls.

She dropped to her knees, staring in horror. Her eyes refused to recognize the warriors, picking their way through the piled limbs, heads, and torsos before charging into the burning town in search of a vanished enemy. Instead she stared at the dead, who watched her from drying eyes, expressions slack, mouths hung wide. And in the pile, the dying writhed, groaned, and twitched, their bodies intertwined with the dead.

The odd question formed: Why are so many killed with our own arrows?

But then, where else would the enemy resupply but by robbing the houses before they fired them?

Later she remembered disembodied voices saying, "They came from the river. Swam in." "They've taken our canoes." "At least eight prisoners, probably a lot more."

Someone else told her, "No one has seen the high minko or Screaming Falcon."

When they came with questions, she just waved them off, saying, "You decide."

The rest of the day became a walking Dream—like looking at the carnage through rippling water. Somewhere in that glassy quivering memory, she found Sweet Smoke's body. Half charred by the heat from her burning house and clothing, she looked like clay—and with her coating of gray ash, not quite real.

Is this how the world ends?

Sixteen

A fit of shivering brought young Crabapple awake. In the name of the Ancestors, had he ever been so cold? He groaned, teeth chattering, as he sat up. Most of the leaves he'd piled over him the night before fell away; the rest, brown and crackling, stuck in his hair, and some slipped down his collar, scratching his goosefleshed skin.

Around him, the forest was waking, birds chirping, squirrels chattering. He could hear the breeze whispering in the trees overhead. The morning looked gray and cold, though the sun was casting its light through the high lacework of branches.

He stood, relieved himself, and scratched at the bug bites that had raised welts on his skin. His urine steamed as it spattered on the leaf mat. Dropping his shirt, he studied his hands, crisscrossed now with red scratches; they were mud-caked from where he'd floundered through streams. His feet, clad in sandals, were black and swollen. What had once been a clean brown hunting shirt had been turned into a pattern of smudges, mud spatters, and holes where thorns had ripped the fabric. He'd watched his mother weave the material. She'd spent a fortune—two sacks of corn—for the silky hemp fibers. Now the garment looked like something the Chikosi had thrown away.

When Paunch had asked him to make this trip, he'd dressed his best, determined to make a good impression on the Chahta. Now, when he arrived, *if* he arrived, he'd look like an escaped slave.

Hugging his arms to warm himself, he listened to his belly growl angrily. The last of the food he'd packed— enough for three days—had been breakfast two mornings past. Fallen nuts, dried rosehips, and withered plums had made for poor trail fare. How could things have gone so wrong? He stared around at the trees, thankful for once that he knew where east was.

"Stay off the main trails," Paunch had told him. *"You don't want to run smack into Smoke Shield's war party. But if that should happen, you tell him you're lost. Do you understand?"*

He'd stayed off the trails, all right. Then, somehow, in the rain, clouds covering the sky, he'd gotten turned around. Following a creek down from the ridges, he'd found himself right back on the Black Warrior River. Retracing his path, he'd become confused among the interlacing valleys.

"I'm a farmer, not a hunter," he muttered under his breath just one more time. But the sun came up in the east. White Arrow Town was west. For the moment, his direction was clear. He worked his mouth, anxious for a drink of water. Five days! Who knew how long it would take Smoke Shield's war party to reach White Arrow Town?

"Got to hurry," he muttered. "If I don't get to White Arrow Town, Smoke Shield will have the place turned to ash before I get there."

He made ten paces before a warrior stepped out from behind a tree. In fluent Albaamaha, he asked, "But what will you do if Smoke Shield has already burned it?"

Crabapple turned to run. He made it five whole paces back the way he'd come before a war club smacked him in the spine. He felt the blinding pain; then his lower body went limp, tumbling him facefirst into the leaf mat.

For the moment, he could only gasp, his legs tingling. He blinked at the leaves, so close to his face. Then the warrior leaned into his field of vision, asking, "So, who are you? And why would you want to get to White Arrow Town before Smoke Shield burned it?"

"Now," another voice—this one Chikosi—stated, "there is a good question."

"I'm a farmer," Crabapple gasped, rolling painfully onto his side. "I got lost." He looked up, and his souls froze. Coming through the trees was a large party of warriors. He knew them for Chikosi by the white swans' feathers they had tied to their arms and run through their hair. All carried weapons, while the grisly pelts hanging from their belts were easily recognizable as scalps. Behind them, flanked on both sides, came a line of captives in single file, their arms bound; a rope ran from neck to neck, looped about each.

"We don't have time to dally," Smoke Shield said, staring down at him with a terrible interest. "Bring him."

The warrior who'd captured him dragged him to his feet. Crabapple wobbled, but managed to keep from falling.

The warrior pushed him to the rear of the line, saying, "You're going to join the rest. If you fall, you'll get a taste of this." He lifted a blood-caked war club in front of Crabapple's nose.

By the time they'd bound his hands and roped him into the procession, enough feeling returned to his legs that he could stagger along behind the other captives.

His hot tears quickly cooled as they rolled down his dirty cheeks.

Trader sat in a backwater and scowled. Swimmer rested on his fabric bed and watched him with questioning eyes. His black dot of a nose rested between his paws.

"What?" Trader asked, then stared out at the water. He needed time to think. Gods, how had this happened to him? Behind the willows where he sat in his gently rocking canoe, thick trees betrayed the location of the bank. Like gray fuzz, their winter branches mixed with the cloudy sky. Somewhere a crow called, and a squirrel chattered in return.

Long before dawn, Trader had slipped from his bedding, rolled it, and packed it to his canoe. Then he had taken his packs, one by one, walking on tiptoes as Swimmer followed him curiously. Finally he had lifted his heavy copper and turned to leave.

The voice from the shadows had startled him. Two Petals—eerie creature that she was—said softly, "Never see you again."

And he had left, picking his way, had loaded his copper, and after gesturing Swimmer into the canoe, had pushed off into the creek.

Now, a day later, the words burrowed like beetles through his souls. *"No matter who you've killed, that piece of copper will buy you forgiveness."*

"No, you don't want to go back. Not Trader. He's happy traveling alone, with no name, and no place to call home."

But the words that stung like cactus thorns were, *"She never thinks of you. You are gone from her memory. The wistful smiles she has in the quiet moments are for someone else."*

"She can't know that. Contrary, or not, no one could know what an unknown woman, half a world away, thinks and feels." He knotted his fist, watching the tendons in the back of his hand. After all these winters, her memory still clung to him. How could any man love a woman that much?

"That piece of copper will buy you forgiveness."

Could it? How could his uncle ever forgive? Sure, the clan would forgive him, happy to make a place for a murderer who handed over so much wealth to pay for redemption. How did *she* forgive what he'd done? He could see her eyes. They'd pin him like a bug on a bone awl. *You killed your brother.* That fact could never be burned away, not even by the reflected glare of sunlight off copper.

How do I forgive myself?

He stared numbly at the water. Sticks and bits of flotsam bobbed on the waves. Overhead a bald eagle wheeled, searching for fish. Filling his nostrils, Trader took in the smells of the river: water, mud, the vegetation. If he did return home, would this ever be far from his blood?

Oh, yes, there were the dangers. Old White hadn't lied when he talked about the snags, driftwood rafts, and bobbing trees that could capsize a canoe and drown a man.

Nor had he lied about the chieftains up and down the river. The Power of Trade was waning. Stories trickled up and down the river about how some chiefs had seized loads, killed Traders, and quietly set their canoes adrift on the current.

For the most part, he'd dismissed them. But the fact was, he had never carried such goods as the ones in his canoe now. And the lesson taught by Snow Otter remained fresh in his mind. Sometimes he tried to talk himself into believing that Snow Otter hadn't meant him harm, but the man's entire nature had changed after seeing that copper. And just why would a fellow who had guarded his daughter's virginity with a war ax insist on sticking her in a stranger's bed? Nor had the expression on Snow Otter's wife's face given him any cause to think otherwise. She had been clearly alarmed that night, shooting uneasy glances at her too-jovial husband.

No, the old world was breaking down. The lords of Cahokia, with their insistence on the safe passage of Traders, were long vanished, like smoke on the wind.

He considered the route downriver. South of the Mother River's mouth, the Michigamea had built several fortified towns in the west-bank lowlands as well as a high city on the east bank where they could watch all travel. He had been stopped every time he made the trip, offered food and drink in return for Trade. While he had always complied, the demands had been ever greater, sometimes to the point of being uncomfortable.

"The plan," he told Swimmer, "was to pass in the darkness. To time it so that I would be downriver by sunrise."

Swimmer thumped his tail.

"But what if I run into a group of warriors traveling on the river?" More than once just such a party had insisted that he return with them to their town. And there were so many towns. Most, of necessity, were built on high ground, back from the floodwaters. But even those sent out fishing, war, and Trading parties. Figuring that on average he passed three towns a day headed downriver, even if he eluded the surly Michigamea, somewhere the odds would overtake him.

"So what was I thinking?"

Unbidden, he could imagine Old White saying, *"You were living in the Dream of wealth."*

That bothered him. He liked to believe he was the canniest Trader on the river. For the most part, he got away with it. Discretion being the smartest way of living, there were times he lost a nice shell or bag of medicine herbs in return for a nondescript pot that nobody would want. But other Trades made up for it. Part of the art was knowing who desired what along the river.

Everyone craves copper.

His scowl deepened.

Home. The word popped between his souls like a turtle rising from the deep. In that moment, he could see the green grass, hear the songs of the Albaamaha as they worked in the fields. Images of the Green Corn Busk crowded each other in the eyes of his souls. He could almost feel the stamping feet of the Dancers, smell the feast cooking on the smoke-scented air.

Her eyes gleamed, a smile lighting her lips.

Then came the memory of his war club, its copper-sheathed blade whistling as it dove toward his brother's head.

"Gods," he whispered.

Swimmer, sensing his upset, rose stiffly, stretched, and prodded his hand with a cool nose. The soft tongue licked tentatively at his hand.

"In all the world," he said gently, taking the dog in his lap, "you're the only friend I have."

"Trader," the Contrary's voice haunted. *"He's happy traveling alone, with no name, and no place to call home."* Somehow, he had thought he was, until she had said that. Now an uncertain and dark future opened before him.

Swimmer remained happily in his lap, licking his hand in reassurance as Trader petted him. Two lost beings, they had only each other and impossible Dreams.

For generations, peoples had congregated around Cahokia. Far from discouraging it, the lords of Cahokia had enticed people to settle in their environs. They pointed out where fertile soils could be had, and extended their knowledge of planting, field management, and crop production. Then, as the soils slowly exhausted themselves and harvests grew ever smaller, the Power of Cahokia and its lords had dimmed.

That same mismatched stew of peoples who had once flocked into the countryside surrounding Cahokia and adopted its ways began to trickle outward.

The territory around the confluence of the Mother Water with the Father Water was dotted with towns. The Michigamea held the lands to the west, and High Town on the bluff overlooking the river. The Illinois Confederacy held the river's north bank, while the Miami resided farther east, controlling the confluence of the Sister River, as they called the Tenasee.

Old White considered this as he used his paddle to keep them centered in the current. Silver Loon had warned him about hostilities in the area. In the bow of the canoe, Two Petals sat, facing him. From the moment they'd left Cahokia, she'd tried to paddle. Problem was, she took this Contrary thing to heart, absolutely infuriating him as she insisted on facing backward and paddling against him. In the beginning, they'd just gone around in circles. In final frustration, he'd hollered, "Stop it!"

At which command, her brow had furrowed, and her tongue protruded from the side of her mouth. She had attacked the water with her paddle; the fury of it only drove them backward in a circle—and splashed him with enough water to thoroughly soak him.

"Go!" he finally cried in defeat. "Paddle your heart out! Paddle, curse it."

And she'd stopped cold, head tilted as she inspected him curiously, the paddle gripped in her small hands.

That she seemed incapable of working to their benefit was of little consequence on the way downriver, but what was he going to do when they turned into the Mother River's current? True, he'd paddled all the way upstream from the Natchez lands, but the Father Water was a wide thing, full of backwaters. The Mother River was a whole different matter; entrenched as it was between high banks, the current flowed swiftly. Could he propel them both?

Oh, such interesting times, Silver Loon had promised.

As they neared the confluence, the highlands off to the east narrowed to a point. There, visible for some distance, he could see the first of the Illinois towns.

"Do we have trouble up there?" He indicated the distant town. Several large buildings could be seen above the palisade.

"Never any trouble. Not for us," she declared.

"I see." And he eyed his packs, wondering how much passage was going to cost him. On the journey upriver, his canoe had been empty, only carrying provisions. Now, however, the gifts bestowed on them by Silver Loon would pique any chief's interest.

"Keep it all," Two Petals told him. "We need every bit of it."

He chuckled, amused by his sudden instinct to hoard. "You're right. They're just things. I suppose it was spending a night with that Trader. His greed must have rubbed off."

A traveler who had nothing was of no interest to petty chiefs. And he was, after all, Old White. As he had done for years, he could barter stories in return for a hot meal, a dry bed, and a roof. Sometimes he could perform a Healing, or dispense some of his medicine herbs. On other occasions his magic tricks would do the job.

He glanced at Two Petals. She might be a real problem. Who knew what might fly out of her mouth at the most inappropriate time? Or, did it matter? Was her Spirit vision so precise that she knew the ramifications of what she said? Thinking back to the discomfort she'd driven Trader to, he wasn't sure. The man had been long gone come morning.

That, he decided, was a shame. The young man was from Split Sky City. Like himself, condemned to a life of running. He would have liked to have known Trader better. Who knew, perhaps they were of the same clan? Trader likely would know the fates of family, old friends, clan leaders, and the like.

"Different," Two Petals told him. "Totally different."

"Who, me and Trader?"

She glanced up at the cloudy sky, her hands making those intricate patterns she seemed disposed to. "Do you think it hurts when clouds run into each other?"

"Maybe. I don't know. I've never been a cloud."

"We are all clouds. Puffy, white, and sailing through blue time."

He knotted his souls around that, trying to find the relationship, and finally gave up. The gods alone knew what twists and bends a Contrary's thoughts took.

"I don't want to hear about the bearded white man," Two Petals said offhandedly.

That caught him by surprise. "Well, I saw him. He's a man, just like any other, but his skin is definitely white. And I swear, he did have dark brown hair all over his face. His eyes were blue, funniest thing. He was about my size, but his hair was a light brown. Unlike any hair I've ever seen. He was pleasant enough—a bit sad, though. Because with his boat wrecked, he could never go back across the sea. He'd taken a Pequot wife . . . had two children."

Old White chuckled. "One of the old men translated for me. You wouldn't believe the stories he tells. Weapons that clap like thunder and shoot fire. Great wooden boats with hundreds of men aboard. He told of how his people ride big animals, sort of like buffalo." He shook his head. "Now, I've seen some things, believe me. But the things he said were beyond belief."

"Lies, all lies," Two Petals told him.

Old White studied her thoughtfully. "Too bad no one can cross the sea. I'd like to see those things."

"Yes, you would. Such friendly people." She trailed her fingers in the water. "How does it do that?"

He dismissed that latter. "I don't know. That white man seemed all right."

"They'll never come here."

He raised an eyebrow. "Indeed? Given the fact his boat wrecked, it doesn't bode well for their abilities to cross the sea, either. Now, that I'd like to see. One of their big floating boats."

"Oh, you will."

"Too bad." He sighed. "Besides, there's other white men. I've seen some on occasion. They've got red eyes, can't see very well, and most avoid going out in the sun."

"Just the same," she told him, frowning down at the water. "Just why does it do that?"

"What?"

"It's always standing still."

"We're moving." Then he thought about it. "But so is the river."

"It always stays in one place."

"What about a lake?"

"The waves are busy trying to stay home."

"Maybe it's happy." He tried to put a Contrary's twist to the idea.

"That's crazy." She gave him the sort of look she'd give a backward child.

He sighed, turning their bow toward the lowlands that marked the confluence of the rivers.

With plenty of time to consider her words, he stroked them forward, but cast occasional glances at the high town. He could only catch glimpses between the trees now.

So, one day the white men would come to his world. But he wouldn't live to see it. Could the stories the white man had told him really be true? Two Petals said they were. Imagine the things they could tell him.

And her notion of water—it had never occurred to him before. Were waves just water trying to escape from a lake? When he thought about it, water was always moving. Springs seeping from the ground, rivers running to the sea. The only time water was still was when it was captured in a pot, caged.

Suddenly, he burst out laughing. Two Petals gave him a probing look.

"Even at my age, I'm still learning about myself."

"You know everything," she agreed.

"Yes, I do. The world is still full of surprises. Two Petals, you make me young."

They were rounding the point now, and far to the south, past the trees, he could see the southern bluffs. That was Michigamea territory, and it would be wise to avoid it. His paddle working rhythmically; he nosed them into the broad waters of the Mother River, seeing the color change: clearer, greener.

He was still feeling lighthearted when the canoes emerged from a creek mouth in the riverbank.

"They'll never catch us," Two Petals said softly.

"Should I be worried?" he asked, checking to see that his Trader's staff was handy.

"Not you." She clapped her hands to her ears. "This is just the beginning. Later, I'll be in the middle of a swarm. If only the sound wasn't so loud."

"Great." He lifted his staff as the canoes approached: four of them, each manned by four husky young men. Their hair was cut in roaches, tattoos marking their faces. Several had copper ear spools in their earlobes. Wolf and bear hides hung from their shoulders. While Old White couldn't see weapons, he imagined they'd be ready to hand just below the gunwales.

Old White called out in Trader Tongue, "We travel under the Power of Trade."

"Good," the man in the lead canoe called back. "We have need of Trade."

Old White shot a measuring glance at Two Petals. She was staring thoughtfully at the clouds, a puzzled look on her face. If it was trouble, she didn't seem concerned.

He cupped hands to his mouth, shouting, "I was thinking of traveling farther upriver."

"We could help you." The first canoe had pulled abreast. The leader stood, balancing easily in the rocking craft. His gaze surveyed the packs, and a ghost of a smile crossed his lips. He turned, saying something in a tongue Old White didn't understand. They talked back and forth for several heartbeats, one man gesturing. Several of his men shipped their paddles, and one produced a coil of rope. Holding one end, he tossed it across to Old White.

"Have the girl hang on," he ordered.

Old White sighed, fingering the fine basswood rope. "Don't take this." He tossed it to Two Petals. "And now, whatever you do, be sure you let go of it."

He could see the puzzled looks in the other canoes.

"We're going to go fast," the warrior told him. "We don't want to linger in these waters."

Old White laid his Trader's staff down as the canoes lined out. The warriors weren't joking. Two Petals grunted as she took the strain of the line. Then she was smart enough to take a wrap around her body.

As his canoe slipped along, Old White noted that the warriors kept looking back behind them. Whatever they'd left back there, they were making fine time getting away from it.

"What are we into now?" he wondered. The fact that the four canoes surrounded them in a diamond formation had disturbing implications.

At the end of the second day, with a light rain falling, Smoke Shield called a halt. He passed orders to build fires and shelters. His weary warriors pitched into the task, raising lean-tos, cutting vines, and weaving them through the poles. Then they piled leaf mat over the frameworks. Deadfall was brought for seats, and their single fire bow was taken from its pack. Within moments, blue smoke rose from the tinder that Scaled Bird had placed next to the cherrywood dowel. No warrior would blow on embers while on the war trail, so he used a section of eagle wing they carried specifically to fan the fire.

Smoke Shield walked along the line of captives, huddled now for warmth, their hair and clothing soaked, their skin pimpled. He knew Morning Dew by the ridiculous dress she was wearing. It was a gorgeous thing, dyed a bright red from bloodroot and dogwood bark. Chevrons of porcupine quills in black, yellow, and white made patterns reminiscent of tents over drilled oyster-shell beads. The effigy of a falcon had been rendered with small white pearls, each drilled and carefully sewn in place. Many were now missing, the threads hanging like forgotten hairs.

"Enjoying your walk in the woods?" he asked.

Morning Dew might not have heard, her gaze fixed on the ground.

"We enjoy nothing in your presence," Screaming Falcon said thickly. The blow that had broken his jaw left his face swollen; a large bruise discolored the left side of his chin.

"More's the pity." Smoke Shield cocked his head. "I wonder if you'll be so arrogant after a couple of days tied in the square?"

"I am a warrior," he spit.

"Yes, I can see that."

. He walked on down the line, seeing the fear in Biloxi Mankiller's eyes. The high minko swallowed hard, averting his eyes. Yes, that one would provide sport. How could the White Arrow have elevated such a man? The women, Biloxi's wives, wouldn't even look up. Dancing Star, the White Arrow *Alikchi Hopaii*, had no expression at all, as if disbelieving his Power could have been so easily broken. His nephew, Daytime Owl, who would have followed him, spent most of his time trying to care for the old man.

Last in line, the shivering Albaamo looked up with eyes that reminded Smoke Shield of a mouse caught in the bottom of a bowl. When he smiled, the Albaamo's chin quivered, and it wasn't just the cold.

Smoke Shield checked their ropes, then ordered, "Tie them between two trees, the rope tight between them so they can't get to each other's knots. I want two guards on them at all times. You are to check their bindings frequently. The rain might loosen them."

"Yes, War Chief."

While he made a round of his camp, his second, Blood Skull, passed out food and water to the warriors. Seeing that all was well, Smoke Shield retired to the small fire in the lean-to Blood Skull had constructed. After carefully placing the war medicine box on a square of sticks that Blood Skull had erected for it, Smoke

Shield extended his cold hands to the fire, grateful for its warmth. Their other packs, containing booty—including the White Arrow scalps, trophy heads, and collected weapons—were laid to the side. To the right rested a mysterious fabric bag that Blood Skull had burdened himself with. When first asked about its contents, Blood Skull had only given him a knowing grin, saying, "All in good time, War Chief."

From a small sack, Blood Skull removed a piece of dried turkey meat. This he offered to the fire, a gesture of respect for the gift of food. Then he extended the sack to Smoke Shield, who also tossed a piece into the fire before eating.

"I would never have believed we could do such a thing," Blood Skull said. "I thought you were mad to suggest it."

"Then why did you agree to the plan?"

Blood Skull shot him a sidelong glance. "In all honesty, it was to see if I could save anyone when it went wrong."

Smoke Shield chuckled. "I'm glad to know you think so highly of me."

His second shrugged. "When you changed the plan, I thought surely we were doomed." He glanced out at the warriors in their shelters. "I thought one of them would panic, flounder, start to drown and scream."

"They didn't."

"No. And for that, I'm very proud of them."

"Since we are speaking honestly . . ."

"Yes."

"You don't like me, do you?"

"No." Blood Skull paused. "But in the grand pattern of things, I don't suppose we have to like each other. Our duty for the moment is to work together for the best interests of our people."

"Can we do that?"

"It depends." Blood Skull took the offered turkey meat and chewed reflectively. Swallowing it down, he took a drink from the water gourd. "When it comes to war, no man can doubt you. I hope your leadership is equally as competent."

"But?"

"As a man you worry me."

"How?"

"I'm not sure your 'appetites' won't cause trouble." Blood Skull shot him a wary glance.

"I shall be careful where I eat."

"I pray that is so."

After the awkward silence, Smoke Shield shifted on the log. "I compliment you on the way you captured Screaming Falcon and the woman. No one could have managed that better."

Blood Skull grinned. "Me? I only had to deal with a dwelling and the Men's House. How you got Biloxi out of his palace, that was a miracle if I ever saw one."

"I've worked harder getting quail out of a bush."

"Well then, bird hunter, I have saved the best for last." Blood Skull reached for the fabric pack and pulled the covering from a beautifully carved wooden box. Inset shell, mica, and pearls glistened in the firelight. The image of a falcon stared at Smoke Shield with a single glowing pearl eye.

"Gods! Is that . . . ?"

"The single crowning achievement of our raid: White Arrow war medicine, War Chief." Blood Skull's wide smile split his face. "With this, our victory is complete!"

"Why didn't you tell me?" Smoke Shield gazed raptly at the captured war medicine taken from the White Arrow Town Men's House. "With that, we have captured their heart, as well as their rulers."

Blood Skull ran his fingers over the carved wood. "This is the same medicine young Screaming Falcon carried on the Alligator Town raid. Perhaps it makes up for the loss of our war medicine when Makes War was captured so long ago."

"Perhaps." Smoke Shield gestured dismissively.

"But, returning to your captives, it was brilliantly done. I have been thinking . . ."

"Yes?" Blood Skull shot a suspicious glance at him, as if surprised that he wasn't more enthused about the war medicine.

"When we return to our glory, I would like to make a present of High Minko Biloxi to you."

"That is an extraordinary gift, War Chief. What could I possibly offer in return? It is tradition that the war medicine be placed in the Men's House where—"

"I think it would please my uncle if you were kind enough to offer Screaming Falcon to him. He would be eternally grateful."

"And you." Blood Skull's voice dropped. "What would you be grateful for, War Chief?"

"Perhaps one of your captives . . . ?"

Blood Skull gave him an evaluative stare. "Of course." He chuckled. "Then, I suppose it wasn't just happenstance that you picked me to capture the great White Arrow war chief and his wife."

"Never accuse me of happenstance."

"From this moment on, War Chief, I assure you, I shall never make that mistake." He watched Smoke Shield through veiled eyes.

What was going on behind that thoughtful face? Smoke Shield could almost see the man's roiling thoughts. It was as if he were rethinking a great many things.

Finally, he begins to see me for the brilliant leader that I am. He fought to keep a smile from his face.

Rain continued to patter on the shelter. Smoke Shield bit the last piece of turkey in two and dropped the final morsel into the flames. "Thank you, Turkey, for sharing your strength and sustenance with us."

Blood Skull, too, offered his last piece to the fire. "Think they're behind us?"

Smoke Shield rubbed his hands before the flames. "I doubt it; but that's why I left three scouts to keep an eye on our backtrail. Even if the Chahta should kill one, the other two should give us time to flee."

"They must think we hit them with hundreds of warriors. In all my life, I've never seen such a panic. You should have seen the palisade gate; it was like shooting deer in a surround."

"I would have liked to have seen that." He shrugged. "Someone had to stay behind and blow the horn."

"I have to tell you, I was sorry to hear the sound of it. I think that if we had kept after them, we'd have run them clear to the Natchez."

Smoke Shield shook his head. "We would have lost someone. Maybe more. When our warriors got into the trees, they'd have been split up. Some Chahta would have had sense enough to stop, step behind a tree, and kill one of ours when he ran past."

"I would hope that in your position, I would have had the same good sense."

"I'm sure you would," Smoke Shield said smoothly. "Now, our bellies have something to chew on; so why don't you and I go see what this supposedly lost Albaamo was doing? I want to know why he wanted to get to White Arrow Town before we burned it."

"That is a good question." Blood Skull asked, "Do you think he'll talk?"

"Oh, I'm sure. I don't plan on doing anything to his tongue."

Seventeen

Old White's Illinois escort led them to a town that had been built on high ground above the north bank of the Mother River. The canoe landing was little more than a narrow sand strip a bow shot up a small creek. As the men piled out of their canoes, Old White wasn't surprised to see each carried a war club of the type common in the northeast: a curving thing with a heavy wooden ball on the end. Bows, arrows, and a bloody—very fresh-looking—scalp accompanied the party.

"Welcome, Trader," the leader cried as he helped to pull Old White's canoe ashore. "I am Three Bucks, war chief of Lightning Oak Town. We are the Crane band, of the Sky Moiety. You have probably heard us referred to as the Illinouiek, or Illinois. We call ourselves the Inoca." He shook the bloody scalp. "As you can see, it was a good day."

"Not for someone," Old White pointed out.

Three Bucks laughed again, turning. Evidently he translated for his warriors, because they burst out in guffaws.

"I am called Old White. Some know me as the Seeker. The woman with me is Two Petals." He paused, aware that their absolutely male attention was focused on Two Petals as she stepped out of the canoe. "She is a Contrary. A woman of great Power." He raised his voice. "Do you *understand*?"

"Yes, yes." Three Bucks seemed puzzled, then added, "Ah, a *manitou*."

"That is correct. We have come from Silver Loon, at Cahokia."

That got the man's attention. "You had dealings with the witch?"

Old White lifted his Trader's staff. "Three Bucks, I want you to understand, it might be wise if we did not stay long. This woman draws Power."

Three Bucks nodded, translating to his men. Someone asked a question.

"Is she your wife?"

"She is." The lie might serve him well here. Prestige accrued to a man married to a *manitou* among most northeastern peoples.

"Yes, I am," Two Petals agreed in a singsong voice. "Wife, wife, wife, forever."

"You must be great to marry a woman with Power." Three Bucks seemed slightly incredulous.

"So it is said. You indicated that you would like to Trade?" Old White reminded.

"This way."

Old White reached into the canoe, removing one of the smaller packs Silver Loon had given them. Without a word, he handed it to Two Petals. To his relief she shouldered it, though she kept working her hands. Cramped no doubt from the death grip on the rope.

People were already running down the hill, calling in excited voices. Shouts of glee went up as Three Bucks lifted the scalp.

"Bees," Two Petals whispered. "Swarming around. Please, don't let them sting me."

"Not if I can help it," Old White muttered.

In reply to the shouted questions from above, Three Bucks turned to Old White. "They want to know if you are captives."

He shot Three Bucks a sidelong glance. "Have they never seen a Trader's staff before?"

"Be at ease. I have told them you are guests. In our town, all are treated with respect once they pass our gates." He shot Old White a sidelong glance. "That is, if they come in peace."

"Oh, we do."

A steep forest path led up the silty slope to a cluster of cornfields on a high terrace. The town itself had been constructed on a small knoll. To defend Lightning Oak Town, a log palisade rose behind a deep ditch that forced attackers into the unenviable position of having to attack uphill while the defenders rained arrows down on them from gaps between the logs. Entry was through a narrow passage that forced attackers to run a gauntlet of arrows released from no more than an arm's length.

Once inside, the town consisted of forty houses, several granaries, a charnel house, men's house, several menstrual lodges, and what passed for the Council House. A tall log structure with bark-covered roof had been erected atop a low rectangular earthen mound. From its ridgepole a rudely carved eagle glared out at the world through painted wooden eyes. Even in light of the dilapidation of Cahokia, the place was shabby at best.

They were greeted by a larger crowd, the women dressed in deerskins, fox and wolf capes hanging from their shoulders. They had pulled their hair up tightly to their heads. The men, hair shaved in roaches, their skin dabbed with red or yellow paint, had deer- or buffalohide hunting shirts, some with bear-claw necklaces, others wearing bone beads dyed different colors. Dogs ran about, barking, wagging tails, and sniffing. To the rear, an unadorned collection of women and girls—slaves, no doubt—wore simple brown dresses, their expressions wary. Most stood with arms crossed under their breasts.

Shouted questions brought laughing responses from the men. The Inoca women immediately began singing, clapping their hands, and Dancing. The men took up the chorus. Someone brought a sapling, perhaps the height of a man, and Three Bucks tied the scalp to it. He led his war party forward in a shuffling half step; his voice, too, added to the song.

"Happy, aren't they?" Old White asked Two Petals.

"Sad. Their hearts are like a stormcloud on a sunny day." She looked to the side, saying, "I wish you wouldn't say things like that."

"Like what?" Old White asked.

"I was talking to her." She pointed over by the side of the palisade. "To that old white-haired woman."

Old White saw no one of that description. In fact, no one stood where she pointed. "You see a woman there?"

"Yes, that one. That old woman. She says that the In-oca are rootless. That's silly. People don't have roots. Not with feet like those." She pointed at the Dancers who were rising, ducking, and prancing.

"Just between the two of us," Old White offered dryly, "I wouldn't mention to the Inoca that you see people they don't."

Two Petals gave him an annoyed look. "How am I supposed to tell the difference?"

"Just ask me if I can see the same person you do before you start talking, all right?"

"It's hard to think," she told him, pressing her hands to her ears and squinting. "How can you even hear with all these thoughts in the air? They keep pulling at me, buzzing all the time. They're all bees. So busy, so happy."

All eyes turned toward the Council House when an elderly man stepped out of the doorway. A clutter of feathers stuck out of the roach atop his head; both sides of his shaved scalp were tattooed with parallel lines of circles. His long shirt was made of finely tanned buffalo calf hide adorned with brightly dyed quillwork. The man's arms and legs were tattooed with bands and flattened chevrons. He lifted a long-stemmed pipe high over his head. The crowd went silent as he began chanting a Song of thanksgiving, his voice rising and falling in the cool air.

At the conclusion, the people took up the Song, women and men forming concentric rings around the war party. They Danced and clapped in unison, all the while casting curious glances at Old White and Two Petals. Every so often, one would break ranks, trotting forward. Three Bucks would lower the scalp so that they could touch it. Many grasped it just long enough to spit on it, or revile it with a curse.

After every man, woman, and child had taken their turn, Three Bucks threw his head back in a long ululating cry and headed toward the Council House. People fell into ranks, men separate from women, and the whole procession marched along.

Old White followed the war party, waiting as Three Bucks climbed the low earthen ramp to face the old man. In a loud voice that all could hear, he began a long narrative, periodically emphasizing each warrior in his party. Gestures added to his oratory, bringing hoots of delight from the people.

"Recounting the raid, I would guess." Old White glanced at Two Petals. She seemed to be engrossed in the performance, her eyes wide.

"They have sparks flying around their heads," she said. "Why don't they catch fire?"

Since he saw no sparks himself, he shrugged. "Just their nature, I would guess."

She clasped her hands to her breast, spinning around in a circle. "So many souls, all crowding around! They are a wave. I'm riding on top of a wave!"

Old White glanced nervously at her, wondering what fed this sudden, heady joy.

Finally, Three Bucks pointed to them. From the gestures, a man throwing a rope, other men pantomiming furious paddling, and the laughter, Old White caught the gist of their rapid journey upriver. Three Bucks pointed back and forth to Old White and Two Petals, the word *manitou* cropping up both times. When it did, the crowd uttered a hushed, "Aahaa." Expectant looks were cast in their direction.

When Three Bucks finished with a barked, "Whoa!" the crowd was silent.

The old man lowered his pipe and turned his attention to Old White and Two Petals. In Trade Tongue, he said, "I am High Buffalo, leader of these people. You may call me Chief. You are welcome in Lighting Oak Town, Traders. Your arrival has come on a very auspicious day. We have avenged ourselves on the sneaking cowards at Flat Board Town. Just a moon past, they ambushed and killed a young woman at the canoe landing when she went down for water." He indicated the dangling scalp. "Now they know the price of their actions."

"We are honored to arrive here," Old White replied. "We are Traders, traveling under the Trader's Staff." He lifted it high. "We come only in peace, and would Trade with the people of Lightning Oak Town."

High Buffalo cocked his head. "Why would my war chief call you *manitou*?"

Old White pointed at Two Petals. "This woman, great chief, is a Contrary. When she speaks, it is backward of what she means. When talking to her, she will do opposite of your words. Power rides her shoulders. Because of that, and because we are strangers, we would not wish to have misunderstandings with your people."

High Buffalo turned his inquisitive eyes on Two Petals. "Is this true?"

"Not a bit," she answered, a pained look on her face as she glanced around at things Old White couldn't see. "He lies. No truth will come from Old White's mouth. Mine, either."

"I shall send for our Priest. He is secluded in the woods close by, praying for the success of our warriors. He will be most interested to meet you." Then he addressed the crowd in his own tongue, pointing back and forth between Old White and Two Petals. The word *manitou* kept repeating.

Nods and softly uttered words met each proclamation.

When he had finished, High Buffalo gestured for them to come forward. "We extend our hospitality. Tonight, we shall feast. Come, join us."

Two Petals immediately turned, heading back for the gate. People scurried out of her way. All except a couple of dogs who obviously didn't know any better. Mutterings rose from some of the people as they scattered, none wishing to be too close to the *manitou.*

"Two Petals," Old White called. "He wants you to go away. Far from the interior of the Council House." She immediately stopped, nodded, and retraced her steps.

"This is true?" High Buffalo asked. "She is truly *manitou?*"

"Oh, very true," Old White told him.

High Buffalo scrambled out of her way as she walked through the door. Old White hurried after her, pausing only long enough to ask High Buffalo, "Is there anything you would like her to do? Any Power objects she should stay away from?"

"Ask her to sit on this side of the fire, please."

Old White ducked into the Council House. The large room was illuminated by a crackling fire. He caught a quick glimpse of deer horns; the splayed hides of birds, foxes, and raccoons; and lines of animal skulls hanging from the walls. War shields, weapons, and a line of scalps also could be seen. He hurried past Two Petals, who was staring around at the walls, and pointed to a place on the rush matting beside the hearth. "Do not sit on this spot."

Two Petals obediently sat there, her eyes still on the stuffed birds, shields, bows, arrows, and buffalo and deer skulls that lined the walls. "Listen to the noise they make." She pointed at a flattened cougar hide pegged to the wall. "He says he can't hunt that way. Anything he eats has to be flat, too."

Behind him, people were crowded at the door, watching with wide eyes. High Buffalo had managed to squeeze through the pack and stepped forward. All the time he was issuing instructions to his people. Many slipped away, leaving room for Three Bucks and his warriors to enter.

High Buffalo recovered quickly, bearing his long-stemmed pipe and taking a place on the bear rug behind the fire. He took a moment to drape his knee-length shirt, glanced thoughtfully at the pipe he held, and said, "Food is being prepared. We must attend to our victorious warriors, and then, Trader, we must hear the story you have to tell."

Old White settled himself beside Two Petals. Her eyes were shining, a rapt smile on her face. She giggled as she watched the flat cougar hide, hearing some inaudible voice as the creature's Spirit spoke to her. Her hands were fluttering, and she bubbled with an excitement beyond his comprehension. A sudden burst of laughter passed her lips.

So far, so good. But he fervently hoped that when the time came, no one would tell Two Petals to go outside to relieve herself.

Split Sky City had to be close. That morning the warriors had opened their packs and donned their finest regalia. They took time to paint their faces in red and black, to fix feathers and clean their weapons. Using grease, they glued swan's down to their heads. Only when each was satisfied had they started the march.

Morning Dew had stumbled through most of the long miserable trip in shock. Her tumbling souls might have come adrift from her body. She had lost herself. Become some elemental animal. Each step she took was without thought, goaded on by the guards. From some distant place, she wondered how a human body could shiver so hard and still have the energy to continue. Her feet had lost feeling, so cold she could have been walking on clay.

Nothing seemed eternal but suffering—and the endless winding forest trails. Images, disjointed, like flashes in nothingness, popped into focus, then as quickly were gone. She remembered scenes from her childhood: a cornshuck doll; a delicious odor rising from a warm bowl of food; glimpses of her comfortable house, firelight flickering; snatches of Song from a faceless elder. Each was nothing more than a fragment of a life that might have been a fevered Dream.

No matter how much she hurt, nothing could compare to what Screaming Falcon endured with his broken jaw, yet he stumbled on with stoicism that she was forced to emulate. When she would have given up, he sensed it, looking back with his hard eyes, slurring past his broken jaw, "We are Chahta. Remember that. We can only be better than these dogs by showing them how real men and women behave."

And then, when she would have thrown herself down, weeping, waiting for the blow that killed her, his words had summoned courage from some unknown well.

Other times, like forest birds, fantasies had flitted through her head: White Arrow warriors were even now setting an ambush that would free them. Because of her status as a future matron, the Sky Hand would release her. Emissaries from her people would arrive moments after the war party reached Split Sky City with ransom. Some daring warrior would sneak into the city to rescue her.

Then the reality of her situation would come crashing down. Tears would streak her cheeks, and the rope would chafe where it rubbed raw flesh on her neck. Only Screaming Falcon's whispered encouragement gave her the will to proceed.

As Morning Dew's uncertain feet followed the trail, she forced herself to believe that Mother was only wounded, playing dead to avoid capture. Her spinning hopes fastened on the idea that Mother was already planning how best to effect her release. Then, in the cold wet night, when she shivered and curled into a ball for warmth, Mother was really dead. In those darkest hours,

while rain soaked her beautiful dress and trickled down
her icy skin, her mother's death couldn't be denied.

I just want to die.

She blinked, coming back to herself. The forest was
endless. The world had funneled down to the back of
Screaming Falcon's head; her link to it was the bobbing
rope running from his neck to hers. She needed but to
glance down to see her bound wrists. As she looked to
the side, the line of warriors paralleling her was impos-
sibly real.

Biloxi was pleading again, begging for mercy and
freedom. "I'll give you anything! Don't you know who I
am?"

Blinking, she wondered, *Is that really my brother?*
Could the grand Biloxi Mankiller, high minko of the
White Arrow, have become this groveling lump of a
man? She barely recognized the naked man as her
brother—not the Biloxi she knew. He wouldn't be whimpering, seeking to curry favor from the guards, promising
them women, wealth, lands, anything to let him loose.
Then, later, his begging was for a drink, for food, or a
wrap of cloth to warm himself in.

Better that Mother was dead. It would wound her
souls to learn that Biloxi had become this broken creature. His three wives, including Water Lily with her broken arm, bore up with more grace and resolve.

"What's going to happen to us?" she finally asked as
they descended a slope. They passed through the last of
the forest to enter a cornfield.

Screaming Falcon turned his head, a hard certainty in
his eyes. "Blood Skull captured us. He will decide." The
words were slurred. She knew it hurt him to talk.

"He will give us away, won't he?"

"It is . . . custom." Screaming Falcon turned his eyes
back to the path they followed around one of the cornfields.

The implications settled coldly around her heart. A
warrior who captured an enemy traditionally made a

gift of the prisoner to another clan, thereby incurring that clan's favor and obligation. No higher honor could be bestowed.

She closed her eyes, heart pounding. Prayed that Blood Skull offered her to any clan but Smoke Shield's Chief Clan. The way the man looked at her sent a chill through her souls that was colder than the night rain.

"We may be all right," she insisted, forcing herself to watch the trail. When one captive fell, he jerked the others down, choking them. Then came the warriors, wielding their clubs to get everyone up. It was an awkward process with bound arms.

The rope jerked, biting into her throat, causing her to stumble. She coughed, fought to keep her balance, and managed.

"Sorry," Juggler managed hoarsely. "It was the *Alikchi Hopaii.* He tripped but didn't fall."

Still coughing, Morning Dew cast a glance behind her. Down the line she could see Dancing Star, the *Alikchi Hopaii,* the Spirit Healer, the greatest of their Priests, wobbling on his feet. His nephew, Daytime Owl, had rushed forward to steady the man.

"Keep the line," one of the warriors barked from the side. The man pointed his war club.

"My uncle is weakening," the young man explained.

"He doesn't have far to go." The warrior seemed to relent. "The way is flatter now."

They took us all. The lonely thought echoed between Morning Dew's souls. In one daring blow, Smoke Shield had captured the high minko and his wives, taken her and Screaming Falcon, killed the Chief Clan matron, and captured the *Alikchi Hopaii.* Screaming Falcon's young brother, a boy who would never see manhood, walked last in line. He claimed to have seen the tishu minko's body outside his house. With Bow Mankiller's death, White Arrow Town's leadership was either dead or captive.

A shout caused her to raise her head. An Albaamo

farmer and his family stood beside their thatch-covered house. The man was waving, smiling. As the warriors passed, he ran out, offering each of them ears of corn. These the warriors accepted, but without the enthusiasm she would have expected.

The words of the Albaamo spy are ringing in their ears. She swallowed hard, remembering the man's unearthly shrieks as Smoke Shield alternately cut him apart and pressed burning branches to his naked, bound body.

She had tried to close her ears, but his screams had pierced the very bones in her head. "Paunch!" the man had cried. "Paunch sent me!"

Every time Smoke Shield had asked who else was involved, the young man had pleaded, sometimes in Albaamaha, sometimes in Mos'kogee, that he didn't know. It always came back to the man called Paunch.

She had tried not to look as they passed the young man's remains the following morning. But a quick glance had etched itself in her memory. Could that piece of charred and butchered meat have once been human?

The final leg of the journey passed in misery, more people crowding around, watching them pass. She flinched the first time someone threw wet garbage at her. After that, the periodic pelting of feces, urine, and turkey intestines became commonplace. So, too, did the Dancing Albaamaha. Several shouted, "This is for our kin, butchered at Alligator Town!"

They skirted the last cornfield, winding down to the Black Warrior River. There, for the first time, she glanced up, seeing the high palaces atop the bluff opposite them. She stared for a moment, openly amazed. "Mother, you never told me."

But she had. So had Old Woman Fox. From the size of the city and the huge crowd on the opposite bank, she began to realize the folly she and Screaming Falcon had proposed. Not even her marriage had drawn such a crowd. The Sky Hand and their Albaamaha allies were like the leaves of the forest.

Canoes were waiting at the river's edge. Still more people crowded around them; the shouts and whoops must have shaken the sky, but when she looked up, it was to see the endless blue unmoved.

The rope binding them was cut, other warriors holding the crowd at bay. She tried to understand the scope of the people's joy. *How can so many Dance, smile, and shout when we are so miserable?*

Smoke Shield seemed to swell, his face painted in triumphal red. His white swan feathers waved with the breeze. She fixed on the nasty scar that marred the side of his face. Then he turned, eyes fixing on hers. He smiled, and it hinted at things too terrible to believe.

"Into the boats! Now, you filthy Chahta!"

One by one they clambered into the canoes, taking seats as warriors piled in behind them. She felt the craft pushed off, watched paddles flashing in the sunlight as they were borne swiftly across the river.

I could jump. The thought came from nowhere. *Down there, in the depths, I could suck water into my lungs. I would die before they pulled me out.*

But she didn't—wondering if she was a coward, or a fool, to hope for a better fate. Then it was too late; the canoe speared onto the black beach—just one among tens of others.

Hard hands pulled her out. With smacks of the war club, the prisoners were lined out, and Smoke Shield— the wooden war medicine on his back—raised his hands and shouted, "Yo hey hey!"

The warriors broke out with cries of, "Wah! Wah!"

"We bring the White Arrow war medicine!" Blood Skull shouted, lifting the ornately carved box high over his head.

The crowd went wild, screaming until the veins stood out in their necks, faces contorted with the effort as their hands clapped and feet stamped.

The warrior called Fast Legs raised a pine branch cut from along the trail. A second warrior raised another.

Both were bent from the drying scalps of her people. The roar bellowing from the crowd deafened her. She flinched from the sound of it, and would have taken a step back but for Biloxi crowding behind her, attempting to be as small as he could.

Then the procession started forward, the warriors Singing "Yo hey hey!"—the time-honored call of victory for the Sky Hand People.

Fear, like a thing alive, twisted around her souls. Despite her raging thirst, sweat broke out on her skin. On trembling legs, she made the climb from the landing up the long ridge inside the high palisade. From the archers' platforms, children watched, waving cloth, shaking small bows. Around her, the crowd surged along, Singing, Dancing, clapping their hands. Like a flood, the people washed around houses, the press of their bodies shaking ramadas, feet overturning baskets and boxes.

Above it all, Morning Dew could see the high palaces, buildings that made her own small and shabby in comparison. Then they spilled out into the plaza. Smoke Shield, war medicine on his back, led the way to the tchkofa. At the northern extent of the mound, he circled to the right, opposite the path of the sun.

Morning Dew shot panicked glances at the faces in the crowd, seeing the mixture of exultant joy and downright elation. Distinct in the jumble of sound, she heard them talking of their Power, of the might of their warriors, how not even the lords of Cahokia had lived through a day like this. Through it all, the warriors' shouts of, "Yo hey hey," were answered by chants of, "Wah! Wah!"

She staggered, terror sapping her legs, as she was prodded around the circumference of the tchkofa. Then they headed north past the red-and-white Tree of Life. The crowd parted. There the towering high minko's palace stood atop a mound that scraped the sky. Then she saw the bare frames of the squares: one each for Screaming Falcon, Biloxi, Dancing Star, Juggler, and Daytime

Owl. Facing them were tall wooden poles, each topped by a carving of an animal representing the captor's clan.

Her knees buckled. She hit the ground hard. Behind her, Biloxi was sobbing. Hard hands grabbed her from behind. She heard Biloxi's squeal as a blow landed. While she was dragged like a limp deer to a pole, two warriors drove her brother before them with smacking blows of their war clubs. The crowd shrieked, whistled, and jeered.

"It won't be so bad," mocked one of the warriors dragging her. "At least you don't have to hang."

Numb with terror, Morning Dew shivered as they bound her to a pole capped with a raccoon head. As tears streaked down her face, she watched Screaming Falcon as he was tied spread-eagled to the square opposite her. The rhythmic chant of the crowd became clear: *"Burn them! Burn them! Burn them!"*

She choked on the sobs in her throat. Her vision narrowed, as if she stared down a long tunnel. Gray haze closed in from all sides. Her last thought was of falling. . . .

Eighteen

Old White blinked his eyes open and found them gummy. The Council House had been smoky, and the feasting, stories, and Dancing had lasted until late. He yawned, shifted in the finely tanned buffalo hide he'd been provided, and stared up at the smoke-hazed ceiling. The Inoca had been exemplary hosts, and memories of the evening played between his souls.

After the smoking of the pipe, invocations had been made to the "Master of Life," as they called the Creator, and to the numerous *manitous* that filled the Inoca's Spirit world. Three Bucks had given a long oratory about the raid, and the scalp had been passed from hand to hand before being given to the murdered woman's bereaved family. Then endless bowls of stewed puppy—an Inoca favorite—had been followed by boiled squash, sunflower soup, roast venison and duck, hominy corn, and berry bread made of white acorn flour.

His Trade had been brisk as he dispensed pieces of worked shell, quartz crystals for scrying the future, and pieces of mica from the goods Silver Loon had given him. In return, he had amassed a collection of the striking wooden bowls the Inoca crafted. Each was thin walled, the deep dish carved in the shape of an animal. His favorite was the rendition of Beaver, its eyes inlaid with mussel shell. The booty had filled a large net bag.

Two Petals had been a sensation, the center of attention. Possessed of a frantic energy, she had almost vibrated, smiling, laughing while people asked her questions to hear the backward response. One by one they listened in awe, trying to decipher the meaning of her words. Things like, "The answer lies in the heart of a blue stone" or "Do not fly when the rain is falling." Each of Two Petals' pronouncements seemed to have great meaning as they were translated for the Inoca.

Old White had been awed himself, amazed at the Power that energized her. The look on her face had been euphoric.

For once, no one seemed interested in the stories the Seeker could tell about strange peoples he had visited, or the things he had seen. In retrospect, it had been rather pleasant to just sit, listen, and watch the rapt faces of the people.

Now fatigued from having slept poorly, and not for long, he stretched, yawned, and sat up. Scratching under his stringy gray hair, he looked around and froze. Two Petals' bed had been rolled and was missing. The net bag filled with carved bowls was also gone. Not quite in a panic, Old White climbed stiffly to his feet, slipped his wooden pack over his shoulder, and retrieved his Trader's staff.

He emerged into the day, the stone in his cloth bag banging reassuringly against his thigh. The sun was already high, and as he looked around the village, he could find no sign of Two Petals. Anxiously, he made the rounds inside the palisade, greeted only by several curious dogs and two wide-eyed little boys who giggled, then ran.

Old White hurried to the gate, passed through the narrow gap, and then down to the canoe landing. He couldn't shake the memory that not a moon past, a young woman had been killed by raiders there.

As he stepped out of the trees, he slowed. Two Petals was sitting primly in the canoe, facing backward, the net bag with its bowls rising prominently atop the load.

"What are you doing here?"

"This is not the time to leave," she told him, not even

turning her head to look at him. "No indeed, I think we should dally all day. Eat their food, laugh, and drink."

"Why? Are we in trouble?" He searched his memory for anything they might have done to sour their welcome.

"With the Inoca? Oh, yes, terrible trouble. That's why we should stay. We should just be late, and forget journeying to Split Sky."

"We should?"

"If we don't stay, the Inoca will want to be rid of us forever."

Confused, Old White muttered under his breath, "Just once, I would love to have a straight answer out of you."

"All of my answers are crooked."

"Ha! Got you. For once, you told it just the way it is."

She gave him the same look she'd give an idiot.

Old White hesitated, glanced back toward the village. "It is considered rude to just up and leave."

"Of course. No one thinks the ways of the *manitou* are mysterious."

Well, that was a point. He could imagine how the story would grow over the coming moons. *"The manitous came. Spent the night performing wondrous deeds, and in the morning, they were gone, leaving only their gifts."*

Old White bent down, arched his back, and began shoving the canoe. "You don't want to get out and help an old man, do you?"

With Two Petals' help, he pushed the craft into the slow waters of the stream. Stepping in, he took inventory. Nothing seemed to have been disturbed. Too many times, he had returned to one of his canoes only to find it stripped. Here, the Power of the *manitou* seemed to have been all the protection they needed.

As they nosed out into the Mother River's current, Old White bent to his paddle. Today, he would miss the strong warriors and their rope.

"Too bad," Two Petals told him from the bow. "We just missed him."

"Who?"

She pointed over his shoulder. "Not that man."

He shot a glance behind him, seeing a solitary canoe hugging the bank as its occupant paddled upriver. A black-and-white dog stood atop one of the packs, ears pricked, watching them with interest.

"Trader?" Old White said aloud.

"No, he's long gone. Headed to the gulf."

Old White stroked only hard enough to keep them stationary with the bank as Trader closed the distance. When he finally drew up, it was to the accompaniment of Swimmer's happy barking. The dog bounced from pack to pack.

"Hush," Trader ordered, and Swimmer, good dog that he was, stood with his tail waving.

"This is a surprise," Old White said by way of greeting. "I figured you'd be in a Michigamea Council House about now, trying to figure out how you were going to keep that copper from staying behind with the chief."

Trader refused to meet his eyes, instead focusing on one of the packs in his canoe. "I spent a lot of time thinking about that." He frowned. "And I thought a lot about how Two Petals knew where to find my camp that night . . . how she knew about the copper. All of it . . . it just doesn't make sense." He looked around, eyes settling on the far bank. "I've been up and down the river, seen a lot of things. Heard a lot of stories, but nothing like this."

"I've been a lot of places, too," Old White replied. "More than you. For some years I was even able to talk myself into believing that Power didn't exist. That everything that happens in life is just random, luck, or coincidence. The truest of things are those that we try so hard to discredit, but cannot. For reasons I do not understand, we've been chosen. Something's happening, something that wants us to go home, Trader."

"Not you two," Two Petals interjected. "Split Sky City is the last place you have to go."

Trader glanced at her for the first time, then lowered his eyes. "I killed my brother. That's why I left." He sighed. "I'm Chief Clan—expected to set an example for the rest of the people. From the time we are children we're taught to control ourselves, to act with restraint, and to be virtuous. We are supposed to balance rage with thought."

"And you were only human?"

"My brother . . ." He hesitated. "We were twins. Not identical, mind you. Not in looks or behavior. We were completely different. He was the one who could never control his passions. He was the red brother, the plotter and schemer. Everyone looked up to me."

Old White nodded. "Oh, I know about twins. They tend to run in the Chief Clan." He didn't want to ask yet, didn't want to hope. There would be time for that.

Trader gave him a hesitant look. "I suppose you are thinking about heading down the Tenasee, past the Kaskinampo to the Yuchi towns? Trading for a portage into the head of the Black Warrior?"

"It would be a little easier to portage to the head of the Horned Serpent. Follow that down, then back up the Black Warrior. We'll see when we get there." He glanced at Two Petals. "Is there any special way you *don't* want to go?"

Two Petals had been making faces at Swimmer. "No way at all."

Trader glanced over his shoulder. "Well, we might want to be at it. I spent most of yesterday afternoon hiding in the rushes. Something happened back there. It was like kicking a wasp's nest. Warriors were canoeing back and forth, searching the trails. I waited until dark to make my way upriver."

"A warrior was killed in a raid. We spent the night with the happy raiders."

"Then it might not be smart for a couple of canoes full of strangers to be caught in these parts."

"Might not indeed."

Trader shot him an uneasy look. "I don't know how this will turn out, but I'm with you."

Two Petals' voice came low and ominous. "Don't worry. We will be *perfectly* safe."

Trader looked sick. "I feel so much better."

A low call from the darkness outside his house brought Paunch awake. He blinked, tried to pull his wits from the Dream where he'd been casting a net from his canoe, and sat up. To his surprise, the fire in the hearth was crackling; yellow tongues of flame illuminated the inside of his humble sapling dwelling.

Sitting demurely before the fire, Whippoorwill wore a plain brown pullover dress. Her long hair hung about her like a cape. She held a stick with which she prodded the fire, but showed no reaction to having heard a thing.

Did I Dream it?

But no, another call came from outside. "Paunch? Are you there?"

"Yes. Here. Who is it?" By Abba Mikko, he could see only darkness between the gaps in the door hanging. At that moment, Cherry Root, Amber Bead's nephew, ducked through the door. He wore a thick blanket around his shoulders. His feet were wrapped in fabric against the chill. He puffed, like a man who was very cold.

"What time is it?" Paunch demanded.

"Middle of the night," Cherry Root told him, panting and rubbing his arms. "I have a message from my uncle. He said to tell you: There's news. Crabapple was caught. Smoke Shield tortured him. They know everything."

A terrible emptiness opened in his gut. "Everything?"

"That's what my uncle said. He told me to repeat every word so that I got it right. Oh, and he said one other thing."

"What was that?"

"Run."

Paunch closed his eyes against the sick sensation. "Whippoorwill, get your things. We must warn your mother. She and Berry must hide. They will search each of us out."

"Why?" Cherry Root demanded. "What is this all about?"

"Your uncle didn't tell you?"

"No, no one has told me anything."

"Trust me, boy, you don't want to know." Paunch tried to make his sleep-foggy head work. "Does anyone know you came here?"

"Uncle swore me to secrecy. He just said to hurry."

"And well you did." He paused. "Did anyone see you?"

"No! It's the middle of the night!"

"Then be home and in bed before morning. And don't let anyone see you getting there, either."

"But I'm cold. Can't I just warm up before—"

"No. Go now, and quickly." He stood, reaching for his breechcloth. "And for your sake, Cherry Root, if anyone asks, you were home asleep. All night. You know nothing about me. Do you understand? Your life may depend on it."

"But what is this—"

"I *told* you. You don't want to know!" He hurried to the baskets at the side of the room. Frantically, he stuffed his things in his pack. Any article that he might need. "By Abba Mikko's breath, boy, believe me, you'll live a longer, far happier life if you forget that this night ever happened. Now, go!"

He was fumbling, dropping things in his panic. Cherry Root's exit went almost unnoticed. "Whippoorwill, you must pack, too."

"I was packed long ago, Grandfather. From the moment I learned of your foolishness."

He paused. "Why are you here?"

"To fulfill the vision." She looked up at him, eyes like pools in the firelight.

"You . . . knew?"

"I have made a hot fire. By the time they get here, it will appear that we just left. Grandfather, this was not our time. It wasn't meant to be."

"Well, when will it be?"

"When the Power is right."

"Well, if it has any pity for me, the time is now."

She laughed, voice like a songbird's. "Oh, Grandfather, how silly of you. Power has no pity."

He finished sorting through his things. "Where shall we go?"

"West, Grandfather. Into the hills beyond the river. To the old places. There we can Dance with the ghosts of our Ancestors."

He stuffed his pack full, tying it closed. Smoke Shield! If he knew, it would only be a matter of luck that kept Paunch from the square. And should that luck not favor him, he'd be seeing the ghosts of the Ancestors himself—and after a most unpleasant death.

"How funny of you, Grandfather. Luck is as fickle as Power."

He knew he hadn't spoken. When he looked at her, her eyes gleamed with hidden knowledge.

"You should be married, not running like a frightened deer in a drive."

"Oh, I'm married already," she answered, rising lithely to her feet. "I consummated myself to destiny long ago."

Button snakeroot contained a powerful cleansing medicine. The bitter root was chopped fine, boiled in water to release its Spirit, and drunk when just cool enough to keep from scalding a man's throat. Within moments, its Power was released. The effects were immediate.

Smoke Shield felt the telltale tickle in his throat. His mouth began to water, and he crouched over the bowl. Within moments, his stomach pumped, and he vomited forcefully. Again and again, his gut convulsed. Gasping for breath, he used a rag to wipe his face and leaned back on his haunches.

"That is good," Pale Cat told him.

The *Hopaye* inspected the bowl, and when Smoke Shield's vision cleared, he could see a worm wiggling in the bottom of the milky fluid.

"The purging brought this up. At some time in the fighting, some Chahta witch shot this into you."

"Did he?" Smoke Shield sighed, raising his head to stare at the roof of the Men's House. Around him, additions had been made to the relics of war that lined the walls. Some Chahta arrows, a shield, several medicine bundles, but most prominent of all, Blood Skull had placed the White Arrow war medicine atop a wooden stand. There lay the heart of White Arrow Town's warriors, as surely as if Blood Skull had cut it from their breasts.

For three days now, Smoke Shield and his warriors had been fasting, drinking button snakeroot, and purging themselves. They had alternately steamed in the sweat lodge, and offered their prayers to the gods. The blood and rage of the war trail had to be purged from their bodies and souls. The process of balancing Power was both grueling and difficult. It took sacrifice and stoicism.

Pale Cat had overseen every aspect, ensuring that no man shirked his duty in following the rituals. The very health of the people depended upon it. As each ritual had been finished to Pale Cat's satisfaction, he had ordered the warriors to leave the building. There, on cue, their wives and mothers had met them, forming two par-

allel lines. As the men emerged Singing and waving
eagle wing fans, the women Danced, calling out their
praises. Only then did the warriors reenter the Men's
House and begin the next phase of the rituals.

The whole thing is tedious, Smoke Shield thought. He
had his own suspicions as to where the worm had come
from. The *Hopaye* carried several small pouches of
"medicine" tied to his waist, and Pale Cat was a well-
known magician, the best sleight of hand Smoke Shield
had ever seen. But he saw the effect it had on his men
when bits of bloody feathers, old arrowheads, crystals,
and other objects appeared in their vomit.

Were it up to him, he would have skipped most of the
ordeal; but, being a leader, he endured. He was the first to
fast, to sweat, and to drink the sacred tea. When this was
over, let no man say he was not dedicated to the well-
being of his people, or the Power that they cherished.

Smoke Shield looked up when the high minko entered; cheers broke from the warriors' throats. Flying
Hawk strode grandly across the floor, dressed in his ritual finery, white apron flashing. He had feathers tied to
his arms, his copper headpiece shining atop his head.
The turkey-tail mace was clutched in his right hand, and
all of his small white arrows had been poked through his
tight hair.

"I bring greetings to each of you," he said as he
walked up to the White Arrow war medicine box. Tapped
lightly with his stone mace, the wood elicited a hollow
sound. Then he turned, addressing the *Hopaye.* "I have
taken the liberty of calling the people. I assume all has
gone well?"

Pale Cat clasped his hands before him, bowing
slightly. "It has, High Minko. These great warriors have
approached their purification with the same dedication
they have shown on the war trail."

Flying Hawk glanced around, meeting Smoke Shield's
eyes. "We have much to do. A great feast has been
cooked. The tishu minko has sent runners. The Council

has been called." He glanced at the *Hopaye*. "Would it be inappropriate if I led the warriors out myself?"

"It would be an honor," Smoke Shield cried, hoping to forestall any last-minute "purification" that Pale Cat might want to inflict.

"And you shall walk by my side," Flying Hawk said. "Has your slave brought you your things?"

"Thin Branch delivered them this morning."

"Then by all means, dress!" Flying Hawk said jovially. "And I warn you all, look your best."

Hoots and laughter burst out as the warriors flocked to the bags their relatives had brought. Fine aprons, feathers, copper jewelry, shell gorgets, paint boxes, and palettes appeared.

As Smoke Shield began to dress, Flying Hawk stepped over, lowering his voice. "The Council may be called upon to do more than praise your success. I have sent word out about the Albaamo you discovered, and his confession. As we speak, warriors are seeking the elder known as Paunch. I am hoping that we will have him before any alarm can be raised."

"Good." Smoke Shield considered. "How did you plan on handling this?"

"If found, he will be dragged in and made to talk. I want everyone to hear his treachery." Flying Hawk gave him a disapproving look. "It would have helped if you had brought this Crabapple back alive."

Smoke Shield waved it off. "I had other reasons."

"Not just your joy at hearing him scream?"

"No, I . . ." What? He thought furiously. Of course it would have been better to bring the man back. But in the forest, despite Blood Skull's wiser counsel, he'd wanted the man to pay. "I was thinking of the effect when the Albaamaha saw one of their own among the captives. It would have spread like fire in a dry field. The plotters would have been warned."

Flying Hawk nodded, expression blank. "Perhaps you were right."

"What of the captives?" For three long days, his mind had been fixed on Morning Dew. Perhaps not tonight, but soon, he would be living his Dreams of her. "Were the women guarded as I instructed?"

"I, myself, appointed the guards. The crowd has been at the men, though. I made sure that the guards tempered their enthusiasm. For the most part, the people have shown remarkable restraint."

Smoke Shield nodded. His sore stomach made a rumbling as he tied his best white apron to his hips. Food would calm any last upset from the button snakeroot drink. Slipping on moccasins, he tied white swan feathers to his shoulders. Finally, Smoke Shield removed his honorary arrows from their otterhide case and slipped them through his hair.

"Let me help you with the paint. On this day, it will be my honor." Flying Hawk took the paint box, opening it. The bright colors—yellow, red, black, blue, green, and white—had been mixed with bear grease.

When all was ready, the *Hopaye* watched them form up in two lines; then he exited the door. The growing murmurs of the crowd went still with anticipation.

Smoke Shield's heart had begun to pound. Flying Hawk, noticing his excitement, said, "Yes, heady stuff this. In memory, no one has achieved such a victory!"

The *Hopaye*'s voice carried on the cold air. "My people, the balance of Power is restored. I ask you to greet your brave warriors."

A shout went up as Flying Hawk and Smoke Shield stepped into the sunlight. The plaza was crowded; people, wearing clothing in all the colors of the rainbow, waved, jumped, and shouted. As they emerged, Tishu Minko Seven Dead and the clan chiefs fell in behind them. Warriors called to their wives and families. Smoke Shield saw that Heron Wing and Violet Bead stood at the front of the crowd. Unlike the others, they only smiled, acting the part of proper high-status wives. Well and fine—at least they were good for that.

In the rear, handpicked warriors carried the spoils of war. Some brandished scalps, fleshed now and stretched in willow hoops; another bore the White Arrow war medicine; then came warriors carrying the shields, bows, and other trophies, all held high so the crowd could see them.

They made the ritual walk north to the base of the tishu minko's mound, then east, toward the great mound.

People parted as they neared the captives. Smoke Shield, head high, chin up, studied them from the corner of his eye. As expected, Biloxi looked the most pitiful, weak like a wounded puppy. Screaming Falcon, however, maintained an air of dignity, studiously ignoring the proceedings. But Smoke Shield had eyes only for Morning Dew. She hunched on the ground at the end of her rope, head down, face hidden by her dirty long hair.

Soon, my little bird. Very soon, he promised himself.

The route turned south past the Tree of Life with its red and white spirals, and proceeded to the tchkofa with its guardian posts.

Smoke Shield's stomach growled as he caught the scent of food over the packed odors of humanity. Then he was climbing the steps, passing the guardian poles, and entering the recesses of the tchkofa. Inside, the blazing fire's heat came as a relief from the cold. He directed his warriors to places of honor beside the fire, the clan chiefs taking their positions behind them.

When all had assembled, Flying Hawk lit the Eagle Pipe, calling the invocation. One by one, Smoke Shield and his warriors took a pull on the pipe, blowing the sacred smoke to the heavens.

The prayers and rituals seemed endless, but finally food was brought in—one fragrant bowl after another—and placed before the warriors. Each man reached in, tossing some morsel into the fire, sharing his feast and appreciation with Power.

Before he could so much as take a bite, Smoke Shield was called upon to relate the story of the raid.

He stood, all eyes fixed on him. The Eagle Pipe was lit, and he took a deep drag of the sweet smoke and blew it out through his nostrils. Raising his hands, he said, "Makatok! I shall tell you the story of how, blessed by Power, we have broken the hearts and souls of the White Arrow people!" As his men ate, he related their reasons for war, told of their preparations, and of the journey to the White Arrow lands.

"And then I reconsidered," he told the rapt audience. "From my scouts, I learned that the marriage was over, and that all manner of people had begun to leave White Arrow Town."

"Wah! Wah!" came the cry from Blood Skull. His warriors nodded in agreement.

"The problem was: With so many people on the trails, how were we to pass? Surely, such a large party, dressed as hunters, would be questioned. And who knew? Even if the Chahta believed we were who we said we were, what was to keep them from sending a runner to inform White Arrow Town that meat was coming? The simple fools might have sent people out to help us carry our burden!"

"Wah! Wah!" came the assent.

"That is when I remembered crossing the river."

His warriors nodded happily.

"A plan—like the gift of Breath Giver—came to me." He paused, letting the expectation build. "What if we floated down the river? We didn't need to steal canoes and take the chance that a warning might be given upon discovery of the theft. No, we could wrap our weapons in deer hide, paying particular attention to the bindings, and float downstream in the night."

Pale Cat stared. "Didn't you think of the Horned Serpent? The tie snakes, and water cougars? They come out at night, prowling the river depths."

Mutterings of unease could be heard; people whispered nervously to each other.

Smoke Shield spread his arms wide. "You, O great *Hopaye,* drove that fear from my souls."

"I did." Pale Cat looked confused.

"How could warriors purified and prepared by the greatest *Hopaye* alive fall prey to Horned Serpent, or any other Underworld creature?"

"Wah! Wah!"

Yes, he had them. "I told as much to our warriors." He indicated the seated circle. "These are not some *brave* Chahta . . . like the ones we passed hanging from the squares." Laughter erupted. "No, these are Sky Hand warriors! They mustered their courage, believing in the Power of our *Hopaye*. In the darkness, after making all ready, we waded into the river, pushing our bundles before us. We floated down to the high bank beneath White Arrow Town." He chuckled, asking the warriors, "Do any of us wish to be that cold again?"

"No!" they shouted in unison, laughing all the while.

"We huddled there in the darkness and made our plans. Blood Skull—in honor of his bravery—I sent to capture that foul Screaming Falcon. I took three other warriors to capture their high minko in his palace. Black Hand went with Bobcat to capture Tishu Minko Bow Mankiller, and Panther Hide sought the matron, Sweet Smoke. The other warriors fanned out; their duty was to instill panic when we were discovered. Those warriors were to set fire to every house, and like a deer drive, herd the foolish Chahta toward the palisade gate."

He enjoyed the wide-eyed stares of the clan chiefs. They hung on every word.

"The White Arrow had been feasting, Dancing, and entertaining. They were weary, exhausted, thinking themselves safe. The camp dogs, after days of guests walking among them, had no reason to bark at strangers. Our surprise was complete. No one guarded the palace. My warriors and I crept into the great hall, then passed into the rear. There we found Biloxi sleeping with one of his wives. He had no idea anything was wrong until I pressed a gag into his mouth. He was tied up before he could even blink. Only one of the wives fought. After a war club broke her arm, she, too, was subdued. Then, as we left, we found torches conveniently stacked by the wall." He grinned. "We lit them from their sacred fire, splashed oil on anything that would burn, and set the place on fire."

Wild applause broke out.

"When I am finished, the others can tell you of their actions that morning, but I stayed atop the mound. My duty was to use the conch-shell horn from Biloxi's palace to call my warriors back when the time came. True to their war chief, my men came when I blew the horn. Together we retreated to the canoe landing and loaded our prisoners. Any boat we didn't need was set adrift so that pursuit could not be easily launched. Then we floated downriver, out of sight, and landed on the east bank. From there, we made our way home."

He seated himself amidst a clapping of hands and gleeful shouts. He looked around the room. *You poor fools. Do you really think I'd risk my neck that way just to avenge our honor? I went for Morning Dew. And now I shall have her.*

Blood Skull then took the floor. As he talked, Smoke Shield turned to his food. For propriety's sake, he tossed yet another scrap of the roast venison into the fire before sinking his teeth into the succulent meat.

One by one his warriors told their tales, each approved by calls of "Wah! Wah!" Smoke Shield fidgeted. Would they never get to the end? He tried not to squirm as he waited for the exchange of gifts. Curse it all, since the moment he'd seen Morning Dew, he'd waited for this day.

Belly full, after days of travel and purification, he should have been lethargic by the time the last warrior finished. Instead, he was quivering with anticipation. He'd felt like this as a boy: giddy with excitement to receive a new gift.

Flying Hawk asked, "Does anyone have anything to say?"

Smoke Shield felt ready to burst as he leaped to his feet. "I have told of taking the high minko of the White Arrow People. At the same time, I took his three wives."

Calls of assent arose.

Smoke Shield fought to keep his rising excitement at bay. "Some have said this is the greatest victory our people have had since settling in this valley. I do not know that to be the case, but I do know that I could not have done this thing without the unwavering support of Blood Skull. Acting as my second, he could have refused to attempt any plan as ridiculous as floating down a dark river. But he didn't. Acting with bravery worthy of Eagle Man, he followed without complaint. In reward for such service to me, and to my people, I wish to give the high minko, Biloxi Mankiller, and all of his wives to Blood Skull as a representative of the Raccoon Clan."

For a moment the room was silent, then burst into cheers.

Blood Skull stood, nodding respectfully to Flying Hawk, the *Hopaye,* and Tishu Minko Seven Dead. "Raccoon Clan and I are most honored by the war chief's gift. We humbly accept, and find ourselves speechless at his generosity."

Come on. Smoke Shield struggled to keep his expression blank. The man would do it, wouldn't he? Fear, like a dousing of cold water, ran down his spine. He remembered Blood Skull's reluctance that night under the lean-to. His heart began to pound. *No, it would be impossible!*

Blood Skull turned to Flying Hawk. "When the White Arrow attacked Alligator Town, it was the work of one man: the war chief, Screaming Falcon Mankiller. I was the warrior who captured him." He hesitated. "Speaking for my clan, I would humbly offer him to High Minko Flying Hawk and the Chief Clan. Would you do us the honor of accepting this gift, High Minko?"

Flying Hawk nodded gracefully. "The Chief Clan is honored by your gift, Blood Skull. We are under obligation to you and your clan for bestowing such an honor upon us."

Smoke Shield shifted uncomfortably. *What about Morning Dew? Come on! Or are you just playing with me?*

Blood Skull shot him an evaluative stare. Smoke Shield couldn't seem to breathe. Blood Skull turned to the door, raising a hand. At his gesture, all eyes turned.

What is this? If I am double-crossed, so help me . . .

Two young men entered the room. Between them, a disheveled Morning Dew stared frantically at the faces surrounding her. She still wore her fine dress, though it was smeared with mud and had lost some of the gleaming pearls.

Smoke Shield started to rise, but caught himself. Every fiber of will was necessary to seat himself again. Fortunately—with all eyes on Morning Dew—no one had seen his lapse of control.

"Then there is the matter of this woman," Blood Skull said. "She was once the new wife of Screaming Falcon Mankiller. She is the daughter of Sweet Smoke, and Old Woman Fox before her. With Sweet Smoke's death, she is now the White Arrow matron. As representative of the Raccoon Clan, I have given long and careful thought to the matter of giving her away." He frowned pensively. "So many are worthy. To make such a gift, however, is a special honor to bestow. For that reason, I have had the woman brought here. That you all might see."

Smoke Shield's blood was pounding. He'd knotted his fists, a rage beginning to burn between his souls. *If you do not give her to me, Blood Skull, I swear, if it takes me forever, I will see you bleed.*

"War Chief," Blood Skull said, "you have led our people to the greatest victory in memory. In return for your leadership and courage, we offer this woman, Morning Dew, matron of the Chahta Chief Clan of the White Arrow Moiety of the Chahta people. Will you do us the honor of accepting?"

At the pronouncement, Smoke Shield saw Morning Dew's legs buckle under her, almost toppling the two men who held her.

"I will," Smoke Shield said hoarsely, and struggled to maintain his composure. Could they see how close he was to screaming his victory? When he looked down, his arms were shaking. The young men dragged her through the press, dropping her among the empty dishes in front of Smoke Shield. She lay like a dead fish.

He realized he was panting from relief; it blew through him like a cool wind. Licking his lips, he managed to say, "From this moment forward, I am in your debt, Blood Skull." He looked back, seeing Thin Branch by the door. "Thin Branch, take this woman to my wives. Have them wash and feed her. I want her dress repaired and cleaned. Her hair should gleam in the light."

Morning Dew raised her head, staring at him through glazed and disbelieving eyes.

To keep from betraying his frayed control, Smoke Shield bowed his head, shoulders slumping. The room burst with cheers. Then it came to him: The fools misread his distress. They thought he was overwhelmed with the incredible honor just bestowed upon him.

Nineteen

Smoke Shield! I am to belong to Smoke Shield! Morning Dew's world had stopped, the sounds of the tchkofa grown distant. The universe shrank to the thunderous beating of her heart. A numbness, like a smothering blanket, settled on her souls. Her body had ceased to exist. She heard nothing, felt nothing, souls floating, disjointed and loose.

Morning Dew was barely aware that two young men grasped her ams to carry her from the smoky tchkofa's interior. The laughter and jeers at her expense had no meaning. As if through another's ears she heard the slave Thin Branch say something to two women who waited just beyond the tchkofa gate. The sight of them hurrying off through the crowd might have been through a stranger's eyes. The crowd parted as the men dragged her after them, her senseless feet scuffing the grass.

For three long days she had longed for death, her situation little better than an animal's. From where she'd been tied to the post, she had watched Screaming Falcon as the Sky Hand abused his body. Some had brought sharpened sticks to pierce his flesh; others jabbed at his belly and chest. People had delighted in slapping Screaming Falcon's broken jaw. That afternoon Morning Dew had watched in horror as a young woman used a burning branch to singe the hair from his groin. Afterward his genitals had turned red, blistered, and swollen.

Somehow, she had forced herself to watch, her anguish a mirror of his own. When he had blinked back tears and called, "Be strong!" a guard had smacked his swollen and bruised jaw with a war club.

If only they would kill me! The pain would be merciful in its swiftness. She prayed that they might do it before they tortured Screaming Falcon to death. More than anything, she hadn't wanted to watch that. His continued screams would have been like burning thorns in her souls. The sight of his wounded body, bleeding, blistered, and slowly cut apart, would have broken her.

But nothing had prepared her for the tchkofa. When two men had appeared in the darkness, whispered to the guards, and untied her, she had stumbled along. A desperate hope that ransom had been received from her people imparted a frantic belief that within a hand's time she would be in a canoe, heading swiftly downriver toward freedom.

Only when she had heard Blood Skull's words did she begin to fear. But even then, as he talked about carefully selecting whom he would give her to, hope had flickered like a tiny flame. With all the multitudes of Sky Hand to choose from, surely she would go to some influential clan, to some family of special merit.

And then the very sky had come crashing down on top of her. She remembered her legs giving out and the derisive hoots of the Sky Hand. There, among the plates, she had lost all of her wits, the words, *No, not him!* echoing in the hollow between her souls.

As the men pulled her limp body across the beaten grass of the plaza, she remembered Screaming Falcon's slurred voice as they took her from the stake: *"Be brave! You are Morning Dew! Matron of the White Arrow!"*

His cry still rung in her ears.

No, my husband. I am not brave. I have nothing left. Even the wells of her tears were empty.

Heron Wing hurried through the crowd, Violet Bead behind her. The news had come before Thin Branch appeared at the tchkofa gate. Blood Skull had given the White Arrow matron to Smoke Shield. The news was whispered from lip to lip, so she was prepared for some instruction; nor had Thin Branch's tersely worded orders taken her by surprise. She quickly asked her cousin to care for Stone, then caught Violet Bead's eye.

Oh, I know you well enough, Husband. From the time he'd returned from White Arrow Town the summer before, she'd seen the obsession in his eyes. She'd heard rumors of how he asked any traveler from the Chahta lands about young Morning Dew. The miracle was that he had actually managed to obtain her.

"Do you think he planned this entire raid just to take that woman?" Violet Bead asked when they had progressed beyond earshot of the crowd.

"In all the world," Heron Wing said, "only you and I know the lengths he would go to in order to warm his rod." She laughed heartlessly. "This wasn't about revenge. It was about her."

"And now, he'll make the most of it," Violet Bead mused. "Nothing will stop him from being named high minko after Flying Hawk's death."

Heron Wing shot a sidelong glance at her co-wife. "The only thing different now is that it will be that much harder for him to ruin that chance."

"You underestimate our husband's ability to destroy himself."

"Underestimate Smoke Shield? Not for a heartbeat." She remembered how he'd managed to marry her. He might have taken a scar for it, but over the years she had wondered if he hadn't planned it from the beginning. What Smoke Shield envied—no matter what hurdles stood in his path—he always found a way to obtain. "For the time being, he will be occupied with his new bed toy. His women are like copper. After a while he will grow tired of shining it. This one, too, will eventually corrode. Morning Dew doesn't know it yet, but all she needs to do is endure for a couple of moons. After another woman catches his eye, he will no longer call her to his bed."

She glanced over her shoulder. In the half-moon's light, she could see Thin Branch a stone's throw behind them. The men dragging the slave were making hard work of it. "From the looks of her, she's half-dead, or her souls have fled. We both know he doesn't like a limp woman under him."

"That's his problem. Ours is to make her presentable. And fix her dress? Did you see what she's wearing?"

"I looked at her when she was tied to the pole. She must have been a vain one, to wear a dress like that just to be captured in."

"We'll need drilled pearls."

Heron Wing considered the problem. "Singing Moon has some. She's admired my quill cape often enough that I think she'll trade."

"That's a beautiful cape."

"What do I care? It was a gift from Smoke Shield."

They walked in silence for a while. Then Violet Bead asked, "You still think of him, don't you?"

"Who? Smoke Shield? He's hard to forget."

"I mean his brother."

Heron Wing shot a glance at Violet Bead. "What on earth could have made you bring that up?"

"I suppose it's this new woman. Just another in a long line. Don't you wonder what would have happened if Smoke Shield hadn't told that lie? Or if Green Snake's hand had been a little steadier that day?"

Of course she did. For years she'd brooded over it. "It's all gone, Sister. Long gone. But if Smoke Shield hadn't lied, he wouldn't be the scheming Smoke Shield we both know." She shook her head. "Sometimes the world turns on a decision. Just a word, or a gesture, and from then on, everything is different. Perhaps only a single person's life changes; or it can lead to the rise and fall of nations. That is the realm of Power, of the balance of harmony."

"So, after all that, just why did you marry Smoke Shield?"

"Because I didn't know what happened that day. It was only later that he told me. He was in one of his rages." The words came back to haunt her. *"You know why he did this to me?"* Smoke Shield had pointed to the ugly scar on the side of his face. *"It was because I told him I'd lain with you. I taunted him—my precious, perfect brother. And he did this!"*

To Violet Bead she said, "He lied. And after Green Snake left, no one would speak the reason of it. By then it was too late to matter anyway." She shook her head, clearing her thoughts. "I don't want to talk about it anymore. What is past cannot be changed."

They walked along in silence again. Violet Bead, however, wouldn't let it drop. "But he could still be alive." She gestured to the darkness. "Out there, somewhere. Perhaps still thinking of you."

"I said let it go. We are done speaking of this."

"Forgive me."

Heron Wing relented at the tone in Violet Bead's voice. "No, it's all right. And yes, I do wonder sometimes. Mostly when I'm alone. But wherever he went, he has never sent word. If he still lives, I hope he's happy. And now, that is the last word I'll speak."

She wondered why she'd even let her guard down that much. Curiosity overcame her. "Why did you even ask?"

"Because, Sister"—Violet Bead used the honorific between wives—"I know that you still love him."

"And what does that matter to you?"

She laughed humorlessly. "Because at least you can still love."

They had reached her house. Inside, a low fire was burning, the scent of wood smoke on the air. Wide Leaf, her Koasati slave, hunched over the fire. She had propped the food-encrusted ceramic pots from the feast so the flames would burn the contents out of the vessels. The old woman had worked most of the day, cooking for the victory feast.

"Wide Leaf," Heron Wing called as the older woman looked up. "We have orders from our husband. We need warm water, soap, and a comb."

"Of course." Her expression narrowed as she used wooden tongs to remove the pots, reached for a water jug, and poured it into a bowl. "He's coming here for a bath, is he?" She eyed Violet Bead suspiciously.

"No, it would seem he has been given a new slave. We are to clean her up and make her presentable for his bed."

"Huh," she grunted. Then she squinted. "Don't expect him too soon."

"Ah, what have you heard?"

"Loose talk."

"About what?"

Wide Leaf shot another glance at Violet Bead, then added, "Trouble with the Albaamaha. They found a runner on the trail. Someone sent to warn the White Arrow that they were about to be attacked."

Heron Wing shot a look at Violet Bead, who shook her head, indicating she'd heard nothing of it. That slaves often knew more than she did was no surprise. Wide Leaf was her greatest source of information on whom Smoke Shield was bedding, and when.

"Do they know who sent the runner?" Violet Bead asked.

Wide Leaf shrugged, but from long association, Heron Wing could tell she'd heard something. "It's all right. Tell us what you know."

Wide Leaf hesitated for a moment. "Some man named Paunch."

"I've never heard of him."

With the arrival of Thin Branch further talk was impossible. The man would tell Smoke Shield anything he overheard. He held the door hanging aside while the burly young men muscled the limp Morning Dew through the doorway.

"Place her there." Heron Wing pointed to the cattail matting near the fire. They watched as the men lowered the woman's limp body to the floor. She might have been dead for all the life she exhibited. Through matted hair, Heron Wing could see the young woman's eyes staring fixedly at nothing. Gods, had her souls fled?

"We are to stay close," one of the young men said. "In case she runs, we are to chase her down and bring her back."

"Thank you." Heron Wing reached for one of the jars, lifting two acorn cakes from it. "Here, this is for your time. I imagine you haven't eaten."

"No," one replied. "We thank you for this. If she makes a break, we won't be more than a stone's throw away." Both nodded politely and stepped out.

"Do you need anything?" Thin Branch asked, looking from one to the other.

"Nothing we can't find on our own." Heron Wing cocked her head. "And you, Thin Branch, have you eaten?"

"No, mistress." He glanced back toward the tchkofa. "But I'd best be getting back. He might need me."

She removed another cake from the jar. "You can wolf it down on the way."

"My thanks." Then he turned, ducking out into the night.

The three women stared down at the captive for a moment, contemplating the listless Morning Dew.

Wide Leaf, as usual, was the first to break the silence. "She sure doesn't look like much. The story is that she's the White Arrow matron. If that's a matron, I'm a chief."

Irony laced Violet Bead's voice. "She might be a matron, but now she's just a slave."

Wide Leaf's jaw muscles tightened the way they did when she knew better than to say what was on her mind.

Heron Wing slapped her hands to her hips. "Let's get her out of that dress."

"Indeed," Violet Bead replied. "I want to see what kind of prize would drive our husband to risk his precious neck on a Chahta square."

Morning Dew didn't resist as they sat her up and pulled the dress over her head. That she was young, with a ripe body, came as no surprise.

Wide Leaf inspected the dress, her critical eye absorbing the quill work and the patterns of pearls. "Good workmanship. As good as my own."

Violet Bead bent down, wet a cloth, and extended it to Morning Dew. "You can wash yourself, can't you?"

The woman gave no response, her face slack and listless.

"Gods," Wide Leaf muttered, reaching over to pull the woman's hair out of her face. "Hey! You in there?" She lightly slapped Morning Dew on one cheek. "Come on. Is that all they breed into you Chahta bitches? You could be a lump of mud for all I care. Pampered matron!"

For the first time, Heron Wing saw the eyes flicker. They cleared, and glared for a moment before going blank again.

"Well, lay her out flat," Heron Wing decided. "We'll just have to do it the same way the *Hopaye* cleans a corpse."

Trader stood in the doorway and stared glumly out at the slanting rain. Just down the slope, their canoes were pulled up and hidden in the tall grass. What once had been a canoe landing was overgrown and almost invisible.

Shelter had come in the form of an abandoned village a half day's journey up the Tenasee, or the Sister River, as the Illinois called it. As the first drops had fallen from the brooding sky, Two Petals had pointed, saying, "That's no place to make camp."

With the storm brewing, no one had objected. They had searched the abandoned village, checking the repair of the houses that still stood. Then they carried the packs up to the house that remained sound. The roof seemed to be good; and its bark construction suggested that it had once belonged to either the Illinois or the Miami. The place was strewn with trash that they swept out, and once a fire had been kindled in the old hearth, it was almost homey.

Then Two Petals had surprised both men, saying, "You know, the last thing I need right now is a woman's lodge." She'd stared through the pouring rain, pointed, and declared, "I definitely don't want that one."

So saying, she had picked up her bedding and strode off.

Now Trader could crane his neck and see a faint blue smoke rising from around the cracks in the bark roof.

"I just wonder why it didn't happen sooner," Old White said from where he nursed their fire. "Of course, sometimes starvation, hard work, or tough times can make a woman miss her moon. I knew of an A'khota woman warrior once who kept herself so fit she claimed she didn't have to go to the Women's House except on rare occasions."

Trader crossed his arms, watching the patterns of rain on the river. "To be honest, I've never studied the problem much." He turned. "The way I was raised, women were kept strictly separate. You know our ways. Men do the things men do, and women do theirs. Then, once I got out on the river, I ran into many different beliefs, most of them contradictory to what our people accept as normal. Where does the truth lie, Seeker?"

The old man poured water into one of their bowls, setting it on three stones over the fire to boil. "That I can't tell you, Trader. There are as many ways of believing as there are people, and each and every one of them thinks

their way is right and proper. Most of them think that
their gods have given them the true and correct rules of
behavior. Up in the northeast, and among the Charokee,
it's the women who really rule. In other places kin is
traced through the men, and the men rule. Or, take the
Sky Hand; we trace our lines through the women, and
the men still rule. I think it depends on what you learn as
a child."

Trader considered that as rain pelted the forest
around them, dripping from the bare trees. In a lower
voice, he asked, "What about Power?"

"Now, there you have me."

"Do you think Power remembers?"

"I think it just is."

"So, Power doesn't hold a man's actions against
him?"

"You thinking of this man you killed?"

"My brother. That's a pretty serious burden to bear.
To have killed one's brother—no matter where I've
traveled—is considered very wrong. To many it is the
most hideous crime a man can commit outside of in-
cest."

Old White's voice lowered. "Trader, tell me: Did he
deserve it?"

He shrugged. "I don't know. All of my life, up to that
moment, I had done everything I could to be different
from him. We are taught that life is a balance of opposites: the white and red forces of nature, constantly in
opposition. Different yet equal. Rattle and I were like
that: twins—equal, and completely opposite of each
other. I sought harmony, goodwill, and acts of kindness;
while he plotted, schemed, and envied. I never understood. Rattle always got what he wanted; but it was
never enough to satisfy his cravings. If I received a gift
because of a kindness I had done, he would stare at it.
He would be obsessed with possessing it. I knew how it
consumed him, so I always put up with his scheming,
letting him talk me into something lesser in exchange

for that thing . . . perhaps a toy bow, or a little clay sculpture. In return, I'd let him concoct his intricate lies.

"Once it was a whelk shell gorget I was given by the *Hopaye*. I had run to fetch his medicine bag when a man was dying. The *Hopaye* saved the man's life, and in gratitude he gave me that gorget. It was a beautiful engraving of two rattlesnakes circling, the center open to represent the passage from this world to the Underworld. The cord it hung on was strung with polished shell beads. It became my prized possession." He paused. "Oh, how Rattle wanted it."

"What happened?"

"Well, he couldn't steal it. Not and be able to parade around with it on his chest. So he started offering things in Trade. First it was a crudely carved stick that he claimed our uncle had given him. He told me wondrous stories about how it was filled with Power to call the lightning. Once, he said, he had thrown it into the air, and an eagle appeared, grabbed it in its talons, and dropped it back to him. He even showed me the imprints the talons had supposedly made in the wood. I refused. Just that once, I wanted to keep that gorget."

"But he kept at you?"

"Oh, yes. Rattle did terrible things after I refused. He made it look like I'd broken one of Uncle's prized ceramic pots, one that supposedly came all the way from Cahokia. He slipped some of the medicine herbs into my tea from a bag we were never supposed to touch. He tied the knot wrong to make it look like a clumsy child had done it. I was sick, throwing up and fevered for almost a week. As bad as the sickness itself, I was whipped for getting into the medicine until my skin was raw with welts. In the end, I gave up and let him have the gorget in return for a woodpecker wing fan someone had given him. After he spilled grease on the feathers, he had tired of it. The grease, he told me, came from a tie snake he'd found one of the Albaamaha cooking. The story he told was that it would enable me to fly."

"Let me guess. It didn't?"

"No. When he finally tired of the gorget, he gave it back to me in Trade for something else. But by then, it had lost its special magic. As if by owning it, he had sullied it."

"Did your family know all these things?"

"Sometimes. Uncle always told me to understand that Rattle was different. He counseled patience and forgiveness. But he had had trouble with his own brother, and it affected his dealings with us. He didn't want my brother to make the same mistakes he had. But in the end, it was I who lost myself in rage."

"That was where the woman entered the picture?"

Trader nodded. "I loved her from the moment I first saw her. She was the *Hopaye*'s niece. Her brother was my best friend. Because I spent so much time with him, I got to know her very well. As she grew up, she became even more beautiful. We tossed pebbles at each other when no one was looking, sharing smiles and secret conversations. We both knew we would be married one day. I had spoken to Uncle about the girl, and he thought it would be a good match when I came of age. In one of those twists of fate, I won war honors before my brother did, and was sent to the Men's House. For four days I went through the training, rituals, and purification. Meanwhile, Uncle sent one of his cousins to see the girl's family."

Trader glanced at the old man. "Can you imagine how my brother felt? Once again everyone was fawning over me. Uncle was telling people that as a man I would begin taking my place at his side in the tchkofa during Council meetings. Feasts were being prepared for the day I left the Men's House; my clan was negotiating marriage for me with the *Hopaye*'s niece." Trader paused. "I think it drove him half-mad."

Old White listened intently, adding cornmeal, acorns, and pumpkin seeds to the stew.

Trader rubbed the back of his neck. "Rattle came on the first day. As a child, he couldn't enter the lodge, but called me over to the door, saying that he saw my girl sneaking down to the river."

Trader hesitated, wondering why he would confess his innermost secrets to a stranger. "Fool that I was, I asked him to spy on her. He left, promising that he'd be right back as soon as he found out what she was doing." He paused. "It was three days. *Three days!* I was half-frantic, and of course, I couldn't ask anyone. I was in the middle of my initiation. When he finally came back it was the middle of the night. He had waited until I was alone and called me to the door. By then I was being devoured by worry."

"And he told you what?"

"That she met an old Albaamo. That she asked him for a drug that would make her passionate on our first night together. My brother said that she took the drug, and on the trail, he stopped her. She thought it was me, called Rattle by my name. He said that she took his hand, led him off into the bushes, and laid with him, over and over and over again. He said that when the drug left her, she was so pleased with him that she no longer wanted to marry me."

"And you believed him?"

Trader stared at the rain-slashed river with empty eyes. "About her? No. The only thought in my head was, 'He's doing it again!' Everything in my souls broke loose. I knew that Rattle wouldn't give up, that he'd figure some way to ruin it all. He would come between me and my wife with some lie about other women, or fix it so that I got the blame for some terrible thing. I just couldn't let him."

Trader swallowed hard. "He saw it coming . . . saw the rage, and realized he'd gone too far. He started to say it was all a lie, but I'd taken one of the war clubs from the wall. He tried to duck, but my blow took him in the side of the head.

"I remember looking down at him, seeing the terrible wound. Blood was pouring out of his head, his eyes fixed in death. I realized what I'd done. By then I was outside the lodge, having ruined my initiation. Worse, when the story got to the woman I loved, she would think I had believed my brother's lies, and that I had killed him for that reason. Even if she still married me, that terrible knowledge would lie between us like a wall. Worse, I had brought shame down on my clan . . . the same shame that my uncle had worked years to overcome. I couldn't stand the thought of looking into people's eyes, seeing their disapproval and disgust. Everything I had worked so hard to overcome was gone. So I ran . . . stole a canoe, crossed the river, and never looked back."

Old White dropped crushed mint into the stew. "During my years on the river I heard rumors. Your uncle, he killed his brother, too, didn't he?"

Trader nodded, looking down where Swimmer lay on his folded blanket inside the door, happily asleep. Dogs didn't bear the burdens of conscience.

With a peeled stick, Old White stirred the stew. "I think madness runs in the Chief Clan. That and dark violence. It passes from generation to generation."

"I was going to stop that."

Old White stared up from under lowered brows. "Power works on us for reasons of its own. Perhaps that is why the Contrary led us to you. The time for running may be over."

"Is it?"

"When we return to Split Sky City, we will see. I have only heard bits and pieces of the doings there. According to the rumors, your uncle has expanded the territory over the years. That is when he's not been obsessed with keeping his own prestige. You're right. He has had to work hard to keep his position. I've heard that it took years before the Council accepted his leadership without reservation."

"He and the Raccoon Clan almost went to war with each other when I was a child. The tishu minko argued that the time had come to spread leadership among the clans, to perhaps elect a member of the Council to lead."

Old White—satisfied that the stew was bubbling—sat back, removed his pipe from its sack, loaded it with tobacco, and lit it from the fire. "Somehow, your uncle managed to keep things as they were."

"Only because of attacks by the Yuchi. An outside enemy works wonders to salve internal strife." Trader shrugged. "But for the timing of one of their raids, my brother might have won war honors before I did." He sighed. "Had he, perhaps all of this might have been avoided. He would have been the center of attention; his marriage would have come first."

A blue wreath of smoke puffed from Old White's pipe. "You delude yourself. The confrontation between the two of you might have been delayed, but never avoided." He pointed with the pipe stem. "Unless, that is, you had decided to forever let him win. Would you have given up everything for him?"

"Didn't it work out that way in the end?"

"Giving up for something is very different than giving up *because* of something."

Trader considered that. The old man might have a point. He chanced the rain to crane his head out, seeing that smoke still rose from Two Petals' seclusion. "Why do you suppose the Contrary picked this time to find me?"

"I don't know. But whatever the vision was that she had at Silver Loon's I think it was most remarkable."

Trader turned. "Very well, that's my story. What about yours?"

The old man's eyes hardened. "All in good time, I imagine. For now, for reasons of my own, I think I'll keep my secrets." To change the subject, he pointed at the stew. "One of us is going to have to take a bowl of this over to Two Petals."

"One of us? Why do I suppose it isn't going to be you?"

"My skin is made of old leather. It hardens and shrinks when it gets wet."

"Maybe it will squeeze some of those secrets out of your reluctant souls."

But the old man didn't seem to hear. His eyes were fixed, as if seeing back into the past, to some terrible event. Bitterness had formed around his mouth, his brow pinched as if in pain.

No matter what he knows, when we finally reach Split Sky City, it will be the most unpleasant moment in my life.

Twenty

The delicious smell of food built a craving in Morning Dew's souls like nothing she had ever known. Her first insistence was that she would refuse to eat. By dint of will she would starve herself to death rather than allow a single morsel of Sky Hand food to pass her lips. In the beginning she thought she could stand hunger, but thirst had been unbearable. The first mug of water pressed to her lips brought her arms up, and she gulped it ravenously.

As she sat on the cattail matting, however, saliva pooled around her tongue; the fragrant odors of sweet corn, acorn-and-hickory-nut bread, and roasting fish ate at her resistance. Then, too, the foul old slave, Wide Leaf, managed to needle her like poison ivy rubbed on raw skin.

The process of bathing hadn't humiliated her as much as she had thought it would. Cleaned like the dead, the Sky Hand women had said. Most appropriate. Their warm cloths had massaged her, starting at the toes, working up her calves, thighs, and belly. They had soothed her breasts, chest, and shoulders. Then the warm relief continued down her arms to her hands.

She actually helped to roll herself before they placed their warm cloths to her backside. While she lay there, her souls remained as wilted as mayapple leaves in winter.

Images kept replaying of the days since her arrival. She saw snippets of the mocking Sky Hand and

Albaamaha who had come to jeer, peer, shout, or throw insulting things at her. She had heard them laugh, seen their pantomimes of how the captives would be treated.

Was it so long ago that I did the same? She remembered the captives in their squares in her own plaza. How could the earth have turned upside down so quickly? A sob tried to choke her as she remembered the lingering deaths of the captives taken from the Alligator Town raid. The memories of how her people had burned, cut, and beat the helpless men in the squares was now too real.

The same is happening to my beloved Screaming Falcon. She had forced her thoughts away from the inevitable—tried to still the horror and pain in her souls.

The process of washing her hair had touched her for some reason and brought her back from the misery inside to the external world. She was able to make an assessment of her surroundings. The house was well made. The wall poles were set upright in a trench, the roof high and pitched. Unlike so many houses, the plaster here was clean, as if freshly done. Sleeping benches on either side were neat with folded hides and brightly dyed fabric blankets. Beneath the benches, pots, jars, and baskets had been placed in orderly rows. The wooden plank boxes were all carved, inlaid with shell, the wood polished to a fine sheen. Cooking vessels had their own place, each capped with a wooden lid to keep rodents out. The matting, though worn in places, looked clean. On the rear wall a carved wooden image of a panther had been hung. The workmanship was excellent, the panther reaching out with one clawed paw, its mouth open to expose white teeth. The single eye—made of polished oyster shell—gleamed in the firelight. To its right a doorway led into a small storeroom where she could see larger baskets and boxes.

As the women continued to scrub and rinse her long hair, she closed her eyes. Just for a moment, she could imagine she was a girl again, and it was Old Woman

Fox's fingers that she felt. What had happened to Grandmother?

"The world is a cruel place," the old woman's voice came back to haunt her. *"You must never forget that. Breath Giver made it that way so that only the strong would survive. No matter what, you must always be strong, girl."*

But she wasn't. *Oh, Grandmother, you would be so ashamed of me.*

She wished for death—anything to avoid this horrible new reality. No matter what ministrations these Sky Hand women did, it was only preparation for the moment she was led to Smoke Shield's bed.

When would that be? How would she endure? Would it be smart to just lie there? Could she pretend that it was Screaming Falcon who climbed onto her? Could she make herself fly away from her body? Perhaps send her souls to some happy place where her mother still smiled?

It will only be my body that he possesses. And if she lay like unresponsive meat perhaps he would simply get it over with, strangle her, or break her neck.

"Oh, she'll make Smoke Shield a happy man," Wide Leaf growled, as if hearing her thoughts. "Don't see what he wants with this one. He'd be happier with one of the slaves. At least they pant at the thought of his touch."

"That will be enough," Heron Wing had warned.

In the end, they had finished, leaving her in a seated position, inspecting their work as her hair dried by the fire. "That will do for now," Violet Bead had decided. "I wouldn't worry about the perfume until just before he calls for her."

"And we have to get that dress cleaned and repaired," Heron Wing had said.

"I'll attend to it." Violet Bead had yawned. "Pine Needle can wash it first chance she gets. She should almost be finished cleaning up." She grabbed up Morning Dew's soiled dress. "Oh, the cape."

Heron Wing stepped over to one of the cedar-wood boxes, lifted the lid, and removed a fine quillwork cape. This she handed to Violet Bead before the woman ducked out into the night.

"Gods," Heron Wing had said, "I'm tired."

"Too many days without sleep," Wide Leaf agreed, her scowling eyes still fixed on Morning Dew. "We going to leave her just sitting there, naked?"

"Give her one of my work dresses. Smoke Shield will be busy. After the celebration the Council will break for a couple of hours' sleep, and then they'll want to get into the Albaamaha trouble and discuss the political situation with the Chahta."

Political situation? A flicker of hope grew in Morning Dew's breast. Then perhaps ransom was still not out of the question? For that she could endure. Once back in her own lands, she would dedicate herself to the destruction of the Sky Hand if it meant selling off her territory piece by piece to the Natchez, the Yuchi, and the Pensacola. Forge a grand enough alliance and even the stunning magnificence of Split Sky City could be brought to its knees.

Wide Leaf dropped an old brown dress in Morning Dew's lap. "In case you get cold, *Matron,* you can put this on." The old woman leaned close, imposing herself in Morning Dew's vision. "And if you run, they *will* bring you back. You're going to be on your back, given what Smoke Shield wants you for. He won't care if the tendons in your heels are still in one piece."

Slaves who insisted on running often had the large tendon severed above their heels. From then on, they walked in a curious, slow, wobbling gait. The idea of it sent a chill down her already-numb souls.

Morning Dew hadn't expected to sleep, but she came awake the next morning, her body resting on a blanket she didn't remember from the night before. In her sleep, she had pulled it gratefully around her, and now she blinked in the light of a new day.

Sitting up, she had clutched the brown dress, wrinkled now, and wadded where she'd hugged it to herself in the night. For long moments she considered it before finally pulling it over her head. Her bladder was full, and she glanced suspiciously at the two women sleeping on the pole beds. It would serve them right if she pulled a jar of food over and urinated in it, but doing so might awaken them.

With all of her stealth, she rose to her feet, stepping to the door and looking out. The sun was high in the sky. Gods, how long had she slept? Two men—different ones from the night before—sat at a fire beside a ramada. Their attention was on bone dice that they tossed on a blanket. Piles of counters lay beside them.

Looking beyond that, she could see log mortars with long pestles propped to one side, then the endless mass of houses and granaries that crowded between her and the palisade. People were everywhere. What were the chances that she could just walk through them, make it to the canoe landing, and push off?

"Going somewhere?" a muzzy voice called from behind.

"Do you want me to wet your floor?" Unbidden, her voice reeked of sarcasm.

Heron Wing blinked, yawned, and stretched her arms. Then she stepped from her bed and scratched. "I could have slept for a moon."

Morning Dew glanced at Wide Leaf. The old woman's mouth hung open, exposing gaps in her teeth. She seemed dead to the morning.

Heron Wing remained an attractive woman, her body athletic, high breasted, and with a slim waist. She pulled her hair back, reached for a dress, and pulled it on. She slipped her feet into sandals and beckoned to Morning Dew as she led the way through the door. At the side of the house a chest-high screen had been built around an old storage pit. From the odor, Morning Dew knew exactly what it was now used for. Heron Wing stepped behind the screen, pulled her dress up, and squatted, saying wryly, "You won't mind if I go first? That way, if you run, it will be on a full bladder. It should slow you down."

When the woman finished, Morning Dew took her turn, pleased that Heron Wing ignored her, her face turned up at the winter sun. The woman's breath fogged in the cold air.

"Why did you marry him?" Morning Dew asked. "He's a weasel."

"He is all of that," Heron Wing surprised her by saying. "Unfortunately, at the time, I wasn't thinking very well. There were political considerations, gifts had been exchanged, and given the events of the time, I consented."

"Then why haven't you divorced him?"

"We are not Chahta." She smiled wearily. "Though at times I wish we were."

The wistfulness in her tone caught Morning Dew off guard. "You are not like him."

Heron Wing actually smiled at her. "I know. Thank the gods."

Morning Dew stood, unsure what to do next.

Unexpectedly, Heron Wing turned to her. "Listen to me. Hear what I say and take it to your souls. I cannot undo what has been done. One cannot stop a river and reverse its flow. But this is my advice: Do not run. Even if you make it to the river, they *will* bring you back, and they *will* hurt and humiliate you." Heron Wing's hard stare emphasized the point.

Having nothing else to do, Morning Dew nodded.

"When Smoke Shield sends for you, just submit. Do nothing to anger him. Whatever you do, don't fight him. If you make him mad, he will hurt you. Badly. If you resist in any fashion, he will consider it to be a challenge. He will make it his duty to break you. If will be fun for him, a grand diversion. Should that happen, you will be the center of his attention for a very long time. Do you understand?"

She did.

"The best thing for you is to do as he says; but the trick for a smart woman—and I think you are that—is to find the balance. Comply with his wishes, but do so without enthusiasm. As soon as he grows bored with you, he will set you aside for other diversions."

"Why do you tell me this?"

Heron Wing smiled humorlessly. "Because I believe in Power. I know how capricious it is, how happy a person can be one moment, and then find she has nothing but broken hopes the next. I don't know why the just can be made to suffer, but it can happen to the best of us." She glanced knowingly at Morning Dew. "And because once, though not a captive, I was in the same situation as you now find yourself."

How could you have been?

"Come," Heron Wing said. "Let's roust that lazy old Wide Leaf and see what sort of meal she can make us."

"I'm not hungry," Morning Dew had insisted as they entered the house. She had refused the first meal. That had been hands of time ago. Now the smell of the food was wondrous.

For the most part, Heron Wing ignored her. She and Wide Leaf attended to various domestic duties. Every so often people arrived, asking for an audience. Each time, Heron Wing stepped outside. Most of the visitors came with the express purpose of catching a glimpse of the famous Morning Dew. They all offered their congratulations on the singular honor bestowed on Smoke Shield. Each time, Morning Dew sighed with relief when Heron Wing used her artful ways to turn the curious away. More than once, however, the visitors wanted to discuss personal problems, or disagreements within the Panther Clan. To those, Heron Wing gave thoughtful counsel, though Morning Dew had no idea of the personalities and troubles involved.

The thought came to her: *Heron Wing is a respected leader.*

When the women finally took a break and dished out the savory fare, Heron Wing said, "A bit of bread won't hurt. It can keep the hunger pangs at bay while you starve yourself. Hold out your hand."

Morning Dew remained motionless, unwilling to risk losing her nerve.

Heron Wing reached out, took her hand, and placed a piece of walnut-laced acorn bread in her palm. For long moments Morning Dew fought with herself.

In the end, rather than look like a fool, she lifted the bread to her mouth. After the first bite, she ate ravenously.

Just submit. Heron Wing's voice echoed over and over in the hollow between her souls.

Smoke Shield blinked awake. How long had he slept? He glanced at the dim light and climbed to his feet. Gods, every muscle ached. With his foot, he slid the chamber bowl out from beneath his bed and relieved himself. Leaving the bowl in the middle of the floor for Thin Branch to attend to, he wrapped an apron around his waist and pulled his hair back. Finally he tugged moccasins onto his feet and grabbed a neatly folded blanket from the pile Thin Branch had left him.

Stepping into the palace hallway, he made his way to the main room with its hanging masks, trophy skulls, and the great hand-eye carving. A fire burned in the hearth, and Flying Hawk sat atop his three-legged chair. He was listening to a scout give his report. Seeing Smoke Shield, the high minko motioned him over and dismissed the man.

"You slept well?"

"I did. What time is it?"

"Late afternoon, I'm afraid. I'm surprised you're up this early." The high minko's keen eyes hid a smile. "But then, I suppose you have things to see to?"

Smoke Shield deflected the question. "Who was that?"

"A scout. Freshly come from the Chahta lands where he's been nosing around."

"And?" A slow smile crept onto Smoke Shield's face.

"Where are you off to?" Flying Hawk tried to distract him by pointing to the blanket.

"The river . . . and a bath. I smell of sweat and the tchkofa's smoke. Then I'm ordering a fire kindled in my room and a meal delivered." He paused, conjuring a confused look. "Oh, and I think there's a slave that I need to inspect."

"Drawing it out, aren't you?" Flying Hawk asked as he stood from his stool. He winced, massaging his left knee, the one that pained him so often these days.

"The best things in life are taken slowly. I have waited a long time for this."

"I'm sure you have." He walked over to pick up a buffalo robe. "Mind if I accompany you? We need to talk. And not just about the scout's report."

"I am always honored, Uncle."

Together they walked out into the day. Thin Branch was sitting in the sunlight, one of Smoke Shield's copper pieces in his hands. The slave used a piece of cloth to polish the beaten metal. Seeing Smoke Shield, he leaped to his feet.

"My pot is full. Oh, and I would like a feast delivered to my room. I want a good fire, with a bed of coals. Make sure everything is in order and looking its best. Then, when you are sure I will be pleased, send for the slave."

"Of course." Thin Branch nodded, taking his work and hurrying inside.

Passing through the northern gate, Smoke Shield could see the long shadow cast by the great mound and high palace. It fell like a gloomy spear point across the north plaza and the steep-walled gully that cut to the east. Beyond it, the river looked cold and dark. The fields in the floodplain beyond lay brown and winter fallow. Wisps of blue smoke rose from the lonely Albaamaha farmhouses.

The view never ceased to astound him. From this height, Split Sky City seemed to dominate the entire world.

As they made their way down the long stairway, Flying Hawk said, "The scout tells me that the Chahta are in complete confusion. There is talk that they might abandon White Arrow Town completely. Some argue for immediate retaliation. To discourage that, I have sent additional scouts out with the orders that they are to be seen at places such as high points, or from across the river. Then they are to vanish, leaving the Chahta with the knowledge that we are watching, and any attack will be discovered the moment it's launched. After the bloody nose they've just received, I don't think they want to chance another."

"What else are the Chahta saying?"

"Others are clamoring for a peace initiative. They would like to see some settlement reached whereby we leave them alone. I imagine that over the next moon they will extend feelers to see if we are amenable to such doings."

"Are we?" He remembered the long Council session. His own clan leaders had sounded as fragmented as the Chahta appeared to be.

"That depends," Flying Hawk mused as they stepped onto the plaza. "The third thing being bandied about by the Chahta is an alliance with either the Natchez or the Yuchi. Obviously they would prefer an alliance with the Natchez. That faction is hoping they can talk them into mustering enough warriors to seriously threaten us."

"And again, what do you think?"

"I think the Great Serpent—the Natchez ruler—would be a fool to attempt any such thing. To seriously hurt us would take a large number of warriors. He would have to send this large war party all the way from the Father Water to attack us. They would need to capture one of our towns with its supplies intact just to keep such a large force fed. That attack would have to come as a complete surprise."

Smoke Shield grunted. "Most improbable given that they'd have to send at least a couple of hundred warriors. Moving such a large party of men quietly and quickly would be very difficult."

"And if they didn't succeed," Flying Hawk continued, "warriors would get strung out on the trails, making them easy prey for an ambush. No, I think the risks are too high, and the Great Serpent knows them full well. When it comes right down to it, why would he wish to involve himself in a war with us? We've offered no threat, no reason for him to pick a fight with us."

"I agree. I also don't think he'd want to weaken his towns by stripping them of warriors. Assembling that large a force cannot be done in secret, and he has his own problems with the Tunica and Caddo. They'd take the opportunity to raid."

"I think you're right." They passed the burial mound where, for generations, the Chief Clan had laid their dead. "Bless us, Ancestors," Flying Hawk called, and touched his forehead.

At the end of the ridge they followed a winding path that descended the steep slope to the river. "What of the Council meeting?" Smoke Shield asked.

"What of it? You heard. Most want to take a wait-and-see approach to the Chahta. After thinking about it, I agree. What point is there to risk more of our warriors in raids? The Chahta are warned now, wary, and have scouts of their own out and about. We won't catch them by surprise again; and trust me, they would make us pay if we sent even a large force into their territory."

Smoke Shield shrugged as they descended to the confluence of a small creek with the river. "I have no need to prove anything else to the Chahta."

"No," Flying Hawk said dryly. "You have what you went for." He paused, eyeing Smoke Shield as he stripped. "I just hope you don't see some pretty Yuchi girl next week."

"I don't need any Yuchi girl." Smoke Shield laid his

clothing atop his blanket; the chill immediately caressed his bare skin. He stepped into the water and lowered himself. Cold leeched into his muscles and bone; his scrotum tightened into a hard knot.

Flying Hawk laid his clothes to one side and splashed in, whooping as he settled in the water and began rubbing himself with handfuls of sand.

"What of the Albaamo traitor?" Smoke Shield asked.

"No one can find this Paunch. His entire family has vanished like smoke." Flying Hawk scrubbed his face. "I'd give a copper gorget to find whoever warned him."

"There is always his lineage. If we put the coals to some cousin's balls, I bet he'd sing loud and hard. Then he'd tell us where Paunch went to, or at least who would know."

Flying Hawk ducked his head, rinsed his face, and sputtered as he wiped the water away. "I considered that. Too much chance of spreading animosity. We'd get too many innocent . . . Correct that. We'd get too many who weren't part of the plot. Doing so would just incite their relatives and drive more Albaamaha into the ranks of the dissatisfied."

"We have to do something."

"In time, War Chief. For the moment, the Albaamaha are satisfied. We have done what we are supposed to: We killed the people who killed their people. And, you did it in a most impressive manner. Any doubts the Albaamaha had about our strength, cunning, and prowess are laid to rest. The tishu minko has had warriors seeing to the redistribution of food to Alligator Town. Depending on the length of the winter, some bellies might be pinched, but we'll do what we can." He wagged a finger back and forth. "Even if it means emptying some of our own granaries to put food in Albaamaha bellies."

"And the traitor?"

Flying Hawk studied him with keen eyes. "You want him, don't you?"

Smoke Shield narrowed his eyes. "He could have gotten us all killed. He could have spoiled everything."

"Ah. Then I give him to you. Find him and do what you will with him. But quietly, Smoke Shield. I said, *quietly*. You're the clever plotter. I don't care what you do. Just don't set off the Albaamaha in the process."

Smoke Shield grinned. Oh, this would be grand fun. "What do you think about this Red Awl? I've always had my suspicions about him."

"Why not Amber Bead, if you're going to look that close to the Council?" Flying Hawk wiped water from his face.

"I think he's an old fool. He has been part of us for so long, I think he considers himself half Sky Hand. No, if I had to choose between the two of them, I'd suspect Red Awl."

"Just be careful."

"Always." Smoke Shield cupped water in his hands to rinse the last of the sand away. Then he stood and sloshed to shore, using the blanket to dry himself. He fought shivers as he wrapped his clothing around him. How odd. He should be tingling with excitement. Instead, a calm assurance possessed him. Had that come with age? Or the knowledge that now, having won, he could take his time, anticipate every delightful joy that Morning Dew was going to provide him?

And then there was the matter of the traitor. That would take some thought. Hate it though Smoke Shield might, Uncle was right: It would have been far better to have kept Crabapple alive for the moment.

He watched Uncle dry and dress himself. Only when one saw him naked like this, shorn of his finery, did the old man seem frail. Skin sagged from muscles gone slack. The old man's ribs could be seen, and his belly had sagged. Not like on some, but it hung out far enough to hide his genitals. The legs, once muscular, looked more like desiccated juniper, curving and angular.

Someday soon, I will be high minko. And when he was, changes would be made. Certain members of the Council had served beyond their time. And yes, Uncle might counsel patience for the moment, but there was no reason Sky Hand chiefs couldn't eventually sit atop Chahta mounds. *And I will appoint them.*

What was hereditary leadership for, if not to use?

He turned, staring up the trail where yellowish sandy dirt was exposed in the cuts. How much time would Thin Branch need? From long experience the slave would see to the chamber pot, fire, and feast first. Only when he knew everything was just so would he send for the slave.

When she arrived, he would be waiting.

"War Chief," Flying Hawk said after he draped the buffalo hide over his shoulders, "I was thinking. About the—"

"Uncle, if you will excuse me, I have to go."

"I see." Flying Hawk was watching him through knowing black eyes.

Smoke Shield turned. As quickly as the excitement built he was on his way, legs pumping as he started up the trail to the great mound.

He cast a glance back, aware that Uncle was still watching him. The old man's sharp gaze had never wavered. He knew that look. It had always communicated disapproval.

Twenty-one

Sunset cast dying light over Split Sky City. The palaces, high atop their mounds, glowed in the ruddy light. Smoke from a thousand fires rose into the still air, creating a haze. A chill had spilled over the city, rolling down from a cloud bank in the north. The high thunderheads had been painted with yellow, orange, and deeper purples.

Morning Dew was vaguely aware of this as she cast occasional glances out the doorway. She sat like a statue, thankful for every breath, every heartbeat that she was spared what everyone seemed to believe was inevitable. She had used that time to reflect.

On a full stomach, with her body clean and her long black hair combed to a sheen, a part of herself had returned. Once again she could think, and Heron Wing's words that morning had taken root. *If I am not amusing, challenging, or difficult, he will grow tired of me.*

She had known men like that. Seen them, full of joy with some new adventure, or love, and then watched that excitement fade as it grew commonplace. Her beautiful dress, the red fabric clean, the pearls replaced and the quillwork bright, lay folded atop one of the sleeping benches.

If only I had donned something else that morning.

But as Heron Wing had said, no one could reverse a river's flow.

She waited until Wide Leaf stepped outside, then asked softly, "Why did you help me?"

Heron Wing—inspecting her son's breechcloth for holes—raised an eyebrow. "Power ebbs and flows. As you have so recently discovered, fate can change in an instant. Once, years ago, it might have been me who was carried off during the worst of the Yuchi raids. I don't know the ways of Power, of fate, and why things happen, but they do. I once knew a man who was the exact opposite of Smoke Shield. I try to live my life in a way he would approve of." She smiled wryly. "And perhaps it is because I just don't like my husband."

"Thank you." Her voice still sounded small.

"Morning Dew," Heron Wing added, "you are a slave. But remember that you are also a matron. There are things you owe to yourself, to your clan, and your people. To be a good matron, a woman must use all the talents at her disposal. She must be responsible, first and foremost. Especially to herself. I have given you the best advice I could."

"I have thought about that."

"Good. I hope you have more courage and intelligence than your brother." She raised her eyes, meeting Morning Dew's across the low fire.

Morning Dew swallowed hard.

"Greetings," a voice called from outside. "It is Thin Branch. I come with a request. The war chief would see his slave."

Morning Dew gasped in spite of herself. Her heart began to pound.

"If you will wait, Thin Branch," Heron Wing called, "she will be right with you."

"Of course," he said easily.

Heron Wing placed the piece of clothing to the side, standing and rounding the fire to pick up the dress. "It would be easier to dress if you were standing." She said it so reasonably.

Morning Dew swallowed hard, climbing weakly to her feet. She fumbled at the brown dress as she pulled it off. Heron Wing exchanged it for her repaired red dress.

Morning Dew's hands shook as she tried to pull it over her head. It took her two tries, but she tugged it down over her hips.

Heron Wing straightened it on her shoulders, then took a tortoiseshell comb and did her hair, fluffing it so that it spilled down her back, full and glistening.

"You are a matron, and a woman," Heron Wing insisted. "Remember what I have told you."

"Yes."

"Go do what you must."

Morning Dew nodded, hating the way her muscles trembled.

She stepped through the door, seeing Thin Branch standing with two muscular young men. He obviously expected to have to drag her again.

No. I will walk on my own. She swore that, and somehow managed to walk past him with her head up, teeth clenched to keep her chin from quivering. She took the lead, heading toward the plaza, walking along its northern edge. Thin Branch and the guards followed close behind her. She could see the high palace, the last of the sunset having bled away to leave it purple in the light. By taking the route she picked, she could avoid the squares, could avoid Screaming Falcon's glazed eyes.

Behind her, she could hear Thin Branch's footsteps. It seemed but the blink of an eye before she stood at the foot of the long stairway. She hesitated, heart pounding, breath short in her lungs. When Thin Branch stepped up and placed a hand on her arm, she shook it off, and took the first step.

She had never climbed anything so high. Her mouth was dry, lungs half out of breath at the top, but she forced herself to step through the gate and into the yard. The guardian posts, with their eagle heads, seemed to glare at her. Above them, the palace rose to a high point. She started forward, trying to muster enough saliva to swallow.

At the great door, Thin Branch hurried past her to take

the lead. With knotted fists she followed him through the great room with its crackling fire. She barely registered the tripod seat with its cougarhide coverings, or the huge Seeing Hand with its single staring eye hanging on the back wall.

Thin Branch led her into a long hallway and stopped at the first door, calling, "War Chief. I bring your slave as requested." Then he held the hanging aside.

From some unknown well, she spurred her muscles and managed to walk into the room. It was large, filled with pots, ornately carved boxes, and the trappings of an influential and highborn man. A crackling fire burned in the clay hearth in the center, bowls of food arranged beside it. Smoke Shield stood beside the bed built into the north wall. The white apron he wore was stainless; his hair, freshly washed, hung loose about his head. His face was unpainted, the tattoos around his eyes and the black bar across his cheeks denoting his status. Firelight cast a black shadow over the scar on the side of his face. He stepped over and seated himself cross-legged on folded deer hides near the fire. Two drinking gourds sat to either side of the bowls of food.

"Leave us," Smoke Shield ordered. The door hanging dropped as the slave left.

For a long moment, Morning Dew waited, arms straight at her sides, her stomach tied like a terrible knot. She had locked her knees to keep from trembling, every muscle in her body tight.

"You are even more beautiful than I remember," he said, getting slowly to his feet. He walked around her like a Trader inspecting a prize copper plate. She couldn't stop herself from flinching as he fingered her hair.

"Relax," he told her. "We have all the time in the world."

Her hard swallow was audible.

"Do not be afraid."

She made herself nod.

When he stepped around in front of her, a gleaming

curiosity lay behind his eyes. She could see the anticipation, the excitement he could barely control.

A voice in her head said, *This is a very dangerous man.*

"Do—do you want me before or after you eat?"

He laughed. "Oh, I've waited long enough for this night. I think we can eat first." He gestured. "Please, be seated."

She sat too quickly, hurrying so her legs didn't buckle. He laughed again, fully aware of her fear. He seemed to savor every moment as though feeding on her distress as surely as he would on the food before him.

She bowed her head, eyes on the floor.

"Hard, isn't it?" he asked. "One moment you're the great Screaming Falcon's wife, matron of the White Arrow. The next you're here. Slave to the man you wouldn't even deign to look at, what? Six moons ago?"

"Things change," she said simply.

"Oh, indeed they do."

She closed her eyes, and her lungs felt starved. Unbidden, the memory of the slave women kneeling before her in White Arrow Town filled her souls. What had she sworn that day? That she would never become someone like that? She ground her teeth and made herself look up. "What do you want with me?"

He was toying with a deerbone stiletto, rolling it between his fingers. "That's a good question. But it seems to me that I already have everything of yours. Your husband, your brother, your holy man. And," he added, "you."

She nodded, stilling the panic that ran like terrified mice through her bones. "Very well, what would you like me to do?"

Again he laughed. "You could tremble, or maybe scream. That would be entertaining." He paused, and seemed to be thinking hard. "No, how about this: I want you to fall madly in love with me. I want you to worship me. Yes, that's it. I want you to look at me with eyes that tell me I'm the only man in the world for you."

She managed a shrug. "I'll try to the best of my ability to do as you wish."

Smoke Shield gave her a sidelong glance. "I'd expect more from a conquered matron. Seems to me you should be plotting revenge." He lifted the stiletto. "Perhaps, in the throes of my passion, you could slide this between my ribs?"

She gave him a slight smile. "No, I don't think so. It wouldn't be prudent. Your people would burn me to death in retaliation."

"So . . . what then?"

"I shall try and fulfill your wishes. That's all. I will do whatever you tell me to."

A cunning smile bent his lips. "When I lay with a woman, I want her to scream. I want to hear her moaning with passion."

"Then I shall scream and moan." *But not in passion for you, beast.*

He dimpled his thumb with the stiletto tip. "I remember one time, I wanted a woman . . ." Moving like a panther, he slipped next to her. She tensed, feeling the point of the stiletto pressed at the angle of her jaw. "I had to keep a knife tip at her throat the entire time."

She took a deep breath, flutters of fear at the pit of her stomach. "I am yours to take however you wish."

He backed away, slapping her hard. The force of the blow knocked her onto her side. She blinked at the hot sting in her cheek. Gods, how she wished she could just cry, let herself sink onto the mat, and sob like a wretch. Somehow, she propped her arm under her, straightening to see the rage on his face. She clawed her hair back, turning her other cheek, waiting for his blow.

He chuckled, tossed the stiletto to the side, and crawled back to his place. "This is not the way I imagined it would be."

"Tell me what to do."

"Fill my bowl."

She ladled cornmeal, roast rabbit, and some squash

as he pointed to the dishes. Then she sat, eyes focused on his muscular chest as he half lifted the wooden bowl. "Go ahead," he said. "Eat."

At his order, she helped herself to several of the bowls, taking small bites. "This is very good," she told him.

"I ordered the best."

"I thank you for sharing it."

His probing stare carried its puzzlement. Finally he said, "You're not what I expected."

"What did you expect?"

"That woman I saw last summer in White Arrow Town."

"I am no longer that same woman."

"So, who are you?"

"Your slave."

"Please look into my eyes when I'm talking to you."

"Is that better?" The effect was like looking into the eyes of a lustful cougar. After the first moments, she began to see the thoughts racing there.

He asked, "Tell me, how do you think your husband is going to die on the square?"

She knotted her fists, saw his smile at her discomfort, and made herself relax. "He will die well. He's a strong man, and will do everything he can to make sure you know it as you burn, beat, and cut him." Gods, how could she say this so matter-of-factly? "He knows what is coming, and will make it a contest between you and him."

He reached under his bed, withdrawing a long slender object the length of his arm. A narrow sleeve of weasel hide encased a slim stone sword. Smoke Shield held it up, inspecting it in the light. "Only the finest flint knappers can make these. Do you know what it is?"

He held it up in the light. The blade had been chipped from a single piece of stone and was as long as his forearm. Firelight gleamed in the riffled surface. The handle had been crafted from a section of human arm bone, and was engraved with intertwined rattlesnakes, their

sides spotted with circles that represented doorways
into the Underworlds. She suddenly realized that the
dark stains in the binding were from long-dried blood.

Smoke Shield ran a finger down the deadly length of
stone. "It's only made for one thing: the ritual execution
of prisoners. A blade this long is too brittle to be used for
anything else. I have been keeping it handy." He smiled
into her eyes. "I think I'll use it on your husband."

She had seen such a thing before. Biloxi had used the
White Arrow ceremonial sword on the day he was made
high minko. He had killed a Biloxi that he had allegedly
taken captive on a raid. From that act, he had received
his name.

"I think I'll slice off his penis and balls first." His
measuring eyes were on hers. "Would you like them
when I'm done? You know, a sort of memento of the
times he lay with you?"

To keep from screaming, she bit down on her tongue.
"You can give me whatever you wish."

"Is this hard for you?"

"He was my husband. What do you think?" The trembling started in her gut, a sickness that grew and expanded.

"Then perhaps I'll make you come with me. Knowing him as you do, you can tell me what his weaknesses
are."

Blessed gods, what do I say? A scattered thought
landed, and she said, "If you order me to, I will." She
struggled to keep her breathing normal. "Actually, it
will help him to endure. Seeing me, he'll want more
than ever to prove his bravery."

She could sense the disappointment behind Smoke
Shield's eyes. "What about your brother?"

She gave him a dead stare. "He will die poorly. There
is nothing I can do to change that. I will weep, and my
heart will break; but he is who he is."

"And you?"

"I have recently discovered that I, too, am who I am.

Isn't that true of all of us, War Chief? You will be what your souls make of you?"

"You sound like my wife." He carefully slipped the sword back into its sheath and replaced it beneath the bed.

"Is that good or bad?" she asked as he picked up his bowl and scooped the last of his meal from the bottom.

"Bad," he mumbled though a mouthful of food.

"Then I will say no more."

"The last thing I need to think of tonight are my darling wives." He threw the empty bowl across the room. The wood split when it hit the wall.

He narrowed an eye, belched, and took a drink of water. She set her plate down when he gestured to her. She stood, stepping around the food bowls, and lowered herself to her knees where he indicated.

What is happening behind those half-lidded eyes? What twisted thoughts are lodged there?

His hand settled lightly on her arm. She flinched, then said, "I'm sorry. This will be difficult for me, but I will do my best."

He traced a finger down from her shoulder to the tip of her breast. He was watching the leaping pulse in her neck.

The corner of his lip quivered as he grasped the neckline of her dress with both hands. Muscles bulged as he strained against the fabric. It gave with a loud rip, pearls pattering off like raindrops. Then he was on his feet, lifting her, spilling her out of the ruined dress. She flopped on the floor, naked and frightened.

She lay panting, staring up. Her wits had scattered like quail before a hunter. His smile victorious, he reached down and untied his apron, letting it fall away. Unable to help herself, she fixed on his penis, watching it rise and stiffen.

Submit! Heron Wing's voice seemed to call from the very air.

This is it. Taking a deep breath, Morning Dew lay

back, spreading her legs among the overturned dishes. Warm food slipped beneath her skin. She fixed her eyes on the soot-stained ceiling, fully aware that he had dropped to his knees between her legs. His hands stroked down the length of her thighs. The shudder that ran through her body was involuntary, and she tried to breathe deeply.

Think! What do you do next? "I'm sorry, War Chief. I'll be dry."

"Oh, I'll fix that," he told her hoarsely.

She stiffened when his finger speared into her, probing.

It's only my body. He's doing nothing that Screaming Falcon has not done before.

She pulled her head to the side and concentrated on one of the knots in the logs overhead, centering the eye of her souls on it as he settled his weight onto her. He drove himself into her as though trying to hammer her hips through the floor.

The knot. All that exists is the knot. She imagined the branch that had once grown from that dark eye, willed her souls into it the way an *Alikchi Hopaii* sent his souls through portals into other worlds. The branch was firm, the leaves it sprouted green, full with life and sap.

She was still lost in the knot when he gasped, moaned, and went limp. From under his stifling weight, she stared vacantly upward, wondering if laughter still lived anywhere on earth.

Two Petals sat backward in Old White's canoe, her stumbling thoughts spinning like a whirlwind. The river flowed around her, buoying her weight, spilling over her fingers when she reached over the side. Even the chilly breeze slipped effortlessly around her, as though in reluctant avoidance.

Why do I feel so desperate? Something terrible was coming. The Watcher loomed somewhere over the horizon. She could feel him, looking in her direction. A great black void was opening, lost somewhere in the days upriver.

The time Two Petals had spent in seclusion during her moon had been refreshing. For those precious moments she had sat in the dim interior of the abandoned house, bothered only by the voices and the disembodied Spirits that came to visit. The visions from her Dance with Sister Datura played between her souls in glowing images of light and color. The voices that whispered in the air around her were calm. And best of all, the world was no longer moving. Not like now. Not like on the river.

Movement made her ill. Her senses would swim, and she could feel herself becoming one with the current. Water was alive. It always sought to move. In growing desperation, she had tried to feel it, sense it, the way she would an animal. But no matter how she extended her senses, she couldn't seem to reach the spirit of the water. When she called out to it from the canoe, she would catch Old White's curious gaze on her as he paddled laboriously upstream. That he seemed to accept her eccentricities didn't lessen the effect his evaluative stare had on her wobbling peace of mind.

At times she would feel the Watcher. She wasn't sure who he was, only that he was aware of her. Sometimes, in the twilight, she'd catch a glimpse of his crystalline eyes. From the shadows, they'd stare at her, glittering and transparent. When they did, she could sense his curiosity and concern.

"Where are you?" she asked more than once, but the phantom image remained mute.

She had first seen him while Dancing with Sister Datura. From a whirlwind, she had looked down upon his wrapped face. He had glanced up in surprise, gazing at her through the cloth that covered his quartz eyes. Uttering a cry in a strange language, he had clutched at a shell gorget on his chest and held it up. She'd seen the design, three spinning triangles in the center surrounded by concentric circles, and a lobed margin that reminded her of flower petals.

She'd felt the force of his Power before it masked him from her gaze. Where he had been, only a curtain of black haze remained. It made no sense, but many things in the vision remained incomprehensible.

Memories out of time slipped between her souls. She had seen incomprehensible fragments of people, events, and heard scattered statements uttered by unknown mouths. The faces of the people, the places they inhabited, were all strange, foreign to her. She had seen herself as if from above. Watched her body undulating on Trader's, heard her soft intake of breath as her loins burst with pleasure. She had seen the Seeker staring thoughtfully into a campfire burned low in the night. A circle of warriors seemed to appear magically from the forest, their weapons held at the ready. And then she would feel the terror. Fear would wash over her, drowning her in an ocean of disembodied souls. Then had come a blackness, a gap in events. A place she could not see—like a huge hole in the vision she had shared with Sister Datura. The rest had been like daydreams, all disjointed and thrown together.

Finally it would all come to an end. Distant murky water, a great Horned Serpent, and the dark-souled man awaited her just over the horizon of future-past. The terrible dark-souled man's gleaming eyes stared at her from the future. They would Dance, surrounded by the shining scales of the great serpent. Around and around they'd go, and then down into the eerie light of another world.

She need only wait until the image became real.

I am backward in time. She had lived those things sometime in the future before her souls had been sent back, to see it all again. The sense of doing it all in reverse disoriented her, as if events had been turned upside down. It left her consumed with confusion.

Gods, if I could just keep it all in order! But control was beyond her abilities.

Traveling upriver, however, was moving backward, going counter to the flow. Doing so helped her to structure her thoughts. Things were calmer when she went backward. The sense of rushing toward inevitability lessened.

She clamped her eyes shut. If only the world wouldn't move. She desperately wished she could stop the clouds in the sky, stop the movement of the sun. If the wind would freeze in place, if fire wouldn't flicker, she could finally find herself.

What had been so normal when she was a child now left her senses reeling. Worst of all were people. They moved faster, like a juddering swirl of partially seen images. When they did, her confusion was complete. It took all of her willpower to keep from slapping both hands to her ears, pinching her eyes shut, and shouting, "Stop!" at the top of her lungs.

She had tried that when the disembodied voices came in a flurry. But to no avail. With real people, she could at least mute the sounds. The Spirit voices, however, seemed to come from inside her head. Sometimes they told her the most ridiculous things, like Trader and Old White were conspiring against her. That they would drug her food, or that one of them was urinating in her water bowl.

She couldn't believe the voices. Sister Datura had shown her none of those things. When she watched Trader and Old White, it was to observe no nefarious actions on their part. Instead, they simply seemed to accept with mild amusement when, with no proof, she lifted her water jar, took it out, and poured it on the ground. Once she had heard Old White say matter-of-factly, "She's a Contrary."

As much as she missed home, and her family, she wouldn't Trade being back there for her time on the river, as confusing as it was. Here she could listen to the voices, dump her water bowl, refuse food the Spirits told her had been poisoned, and fight to keep the world at bay without hearing anger in people's voices or seeing the fear in their eyes.

Now she sat, facing backward, watching the river rush away from her. She was going backward, trees creeping into the corner of her vision, slowly moving away from her. And today, with a south wind, the few fluffy clouds, too, were acting correctly.

"You are the only constant," one of the voices told her. *"It is you who is in place. The rest of the world is moving around you."*

Stopped in time, she thought. But what anchored her? What terrible thing pinned her in place so that she was rooted while the earth, sky, and water flowed steadily past? Sister Datura hadn't told her the how of it, only the why.

"Be who you are," Sister Datura whispered from her memories. *"The rest shall come to you."*

The fear that came from that knowledge was lessened only because she had seen and lived through it in her Vision. Time was alive. She had entered it, lived within it. Then that morning when she had awakened in Silver Loon's temple, she had somehow slipped outside of its breath and being.

"Not everyone has received a gift like this," one of the voices in her head said.

"But I don't want it!"

She realized that Old White had heard. He cocked his head, as if waiting for more.

She looked away, fixing instead on the packs between them.

After a while, Old White asked, "We're coming up on the first rapids. There's a Kaskinampo town there. Anything I should know about it?"

The coming sights and sounds played through her. People haggling, Trader offering packs of prime beaver. She could sense the growing confusion, the smoky air of the Kaskinampo town, and a thousand questions buzzing around her like an angry swarm of churning insects.

"It will be terrible," she said of the swelling panic within. "No laughter. None at all."

"We were thinking about hiring a couple of canoes. Remember how the Inoca towed us upstream?"

"Yes, slow us down immeasurably," she replied, dreading the idea of the world moving even faster around her.

She sighed, bending over to trace her fingertips through the water. The feel of it passing added to her sense of unease. "I still don't know how it does that."

"Because it is running away from you. Trying to get as far away as possible before you reach Split Sky City."

She closed her eyes, seeking the Spirit of the river, only to feel it shift ever so slightly, just beyond her ability to touch it. Why did it elude her so? What did the river have to fear from her? She wouldn't even be near its waters when they reached Split Sky City.

"Can you hear me?" she called into the depths. "Why won't you talk to me?"

"Maybe you're not asking the right question," Old White said from his seat in the rear. "Myself, I've never talked to rivers. But then, perhaps I wasn't smart enough to know that I should."

"It has such a short Spirit," Two Petals told him. "All compressed, bursting to be longer." In the end, her time with this river would be so brief. Shorter now that Yuchi paddlers would speed up the entire world. Did they know that by dint of their muscles, they were moving the entire earth? If she told them, would the knowledge sap their energy?

She said, "The only time a man can move the entire world is when he isn't aware that he is doing so."

Old White nodded, his expression turning pensive.

She glanced past him, seeing Trader in his birch-bark canoe following in their wake. The rising and falling of his paddle was regular as a heartbeat. With each stroke, it captured a bit of sunlight on the blade, and sank it into the river. She could see sunlight sparkling on the water, and wondered if that, too, was reflected from beneath the surface, from the thousands of paddles over the years that had stirred captured bits of light into the water.

She studied Trader over the distance and remembered the image of their naked bodies locked together.

Not yet. But the time will come. He has much to teach me.

Trader was still far back in time, consumed by his worries and guilt. She had seen his interest in her. He was a man, after all. But the wariness behind his eyes had built a wall between them. She knew how it would slowly come unraveled, to fall with one last surprise.

Oh, I know you well, Trader. She both anticipated and dreaded the moment their paths would finally intersect. In her souls' eye she saw two rocks, flying through the air, clacking loudly, and then glancing off in different directions to land in the hands of their throwers.

From his perspective, however, he was but moments from the initial throw, just beginning his whistling path through the air. Like a stone, he had no idea what he would hit, or where he would finally fall to earth, or the shape he would be in when he landed. Seeing from the last to the first, Two Petals could pity him.

"Yes, we'll see terrible times," she said.

"Good," Old White answered, thinking she was still speaking of the Kaskinampo.

Twenty-two

Old White glanced back at Trader as they nosed into the canoe landing below the rapids. A child had already spotted them, and ran toward the nestled houses calling a warning. The settlement had been built on a low terrace just above flood stage. People emerged from dwellings, or looked up from the cook fires, mortars, and other tasks they were occupied with. Others stepped out of a fortification behind the village.

Trader seemed only slightly nervous, obviously having at least a little faith in Old White's sleight to protect his copper. During the days when Two Petals had passed her moon, they had laboriously chipped away most of the stone, hammered nodules flat, and beaten the metal into a thick square sheet. For the time being it was wrapped in a durable cloth bag with heavily stitched shoulder straps.

Well, now we see if the story we concocted works.

The Kaskinampo were a Mos'kogean people. Like the Sky Hand, they had invaded this country, taking the three falls of the Tenasee River from the original inhabitants. Those unlucky folk had fled farther east, only to be crushed and enslaved by the Yuchi and Charokee. Their name was no longer spoken. As to the Kaskinampo, some still lived in the old towns west of the Father Water. Contact, Trade, and communications continued to be maintained between the groups.

Because of their location on the Tenasee—and the heavily fortified towns they had constructed on the heights—they controlled all Trade up and down the river, offering their services to portage around the rapids for a reasonable fee. For the most part the ambitious Yuchi, farther upriver, left them alone. It didn't hurt to have the Kaskinampo to take the brunt of Miami, Illinois, and Shawnee war parties headed upriver; and for their part, the Kaskinampo never got too greedy about the Trade. They took a fair share for their services, and did their best to facilitate the movement of goods up and down the river. They believed that a smaller share of a lot of different goods served them better in the long term than a discouragingly large cut from fewer and fewer canoe loads.

The Michigamea should be so smart.

By the time Old White's canoe nosed into the beach, a dozen helping hands were waiting to pull the craft up onto shore. Others performed a similar task for Trader, though wary of Swimmer where the dog perched atop the packs.

"Greetings," Old White called, raising his Trader's staff. "I am Old White, sometimes called the Seeker. The woman is Two Petals, a Contrary. This other man is Trader. We come in need of portage past the rapids. For this service, we offer Trade."

One of the older men stepped forward, touching his breast by way of greeting. "I am Buffalo Mankiller, of the White Earth Clan. My lineage has charge of the lower landing. What can the Kaskinampo do to help you?"

Old White grimaced as he stood stiffly. "I'm not as young as I used to be." He could feel the ache up and down his body. His lower half was cramped from sitting, his upper body pained from paddling.

"None of us are," Buffalo Mankiller told him with a smile.

Trader stepped out of his canoe, trying as best he could to swing his heavy cloth pack onto his shoulders in a way that made it look light. He added, "We need to Trade for passage up past the third rapids. Is Long Hand still chief here?"

"It is with sorrow that I tell you that he has passed to the Sky World two winters past." Buffalo turned his appraisal to Trader, and the obviously heavy pack he carried. "You knew him?"

"I used to travel this way often."

Buffalo Mankiller indicated Trader's tattoo with a finger. "That looks like a minko's tattoo, but unfinished."

Trader smiled humorlessly. "To have finished it, I would have had to have completed my initiation. Some things in life are disrupted by Power, fate, or destiny. In my case, the disruption was from the Hichiti. I was lucky to escape with my life."

Old White thought it was a smooth lie.

"And your town?" Buffalo Mankiller asked.

"It is gone," Trader said with great facility. "Most were taken by the Hichiti. Some fled to the Ockmulgee. Me, I turned to the river, and to Trade." He made a throwing-away gesture. "Living in the Trade is so much better than serving as a slave, don't you think?"

"It is so." Buffalo shot an evaluative stare at Two Petals. "You said the woman is a Contrary? This is true?"

Old White nodded. "It is. Two Petals is from the far north. She has no understanding of your culture, and all that she does is backward. Power rides on her shoulders like no woman I have ever known. For that reason I would warn you, and ask you take any precautions necessary around her. We are here in peace, and for the Trade. We wish only to pass through your country as quickly as possible, without incident."

Buffalo's scrutiny intensified as he stepped unconsciously back from Two Petals. "If she is so Powerful, how do you travel with her?"

"We carry our medicine to protect us." Old White indicated the heavy pack on Trader's back, and his own wooden box. He reached down, lifted it, and swung it onto his shoulder. Then he grabbed up his weighted bag and shouldered the strap. His pouch of herbs he tied to his waist.

"What medicine is that?" Buffalo asked, pointing to Trader's sagging bag.

"It is a slab of carved stone," Trader told him straight-faced. "It contains Spirits in each of the carvings on its surface. As long as it is covered, none of those Spirits will wake. This is another reason we wish to pass as quickly as possible through your country."

Buffalo rubbed his chin, thoughts racing behind his eyes. "Where do you go with this Contrary and this terrible Spirit Power?"

"Split Sky City. Once there, we can divest ourselves of our charge, and return once again to our normal lives," Old White said honestly. "We were wondering, would a half pack of prime northern beaver hides cover portage past the rapids, and perhaps two canoes filled with young men to pull us upriver?"

Buffalo thought, then shook his head. "No, for that many men, I would need much more than that." An eyebrow raised. "And being around both a Contrary and such Powerful medicine would mean that they would have to be secluded, purified by our *Hopaye,* our greatest Healer." A pause. "Then, too, we have plenty of beaver in our own country."

"I see." Old White let his gaze run over the packs.

Trader interrupted his thoughts. "I have something that Kaskinampo have not seen often."

"We have seen many things," Buffalo Mankiller said, affecting boredom.

"Have you seen a white fox skin?" Trader asked, crossing his arms against the weight of the copper.

"Sometimes—rarely, I'll grant you—a fox is born white. They don't live for long."

Trader bent over, the pack swinging awkwardly on his back and banging his elbow. Old White smiled at that, having been bruised by his own stone-weighted sack over the years. The young man finally managed to find the right bale and untie the straps holding it. From under a press of flattened mink, lynx, and wolverine, he brought forth a gleaming white fox skin, rubbing the thick long fur to make it stand. He handed it to Buffalo Mankiller, asking, "What do you think of that?"

Old White watched the Kaskinampo's expression as he inspected the fox skin. Buffalo Mankiller was no novice given the amount and number of goods passing through his hands, but the look of fascination overcame his control. "Where did this come from?"

"The far north," Old White added, having seen the beasts in his travels in those distant lands. "The white fox doesn't live below the tundra. You'll notice its ears are smaller than any fox ears you've ever seen before. Being small keeps them from freezing in the miserable cold."

Swimmer was already out of the canoe, having found children who would pet him and scratch his neck.

"How many of these do you have?" Buffalo Mankiller asked, trying to peer into the partially uncovered pile.

"I would Trade four. One for you, one for the chief here, and one for each of the chiefs who control the rapids upriver."

"And for the men who paddle us upriver," Old White added, "I will throw in a shell gorget apiece for their labor and the discomfort of cleansing, as well as a large crystal for the *Hopahe* who must conduct the rituals."

"I shall see what can be done," Buffalo Mankiller relented. "In the meantime, we still have daylight left. Do you wish your canoes and packs carried up to the landing above the rapids?"

"That would be fine." Old White inclined his head. "We would offer a sack of wild rice to the porters. I suspect that you don't get much of that here."

"Your gift is most generous." Buffalo Mankiller gave a signal. His strong young men began unloading packs.

Old White told Two Petals, "If you don't want to walk, stay in the canoe."

She immediately climbed out, a frown on her forehead as she watched the porters swing the heavy packs onto their heads and start up the trail. "Just keep me away from the flies." She batted at the air around her. "It's like kicking a carcass. Confusion everywhere."

Old White glanced at Trader, who shrugged. The unpacking, shouldering of the packs, and lifting of the canoes onto strong backs was finished before Old White could cinch his packs tighter on his back.

"One thing," Trader asked of Buffalo Mankiller, "would you have an ornately carved box? The sort of thing war medicine is carried in?"

The Kaskinampo thought for a moment. "I might." A pause. "Why?"

Trader indicated the fabric on his back. "It was the best I could do at the time, but fabric can rip. To keep Powerful Spirits like these, I would prefer something sturdier."

Buffalo Mankiller took a quick measure of the size with his eyes. "We have something. A box of great Power. It comes from down south, and those who have owned it have all suffered terrible misfortune. Our Priests have decided that it should be sent from our lands. But it will cost you."

"Somehow I expected that."

"Just promise me you won't let that Power loose in the process of transferring your Spirit Stone."

"I will be as careful for my sake as for that of your people," Trader promised. Then he whistled. "Come on, Swimmer. Leave the children alone. Let's go."

Trader hummed a tune to himself as he reclined before the fire. Swimmer curled beside him on his blanket, allowing Trader to stroke his silky hair. Periodically the dog sighed in contentment and shifted himself so as to expose other parts of his body to petting.

The night was cold, but one thing Trader wasn't short on was furs. That the heavens were clear, literally frosted with stars, was a blessing. The alternative would have been either cold rain or swirling snow. He'd take the stars, and with pleasure, thank you.

Buffalo Mankiller had made the decision that, due to the Power they represented, it would be unwise to lodge them in one of the guest houses before the main town's palisade. Instead, they had been asked to camp here, on the sandy canoe landing above the rapids.

Just by lifting his head, Trader could see his birch-bark canoe—reloaded to his specifications—ready to be pushed off at a moment's notice. Old White's finely made dugout sat beside his, mounds of packs visible. The river ran black, its surface reflecting the faintest sheen of starlight.

"Cheaper than I expected," Old White said as he used sand to scrap out the cooking bowl. Supper had been a thick fish stew flavored with hickory and beechnuts. Afterward they had nibbled on a local cornbread.

"White fox is a powerful incentive."

"You must have been in the north a while."

"Trade was good." He grinned. "And I wanted to do a little digging of my own."

"Paid off," Old White noted, glancing at Two Petals.

Trader turned his attention to her. She'd seemed pre-occupied of late, as if a great depressing weight had settled on her since she'd been in the moon lodge. Trader considered her features: definitely comely. She kept cropping into his thoughts. Watching her brought the constant reminder that she was an attractive and single female with a charming body. But just when his thoughts began to dwell on her full breasts, or the way her dress clung to those round hips, she would look at him, and say something spooky enough to snuff any sprouting desires.

"Nice to be among Mos'kogee speakers again," Old White noted.

"It is," Trader agreed, rubbing Swimmer's ears. "But I have to concentrate. Enough words are different that you get lost if you don't pay attention."

From the darkness, a voice called, "Hello the fire."

Trader could see Buffalo Mankiller approaching, a dark square object in his hands. As he walked into the firelight, it formed into an intricately carved wooden box, red cedar, if Trader was any judge.

"Mind if I join you?"

"We would be honored," Old White said, moving to make a place by the fire. He indicated a fold of matting. "Here, keep your bones off the cold ground."

Buffalo Mankiller seated himself, extending the box to Trader. "You said you were going to Split Sky City? See if this will do?"

Trader disengaged himself from Swimmer, who had sat up to inspect the newcomer; his nose sifted the air for the man's scent.

The box had been carefully crafted, lightweight but sturdy. Two thick straps had been run through slits in the bottom and then double sewn over the shoulders. The bottom side, visible when carried, had been carved with images of rattlesnakes, water cougars, and snapping turtles. The sides were done in relief with buffalo, deer, raccoons, and turkeys. The top had a depiction of Eagle Man, his turkey-tail mace in one hand, a rattlesnake in the other. The back, or lid, brought a cold shiver to Trader's souls. There, perfectly rendered, was the eye-hand symbol of his people.

Old White gasped, as if shocked. His eyes were wide, fixed on the box. An expression of disbelief filled his face. He reached out, as if to touch the box from across the fire, but his hand froze midway to its goal. Two Petals, however, had a knowing smile on her face, as if something had just come clear in her odd souls.

Trader stared at the symbol, running his fingers over the relief. "Where did you get this?"

"It's been around for a long time," Buffalo Mankiller said, shrugging. "According to the stories, a young Yuchi, who had been disgraced, stole it. The young man brought it here, thinking he could obtain enough wealth to become a Trader. It has passed from hand to hand, each of its owners falling on bad times. Since you travel surrounded by Power, perhaps it would be best to send it away with you." He lifted an inquiring eyebrow. "Assuming you can meet my price."

Trader swallowed dryly, and managed to say, "What . . . What would you want for it?" Gods, what had gotten into Old White? He looked as if he'd seen a ghost.

"We both know the value of that box. Do you have Trade of equal value?"

Trader carefully set the box to one side, standing and walking down to his canoe. He fished around in one of his packs, finding the thing he sought. Returning to the fire, he dropped the heavy object into Buffalo Mankiller's hand. The man frowned, holding the shining stone up to the light. "Is this what I think it is?"

"Silver," Trader told him. "From the far north. I got it from an Ojibwa Trader. It cost me two bundles of yaupon tea. They don't get much black drink up there."

"And we get even less silver here," Buffalo Mankiller said softly. He tightened his fingers around the small stone. "It is a Trade. But I have to tell you, we have waited for years to get fair value."

"I follow the old ways," Trader told him. "I'm just as happy as the next man to get a good deal, but when it comes to Power, I give value for value."

Buffalo Mankiller clutched his silver close to his breast. "It is a mark of the times that such a thing as silver is so rare. Each year, fewer and fewer canoes pass from distant lands. These days people look in, rather than out. Stories of warfare are heard more than those of peace."

"Have you seen an increase in raiding parties?" Trader glanced at Old White. The man appeared speechless, disbelieving eyes still fixed on the medicine box.

"More this last season than usual." Buffalo Mankiller stared into the fire. "We will stay in these lands as long as it is profitable, but we do not have the numbers of the

Yuchi, or the Charokee. The Iroquois, too, have begun to make incursions. Last year we saw the first Shawnee raiding party. They stopped here in peace, Traded, and went back east to raid, but it is a sign of the things to come."

"What . . . What of the Miami and Illinois?" Old White physically tore his gaze from the box and forced himself to rejoin the conversation. He had withdrawn his quavering hand, knotting it into a fist in his lap.

"We have bloodied them often enough that they prefer to kill each other for the time being."

"And if things continue to grow more dangerous?" Trader asked.

"That will depend on the Trade." Buffalo Mankiller removed his own pipe from a pocket. He took a moment to load it, lighting it from the fire and puffing. "Should the Trade dwindle to almost nothing, and the dangers grow, we will return to the west and rejoin the rest of our people." He smiled wistfully and fingered the silver nugget, holding it up to the light. "It seems that the world is slowly turning to madness."

"We live in the fading shadow of Cahokia." Old White spoke as if his souls were elsewhere, his gaze returned to the wooden box with an odd intensity. "In times past, the lords of Cahokia would have sent envoys to people like the Michigamea asking them to cease and desist. Once, that was all it would take. Even the threat of their warriors was enough to make any chief—no matter how great he deluded himself into believing he was—find an excuse to make peace rather than disrupt the Trade."

"Those days are long gone," Buffalo Mankiller muttered.

Old White shook his head as if to clear his thoughts. He glanced at Two Petals, at the box, and then at Trader as if fitting some puzzle together. Finally he blinked, rummaging in his belt pouch for his pipe. "Smoke? It's northern narrow leaf."

Buffalo Mankiller smiled, unhooked a bag from his own belt, and tossed it over. "Try mine. One of the things we pride ourselves on—besides war and Trade—is our tobacco. It's a mixture of broad leaf with a hint of sweet sumac from my own garden."

"Tell me, good chief," Trader asked, trying to decipher Old White's stunned expression. "Aren't you afraid you'll be tainted by our Power?"

As Old White loaded his pipe with trembling hands, Buffalo Mankiller chuckled. "I am responsible for the Trade at Lower Town. Because of that, I am a constant preoccupation for the *Hopahe*. He ensures that I take a great many precautions. Because of the unique nature of your visit, I have taken responsibility to see that you pass safely . . . both for yourselves *and* my people. While I am with you, my son will handle any other business that should come our way."

"He must be a fine—" Old White stopped short as Two Petals began to Sing in a soft voice.

Trader cocked his head; the Song was a lullaby he'd first heard as a boy. "Where did you learn that?"

Two Petals seemed not to hear.

Trader reached over with his foot, prodding her. She blinked, and appeared to have trouble focusing on him.

"I said, where did you learn that Song? Your people are Oneota."

Her expression grew confused. "It's her voice. Clear as silence . . . and so beautiful. She Sings as he marches off to war, knowing all the while that she has driven him to this."

Trader shivered again, eyes fixed on the box. Old White's pipe lay forgotten in his hands, a look of horror on his face, as though terrible memories were creeping out from dark places in his souls.

Buffalo Mankiller glanced uneasily away from the box, a new comprehension in his calculating gaze. "I think," he said softly, "that I shall accompany you upriver to the boundaries of our lands." He paused. "Just to be sure that there are no . . . complications."

"Your company would be a pleasure," Trader said

absently. Now Old White was gaping at Two Petals, oblivious of everything else.

Buffalo Mankiller recovered his composure, turning to Old White. "I also asked around. You are the one they call the Seeker?"

"I . . . What did you say?"

"I asked if you were the Seeker." Buffalo Mankiller smiled as if to chide himself. "Are even half of the stories they tell about you true?"

"What?" Old White shook himself as if from a chill. His hands were still trembling as he lit the pipe, drew, and exhaled the blue smoke. His eyes were closed, lips moving as if offering a prayer with the smoke. "Oh." Then he sighed. "The stories about me? It depends entirely on the tale. But the short version is that I have traveled most of our earth. No, I do not fly, or shape-shift into animals or birds. I do not consort with the dead. I have no mystical Powers, though I am skilled at the magician's craft and the arts of illusion. I know the use of herbs. And, no, I cannot kill with just a glance. Mostly, I have gone from place to place, searching." He stared hollowly at the box. "And now, I wonder for what?"

"And you, Trader?" Buffalo Mankiller asked. "Somehow I don't think you're as simple as you pretend, either."

Trader smiled sadly, running his fingers through Swimmer's fur now that he'd resettled on his blanket. "Are any of us simple, clan leader?"

"I am," Two Petals said into the silence. "There is no one as simple as me."

Buffalo Mankiller studied her through the smoke rising from his pipe. "In my old age, I expect that I shall look back on these next few days with disbelief and wonder. My grandchildren will either look up at me with awe, or terror."

"Oh," Two Petals answered, "no one will speak of us . . . or this journey. We will vanish like the breeze in the morning, only to be heard in the distant trees."

Why don't I believe a word of that? Trader let the fingers of his other hand trace the carefully carved wood of the medicine box. He would have sworn it vibrated under his touch.

Twenty-three

Morning Dew endured. Her universe had contracted to Smoke Shield's room. She finally had some respite when the high minko called his war chief to conference with one of the clan leaders. Smoke Shield had washed himself, dressed, and ordered her to clean up the room.

Dutifully she wiped up the spilled food, collected the bowls, and placed them outside the door. She supposed it was Thin Branch who removed them. The same thing happened with the chamber pot when she set it out.

She prized each second that he was gone. During that time, she set her souls loose, allowing them to travel to fantasy places where she and Screaming Falcon lived alone beside a broad river. They had a snug house, and walked hand in hand through the forest, collecting berries, grapes, and fallen nuts.

But Screaming Falcon would never go to those places. He hung from a square, just beyond the base of the great mound. Pinching her eyes shut, she forced her imagination away from what he was enduring.

If only I could . . . But no option remained. Only endurance. Heron Wing's words echoed hollowly within her. The only thing she could cling to.

She lost track of time, and sleep crept up on her with stealthy feet. She and Screaming Falcon stepped out of the forest and passed the houses and fields to enter White Arrow Town. Mother was waiting for her, two stickball racquets in her hand. "About time you returned. A matron owes more to her people than you've been showing them."

"I'm married, Mother. I have my own life now."

"You always were a selfish girl," Sweet Smoke said sadly. "Only you can save yourself, your husband, and your people." Mother cocked her head in that old familiar appraisal. "Are you up to it? Are you strong enough? Can you defeat the Sky Hand, and win them at the same time?"

"I don't understand," Morning Dew complained. "You never say things straight. We're prisoners! How can I defeat and win the Sky Hand at the same time?"

"Pierce the heart of your hopes and love. Kill what you seek to save. Surrender yourself, Morning Dew. Become the tool of your people." Mother offered the stick-ball racquets. "Can you accept your responsibility?"

As the familiar handles were extended toward her, Morning Dew could see the polished wood, stained dark by her sweat. She started to reach for them, but a terrible premonition grew as her fingers hovered above the wood. If she touched them, it would bind her to some awful promise, something she couldn't quite perceive, but knew lurked down there in the familiar wood.

Her fingers curled, on the verge of seizing the handles.

"Gods! You'd think these clan chiefs were geese the way they honk and flap their wings." Smoke Shield's irritated curse brought her bolt upright, blinking as the fragments of the Dream slipped away. She couldn't help but glance down at her hands. Had she taken the racquets?

"Glad to see you are still here," he told her as he stepped into the room. "I didn't think to post a guard." He tossed a bit of meat onto the matting beside her. She stared at the bloody thing. Gods, was that a toe?

"Your friend," he told her, stripping off his apron, "Reed Woman."

Morning Dew gaped at the thing, then stared her incomprehension at him.

"She ran," he told her. "When they dragged her back, she was fixed so that she couldn't run again. I thought you might like a little keepsake. Something to remind you what would be in store if you ran, too."

She swallowed hard. *I won't give you that pleasure.*

"It's as dark as a pit in here. Fix the fire."

She mustered herself, scuttling to the small pile of wood and adding some to the coals. She blew, managing to coax yellow flickers of light from the wood.

He pointed to the bed, the meaning clear.

She lay back on the soft furs and raised her legs. As he fondled her body, she fixed on the knot again, just visible in the dim light cast by the fire. She winced as he forced himself in and began battering at her sore sheath.

"Is it always going to be like this?" he asked.

"I do my best."

"Then do better."

"Yes, War Chief."

"Tomorrow I'll bring you your husband's penis. You can run a stick up the middle to stiffen it and practice."

His head to the side, he couldn't see her tightly closed eyes, couldn't read her sudden panic.

"I would have brought it to you tonight. Another gift to go along with the toe. But the god-cursed Albaamaha and their schemes took up too much time. That and the fog moved in. A man can't see ten paces in front of him . . . and that's before it got dark."

Fog? She swallowed her disgust as he gasped and his seed jetted inside her. He sighed contentedly and breathed in her ear. "I mean it. You *will* make yourself ready for me next time. If you don't I'll cut your precious little sheath out of your body."

"Yes, War Chief."

But how? Then she remembered that he kept a grease jar beneath his bed.

He rolled to the side, pushing her away. She carefully slipped from the pole bed and retreated to her corner. He yawned and reached for the chamber pot. She stared at the matting as he squatted over the pot.

When he finished he crawled back into bed. For long

moments he stared at her, firelight like sparks in his dark eyes. She could see fatigue heavy in his eyes. "Go find Thin Branch. Tell him you need something to wear."

She nodded, climbing to her feet.

"When you're dressed so that all the men in the palace don't gawk at you, empty that chamber pot. You ought to have some use besides being a receptacle for my seed. I'm tired. *Don't* disturb my sleep."

Morning Dew slipped to the door hanging, glanced out into the hallway, and tiptoed to the great room. Carefully, she peered around the corner. The place looked empty. Where in the name of the gods was Thin Branch?

"Can I help you?" a voice asked from behind.

She whirled, modestly crossing her arms over her naked breasts. The high minko stood in the dim hallway. He looked her up and down, an eyebrow rising curiously.

"I—I mean no . . . The war chief . . ."

"Yes, the war chief?" Flying Hawk asked woodenly.

"He wanted me to find Thin Branch. To get me a dress."

"And the one you wore in here?"

"Ruined. It's . . . torn."

Flying Hawk sighed. "I can imagine. Just a moment." He walked back the way he had come, only to reappear a moment later bearing a folded dress. "My wife was about your size. This should do."

"Thank you, High Minko."

"If you do find Thin Branch, tell him I have retired for the night."

"Yes, High Minko."

"Gods, *if* you can find him. The fog out there is as thick as muddy water."

He watched her as she pulled the garment over her head. She was long past embarrassment. As she slipped past him, she could see the old man shaking his head. Then Flying Hawk turned, heading back to his rooms.

Morning Dew leaned against the wall, her heart pounding. *I live in madness.*

As she glanced out at the great room, the fire cast its light on the carvings, the stool, and hanging skulls. On silent feet she hurried to the great door and peered out. The thick mist carried the damp odor of Split Sky City, rich with smoke and the dank smell of humanity. The darkness was complete. Not even the guardian posts were visible.

No one would see me in this. But did she dare run?

Morning Dew retreated to Smoke Shield's room, finding the war chief already asleep. He lay on his back, an arm over his head. His mouth hung open, chest rising in deep sleep.

She bent for the chamber pot, staring at the collection of items beneath his bed. The long chipped stone sword seemed to mock her. Soon that sharp point would drink of Screaming Falcon's life.

Then she glanced at the severed toe. *Gods, he enjoys this.*

What would she do when Smoke Shield returned the following day to present her with her husband's genitals?

I'll break like a shattered pot.

She bent her head, heart pounding at the terrible images down in her souls. In a soft whisper, she said, "Help me, Breath Giver. I ask only for a little courage. Help me to see this thing through." She raised her eyes, mouthing, "*Please!*"

Paunch and Whippoorwill had made their way for two days' travel westward to the Horned Serpent River Divide. They had slipped silently through the trees, avoiding the trails. Paunch had labored up the long slopes, stumbling over roots, catching his clothing on greenbriar and spiny walking stick. When they finally had reached the crest, Whippoorwill had told him, "We must camp here for a while."

When exhausted Paunch had awakened the next morning, Whippoorwill was nowhere to be found. Though he had waited anxiously, the girl had been gone for two long days. Paunch was near panic. Twice he had doused their little fire and started east, headed for Split Sky City. Each time, he had stopped, staring uneasily at the trees and listening to the silence. And each time he had talked himself into returning to their little camp. When she returned, *if she returned,* she would seek him there. Now he was just as glad he'd stayed. That morning he had awakened to find the valley below filled with a dense fog that lay like a blanket on the lowlands.

He had walked down the slope, peered into the obscure white haze, and shaken his head. He wouldn't be able to see beyond the next tree if he got into that. He'd lose his way as sure as the rain fell. Even if Whippoorwill was out there, somewhere, in that mess, he could walk right past her and never know.

Where is she?

It was madness. Why hadn't she told him she was going away? But then Whippoorwill had always been odd. She had had Dreams from the time she was little. Then, as she grew older, she would often disappear for days into the forest, only to reappear as if it were the most normal thing in the world.

She often knew things he didn't; and for reasons he had yet to understand, he trusted her instincts.

As well you should have when she counseled you not to send Crabapple on that idiotic mission to warn White Arrow Town.

So, what should he do? Go back and see if she'd returned to Split Sky City as he suspected, or stay close to their little camp? Curse it all in the Ancestors' names, she'd expect to find him at camp.

He teetered with indecision, then reluctantly turned to climb back to his little fire. The fact was, if she'd returned to Split·Sky City, she was either hidden, or the Chikosi had her. If the latter was the case, there was nothing he could do for her. And he just might be caught himself.

Fretting, sick with worry, he hurried back up the trail. He didn't like traveling in haste. Movement was the first thing spotted in the forest, and Chikosi scouts were everywhere, keeping an eye on the trails in case Chahta war parties were headed their direction in retaliation for the White Arrow Town attack.

Heart hammering in his chest, he staggered up the last rise to the sandstone outcropping where they had camped. Gasping for breath, he settled himself on a rock and dropped his pack to the leaf mat. Overhead, the sky was a patchwork of interlaced branches against a hazy blue. The only clouds were below him.

"Are you ready to leave, Grandfather?" Whippoorwill asked, climbing up the trail he had just ascended.

"In Abba Mikko's name! Where have you been, girl?" he exploded.

She cocked her head, as if nonplussed. "Communing with the victims of the Chikosi. Among other things."

He looked her up and down, seeing the dew in her straight black hair. By the Ancestors, she'd been down in the fog for sure.

"What's that on your hands?"

"Blood, Grandfather."

He started toward her, a terrible fear brewing inside him.

"Stop where you are," she told him. "You don't want to get near me until I can wash. There is woman's Power in this." She lifted her hands, staring thoughtfully at the red stains.

Did she just go away to spend her moon . . . or is there more to that blood on her hands? He backed away, wary of her.

"Come," she said, passing wide of him. "We have only been delayed a little while."

Paunch picked up his pack to follow her and shot a

final glance back at the Black Warrior Valley. *What on earth happened back there?*

Loud voices brought Smoke Shield to wakefulness. He pried his eyes open and glanced around. Lazy smoke rose from the fire pit, and Morning Dew, in a gray dress, sat in her corner. She stared listlessly at her hands, turning them this way and that, as though transfixed.

Gods, he was growing tired of her. For moons he had looked forward to beating her down, breaking her. Instead, she'd simply been compliant. Nothing he did brought more than a nod and submission. In the face of threats, she had numbly accepted that she was his to do with as he pleased. What a disappointment. Even his troublesome wives were more entertaining.

He tossed to his back, flipping the thin hide from his body. The voices down the hall were louder now.

"What is all that?" he growled. But Morning Dew remained oblivious. Well, he'd relieve himself and provide her with a reason to be animated. Then, later, he'd bring her Screaming Falcon's male parts—see if that final humiliation provoked some response. He wanted her in tears, or perhaps rage—anything but this emotionless obedience. Mulling his dissatisfaction, he had just stepped to the chamber pot when Thin Branch called, "War Chief? We need you."

"Coming," he barked, lifting the bowl to take his hot urine. He finished, grabbed up his apron, and ordered, "Empty that." He cast one final glance at her wooden expression, growled to himself, and ducked into the hallway. A pile of cloth would have been more responsive.

In the main room, Flying Hawk was listening to a distraught Blood Skull. From the high minko's posture, whatever had happened wasn't good.

"What is it? The Albaamaha?" Smoke Shield demanded as he stalked into the room.

"Perhaps, War Chief." Blood Skull shot him a glance, his face livid. "The prisoners . . . they're all dead!"

"What?" Smoke Shield came to a sudden stop. "How?"

"Stabbed in the heart." Blood Skull's fists were knotted into hard balls. "It looks like an angry warrior did it. Someone with vengeance on his mind."

"The Albaamaha wouldn't dare!" Flying Hawk sputtered.

"What about the guard?" Smoke Shield demanded.

Blood Skull worked his fists. "He saw nothing but fog, War Chief. You still can't see more than a man's length in any direction."

"Tracks?" Flying Hawk demanded.

Blood Skull shook his head. "By now so many people have tracked through the blood that you can't see anything."

"When I find out who did this, *they will pay*!" Smoke Shield roared.

Flying Hawk sighed. "Perhaps some Chahta sneaked in to rob us of our victory."

Smoke Shield shook his head. "No, they would have cut the bonds, tried to rescue their leaders." He glared at Blood Skull. "Five of them! And the guard didn't see a thing?"

"He did not, War Chief." Blood Skull's jaw muscles had bunched like angry mice. "He swears that he walked back and forth all night long, but that he couldn't see a thing. He only became suspicious when he noticed the blood with the first faint light. Then he checked each of the captives and came running to me."

"You know this man?" Flying Hawk asked.

"My cousin. He's a good man. Not given to laziness or sloth."

"I'll take a piece of his hide for this!" Smoke Shield roared.

"With all respect, War Chief," Blood Skull shot back, "discipline is mine. He's of *my* clan. We will attend to it."

Before Smoke Shield could draw breath, Flying Hawk had lifted a hand, stilling any further outburst. "We do not need this. Someone has played the fox to our rabbit. We need not turn on ourselves."

"This cousin of yours, he must have heard something?" Smoke Shield asked.

"I asked the same thing," Blood Skull replied. "He said he often heard groans, gasps, and cries. What do you expect? The men hung in the squares. Some had been burned, others cut."

"And the sudden silence?" Flying Hawk asked.

Blood Skull shook his head. "Sometimes there are periods of it. Men faint. Sometimes they nap." He raised his eyes to Flying Hawk's. "In the end we can say that they are dead, that's all."

"Gods," Smoke Shield muttered, drawing his breath. "First the Albaamaha send a runner to warn the White Arrow, and then they do *this* to us?"

"If it was the Albaamaha," Blood Skull reminded.

"Oh, it was them," Smoke Shield said firmly. "You can bet on it. This is a provocation. They are pushing us, testing our limits."

Boiling with anger, he turned, stomping toward his room. At the door hanging he ran full into Morning Dew on her way out. In the collision, the bowl she carried sloshed, spilling his urine down her front and over his arm. Shaking droplets in every direction, he glared at her, grabbed her by the collar of her dress, and tossed her rudely out into the hallway. The chamber pot shattered into fragments that bounced and pattered. Morning Dew slammed facefirst into the far wall, bounced off the matting, and sprawled atop the potsherds and urine.

Smoke Shield whirled as a frightened Thin Branch gaped, eyes wide. Smoke Shield jabbed a finger at him. "Bring my war club!" Then he stalked into his room to throw things as he searched for his bearhide cape and slung it around his shoulders. As he burst out into the hallway, Thin Branch was helping Morning Dew to her feet; the slave woman had a bloody nose. She was dabbing at it, crimson smearing her fingers. Thin Branch was staring at the urine stains and broken pottery. "Clean up this gods-cursed mess! And someone get this woman *out of my way!*"

"Where should I put her?" Thin Branch asked meekly.

"Send her to my wife, for all I care!"

Then he bulled his way out into the fog-shrouded morning to make his own inspection of the dead captives.

Flying Hawk watched Smoke Shield's actions through narrowed eyes. Gods, would he act that way when he was finally confirmed as high minko? His own anger was stewing like an overcooked broth. He ground the few teeth he had left and flexed the muscles in his arms. Then he shot a glance at Blood Skull, who stood, gaze averted in embarrassment.

After Smoke Shield's exit, Flying Hawk took a breath to calm himself and stated, "You would think Screaming Falcon was *his* captive, wouldn't you?"

"The war chief is distraught, High Minko."

"So are we all." Flying Hawk walked over and retrieved his cougarhide cape. "Come, let us see for ourselves what has transpired. And perhaps together we can calm Smoke Shield before he breaks something more important than a chamber pot."

As Heron Wing walked through the cold white haze toward her house, her son at her side, she considered what she had seen. The captives had been killed with a single deep thrust to the heart. The act had been simple execution. What perplexed her wasn't the why of it, but that each of the captives had been castrated, apparently after the fact since the guard had heard none of the men screaming. And men—no matter how battered, cold, and weak—screamed when their male parts were sliced off.

Even more surprising, the missing pieces were nowhere to be found. Usually they were stuffed in the man's mouth, stomped on the ground, or somehow publicly mutilated. The bodies had shown none of the usual signs of such degradation.

What sort of person would take the genitals from all five men? That single fact would seem to indicate that the killer had sought some sort of revenge, but for what? The rape of a wife or daughter by a Chahta sometime in the past?

Warriors, when raiding, studiously avoided any sexual activity while on the war trail, fearing it would diminish their war medicine. Once a captive woman was taken, however, she was considered property. Everyone accepted that she would be used sexually. No, this was more serious—it pointed to a soul sickness, a surrender to the forces of chaos.

Or witchcraft. And that thought sent a shiver down her spine. She glanced uneasily at the surrounding fog as she left the plaza and approached her house. Witches liked fog. They could travel about in secret and work their evil without fear of discovery.

She glanced down at her son, thinking about what he had seen. She had wanted him to view the bloody bodies. One day he would be a warrior, and knowing the realities of war and death at an early age left a child with no illusions about life and the ways of Power.

What concerned her was how he perceived the reaction of the crowd. They had been enraged, frightened, and dismayed. The idea that unknown enemies could walk in their midst, flout the authority of the Sky Hand People, and commit such an atrocity put everyone on edge. Such passions, when mixed between the people's souls, could burn out of control. Would that knowledge frighten Stone?

"Are you all right?" she asked.

Stone nodded. "It was scary."

"Yes, it was."

"Whoever did this must be punished."

"They must," she agreed. "Do you understand why?"

"Because they defied us."

"That's right. But there is more to it."

"It's because of Power?"

"Why would that be?"

Stone's forehead lined. "Because killing the prisoners shifts Power out of balance. It encourages chaos and disorder."

"That it does. What did you think about the way people responded?"

"They were mad. Just like Father."

She had stood with one hand on Stone's shoulder and watched Smoke Shield pacing in anger, his war club swinging dangerously. Finally, Flying Hawk, Blood Skull, and Pale Cat had arrived and taken her husband to the side. The four of them had talked, heads together, nodding occasionally, before the tishu minko arrived. Moments later, Seven Dead had walked out, calling for the Council to assemble in the tchkofa. In the meantime, more guards had been posted to ensure that the angry crowd didn't do more damage to the bodies.

"I want you to stay close to the house for a couple of days. If you want to go and visit Grandmother, you come and tell me first. If your friends want you to go play, you tell them you can only play where I can see and hear you. Do you understand?"

He looked up at her, his dark brown eyes large. The black thatch of his hair was mussed. "Do you think there are witches loose like the people in the crowd were saying?"

"I don't know, Stone. But you stay close just the same.

And if you see anything strange, you come and tell me. One of the captives belonged to your uncle. We might be targets, too."

He gulped, nodding.

As her house emerged out of the thick mist, she could see Violet Bead and her two daughters. They waited by the door, talking with Wide Leaf.

"Is it true?" Violet Bead asked. "I just heard the news and thought I'd see if you knew anything before I walked over to see for myself."

"It is true indeed." Heron Wing looked back the way she had come. Shadowy figures could be made out moving through the fog. "No one knows who did this thing. Smoke Shield is mad enough to do something foolish. Charges of witchcraft are flying around like screech owls in the night. The Council is called. This could turn ugly in no time."

Violet Bead looked toward the plaza. They could hear angry shouts and something that sounded like a scuffle.

"Maybe I should take the girls home."

"That might not be a bad idea." Even as she said it, Thin Branch appeared out of the haze, Morning Dew walking a half pace behind him. "Now here's something."

Thin Branch called, "Greetings. You have heard?"

"And seen," Heron Wing told him. "Can you tell us anything?"

"Only that no one knows who did this thing. The war chief suspects the Albaamaha."

"These days he sees the Albaamaha behind everything." She shook her head. "I swear, if he tripped over a stone in the trail, he'd be pulling up the grass, suspecting an Albaamaha of hiding there to roll it into his way."

Thin Branch grunted noncommittally, and then asked, "You don't think they'd do it?"

"For what purpose?" Violet Bead asked. "They have nothing to gain by angering us."

"Perhaps the intent was to give them heart," Thin

Branch suggested. "This defiance might be a way of proving our vulnerability to less-radical leaders among them."

"Then it has turned against them," Violet Bead said darkly. "I, for one, say that we replace the Chahta in the squares with Albaamaha mikkos if it turns out that some of their people were responsible."

Heron Wing shook her head. "Do that and our land will be burning within the moon. We will be so busy trying to keep the Albaamaha subdued that Yuchi, Chahta, and Talapoosie war parties will be slipping down every trail to take advantage of our confusion."

She watched her words strike home. Weakness was the last thing they could afford. Every chiefdom in the surrounding regions would smell it, and their warriors would be close behind, seeking to exploit Sky Hand confusion for slaves, scalps, and booty. Should another town suffer the fate of Alligator Town, and have its granaries burned, the ensuing food shortage would fan the flames of chaos, leading to famine and intervillage raiding that would follow as neighbors turned on each other to feed their families.

Heron Wing glanced at Morning Dew to see her reaction. The woman had a stunned, disbelieving expression on her blood-smeared face. No wonder. She'd been in Smoke Shield's bed for days. That would be enough to stun anyone. On top of that she had just learned that her husband was dead. The wonder was that she could muster the energy to walk.

Heron Wing asked Thin Branch, "Why have you come?"

"The war chief has sent you this woman. He asks you to keep her for him."

Wide Leaf made a hissing sound, her expression turning sour.

Heron Wing shot her slave a reproving look before asking, "And what am I supposed to do with her?"

"Whatever you need her to do. I will come for her whenever my master sends for her."

"I take it the war chief will provide food for her from his stores? Or does he expect her meals to come out of Panther Clan granaries?"

"My master didn't say, but were I his wife—the slave being his property—I would imagine the answer would be self-explanatory."

"You assume a great deal."

Thin Branch shrugged noncommittally. "If you have no other use for me I will be off to the tchkofa in case my master has need of me." With that he bowed, and turned on his heel.

Heron Wing shot a dubious glance in Morning Dew's direction, then turned back to Violet Bead. "With charges of witchcraft on the air, I would be most cautious."

"Indeed, I will." She gathered her daughters. "Come, let us be off. There's no telling what might be flying around here." She cast a glance at the fog, shuddered, and marched her girls toward home.

Heron Wing lifted an eyebrow. "Have you eaten today, Morning Dew?"

"No." The woman kept her gaze fixed vacantly on the ground. She kept rubbing her hands together, as if subconsciously trying to clean them. Heron Wing usually had the same impulse after touching Smoke Shield.

"We have some of that pumpkin bread left over from this morning's meal." Heron Wing gave her son enough of a shove to start him toward the door. She watched Stone and then Wide Leaf step inside. To Morning Dew she said, "I'll say this. You're back in record time. And walking on your own two feet, too." She studied the woman. "Your nose is still bleeding."

"He threw me against the wall."

"I don't see any bruises or cuts."

"He didn't beat me." She was scrubbing at her hands again.

Looking closely, Heron Wing could see blood in her cuticles. She gave the woman a sly smile. "That he has lost interest so quickly is most unusual, but then, perhaps he underestimated you. You should be proud."

When Morning Dew looked up, tears were welling in her eyes, her jaw trembling. "After the things I . . ." In a broken voice she whispered, "I'll never be proud again."

Twenty-four

Two Petals stood, her feet on the sandy shore. Small waves from the Tenasee reached for her before sinking back into the river. She stared after the Kaskinampo. They were wasting no time on their journey home. Their paddles rising and falling, the Kaskinampo rounded a distant bend. When the last canoe vanished, she was alone with the river, aware of its Spirit winding back and forth across the muddy bottom. She could sense it fingering the rocks, moss, and mud as it slipped this way and that within the confines of its banks. Did it long for freedom from the imprisoning shores? Did it chafe as it rubbed against the banks?

The world slowed. The Kaskinampo were gone. She closed her eyes, breathing more easily, thankful for the respite.

I need to be alone.

The disembodied voices whispered around her, just beyond her hearing for the moment.

"The northern Yuchi outpost, a place called Cattail Town, is a half-day's paddle upriver. You should reach it by high sun tomorrow," Buffalo Mankiller had told them after landing at the sandy beach. The sun had been low in the west, casting the shadows of trees into the murky river water.

"You could camp with us," Old White had offered. "I know your men are tired." Fatigue had lain like a map on the old man's face.

Two Petals understood. Their travel through the

Kaskinampo lands had been like a flurry. Buffalo Mankiller had pushed his young men—marching like a war chief during the portages, timing their travel so that camp was made at a distance from the towns, and always in isolated locations.

Two Petals knew why: The Kaskinampo feared them.

What do they know of fear?

Images of the visions slipped through her souls. She closed her eyes. Her souls twisted inside her, struggling to be free. But they, like the rest of her, were bound as if by rawhide. She relived a vision of water closing over her, her body riding down into the depths. Around her, rainbow colors shone and blazed as sunlight played through the water.

Voices hissed and laughed, urging her to run.

"You must survive the trial, if you are ever to find your husband," one of the voices said.

She opened her eyes to see the half-man–half-deer figure of Deer Man standing on the water. He was watching her, eyes glowing yellow, antlers rising from the top of his head. He stood on the moving liquid, waves washing through his feet.

"I know."

"Are you strong enough?"

"I have seen the end. I know the final Dance."

"But is your husband real? Or illusion?" Deer Man asked.

"I don't know."

"Beware of the blind man. He has Power all his own."

A tendril of fear wound around her. For a moment, she felt lost, disconnected. Her souls floated like a canoe cast adrift on the current.

She started, hearing Trader's voice behind her. It intermingled with the whisperings of Power that hovered around her. She bowed her head, souls crying silently within her. It was all so impossible. Power lied. She knew that. But truth and falsehood were woven through the universe like threads in a fine fabric.

When she looked up, Deer Man was as gone as the Kaskinampo.

She had felt incredible relief as Trader and Old White had doled out the Trade, handing each piece to Buffalo Mankiller before he extended it to one of the young men who had labored so hard to pull them upriver. Each piece had been valuable—enough to compensate the men more than fairly for their labor and danger.

She shivered, aware that she was being watched. For a moment she thought it was Deer Man, but no such figure stood upon the water. Looking around, she could see no one. Behind her, in the camp, Trader and Old White huddled over a fire. So who had eyes upon her? Cocking her head, she listened as the rustling whisper of the voices grew still. She sniffed, reached out, and fingered the air as if to touch the Watcher's presence. Then she placed the familiarity.

She turned her head, looking upriver. *The blind man has Power all his own. He is there, watching you.*

Deer Man's warning, however, wasn't unexpected. In the Dream Vision, she had seen the blind man and felt his startled reaction to her awareness of him. He was old, gray haired, and wore a cloth tied around his sightless eyes. The skin that she could see bore hideous burn scars, and the fingers were missing on his right hand. When he had looked up, Power came swirling out of the Dream to obscure his form. The last thing she saw was the beautiful shell gorget that he wore around his neck. In the middle was a circle that contained three spiraled arms that curled together in a point. The surrounding ring had been divided and contained eight smaller circles. The spaces between them were dotted, like stars. The edge had been scalloped, as if portraying clouds.

"Who are you?" he had called out from the shining haze that hid him.

"I am Two Petals," she had told him in return.

His Power had grown, and with it, he closed the portal through which she had seen him.

Sister Datura had just Danced away and clapped her hands.

He was close now. She had felt him as they traveled ever southward, but not like this. His presence hung there, just below the horizon, like a gathering black storm. Men were coming, warriors, their hands caressing weapons. Fear and worry burned brightly around their hearts. They were the Watcher's arms, reaching out to enfold her.

"Are you there?" she asked the empty river. "Can you hear me?"

She turned her head, listening, but for once the voices were silent. She could feel the Power in the world around her, changing, ebbing and flowing. The future that she knew as the past was moving inexorably around her. Something was coming, going, receding as it roared ever closer.

Swimmer's sniffing nose prodded at her leg, and she looked down to find warm brown eyes and a wagging tail. "There is no time for us, is there?"

Swimmer seemed happy with the moment.

Why can't I?

Her fingers reached out, curling into a tight grip. Try as she might, she could no more grasp the present than she could the very air around her.

Fragments of Song filtered through her souls, unbidden. Had the medicine box reacted to the blind man's attention? She remembered her amazement when she first heard the Singing. The lovely voice had risen on the night air, brought to life by Trader's gentle touch.

It knew it was going home.

She thought back to what had been; her gaze shifted longingly to the north, replaying the unwinding of the rivers she had traveled. In the eye of her souls, she imagined her house, Father, the familiar forests and fields where she had lived.

I will never go home.

A shiver washed down her spine, and someone's hard

gaze burned into her back. Wheeling, she turned, staring upriver, fully expecting to see the blind man standing there.

The riverbank was empty but for Swimmer and the beached canoes.

Old White glanced at Two Petals where she stood outlined against the river, her slender body no more than a silhouette. He sighed and inspected the camp, an aching weariness in his bones. Buffalo Mankiller had worn him out as he pushed from dark camp to dark camp. Rations had been one hastily cooked meal at night and cold dried meat, nuts, or whatever he could pull out of the sacks during the day.

"You'd think he didn't like our company," Trader said as he laid out tinder and used his fire bow to create a smoking ember. This he carefully scooped into the twigs and crushed leaves, blowing to coax a flame.

"It must have been something I said." Old White stepped over, then groaned as he lowered himself onto one of the packs. He stared at the medicine box, remembering how Trader had been able to lay the heavy copper plate inside it.

Which had been formed to fit the other? The copper that they had pounded into a square could not have been more perfectly fitted had they measured it. The box was the last thing he had expected when Buffalo Mankiller had come walking out of the darkness. How long had it been since he'd seen the box last? Fifty winters? More? He'd been so young that day.

"You want to tell me about that box?" Trader asked, looking up from the fire. "Your eyes have been on it constantly, your expression like you were watching a live tie snake." He pointed a finger. "And how could Two Petals hear it Singing?"

Old White stared at the wood, tracing its patterns with his gaze. He began in a soft voice: "The last time I saw that box it was on my father's back when he marched away to war. It was a grand spring morning. He led a party of forty warriors north to drive the Yuchi out of our lands. The women were Dancing, clapping their hands. The Power of war filled all of us. We were so certain that Power favored us. I had no idea that my life was about to be turned upside down. None of us did."

"Ah, so your father was a war chief? Finally, the Seeker speaks."

"Two of his party returned. My father never did." He paused, seeing Trader's pinched expression. "That was but the first of a series of calamities."

"As a child, I remember hearing about a lost medicine box."

"Many have been lost over the years. This was not the first, and I'm sure it won't be the last."

Trader was figuring in his mind, adding the years up, no doubt. He finally asked, "How old were you?"

"That is the earliest memory I have. I just recall the sunlight shining on that seeing eye in the middle of the hand. I remember thinking that I would be a great warrior one day; and that I, too, would carry this box off to war against our enemies." He chuckled, feeling the weariness riding his bones. "Children have such limited understanding."

"Want to tell me the rest?"

"When the time is right."

"Ah, yes," Trader said sarcastically. "I should have known." He shook his head, tired too. "This whole silly venture is mad."

"Madness is only the other face of sanity."

"Gods, you're starting to sound like Two Petals."

"I wish I could see it as clearly as she does."

"That's it. I'm going to go drown myself in the river." Trader lurched to his feet, stalking off toward the forest.

"River's the other way," Old White offered.

"Don't remind me," Trader called over his shoulder.

Old White stared at the box, hearing branches snapping in the darkness beneath the trees as Trader gathered wood. Somewhere an owl hooted to greet the coming night.

Firelight bathed the medicine box. It accented the carvings, casting shadows into the grooves. The images on the wood wavered and Danced in the warm light. The Seeing Hand seemed to watch him with a penetrating stare.

You have come back to me. Why?

Tomorrow they would land at a Yuchi town. He realized that they would know exactly what the medicine box was, and what it signified.

Two Petals walked up. Swimmer—feet and legs wet—wagged his tail by her side.

"Are you as worn out as I am?" he asked.

"Wide awake," she told him. Her head tilted. "I can see that you're not worried about the Yuchi."

"Oh, not at all." He glanced up. "Got any advice?"

She paused, her eyes going vacant. "The Watcher's arms are reaching out for us. A thousand souls will be unleashed. Can souls float on a flood?" She winced, as if pained. "You can see them, can't you?"

"Who?" he asked.

She pointed upriver. "The blind man's fingers. Right there. Reaching out."

"What blind man?"

"The one who is watching me."

He sighed. "What about Trader's medicine box?"

"No medicine in that."

"Oh, yes. There's a heap of medicine there."

"The box Sings of want and desire, fear and anxiety. Like keeping a rattlesnake for the sole purpose of admiring its colors. Is it safer to keep it in a jar, or let it loose to be encountered who knows where?"

"That's what worries me." The notion of finding the box and losing it again was more than his souls could bear.

"It's using you for legs," she told him cryptically.

"Legs? Me?" He stared down at his withered shanks.

Her eyes cleared, and she gave him a weary smile. "We had best give it to them. Hand it right over. We're not Traders, after all. Too meek. No courage here."

"So, if I get this straight, we just bluff our way through? Act like we're high minkos and demand respect?"

"Not even arrogance can Dance in the future without getting thorns in its feet," she told him positively. "We've got to be meek. Like mice in a jar. Scrambling, hiding. Don't want anyone to see us when the blind man closes his embrace."

Old White sighed and looked up as Trader appeared out of the gloom. "I've been talking to Two Petals."

"Glad I missed it."

"She's got a plan for the Yuchi."

"Better than drowning in the river?"

"Well, I guess that remains to be seen."

Trader dropped his armload of wood. "I can't wait to hear it."

"We're going to be the cockiest Traders on the river."

"Oh, really?"

"Absolutely." Old White swelled his chest. "After all, I'm the Seeker." He grinned with a confidence he didn't feel. "You know, I've been waiting all my life to boss a bunch of Yuchi around."

"Didn't your father go off to boss a bunch of Yuchi around once?"

Old White deflated like a punctured bladder. He stared up at Trader from under lowered brows. "You're as charming as a windstorm. Gods, let's get some supper cooked. Then I'm going to sleep until I wake up."

"Good," Trader noted dryly. "I'd hate to see you break old habits."

A thousand angry thoughts whirled around Smoke Shield's souls as he glared around the tchkofa's smoky interior. He could see the stewing anger in the other chiefs' eyes, could read it in their stiff expressions. The Power they had drawn to them with the success of the White Arrow Town raid was dissipating, robbed away by the murder of their captives. Action was demanded.

At his station, the tishu minko, Seven Dead, betrayed a poorly harnessed fury. Biloxi Mankiller had been his captive, and Smoke Shield knew the tishu minko had been looking forward to killing the whimpering fool at solstice. Now he only had body parts to pass around to his worthy Raccoon Clan warriors. Such trophies were carefully cleaned, sometimes turned into ornaments, and often buried with the dead as mementos of their valor on the war trail. Whatever was left over of Biloxi Mankiller would still be prestigious, but always tainted, the Power diminished by the premature murder of the captives.

The *Hopaye,* Pale Cat, stepped forward, a large whelk shell cup filled to brimming with steaming black drink. This he carefully placed beside the Eagle Pipe, and then prepared the latter, filling the bowl with tobacco and placing a punky stick in the fire. "Sister Tobacco, carry our words to the heavens, that all Powers may know the truth of what we say." Then he nodded to the sacred fire where it burned in the center of four logs. That seen to, he retreated to his station.

Flying Hawk, as high minko, was given first right to speak. He paused, leaning close to Smoke Shield, speaking softly. "I would remind you, Screaming Falcon was *my* captive. I would ask you not to act in Council as if he were yours."

Smoke Shield ground his teeth, jerked a terse nod, and watched his uncle step forward. The high minko knelt, drinking from the shell cup. Then he lit the pipe with the smoldering stick and drew smoke deeply into his lungs. When he exhaled, he called a prayer to the Spirits, and turned, looking from chief to chief.

"We know what has been done. Before coming here, I asked some of the warriors to patrol the city. In small bands of two and three, they are searching for any strangers, seeking anything out of the ordinary. I have already sent spies to inspect the few Trader camps at the canoe landing. I only know of a couple of Pensacola Traders up from Bottle Town. They came with loads of shell to Trade for sandstone paint palettes and fabrics. Another Trader, a Tallapoosie, left the day before the fog rolled in. I have sent a fast runner to see if he can catch the man. In this fog, I doubt the Tallapoosie made it very far. These things I have already done. Does anyone else have anything to offer this Council?"

Smoke Shield cleared his throat hoping to be recognized, but Flying Hawk nodded to old Night Star. The dwarf woman stepped forward, drank from the shell, and took a pull from the long pipe stem. She turned, but ignored Smoke Shield's simmering eyes as she surveyed the Council.

Her reedy voice rose. "If we are searching for culprits, I say that we send a large party of men to comb the territory between us and the Chahta. Looking at this as calmly as I can, I can think of no one else who would have reason to rob us of the captives' lives. I think we can dismiss the Pensacola Traders. They honor the Power of Trade, and they could care less who we torture, as long as it isn't their people." She looked around, sharp old eyes taking in the chiefs. "Some here might say the Pensacola have an interest in keeping good relations with the Chahta, and such an interest might have urged them to take such drastic measures. Yes, they do considerable Trade with the Chahta, and yes, the Chahta might think kindly of them for doing this thing. But, think a little further and you will realize—as I'm sure the Pensacola would—that eventually it will get back to us. Someday in the future, some foolish Chahta would brag about it. When that day came, the Pensacola are fully aware that we would turn our wrath upon them. So, while yes, the Pensacola Trade with the Chahta, they Trade more with us."

She gave them a thoughtful expression. "Again, if you are searching for a motive behind these murders, look no further than the Chahta. Do not waste your time looking for a large party, but for a single warrior, a lone man. He will be someone who could pass unseen, sneak into our city, do this thing, and slip away again."

Once again Flying Hawk ignored Smoke Shield by acknowledging Two Poisons. The Deer Clan chief drank, smoked, and offered his prayers. Then he said, "For the most part, I agree with Night Star. The Chahta have the most to gain from this. And if one of them did kill the captives, we will eventually learn of it. No man who has accomplished such a deed will be silent upon his return to his people. I know the Chahta. They are a proud and boastful people. The man who did this will be feted, feasted, and honored in many ways. Committing this crime against us is almost meaningless if it is not rubbed in our noses. My counsel is to wait. Within a moon, word will reach us one way or another. When it does, we can prepare properly. When the Chahta have grown complacent, we strike, sending a large war party to attack the town where the culprit lives. We may not be able to fill the squares with a high minko, a Priest, and a war chief, but where five squares now stand, we can fill ten or twenty." He looked around. "Consider this, my chiefs. Think carefully about it. Thoughtful planning will give us much more in the end than a rash act committed in a moment of rage."

When he sat, Flying Hawk acknowledged Wooden Cougar. The Crawfish Clan chief took his turn at the black drink and the Eagle Pipe. Only when he had offered his prayers did he face the Council. "Many of the dead at Alligator Town were Crawfish Clan. We rejoiced in the success of Smoke Shield's raid, and my people heaped indignities upon the captives, calling to the dead to come and see, to watch what we do to those who would kill them without provocation." He considered his next words. "I, too, suspect the Chahta first and foremost, but I have been a chief too long not to look for other explanations. I notice that this Council is called, but the Albaamaha are absent. Is there a reason for that, High Minko?"

Flying Hawk nodded. "Some have hinted that the Albaamaha might have been complicit in the killings. I made the decision that we should discuss this among ourselves."

It's about time the Albaamaha were brought up, Smoke Shield fumed.

"I wondered that very thing," Wooden Cougar said. "But if they are accused, should not their representatives be here to answer to the charges? I myself—though never completely trustful of Albaamaha—have doubts about their reasons for attempting such a thing. While many of the dead at Alligator Town were Crawfish Clan, a great many Albaamaha were killed there as well. How would it serve the Albaamaha dead to have their killers escape justice?"

Smoke Shield bounced from foot to foot, clearing his throat.

Flying Hawk turned. "It would seem that the fog has clogged my nephew's throat. Does he wish to speak as a means of clearing it?"

Smoke Shield stepped forward on charged muscles, bent, drank of the bitter black drink, and took a pull of the sweet smoke. He offered his fervent prayer and stood, letting his audience absorb the rigid muscles, his stiff posture. "I will tell you what races through the minds of the Albaamaha: the same thing that urged them to send a runner to warn White Arrow Town that we were about to attack. They chafe under our leadership, and would rather see themselves at the mercy of the Yuchi, the Pensacola, or the Chahta than protected by our warriors. When they come to Split Sky City, they do not see the grandeur of our works, but only note a blot on a land they think of as their own."

He stalked around in a circle, feeling the heat build inside him. "The time has come for us to wake up! The Albaamaha have been brooding long enough without a response from us. We have a choice. We can remind them of their position, or the next time they strike, it will not be to murder captives." He thrust a hard finger at each chief in turn, saying, "Will it be you? Or you? Or you? Which of us will be awakened from his sleep by a stab to the heart? They have proven they can slip through the night in obscurity, murder, and vanish again."

"What do you suggest we do?" Flying Hawk asked uncomfortably.

"I say we hang five of their mikkos in the squares until the person who did this comes forward. Let them see that Sky Hand vengeance is a thing to be reckoned with." He glanced at the worried chiefs. "You doubt me? Oh, no. I doubt it will take longer than a day of hearing their beloved mikkos moaning in the squares before the cunning Albaamaha offer us the perpetrator of this foul deed." He nodded firmly. "*That* is a language they will understand."

Flying Hawk appeared to be controlling his voice when he asked, "Does anyone wish to take the floor and add anything to this suggestion?"

Vinegarroon nodded, stepping forward. Smoke Shield gave him a piercing glare before yielding. The Skunk Clan chief knelt, sipping the black drink, then puffed from the pipe. When he turned, his ugly face was awash with uncertainty. He ran a hand through his bristly hair. "I am concerned by what I have heard here today. Concerned not only that someone would kill our captives, but by some of the suggestions as to who has done this thing. I do not question the suspicions about the Chahta. That I can understand. The Traders? No, I don't think so. They would never profit by such doings.

But I find myself most upset by the accusations against the Albaamaha."

Smoke Shield growled loudly enough that everyone could hear. It was rude, but he couldn't care less. Didn't the fool understand what was happening under his nose?

Vinegarroon took a moment, then said carefully, "Yes, an Albaamo was implicated in trying to warn the White Arrow. But that man is dead, killed before we could question him." He pointedly avoided Smoke Shield's burning gaze. "Myself, I have given this a great deal of consideration since we discussed the Albaamo traitor here last time. That he named only one accomplice, I think, tells us something." He paused. "This is not some grand Albaamaha conspiracy. Rather, this Paunch, for reasons of his own, dispatched young Crabapple to warn the White Arrow."

Smoke Shield snorted, receiving disapproving glances from the others.

Vinegarroon ignored him. "I believe this because had the Albaamaha mikkos been party to treachery, they would not have sent some foolish young man on a mission of such great importance. The Albaamaha are not stupid, and those who think them so do it at great risk."

Smoke Shield crossed his arms angrily.

"Do the Albaamaha chafe under our rule?" Vinegarroon looked calmly around the room. "Of course. Why wouldn't they? But they also realize that we are the ones who stand between them and the Yuchi, the Chahta, and the other chieftains. Rather than hang their elders in the squares, I would ask them to Council with us. If they have grievances that are so pressing as to lead them to revolt, perhaps we can come to a mutual satisfaction."

"When they live in our palaces," Smoke Shield muttered under his breath.

Vinegarroon narrowed an eye, having heard. "The Albaamaha are a large and diverse population. Some, a few, are no doubt delighted to see us suffer any calamity. But most of the Albaamaha no more wish to infuriate us than we wish to infuriate them. If we overreact to the killing of the captives and it turns out that it was a Chahta who committed this crime against us, we will have played into the hands of the few. Why should we do the work of the malcontents?"

Vinegarroon looked around reasonably. "I have heard good counsel here today. Rather than act rashly and give the Albaamaha real reason to rebel against us, I urge this Council to show restraint. Let us wait, think this thing through, and allow all other trails to be followed before we commit some act that would turn even the most reasonable of the Albaamaha against us."

Smoke Shield ground his teeth as Vinegarroon took his seat, and Flying Hawk recognized Black Tail. The Hawk Clan chief attended the rituals and offered his prayers. Then he stood and looked around the Council. "The killing of the captives cannot go unpunished. On that I think we all agree. To allow this to pass without response would be an affront not only to our people, but to the brave warriors who ransacked White Arrow Town. But we must act with prudence and foresight."

Black Tail inclined his head when he met Night Star's gaze. "I personally think the Panther Clan chief is correct when she says that this was done by a Chahta. I would urge the Council to wait, to listen, and to learn. Then, when we discover who really murdered our captives, we must act swiftly, surely, and ruthlessly to punish the offender."

He turned to Vinegarroon. "However, I do not discount the possibility of Albaamaha perfidy. If, in the end, it turns out that the Albaamaha were responsible, we must take the appropriate measures." He lifted a hand. "However, we must also remember how we came to be here. When our Ancestors came to this land, we did it with Albaamaha support. Some welcomed us with open arms; others resisted. For generations we have ruled here, but we have done so through wisdom, strength of arms, and justice. The Skunk Clan chief speaks with wisdom."

Smoke Shield made no attempt to hide his irritation. Flying Hawk shot him a look of warning.

Black Tail added, "Let us say that it finally turns out that an Albaamo really did kill the captives. I doubt this, but let us assume it so for the moment. The Albaamaha expect us to act with wisdom, restraint, and justice. I said justice, my chiefs. If we are to avoid a calamity, we must punish only the culprit. Should we punish all the Albaamaha, or the wrong ones, Vinegarroon is right: We will incite a revolt."

Flying Hawk took a deep breath when Black Tail resumed his seat. "Is it my understanding that the consensus of the Council is to wait and learn what we can before making any decision?"

One by one, the chiefs nodded.

Smoke Shield's eyes narrowed. *Fools; by the time they come to a consensus, the Albaamaha will think themselves invincible.*

"Then we will wait, listen, and learn." He glanced around the room, finally ending with Smoke Shield. "Any final action will be taken with the approval of this Council. Is that understood by all?"

"It is," came a chorus of replies.

"Then, in the name of the gods, so be it," Flying Hawk concluded, his hard gaze fixed on Smoke Shield.

Twenty-five

In Trader's Dream Two Petals was Dancing, her naked body weaving in time to the lilting Song of the medicine box. As the melody rose and fell, she swayed and stepped to the music. Her smooth arms flowed with graceful movement, and her long black hair swirled and gleamed in the light. When she cast a glance over her bare shoulder, her eyes were sparkling. She whirled then, her gaze locked with his. Despite that, his attention was drawn to her breasts. Next he fixed on the dark dot of her navel. Her belly was flat, and each movement she made emphasized the thick tuft of her pubic hair. He let his eyes trail down her shapely legs. She Danced closer to him now, a knowing smile on her lips. As she circled him, hair swinging, hips gyrating, her fingertips traced the air around his body.

Trader's heart began to pound, blood racing in his veins. She flipped around in front of him, fully aware of his erect penis. Her agile hands began caressing the air around his hard shaft.

He gasped, raising his eyes to hers and finding them full of promise. The tingle began deep in his pelvis, anticipating the explosion of his loins.

It was at that moment that Swimmer barked, bringing him back from the brink to groggy wakefulness. The Dream shattered and fell away.

Trader opened his eyes and stared around. They were in camp, on a low tree-covered knoll. Blue hazy smoke rose from white ash in the fire pit. Swimmer was barking, growling, his back hair standing on end, tail like a lance as he fixed on something out in the forest.

Trader sat up, reaching for his weapons, and froze. Two Petals sat across from him on a log, her wide dark eyes fixed on his. He gulped, flushed with embarrassment. "Gods, did you do that to me?"

Her lips parted as if in anticipation. Then she said, "The blind man is embracing us."

He shook himself, breaking the gaze and turning his attention to Swimmer. "What's wrong, boy?"

Swimmer growled, barked, and retreated to Trader's side to stare out at the forest.

Old White muttered as he sat up, asking, "What's all the racket?"

"I think someone is out there," Trader told him, trying to shed the last fragments of the Dream.

"None of them are real," Two Petals said, her eyes now unfocused. "We can ignore them all. They're of no consequence."

"Who?" Trader asked, whipping his blanket off and standing. The morning sun was no more than finger high over the southeastern treeline. He searched the shadows, letting Swimmer bark to his content. Then he saw movement, the briefest glimpse of a man's head as he peered from behind a tree.

"At least one man," Trader noted as Old White stood, shivering in the cold air. The Seeker grabbed up a buffalo cape and hung it over his shoulders, then lifted his Trader's staff, with its long white feathers.

Walking to the edge of the camp, Old White held up his staff, shouting, "We travel in peace under the Power of Trade. Come, warm yourselves at our fire and share our hospitality."

For a long moment, the forest was silent. Then an order was barked. Trader had no idea what language it was. To his dismay, figures appeared—a lot of them. He glanced around, seeing movement in every direction.

"Hope they're friendly," Old White noted as warriors magically stepped out from every tree and bush.

"Who are you?" a voice called in Trade Tongue.

"I am Old White, often called the Seeker. With me is Two Petals, a Contrary, and the man is called Trader. We travel from the north with Trade."

A broad-shouldered warrior, short, with the body of a bear, stepped to the forefront, an arrow nocked in his bow. He wore a red war shirt, his face painted in red and black stripes. Oversize copper ear spools filled the lobes of his ears. A large bun—the hair wrapped over a bundle of cloth—stuck out from the back of his head. The cross-shaped sun symbol that decorated the chest of his war shirt was painted in bright red.

"Yuchi," Trader noted dryly. Just at first glance, he figured they were surrounded by no less than thirty warriors.

"Yuchi," Old White agreed.

The burly warrior was approaching slowly, his suspicious eyes darting this way and that, as if in anticipation of an ambush.

"There are only the three of us," Old White said reasonably over Swimmer's frantic barking. "By the Power of Trade, I swear that we are no threat."

"That remains to be seen," the man said warily. "I have been sent to find a Powerful witch that is coming to our country."

"You will find no witches here." Old White kept a smile on his face.

It was then that Two Petals stood, walking straight toward the warrior, saying, "He is calling for me."

The warrior pulled his arrow back, expression sharpening. "Come no closer!"

"Two Petals!" Old White cried in horror. "No! I mean yes! Um, go, run. Gods, do something!"

She stopped short, head tilted as she studied the wide-eyed warrior. "When your arrow pierces my chest, the blind man will be so pleased with the answers to his questions. He hasn't seen me yet."

"What blind man?" Trader asked, his hands held wide so that no warriors would get the wrong idea.

The burly man swallowed hard, barking another command. His warriors stood like statues, eyes flint-like, arrows drawn.

Old White growled under his breath, stepping out to place himself between Two Petals and the thick warrior. "She is a *Contrary*! What she says is backward. It's the Power that fills her. You do understand a Contrary, don't you?"

The burly warrior nodded, swallowed hard, and released the tension on his arrow. "What is your purpose in our lands?"

"We come bearing Trade. Nothing more. We wish only to pass through the lands of the Children of the Sun, and we will be gone to the south. To do so, we offer Trade, and would hire some of your young men to pull us upstream, and perhaps pay for portage into the head of the Horned Serpent River. That is all."

The man hesitated before asking, "How do I know that you will not witch us?"

"We are *not* witches," Trader cried. "By the gods, see the staff that Old White holds? Why would you think we are witches?"

"Because we have been sent to find a witch," the warrior replied. He glanced past Old White at Two Petals. "And we seem to have found the woman that our Kala Hi'ki described."

Old White turned, looking at Two Petals. "Is this right?"

"Their blind man saw me." Her eyes had lost focus. "I saw him when he disappeared." She reached out, fingers caressing the air in a way that made Trader flinch—it was hauntingly similar to what she'd done in his Dream.

"There," she said. "You can touch him."

Old White glanced at the warrior. "This Priest of yours, he is blind?"

The warrior nodded. "He sees the Spirit World. He has seen this woman coming."

"We wish the Children of the Sun no harm," Old White insisted.

The warrior ground his teeth, muscles in his jaw flaring. Then he came to a decision. "I think it would be best if we kill you here. That way there is no chance that you can work evil on us."

Old White drew himself to his fullest and tapped his Trader's staff on the ground. "If you do that, you will break the Power of the Trade." He lifted a finger, pointing. "If this Prophet of yours is so Powerful, take us to him! If he is truly a man of Power, he will know who and what we are."

Gods, the old man has lost his souls to madness! Don't anger them more!

The warrior continued to hesitate. Trader's heart skipped as he glanced sidelong at the ring of warriors. What couldn't have been more than a couple of breaths' duration seemed like half of his life.

The warrior turned, barked an order, and a young man spun on his heel, leaving at a high run. "Very well, you will get your wish. The Kala Hi'ki will decide what to do with you." A hard smile curled the man's lips. "But if you are wrong about this, you might end up longing for a quick death here in the forest, rather than what awaits foreign witches in our captivity."

"You are a wise man," Old White said with relief.

One of the warriors off to Trader's left gasped, pointing at the medicine box. The war leader glanced, squinted, and paled. He spoke in Yuchi, and the rest of the warriors replied in awe.

"Where did you get that?" he asked.

"In Trade from the Kaskinampo."

The war leader's eyes narrowed. "We know that med-icine. Once it was ours, and then stolen. Now it seems to have come back to us."

Trader felt his gut sink. The copper, the box—all of it was gone. He considered his bow where it lay just out of reach. "The box is mine," he said through gritted teeth.

"All in time, Trader," Old White remarked sternly. "Let this wise war leader take us to his Prophet. If the man is as Powerful as they believe, he will understand the reason why we have to take it south."

"Oh, I am a very wise war chief," the burly warrior assured him. "We will watch as you load your posses-sions into your canoes. You will wear only your cloth-ing, with no pouches, bundles, or fetishes with which to curse us. At the first sign of witchcraft, we will kill you and throw your bodies into the river. There, your pollu-tion will wash down to bedevil the Kaskinampo."

Old White turned to Two Petals. "Do you understand what he is saying? You must be very careful. Your life, and ours, will depend upon it."

Two Petals' voice carried a deadly calm. "Power Dances—but ever so carefully—to see what will hap-pen."

"Move," the war chief ordered. "And please, make a mistake. I am already regretting this decision to carry you and your pollution any farther into our lands."

W ell," Old White mused, "that wasn't so bad."

He watched the Yuchi archers watching him. He could have given a halfhearted toss of a pebble and landed it in their canoe. The war chief had taken no chances, hav-ing them load their packs into the rear of the canoe, leaving only enough room for Trader, Two Petals, and himself in the front of Trader's birch-bark vessel. Ahead of them, at the end of a rope, the Yuchi warriors bent their backs to the paddles, heading south along the backwaters.

"My copper," Trader sighed as he stared listlessly at the gray forest passing slowly past. "I have searched all my life for a piece like that. Then I find the medicine box, and lose them both." He paused. "I didn't even put up a fight."

"Breathing has something to be said for it." Old White glanced at the canoe full of warriors paralleling them. "Like the joy of being able to continue doing it."

"We're moving so slowly," Two Petals added where she perched on a pack.

"They don't even trust Swimmer," Trader noted, reaching back to scratch his dog's ears.

"I wouldn't refer to him as Demon Dog," Old White said dryly.

"There's a reason I called him Swimmer."

"And to think I considered you slow-witted."

"Well, if it were up to my wits, we wouldn't be in this situation."

"I didn't notice you coming up with anything back there."

Trader gave him a scowl.

Old White turned to Two Petals. "I would know about this blind man."

"He appeared in the Dream," she said absently. "He only wore Power. Shimmering and shining. He looked up through his blindness and saw me. He watched me all the way upriver."

"A blind man watched you?" Trader mused. "Let's see, in Contrary talk, that means a man with sight didn't see you, correct?"

Two Petals glanced at him. "You know everything."

Trader sighed, his gaze fastening on his canoe where his precious copper rode.

Old White allowed his own attention to focus there. What was Power's purpose to give them the medicine box, only to take it away again? None of it made sense.

"Two Petals, describe this blind man."

She looked down at her hands. "He lives in the light; it shines in his eyes. He has come through fire and water, his flesh alive. I could feel his gaze from a great distance."

"And you didn't tell us?"

"None of this was meant to happen," she replied. "You didn't have to be arrogant when the warriors arrived. We could have been meek. Like little voles hiding in the grass."

"Yes," Trader said mockingly, "we didn't have to be sound asleep when they arrived, either."

"Dying is a different way to live," Two Petals said softly. Then she looked out at the water. "I don't know how Deer Man can stand out there." She cocked her head, eyes fixed on a spot on the water. Then she frowned as if listening to some voice beyond their hearing. "Only Dancing keeps you from sinking?" She smiled. "That's why you're skipping your feet." A pause. "That's right. Kick out the droplets of water."

Trader shook his head. "We're all going to die."

Two Petals ignored him, expression on the swirling waters. "Is it going to be bad?" Then she nodded, her shoulders slumping.

"Two Petals?" Trader asked. "What's going on?"

Old White arched an eyebrow. "Whomever she's talking to, this is Power, Trader. Let it play out."

"Power is known to be capricious at best." Trader snorted derisively. "But for Power, I would have a wife, home, and position." He paused, adding bitterly, "Why am I even here?"

"To set things right," Old White answered. "That's why we're all here. You just have to trust yourself, that's all."

"I'll trust myself before I trust to Power."

Old White winced at the anger buried in the young man's voice. "Trader, you wish to possess what is not yours. Nothing, especially copper, ever belongs to you. It only passes through your hands to another."

"I could be buried with copper," he shot back. "I could have it with me forever."

Old White let him stew for a while before he said, "I saw a grave once, in the bank of the Red Earth River down in Caddo country. The river had changed course, eating away at an abandoned mound. The graves were all spilling into the river. Bones, stone and shell ornaments, fine fabrics—they were all washing away. Even the copper."

"This is supposed to make me feel better?"

"It is supposed to remind you that the only possessions you ever really have are your souls. Eventually, even your bones will vanish as if they'd never been."

Trader narrowed an eye. "Then how can you even be sure of the souls?"

"I can't. Which is all the more reason to live well while you are living."

"Like Trading my copper among the Natchez or Tunica like I had originally intended?"

"Assuming Power meant for you to do that." His voice turned mild. "I suspect that we are where we are supposed to be right now."

"Is it all so simple for you?"

Old White couldn't help but notice how worried Two Petals had become. She had lowered her gaze to her hands, where they fluttered in mirror motions. The Spirit she'd seen Dancing on the water had warned her of something unpleasant. No doubt about it.

To Trader he asked, "Did you ever see a Healer perform a sucking cure? You know, when he places a tube to a sick man's side and sucks on it?"

"Don't be a silly rabbit," Trader muttered. "Of course I have. He uses sleight of hand to drop some object—a bloody feather, a bit of bone or something—into the bowl so that the sick man thinks it was drawn out of his body."

"Do you know why?"

"To make the man think something was shot into him

to cause the sickness." Trader gave him a hard look. "They've done it to me on occasion. It's just a trick."

"No," Old White insisted. "It isn't." He made a dismissive gesture with his hand. "Oh, I thought so, too, once upon a time. But I didn't understand. Not until I was trained by a Tlingit shaman."

"Ah." Trader rolled his eyes. "Then, you'll enlighten me?"

Old White glanced thoughtfully at the water off to the side, where Two Petals had seen her mysterious Deer Man. "Where we see one world, there are two. Our world—the one we see, touch, smell, and taste—and the Spirit World, where Power flows and Dances. We live separate from the Spirit World, Trader. It is parallel to our own, surrounding us, intermixed with ours."

"So what does that have to do with a shaman sucking a bloody bone from my thigh when I have an ache in my leg?"

"A Healer has to trick the Spirit of the ache into leaving you. That's what the tube is all about. He places a bit of bone in his mouth, then bites the inside of his lip to make it bleed. Washed in blood, the bone becomes an enticing home for the Spirit. Don't you see? He uses it as a lure, a more tempting prize for the pain. By drawing it from you to the bit of bone, he can remove it, and then dispose of it in a fire, or bury it."

"Then why doesn't he just tell the sick man that's what he's doing?"

"Because he believes, and you don't. So he gives you a reason to believe. Your souls can overcome their reluctance to heal. That's why Two Petals can see Spirit People, because she isn't blinded by this world. She accepts the reality of the Spirit World around her. She does not question."

"But I do? Is that what you're telling me?"

"Don't you?" Old White asked.

Trader snorted to himself and crossed his arms.

Old White sighed, leaning back. *We're quite the companions, aren't we?*

He tried to still his souls, to find the peace he needed. From Two Petals' depressed and worried expression, her invisible Deer Man had told her something terrible was coming. Old White need only look to the side where the wary Yuchi paddled to have an inkling of just what the terrible thing would be.

The Yuchi warriors did not stop at Cattail Town, but hustled right past it, the warriors waving off any inquisitive canoes that came out to inspect the armada. From there on, they were in populated country; the river terraces had been denuded of trees, occasional farmsteads just visible above the banks. Here and there patterns of stakes marked fish weirs, and canoes of fishermen waved warily as they passed, then went back to casting their nets in the shallows.

They passed more towns, the settlements fortified with palisades and one or two platform mounds with square, thatch-roofed buildings visible behind the stockades. Any patch of arable ground had been cleared, and one or two houses were always in sight.

"The Yuchi are doing well," Trader observed, recovered from his irritation. "I don't remember so many people the last time I went through here."

"How long ago was that?"

"Ten years?" Trader studied the fields. "When I was a child, the Yuchi were a force to be reckoned with. They must be a real threat now."

"Like fluff in the wind," Two Petals told him emotionlessly. "You aren't meant to see this. Forget it . . . cast it from your thoughts. The Children of the Sun are meaningless."

Trader's expression hardened. "I'll keep that in mind."

She stared at him, head cocked expectantly. "Forget, forget. Do that and you won't have to remember anything." She grew puzzled. "Remembering, it's like cutting squares in old fabric." Then she laughed ironically. "You can put your fingers through the holes."

Trader didn't look happy as he turned his attention back to Old White's canoe, where his precious medicine box and its wealth of copper lay.

Daylight was a fading memory when they finally passed the mouth of a large creek, its swampy confluence thick with young bald cypress. A short distance beyond, a section of the high bluff had slumped and was used as a landing. Tens of canoes were pulled up below a cluster of houses, granaries, and ramadas. In every direction the land was bare, denuded for either cornfields, firewood, or building materials. On the breeze coming from the southwest, Old White could smell the familiar odors of a city: smoke, cooking food, human waste, and humanity.

"What is this place?" he called to the Yuchi as they were brought into the landing.

"Rainbow City," the war chief called back. "You will wait in your canoes until I receive instructions from the Kala Hi'ki."

Old White sighed, wondering if he'd end up bristling with arrows should he try to stand to ease the cramps in his old legs.

Two young men, dressed in white aprons, appeared from the gloom. In the torchlight, one walked up. He was tall, with clear eyes, his face painted in black and yellow. A long copper pin ran through the twist of hair on the back of his head. Holding up a beautiful quill-work bag, he muttered a slow incantation, then watched for some reaction.

Old White lifted an eyebrow as the young man studied him. In Trade Tongue, he said, "Whatever the warding was, it didn't work."

The young Priest lowered the bag. "What sort of beings are you?"

Old White grunted as he clambered out of the beached canoe, offered his hand to Two Petals, and let Trader climb out by himself. Turning, he reached back for his staff. When finally composed, he said, "I am Old White, known as the Seeker. With me is Two Petals, a Contrary. The man is known along the rivers as Trader. Under the Power of the Trade, I swear to you that we are here to commit no mischief. Our goal is to Trade, hire labor to carry us upstream, and make a portage into the Horned Serpent River."

"You are bound by the Power of Trade?" the man asked.

"I am. So are my companions."

He turned his eyes on Two Petals. "And you are the Contrary?"

"Not me," she muttered darkly. "It's everyone else who is confused." She stepped toward him. The young man must have trusted his medicine Power, for he did not back away. She looked into his eyes. "You have no idea what is happening, do you? You're all staring backward. Everything is moving." She pointed out at the dark river. "Can't you see them Dancing out there?"

His expression didn't change. "Beings with great Power have come to my land. My master, the Kala Hi'ki, and I would know why."

"A drop of blood leaps to the sky," she said. "I'm sure you would have no fear of that."

The faintest flicker showed at the corner of his mouth. "We would return to our mother."

"Your direction is forward. Mine is past. Front has become back, and your mother scrambles from the west. Even she seeks to return to the womb." Two Petals smiled. "I died when I became Contrary. I grow younger by the moment." She hesitated. "There, his gaze is sharpening. Even now I am the center of his vision." She raised her voice and called out, "You cannot know me through your sight."

"Who do you talk to?" the young man asked, refusing

to stare around at the air like the nervous warriors were doing.

"I talk to the blind man with such sharp eyes." She laughed. "Things are so much clearer in darkness." Then her expression changed to wonder. "I think he is the most beautiful man I have ever seen."

Old White and Trader cast nervous glances at each other.

The Priest nodded to himself. "Bring them. I will take them to the Kala Hi'ki."

"Are you sure that's wise?" The muscular war chief pointed at the canoes. "They have brought many things. Some of them might be dangerous, vehicles of sorcery and witchcraft." He licked his lips. "And they have the Split Sky war medicine that vanished from our War House."

The two Priests conferred in whispers. The speaker nodded before ordering, "Bring their packs. Everything. The Kala Hi'ki and I shall investigate each one."

The warriors hesitated.

"Do it!" the Priest ordered. "If you are worried about being polluted by the strangers, it has already happened. The Kala Hi'ki and I can't treat you until we know what medicine they have used and what cleansing is appropriate. Before you go home to your families, you will seclude yourselves in the War House. See no one, talk to no one, and wait for our word."

Old White gestured to Trader and Two Petals; she seemed preoccupied, as though listening to the voices they could not hear. Taking a position behind the Priests, Old White followed as they wound up through the landing settlement. The houses here were a mixture of new and old. People had flocked out, standing back to watch the show. Some carried cane torches that lit the way.

The beaten trail wound past houses, through a low cut, and onto the flats. Old White was aware of fields to either side, farmsteads consisting of two or three houses clustered here and there. Trader had bent down to scoop

Swimmer into his arms when the local dogs came too close.

Glancing over his shoulder, Old White could see the warriors struggling along behind them, heavy packs turning them into ungainly caricatures.

"What are we into now?" Trader wondered.

Old White shrugged. "We are going to meet a beautiful blind man who can see across great distances."

"I just hope he can see even better up close."

"Oh?"

"I want him to look inside me and see the purity of my souls."

"Gods, you're a brave man."

"I'm not feeling so brave. Why would you say that?"

"Only a braver man than I would want a Powerful *Hopaye* looking so closely at his souls."

Trader looked like he'd just swallowed mold.

Old White shot an evaluative look at Two Petals. She kept closing her eyes, and periodically, when passing knots of people, covered her ears.

"How are you doing?" he asked, leaning toward her.

"So noisy," she whispered. "Everything is screaming."

Old White cocked his head, hearing only the low mutterings of the warriors, the soft padding of feet on the trail, and the distant barking of dogs.

This could all go wrong. If the Yuchi Kala Hi'ki was the wrong kind of man, the sort who was preoccupied by his own petty concerns, it might give his reputation a huge boost to declare them enemies. Such an individual could gain prestige among his people, creating theater with the bloody, drawn-out executions of foreign witches.

Old White tightened his grip on his staff. *Let us pray the Power of Trade still holds here.*

Twenty-six

Two Petals stumbled, trying to protect herself from the onslaught. Keeping her feet took all of her concentration. If only the confused voices babbling around her souls would be still! Some cried out in panic; others hissed warnings. Beyond those, a growing chorus of sounds and images spun around in the darkness. She glanced this way and that, catching phantasms of colored light in the darkness. At the peripheries of her senses, she could feel the blind man, could almost make out his bound eyes as he watched them approach. They were closing the distance between them with each step; his Power drifted through the very air, carried on the evening breeze. It lingered like a recent touch, hidden there in the odor of smoke, waste, and human sweat.

Panic rose, bubbling around her confused and frightened souls. She clapped hands to her ears and threw her head back, filling her lungs to scream.

A shimmering darkness slammed down around her. The sensation was akin to being slapped with a wet blanket. Mercifully, it blocked the circling sights and sounds. "Go away," she pleaded. Old White's question came through as an incoherent babbling.

"He's right here, with us," she tried to explain. The dark veil—thicker than any night—pressed down around her. She peered out at it, aware that it blocked anything beyond her immediate surroundings.

He's placed a wall around you, a disembodied woman's voice said in her head. *He fears you.*

Fears me? The very notion of it left her unbalanced. Why would anyone fear her, of all people? Her own terror was all consuming.

He doesn't want your Power to run free.

After climbing a steep slope, they passed through a gate in a tall palisade that perched on the edge of the bluff. Two Petals imagined it in greater detail than she could see, given the gloom.

What place was this? She reached out with her hands, trying to part the gloom. In her fingers, the sooty darkness felt like soft fabric. Desperately, she ripped it aside.

Sensations, like a rupture in a dam, poured through. A howling of sound, like a great wind, blew over her. She stumbled. Thousands of souls rushed toward her from every direction. The people, gods, *thousands* of people, they all hummed with thoughts and life. She clamped her hands to her ears, tried to shut out the buzzing activity that swarmed around her like an impenetrable fog of insects.

Let it go, a voice told her. *See them. Hear them. Become them. You only need to set yourself free.*

She took a breath, frightened and horrified, reaching out with her senses in an attempt to escape the press that threatened to drown her. Bits of her souls were batted this way and that. Visions—the compressed memories of a lifetime—whirled around her like autumn leaves in a gale: a woman feeding a baby, two men arguing, a wife scolding her husband, a teenage girl cooking a pot of beans, a warrior in a sweat bath, a man coupling with his woman, a child crying from fever, and a thousand other images flooded through her.

"Too much! Too much!" she cried, seeking desperately to block it all out.

She blinked, trying to absorb it all: swirling lights, faces, bodies, souls. So many demands. Too many. Her world whipped around, ever faster and faster, spinning like a top. She felt herself whirling in the tornado. Whirling, ever faster, falling . . . into gray oblivion.

What happened to her?" Trader demanded, dropping to one knee beside Two Petals. The Contrary had crashed to the hard ground with a soft thump. She lay with one leg bent, an arm sprawled out.

"I don't know," Old White said, crouching beside him. "She just said, 'Too much,' then seemed to lose her balance and fall."

The Priests had turned, looking back in the light of the torches.

"Carry her," Old White ordered as he glanced around at the muttering warriors and growing crowd of locals. "Here, I'll take Swimmer."

"Is she ill?" one of the Priests asked.

"I don't think so," Old White told him as he took the squirming Swimmer from Trader's arms. "She was complaining of the noise, but I didn't hear anything unusual for a city at this time of night. My friend can carry her. Let's go find your Kala Hi'ki; perhaps he can determine what's wrong with her."

Trader heard the warriors growl darkly behind him. Gods, this was turning into a nightmare. He scooped Two Petals up and tossed her easily over his shoulders. The feel of her awed him; her muscles were locked, rigid. Her body barely flexed in reaction to his hurried steps. Catching a glimpse of her face, he saw a frozen rictus, her eyes rolled far back in their sockets.

Two Petals' collapse had taken him by surprise, his attention on the city itself. The fortifications atop the steep bluff were tall, well made, and capable of withstanding an assault. The high archers' platforms gave good fields of fire down the incline surrounding Rainbow City. Around him were bent-pole thatch-roofed houses, looking like overgrown mushrooms atop thickly plastered walls. People were flocking out, watching, and talking to each other in low voices.

Trader gave a quick nod to Old White and resumed his pace. Their route took them west along the northern edge of the plaza. Passing a high moiety house, the Priests led them to a grand building atop a square earthen mound on the northwest corner of the plaza. Perhaps three times his height, the mound was coated with a layer of light-colored clay that looked pale in the torchlight. The Priests led the way up a ramped stairway, passed through a low palisade and into a yard. Fierce panther heads had been carved from the guardian posts on either side of the entrance.

As the warriors ducked through the gate, the Priest gave them strict orders, pointing to either side. The warriors hastily divested themselves of their loads. "You three, come with me," the Priest added.

Trader managed to linger long enough to see a sweating warrior carefully set his medicine box on the ground beside Old White's pile of Illinois bowls in their net bag. Then, like water through a hole in a cup, the warriors vanished through the gate.

Did he dare try to scoop up the medicine box?

"Trader?" Old White called from the temple doorway.

He turned, reluctantly, casting glances behind him as he carried Two Petals' wood-stiff body.

Inside, the temple was elaborately furnished. A fire crackled, and illuminated masks that hung from the walls. Hide-covered benches lined the walls; beneath them beautifully carved wooden boxes, burnished clay jars, and intricately woven baskets had been placed. A low wide clay altar rose behind the fire; and on the back wall hung a beautifully crafted image of a warrior, a turkey-tail mace in one hand, a severed head in the other. The relief had been crafted from a great single piece of wood, the image carefully painted. Parts of it were clad in copper. Shells and pearls had been inlaid. Real feathers hung from the apron.

The wall to the left was dominated by a huge wooden relief, the center of which was a spiral: three spinning wedges within a yellow sun disk. The spaces between the curving wedges had been left open. Surrounding the spiral was a ring that contained six copper moons evenly spaced; the area between them had been painted black and was dotted with white stars. The perimeter was a series of oblong white circles.

A competing relief hung on the opposite wall; this one consisted of two great rattlesnakes carefully carved from wood, their bodies intricately detailed in yellow, red, and white bands, while oval-shaped black portals—the doorways to alternate worlds—had been rendered along the serpents' sides. In the center, the two snakes faced each other, large eyes done in copper, mouths gaping and filled with sharp teeth. Long tongues flicked out into the empty space between them that represented the opening to the Underworld.

The floor was of packed white clay covered with fine rush matting that had been interwoven with strips of fur. On either side of the doorway they had entered was an image of the sun carved from wooden planks, each clad in shining copper that reflected the firelight like rays of reddish gold light. Just below the ceiling, all the way around the room, shelving held a line of human skulls.

Just so mine doesn't end up there.

He walked forward, lowering Two Petals' wood-stiff body to the floor before the great fire. The war chief had taken a position guarding the exit. One of the Priests disappeared into the hallway leading to the back. The other stood watching, his arms crossed over his chest. The expression on his face was anything but friendly.

Blood and dung! There's no escape from this place.

Trader placed his hand before Two Petals' nose, feeling her warm breath. He could see the whites of her eyes behind her thinly slitted lids. Her hair draped the floor in a swirl.

"Two Petals?" he asked, patting her cheek. "Are you all right?"

"She is not," a raspy voice said in Trade Tongue.

Trader looked up. His eyes widened, and he swallowed hard. An old man had stepped out from the rear. While he wore a white triangular apron, the exposed skin of his bare chest was covered with scar tissue, the glassy kind that came from fire. A piece of neatly folded white fabric had been tied around the ruin of his eyes. Sometime in the past, his nose had been sliced from his face, leaving two oblong holes for nostrils. No fingers remained on his right hand. The gray hair, pulled back, was pinned to hold a shining copper headpiece that depicted a stylistic rendition of a tall mace or war club.

The old man stepped forward, sure of his footing. Blind he might be, but he walked right to them and stopped an arm's length from Old White. He seemed to inspect the Seeker, his head held high. "Who are you?"

Old White set Swimmer on the floor, and Trader called him over, gesturing for him to lie down. Old White, his staff unencumbered, replied, "I am Old White, sometimes called the Seeker."

"Ah, the Seeker! I have heard of you." The blind man cocked his head. "What have you found?"

"A great many things. Some are wonders, others more terrifying than your worst nightmare."

No humor filled the blind man's voice when he said, "You would do well to avoid my nightmares, Seeker."

From the looks of the man's body, Trader could agree.

"Accompanying me is Two Petals, the young woman lying on the floor. She is a Contrary."

The blind man stood silently, digesting that. After a time he said, "That might explain a few things." A pause. "She has a poor handle on her Powers."

Another silence, then Old White said, "The third person in our party is only known as Trader. We come here under the Power of Trade; upon that I swear and bind us."

"What is your purpose with the Tsoyaha?"

Old White shifted. "Only to Trade for strong bodies to paddle us upriver and then to portage into the head-waters of the Horned Serpent River."

He considered that. "A traveling man must have a destination."

"We do, Kala Hi'ki."

A faint smile crossed his scarred lips. "Do not treat me like either an idiot or a simpleton. My body might be a wreck, but I assure you my wits are as sharp as they were when I was young. Your young woman called to my Dreams over a moon ago. I have had glimpses of her from Cahokia all the way to just inside the palisade. Why have you brought her here?"

"I spoke the truth, Kala Hi'ki. We are just passing on to the south."

"To a mysterious destination. And, I am told, with the Split Sky war medicine box and some heavy content."

Old White's eyes narrowed. "The box came to us in the Kaskinampo lands."

The blind man turned to Trader. "And do you have a tongue, Trader?"

"I do."

"Where are you from?"

"The far north. I have brought packs of furs, medicine plants"—he winced—"some copper, and other things."

The old man considered. "You are Sky Hand."

How does he know that? Trader felt his stomach fall. "I was born there. I have been away for many seasons."

"How many?"

"More than ten winters."

"Why did you leave?"

"I had my reasons."

"And I have mine. Why did you leave?"

Trader swallowed hard, his heart racing. He could see

the warning look on Old White's face. "I killed a man," Trader blurted.

"Ah, there." The blind man made a tsking sound with his tongue. "So, you come from the far north, a Chikosi man, with goods to Trade, and a secret that causes your heart to hammer."

Gods, does he see into my souls?

"Maybe I see more than you think," the blind man told him. "A good reason not to tell lies."

Trader's loud gulp carried.

"We are concerned about the Contrary," Old White said. "Just past the palisade gate, she lost her balance and fainted."

"Sister Datura doesn't train a person to their Powers; she only grants Visions of the potential. Has she no trainer?"

"At the time, we didn't know she needed one."

"This Chikosi Trader told you that, Seeker?"

"We had not encountered Trader at that time."

"Then *you* sent her to Dance with Sister Datura?"

"A medicine woman did."

"Who?"

"I knew her under the name Silver Loon."

"Ah, the Cahokia witch."

Old White evidently saw no need to reply.

"Curious, isn't it, that she would simply help a Contrary to find her path, then set her free to blunder through the world?"

"There were complications."

"Aren't there always? Describe these . . . complications."

"Black Tooth had designs on the Contrary. Unfortunately, none of them conducive to helping her with her Powers."

"And Black Tooth is dead?"

"He is."

"One shouldn't treat Power with disrespect."

"I agree."

The blind man stood so still he might have been carved of wood, no expression on his ruined face. But Trader had a sneaking suspicion that his souls were in a frenzy behind that calm exterior.

"We wish no trouble," Old White finally said. "Our business lies in the south."

The long silence continued.

Trader had begun to fidget. Swimmer, reading his unease, had started to creep along on his belly, eyes fixed anxiously on the door. *You and me, dog.*

"Tell me why you are going to Split Sky City, Seeker. Tell me plainly, under the Power of Trade that you claim you are bound by. This thing I would know."

Old White took a deep breath. "Power is calling us there."

"Did the Contrary tell you that?"

"No. I first heard the call from the *Katsinas*. They are a—"

"I know who the *Katsinas* are."

Old White turned curious eyes on the blind man.

"Tell me, Seeker, after all that you have seen, do I really surprise you that much? Rainbow City is tied to the world as thoroughly as any other place. Traders still pass through here with great regularity, and have for years. My body does not let me travel, but other men, such as yourself, do; and they impart a great many things. Did the *Katsinas* tell you to find the Contrary?"

"No, they only told me to go home. That the way would be long, and I should follow the route I was required to."

"Then where did you learn of the Contrary?"

"She called to my Dreams. At the time I was in the Caddo lands. To obtain more information, I stopped to ask the Forest Witch her opinion. She thought I should go north, though it was several seasons out of my way."

"Now the Forest Witch appears in your story. You know a great many Powerful women, Seeker."

"I have had an unusual life," Old White said dryly.

The blind man asked, "Why does Power want you, a Contrary, a murderer, and the Chikosi war medicine in Split Sky City?"

"I can only guess at the reasons."

"Tell me your guess."

Old White straightened, evaluative eyes on the Kala Hi'ki. "I think we are called there to right an old wrong. For reasons I do not understand, Power is out of balance. We are being called there to restore the harmony."

"Why, out of all the Dreamers, *Hopaye,* and chiefs available to it, would Power call you from across the world?"

Old White nodded as if he'd anticipated the question, a wistful smile on his lips. "Because I have seen the many ways and forms of human beings. I have lived at the edge of the ice with the Inuit. Among the Azteca I watched the construction of a great mound of human bodies. I have talked with the Chumash about Traders from across the western ocean, and seen the bearded white man among the Pequot. While with the Tequesta, I watched them hunt whales by driving stakes into their blowholes. My feet trod the ruins of the White Palaces in the land of the *Katsinas,* and these eyes saw the To'Odam canals filled with roaring floodwaters. Dead Cahokia has cast the shadow of its great mound upon my souls. I know the hearts of the poorest farmer and the greatest rulers." He hesitated. "Something terrible is about to happen at Split Sky City. For reasons I will not share—even with you, great Kala Hi'ki—I must restore the harmony." He paused, then added softly, "Power has called me home to die."

Trader stared, aware that his mouth hung open. *Who is this man?*

A runner dressed in a brown shirt appeared at the door, whispered to the war chief, and stepped out to wait.

The war chief motioned the man to stay and crossed

the room to whisper a terse question into the Kala
Hi'ki's ear.

The blind man nodded; then he turned his head toward Old White. "My chief is anxious to know how we
should dispose of you."

"We mean the Children of the Sun no harm," Old
White insisted.

"Meaning and doing are two different things."

Trader felt fear sweat growing clammy on his skin.
This could turn either way. The blind man's face
showed no emotion as he spoke rapidly in his tongue.
The war chief barked a sharp reply, and turned, walking
out of the temple.

"For the moment," the blind man told them, "you
shall live. But I warn you: Be very, very careful."

Smoke Shield's canoe floated on the calm backwater.
He had chosen a partially silted-in channel of the Black
Warrior River for this rendezvous. Stands of cane surrounded him, many of the stalks showing scars where
they had been cut and carried off for building materials.
People tried to keep from cutting all the cane, but year
after year there were more people, and fewer canebrakes to go around.

A cold wind had blown down from the north, and his
breath frosted before his mouth. He had wrapped his
body in a warm beaverhide hunting shirt tanned with
the hair on. Thick moccasins hugged his feet and calves.
A bearskin cloak lay folded on the canoe floor; weapons
were laid close at hand atop it. For this outing he had
left his war shield behind. Should the high minko ask,
Thin Branch was to tell him that his master had gone
hunting as a means of working off his anger.

"You heard the Council." Flying Hawk's words lingered like the bitter taste of juniper berries. *"You heard*

me. I am your high minko. We will wait, learn what we can, and then act. In the meantime, I do not want you kicking the Albaamaha anthill."

"Oh, no, Uncle," he whispered to himself. "But you did once tell me that the Albaamo traitor and the mysterious Paunch were mine to hunt."

Hunt him, Smoke Shield would. In that process, who knew what might be uncovered?

Memories of the Council session replayed between his souls. They had humiliated him. To be sure, it was done with the Council's usual polite tact, but they had thrown his insight to the dogs. How soon they forget. The victory at White Arrow Town was a thing of rapidly fading memory.

"How did I get in this position?" He frowned at the gray day. Once given, the high minko's word was final. That the Council had gained such authority over the years was a weakness. How could a people maintain their strength if they succumbed to the notions of six different chiefs in addition to the high minko? That led the people in six different directions. In this case, they were pandering to the Albaamaha—the same Albaamaha who were plotting to cut their throats.

He frowned up at the scudding clouds. Flying Hawk would not be high minko for much longer. The man was old. The years now weighed heavily on him. Where had the fiery Flying Hawk Mankiller that Smoke Shield had once known gone to? He remembered his uncle stamping furiously around the palace. And, in those days of rage, people listened, nodded, and obeyed.

I always wanted to be like him: Strong. Sure of myself. Well, now I am. But what has become of him?

Leadership had faltered in the days after the great fire. Flying Hawk and his brother had been little more than boys. A cousin, Fire Sky, had been made high minko. He had been chosen because he was weak, easily manipulated. It was during his rule that authority had shifted to the Council. Then Flying Hawk had killed his brother.

For years after he had finally come of age, the Council had rejected him for high minko. Only after a daring defense of Split Sky City, when Flying Hawk destroyed most of a Yuchi war party and captured their war chief, had Flying Hawk finally been considered for the position. That, and they were running out of old men in the Chief Clan to fill the position.

The Council didn't want strong leaders sitting on the high minko's chair. Only after offering assurances had Flying Hawk finally been installed as high minko. The Council had considered him as a short-term solution.

They wanted my brother. The memory stung Smoke Shield. He reached up to finger the deep scar in the side of his face, remembering the blow that had come with such fury. How he had tried to duck, realizing too late he had pushed too far.

For four days he had lain, his souls fluttering away into nothingness before returning to his body. Then had come the slow healing. He chuckled hollowly. All his plotting, his carefully laid schemes, and in the end all it had taken was a blow to the head. When he finally came to, it was to inherit everything that was due him.

He considered Flying Hawk. Was the old man still on his side? The Council session left him wondering. Gods, what could his uncle be thinking? Why—in the wake of Smoke Shield's success against White Arrow Town— would the old man turn against him now?

A low chirp sounded in the cane.

Smoke Shield cupped hands around his mouth and chirped back, sounding like a mockingbird.

A canoe edged around the bend, Fast Legs paddling slowly forward. "War Chief," he greeted softly.

"Is all ready?"

"It is. I found a stupid Albaamo farmer to deliver the message. Red Awl was packing when I left. If I'm any judge, he's already headed upriver."

"Then we should position ourselves. We don't want to miss him."

"Yes, War Chief." Fast Legs glanced back over his shoulder. "You're sure he had something to do with the traitor?"

"I have my sources. I am looking forward to speaking with Red Awl. Being the *good* Albaamo that he is, he'll welcome our company on the way upriver. Then, at Clay Bank Crossing, we order him to shore. Most of the hunting parties have trickled back from the high country. Sandstone Camp will be secluded enough for our little visit."

Fast Legs glanced up at the sky. "This weather is closing in. We'll have a little cold rain, then who knows? Snow?"

"That will be fine." Smoke Shield reached for his paddle. "Come, we don't want to miss the loyal Red Awl when he passes."

They took positions at the mouth of the backwater.

Smoke Shield could feel the cold settling on the river; a worried breeze blew down from the north. Rippling waves marched across the swirling water.

"I would never have guessed Red Awl," Fast Legs muttered, blowing into his hands to warm them.

"His rise among the Albaamaha wasn't by accident. He's a hothead, promising more than he can deliver."

"I would have suspected Amber Bead before Red Awl."

Smoke Shield smiled grimly. "My guess is that we were all supposed to. But think about it: Amber Bead is an old man. He's been cowed for so long all he wants to do is keep the peace."

"Shh!" Fast Legs raised a finger to his lips. "Here he comes."

Smoke Shield craned his neck. Emerging around the downriver bend, a low dugout canoe could be seen. A man was paddling. But that was definitely a second figure in the bow.

"Who's with him?" Smoke Shield asked.

"Chaos! He's brought his wife."

His wife? Yes, that's undoubtedly who it was. Lotus Root was a pretty woman with long legs and a narrow waist. A quick spirit flashed in her dark eyes, and her smile was backed by straight white teeth. The ribald saying was that Red Awl had everything: status, prestige, the respect of both his people and the Sky Hand—and the saucy perfection of Lotus Root in his bed to boot! Smoke Shield remembered her well; perhaps her fiery spirit would provide what that limp-spirited Morning Dew had not.

"Oh, so he brought his wife," Smoke Shield said mockingly. "Too bad." Then he smiled. "Well, if it gets as cold as you think it might, we'll have someone to warm our blankets up in that cold camp."

"Two of them?" Fast Legs asked dubiously. "That's twice the risk."

"I think we can handle an Albaamo woman. And what if she does get away? What's her word against ours?" But Smoke Shield didn't think she was going to get away to anywhere. "Come, let's go and see if they'll travel upriver with us."

He lowered his paddle, pushing out into the sluggish winter current. Overhead, the sky continued to darken. A lighthearted joy filled Smoke Shield's breast. How fitting—a storm really was coming.

Twenty-seven

Old White chewed thoughtfully; then he spooned up another mouthful of beans. He glanced across at the pole bench where Two Petals lay sleeping, her Dreams disturbed. She whimpered on occasion, and tossed under the deerhide blanket that one of the Priests had spread over her. Trader sat to his right, picking meat off a turkey carcass, tossing occasional scraps to Swimmer.

The dog watched them with that rapt attention that could consume the canine soul. His ears were pricked, the brown eyes pleading. Swimmer's tail betrayed the barest twitch of anticipation. The faintest sliver of drool escaped the corner of his mouth.

The Kala Hi'ki was seated opposite them, his ruined body composed, the binding over his eyes pure and white against the corruption of his face.

Old White could see the question in Trader's eyes, but the answer was self-evident. Only one circumstance could leave a man looking that way. He'd been hung upon a square once upon a time. For whatever reason, he had either been cut loose, rescued, or somehow managed to impress his captors with such resourcefulness and bravery that they had let him live. Those events were as rare as turkey teeth.

"Has the Contrary been in such a large city before?" the Kala Hi'ki asked.

"Cahokia," Old White said after swallowing.

"Cahokia is abandoned," the Yuchi said. "It lies in

ruins with only small villages clustered around it. Has she ever been close to so many people?"

"We have stopped to Trade only in small villages. The Kaskinampo labored like slaves to get us through their territory."

"Wise of them." The Kala Hi'ki nodded. "She has lost her souls for the moment. They fled in panic to find shelter from the people. I had cast a Spirit wall around you, a way of containing any witchery that you might consider. It shielded her for most of your walk up from the landing. I didn't understand what she was, or how Powerful she could be. She broke the barrier down. Can you imagine suddenly touching all those souls? Hearing their thoughts, longings, and passions? It was too much."

"Too much. That's what she cried out before she fell," Trader added.

"She must learn to focus." The Kala Hi'ki fingered his ruined right hand with his left, touching the pad of his fingers on each stump. "I cannot understand why the Cahokia witch would just set her free like that." He turned his head in Old White's direction. "This complication with Black Tooth . . . it turned out badly, didn't it?"

"She killed him," Old White said softly. "She blew the souls out of his body. Just a puff of her breath and he fell from his tripod like a stone. I've seen the like before. Sometimes people survive with parts of their body paralyzed, or their speech slurred. Some can live for years afterward. He just hit the floor with a thump . . . dead."

The blind Prophet nodded. "Black Tooth mocked the lords of Cahokia. He abused what Power was left to that place. Cahokia may be an empty husk, but one should not enrage the souls of the dead who walk there." He paused. "Sometimes I think we are all losing our Power. Perhaps it has been drained away. Or, like good farmland, it loses its fertility over time, only growing stunted crops."

Old White chewed his beans and said, "The center that was Cahokia has spread out; people of different nations and languages have taken its beliefs in all directions. Perhaps what was once concentrated is diffused."

The blind man smiled. "We are the Children of the Sun, the Tsoyaha. This has always been our land. Our home is here on the Tenasee River and in the hills to the east. Our stories tell of the coming of the Cahokian Traders. Some of our chiefs went there and we learned their Power. Many of their teachings were incorporated into our own. We took their Power, and mixed it with our own, growing stronger. That is the strength of the Tsoyaha." He paused. "But perhaps as different people took the Power, Cahokia faded. It is a lesson for all of us."

"If you believe that there is only so much Power in the world." Old White added, "That it is like water in a jar. You can only pour so much out before it is all gone."

"Do you believe this?" the Kala Hi'ki asked.

Old White shrugged, setting his plate aside. He fished for his pipe, happy that at least it had been returned to him. "I'm not sure. But I have come to believe that those who hoard Power are finally destroyed by it. You have heard the legends of Tharon?"

"The great lord of Cahokia who sent warriors out around the world to obtain Power objects. He became a witch, and in the end his own people burned him to rid the world of his evil."

"Power must always be treated with the greatest respect," Old White agreed. "It is to be used with the utmost care, allowed to flow through us."

"Perhaps that is why the Tsoyaha are still strong," the Kala Hi'ki said thoughtfully. "Our people must ever be obedient to our promises to Our Mother Sun and the forces that have made us." He fingered the shell gorget on his chest, another of the three-winged spirals surrounded by a circle containing what looked like moons and stars. The edge looked like round flower petals.

"The Tsoyaha manage," Old White granted.

"But it is difficult," the Kala Hi'ki continued. "Our stories tell us about the coming of the Mos'kogee. We watched them flood eastward, and they washed around us, conquering, settling, and moving on again. To the north are the Kaskinampo, to the south the Chaktaw, and Chikosi. East of them are the Talapoosie, the Ockmulgee, and others. While others have been swept away, we remain."

Then he glanced at Two Petals. "For the moment, I worry about her Power. She is dangerous, unfocused. If she lashes out instead of fainting, the consequences could be severe."

"Split Sky City, I'm afraid, is even larger than your city is. She will be overwhelmed."

"You have never seen a Contrary trained?"

"No, I haven't. Most of the Contraries I have known are older, and often just people who affect the ways and manners to touch the Power. I've never known one as young as she."

"That is the problem." The Kala Hi'ki turned his blind face to Old White. "I could help her."

"Why would you offer to do that, great Kala Hi'ki? Even I, who am in the middle of this, have no real idea of Power's purpose with her."

"She appeared to me," he said. "From far-off Cahokia. Perhaps she came here for a reason. Came to me. Perhaps I am part of Power's purpose." He paused. "You have claimed, under the Power of Trade, that you wish us no harm. Do you still bind yourself to that?"

"I do," Old White answered.

"Trader?" the Kala Hi'ki asked. "You, who are an enemy of my people, do you so swear?"

Trader nodded. "I do. I have no reason to wish the Tsoyaha ill."

"Why would that be? Our warriors have killed your people, and you mine. We have been enemies from the time your people conquered the Albaamaha."

"We have also made peace between us at different

times in the past," Trader responded. "I'm a Trader first, and I've seen many peoples. The ones at war do the least Trade."

"But warriors often capture good farmlands after they have weakened their enemies or destroyed them," the Kala Hi'ki countered. "War strengthens the young men. Makes them fast, quick of thought and action. It hones them to aspire to their best."

"And it often leaves them dead," Trader responded woodenly. "There are better ways to make young men quick of wit and skilled. Personally, I would see them play stickball, or learn the ways of the hunt."

"Some would say you were a coward, Chikosi."

"What do you think, Kala Hi'ki? Do you think I am a coward?"

"I think you are often afraid."

"Being afraid and being a coward are two different things."

"What is the secret that you hide, murderer? Are you afraid to tell me?"

Old White watched Trader lower his eyes. The man glanced at Swimmer, then at his hands. "I have found no reason to tell you."

The Kala Hi'ki nodded slowly. "I see. Well then, let us try this: Your life rests in my hands. My chief would like to burn you alive in the square at the height of winter solstice. He thinks you would make a good sacrifice to Tso, our Mother Sun. He sees no reason to let an enemy of his people return to home with such a wealth of Trade. In principle, I agree with him; however, I am curious about why Power is calling you to Split Sky City. If there is advantage in this, I would know it. Unlike so many, I have a healthy respect for Power. But I do not want to see my enemy strengthened. Especially when he grows stronger by the season."

The Kala Hi'ki rubbed his maimed hand. "So my proposal is that we all be honest with each other. Power is at work here, and while I do value the Power of Trade—and its guarantee of safe conduct—no Trader would blame me if I accused a self-confessed murderer of witchcraft and let the *yu bah'le,* my high chief, burn you alive at the solstice."

The grin he gave Trader was a gruesome thing. "The Kaskinampo could easily be persuaded to support such a claim, given their haste to see you out of their territory. So, Trader, knowing that your lives are in the balance, will you be totally honest with me, assuming I am totally honest with you?"

Trader looked doomed. "My uncle is called high minko among the Sky Hand. The man I killed was my brother."

Old White chuckled, aware that attention switched to him.

"That is funny?" the Kaka Hi'ki asked, a terrible passion in his voice. "Are you so blind you do not see these scars? I received them at the hands of the Chikosi high minko! Flying Hawk did this to me while I hung in the square. Now, his nephew sits before me? Do you know how desperately I have wanted to repay them in kind?"

"Power plays us for fools," Old White said, still chuckling. "This grows ever more intricate in its weave. Just when I begin to perceive the pattern, I encounter yet another thread. Very well, Kala Hi'ki, if we pledge ourselves to honesty, what will you do now that you have such a prestigious person in your hands? We are being tested. Each of us is being granted their heart's desire. Mine—and Trader's, I suppose—is to return to our land. I wish to correct an old wrong before I die. Trader wishes to regain his name and honor. You wish to repay pain with pain. Power has sent us down this trail, and now we all face choices. What will yours be?"

The Kala Hi'ki sat silent as a stone, head back. The muscles in his face quivered with the passions that burned inside him. "Flying Hawk laughed as I screamed."

"I am not that man," Trader insisted doggedly.

"You are Chief Clan. Of his lineage. Give me one

good reason why I should not have you dragged out of here this moment and tied into the square."

"Because Power has brought us all together here," Old White replied as if they were discussing the strength of a mint tea. "You are meant to be tempted with the revenge you thirst for. Power gives, and it takes."

"I feel like taking," the Kala Hi'ki said through gritted teeth.

Trader had turned sickly pale, wide eyes on the Yuchi priest. "But you did not die on the square. Somehow you got loose."

"A boy untied me in the middle of the night. In that disgusting tongue of yours, he told me to run. My legs failed me, and I lay writhing and bleeding on the ground. He laughed as he ground my right hand under his foot. When I could finally hobble, he told me to never come back. That his name was Green Snake."

Trader sucked his breath in. "I *never* cut you loose!"

The Kala Hi'ki jabbed out with a pointing finger. "You are *Green Snake*? The man who freed me, stamped on my hand, and *urinated* into my wounds?"

"No." Trader dropped his head into his hands. "I never did these things you speak of. Not me. But, my brother . . . Gods, the things my brother did."

Old White puffed his pipe and nodded. "There it is. You see, it all fits the pattern. You have been tormenting yourself for years, punishing yourself for the murder of your brother. This is just another proof that killing him was not without justification."

Trader hung his head. "There is a terrible ugliness that runs in my family. Flying Hawk killed his twin brother in a blind rage." He drew a deep breath. "And I had sworn all of my life that I would never be the same kind of man Flying Hawk was. His souls were out of balance, stained with red, possessed of chaos, anger, and rage. My brother was the same sort of man. But it was I—also in blind rage—who struck him down with a club.

"Gods, it all makes sense." Trader knotted his fists.

"You asked for honesty, Kala Hi'ki? I think I know when this happened. I was told that when I finished my initiation into the Men's House, my uncle had a special present to celebrate the occasion. I think I was supposed to finally kill you."

The Kala Hi'ki hadn't moved, his slow breathing whistling through the holes in his face.

Trader laughed bitterly. "So, there it is. The circles have turned. If you were that Yuchi warrior in the square, Power has played its game. Now I am yours. If it will bring you peace, Kala Hi'ki, tie me to your square. I can only hope that I face it with the courage and honor that I heard you showed."

"Trader," Old White warned, but the young man waved it down.

"No, it is all right. Perhaps this is what I was brought here to do, Seeker. To make this decision. If my death on the square restores the balance, if it brings harmony between the white and the red, I will do this thing. From the night I left, I imagined my brother's souls, angry and wailing, unable to travel to the Land of the Dead. He cannot rest until I have paid for his murder. If I die here, his souls can finally take the route westward and make the leap through the Seeing Hand when it meets the western horizon."

He is a fool! Gods, how am I going to get him out of this? Old White considered the wealth of their Trade. It might just be enough to buy the young idiot's life. Though the gods alone knew how they'd manage to finish the journey. Traders without Trade cut a rather ridiculous figure.

He studied the Kala Hi'ki. The time would have to be right. Now was not the moment; the man was reliving those terrible days on the square, feeling the pain as burning cane torches were being pressed against his naked flesh, remembering the horror of having his eyes ripped from their sockets. But later, when he was over the first crashing waves of rage, yes, that would be the time.

The Kala Hi'ki surprised him when he climbed unsteadily to his feet. "I must consider this. Neither of you is to leave this room. If one of you runs, I will have you hunted down. Then the three of you will hang from the squares together. At the solstice, we will burn you, one by one." With that he turned on his heel and left them to stare hopelessly into the fire.

Twenty-eight

The nagging ache in her bladder finally forced Two
Petals to claw her way through the spinning images in
her head. The action of coming back to her body was a
misery. For days she had been overwhelmed, panicked
at the visions of her future. Deer Man had assured her
that a terrible trial was coming.

I don't want to do this anymore. Seek as she might,
there was no way out. For the rest of her life, she would
be Contrary.

The whispers in her head told her terrible things.
Images of murky water, gleaming rainbow scales, and
sunlight flashing on copper left her confused. Angry
black eyes bored into hers, seeking her souls. She
could see the ugly scar on the side of his head as his
hands slipped over her bare skin. Images of a room, a
ceiling of knot-filled poles, and a flickering fire were
tinged with darkness. His muscular body settled on
hers. She could almost feel his hot shaft driving into
her.

I will be at his mercy. . . .

Before that, people would stare at her, whispering
about her, plotting terrible things. They would call her a
witch. Then, sometime when she least expected it, they
would sneak out of the night, smack her brains out, and
burn her body.

Why can't they just leave me alone?

She opened gummy eyes, aware of a terrible headache
and the pressing needs of her bladder. Her stomach

rubbed like a hard knot against her backbone. How long since she'd eaten?

She sat up, confused. The room was small, a low fire sending tendrils of smoke to pool against the poles of the ceiling. Someone had placed a beautifully woven blanket over her, and soft hides cushioned her from a pole bed built against the wall. With trembling hands, she pulled the blanket aside and swung her legs out.

"I was wondering when you would awake."

She gasped, aware that a man crouched to one side of the fire. She knew that ruined face, had seen it in her Dreams. He wore a fold of cloth over his eyes, and the two nostril holes reminded her of a snake's.

"Where am I?"

"In the temple of the Yuchi, as we are called. The name is wrong, of course. We are the Tsoyaha. In Trader Tongue we are the Children of the Sun."

"What do they call you?"

He chuckled. "I am called Kala Hi'ki. It began as a joke. It comes from one of our most prized stories. It seems that once, long ago, a stranger with great Power came down from the rainbow. This mysterious being lived among the Tsoyaha and taught us many of our rituals: the arts of Healing; the proper ways for the Yuchi to behave; and how to find the path eastward to the Sky World, a place where our Ancestors live that we call Yubahe.

"After the mysterious stranger lived among us for some time, Mother Sun began to act strangely. She would arise from her home in the east, then race up into the sky before hanging there, as if afraid to move.

"This miraculous sky being was called Kala Hi'ki. He told the bravest warrior, 'Something is wrong with Mother Sun. Are you brave enough to go to the end of the earth and see what is frightening her? I warn you now it must be a terrible sorcerer, one who has Power enough to frighten your Mother. Do you have the courage to slay this sorcerer and bring his head back?'

"Being the greatest of the Tsoyaha, the warrior agreed that he did. Kala Hi'ki gave the warrior a special war club made from a turkey tail. And he said, 'With this you must strike the sorcerer. The club will only work if you aim your blow at the back of his neck, for that is the only place such a terrible sorcerer is vulnerable. Should you hit him anywhere else, he will turn and kill you in a most dreadful way.'

"For days the warrior traveled, forever to the east, until one day he reached the edge of the world. There he spied two caves. Hiding in some bushes, he settled down to watch.

"Sure enough, night came, and he was frightened, for monsters exist at the edge of the world. But he was the bravest of our people. That next morning, as he had been told, Mother Sun emerged from her cave. Her light was brilliant, and warmed him after the cold and terrifying night.

"That was when the sorcerer popped out of the second cave. He prepared himself, then sprang out at Mother Sun, waving his arms and screaming in a most hideous manner. Because of his Power, Mother Sun fled up the sky until she was out of his reach.

"The warrior saw his chance, for the evil sorcerer was so preoccupied and gleeful at his Power, he did not watch what was behind him. With one mighty blow, the warrior struck the sorcerer in the back of the neck. As Kala Hi'ki had promised, the sorcerer's head tumbled from his body. The warrior stared, afraid to believe his luck.

"Now he had to bring the head back. But when he went to pick it up, the head blinked, the mouth moving like a fish's does when swallowing air. The warrior's courage fled. Three times he tried to pick up the head, and three times he couldn't summon the resolve to touch it. Finally, on the fourth attempt, he steeled his heart, reached down, and knotted his fingers in its hair.

"Then the most terrible part of the journey began.

You see, every night the severed head would talk to the warrior. It would tell him, 'You must leave me and run home, for your wife is lying with another man.' The next day it would say, 'You must leave me. Your mother is sick and dying, and only you can save her.' Day after day, the head told him terrible things. Once it was that Kala Hi'ki himself was an evil Spirit that was poisoning his people. But the warrior kept to his task.

"Finally, he returned to the Tsoyaha in triumph, and discovered that his wife had lain with no other man. That his mother had never been sick, and so on. That first night they buried the head, thinking it would die in the ground. But imagine the people's surprise when they awakened the next day to find the head lying atop the grave, still spouting lies.

" 'Throw it in a fire and burn it up!' the people cried. So they went and found wood. They kindled a great bonfire and threw the head in. There it burned for the entire day. So imagine their consternation when they awakened the second morning, and found the head atop the ashes, still spouting lies.

" 'Tie the head to the tallest tree!' they shouted. Once again they tried, climbing the tallest oak in the forest. They went to bed that night knowing that the terrible head was finished. So, imagine their surprise when they awakened the following morning to find the head on the ground beside the dead oak. That is why even today, acorns fall from the oak. If you look, acorns still have heads of hair like the sorcerer's.

"In despair, they went to Kala Hi'ki and said, 'What do we do to kill this sorcerer's head?'

"Kala Hi'ki thought, and said, 'You are tying it to the wrong tree.' He gathered them together and led them to the cedar tree. 'There, tie the sorcerer's head on the highest branch.' This the people did, and that night they went to bed hoping that Kala Hi'ki was right. Now, the next morning they awakened, and one by one, filed out into the forest. There, the cedar stood still vibrant and alive, and on its highest branch, the sorcerer's head was dead. Then they looked at the tree and saw that it was streaked with the sorcerer's blood. That is why to this day the cedar is sacred, and its wood still red, stained forever by the sorcerer's blood."

He smiled slightly. "My people called me Kala Hi'ki because I once left to go to war. When I finally came back to them it was as a mysterious stranger. Not the handsome young man they had known, but the one you see before you. Nothing was left of the brave warrior they had known. Not his name, nor his laughter, nor even his souls. What came back was entirely different. Power had come to live within me, and I have belonged to it ever since. I am indeed the mysterious stranger to them."

"Do I know this place?" She looked around. "Oh, yes. Been here before. Like leaves blowing through the forest."

"Your souls were overwhelmed when you broke through my protection. Your companions carried you here on my orders."

"Does your bladder hurt, too?"

"Use the pot there beside the bed." He laughed. "I won't watch."

"You won't hear, either."

"Contrary, there are few secrets left for me. We are as we are made, and no more."

She used the pot, staring hesitantly at him. "I have nothing for you."

"You are a Contrary. You have everything." A pause. "Hungry?"

"Couldn't eat a bite."

He stood, walked to the doorway with the same assurance as a man with sight, and returned moments later with a warm corn-and-bean stew laced with bits of meat. A horn spoon stuck up from the fragrant gruel. "There is more where that came from."

She attacked the bowl ravenously.

"Can you hear them?" he asked.

"I can't even hear you."

"You are distracted for the moment. It's worse when you think about it. When your senses are lowered." He hesitated. "Two Petals, when you finish your stew, I will need you to drink this tea I have made. It will help you to focus, to enter my world for a time."

"I don't want to know what's in it."

"It is a weak mixture of herbs, but mostly chopped licorice root, blackhaw, and an infusion made from pipe plant root. I have added a little sassafras root for taste."

She took the cup he indicated, sniffed it, and drank the concoction. "Aren't you glad I'm not interested in what this is supposed to do to me?"

"I am hoping it will calm the voices."

"Why would you care?"

"Because you are so Powerful." He paused. "Tell me about the voices."

"Some are real; others aren't. Just like you're not real, and then I wake up and here you are. Dreams become real; the real become Dreams. As if there was a difference." She cocked her head; one of the voices in her head was whispering just below the threshold of her understanding. Was it trying to warn her of something?

He asked gently, "What is going to happen at Split Sky City, Two Petals? You can tell me backward if you like."

She sighed. "You can't know about that. It's in the future, and you're all backward."

"But I do know. I saw you, remember? When you Danced with Sister Datura at Cahokia, you saw me."

"I remember. You turned into a shimmering darkness, slipping away from me."

"I didn't know who or what you were."

"Me. I'm just plain old me. Nothing here. Emptiness that's full of everything."

"Oh, I'm well aware of that. The Power ebbs and flows through you." He tilted his head, as if straining to hear her. "Is the tea beginning to take effect?"

"How will I know?"

"Hopefully you should relax. You worry a lot, don't you?"

She glanced down at the food bowl. "Sometimes, like at Lightning Oak Town, I'm so excited. I feel ready to burst from my bones. Then, like now, I see nothing but darkness, and death. Sometimes the invisible voices tell me terrible things. Other times they tell me wonderful revelations about secret things, like the bugs under leaves."

He nodded, as if understanding something. "I think I understand. Great happiness that lasts for a while, followed by periods of misery."

"Up and down. Up and down." She laughed. "I want to be a log lying in the forest, covered with moss. Old logs move very slowly. They just grow flat and hollow. Instead I'm a canoe rising and falling on huge waves, like Old White tells about on the great oceans." Her voice rose in desperation. "I want the world *to slow down*!"

"The tea will help." A pause. "Did you always hear the voices?"

"No. When I was little, everything was all right. It used to be I could do normal things. Gather wood, cook food. Then the voices started to speak inside my head. I remember the first time: I was fleshing a deer hide for Father. You know, chopping the tissue and meat away with a bone flesher. Then, as clear as anything, the deer's voice told me to keep chopping. I remember it saying, 'Harder! Harder! You'll never clean me like that.' And the harder I chopped at the hide, the more frantic the voice became. 'You'll see sunlight through the hide,' it told me. I hammered a hole through the skin, and it said, 'The hole isn't big enough." So I kept at it even though my arms were aching, and I was out of breath. I was frantic to see the sunlight shine through the hide."

She paused, remembering. "Father came in. I remember him shouting at me, dragging me away. He was so mad." She gave the Kala Hi'ki a sad look. "I never did see the sunlight that deer's Spirit promised. I just got a beating from Father. He didn't believe that deer's voice told me to do it."

"And your mother? What did she do?"

"She was killed. The A'khota killed her when she went out to collect firewood. I saw her body. All chopped up like that deer hide. She was bloody. They had taken her scalp. I remember screaming, wanting to die so I could go looking for her souls. I couldn't imagine what living would be like without Mother. That night she came to my Dreams, telling me that the world was all backward." Two Petals nodded to herself. "That's when it all started to make sense."

"Make sense how?"

"Mother was good. She never hurt anyone. People came from all over to have her treat them when they were sick. Father and the rest of the men listened to her counsel. She had so many friends. People brought her gifts, and our house was always full of visitors. She loved everyone, and always had food for them. Even the A'khota, after they heard she had been killed by one of their warriors, sent gifts to Father. They did that because she had Healed A'khota. They said they were sorry."

"And that made the world backward?"

Two Petals nodded. "Why else would someone who always tried to do good be killed like that? I knew lots of mean and angry people. None of them died that way. Well, sometimes they did. It was always the good ones who got killed, or sick. Then one of Mother's souls came and told me why it was. Backward. Everything was backward. That's why I didn't fit anymore. That's why I started hearing the voices." She nodded to herself. "Sometimes I would see people . . . just as clear as I see you now. They'd tell me things and I'd answer. It made other people in the room scared because they couldn't see who I was talking to."

"So what did you do?"

"I stopped talking to them out loud. But I'd listen."

She looked down at her hands. "I just couldn't get anything done. I'd start cooking. Maybe boiling corn. Then I'd see someone, or the voices would start talking about things like why sunlight could shine through cracks in the wall, and next thing I'd know, the corn was boiled dry and burning in the pot. It made Father so mad. Other times I would be doing something like weaving matting for the floor, and the voices would tell me to look outside. Then they'd tell me something was outside the palisade. When I finally followed their instructions, I'd find a woman standing in a clearing. We'd sit and talk, and Father would show up sometime later, angry and frightened that I'd disappeared. But when I explained I was talking to the woman, he'd insist she wasn't there."

"It must have been very disturbing."

She nodded, staring at his ruined face. "Things didn't make sense until Mother told me the world was backward. Then I finally understood. I was the only one who saw things correctly. If I said things backward, I could make sense of it all."

He nodded, as if understanding. "That explains a great deal." He fingered the stumps on his right hand. "Why did the Seeker want you? Did he say what his purpose was?"

"He says I called to him in his Dream. He told me he searched up and down the river until he found me."

"Did he say why that was important?"

"Something terrible happened at Split Sky City. He thinks he needs me to make whatever got turned around right again. Power is calling us there. I've seen . . ."

He waited before prompting, "Yes? It's all right. I need to know these things if I am to help."

She blinked, staring at the tea cup. She could sense the herbs working within her. Her thoughts had slowed, and she felt more relaxed, almost at peace. For the first time in seasons, she could concentrate without her souls fluttering around like butterflies. "I've seen fire and blood. If we don't make things right, balance the Power, a great many people are going to hurt."

The Kala Hi'ki took a breath. "Did either the Seeker or the Trader say anything about the Yuchi?"

"They have been worried about crossing your territory. I had seen images, things that happened . . . I mean things that *will* happen."

"What were they?"

"One way, Trader hangs from the square. It will take him a long time to die, but in the end, people will admire his courage. In another vision, I have seen Trader playing chunkey with a warrior. I think it's at the solstice ceremony. The weather is cold, the ground frozen. People are watching, cheering. Something about the counting sticks is very important to you and your people. And to Trader, too."

"How do they mean to hurt us?"

She blinked, frowning. "Hurt you? Neither Trader nor the Seeker mean to harm your people. In one vision, the Yuchi are part of the future. Part of fixing the problem. Trader can stop the war."

"Stop the war?"

"The one that's coming. He doesn't know. I haven't told him. I think it would scare him."

"What happens in the war?"

"Chaos is let loose. Everything is ruined. War washes like a red wave across the land. The sky is black, even during the day. When people aren't looking into the forest for raiders, they are staring at the black sky. I see death everywhere, and the ghosts wander, seeking peace they can never find."

"Does Trader lead this war?"

"No. If the war happens he will be long dead in your square. A terrible chief, a man with a scar on his head, will lead it. He will spare no one. Not even his own people."

"Does Trader know this scarred man?"

"He does . . . and he doesn't." She cocked her head. "How odd that it works that way."

"And if Trader lives? What will become of Split Sky City?"

Tell him the rest, one of the voices in her head prompted. She took a deep breath. "You should know this: One way or the other, your city here will be abandoned. Where your fields now stretch, only forest will grow. Whether you like it or not, the future of your people is tied to Trader, and whether he survives the return to his people. If Power is not restored, the Children of the Sun will be broken, scattered, and those not killed in the fighting will be absorbed by the Charokee, Shawnee, and others."

The old man nodded wearily. "I feared as much, Contrary."

"Ask yourself this: Was the pain of becoming the Kala Hi'ki worth the gift of wisdom? Would you Trade your Power and true vision for a whole body? You are scarred, blind, and bitter, but Power fills your life in a way it never would have had you remained whole. No gift comes without a price and terrible sacrifice. By surrendering what you most desire for yourself, you will achieve what you sincerely want for others."

"I think I already knew that."

"So does the Seeker." She smiled. "Trader will discover this, but he has yet to face his trial."

"Am I not 'his trial'?" the Kala Hi'ki asked dryly.

"Dying on the square isn't his choice. You, like everyone else, see the world backward. You are not Trader's trial; he is yours." She smiled at the irony. "How will you choose: to feed your rage and lust for revenge, or gamble on the future of your people?"

"So, if I let him go, my people are safe? I don't understand."

"Power didn't make your choice simple. Killing Trader is quick and certain. He will die on the square, and you

will enjoy his suffering. Letting him go is a gamble—not
only on him, but that Seeker and I will succeed in restor-
ing the harmony. I have had glimpses of the different futures. You are but one thread of the weaving."

"And if I choose wrong?"

"Choose one way and the Tsoyaha continue for a
long time to come. Choose another, and they will be forgotten within two generations."

"Which choice is which?"

"You know the ways of Power. Do you even have to
ask?"

As snow swirled out of the night sky beyond the door
of Heron Wing's house, Morning Dew added a stick to
the fire and then retreated to her place along the wall. In
the days since Thin Branch had led her to Heron Wing's
house, some of the numbness had leached out of her
souls. Slowly, inexorably, she was becoming part of
Heron Wing's household. Even sour old Wide Leaf had
grudgingly offered her an occasional kindness.

Little Stone, however, had immediately made her
welcome, showing her his toys and telling her detailed
stories about each of his possessions, and who had
given them to him. Somehow it had devolved on her to
keep track of the boy.

She glanced across the room at Heron Wing, who
was stringing shell beads onto a necklace. The woman
had been considerate, almost indulgent during those
first few days when Morning Dew had sat in shocked silence by the fire. Without comment, Heron Wing had
placed the tripod and hung a bowl over the fire to heat
water. After checking it with a finger, she had calmly
said, "You will want to wash yourself." And she had
handed Morning Dew a cloth to sponge herself.

She had stripped off the dress Flying Hawk had given

her and scrubbed. She began halfheartedly, then with ever-increasing vigor. She had ended in a manic flurry, as if to remove the very skin from her body. She persisted, even when the bowl was empty. Only when Heron Wing bent over, placing fingers on her hand, did she slow, stare up at the woman, and burst into tears.

"Where is your other dress?" Heron Wing had asked. "The one you wore."

"Ruined," she had managed. "He . . . he tore it."

Heron Wing had inspected the gray dress. Droplets of blood and urine stains speckled the front. "He gave you that one?"

"No. The . . . the high minko."

"Looks like the one Flying Hawk's wife used to wear," Wide Leaf noted, her usual gruffness tempered after Morning Dew's frantic ablutions.

"Wide Leaf," Heron Wing had asked, "would you take this and wash it?" The tone in her voice was firmly controlled.

The slave had taken the fabric, then vanished into the fog.

Heron Wing had rummaged through a box, procuring one of her own dresses. "It will be a bit large, but it will do until yours is clean." In the firelight, she had turned knowing eyes on Morning Dew. "We all heal, Morning Dew. Even you."

An image of Screaming Falcon's face had flashed down deep between her souls. She had closed her eyes, unashamed at the continuation of her tears. The woman had no idea. Some things would never heal. She had glanced down at her hands, staring at them in disbelief, as if they belonged to another.

The days had passed, and while the horror of what she had done lingered, some semblance of life returned. She found it in cooking, carrying, mending, sewing, and cleaning. Every task she attacked with total and intense concentration. Anything to keep the memories from creeping out. *I have buried the memories,* she told herself. *They are in a box, deep down inside, covered over with a rock. They are forgotten.*

But they weren't. She couldn't control her Dreams, and more than once, in the night, Heron Wing would wake her, a reassuring hand on her shoulder, and say, "You were having a nightmare. All is fine. Go back to sleep."

Now as she sat with her back to the wall, she wondered, *Who have I become? What have I become?* And once again found herself staring at her hands.

"Greetings!" a male voice called from the snowy night.

In that instant, Morning Dew's heart skipped, fear shooting down her limbs. *Please, Breath Giver, tell me they're not coming for me!*

"Pale Cat!" Heron Wing called with delight. "Come warm yourself. It's not a fit night for beavers to be out in, let alone you."

The *Hopaye* ducked past the door hanging, smiling, and grabbed Stone up as the boy shot across the room and into his uncle's arms. "How's my boy?" Pale Cat asked.

"Fine, Uncle. Look! Morning Dew made me a clay gorget! See? She carved a circle with a cross inside. You know what that is?"

"I do. It's the sacred fire at the center of our world." Pale Cat glanced at her. If he saw her fading panic, he didn't remark on it, saying only, "Thank you. It was a kind gift."

She nodded politely, averting her eyes.

"What brings you?" Heron Wing asked. "That wife of yours not feeding you well? We have a bit of stew left. Buffalo tongue. It seems that some of the hunters found a little herd of yearlings along the divide to the east."

"I've heard of several buffalo that have been killed this season. Old Broken Thumb killed a couple of cows. They've been packing the meat and hides in. Made it just before the storm." He settled himself before the fire.

"Smells wonderful, and while yes, I'm well fed, Sister, I could stand a taste of delicacy. That's why I came. Solstice preparations begin. I'll be fasting and sweating, preparing for the ceremonies."

Morning Dew drew her legs to her chest, trying to be as small as she could. She ached to ask after her brother's wives, but couldn't muster the courage.

Imagine that? After what you've done, you can't find the courage to ask about some slave women? The notion surprised her.

"What is the news?" Heron Wing asked.

"People are preparing for the solstice, cooking, planning, getting ready. A few relatives from the outlying towns have already arrived. If the cold doesn't break, we may not have as many people as originally anticipated, but these snows don't last long. Cousin White Fish is bringing his entire family. I don't know where we'll put them all, but it's the first time in four years they've come down from Bowl Town."

"I heard you went to look at old man Bittern," Heron Wing said, a careful eye on Stone, who concentrated on ladling out buffalo tongue stew with a wooden spoon.

"There is nothing to be done. Some malignant Spirit has fastened itself in the bowels. He's burning up with fever, passing blood and pus. I've seen this before. I think his souls will leave within the next couple of days." Pale Cat took the bowl, thanking Stone, then cast some into the fire, asking the buffalo Spirits for forgiveness.

"I'll send Wide Leaf over with a bowl of something for the family."

Pale Cat glanced around. "Where's Wide Leaf?"

"She has a new man. Builder, they call him. An Albaamo. He has a farmstead just beyond the palisade."

Pale Cat grinned. "At her age? You know, some say you allow her too much latitude."

Heron Wing arched an eyebrow. "A woman in my position doesn't begrudge another a little companionship.

Besides, it's early yet, but they both seem most taken with each other." A pause. "And she still serves me."

"And what if he wants her for good?" Pale Cat tasted the stew. "This is excellent!"

"Thank Morning Dew. She made it." Heron Wing flipped her hand absently. "Gods, Brother, if Wide Leaf wants to go, I won't keep her. I'll find some sort of Trade, maybe a new room on the back? Whatever we work out, Builder and I can come to an arrangement so that it all looks proper." Heron Wing laughed. "Assuming he wants to keep her after he gets to know her."

Pale Cat had cast an evaluative glance at Morning Dew. He didn't bother to say, "That's all right; you have another, younger slave. One who also makes excellent stew." Morning Dew tried to keep her face blank, but couldn't help grinding her teeth.

"Any other gossip?" Heron Wing asked.

"Your husband is still missing. Thin Branch claims he's hunting." Pale Cat glanced at the door, where jets of cold air crept in. "In weather like this?" He shook his head. "Whatever he's hunting, it's going to end up as trouble."

Heron Wing grunted. "Maybe this time her husband will come home unannounced from a hunting trip with all of his brothers in tow. Armed and angry."

"Do you think we could get that lucky?"

"Haven't yet," Heron Wing replied lightly. "But I still have faith in Power. It can't always be looking the wrong direction."

"Sister," Pale Cat warned, admonishing with his spoon.

Heron Wing chuckled. "We've had this discussion before."

"Power will have its due," Pale Cat replied kindly.

"And the Albaamaha situation?"

At that Pale Cat frowned. "A lot of people are concerned. And not just among the Sky Hand. I have had Albaamaha coming to see me when no one is looking. They're worried. Word got out—as it always does—about the last Council. I've had private assurances that no Albaamo killed the captives."

Morning Dew closed her eyes, heart sinking. Her people . . . The hurt tried to seep out from her souls.

"But there's been a new complication," Pale Cat continued. "Red Awl and his wife have vanished. The story is that someone sent word that they were needed upriver at Bowl Town. The next morning, White Fish's messenger arrived with news that he'd be at the solstice ceremonies. When I asked him about Red Awl's sick mother, he replied that she's fine. No sooner did that get out than tongues started wagging. People are wondering just why Red Awl vanished when he did."

"Think he's involved?" Heron Wing asked.

Pale Cat finished the last of the stew, saving one piece as an offering to the fire, and laid the bowl aside. "Red Awl? No. I can't see it. He's always been the voice of reason. I've talked to him several times about our relations with the Albaamaha. My impression is that yes, he wants the best possible for his people, but he's a realist. He doesn't like the idea of trouble between the Sky Hand and the Albaamaha. He knows it would go nowhere but wrong for everyone. What do you think?"

"I agree." She considered for a moment. "He has always impressed me with his reasoning and tact. I like him. Respect him." She lifted an eyebrow. "Amber Bead, however, is a different story. He comes across as a fool." She waved off his look. "Oh, I know. Everyone thinks he's harmless. But there's something about his eyes, as if he thinks one thing, and says another."

"Amber Bead? A plotter?"

Heron Wing studied her hands for a moment. "Only until the situation begins to get serious. He doesn't have the stomach for the consequences if things go wrong."

"The Albaamaha are nervous." Pale Cat agreed. "Few think anything will come of Smoke Shield's accusations, but they see this as a sign of things to come. There is already talk in the villages that when Smoke Shield becomes high minko, the Albaamaha will suffer for it."

"He is not fit to be high minko." Heron Wing tried to shrug it off. "But then, for years people said the same thing about Flying Hawk. Maybe Smoke Shield will show some sense when the responsibility falls on his shoulders."

Pale Cat reached out to ruffle Stone's hair as he watched the fire. "Flying Hawk spent years recovering from his brother's murder. How many times has he said that if there was one thing he could take back, it would be that?" He paused. "Have you ever heard Smoke Shield regret anything he's done?"

"No."

"Maybe it's just bad blood in the Chief Clan."

"They weren't all bad," Heron Wing said softly. "Just the ones who are left."

"Well, if something doesn't bring Smoke Shield to his senses, his leadership could be a disaster. If the Albaamaha revolt, this entire land will go up in flames and smoke." Pale Cat sighed. "If we turn on each other, the rest of the world will turn on us. No one will be safe. And you can bet the Yuchi will be out to make the most of it."

Morning Dew listened, wondering, *How can the Chahta turn this to their advantage?*

Twenty-nine

How will I die? The question continued to run through Trader's head as he stared out the temple door to the snowy compound enclosed by the mound-top palisade. The cold ate into his skin, a sharp reminder of what was to come. Cold, and pain, and unbearable heat. If the gods were merciful, he would freeze to death the first day.

From the time Trader was a little boy, Uncle had trained, coached, and tested him. From the first dunking in icy waters, to holding his hands out to flames, the goal had always been to harden his body.

"You must learn to ignore pain. It is only a discomfort, not the end of the world. Like casting a lance, the body can learn to bear pain. Unpleasant, but necessary." Uncle's words carried across time and distance. *"You, Nephew, represent our people. Should you ever be captured, you will become the heart and Spirit of our people. Some lowly farmer, or potter, or stone carver, can weep, plead, and wail on the square. People will just laugh and spit on him. But you are Chief Clan. Should you ever face the square you will become us."*

Trader took a deep breath, his blood charged with worry. He had spoken brave words to the Kala Hi'ki. Now creeping doubts began to fester. *What if it is too much?*.

It was one thing to just be dragged out, not to have time to think about the coming agony, but this way he had plenty of time to anticipate it. The worst would be the burning. Fire seared the flesh, cooked it onto living bone. They would take his eyes among the first things, because that had been done to the Kala Hi'ki. The old Priest would be sure of that.

Trader shook his head. It seemed like no more than a short breath past that his greatest concern had been how to protect his marvelous wealth in copper. Now, just the knowledge that he'd still be breathing come the next moon overcame all other preoccupations.

"You look cheery," Old White said as he came to stand beside him. "Could I get you a coat? This is freezing here."

"No. I had better get used to it."

Old White lowered his voice. "You could run. And, as to me, don't think twice. I'm an old man with a considerable reputation. I'll take my chances. As far as Two Petals is concerned, I think it's an empty threat on the Kala Hi'ki's part. She's too Powerful."

"Thank you, Seeker. But it is out of the question." He gestured to the snow. "They couldn't ask for better tracking weather—assuming I could even get out of the city. No, I am bound. I am a Trader, and born of the Chief Clan. This is now a matter of my honor, and the honor of the Tsoyaha. I will not break the Power of Trade, or my promise to the Tsoyaha. If this is the price of being who I am, I will pay it to the best of my ability."

"All is not lost," Old White said. "When the Kala Hi'ki's anger ebbs, I will make the offer to buy our freedom. It will leave us with nothing . . . but they are only goods." He shrugged. "It won't be the first time I have started with nothing."

"If we can do that with honor, I agree." He frowned. "I have recently been forced to reevaluate my priorities. A wealth in Trade is no longer as important as it once was."

"I repeat, you do not have to do this thing because of me and Two Petals."

"The stakes have gone beyond that." He smiled sadly.

"No, if this is what Power has planned for me, I will endure to the best of my ability. My decision is bigger than just us. We serve Power on this journey, Seeker. Not ourselves or the interests of our people."

"Then perhaps you are worthy," a guttural voice said from behind.

They both turned to see Kala Hi'ki standing no more than a pace behind them. How did an old blind man move so quietly?

"I will be worthy," Trader said with a confidence he did not feel. "Even if it had not snowed, even if you had no hopes of capturing me, I have come in peace, asking only to purchase labor to cross your lands. I serve the Power of Trade. No matter what was done to you, it wasn't anything you have not done to my people in turn. That is the way we have been given, so I do not seek any explanations. But when you finally cut my corpse from the square and give pieces of my body away, you will live with the knowledge that you, not I, have broken the Power. From that moment on, you will know that if there was treachery, it was at your hand, and not mine. Word will travel. Traders will know. A witch—if that's what you decide to portray me as—would not willingly walk to the square and die with the dignity and courage that I will."

Kala Hi'ki listened intently, saying nothing. For a long time, he stood as if carved from wood. Finally he said, "You are no witch." He sighed. "You are free to go. Along with all of your Trade." He paused. "Including the wealth of copper you carry in the Chikosi war medicine."

Trader stiffened.

"You didn't think we would look?" He shook his head. "I've had quite a time silencing my Priests, but they have a great deal of respect for me. I have told them that despite the wealth it represents, keeping it would bring us ill fortune. So far, they are heeding my words. However, I must know something. Tell me, man of honor, why should I allow you to take the war medicine back to your people, where it will eventually be used against us?"

Trader nodded. A fair question. "Power sent the war medicine box to us, entrusted it to our care. I know my people have a new war medicine. This one was lost long ago. Perhaps it is time that it is used for something besides war. Perhaps, like the Seeker, it only wishes to go home to die. It shall be my request that when I am buried, the box will be buried with me. I cannot promise you things beyond my ability, but I shall do whatever it takes to keep that war medicine from ever being used against the Tsoyaha."

"I take your oath, man of honor." The Kala Hi'ki paused. "As to the Contrary . . ."

"Yes?" Old White asked, curiosity growing.

"She responds to certain herbs. I think over the coming days I can help her to deal with her Power. If you can wait for a time, she may find a way to focus, to control her fear, and handle the Power that now consumes her."

"We would be honored, Kala Hi'ki." Old White glanced at Trader. "Power brought us here for a reason." He smiled cunningly. "And we do serve the Power of Trade. We have things from the north. Perhaps the Tsoyaha would be interested in some of them?"

"Perhaps they would." He raised his ruined hand. "We are preparing for the solstice ceremonies—one of our most important observances. This is the time that we call Mother Sun to begin her journey northward. You will be welcomed among our people, though I suppose our high chief will wish to see you and hear your story. He is most interested in you. I have had to fend off runner after runner seeking information."

"We thank you, Kala Hi'ki." Old White bowed to the blind man.

"I ask only that you heed our ways, and respect our customs."

"It is done," Trader agreed. "As I recall, you make offerings to Mother Sun at this time. We are Traders, of an enemy people, but might we make a gift and offering in the name of the Tsoyaha at the solstice?"

"Why would a Chikosi do this thing when it benefits the Tsoyaha?"

"Because all Power is shared," Trader said, images of a Yuchi square filling his head. *Was he really spared?* "I may not have seen as many peoples as the Seeker, but we all share a respect and reverence for Power. Perhaps this is a lesson that has faded along with Cahokia. My people may believe they were made of clay from the sacred mountains of the west, but we, too, honor the sun. We are taught that Mother Spider brought sacred fire to earth for all peoples. And perhaps, Kala Hi'ki, just perhaps, seeing a Chikosi offering prayers for her well-being, while in the midst of her children's most sacred ceremony, might bring a smile to her. Perhaps she will think kindly of all of us."

The Kala Hi'ki vented a weary sigh. "I think it is good that you are unique among your people, Trader. I would fear for our continued prosperity if all Chikosi had your sense and courage."

As the blind man turned to go, Old White asked, "Kala Hi'ki, I would know why you have changed your mind about us."

He hesitated, not turning back. "Because I am like you in the end. No matter what the cravings of my heart, and my thirst to repay the Chikosi for what they did to me, I, too, serve Power." He laughed ironically. "I now wonder if that is not why you were sent here. To remind me of that fact." Then he walked steadfastly to the rear and vanished into the hallway.

"A gift, you say?" Old White asked.

Trader shrugged. "I was thinking of that big bag of Illinois bowls you carry. Can you think of a better use for them?"

Everything had worked out the way Smoke Shield had hoped it would. Red Awl and his wife had easily acquiesced to accompanying them upriver. The first frigid drops of rain had started to fall just as they reached Clay Bank Crossing. When they were faced with pelting cold rain, persuading Red Awl to make for shore hadn't been too difficult.

"It will give us a chance to talk," Smoke Shield had said reasonably enough. "I would hear your thoughts concerning the Albaamaha."

They had landed, pulled the canoes up, and climbed the slope to a small shelter built under the trees. It was there that he and Fast Legs had lifted their weapons. Red Awl had gaped in disbelief; then his expression had hardened. His wife, however, had stared in wide-eyed dismay.

"What are you doing?" she had demanded. "Don't you know who this is? He is Mikko Red Awl, representative to the Council for the northern Albaamaha!"

"And I am war chief of the Sky Hand," Smoke Shield had barked back. "You will shoulder our packs and take the trail up the hill."

"Just do it," Red Awl had said. "Mother will be all right."

"Your mother is fine," Fast Legs had snarled. "We had to tell you something to get you out of the city."

Red Awl's expression had fallen. As he had picked up the pack, he asked, "Why are you doing this?"

Smoke Shield had fingered the stone-tipped arrow in his bow. "Because I want to know the truth about Albaamaha treachery. You can avoid a long unpleasant session at Sandstone Camp if you will tell me who is behind the Albaamaha conspiracy against the Sky Hand. Give me the names, the clans, and you can go about your business."

"I know of *no* conspiracy against the Sky Hand."

"Who sent the hunter to warn the White Arrow about my attack?"

"I am told it was Paunch. You know as much as I do!"

"Walk. We'll do this the difficult way."

"Husband?" Lotus Root had asked.

"It will be all right. As soon as we convince them we are telling the truth, they will let us go." But he didn't sound like he believed it himself.

Fine, let him buy time.

The march up into the hills had gone smoothly. Even the weather helped, the cold soggy conditions ensuring that no unwelcome travelers would be lurking along the trail. As Smoke Shield had expected, Sandstone Camp was empty, the quarries there abandoned.

They took shelter in a small hut used by the stone cutters, and Smoke Shield ordered the woman to make a fire while Fast Legs gathered damp wood from the forest. Snowflakes were falling by the time all was in order.

"Tie them up," Smoke Shield ordered, his arrow nocked.

"This will be a terrible mistake," Red Awl predicted. "I have done nothing but try and smooth relations between our peoples. When word of this gets out, you will have done more to turn the Albaamaha against you than any other man. That eye in the middle of the hand you are so proud of shall weep."

"You are assuming word will get out," Smoke Shield had said as Fast Legs pulled the last of the knots tight on the woman's arms. She was trembling with fear, her wet clothing clinging to her body. Yes, a nice body, with shapely breasts and the kind of hips that promised delight.

"Is the fire hot?" Smoke Shield asked.

"Hot enough," Fast Legs agreed.

"Good. Cut the shirt off the man. Let's hear what he has to say when only the truth will save his flesh from the fire and knife."

That had been early afternoon. Now Smoke Shield stared sullenly into the night as he hunched at the low doorway. Red Awl whimpered behind him. Albaamaha had no more guts than certain Chahta high minkos. But no matter where they cut, or what they burned, Red Awl insisted his Albaamaha were innocent.

"Of course my people hate you," Red Awl had said. "Look what you do to us! You even turn on those of us who would find ways to live with you! You, and your Power, are cursed!"

"Then you know nothing of Power," Smoke Shield had replied. "We are strong, and Power flows through the strong like a great wind. With it, the weak are blown away."

"If you are made high minko," Red Awl had said, "you will bring blood and fire to our land. It will end in death and misery for all of us."

"Who killed the captives? Who decided to humiliate us before the gods?"

"I don't know!" he had screamed as Fast Legs applied a burning stick to his testicles.

"Just name the Albaamaha who did this thing, and the pain will be over."

"*I can't!*" Red Awl had cried. "Anyone I named would be innocent! Don't you stupid Chikosi understand? If an Albaamo did this thing, *I don't know who!*"

And so it had continued. Now for a blissful moment there was silence but for the woman's choked breathing. Red Awl had fainted, his souls fleeing from the wreckage of his body. Fast Legs had slapped snow against the worst of the wounds, seeking to draw the man's souls back, but his body sagged limply.

Smoke Shield stared out into the night. A good three inches of soggy snow had fallen, melting from the bottom up. *What will make him talk?* He pondered that idea, thinking of different manners of inflicting pain.

Fast Legs asked, "War Chief? Should we let him rest until morning?"

Smoke Shield rubbed the back of his head. "I suppose. It's late. Maybe when he finally comes to, he'll understand that this will go on and on until he talks.

Maybe that inevitability will do what immediate pain cannot."

"And the woman?"

"Cut her dress off. It's cold. I could use some soft warm relief." He smiled grimly. "Torture is an exhausting business."

Lotus Root turned out to be the best part of the day. She fought like a wildcat when he pulled his beaverhide shirt over his head and settled on top of her. He had to cuff her once, hard, when she bit his lip and drew blood.

Red Awl blinked. Pain, terrible and encompassing, brought him to wakefulness. He bit his tongue to keep from screaming. He gasped for breath and tried to swallow down a dry throat. The deep burns on his body shot white agony through his limbs and torso.

I have never known hate until now. He managed to focus on the sleeping forms barely visible in the darkness. In the rear, huddled against the wall, he could make out Lotus Root. Her hair fell over her head like a shawl, and she clutched her ruined dress around her like a blanket. He swallowed hard, trying to keep from moaning. By the Ancestors, he didn't want to wake the Chikosi.

The act of sitting up left him woozy and reeling. How could a human body hurt this much? "Lotus Root?" he whispered. "Shhh! Lean this way. Maybe I can get to your knots."

She didn't respond, but remained huddled, like a child who had been beaten.

"Lotus Root? We must be very quiet."

"Go away," she whispered miserably.

A hot tear traced down his cheek. What had they done to her? She had always been the strong one.

"If I can reach your knots, I may be able to loosen them."

She remained like a lump.

He bent his neck, feeling burned skin compressing. *Abba Mikko, help me!*

Smoke Shield awakened to the winter song of a robin. He shivered in the cold, blinking to clear his vision. Morning light spilled through the low doorway, the world beyond bright with reflected snow. He yawned, seeing his breath rise in a wispy white streamer. Gods, Fast Legs needed to stoke up the fire. He tried to snuggle deeper into his bear hide. When he made a face his lip ached, which reminded him of the Albaamo woman, and her sharp teeth.

He chuckled. Well, Red Awl should be recovered enough that he could watch while Smoke Shield enjoyed another session with his wife. Yes, that was a great way to warm up while the fire was rekindled.

He sat up, dabbing at his swollen lip, then froze as he looked toward the captives. Gone! Both of them!

"Fast Legs! Wake up!" He scrambled to his feet, searching in the old trash at the back of the hut. The bindings lay in limp piles. He knew Red Awl's; they were stiff with blood, and cleanly cut. The woman's still had kinks in the cord where the knots had been pulled loose.

"What's happened, War Chief?" Fast Legs stood, eyes thick with sleep.

"They're gone. So are my bow and arrows."

"I was sleeping on mine."

"Thank the gods." He leveled a hard finger. "How did they *pick the knots*?"

"I don't know, War Chief!" Fast Legs swallowed hard. "You checked them yourself!"

He gave the man a "You'll pay for this" look. "They can't have gone far. Come, before this snow melts, we can run them down."

He grabbed up his bearhide cape and peeked out the doorway, half expecting an arrow to be loosed in his direction. Nothing. He bolted from the door, sprinting to one of the trees, to stare warily out at the forest.

The tracks headed straight down the trail, making for the canoe landing.

Fast Legs darted out, then to the side, his bow drawn, arrow nocked. "Do you think they headed for the canoe landing?"

"I do. But we'll have to go carefully. I think they've fled, but you can't tell."

"They're not warriors," Fast Legs replied. "I say we forget caution. The important thing is to find them before they reach the river."

Together they sprinted down the trail. How long had it been? Smoke Shield's practiced eye read the tracks. Some, in patches of sunlight, were already melting out. The woman ran easily. The man however, was dragging, stumbling, drops of blood spattering here and there. They were nothing more than pink splotches in the melting snow.

Smoke Shield paused where the man had fallen, then struggled to rise. The woman had come back to help him. "He's weak," Smoke Shield noted before resuming the chase. How much lead did they have? Judging from the tracks, at least a hand of time. But the rapidly melting snow masked the usual clues a tracker would use.

Smoke Shield led the way, careless that his prey might have circled to lay an ambush. At the speed he was running, there was a good chance a weak man, even a good hunter, would miss a shot. And Red Awl was weak. Another bare spot showed where he had fallen.

"He has lost a lot of blood," Fast Legs decided. "Running has opened some of the wounds." Looking closely, Smoke Shield could see clots of it. The surface had dried, crinkling. The quarry had a good lead.

"We have to run," Smoke Shield ordered. "They're farther down the trail than I would have thought."

Curse it! How could I have slept through their escape? A building rage lent strength to his muscles as he pounded down the trail. He slipped on the muddy ground, scrambled for purchase, and regained his feet, running harder.

He noted impressions in the mud where the Albaamaha had slithered and slid as well. The marks where Red Awl had fallen were coming at ever-greater frequencies.

Please, great gods, tell me he has passed out again! The woman wouldn't be able to do more than drag her unconscious husband along.

Hope began to rise between Smoke Shield's souls. There was a chance. Gods, why hadn't he thought to cripple the man last night? Cut his tendons, and he'd never have made it this far.

They slithered down a steep slope where the soil was mostly clay, and found better footing in the leaf mat. Here the snow was reduced to patches, the flat having a slight southern exposure. *Which way? The canoe landing. If they haven't reached there, we can circle back, pick up the trail, and hunt them down.*

He was panting, running easily now that his muscles had warmed. The desperation of the chase sent a thrill down his bones. Yes, he would catch them. Another bloody patch marked the man's latest fall. The leaves here were disturbed as if stone-clad feet had stumbled through.

Back in snow again, the tracks looked fresher, and Smoke Shield fought the urge to whoop with glee. They would catch them; he just knew it!

He bounded down onto the old river terrace, and sprinted along the winding trail. Drag marks in the leaves and snow, coupled with deeply imprinted tracks, showed that the woman was pulling Red Awl now.

"I've got you!" He raced forward, catching glimpses of the river's far bank through the maze of tree trunks. He almost overran the place where Lotus Root had dragged the man off to the side, then scattered leaves to hide the fact.

Smoke Shield skidded to a halt, crouching, panting for breath as he stared into the trees. Fast Legs, a stone's throw behind, slowed, crouched, and took cover behind a thick gum trunk, his careful eyes peering into the forest.

Smoke Shield slipped from tree to tree, and stopped. He signaled Fast Legs to sneak around to the side. A man's form—leaned against the far side of a beech—didn't move, but Smoke Shield could see a muddy foot. That had to be Red Awl.

He waited, glancing this way and that. Where had the woman gotten to?

"War Chief," Fast Legs called, "he looks dead." Fast Legs approached warily, his bow drawn, alert for any movement.

Smoke Shield eased forward, eyes scanning the silent forest for any sign of ambush. *Where is that four-times-cursed woman?*

"Dead," Fast Legs asserted.

Smoke Shield hurried forward, crouching by the dead Albaamo. He touched Red Awl's neck, feeling cold flesh. The man's eyes had begun to dry, the pupils in the first stages of gray. As Smoke Shield raised the man's arm, it felt loose. "Not dead long. Perhaps a hand of time?"

He turned, staring at the trees. "Where is the woman?"

Fast Legs studied the ground around them. Most of the snow was melted, stripelike patches here and there in the shadows of the trees. "There." He pointed at a partial track. "Canoe landing, I'd say."

"Remember, she still has my bow and arrows."

"Even if she reached the canoe landing, she can't have gone far. We'll split up. I'll go upstream while you head down." Fast Legs added, "It would be better if you were seen in Split Sky City sooner rather than later. If she's hiding among her people at Bowl Town, I'll get her in the end."

Smoke Shield bent, got a grip on the dead Albaamo, and hoisted the limp body over his shoulders.

"What are you doing?" Fast Legs demanded.

"Go! Canoe landing. Kill the woman. I'll be along."

Fast Legs left at a pounding run.

Smoke Shield hurried along, aware of blood and fluids leaking down his back and legs. The bear hide would be ruined, but he could always replace a bear hide. The one thing he could not afford was the discovery of a dead Albaamo mikko. He topped the crest above the landing and tossed the corpse to slide down the greasy wet clay. Fast Legs stood there, dark worry on his face.

"Gods!" Smoke Shield cried, seeing only their two canoes resting on the beach. Deep tracks showed where the woman had struggled to push her heavy dugout into the water. He slipped and slid down before grasping the corpse and dragging it to the canoes.

Smoke Shield walked out into the current to see past the thick stand of rushes and cattails on either side of the landing. He stared up and down the river. Nothing broke the smooth surface of the water, either upstream or down. "Her first impulse would be to head downriver," Smoke Shield said. "She would believe herself moving faster, gaining distance."

"That same current will carry you, War Chief. Hurry. Let me push you off."

"What about the body?" Smoke Shield asked.

"I'll attend to the body. You go!" Fast Legs was pushing the canoe as Smoke Shield climbed in. "Here, War Chief! Take my bow." He tossed his bow and quiver into the hull.

"What about you?"

"I'll manage! I'm a warrior." Fast Legs waved as Smoke Shield lifted his paddle and steered into the current.

Foolish woman. He'd be on top of her before she could make any kind of safety.

And when I do, Lotus Root, you are going to wish you were lying back there with your dead husband!

Thirty

After Fast Legs tumbled Red Awl's body into his canoe, he pushed off, reaching for his paddle and driving the craft upriver, close to the bank. As the first fingers of sunlight topped the horizon and cast light on the wavelets breaking on the shore, the rushes just north of the landing parted, and Lotus Root stepped out. She glanced back where her canoe floated, hidden in a marshy stand of cattails.

"You were right, my husband. These are not smart Chikosi." She sniffed against the tears that began to trickle down her cheeks. "They shall hear of this day's work. Upon your dead souls, my husband, I swear it."

She wiped at the tears, stepping out to stare upriver. Fast Legs' canoe was a dark speck at the bend of the river. She had hoped they would be too anxious to take Red Awl's body, that they would rush headlong into their canoes and paddle off, giving her time to retrieve the final conclusive evidence of what they'd done.

Instead, she had only her word, and the Chikosi war chief's bow and arrows. It, along with her status as Red Awl's wife and leader of the Dog Bane Clan, would be enough.

"You have unleashed the winds, War Chief. Now, let us see if you and the Chikosi can ride them!"

Sunlight streamed down between puffy white clouds in the aftermath of the storm that had drifted far beyond the southern horizon. Snow melted into puddles of water on the packed earth of Rainbow City's plaza. People hurried along, bent on various tasks. They were bundled against the chill that blew down from the north. As they passed, they cast curious gazes at Old White, Swimmer, and Trader as they skirted the edge of the great plaza. To their right, the flat expanse was broken by the great Sacred Cedar of the Tsoyaha. In this case, the Sacred Cedar pole was a tall straight specimen, its sides carved to show the long-ago quest of one of their warriors in search of the terrible wizard who was frightening the sun. Old White wasn't certain he'd ever seen such a large cedar log. That the Yuchi had managed to cut it, drag it here, and plant it awed him. It must have been a gargantuan effort.

The plaza they skirted consisted of the gaming ground, oriented north to south so the teams could play before the Sacred Cedar. Meanwhile oriented east to west on either side of the pole were the chunkey grounds, one for each moiety.

The Yuchi were unique among peoples. A child was born into his mother's clan as among other folk, but he was a member of his father's moiety. The Chief Moiety had its Council House on the square mound overlooking the plaza, while the Warrior Moiety lay to the south. Unlike among the Sky Hand and other peoples, the clans acted autonomously, owing nothing to the moieties. Of these, the Bear, Wolf, Deer, and Panther clans were the most prominent and influential. Yuchi houses all bore an emblem of the sun high up on the ridgepole, but each clan totem was displayed just over the door.

The ground between the plaza and tall palisade to the east was packed with thatch-roofed houses, granaries, storerooms, ramadas, and hollowed-log mortars with their associated pestles. A thick veil of blue smoke rose from around the roofs to trail off to the south. Along with the smell of wood smoke came the odors of cooking food. Everyone was busy preparing for the winter solstice. The high point would be the stickball game between the moieties on the final day. Wagers were being cast, with the fortunes of entire clans bet on the outcome.

They passed the Chief Moiety Council House—a high building behind a low palisade. The mound it was constructed on was capped with blue clay that shone in the sunlight. Across the plaza, they could see its opposite, the Warrior Council House atop a similar yellow clay mound. Both structures had been built to impress, but not so much as the great mound rising on the northeast corner of the plaza.

The palace there was the grandest building in Rainbow City. The mound itself was huge, a jutting earthen construction finished in bright red clay that glistened in the sunlight. The palisade at its margins rose straight and true, allowing glimpses of the palace beyond. The high walls were similarly plastered in the bright red of the mound with a white stripe surrounding the walls, and visible just below the overhanging roof. The roof itself rose high into the sky, with effigies of Bear, Wolf, and Ivory-billed Woodpecker protruding from the gray thatch.

"Not as impressive as Cahokia," Old White granted.

"Nothing is." Trader looked around. "Nevertheless, it gives a person an entirely new perspective of the Yuchi. These are a strong and healthy people."

"Most of the southern chiefdoms are." Old White replied. "It makes a person wonder if the Spirit of Cahokia has moved to the south. As if somehow the Power has shifted this direction. Corn grows better here. The Caddo, Natchez, Chikosi, and Chaktaw seem to have inherited Cahokia's heart."

"Go away," Trader said, shooing one of the growling local dogs who approached Swimmer with stiff legs, its back hair on end. "That's it, Swimmer. Relax. We're on our best behavior here. I don't want to end up on a square just because you think you can whip some upstart Yuchi mongrel."

"Speaking of which"—Old White pointed—"there they are. And, blessed be Power, you're not hanging in one."

A series of squares stood along the northern boundaries of the plaza just ahead of them. Off behind them were society houses on low mounds. And behind them rose the city palisade that clung to the edge of the steep bluff.

Trader walked over, running his fingers along one of the poles, staring thoughtfully at the stained wood, knowing full well what gave it that dark hue. "It was a close thing."

"Perhaps," Old White granted.

"You weren't the object of the Kala Hi'ki's wrath."

"It was only a matter of removal. I am still Chikosi, even if I've been gone longer."

"You are going to have to break yourself of the habit of calling our people Chikosi, assuming we ever make it there. It's considered derogatory."

"The Natchez call us the Chikaza. The Chahta are called Chaktaw. It will all become one someday." Old White scratched his chin. "People are funny that way."

"Are you going to tell me your terrible secret now that we've dodged the Yuchi arrow?"

"No." Old White smiled. "Some secrets are best kept until the moment of greatest import. And who knows, we are not at our destination yet. I might die with it, leaving you forever perplexed. That notion entertains me immensely."

"Your idea of amusement is seriously ill," Trader said, straightening from his inspection of the square.

"Greetings!" a voice called from behind them. The burly war chief who had captured them on the river emerged from one of the buildings. He descended the wooden steps fronting the low mound, muscles bunching in his thick legs.

"Greetings, War Chief." Old White gave him a slight nod. "You are well, I hope?"

"Well indeed." He glanced at Trader as he approached. "And sleeping well despite the lack of Chikosi screams coming from the square." He offered a slight bow. "Forgive me. I am not known for my tact. My people find that my other talents offset my brutish manners. I am Wolf Tail, war chief of the Tsoyaha. I ask you to understand my reluctance to name myself the other night. Were you to be witches or dangerous sorcerers, that knowledge might have given you something to fasten your magic upon and done me ill. I have had occasion to deal with witches in the past. It wasn't pleasant."

"You are forgiven," Old White granted easily. "My young friend here will also forgive you, but it takes him longer. He hasn't had quite the breadth of experience I have. Youth and all, you know."

Trader added dryly, "You are forgiven, Wolf Tail. A war chief's first duty is to protect his people from all enemies."

Wolf Tail glanced sidelong at the square. "Personally, I am just as glad that the Kala Hi'ki has offered you his protection. I don't like war . . . or the things that come of it."

"A peculiar notion for a war chief," Old White granted.

The warrior shrugged. "When called upon, my men and I do what must be done. We do it very well, and while some chafe, and wish me replaced so they could seek greater glory on the war trail, I would as soon avoid the fighting." He glanced at Trader. "When it is all finished, win or lose, someone must weep. Children lose parents, and the defeated are always driven to retaliation. Or do Chikosi enjoy weeping for their dead?"

"No one does," Trader replied. "I may indeed be younger than the Seeker, but I have traveled far, and seen many peoples. Warfare, like everything else, must be kept in balance." He paused, studying Wolf Tail. "For a man who claims to lack tact, I think a great deal more goes on inside that head of yours."

Wolf Tail grinned. "It is good to have the respect of one's adversary."

"You have mine, War Chief," Old White added. "Did your warriors receive the gifts we sent?" Small packages of mint tea had been parceled out from one of Trader's packs and sent to each of the warriors.

"They did. I would thank you. It was an unnecessary gesture. They were just following orders. Reluctantly, I'll admit, but they obeyed despite their wishes to simply smack you in the heads and toss your bodies into the river."

"Our arrival caused them inconvenience," Old White added. "It was only fair given that they carried our packs to the temple."

Wolf Tail gave him a thin smile. "My understanding is that the Kala Hi'ki is Healing the Contrary?"

"And making good progress," Old White reported.

"I have also heard that you will be with us until solstice."

"At least," Trader said, signaling Swimmer to stop sniffing at Wolf Tail's leg.

Old White prayed the dog wouldn't mistake it for a tree.

"In that case I hope our hospitality makes up for our welcome."

"It will," Old White said agreeably. "We were just on the way to pay a visit to your chief. It seems he has been most curious about us."

"A great many people are." Wolf Tail paused. "I have only heard vague rumors about Power, the Chikosi, and trouble ahead."

Trader added fervently, "Yes, well, Power has certainly given us a few surprises. As to the Chikosi and trouble, I fall into your camp. I would rather avoid it."

"What do you think about their attack on the Chaktaw?"

"What attack?" Old White and Trader said simultaneously.

"They surprised White Arrow Town in retaliation for a raid. It was remarkably efficient. They swam down the river at night, taking the town immediately after the matron's daughter married the White Arrow war chief. They captured the high minko, the *Alikchi Hopaii,* and many others. A great many were killed. The Chaktaw are reeling."

Old White frowned. "We have heard nothing of it. We have been upriver. We had hoped to descend the Horned Serpent River, Trading all the way. Are the Chaktaw preparing for war against the Chikosi?"

Wolf Tail studied them thoughtfully. "For the moment they are strengthening their defenses. They expect a series of attacks when the weather warms. This new Chikosi war chief, Smoke Shield, is an ambitious man. Now that he has tasted success, with no battle losses, he is going to think about settling old scores."

"This could be trouble," Old White told Trader.

"It could indeed." Trader frowned. "I wonder who this Smoke Shield is? Have you ever heard of him?"

"No. But I have been long gone from these parts. This could complicate things for us." Old White turned to Wolf Tail. "You have taken precautions, I hope."

"Odd words for a Chikosi, no matter how long removed from his people." Wolf Tail lifted an eyebrow.

"War is bad for the Trade," Trader added. "Things have become difficult enough without having armies of warriors marching the trails. You need look no farther than the Michigamea to see the effect it has on the movement of goods along the rivers."

"Who started this trouble between the Chaktaw and Chikosi?" Old White asked.

"The White Arrow. But how does any of this get started? Someone inflicts a real or perceived insult on someone else, or a grieving relative attains a position of authority. A chief believes he can gain prestige and Power by defeating his neighbor. In this case, according to rumors, a young and inexperienced high minko thought he could chastise the Chikosi."

Trader was frowning. "The Flying Hawk I remember would take this as an opportunity to repay old debts. I don't blame the Chaktaw for preparing their defenses." He looked at Old White. "What do you think? Should we stick to the original plan to travel down the Horned Serpent River? Or would it be better to make the more expensive portage from the Tenasee to the headwaters of the Black Warrior?"

"That's a much longer, rougher portage," Old White noted. "Crossing into the Horned Serpent, we cross hills from one watershed to the next. Two days at most depending on the trails. To the Black Warrior? That could take seven to ten days depending on labor, the trails, and weather."

"Figure three times the Trade," Trader decided. "Maybe more if there is news of a Chikosi war party in the area. People will be nervous."

Old White shot him a curious look. "I thought you were the one who said we had to stop calling them Chikosi, that it was derogatory."

"If it doesn't bother you to be insulted, why should it bother me?"

Old White turned to Wolf Tail. "Do the Chaktaw still honor the Power of Trade, or have they grown introspective like the Michigamea?"

"Introspective?" Wolf Tail mused. "I like that. It's a good term for people who are busy staring up their own behinds. But to answer your question, the Chaktaw have always honored the Power of Trade in the past. For the moment, however, they will be very suspicious, worried about spies, and—I don't have to remind you—wary of anyone with ties to the Chikosi."

"Well," Old White said wearily, "Power didn't promise us that this would be easy."

Trader fingered his chin. "What kind of trouble would we be in if we just went back upriver and Traded with the Oneota for a while?"

"Somehow," Old White said dryly, "I don't think Power would let us get away with that."

"There's the Charokee over to the east," Wolf Tail suggested. "If you're bound and determined to deal with barbarians, they can be as rude as Chikosi."

Old White noticed that Swimmer had decided to lift his leg on the corner of the square. Wolf Tail shifted his attention to the dog, one disapproving eyebrow raising.

"It's all right," Trader said, smiling blandly. "I was inclined to it myself."

Heron Wing pounded acorn and hickory nut flour into a patty, slathered grease on both sides, and laid it on a growing stack atop a wooden platter. She kept casting sidelong glances at Morning Dew as she stirred dried pawpaws into a mix of cornmeal and sunflower seeds.

The day was chilly, but bright. The warmth from the fire they worked around had coaxed a fine perspiration from Morning Dew's skin. People were already arriving at Split Sky City from the towns up and down the river. Camps were springing up outside the palisade. All brought food, of course, but bellies—never full for most of the year—always seemed to yearn for more during the holidays.

Among the Sky Hand, the solstice served as the major winter ceremony when people remembered Spider, who had climbed up to the sun after Vulture, Bushy-tailed Opossum, and Many-Colored Crow had failed to bring the fire down to earth. Winter solstice wasn't as important as the Busk Ceremony—when the green corn was sanctified and the people underwent their ritual cleansing before restarting the sacred fire—but it was still one of the major celebrations.

"Smoke Shield returned from his 'hunt' last night," Heron Wing announced.

"I know." Morning Dew continued to concentrate on her cooking.

"Curious thing, he came back with speckles of blood on his clothing, but no game. He's in a surly mood."

Morning Dew ground her teeth, fearing to look up and meet Heron Wing's eyes. *Tell me he hasn't asked for me. Please!*

"I don't know what happened upriver, and apparently he won't speak of it." Heron Wing thoughtfully greased another of the cakes. "I have heard that he returned without his bow and arrows. His bearhide cape is missing, too." Heron Wing wiped at her forehead, smearing it with grease. "Flying Hawk is worried. He didn't come out and say it, but I can see it in his eyes."

Morning Dew glanced down at her hands, absently rubbing her fingers together. She could sense Screaming Falcon's eyes, as if he were watching her from across an immense distance.

Heron Wing hesitated. "Could you look at me for a moment? I need to ask you something."

Morning Dew lifted her gaze, meeting Heron Wing's as the woman asked, "Did Smoke Shield say anything when you were with him? Would you have any hint as to why he went up the river?"

"Who knows what possesses that man?" Morning Dew shook her head. "The last time I saw him, he was in a rage over the captives." She swallowed hard. "And . . . and what happened to them."

"What did he say in particular?"

"He thought the Albaamaha did it." She couldn't help herself, but glanced back at her hands.

"I know that was a difficult day for you." Heron Wing

sat back on her haunches. "The Council gave him direct orders to leave the Albaamaha alone for the time being. But then Red Awl disappears. Now Smoke Shield comes home from a hunting trip without his weapons and coat. And he's in a foul mood on top of it. His clothes have spots of blood, and his lip is swollen and bloody. If you ask me it looks more like it was bitten; but he tells a story about falling in the forest."

Morning Dew said nothing.

Heron Wing was still watching her. "Look at me, Morning Dew. There, that's better. Listen to my words: You are a captive, but you are also a matron. Granted, you are young, but one thing you are not is stupid. I would like to know what you think. Come on, you can do that, can't you? Think?"

Morning Dew met Heron Wing's eyes, saying, "I'm afraid my thoughts would either get me a beating, or worse, sent back to Smoke Shield."

Heron Wing couldn't stifle her laughter. "Well, how about this? For this one moment, let us forget what is between us, and just speak as two women. I can well imagine what goes through your head, because the same thoughts would be in mine were our roles changed." She shrugged. "And who knows, one day they might be. The future is a frightening place, and forever uncertain. But for now, just be honest with me. We can go back to playing master and slave if anyone should happen in on us."

Morning Dew frowned. "Why should I do this? Anything I say could be held against me."

Heron Wing arched her brow. "Oh, I don't know. I suspect that you wish we were all dead. I think you wish you had Smoke Shield hanging from a square in White Arrow Town. That way you could roast his shaft and balls with a cane torch just for the simple pleasure of hearing him scream. What more could there be?"

Morning Dew pursed her lips. *That's about it in a pecan shell.*

"At least," Heron Wing continued, "that's exactly

how I'd feel were I you. And believe me, I know the pleasures of Smoke Shield's bed. But here's the thing: You were raised in the middle of clan politics just as I was. I want to know what you think."

"About what?"

"Do you think he could have gone after Red Awl?"

She glanced at the doorway, running through her options. Caution finally surrendered to the opportunity to vent her feelings. "I think he's the most dangerous man I've ever known. Do you remember what Pale Cat said the other night, about Smoke Shield never saying he regretted anything? He has a soul sickness, Heron Wing. Something is dark, black, and twisted inside him. What makes it worse is that he is Chief Clan. If he fixes something in his mind, he will accomplish it." She winced. "Just like he wanted me."

Heron Wing nodded. "You have no idea."

"Then why does Flying Hawk put up with it?"

"Because the high minko was a lot like Smoke Shield once upon a time. Flying Hawk sees a younger version of himself. He keeps thinking that Smoke Shield will change when he assumes leadership. And, he's desperate. Flying Hawk is the last of his line. If Smoke Shield doesn't follow him as high minko, the leadership will go to a cousin."

"He'll be dead by then. What difference does it make?"

Heron Wing patted out another of the cakes and greased it. "Myself, I think it has something to do with killing his brother. He has spent his entire life overcoming the stigma attached to that one passionate act. My guess is that when he dies, he wants to find his dead brother's souls and say, 'See, it's all right. I kept our family's prestige intact. I was a worthy successor in spite of what I did to you.' And then there's Green Snake."

"Who is he?"

"He was Smoke Shield's brother—the man who gave him that terrible scar. Green Snake was a . . . well, he was a wonderful man. Everything that Smoke Shield isn't. Kind, compassionate, and thoughtful—everyone liked him. Even as a boy there was talk about what a good high minko he would make. Smoke Shield was jealous, and being Smoke Shield, he managed to drive Green Snake into enough of a rage that Green Snake struck Smoke Shield down with a war club, then ran away, horrified at what he'd done."

"So how did that reflect on Flying Hawk? Why would that affect his relations with his brother in the afterlife?"

"Because he was the boys' uncle. He had the responsibility of raising them. And, lo and behold, one brother struck the other one down. Flying Hawk has always seen that as his failure, not Green Snake's. If, on the other hand, he can make Smoke Shield into a good high minko, I firmly believe his souls will rest easier."

"Why would that be?"

"Because he could make the argument to himself that what Green Snake did wasn't important in the end, that Smoke Shield was the right man for the position."

"Then why would you care what I think about all this?"

"Because you and I both know that Smoke Shield will never be the man Flying Hawk hopes he will. It is beyond his . . . how did you put it? Twisted black souls? A most apt description."

Morning Dew laughed bitterly. "Why would I want to contribute to this discussion?"

"Because"—Heron Wing gave her a clear-eyed stare—"if Smoke Shield succeeds in alienating the Albaamaha, drives them into revolt, your people will see an opportunity to strike back. We will be so busy with the Albaamaha that your Chahta warriors will have initial success. They'll burn a couple of towns and go home feeling avenged. Enough Albaamaha and Sky Hand will die, and the threat will seem so menacing, that hostilities will be put on hold. A mighty force will be put together to break the Chahta once and for all."

"They will suffer for it. My people know war as well as yours."

Heron Wing nodded. "But by then, Smoke Shield will be firmly in charge. He will have vanquished the Albaamaha threat, at least for the moment. The bad blood will eventually fester into another uprising. But you know Smoke Shield, how he plans and plots. If the Chahta strike while we're fighting with each other, how do you think Smoke Shield will react?"

She sat back, playing it out between her souls. "He will see it as a terrible affront to his authority. We will become his obsession, and he will be driven to find a way to pay us back for attacking while he was vulnerable. It won't just be war, but personal. Just like blaming the Albaamaha for killing the captives, or taking me because I rebuffed his advances."

"Ah," Heron Wing said, "now you're talking like a matron."

"But he would still have to win the war."

"A matter of time."

Morning Dew bristled. "Don't think that every Chahta town will fall like White Arrow. We were caught by surprise. That won't happen again."

"Think, Matron," Heron Wing said sternly. "You will win some, and lose some. That is the way of war. I agree that Smoke Shield got lucky at White Arrow Town. But think it through. You have six towns scattered up and down the Horned Serpent River within easy reach. Six! We have fourteen in addition to Split Sky City."

"Most of your population is Albaamaha."

"Who support our warriors through tribute. Your warriors live on farmsteads. Granted, your women do most of the work, but men don't like to leave wives and children behind, undefended. The Chahta can't call up a large body of warriors and keep them ready to fight for an extended period of time. Those men won't leave their families out on farmsteads for several moons. And they can't send them to the fortified towns during the growing season or they will lose the crop."

"Gods," Morning Dew said, the implications of it falling into place. "If the Chikosi really committed themselves, they could drive us right out of the Horned Serpent Valley. Reinforcements couldn't arrive in time from the Pearl River towns off to the west."

"Maybe, but whether we drove you west or not, our concerted attacks would leave you severely weakened."

She gave Heron Wing a hard stare. "Why are you telling me this?"

"Because the Natchez, the Yuchi, or the Pensacola would send war parties in our wake to look for slaves and booty. What we started, they would finish."

Morning Dew frowned. *We have alliances with both the Natchez and Pensacola.* But then she knew full well that an alliance only lasted as long as both parties saw the benefit. They could be broken overnight based on some perceived insult, or a wild claim of sorcery.

"If we are destroyed, it will leave a big hole. And who knows who will rush to fill it?" Morning Dew raised her eyes to Heron Wing's. "That's what you're worried about, isn't it?"

"Peoples rise and fall," Heron Wing told her. "Our traditions are full of such stories. When a nation slowly fades away, as Cahokia did, everyone has time to adjust. When they collapse overnight, chaos breaks loose. The balance is broken."

Morning Dew nodded. "The entire region would crack and shatter."

"Prolonged fighting with the Chahta would weaken us. The Albaamaha would revolt again, and the surrounding nations would come flooding in. We would beat them back, becoming ever weaker in the process. Our towns in the north and south would have to be abandoned. We would probably survive as a people, but why take the risk?"

She stared anxiously at Heron Wing. "My people would suffer in the process."

Heron Wing cocked an eyebrow. "Correct."

"I don't understand. It's almost as if you want us to survive."

"Oh, believe me, I do. So does most of the Council. At least for now. Your Chahta have alliances with the Natchez and Pensacola. You pose no real threat to our existence." She smiled. "We came from the same people, have the same gods, the same language. You are distant relatives. Traditionally we have done more Trading than fighting. Screaming Falcon's raid on Alligator Town was a poor choice, based on an impossible ambition. Our retaliation was an accidental triumph. But I do not cast blame. People will be people."

"The problem, you are saying, is that Smoke Shield will make such a mess of things that everyone will lose."

Heron Wing shrugged. "That is one possible outcome." She paused, lowering her voice. "Tell me, with the right enticement, could peace be restored with your people?"

Morning Dew glanced uneasily at the door, ensuring that no one was close. "It is possible. But negotiating it wouldn't be easy. It would take some sort of symbolic gesture first. A lot of people were killed at White Arrow Town. My people will be frightened and enraged. Relatives are grieving. The souls of the dead must be avenged. They have to weigh that against the potential for retaliation. If the Albaamaha revolt, it would make coming to terms very difficult."

"Too bad we're not Charokee," Heron Wing said.

"Charokee? You want to be Charokee?"

"The women have the political authority there. They don't have to depend on men to make the decisions." She sighed. "Here, I can only work in the background."

"Greetings!" a voice called from outside. "It is Cattail! I am coming with Stone. He has finished his practice for the children's games."

"We'll talk later," Heron Wing said softly. Then as her son charged into the room, muddy, scratched, and beaming with excitement, she cried, "Welcome, my son! Tell me about your practice!"

Morning Dew busied herself with her cooking, but her mind was knotted around Heron Wing's predictions. *My people could be destroyed!*

Thirty-one

Trader strode up the wooden stairs that led to the high chief's palisade. Swimmer, who charged up beside him, panted happily, tail wagging. Sunlight gleamed on the bright red clay. He could see little rivulets eating away at the clay coating. Looking back, he saw Old White climbing, muscles not as spry. The Seeker was already puffing.

At the gate, Trader turned to admire Rainbow Town from his high vantage point. The plaza extended in a great rectangle, the corner of the mound protruding into the plaza's northeast corner. The red cedar pole—sacred to the Yuchi—rose straight and tall into the sky. To either side of the pole the chunkey courts had been laid out east to west. The northern one, just south of the High Chief's Mound, served the Chief Moiety, while the southern-most was for the warriors. The courts consisted of long lanes paved with smoothly compacted clay. Between them, and just south of the Chief's Mound, the Council House rose atop its square mound, and beyond that the Men's House dominated a mound at the southeast corner of the plaza.

The eastern half of the plaza, just beyond the moiety houses, had been reserved for the stickball field. There young men darted back and forth, tossing a small hide-bound ball to each other in practice. Each of the mounds had been capped and sealed with a different color of clay, each one of the rainbow colors that held so much meaning for the Children of the Sun. The Temple

Mound across from them on the plaza's northwest corner was a brilliant white.

In the flat to the east, a sea of houses, many on low mounds, extended clear to the distant high walls of the western palisade. He could see ponds created from borrow pits, the water reflecting blue sky. Beyond the city walls, a gray pall of smoke hung above a thousand camps. From every direction along the river, people had flocked to Rainbow City for the solstice celebrations. The city reminded him of a beehive. Individuals could be seen crowding through the gates, inspecting items of Trade that the locals had spread on blankets.

"Should be quite a party," Old White observed as he panted his way to the top.

"They will be doing the same at home, you know." How odd that he had started referring to Split Sky City that way. "Everyone will be arriving, canoes laid side by side at the landing until there is hardly room to walk." He closed his eyes, almost able to smell the wood smoke and cooking food. A sudden pang of homesickness, like he hadn't felt in years, filled him.

"I will share it with you this summer," Old White promised. "We will enjoy the Busk together." He sighed. "But for the moment, let us see what this high chief is like."

"He's Yuchi," Trader muttered. "Probably some overblown, self-important old man with delusions of inflated glory."

They turned and stepped through the gate to find a packed clay compound with two guardian poles to either side of the walkway to the palace. One was a rendition of Crawfish, the other of Vulture, his long wings carved down the sides of the log. A log pestle and mortar stood to one side, a ramada to the other.

They walked to the plank door, Old White calling out in Trade Tongue, "Greetings, High Chief of the Tsoyaha! Old White, the Seeker, and the man called Trader would speak with you."

A young woman, her swollen belly marking an advanced pregnancy, swung the door open on its leather hinges and smiled at them. "You are welcome. My husband will see you in a moment. May I get you some tea?"

"That would be appreciated," Trader said easily. He reached into his belt pouch, producing a large copper-clad wooden bead. "May we offer this token of respect for your kind hospitality? You will honor it with your beauty."

She took the gleaming bead, gasping with delight as she held it up to the sunlight. "It's beautiful! Come in! Be seated. I will get you tea."

Stepping into the great room, Trader glanced around. To his surprise, the structure had two stories, with a ladder leading up in one corner. The room measured perhaps five paces by ten, with a thick pole ceiling. On the wall to the right was a beautifully carved image of a warrior with a long, beaded forelock holding a turkey-tail mace in one hand, a severed head in the other. Finally, the wall to the left sported a flat round plaque consisting of two circling rattlesnakes coiled about each other, the heads facing an open center. Their long tongues protruded, almost touching. A three-legged stool stood behind the large fire pit, a series of raccoon hides sewn together for a covering. Wooden boxes, intricately carved, were tucked neatly under the pole benches built into the walls.

He blinked at the incongruity of toys scattered around the rush matting that covered the floor. Some were corn-shuck dolls; others consisted of deerhide balls, small stickball racquets with net-filled loops for playing the children's version of the game, and little clay figurines of turkeys, dogs, and what might have been raccoons. Weapons—obviously the high chief's—rested on a stand near the door. Trader saw a bow and arrows, several war clubs, and a fine shield with the three-legged spiral surrounded by the rings of circles and the scalloped cloud motif.

Doorways led off to either side, the rooms obscured by fabric door hangings decorated with opposing turkeys facing a spiral-striped pole. The bubbly laughter of children could be heard behind the doorway to the right.

Trader walked to one of the benches. There, displayed in a beautiful open box, were four highly polished chunkey stones, the sides convex with dimples in the center, and behind them lay four perfectly straight lances. He considered the pieces, then stared up at the huge carving on the rear wall. Portions of the three-legged spiral were clad in copper. The central disk had been painted in bright yellow.

"You are looking at the sky," a voice called from behind him.

Trader turned to see a tall athletic man emerge from the right doorway. Several small children peeked around his legs and the door jamb. These, the man shooed back, and then he stepped into the room.

He wore his hair up; a copper headpiece of the familiar lightning design with an arrow splitting a cloud rested atop his head. His face had been tattooed in the forked-eye design with a pattern of lines running down and to the sides from his nose and mouth. Gleaming copper ear spools filled his elongated earlobes. Trader estimated the man's age at less than thirty winters. The coarsely woven apron he wore was stained with what looked like food.

Following his gaze, the man looked down, smiled self-consciously, and shrugged. "I know. A great chief should greet such exalted visitors in his finest, but I don't get much time to play with the children. We are preparing for the solstice ceremonies, and I will be called upon to be very formal during the coming days." Then he saw Swimmer, and a smile beamed as he dropped to his knees. "Hello there! Come here. That's it. Who are you?"

Trader shot a curious glance at Old White, who just

shrugged, apparently baffled. Was this man really the high chief? His hairpiece would have indicated that, but for the moment, he was fawning over Swimmer, rubbing his ears, making cooing sounds, and acting more like a boy with his first puppy than a chief greeting auspicious visitors.

The high chief was laughing, almost rolling around as Swimmer bounced and licked playfully at his hands. The dog's tail lashed the air in absolute joy.

"My dog is called Swimmer, Great Chief. I rescued him from a raft of driftwood far up the Father Water."

"Swimmer!" the chief cried in delight. "Welcome to my palace, Swimmer. New Moon? Bring Swimmer some of that deer meat."

The pregnant woman did her best to hide an indulgent smile and vanished into the children's room.

The chief chuckled, gave Swimmer one last pat on the head, and climbed to his feet. "Welcome. I am Born-of-Sun, the *yu bah'le,* high chief of the western Tsoyaha."

"I am Old White, known as the Seeker." Old White bowed graciously. "My companion is Trader, of whom you have no doubt heard."

"Great Chief," Trader acknowledged, touching his forehead respectfully.

Born-of-Sun walked over, taking each of their hands in turn, meeting their eyes with a thoughtful appraisal. To Trader, he added, "I am glad Kala Hi'ki decided you were a friend. It would have been hard on Swimmer to have endured your suffering on the square."

He is more worried about the dog than me? "I'm sure it would have been."

Old White was grinning, amusement in his expression.

"The carving"—Born-of-Sun returned his attention to the intricate relief hanging above the chunkey stones—"is one of our most important symbols. Do you know the story? What this represents?"

"The sky. The yellow disk in the center is the sun, of

course. I don't understand the three copper triangles spinning on top of it."

Born-of-Sun stared happily at the image. "In the beginning, after Sock-chew, Father Crawfish, brought mud up from the waters to create the land, and Yaw-tee, Father Vulture, flattened it with his great wings . . ." He paused. "You saw the Guardians out front?"

"Crawfish and Vulture," Old White agreed. "Yes."

"After the world was formed, the skies were dark. All creatures lived in perpetual night. They all called out, asking for light. Yo'ah, the star, told them, 'I will make light.' And he did, but his light was very dim. The next to try was Shar-pah, whom you know as the moon. He, too, rose into the sky and shone as brilliantly as he could, but then he grew dimmer and dimmer. He had to rest. Then Shar-pah put all of his effort into it, and glowed brightly again, only to dim.

"Tso, our Mother Sun, finally said, 'I made you all. I can do this.' So she went way off to the east, gathered herself, and rose into the sky. All the earth bathed in her light." He pointed to the three legs of the spiral. "That is what you see in the center. Tso's bright light filling the sky. The reason there are three legs to her spiral is to honor the efforts of Tso, Yo'ah, and Shar-pah. The three great lights of the sky. The stars and moon are present in the next ring. You see Shar-pah in his six phases. One for each full moon from solstice to solstice. And around him, the white dots on the black background are all the Yo'ah, the stars."

"And the clouds?" Trader pointed to the scalloped edge.

"They are the last of the Sky Beings. Clouds are always born at the edge of the sky and move across it. This is the place from which we come. We are Tso's children, born of a drop of her menstrual blood that fell from on high. We carry part of the sky in our bodies and souls."

"And you like dogs," Old White noted.

Born-of-Sun chuckled at that. "I like dogs, Seeker, because they are honest. They will not trick you with cunning speeches, or promise peace one moment, only to attack you the next. If you treat a dog with kindness and respect, he will not murder your people the moment you turn your back." He paused. "My dog, my companion and best friend for years, has recently sent his souls to the sky. I have a softness and envy for those who still have their faithful friends with them." He stared longingly at Swimmer.

Trader nodded thoughtfully, remembering when Swimmer had been his only friend.

Born-of-Sun evidently read his expression, for he said, "That you bring him with you tells me more about your character than even Kala Hi'ki's report."

New Moon had emerged and placed a wooden platter on the floor. The vessel sported two rattlesnakes carved in relief around the edges. Swimmer attacked the pile of meat, wolfing it down.

"It looks excellent," Old White murmured. "You think he'd at least stop and taste."

Born-of-Sun grinned happily. "I know dogs. This one has been very hungry at some point in his life." Then he looked up, eyes clearing. In that moment, he went from warm host to high chief. "Now, let us be seated. I would hear what has brought you to Rainbow City, and what it means for me and my people."

Trader took a seat at the fire, Old White lowering himself beside him. Swimmer, having licked the wooden bowl scrupulously clean, came at a gesture and lay happily at Trader's side.

New Moon provided cups of warm tea as Born-of-Sun took a beautifully carved pipe from one of the boxes, tamped tobacco into it, and lit it from the fire. He puffed, blowing blue smoke into the air, then uttered a short prayer in his own language.

Trader followed suit when the pipe was extended to him. He handed it to Old White, who drew, exhaled, and chanted a soft prayer in a language Trader had never heard. Then the old man handed the pipe back to Born-of-Sun as the high chief seated himself on the tripod.

"We come under the Power of Trade, High Chief." Old White spread his hands. He told the long and involved story of their travels. At times, Born-of-Sun nodded; at others, he might have been a motionless lump of wood, showing no reaction whatsoever. Old White ended, saying, "We would only pass through your country and Trade for portage to the Chaktaw lands."

For a long time, Born-of-Sun studied the pipe he held. "You have heard of the trouble brewing down there?"

"We have," Old White agreed. "It may well be that same trouble is what calls us to Split Sky City."

Born-of-Sun ran a finger down the snake-shaped stem of his pipe. "Let me explain my dilemma. Once, in the time of my grandfather, the Chikosi caused us a great deal of trouble. We were at war constantly. Chikosi warriors, led by a Powerful war chief, caused many of my people to abandon their towns along the Tenasee River east of us. Some moved back north; others came here. Where our fields once grew corn, only weeds and brush flourished.

"My people believed that Power had deserted them. In response, we conducted a great purification here, at Rainbow City. For a whole moon, we fasted, purged, and cleansed our bodies and souls.

"Disaster befell the Chikosi when Power favored us. They sent their high minko to fight us. We captured him and his war medicine. For a time, we persevered. Then the Chikosi raised a new war chief, Bear Tooth. Power favored him in war, but not in life. Some years later their great palace burned in the night; and War Chief Bear Tooth died along with the Chief Clan matron. Their Power was broken, their leadership weakened. In the following years, we beat back the raiders and retook our lands. Once again our towns to the east flourished. Today, I rule those towns. They are my responsibility to care for and protect. Now you want to take the same war medicine we captured back to them and restore the Power?" He paused, giving Old White a hard stare. "Give me one good reason why I would want the Chikosi returned to their former strength?"

Old White spread his hands helplessly. "Great Chief, I can only tell you that Power calls us there. A darkness has been growing in Split Sky City. Now we hear that they have delivered a serious blow to the Chaktaw. Even I do not know Power's ultimate purpose in carrying the war medicine box and the Contrary to Split Sky City."

"And you, Trader?" Born-of-Sun asked. "It is reported that you are Chief Clan, that you are in line to be high minko. Despite the fact that you like dogs, is there a reason I should allow you to assume the leadership?"

Trader ran his fingers through Swimmer's fur. "I have no reason to wish for war with the Tsoyaha. It disrupts the Trade." He glanced up. "I have seen many things during my years on the river, High Chief. Many people believe they can accumulate Power through war. Some do; most do not. I have watched nations eaten away by raids, their numbers dwindling until they are mere shadows of who they once where. Why should I wish that for my people?"

Born-of-Sun spread his fingers, as if letting something go. "We do not live on Trade alone. And no matter what a chief may want, his actions are determined by the will of his people. Are you trying to tell me that if the Chikosi Council demanded that you make war upon us, you would tell them no? Think about that. Your personal desires must come second to the politics of your people. Saying one thing—while you enjoy my hospitality, and surrounded by my warriors—will be far different than what you will say while facing a united Council. If they appoint you at all, they will be suspicious. Until you prove yourself, you will be in a weak position. I am told that you have been gone from them for ten summers. Yes, you have seen much, and learned a great many lessons on the rivers. But they have never left the Black Warrior Valley. They have only your word on these things. Why should they trust a stranger's counsel? What promises will you have to make to enjoy their support?"

Trader sighed. Somehow, he hadn't quite thought that through. "I only know that Power wishes for us to go to Split Sky City."

"Power comes in many forms," Born-of-Sun said softly. "I would be much happier if you gave me your oath that you would take your Trade east along the river, or back north. I will even help you to take it west, to the Father Water. Could you give me such an oath?"

Old White slowly shook his head. "That option is denied us, High Chief. Even your Kala Hi'ki understands that. Whatever Power wishes us to do, it must be done at Split Sky City."

"Then I am back at my impasse, Seeker. My responsibility is to the safety and security of my people. Somehow, I think I would be better served if you were hanging in the squares." He considered them thoughtfully. "But I, too, serve the will of Power." He frowned, lost in thought. "Your arrival here was auspicious. We are Tsoyaha, and you arrived just before the solstice. Perhaps it is best if we let Mother Sun decide."

"How would this be done?" Old White asked warily.

"I will play Trader for your futures," Born-of-Sun replied. "A game of chunkey, at midday on the solstice. We will play to twenty. And Mother Sun shall decide the merits of who should win. If I win, I will know that your journey to the Chikosi is not in the best interests of my people. Should you win, we will know that your actions there will not bring harm to us."

"And the wager?" Trader asked.

"If you lose, you shall forfeit your Trade, the war medicine box—including that fabulous piece of copper I have managed with such difficulty to hear about—and your fates shall be mine to determine." He arched an eyebrow. "Trader? Outside of your possessions and lives, what will you wager for?"

Trader considered that. He had a talent for chunkey. But then those finely polished stones he had seen resting in the beautiful box with their associated lances suggested that Born-of-Sun was no novice, either. What offering would Power favor?

He reached over to give Swimmer a reassuring pat. "Great Chief, I think you are a wise and thoughtful leader, as well as a good man. I don't think that humans can know the many ways of Power; it shifts and flows. The proud lords of Cahokia learned that."

Trader stared thoughtfully at the beautiful carving on the rear wall. What wager would best suit his purposes? Wealth? He had that. He glanced at Born-of-Sun's calculating expression. No, he needed something more, something Power would favor.

And then he knew.

Trader cleared his throat. "If I win, High Chief, this is what I want from you: You will send a messenger to Split Sky City, telling them of this great game of chunkey we played in the name of peace. Once the story is told, the messenger is to announce that Green Snake and the Seeker are returning home to their people to restore the balance of Power. Old White, the Contrary, and I will Trade fairly for labor in making the portage into the Horned Serpent River. And after that, you and I shall enjoy a friendship that lasts until the end of our lives. On that I stake my life and fortune."

Paunch stared at the collection of nuts he and Whippoorwill had looted out of a squirrel's cache. He had cracked the shells using a crumbly piece of sandstone, then dug the meats out with a sharpened stick. That— along with shriveled grapes, some rosehips, and occa-

sional hickory, walnut, and beechnuts—made a thin
stew. Earlier in the morning—using a bent branch for a
throwing stick—he had missed a rabbit by a mere finger's width.

They camped under the trees on a bluff overlooking
the Horned Serpent River. The vantage was possible because a summer tornado had toppled the trees on the
slope below. Deadfall made for an ample supply of firewood, the branches having cracked when the trees fell.

This day the sun shone, warming the forest for the first
time since the snowfall. A breeze blew up from the
south. It teased Whippoorwill's long black hair as she sat
on the Y of a fallen branch and watched him with those
knowing dark eyes.

"It's not as easy as you thought, is it?" she asked.

"What's that?"

"Being free."

He stared at her, seeing her worn dress, smudged
with dirt, torn here and there.

"It beats hanging from a square."

"You needed the wilderness, Grandfather. You have
missed the reality of life."

"Reality? Like that bunch of warriors who barely
missed catching us yesterday?" He winced, remembering how close the Chahta had come. But for a handy log,
nothing would have kept the keen-eyed warriors from
seeing them.

"Power sent them past us," Whippoorwill said easily.
"The time isn't right yet."

"Time? Time for what?" He hated it when she did that.

"Time for us to meet them."

"Them? Them who?"

"My sister comes," she said reasonably.

He stared at her across the tiny fire. It put out just
enough heat to boil the stew, not enough smoke to be
seen, and the smell of it would be carried out over the
valley in a way that wouldn't alert any snooping warriors to their presence.

"Just once couldn't you say straight out what you mean?"

"I always say it straight." Her eyes seemed to expand. "You just aren't ready to listen yet."

"Try me."

"When the time is right, I will." She turned her head, looking to the north. "You are hearing with a clarity you have not had for a long time. Soon you will hear without letting your passions get in the way."

He shot her a nervous glance. "My passions are just fine, thank you. I only hope that no one has placed any blame on Amber Bead."

"He must be who he is."

"As if he could be anyone else."

"Oh, he could be. It's just that he won't."

He grumbled to himself, wishing for a warm house and a bowl brimming to the top with squash, corn, and sunflowers simmering in a venison broth.

Thirty-two

Smoke Shield dabbed at his lip and made a face. The bite was healing; the scab starting to itch and peel. He glanced around at the fourteen chiefs who sat around the tchkofa fire. Twice a year the chiefs made the journey from their towns along the river to Split Sky City: once in the Moon of Greening Corn for the Busk, and then again for the winter solstice. This was their opportunity to air grievances, to collaborate on the divisions of labor necessary for town projects, to hear the high minko's plans for the next six moons, and most important, to settle disputes.

Smoke Shield found the proceedings boring.

Flying Hawk had the floor and had disposed of several of the topics he wished to address.

"Finally," Flying Hawk said, "we must discuss the condition of the Split Sky palisade. Many of the pine logs are rotted out. We have six sections that are in need of replacement."

Groans came from the surrounding chiefs.

Flying Hawk made a calming gesture with his hands. "Yes, I know. The stocks of mature pitch pine have been already harvested from the surrounding forests. One of the tishu minko's clansmen who understands such things has made a survey of the local pitch pine. He thinks only one-third of the necessary poles can be obtained from the pine groves. The other two-thirds, over two hundred logs, must come from somewhere else."

"Where is the best stand?" Wildcat, from Great Corn Town, asked.

"The tishu minko's cousin thinks that a stand in the hills below Alligator Town is the best source. The trees need to be felled, limbed, and carried down to the river. He figures it will take a crew of twelve men per tree a half day to fell, limb, and slide the logs down to the river. Then they have to be floated upstream. With five hundred workers we could do this in three weeks from the harvesting of the trees to their delivery here."

The chiefs looked uneasily at each other.

"Assuming Split Sky could send two hundred and fifty Albaamaha, each of the towns would have to contribute somewhere around ten to fifteen men each, depending upon their populations."

Wildcat frowned. "High Minko, you must know, the Albaamaha are going to resist sending that many men away for hard labor. If we have problems with weather, it could turn into over a moon away from their families."

"And we are already looking at food shortages," War Squirrel, the new chief of Alligator Town, added. "I am the first one here to know the advantage of good fortifications given what we just suffered, but, High Minko, can the palisades last another year? If so, it would reduce the strain on both the food resources as well as the political situation with the Albaamaha."

Smoke Shield cleared his throat and stepped forward before Flying Hawk could find some way to avoid recognizing him. "The Albaamaha do not need to be treated as if they are somehow special. We tell them to send workers, and they send them. Or else." He looked at the chiefs, one by one. "Somewhere along the line we have forgotten that the Albaamaha serve us. They are not here to send messengers to the enemy, or kill our captives under our noses. We *tell* them what to do, and they do it."

Sun Falcon Mankiller, chief of Bowl Town, stood. "War Chief, perhaps you are unaware of feelings among the Albaamaha. Even as I was leaving, rumors were flying around the Albaamaha farmsteads in my territory. Stories that Red Awl—who comes from our town—was lured away, captured, and killed. I did not have time to discuss this with my Albaamaha chiefs to determine the source, but if there is any validity to it, I face a terrible problem."

Sun Falcon looked around at the other chiefs. "Have any of you heard rumors of this? Does anyone here know of such a thing being done to Red Awl? Because if you do, and such a deed has indeed occurred, we must all take measures." He looked at Flying Hawk. "High Minko, as my chief, do you have any information about Red Awl?"

Flying Hawk frowned, his gaze fixed on the four logs that fed the sacred fire. "I do not. While the Council has been concerned about the Albaamo courier we captured, they have ordered—with my blessing—that no one incite the Albaamaha. If anything happened to Red Awl, I swear on my Ancestors that I know nothing of it."

"Thank the gods," Sun Falcon said with a sigh. "Hopefully Red Awl will appear and give everyone an explanation of his absence."

Smoke Shield stood stiffly, a tingling of unease at the base of his spine. "Pardon me, but do we *fear* the Albaamaha? Forgive me, wise chiefs, but who controls our warriors? And what if this is some Albaamaha plot? Red Awl has vanished into the hills, probably to consort with his friend Paunch, and we are to take the blame?" He spread his arms wide. "By doing so, are we not playing into some Albaamaha plot? Who knows? Maybe that was why my bow and arrows were stolen while I was traveling. Some Albaamo will turn up with a silly story. Perhaps it will be that I slew Red Awl, shot him with that very bow, or something equally insane. I say if the palisades need to be rebuilt, we place our demand for the workers to cut and transport the timber. Perhaps sweating Albaamaha with calluses on their hands will have less free time to dream up stories that do nothing but sow discontent."

Wind Town, the northernmost Sky Hand settlement,

lay in the flats just downriver of the fall line. Black Buffalo, the town's Hickory Moiety chief, stood, his hard eyes on Smoke Shield. "War Chief, it is easy for you, who live here surrounded by Split Sky City's high walls, to make ultimatums. We, who survive on the borders, cannot be so brash. Across the mountains from me, the Yuchi are very real. My Albaamaha are my ears and feelers. We depend on each other, knowing that if we are attacked, we have only ourselves. True, I can send a runner and know that Sun Falcon will dispatch any warriors he can spare from Bowl Town; but help from Split Sky City will come too late. By the time a runner travels to you, you assemble warriors, and they run full-tilt up the trails, they will arrive a full two days later. Not to mention exhausted. I *need* my Albaamaha as much as they need me." He looked at War Squirrel. "Some of us rely on that relationship. We have survived only because we work *for* each other."

Calls of agreement came from the other chiefs.

"The Council understands this," Flying Hawk told them. "That is why we have backed off from accusing the Albaamaha of anything, even with proof that an Albaamo runner was sent to warn White Arrow Town." He raised his hands. "For the moment, you must trust us. We are listening, learning. If it does turn out that some Albaamaha plot is discovered, we will not act rashly." He shot a warning look at Smoke Shield. "For the moment, if you could simply broach the topic of the palisade to your Albaamaha, let them consider it for the time being, I think that will be sufficient."

Smoke Shield swallowed the angry retort that was building in his throat. *The old man is placating them!* His eyes narrowed. *There are ways. Even these whimpering chiefs can be made to understand the threat.*

It was just a matter of creating the right circumstances.

Two Petals studied the empty cup she held and waited for the Spirits in the tea to take effect. She stood in the great room of the temple. The Kala Hi'ki—blind eyes wrapped in white cloth—seemed to be observing her, his ruined face expressionless. Outside in the plaza, a hundred drums were thumping while thousands of voices rose in Song to mark the first of the Yuchi solstice ceremonies. She swayed on her feet, as though the rhythm of the voices, the music, and the Dance outside were a physical presence pressing against her. The first soothing fingers of the tea began to massage her souls.

So many people. So many souls. She tried to shut them out, to stop the movement. Her first impulse was to press her hands to her ears. Instead, she concentrated on the intricately carved relief of the two great rattlesnakes on the west wall. The daylight shining through the east-facing door illuminated the red, black, and yellow chevrons, and gleamed off of the polished copper eyes.

"What are you seeing?" the Kala Hi'ki asked.

"The snakes curled about each other." She leaned over the pole bench, running her finger down the wood. "What are the black circles on the snakes' sides?"

"Openings," the Kala Hi'ki said. "The passages that allow Power to slip between this world and the next. Snakes are beings of great Power. They move without legs, and shed their skins. We treat them with utmost respect.

"You are from the north; you have different origins and beliefs than the Tsoyaha. People are like leaves. They come in different shapes in the north, south, east, and west. Among our peoples here in the southern lands, and in particular the Tsoyaha, the snake is a master of water. He calls the rain and coaxes water from the Underworld through springs. Those are the black openings represented by the dark ovals you see on the snakes' sides. Then, finally, the waters flow together, following the Spirit of the great ancestral snakes that crawled over the earth just after it was Created by

He-Who-Sits-Above: the one we call Gohantoneh. When the earth was still wet mud, just after Crawfish brought land up from the bottom of the oceans, the great serpents crawled down from the heights. The land was like wet clay, and where the giant snakes crawled, they called the waters after them. It was in this way that the rivers were formed. Even today, when you look down on rivers from high places, you can see the Spirit of the serpents as the waters flow."

She asked, "Why is there an opening between them? I mean, the way it's cut out around their heads?"

"Ah, that is the passage from this world into the Underworld. Anyone journeying into the Underworld must pass between the snakes' heads. There, they will be judged. The weak, or those who are not worthy, will be devoured. Only the greatest Dreamers can pass."

"Have you done that?" she asked, aware that Old White had entered the room.

The Kala Hi'ki was silent for a moment. Then, in a low and reverent voice, he answered, "I have."

From outside, a great shout could be heard, thousands of voices rising in the morning air. Two Petals turned toward the sound, feeling the weight of those countless souls pressing around her.

"The games have started," Old White noted.

"How do you feel?" the Kala Hi'ki asked Two Petals. "Can you sense them?"

She closed her eyes, nodding, aware of the calming effect of the tea. It eased the incipient panic at the edges of her souls. The movement of the world had settled, slowing. Time seemed to weave around her.

"It is better."

"Good. Now, I want you to concentrate. You are a great boulder in a slow-moving river. Let the world wash around you. We have practiced this; now you must actually do it. Let the world flow around you. Remember that you are the rock. All those thousands of people cannot wash away your sides. Instead, they part, moving to either side, flowing past you. You are not of them, but separate, compact, and impenetrable."

She nodded, falling into the mantra of his soothing voice. *I am a rock. The river of souls and time flows around me.*

"Do not let them distract you." The Kala Hi'ki's voice came from a distance. "You can look at the water, observe it. But you are stone, impermeable, and water can only pass around you."

She nodded.

"Are you a rock?" the Kala Hi'ki asked. "Are you solid, contained within yourself?"

She smiled, saying, "Yes."

"Good, then let us go out. You will be a rock, and observe for me. You will tell me only what you see. For this moment you are my eyes. You are *only* my eyes. Eyes of stone. Eternal, strong, and impervious to the river of sounds. You will allow the souls of others to wash around you. The current of time passes, but it does not affect your great weight."

She nodded, willing her souls to be stone.

"If you are stone, take my hand. Lead me to the doorway."

She reached out, taking his maimed hand in hers. Walking carefully, she passed Old White and led the Kala Hi'ki to the doorway. The sunlight was bright, and she squinted as they stepped outside. The sound of the people smashed against her. She staggered at the weight of it. *I am a great stone. It washes around me.* She swallowed hard, looking inside, feeling herself grow solid like the rock he insisted that she be. *I am a rock.* She took a step. And then another. With each, she let the roar of the crowd wash around her, over her. In the blinding light she made her way to the palisade gate at the mound top.

A sea of people surrounded the plaza. The height of the mound gave her a clear view of the great contest being waged on the stickball field. The sight of it brought her to a stop at the head of the stairway. In all directions, shouting, milling people crowded around the plaza. House roofs seemed to rise from the human mass like islands.

I am a rock. She struggled to simply let herself be.

A rock. Keeping that thought was so difficult. It seemed to slip back and forth like a fish.

"Take a moment," the Kala Hi'ki said. "Remember how strong you are. Solid. A great mass that not even the crowd can move. You are alone within yourself. None of this is real. Only you are. Let it pass by."

She filled her lungs, then let the breath drain away. "I am alone inside myself," she repeated.

"Now look out with your eyes of stone. Tell me what you see. You are not part of it. Only an observer from within a heart of solid rock. What your eyes see is outside and meaningless."

From the distance she had created within herself, she looked out. "People surround the plaza. Inside the square, young men are running, shoving. They are playing a great game of stickball."

As she stared upon the scene from her high vantage, she had a good view of the frantic game. The players were all young men in breechcloths. Some wore white bustles that stuck out from their belts like flowing tail feathers. Their heads were done up in more feathers that bobbed and weaved as they ran. The effect was as if peculiar wingless birds were running, jumping, and shoving. One team wore white, the other yellow. She had seen stickball played in her own country, but there they used only one racquet. Here the players held two, each about the length of a man's arm, the end bent in a loop and webbed with rawhide.

In the north teams consisted of perhaps twenty; here, they numbered in the hundreds as they ebbed and flowed, shouting, running, shoving together in great masses. She caught sight of the ball as it emerged from a mass, flying in a long arc. For a time the human mass continued to shove and mill, most of the players having lost sight of the ball. Then the press dissolved as a hundred men charged off in pursuit.

The goals were at opposite sides of the plaza, the closest just east of the Temple Mound. There two tall posts had been set in the ground; a crosspiece was laid between them twice the height of a man above the ground. From the closest, yellow fabric flagging was draped. At the far end of the field, the goal sported white.

"Who is playing?" the Kala Hi'ki asked.

"A white team plays yellow."

"Ah," he said. "Cattail Town is white and plays Canebrake Town in yellow. They have a score to settle. A dispute over an arranged marriage. A woman from Canebrake Town was promised to a man in Cattail Town. Then her family married her to another. If Cattail Town wins, they will receive compensation. Adding to the fury of the contest, Canebrake Town has won for the last five matches. It is said they have managed to 'doctor' the grounds each time. Cattail has a new conjurer. He is supposed to have influenced the Power so that they will win this time."

The ball was neatly caught by a young man in yellow. With his racquet, he slung the ball toward the goal. There three men in white mobbed the yellow player, knocking him to the ground. The ball was neatly intercepted and pitched south toward the white goal.

Two Petals stared in amazement as the milling players ran together, people grunting under the impact. She watched two players wiggle between the legs of a third, then try to rise between the man's legs, the three of them falling in a pile. The clatter of banging sticks rose over the roar of the crowd and whooping cries of the players.

Another press formed around the ball, people grunting and bellowing, squirming like a mass of earthworms. A single man wiggled from the mess, tossing the ball northward toward the yellow goal. A racquet neatly snatched it from the air, and the man turned, winging the ball north again, where another player leapt, caught the ball, and turned like a bobcat. As he hit the ground, his wiry body curved around and he whipped the ball between the goals.

A fierce shout exploded from the crowd. The force of it staggered Two Petals, and she tightened her grip on the Kala Hi'ki's hand.

"You are a rock," he told her. "You are only my eyes. Eyes can't think. They only observe. To see is passive. Let what your eyes see pass through you."

She steadied herself, forcing calm around her souls.

"What just happened?" the Kala Hi'ki asked.

"Yellow scored a goal."

"Then the score keepers will place a stick in the ground for Canebrake Town. They will play to twenty, placing ten sticks and then taking them down again with each score."

"What does the winner get?" she asked.

"On top of compensation for the woman, the towns have bet most everything they own: pottery, clothing, jewelry, food. Sometimes they even bet the clothes on their backs. Cattail Town has been nearly destitute for over a year now. Perhaps this new conjurer isn't as good as they have hoped."

Two Petals watched the teams re-form. The ball—having been retrieved—was run by a boy to an old man who walked out from the sidelines. He looked frail and small flanked by massed parallel ranks of the opposing teams. In the alley left down the middle of the field, he stopped, glanced back and forth, and then pitched the ball straight up in the air. He wheeled on his feet, sprinting for the sideline. The teams crashed together, and the melee began again, buoyed by a roaring of the crowd.

"Yellow has the ball again," Two Petals noted as it was flung northward. As the mass of players dissolved to sprint after the ball, two men hobbled toward the sidelines. One held his arm; the other's face streamed blood from a broken nose. Only after that portion of the field was left empty could she see the limp body of a third. Two of the Cattail Town players hesitated, then went back and carried their limp comrade to the side-lines, where the crowd took the burden and bore him to the rear.

"They take their play seriously," Old White noted from where he stood beside the Kala Hi'ki. "They hope Power will favor them for their dedication."

"And it is better that the disagreement over the woman is settled here, under the watchful ·eyes of Power," the Kala Hi'ki added. "They hope Mother Sun and the Spirits will grant favor to the side with the great-est merit. Here everyone can see justice done. The towns can take out their grievances without resorting to bloodshed."

Two Petals smiled slightly as a dazed man was left behind the scrimmage, blood dripping from his mouth. She watched as he rolled onto his knees and wrenched his dislocated jaw back in place. When he stood, he al-most toppled, weaving his way on wobbling legs to the side, where his relatives crowded around him, patting him on the back, thumping his shoulders, and propelling his wobbly body back onto the field.

Cattail Town's white-clad players broke the ball free, passing it neatly from player to player, each catching the ball in their hoops and finally casting it through the far goal.

She waited for the roar of the crowd to vanish, then said, "That was Cattail Town's goal."

The Kala Hi'ki asked, "How are my eyes faring? Are you still a rock?"

"I am still a rock." She watched the teams take their places as the old man walked out between the ranks, an-other boy bringing the ball to the elder.

"Do you begin to understand the lesson?" the Kala Hi'ki asked. "Can you see the way of it? How you can just let the world pass? For you, Contrary, none of this is real. The struggle you face is to convince yourself of it. All of your life you have been taught that you must be part of the world around you. You have been directed since you were little to be one of the players. People have encouraged you to interact with them, talk, and participate. Deep inside you is the need to have people respond, to see approval in their eyes. As Power grew inside you, you tried harder and harder to fit in, to be one of them. In the end, you were only fighting against yourself and the gift Power filled you with."

"But I—"

"There is no but!" the Kala Hi'ki insisted sternly. "Surrender yourself. Give up Two Petals. She is no more. The woman you once were, the one you fought so desperately to keep, is faded like a shadow under the clouds. Only the Contrary remains. You are separate. Special. Power has placed you apart. As it has me. Only when you give up trying to be as you once were—forget trying to be like everyone else—will you accept Power, and allow the world to wash around you."

She nodded, swallowing hard. In that moment, she began to lose her focus. She could feel the tremble begin in her jaw.

"You are a rock," the Kala Hi'ki told her firmly. "Close your eyes. Concentrate on being impervious. There, that's it. Feel the world flow past like the river. Allow the noise of the crowd to pass around you. It is illusion. Not of your world, but a distraction to keep you from yourself. Ignore it. Sound is not real. You only imagine it." He paused, letting her concentrate. "Search for yourself inside. Find your souls. They are real. You are real. You are the rock. The world flows around you."

She felt herself still; the trembling fear receded.

"Let Two Petals go," he said softly. "You are the Contrary. You are only the Contrary. Not of this world, but separate."

She nodded, her breathing settling. *I am calm. I am stone.*

She opened her eyes and just stood, letting the sights and sounds flow past. *It is all illusion.*

"Who has the ball?" the Kala Hi'ki asked.

"Yellow again." She watched, forcing herself to be detached. In that state she let herself speak. She simply let the words flow through her. For the first time since her mother's death, she experienced peace.

"Yes," one of the voices in her head said. *"This is the way it is supposed to be."*

I am Contrary. I exist outside the world. The rest is illusion.

In the end it didn't matter that Cattail Town won. It simply was.

Thirty-three

Morning cast a gray luminescence into the eastern sky. Rainbow City was already coming awake—not that it had slept with Dances, feasting, and celebration through most of the night. Frost had settled on thatch roofs and coated the brown leaves of grass where they had been beaten flat. It left a hoar on the posts and ramadas, and turned treacherous the wooden stairways that climbed the mounds.

In the predawn light, Trader studied the cool stone disk he cupped in his right hand. He had Traded for the stone blank many years ago while living among the Caddo. The blank had come from high in the mountains at the headwaters of the White River. Then, over the next year he had laboriously ground concaves into each side, and rounded it to fit a circle he had scribed onto a piece of leather. When he had the shape perfect for his hand, he had used fine sand sifted through fabric to polish it. The process had entailed using ever finer sand on wet leather until the surface was so glossy it reflected his image. The rounded circumference was dull now, having been rolled down countless clay tracks.

He hefted his lance in his left hand and looked around at the awakening city. A smoky pall hung over the pointed roofs. When a dog barked in the distance, Swimmer perked his ears. Stakeholders had already set up shop on the plaza before the Council House. There they would take the wagers on the day's chunkey match as well as for the final stickball game. This was the grand one, played between the Yuchi Chief and Warrior Moieties. It would follow immediately after his chunkey game with Born-of-Sun.

Trader took a deep breath, watching it rise in the frozen air as he exhaled the tension inside him. Then he walked to the starting mark. Swimmer sat to one side, his head cocked. It had been something of a battle to keep the dog from running beside him, barking, and then chasing the chunkey stone as it raced down the clay track.

Trader stilled his thoughts, balanced his lance, and played the cast in his mind. Uncle Flying Hawk's words came back from his youth: *"The trick is to concentrate. You must release the stone true. Knowing how it will roll and where it will stop is to know where to cast your lance. If you understand this thing, you will win. Mastery only comes of long practice, of familiarity with your equipment."*

That Trader knew. After all, what did a Trader do for an entire winter among a foreign people? He didn't have family, friends, and kin obligations. He needn't prepare for festivals, or see to the raising of his nieces and nephews. Instead, he played chunkey. If he was good, he could gamble on his skill; and by winning, fill his canoe with more precious Trade to take upriver.

But I've never wagered my life before. It was sobering knowledge that had plagued his sleep.

Uncle's words came back. *"The trick is to concentrate."*

Trader scuffed his moccasined feet on the hard clay, flexing his thighs, rolling his shoulders. Swimmer perked up, aware of what was about to happen.

Trader crouched slightly, his gaze fixed on the long clay strip. He launched himself, taking four fast steps, bent, and smoothly released the stone. It kissed the ground, spinning off his fingers. Trader let momentum carry him forward, smoothly shifted his lance, and cast at the second mark, sure of where the stone would stop.

He pulled up, watching the lance spin slowly through the air. The stone rolled straight and true. He could feel the rightness of it. As the lance arced, the stone slowed. It curved to the right as he had known it would, and toppled to its side. The lance impacted point first—an arm's length from the stone.

"Well done!" a voice called from behind.

He turned back to see Born-of-Sun kneeling beside Swimmer, mussing the dog's long hair.

Trader shrugged. "I've done better."

"So have we all." Born-of-Sun rose and gestured for Swimmer to stay. He carried his own lance and one of the beautiful stones Trader had seen in the box.

Trader trotted down the clay, retrieved his stone and lance, and jogged back. Born-of-Sun was staring at his stone.

"Nice piece," the chief noted. "Trade for it?"

"Made it."

"Excellent workmanship. And the lance?"

"Cut from a white ash sapling. It took a while, but with judicious sanding I managed to get the balance just right."

The chief nodded, his attention turning to the chunkey court. "I didn't get much chance to practice. The chiefs had a meeting that lasted most of the day yesterday. I didn't even get to watch the game between Canebrake and Cattail Towns. I heard that Cattail pulled it out in the end."

"It was close," Trader agreed. "Canebrake would have had it, but one of their players struck another from behind with his racquet. The judges took a point as penalty."

"Passion can lead men to foolish things." Born-of-Sun hefted his lance, testing its balance. "May I?"

Trader stepped back, nodding. He walked over to Swimmer, stopping to lay his lance to the side and scratch the dog's ears. "Let's see what we're up against."

Born-of-Sun squatted to loosen his muscles, flexed

his shoulders, and took his position. He drew a deep breath, eyes closed. When he opened them, he started forward, neatly bowling his stone down the track. In another four paces, he released, just shy of the mark. Trader nodded, impressed by the man's perfect cast. He stood, watching the lance arc over the speeding stone. It would be close.

"Come on. Let's go see," he said to Swimmer, and together they trotted down the court behind Born-of-Sun. The lance had stuck no more than an arm's length from the stone. "The distance between your cast and mine could only be determined with a measuring string."

"I got lucky," Born-of-Sun said modestly. "It's the first cast of the morning. Generally I'm happy to keep stone and lance inside the bounds of the court."

"I'm sure," Trader noted as the chief retrieved his pieces.

Together they walked back, Swimmer's tail cutting lazy arcs in the morning air.

"That was a good visit we had the other day," Born-of-Sun remarked. "I have given our talk a great deal of consideration."

"And?"

"I would set your mind at rest. When I win this thing, I will not be putting you to death."

"That's a fine thing. When I win this thing, I will not leave with a dark view of the Tsoyaha."

Born-of-Sun chuckled. "I would like to know something: When I win, and your fate becomes mine, will you stay here without resentment, understanding that the outcome was the will of Mother Sun?"

Trader shrugged. "I accepted this gamble in good faith. I am a man of many things: One of them is my word. I am here under the Power of Trade. But, yes, if by some sorcery you manage to win, I will keep my end of the bargain."

"Good. As I will keep mine." He gestured as they reached the starting mark. "Your cast."

Trader put Swimmer in his place, telling him to stay. He walked to the mark, seating the stone carefully in his hand, feeling the cold disk against his palm. From long practice, he stilled himself, running the cast through the eye of his souls. When he launched, it was in fluid motion; he barely broke stride as he bowled the stone, shifted the lance, and released it to arc, spinning through the sky.

The lance nosed over, almost meeting the stone as it toppled onto its side.

"Well done!" Born-of-Sun cried.

In his excitement, Swimmer let out a staccato of happy barks.

As they trotted down the course, Born-of-Sun added, "We talked about something the other day—about how over the last tens of summers, people know less and less about each other. Face it, the Trade is slowly fading away. You, however, know the hearts and minds of a great many peoples, nations that I will never visit."

"I do."

"You and Old White could become valued counselors to a chief who would listen and consider your words."

"Meaning you."

Born-of-Sun nodded. "I think we are entering a difficult time. This thing with the Chikosi, for example—I have no idea how it will turn out."

"If we are to believe Power, then Old White, the Contrary, and I will bring it to some sort of conclusion. Something happened when Old White was a boy. His heart beats at the center of this. I think that's why he ran."

"Who is he?"

"Honestly, I don't know. Nor will he say. And, believe me, I have been searching my souls for the answer." Trader stopped to stare down at the lance. It rested no more than a hand's breadth from the edge of the stone.

"That will be hard to beat." Born-of-Sun raised an eyebrow.

Trader recovered his pieces, and as they started back,

said, "I can't figure it out. Unlike me, he has no tattoos that would indicate he was Chief Clan, but he thinks he is a relative of mine."

"And you heard of no one of his age leaving your people?"

"No one. And if they had, I would have heard. No, he's as much a mystery to me as he is to you. I could almost believe that Power made him up from clay and breathed Spirit into him for reasons of its own."

"He has never given you a name?"

"Only Old White, and of course, the Seeker is known far and wide. When he and the Contrary found my camp that night, I thought it was a trick. The Seeker is almost mythical."

They reached the mark, and Trader stepped to one side. He watched Born-of-Sun curiously. His entire future hung in the balance, and here he was, talking as if to a best friend. Fact was, he really liked Born-of-Sun. This was the sort of chief that people longed for, his authority tempered by a kind and thoughtful humanity. That Born-of-Sun could shift from an indulgent uncle playing with children and dogs to a respected leader was a trait Trader had rarely seen—and never with such deft competence.

Born-of-Sun took a breath, his eyes closed. When the man launched, it was with grace and power. He had bowled his stone perfectly, his cast arcing through the sky. Trader stood, craning his neck to see. It would be close.

Together they trotted down the course, Swimmer bounding along, his long hair rolling with each joyous leap.

"When you lose," Born-of-Sun said seriously as he measured a hand's breadth between his lance and stone, "you would be most welcome to Trade out of Rainbow City. Sometimes that gets in a man's blood. I think it is in yours. You will always have a base here. I would be happy to have you come and go as you pleased.

Consider yourself to be my agent, if you will. It would be good to have someone I trusted bring me information on other chiefs in other lands."

"When I win, I will be happy to send runners to you every now and then. There will be problems between the Chikosi and the Tsoyaha. Not because we wish them, but because that is just the nature of people. When those problems occur, I would see us meet, discuss them, and find a solution that didn't involve war parties, bloodshed, and retaliation."

Born-of-Sun pulled his lance from the ground and picked up his stone. "I have several female cousins who are coming of age, and another, older, who was recently widowed. Perhaps I should introduce you. When Rainbow City becomes your home, it would be good to have a wife to make your life comfortable."

"You've planned this right down to the last detail, haven't you?"

Born-of-Sun looked back at Swimmer. "My brother has a black bitch. When she cycles again, we should put them together. By then I will be ready to raise another dog. I miss mine."

Trader tried to judge their casts. "So far, I'm not sure either one of us is showing any advantage. Our casts seem to be particularly well matched."

"And, I think, so are we." Born-of-Sun looked up at the lightening sky. "I have to go now. On this very sacred day I must make my greetings to Mother Sun as she appears over the horizon. But I want you to think of this, Trader: Power brought you here to me under auspicious signs. Perhaps Rainbow City is truly where your destiny lies. Whatever will happen among the Sky Hand, you have no guarantees that you will survive it. As to the Contrary, I have heard that the Kala Hi'ki has been making good progress teaching her how to handle her Powers. She would be welcome among us, and we could care for her special needs. The Kala Hi'ki is old, and I think his wounds weaken him more with every passing season.

The Seeker, too, would find a place among us, treasured for his knowledge of foreign peoples and events." He glanced at Trader. "Perhaps, when we play for real at high sun, your hand might tremble just the slightest. Should you lose by no more than a finger's width, you know what people will say."

With that, Born-of-Sun gave a knowing smile, turned, and trotted toward the palace ramp to prepare his ritual greeting of the sunrise.

"If I lose by a finger width," Trader mused as he bent to pet Swimmer, "people will say it was a close decision, made by Power, between perfectly matched equals."

Morning Dew panted for breath, squeezing through the press of bodies like an eel through swamp grass. Didn't these stupid Chikosi know anything? Scores were never made while being squeezed in the middle of a pile. The ones who scored were the fast ones on the outside. She broke free of the morass of pressing, kicking bodies and trotted backward, eyes on the mass of battling women.

"Go south!" Heron Wing called.

Morning Dew shot her a quick glance, understanding immediately. The south was unprotected, only a few Old Camp Moiety women there, and those the fat ones, out of breath, who didn't like the notion of fighting for the ball.

Morning Dew turned, sprinting in that direction, her racquets clutched in her hands.

This is madness!

But then she had stared dumbfounded that morning when Heron Wing handed her two well-made stickball racquets crafted of fine hickory. "You do know how to use these, don't you?" Heron Wing had asked, as if she already knew the answer.

I am Chahta, of the White Arrow Moiety. My mother's blood runs in my veins, Morning Dew had asserted in her head as she took the racquets. *What sort of matron would I be if I didn't?* More to the fact, she was Sweet Smoke's daughter; and no woman descended from her mother's loins could help but be trained in the use of stickball racquets. From the time Morning Dew could walk her mother had insisted that she not only know the game, but excel. "You will be the matron one day. Part of earning the people's respect is being among the best."

As a child she had had hours of practice and had been a cherished player in her moiety's girls' team. The women had cheered at the knowledge that she would be joining their ranks after her emergence from the Women's House.

And now, here I am, playing for the Chikosi.

"You are a slave," Heron Wing had said wryly, a secret amusement behind her expression. "Affiliated with our moiety. And, given the pitiful performance of our men this morning, we can use all the help we can get." With that, Heron Wing had given Morning Dew's body a careful appraisal. "I am hoping that you carry your clan's legacy." Then she had winked. "Let's see if you can show us a thing or two."

That morning, the Hickory Moiety men had lost, their defeat humiliating. It didn't help that five of the goals had been made by Smoke Shield. Morning Dew might hate him, but she had to admire his ability on the field. The man had moved like a panther, catching, throwing, fighting through the press when the ball was dropped.

In the end, however, Hickory Moiety had lost by five. Not even Smoke Shield could prevent that. Sensing opportunity, the celebrants from Old Camp had bet their winnings and more on the women's game that followed.

The pile of wagered goods had shocked even Morning Dew: stacks of hides, pottery, shells, blankets, pieces of worked copper, baskets of corn and beans and squash, clothing, and slaves.

It could be worse, she had thought. *I could be there, too.*

Instead she was here, in the midst of the fray, the score tied evenly at fifteen. Only five stakes on each side remained to be taken down as the score built.

Morning Dew slowed, staring back over her shoulder. She felt good, having not run like this since the day of her marriage. Throughout the game she had steadfastly refused to look over at the squares, now hidden by the throng of people watching the game who shouted, Sang, and leapt as the women struggled, gasped, and slammed each other for the ball. Nevertheless, Morning Dow could feel the oppressive presence of the empty squares, and what she had lost there.

So why am I playing for the Chikosi?

Heron Wing, Violet Bead, and several others milled about the edge of the press. In the melee, someone screamed in pain. Morning Dew had lost track of the ones carried or limping off the field, some with broken arms or legs, others streaming blood.

Head butting and striking with the racquets brought penalties. Anything else, provided it wasn't too blatant, was just part of the game. The referees consisted of ten old women on the sidelines. They walked back and forth, each with a feathered stick. Any foul would be called by them raising their sticks, pointing at the offender. Head butting was a nasty two-point penalty here, while a purposeful strike with a racquet lost one. Touching the ball with a hand meant surrendering the ball to the opposing team.

Vigilant as Morning Dew was, she almost missed the ball when a woman eased out of the melee, wobbling on her feet as if injured, only to straighten and toss the ball to Heron Wing, who now stood well clear. Heron Wing pivoted, finding Morning Dew right where she should be. The woman pulled back, using her entire body to cast.

Morning Dew tracked right, leapt, and felt the impact of the ball into the pocket of her racquet. She turned, sprinting east toward the goal. The defenders, mostly to the north, came charging after her. She did a quick evaluation of the fat women in her way, feinted right, dodged left, and shot away from the first, only to follow suit with the second.

From the edge of her souls, she could hear the frantic shouts of the crowd. Glancing around, she could see no other players wearing Hickory's white feathers or short dresses.

Dancing and darting, she slipped through the few women in her path. Closing from the side came no less than fifteen women, seeking desperately to intercept her.

Morning Dew broke left, sprinting for a hole, her breath tearing at her throat. Four red-clad opponents blocked her way. Using a trick her mother had taught her, she let them rush, knowing they would try to knock her off her feet, retrieve the ball, and send it back downfield. Instead, Morning Dew slowed, trying to look bewildered, and at the last moment, tossed the ball high over their heads, well above their reach. They stopped in confusion, eyes on the soaring ball instead of her.

Her speed carried her between them, and she used her momentum to slam one of the distracted women into her companion as she burst past. She had the advantage, well ahead of the others, who had to reverse direction, locate the ball, and retrieve it. On the run, Morning Dew swept up the ball and ran full-tilt for the goal, which filled her vision, ever closer as she raced.

She could hear bare feet pounding behind her, set herself, and with years of practice to back her, flung the leather-hide ball through the goal.

The crowd exploded as she trotted to a stop, chest heaving for breath. Four points left. Winded, she walked slowly back as the jubilant Hickory crowd screamed. Old Camp hissed and shouted insults.

She was still panting as she crossed the center line to

the cheers of her teammates. "Two goals!" Heron Wing grinned. "I was right about you."

"Why am I doing this?" Morning Dew gasped, hardly aware of the women who crowded around her.

"You are a matron," Heron Wing said simply. "It is your calling."

My calling?

She glanced up as one of the old women was handed the ball. The ranks formed up on either side, leaving the old woman to look back and forth between the sides.

"Rest up," Violet Bead said, leaning toward her. "I have a feeling we'll need you again." Then the woman gave her a pat on the back.

Morning Dew watched the ball sail high into the air. She backpedaled, fully aware of the futility of scrambling for the ball amidst that milling confusion of bodies.

She took a position midway back, glancing at the others around her; those fleet of foot, and quick with the racquets. These were the skilled players, the ones who left the bigger women to battle for the ball. The more aggressive women liked close quarters. It allowed them to jab an elbow into a longtime rival's breast or "accidentally" backhand an opponent in a move that didn't seem a blatant strike.

More and more women crowded into the mess. Heron Wing had taken a position on the south, Violet Bead and several other good players filling the gaps, knocking shoulders with Old Camp opponents who were also circling the fringes.

Gods, how long was this going to last? Morning Dew was almost breathing easily again when a woman rose above the confusion, lifted by her friends. She gave a halfhearted toss of the ball to a red-dressed player, who flung it hard at another. The receiver missed what should have been an easy catch, and turned, racing two Hickory women for the rolling ball. In that instant, Morning Dew could tell which way it was going to go. One of the Hickory women trapped the ball with her racquet, scooped it up, and slung it eastward. Morning Dew couldn't see who caught it as the press of women broke apart like a school of fish, racing off to the north.

"Pace yourself," Mother's warning voice reminded from the past. *"Think first; run yourself to death later."* The ball would always come back.

She glanced at the other women around her, they, too, taking the opportunity to prop their hands on their knees, breathing deeply. Her job now was to wait, to be fresh if the ball came back her way. When it did, she needed to intercept and fling it eastward again. In the meantime, she checked the tight cloth binding she had wound around her chest, ensuring it wouldn't slip down.

When the ball came it was rapid, the Old Camp women having established a line, passing one to another. Morning Dew turned, heading to intercept when she was hit from the side. She stumbled, tripped, and hit the ground hard, glaring back. The woman who hit her had also tumbled from the impact. As the woman scrambled to her feet, she yelled, "Sorry, but you're too good!"

Morning Dew found her dropped racquets, climbed to her feet, and charged off, too late to make a difference as Old Camp scored again.

Even up.

Cursing under her breath, Morning Dew limped to the forming line.

"What happened?" Heron Wing asked.

"Got knocked down," Morning Dew said through gritted teeth.

"Take it out on Old Camp," another of the women replied. Some clacked their sticks together in approval.

The game seesawed, point for point. Twice Morning Dew got the ball, passing it neatly. Once a woman dropped it, only to have an Old Camp player scoop it, then sling it west, where a goal was scored. They were tied at nineteen apiece.

"Last point," Heron Wing said darkly. She shot Morning Dew a look. "You rested?"

"I am."

"Go long. If we tag you, *you make that point!*"

Morning Dew watched the woman cast a quick look at the piles of goods wagered on the game. They rose behind the stakeholders like a small mountain.

"Nothing about moiety honor?" Morning Dew asked.

"That, too," Heron Wing asserted as the ball was tossed to open the final play. Morning Dew went south, skirting the massed struggle over the ball. She wasn't even halfway to her position when Heron Wing's shout brought her around. The ball was already in the air, arcing wide.

Morning Dew broke stride, racing, too far away to intercept. Nevertheless, she had one chance before the nearest Old Camp woman would be on it. From a dead run, she batted the ball, half a heartbeat ahead of her opponent's frantic strike. Racing after the rolling ball, she managed to scoop it into the air, run under it, and snag it in a racquet pocket. Then she turned, sprinting for all she was worth. A quick glance over her shoulder let her know the entire mob was racing after her. Before the distant goal four women waited, racquets ready.

How do I do this? Thoughts raced through her. If she could pass them, get within range, the point would be hers.

Why should I? This was Hickory Moiety's game. All of their possessions rested on her. She could throw wide, send the ball out of bounds, or she could bobble a pass, trip, do anything, and the defenders would scoop up the ball. From them it would pass down that most able line of players to the Old Camp goal.

Trip! she thought. Yes, that would be best. For the coming moons, she alone would know what damage she had done to the Hickory Moiety. In her souls, she was plotting the best way of doing it. Simple: overrun, stumble, and fall. By holding the racquet just so, she would make the ball roll straight for her opponent. It would all be over. She could limp convincingly crestfallen to Heron Wing, and there would be no censure.

She was smiling as she ran headlong for the braced woman in her way. Behind her, the pursuing wave of players was pounding ever closer.

At the last moment, she twisted, feinted, and dodged past the defender. Her thoughts had gone silent. Breath tearing at her lungs, she raced for the goal. Driven by something she didn't understand, she bulled her way forward. The last two defenders had backed, just at the edge of range.

At the last moment, an instant before impact, she recognized the Old Camp woman who had knocked her down. Reversing the racquet, she put her weight behind a low cast, firing the ball between the woman's legs. That momentary act confused her opponent, drawing her to stare stupidly between her legs. Morning Dew lowered a shoulder, driving into the woman, knocking her sprawling.

That'll show you just how good I am!

Morning Dew grunted at the impact, stumbled sideways, and saw the ball zipping ahead of her. In three steps she had recovered her stride. Breath coming in great gulps, she raced for the ball, scooped it up, and heard the second woman's bare feet hammering the ground.

Too fresh, she'll catch me. Instinct took over; the racquet went back. With all her might, Morning Dew launched the ball overhand, tripping from the exertion, falling. She hit the ground hard—impact drove the breath from her lungs. Her pursuer tried to jump, snagged one of her legs, and hammered the ground beside her with a sodden thump.

Morning Dew sprawled on her stomach, stunned, sparkles of yellow flickering before her eyes. She felt herself falling, unable to suck breath. A gray twilight hovered at the edge of her vision, and a loud ringing filled her ears. When she could finally draw breath, it was shallow, and the pain came welling up from her body.

Shuffling feet came into vision: two, four, then tens of them. The world consisted of feet and the ringing in her ears. Then she gulped a full breath, her stomach nauseous. Hands lifted her, and she blinked, aware that a sea of women surrounded her. The ringing mixed into cheers as her stunned body was lifted high, borne along as if on a wave.

There she floated, adrift on a sea of supporting hands, buoyed by a press of smiling, shouting women.

"What happened?" she asked herself numbly. "What did I do?" She thought of the immense pile bet on the game. Of the loss she could have dealt Hickory Moiety and her tormentors.

You are a matron, the voice said from somewhere inside her.

Thirty-four

"Five points!" Smoke Shield roared. "Five *miserable* points!" He sat in the seclusion of his dark room. No one would find him here. In the gloom, he could be alone, staring at the empty room around him. He had bet everything: his clothing, furs, paints, boxes, shells, and pottery. Even the blankets and hides on his bed were gone, leaving only the split-cane matting. Through the weave he could see the sheathed stone sword and the little honorary arrows. Had they not been of such great importance to him, they, too, would have been gone. He had even surrendered his shirt, and now wore one of Thin Branch's, feeling the too-tight material almost ripping from the act of breathing.

The roar from the solstice games had been drifting in, reminding him of the women's contest. Now it reached a crescendo. Looking up, he could almost believe the palace was trembling. What more had Hickory Moiety lost? He had seen the Old Camp women practicing, and after the drubbing the men's team had taken this morning, he wouldn't have bet a broken pot on the women winning. Not that he had one to bet.

The tumult beyond the palace didn't recede. If anything it grew louder. He closed his eyes, dropping his face into his hands. Old Camp must have been exultant like they had never been before.

Time to go "hunting" again. The last thing he wanted to do was face all the smug faces, hear the taunts and jibes from the winners.

"Five foul little points!" He rubbed his face. The gods alone know what it would have been without his efforts. Of all the points scored by Hickory warriors, one out of three had been his. Gods, what a bunch of rabbits. He peeked through his fingers, seeing his empty floor. The outlines where boxes had been could be made out in the dust. Round rings marked where the pots had once sat.

He had only matting, the ceremonial sword, his war honors, and a borrowed shirt to his name. Not even his war club was left to him. A stinging reminder of his previously stolen bow and arrows.

"Please, Fast Legs, tell me you have run the woman down, killed her, *and recovered my bow and arrows*!"

The muted roar of the crowd was his only answer.

Fast Legs! There was the problem. During the Busk celebration, Fast Legs had made more goals than Smoke Shield. Fast Legs hadn't earned his name for nothing, and now, when so much was on the line, *where was he*? Blood and thunder, all he had to do was hide a body and hunt down one weasel-like woman. What could possibly be taking him so long? It wasn't even as if he didn't know where the woman lived.

If Fast Legs had just set a diversionary fire in a granary, he could have slipped into the woman's house during the confusion, brained her when she stepped in the door, and been done with it.

He had needed Fast Legs *here*! For the game. In the eye of his souls, Smoke Shield could see Fast Legs catching his throw, turning, and slinging the ball through the goal time after time.

"It's your fault," he mumbled. "But for you, I wouldn't be in this situation."

Just kill that cursed woman, and get back here!

"War Chief?" came Thin Branch's call.

"Yes, I'm here." He straightened, leaning back against the wall. Gods, the last thing he wanted was to deal with his idiot slave.

Thin Branch pushed the door hanging to the side, his face betraying a curious excitement.

"How bad is it?" He couldn't bring himself to look at Thin Branch, didn't want to betray the extent of his depression. "I watched the Old Camp women practice. That relay of outside passing was remarkable."

"We won!" Thin Branch chirped. "You should have seen it. Twenty to nineteen. And, here's the remarkable part: Heron Wing had Morning Dew play for us. She was wonderful! Three goals she made, War Chief. Three *unassisted* goals. It was amazing! She ran like a deer! Outplayed the defenders every time. Tricked them, outran them, knocked them out of the way like they were grouse!"

Smoke Shield straightened. "She did what?"

"She *won* the game! On the last play, she got the ball and ran from half field clear to the goal! You should have seen it! The whole field was chasing behind her, this huge mass of women!" Thin Branch's face was glowing. "She outran them, dodged the defenders, or tricked them. Once she threw the ball between a woman's legs. While the woman was looking between her legs, Morning Dew knocked her flat, ran past, scooped up the ball, and made the most spectacular cast I've ever seen. The ball flew true, perfectly between the goalposts."

Smoke Shield gaped. "My slave did that?"

"Well . . ." Thin Branch looked slightly abashed.

"They must be showering her with gifts!"

"Oh, they are. You wouldn't believe it. Morning Dew took a terrible fall as she made that last cast. Knocked the wind right out of her. Our women picked her up, carried her. They went three times around the tchkofa, laughing and singing; then they plopped her down in front of the stakeholders. As the wagers were handed out, she was covered with pots, pearls, baskets of food, blankets, hides, and copper. We could hardly carry it all away."

Smoke Shield threw his head back, laughter rolling

from deep down in his gut. "Carry it you shall. You take as many men as you need, those selfsame stumbling idiots that lost my wager, and you bring it all up here. Every last bit of it!" He jumped to his feet, flush with excitement and victory. He smacked a hard fist into his palm and let out a whoop of victory. He was giddy, laughing like a child.

When he spun, he could see the look of consternation on Thin Branch's face. He waved at him. "Go on. Like I said, you don't have to do it yourself. Take some warriors. Tell them I ordered it."

Thin Branch swallowed hard. "You said everything, War Chief."

"Yes, yes, everything! All of it. The pearls, the food, the copper, everything!"

Thin Branch swallowed hard. "That's just it, War Chief. I followed your orders perfectly this morning. I did exactly what you told me to."

Smoke Shield stopped short, spinning, muscles bulging. "What are you talking about?"

Thin Branch, looking like a man poisoned, whispered, "You told me explicitly this morning. You had me repeat the order you gave me, War Chief. Word for word. I did exactly like you told me to."

Smoke Shield frowned. "I told you, word for word, to bet everything on Hickory Moiety this morning." He thrust an angry arm out. "Look at this room! Everything."

"Yes. And I did that. Just as you ordered." He winced. "You see, the thing is, everything included Morning Dew. Heron Wing . . ."

Smoke Shield's vision narrowed. "Morning Dew?"

"Heron Wing . . ." Thin Branch wrung his hands. "She took the wager. She bet against her own moiety. Isn't that the most amazing thing you've ever heard? She wagered her entire collection of fine shell necklaces specifically against Morning Dew. As of this morning, your slaves, me included, belong to Heron Wing."

Smoke Shield sat hard on the pole bench, hardly aware that it cracked dangerously under his weight.

"It's not all bad," Thin Branch replied meekly. "The gracious Heron Wing has sent me back to you. As a . . . a gift to her beloved husband!"

The solstice remained cold, the ground hard and frozen for the much-anticipated chunkey match between Trader and the Yuchi high chief. Old White was so nervous he found it difficult to breathe as he watched Trader and Born-of-Sun make their ritual observances. Around them a huge crowd had gathered, literally pressing against each other to the point that War Chief Wolf Tail had to delegate warriors to keep the crowd back, especially downrange where an errant lance might do serious damage to a spectator. A buzz filled the air, all eyes on Trader, the high chief, Swimmer—who sat at Old White's feet—and Two Petals.

That morning, in the ceremony before the first ballgame, people had been amazed that Chikosi would offer gifts to Mother Sun, and had actually fought over the Illinois bowls they had passed out randomly among the crowd.

"I guess we are no longer witches and wicked sorcerers," Old White commented to Two Petals and the Kala Hi'ki. He waved back at a well-wisher in the crowd.

"People are curious," the Kala Hi'ki replied. "That you are here, with me, is most auspicious to them. Their interest in the welfare of the Contrary has passed from lip to lip. And the offer made to your Trader has been buzzing among them like bees among flowers." He turned his blind head toward Two Petals. "Are you all right?"

"I am stone," she said softly, her expression oddly preoccupied as she watched a steaming shell cup of black drink being passed between the high chief and

Trader. "The people flow around me like a river. I am awash with their souls; they lap against me like waves." She looked at an open space near them in the chunkey court. "You don't feel them the way I do." Then she cocked her head, as if listening to an answer. "I will not leap up and grab the chief's lance from the air. You haven't seen this like I have."

Old White glanced in the direction she spoke, wondering what sort of being she saw out there on the naked clay.

A pipe was brought to Born-of-Sun, who took a pull, exhaled, and offered a prayer to the sky, his words spoken in Yuchi.

"He is calling for strength, for firm aim, and for Power to side with him in this most noble of contests," the Kala Hi'ki translated. "He is a good man, this chief. Better than I would have made."

"Better than any of us, I am beginning to think," Old White said agreeably. "And, believe me, I have seen many chiefs. I hope your people continue to be grateful for what they have here."

"Depending on those two men there, Seeker, he may well be your chief soon."

Two Petals unexpectedly said, "I've seen the wood shatter. It cannot penetrate the stone. Rock has a hard and unforgiving heart."

Old White nodded thoughtfully. The Kala Hi'ki had done wonders with the woman. And this time the blind Priest had used just a little of the herb extract. With each dose he had been cutting the mixture, weaning her slowly from the brew. As a result, her backward speaking was increasing and she'd grown detached. She paused more often to listen to voices and talk to beings he couldn't see; but she no longer grew frantic when people crowded around. Sudden noises, like cheers from the crowd, didn't cause her panic.

Old White fingered his chin, reached down to pet Swimmer, and watched as Trader and Born-of-Sun stripped down to their breechcloths in the cold air. Trader raised his chunkey stone to his lips, blowing across it. Then he did the same with his lance.

The crowd went silent as Trader generously offered the first cast to Born-of-Sun. Old White felt his heart begin to hammer as the chief took the first mark, bent to loosen his muscles, and closed his eyes, as if seeing the cast deep inside the eye of his souls.

Why am I so worried? He had seen chunkey before, had often had games played in his honor. This one, however, would determine his future.

He closed his eyes, praying, *Be strong, Trader. May Power ride your muscles and guide your cast.*

Involved in his prayer, Old White missed the first cast, hearing the crowd explode in praise. Downrange he could see the lance and stone. The distance was close. One of the Priests stepped forward and used a knotted string to measure the distance. This he showed to the rapt crowd, and a cheer went up.

People called out encouragement as Born-of-Sun trotted down to retrieve his pieces.

Old White shot a glance in the direction of the stakeholders. A considerable pile had been bet on the Yuchi chief. A rather pitiful pile on Trader. Those few who had, Old White suspected, were hedging their bets. And besides, what good was it to bet everything against nothing?

Trader had taken the mark, did a deep knee bend, and rolled his shoulders. For a moment he looked calmly down the course.

Is he any good? Old White wondered, having never seen Trader play.

Trader launched himself, releasing with the smooth skill of an accomplished player, the stone disk rolling true. Then he cast—the motion smooth. Old White stood transfixed, watching the lance arc toward the stone. Both lance and stone came to rest at the same time. For the life of him, Old White couldn't tell which cast had been closer. The priest measured, holding up the string. "The point goes to the high chief by half a knot!"

Again the crowd roared.

To one side, an elder twisted a pointed stick into the ground.

Twenty casts, Old White thought. *Then at the end of them, my future will be decided.*

In all of his life he had never felt such a sense of futility.

Trader and Born-of-Sun were talking like old friends, each calm, both congratulating each other on their casts. They acted as if they had played thus for all of their lives: a friendly rivalry.

The notion formed in Old White's head. *Gods, does he even want to win?* The rumor had been running through the city like a scalded dog. "The chief would have the visitors stay. He has offered a cousin to Trader for a wife. The Contrary would live with us."

Old White's heart began to hammer, and he looked at Trader anew. The man stood relaxed, no hint of the gravity of their situation reflected in his easy smile.

Do I dare try to stop this?

"Wait for Power," Two Petals said, eyes focused on the distance. "Power knows all."

Born-of-Sun cast again. The crowd cried happily as the lance imbedded at about the same distance from the toppled stone as before. After the Priest measured, he held the string up for the audience. More cheering.

Trader cast, and Old White stepped forward, as if he could will the slim lance to its destination. He held his breath as the priest measured, then called, "Point to Trader, by a full knot!"

Again the crowd shouted happily. Old White could see individuals slipping away, headed in the direction of the stakeholders. If it stayed this close, even more would be slipping away, trying to change their bets in spite of the fact the stakeholders would have declared it closed at the first cast.

"How about you, Seeker?" the Kala Hi'ki asked. "Are you all right?"

"I believe I am a bit anxious."

The scarred blind man drew a breath that whistled through his nose holes. "This is a thing of Power, Seeker. This is done in the light of Mother Sun, on her special day. You do not know the ramifications of your journey. Things may have changed at Split Sky City since you were summoned. Do not fret; if Power wants you to go, it will happen."

How can I tell him? What would make him understand why I must go back?

"You could tell it like it actually is," Two Petals said, again seeming to read his thoughts. "I see a stick in the current. It cannot help but go where the river wills."

He drew a breath. Gods, what a mess!

The points wavered back and forth. One to Trader, another to Born-of-Sun. Each cast was so close, each measured by a knot, or half knot. Old White ground the few teeth remaining in his head. Images of his past were slipping out from between his souls, only to be beaten back by force of will alone.

"I can smell your worry, Seeker," the Kala Hi'ki said. "Perhaps I should have brewed some of the Contrary's tea for you. It calms the nerves, settles the thoughts. Your souls are in need of soothing."

"My souls may jump out of my body if this turns out wrong."

The score was tied at five and five. Old White's mouth had gone dry. Was the entire match going to be this close?

Then, to his horror, Born-of-Sun took two points in a row. The crowd had grown increasingly silent. Now they burst out in gleeful cries. Only to fall silent again as Trader won two.

High above, an eagle floated into view, as if curious about the proceedings. People pointed, sure that the bird signified a blessing for Born-of-Sun. A jubilant mood seemed to flow through the crowd, lifting them upon its wave, only to have Trader make the next point to pull ahead.

Old White's heart leaped. Gods, there was a chance.

Born-of-Sun then tied it.

A chill formed in Old White's bones, creeping out through his flesh as the nineteenth cast was made. Born-of-Sun won by a knot's length.

"Twenty," Two Petals said positively. "It won't be enough."

Old White felt his souls begin to drift. A sodden ache had started deep inside. *Gods, it won't be enough.* What would he do? The voices of the *Katsinas* whispered in his memory. *Home. You must go home. It is time.*

A roar went up from the crowd. The Priest's voice rang high and clear. "Point to Trader! They tie at ten apiece."

Old White staggered, his legs weak beneath him.

"One more! One more!" the crowd began to shout.

Old White stared at them in dismay. People were bounding up and down; Swimmer was barking gleefully, his tail wagging. Old White was too dazed to stop the dog as Swimmer charged over to bark at Trader's feet, his tail swishing, pure delight in his eyes.

To his credit, Trader bent down, rubbing Swimmer's hair, whispering in his ear. Then he rose, calling, "One more! We will break the tie!"

The crowd whistled, stamped, and shouted.

Old White realized that Two Petals had stepped beside him, her hand on his elbow, steadying him. "Power swirls about us. Feel it? Like wings in still air. Beating all around."

"Gods!" *Help me!*

Born-of-Sun took his mark, following his ritual. Then he started, sprinting forward to release the stone, taking another couple of steps, and his arm shot forward. The lance spun in the sunlight, flying like a thing alive as it arched down. It impacted point first, not a hand's distance from the stone.

The shout from the people rose like thunder from the earth.

Trader himself applauded, a look of satisfaction on his face. The people noted it, their exuberance riotous.

"How can he beat that?" Old White cried weakly.

As if lost in a Dream, he watched as Born-of-Sun returned, nodding to greetings along the way.

Trader took the mark, and then, breaking his routine, he looked directly into Old White's eyes, an odd smile on his lips. Old White staggered as if he'd been struck. Only Two Petals' support kept him from toppling. *He's going to throw it. That's what that knowing smile was. He is ready to stay here with Born-of-Sun.*

A sickness began to bloom within his souls. Like a fungus, it began consuming him as Trader took the mark, rolled his shoulders, and sprinted forward. The release was fast, a blur of motion as the stone kissed the ground, shooting forward. Trader shifted his lance to his right hand, took another four steps, and cast at the mark.

Old White watched the last of his life fly away with that gleaming shaft of wood. It spun in the golden sunlight. Then it arced gracefully toward the ground. He had forgotten Two Petals as she supported his weight, could only see the stone slowing, veering to the left.

The lance seemed to hang in the air, and then it dropped. The sharp point slammed into the center of the stone with a loud *clack*. Wood splintering, the broken shaft leaped futilely into the sky, only to fall back and bounce, shivering on the ground.

A terrible silence hung, as if the entire world had drawn breath, afraid to release it.

"A hit!" called the Priest. "Trader wins!"

Even then, the crowd seemed frozen, as if they could not believe what they had just seen. Slowly, first with nods, then a couple of calls, the applause built. People were gyrating on their feet, clapping their

hands, whistling, and screaming. Wolf Tail's warriors
had all they could do just holding them back.

Old White, mouth open, turned to stare at Trader, who
was clasping Born-of-Sun's arm, a warm smile beaming
on his face. Even Born-of-Sun seemed shocked, but was
making the best of it. He nodded, said something polite,
and then reached down to ruffle Swimmer's fur. Standing, he motioned for silence. It took longer than even a
bad chief should have had to wait.

Finally, the crowd stilled enough that he could call
out, "We have had the judgment of Mother Sun! Trader
has won. And in so doing, does us all honor. The stakeholders will release the debts, and then we have a ballgame to play!"

The crowd didn't sound as enthusiastic this time, or
so it seemed to Old White. Many were no doubt realizing how much they had bet.

"Are you all right?" the Kala Hi'ki asked again.

Dazed and drained, Old White swallowed. "I think I
need to go sit down somewhere."

Old White rested in the quiet solitude of the temple,
his eyes on the gleaming reliefs that hung from the
walls. Firelight shone off the copper and made the colors come alive. For the moment, he was just happy to
breathe, overjoyed that he had been able to walk back
here on his own rather than be carried by some sturdy
young man. As to their winnings from the chunkey
game, he had no idea what to do with them. For the moment, the wealth had been placed in a storehouse. They
certainly had no way to take it with them.

He looked up as one of the young Priests led the Kala
Hi'ki into the room. Then the younger man turned,
walking back out into the night.

With the surety of a sighted man, the Kala Hi'ki walked over and seated himself beside Old White. He sighed, remarking, "I am not as young as I once was. The Sunset Blessing almost exhausted me."

"I never want to pass another day like this one." He glanced up at the image of the Yuchi hero bringing home the sorcerer's head. "I should be thankful. But somehow, I'm not."

"Life would have been good for you here. I'm not sure what awaits you at Split Sky City. You said you were going there to die." He hesitated. "If it's just being close to your Ancestors that matters, you could die here. We could ensure that your bones made it home to rest among them."

"I appreciate the offer. The thing is, I have unfinished business there. Something I must see to."

"Ah, your great secret."

Old White nodded, fairly sure the Kala Hi'ki could see it even without eyes.

"Power has mysterious ways."

"Something has been bothering me," Old White said. "How did you make it home after escaping from Split Sky City? I would hear that story. I think I need to know it."

The Kala Hi'ki paused reflectively. "I took a blow to the head during a fight with the Chikosi. When I came to, my skull was splitting with pain and I was being carried on a pole, hanging from my hands and wrists. I thought nothing could hurt so much." He chuckled dryly. "I was so very wrong.

"They took me, paraded me around, and, as is the custom, I was given to Flying Hawk . . . for he was only recently confirmed high minko. And he had successfully beaten off my raid. I, who went to the Chikosi to take captives, had become one."

He seemed to be staring into the past behind his bound eye sockets. "You can imagine what they did to me on the square. People tell me it hurts just to see what they did to my body. Day after day, I was burned and cut. My eyes, well they thought that was the worst, but it helped actually, not being able to see what I had become.

"Then one day, Flying Hawk came, telling me, 'You must live just one more day, and then my nephew—he who will become high minko after me—will emerge from the Men's House. I will allow him the honor of cutting your heart from your body. You will be my gift to him . . . his first act as a man.'"

The Kala Hi'ki nodded his head. "I prayed for that to happen soon. My souls were wandering, passing in and out of my body. Perhaps that is why we have two nostrils. Without a nose, mine could enter and leave freely.

"Then in the night, the boy came, saying his name was Green Snake, and that he was too cowardly to do this thing. He told me he had sneaked out of the Men's House with no one knowing. And he cut me down, ground what was left of my right hand into the earth while I lay there, and urinated on me." The Kala Hi'ki snorted through his open nostrils. "It was without honor."

He paused. "I remember hearing Singing, beautiful Singing. So when I could finally crawl, I headed for the sound of it. I inched along for what seemed an incredible distance, and each time I made a move, my flesh screamed. I remember tumbling down a long steep hill. Talk about pain? It drove my souls from my body."

He took a breath. "When I came back to myself, I followed the Singing again, and splashed into water. Drowning, I thought, would at least be quick, and it would save me recapture when the Chikosi followed my trail. So I crawled into the water, pleading that I be allowed to drown quickly. I went down, sinking, hearing the Singing grow louder all the time.

"I think I was dead, for my body settled into the deep and kept going, downward, ever down. The Singing grew louder, and something rubbed against me. I could feel it take me in its mouth. For a long time it swam, bearing me down into the Underworld. I think it carried me through one of the portals, for I remember lying on moss, seeing the most beautiful creature: a giant horned snake, his body gleaming with all the colors of light. Me, a man with no eyes, I saw this thing, so it had to be with my souls."

The Kala Hi'ki rubbed the stubs of his maimed hand. "Horned Serpent licked my wounded skin, and where he did the scars healed. I will always remember the eyes, like great crystals of quartz backlit by the sun. And the scales, they shimmered, rainbowlike.

" 'Time for you to go home,' he told me. His voice was musical, and I realized this was the being who had Sung me to the river. He picked me up in his jaws, and the next thing I knew, I was on a shoreline. Just lying there, a broken lump of flesh. What was I to do? I had no idea where I was, or which way to go. No strength was left in my limbs. I could barely raise myself far enough off the ground to crawl."

He smiled faintly, the patterns of scars rearranging. "I could sense the people coming. Hear the strokes of their paddles on the water. I heard their voices, and the language was Tsoyaha. I shouted, at least tried to. My throat was raw from screaming curses at the Chikosi while I hung in their square." He made a smoothing gesture with his good hand. "What I did next surprised me. I reached out with my souls and called to them. Touched them, and drew them to where I lay on the bank, all covered with mud."

The Kala Hi'ki sighed. "At first they thought I was some sort of monster. 'No!' I croaked. 'It is Bull Shield Mankiller, escaped from the Chikosi.'

" 'You are dead!' they cried.

"So I told them who I was, who my relatives were, and how I got my man's name. Only then would they believe me. But they still didn't want to touch me, so they carefully loaded me into a canoe by using a coat to sling my body aboard. Then they brought me to Rainbow City, where the Priests interrogated me, heard my story. They were suspicious at first, but I knew things about Horned Serpent that only the Priests know. And I could see through the eyes of my soul. I told them things about the Spirit World, about beings I could see through my new kind of sight.

"Meanwhile the story of my escape traveled along the rivers. It was told how Flying Hawk was frothing with anger. How his nephew, Green Snake, had tried to kill his brother, how the Power at Split Sky had gone wrong that night I vanished. The Chikosi had followed my bloody trail to the river, where they thought I had drowned.

"And I did. The man my people knew, he died that night. I was given a new life, a different existence, by Horned Serpent. Down there in the Underworld, he saved me. Gave me a Vision I would never have had. Now, Seeker, you will see what I rarely show any other man."

With great care, he reached up with his good hand and undid the white cloth binding around his head. As it came loose, the Kala Hi'ki turned to stare.

Old White gasped. Pressed into the scar tissue in the empty eye sockets were two large crystals.

"These were the gift of Horned Serpent," the Kala Hi'ki said. "They are scales that fell from his body onto the moss in that cavern deep down in the earth. When I placed them where my eyes should have been, I could see." He smiled, the effect sending a shiver through Old White's bone and muscles. "It was through these eyes that I saw the Contrary. This is the gift of Horned Serpent to the Kala Hi'ki."

Thirty-five

The world had turned on its head once again. Morning Dew tried to make sense of it. She crouched in the sunlight on the southern side of Heron Wing's house. Just behind her the matting screened the old storage pit where they relieved themselves. What made the odor bearable was the oyster shell that Morning Dew crushed. She used a large river cobble to grind the shell into a fine powder. When she had enough, she would scoop it into a shallow bowl and hand it to Heron Wing. Heron Wing in turn pressed the ceramic bowl down in a bed of hot embers to further process the shell. The resulting rotten-onion stink overwhelmed anything rising from their toilet.

"I'm still a slave," Morning Dew mused. She couldn't help but think about the wealth that had been heaped upon her. Unlike her marriage gifts, this she could keep, although good manners dictated that it be given back to people in the coming days. Gifts came with Power. People who hoarded wealth that was bestowed as an honor offended that selfsame Power. Misers were known targets of witchcraft, illness, and other bad humors.

"You're *my* slave," Heron Wing corrected, shifting upwind from the cloying smell given off by the cooking oyster shell. The purpose of grinding and heating the shell was for use as temper in the production of ceramic cookware. Part of Heron Wing's spoils from betting on stickball had included a sack of oyster shells that had been Traded north through the Pensacola. With it,

Heron Wing could barter for new cooking pots. Clam shell made better ceremonial pottery, but oyster was more durable for everyday use.

Your slave. "I still don't see how that could have happened. Smoke Shield doesn't often let loose of his things, does he?"

Heron Wing chuckled. "He did this time. I'm sure the last thing he would have expected was that I would bet against my own moiety. Nor can he come here demanding anything. I sent that crawling Thin Branch back as a gift. It would make Smoke Shield look like the foul-tempered badger he is if he made a fuss. Fact is, for the time being I expect him to leave. He's not the type to walk around and take it when others can strut."

"Heron Wing," Morning Dew said. "If I am now your property, what do you intend on doing with me?" She glanced around. "It's Wide Leaf, isn't it? She's going to marry that man."

Stone came racing through, a small stickball racquet in his hand. Two of his little friends charged after him. Stone threw the ball; the other little boy missed it. Morning Dew remembered her own lack of skill at that age. Proficiency only came with years of practice.

Heron Wing raised her brow in disbelief. "The gods alone know why, but old Builder seems to like her. So, yes. I'll let him build my room on the back for a Trade, and she can go with him. At least until he throws her out."

A pause, then Heron Wing continued. "As to you, Morning Dew, when the time comes I think you should go back to your people."

Morning Dew stopped short, staring with disbelief. "Back to the Chahta? Gods, why?" She swallowed hard. "I mean, yes. I'd do anything. But, why would . . ." She shook her head. "Why would you do that?"

Heron Wing studied her from under a questioning brow. "I'm so glad you didn't choke up like that on the stickball field. I'd have lost everything."

Morning Dew continued to stare incredulously, her heart pounding.

"It's simple, really," Heron Wing told her. "In the end we're better off having good relations with the Chahta. At first casual glance, you appear to be the only White Arrow woman from the Chief Clan that we have around here. Like it or not, you are the matron. If we can manage to find a way to send you back, you can probably help bring this trouble between us to a conclusion."

Morning Dew shook her head. "This still confuses me. Don't you know what happened to me? What your people *did* to me? What you Chikosi put me through? Do you know what it cost me to . . ." She bit her tongue and looked away, terrified of what she'd been about to say.

"Now you've ceased to think like a matron." Heron Wing turned back to her roasting shell, using a stick to stir it. "Stop thinking of yourself and think of your people. Of course terrible things happened to you. That's the way of war. Tell me that you didn't hang the Alligator Town chief in the square, and that his wives weren't enslaved, raped, and humiliated."

Morning Dew sighed. "We did. And, yes, they were."

"I would really like to know what prompted your people to raid Alligator Town. Looking back, I can't see the logic of it. If you're going to pick a fight, think it through carefully. Sometimes war can't be avoided. Just like once Alligator Town had been destroyed, there was no way the Council couldn't have sent Smoke Shield to strike back." Heron Wing again raised that questioning eyebrow. "So what was the reason behind that raid?"

Morning Dew returned to crushing oyster shell. "I think it just grew. A suggestion from Biloxi: 'Wouldn't it be nice if we could put the Chikosi in their place for once?' An answer from my . . . our war chief: 'Well, there is a way. No one would be expecting a raid at this time of year.' And back and forth it went, growing, gaining possibility." She shook her head. "They didn't know any better."

Heron Wing chuckled dryly. "How often has that been said, in how many towns and villages, for how far back in time? Worse, I don't suppose that it will stop with our lifetimes, either." She shot a speculative look at Morning Dew. "But I suppose that you do know now. I think you have become someone very different from the girl who married Screaming Falcon. Life hurts, doesn't it?"

"If it's lived, I suppose it does." She put her effort into grinding the shell. "Very well, I'm listening, Heron Wing. How do you see this working? What do you want me to do?"

"Be patient. For the gods' sake, don't go speaking of this to anyone! And whatever you do, don't make a run for it. Do that and I'll never get you home. At least not while you're still young and attractive, and certainly not with your tendons uncut above those flying heels. No, for the time being, you just be a good slave. If anything happens, if you get so desperate that you can't stand this a moment more, you come and talk to me. We'll find a way out of it." She made a skeptical face. "Somehow."

"I don't think your Council is going to take kindly to this suggestion."

"Not at present. That's why we wait." She grinned. "Selfish she-bitch that I am, it's going to be tough letting you go even when the time comes. You're a wonder at stickball."

Morning Dew smiled at that. She still ached from that last fall.

Heron Wing jabbed her stick in the stinking shell. "No, things are going to have to play out for a while. But Morning Dew, I won't give you false hopes. This may take some time. Can you work with me, even if it means another winter?"

That long? Her heart sank. "If you are being honest with me, by Breath Giver, yes! Think, Heron Wing. How long do you suppose I'd have remained alive if you hadn't placed that insane bet against Smoke Shield? Putting that in perspective, I imagine I can tote water, cook food, wash clothes, and keep your house." She paused. "And another thing. My moon is starting."

Heron Wing sighed. "Well, at least Smoke Shield didn't plant an heir to your Chief Clan. I'm not sure they'd want his bloodline."

Morning Dew shot her an appreciative glance. "I have to tell you, I'm late. For a while I hoped my husband had caught, then I feared Smoke Shield might have. I think one was early, the other late. The worry and fear probably didn't help matters."

"I'm close as well." She glanced up from her cooking shell. "You belong to Panther Clan now. You will be welcome in our Women's House. Pale Cat will be delighted to have us both gone. He has time to spend with Stone now that the solstice ceremonies have passed. And it is good for my son to spend time with so good an uncle."

Morning Dew nodded, wondering at the changes in her life, at the things she had done. "No matter what, Heron Wing, I shall always be grateful to you. From you I have learned strength and wisdom. I will need all of those qualities when I return to the White Arrow."

The woman smiled wistfully. "I told you, it might be a while."

"Yes," Morning Dew agreed, remembering her vain boasting so long ago in the Women's House. That silly girl had died the day she had been taken from Screaming Falcon's house. This new woman had been born in blood, rape, and suffering. She had survived Smoke Shield, and robbed him of his greatest triumph. In the process, she had paid a terrible price, one that even now she could barely allow herself to contemplate. "But I will return to my people. I just know it. And when I do, I shall be the greatest matron they have ever had."

"You're sure of that?"

"Oh, yes."

Home! The word rolled around inside her. But then, Heron Wing was right. It might be a long time getting there. She shot a sidelong glance at the woman. Going home would come at a cost, but how much would she have to pay?

Whatever I have to.

Paunch made a face as his stomach growled. The smell of roasting fish had the juices flowing in his mouth. He glanced up at the sky, wondering at the cold emptiness of it. Not even clouds floated across the blue dome where he could see it through the naked branches of the trees.

"I'm not cut out to be a thief," he muttered, prodding the fire with a stick. Flames licked up around the rounded sides of the pot where it rested in the coals. Odors of cooking fish mingled with hickory smoke. "I thought my heart would leap out of my chest."

Whippoorwill gave him a sidelong glance. "It took courage to rob that Chahta fish trap last night."

"And I almost froze my balls off!" he groused. "That water was cold. And scary! Wading around in the river at night. What chance would an old man like me have against a water cougar, or, the gods forbid, Horned Serpent?"

"Horned Serpent isn't interested in you," Whippoorwill replied. "He bides his time. And be assured, he will receive his due when the time is right."

"As if you knew what drives a creature as Powerful as Horned Serpent!" he shot back bitterly.

She gave him that eerie smile, her eyes seeming to expand in her head. "Can't you hear him, Grandfather?"

"What? Hear Horned Serpent?"

"He's Singing, even now. The notes so musical they carry up from the river, across the land. It reminds me of drops of rain falling through a rainbow mist." She rose, walking over to the bluff to stare down at the Horned Serpent River.

Paunch muttered to himself, prodding his fire. How long did it take a fish to cook, anyway? Then he looked out at the forest. It waited, silent, and he swore he could feel it, somber, watching him. If he looked sharp, he knew he'd see eyes staring back from the shadows cast by the thick trunks. Patient Spirit beings lurked back among the hanging vines of grape and greenbriar.

"I say this fish is done." He used sticks to lever the pot out of the flames. It would have to cool before he dared to dump the flaking white meat onto his bark plate.

Listening to his knees crack, he stood, wincing at the sudden pain in his back. "I'm too old to be sneaking about like a forest rat. When can we go home?"

"Home, Grandfather?" Whippoorwill laughed. "Are you ready to face Smoke Shield? Anxious to hang in a Chikosi square while they slice the flesh from your old bones? Are you so chilled that the thought of burning cane brands against your skin has grown attractive?"

"I didn't bargain for this," he added, eyes taking in the silent forest.

"Yes, you did," she said thoughtfully. "Bargained, and lost."

He pinched his eyes closed. "Why me? Why not Amber Bead or one of the others?"

"Because you were there." She turned her head, her long hair curling about her shoulders. "Power has made its gamble, picked its players. They have passed the test. Now we need but follow the Dance. One foot after the other, and trust to Power."

"Trust to Power? Look where that got me!" He reached down, angrily throwing a moldy hickory nut at the forest. It bounced hollowly off an oak tree and rattled on the dry leaves.

"It placed you right where you need to be," she said simply. "And we have a part to play . . . assuming you live that long." She turned her attention back to the river. "The brothers are coming ever closer. Blood has been spilled and cries for vengeance. Old fires still burn in men's souls. Power balances on so fine a thread. . . ." Her voice trailed away, her attention fixed on something in the river.

Paunch hurried over, fearful that she was watching a canoe load of warriors making shore just below them. It would be just his luck to have to run—and his pot full of cooked fish too hot to handle! Reaching her side, he peered cautiously over. The steep bank had been under-cut by the current, and a stone's throw below him, the thin section of beach lay empty.

Paunch vented a sigh of relief. "What is it? What do you see down there?"

"See?" she asked absently. "Can't you hear it?"

"Hear what?"

"Singing. The most wonderful Singing. He's there, waiting. Watching the present slipping away."

"Who? Who's watching?" He glanced anxiously back at the forest.

"He knows they are coming."

"They, who?"

"A seed to be planted deep inside me. Copper, and a Contrary. Your new masters, with wealth to humble high chiefs." She gave him a searching glance. "Are you ready?"

"Gods, girl. Do you always have to talk in nonsense words?"

"You shall see, Grandfather. Chaos is about to burst loose on the land. Red Power is swelling. Gods and he-roes shall tremble before this is all over. And Horned Serpent shall have his due."

"Horned Serpent?" he scoffed. And then he followed her gaze to the center of the river, seeing the water swirl. For the briefest instant he thought he heard Singing. The gentle melody played across his souls, too low for ears to hear. Then the water sucked and eddied. Paunch would have sworn he saw a great scaled body slip into the depths, the colors of the rainbow glinting from its sides.

"Bless me! Was that . . . ?"

"Our final hope," she answered. "If we live that long."

Would it have been so bad to have lost?" Born-of-Sun asked as he tossed a stick for Swimmer.

Trader watched Swimmer tear madly after the whirling piece of wood. The dog's coat was flying, his feet pounding the ground like a wild buffalo's while little frantic barks escaped his throat.

They sat at the edge of Rainbow City's steep eastern bluff, just south of the high chief's great mound. The slope here was nearly vertical, dropping the length of a bow shot to the slow-moving Tenasee. There, in shadow, the waters swirled as though listening. Behind them, Rainbow City had settled into a gentle slumber, worn out from the days of solstice celebration. A chill lay on the land, and Trader fought a shiver as his eyes traced out the cloud patterns above the eastern horizon. The winter-bare trees stood somber across the far shore, and he could see open patches where cornfields had been carved out of the virgin forest.

"No, High Chief. It would not have been so bad. I would have served you to the best of my abilities. Old White, however, would have continued on. No matter what, he *must* return to Split Sky City. He's a driven man. Whatever happened there, whatever secret he carries deep inside, it is a thing he must do."

Born-of-Sun nodded. "Power rides his shoulders like a heavy cloak." He shot Trader a sidelong glance. "You don't need to go on, you know. Just because you won our bet, you could still stay here. You . . . and that fabulous piece of copper. You could buy anything you wanted. A clan? Half of Rainbow City? Anything."

Trader smiled wistfully. "Once, High Chief, that was my Dream. Slowly, dimly, however, I have come to understand that Power gave me the copper as a test. A wise man once told me that a person doesn't own copper. He only holds it for a short time, and while men die, copper is forever."

"So, you will do what with it?"

Swimmer was back, literally spitting the slobbery, tooth-marked stick at Born-of-Sun. Then he crouched down, ears pricked, giving the high chief a wolfish stare.

Born-of-Sun casually reached out, taking the stick. Swimmer trembled, every muscle vibrating in anticipation. Born-of-Sun's arm flashed as if in a mighty throw. Swimmer charged off, barking his excitement as Born-of-Sun slyly placed the unthrown stick under his leg. The dog barked to a stop, head up, listening for the stick's fall as he searched the air for the missing prize.

"Grows tiresome after a while, doesn't it?" Trader asked.

"You'd think he had no other calling in life."

"Well, he's a dog. When it isn't stick, there's still food and sleep."

"And the copper?" Born-of-Sun returned to the subject. "You're a Trader. What would you want for it? All of my female cousins?"

"Trying to keep it here?" Trader raised an eyebrow.

"Of course. It's more wealth than I have ever seen."

"And that's the Power of the test I was given." Trader rubbed his cold hands together, watching a canoe pass below them. "I won't Trade it, High Chief. Not for possessions, status, or privilege."

"Then what?"

"The copper was given to me for a purpose. It will be given away when I know the time and place is right."

"Somehow that doesn't surprise me." Born-of-Sun glanced over his shoulder to see Swimmer coursing back and forth, nose to the ground, searching for the lost stick. "You are a better man than I. Perhaps the stuff of legends."

"No. I am only myself. A lesson that has come ten hard years later than it should have."

Swimmer had finally caught on, trotting back to stare suspiciously at Born-of-Sun. The high chief laughed and flung the stick, Swimmer's irritation forgotten in joyful pursuit.

"It is a rare achievement, to know oneself." Born-of-Sun frowned quizzically at the distant clouds. "I can only hope that I, too, might find that realization someday."

Trader shrugged. "I think, High Chief, that you are very aware of who you are."

"I still question."

"We all do."

After a long pause, and several tosses of Swimmer's stick, Born-of-Sun asked, "What of your winnings from the chunkey game? You own half of the Tsoyaha's possessions. It will take all of my people's canoes to haul it out of here."

"We shall give it all back. All but the Trade we brought here."

"There is Power in that. And humility."

Trader met the chief's eyes. "A few days past, I was preparing myself to die on the square. My only hope was that I would have the courage to face the pain and agony." He shook his head. "I was terrified that I wouldn't be able to stand it. Afraid that I would weep and plead. Anything to be released from the misery. The injustice of it made my souls cry out in disbelief. After that, life takes on a whole new meaning."

"As the Kala Hi'ki can tell you." Born-of-Sun took Swimmer's stick, inspecting the gnawed wood while Swimmer panted from exertion and anticipation. "We are flawed creatures, Trader. Caught between the forces of Power. If suffering could be banished, we would invent it again. It is in our nature."

"I suppose."

"And there may be a great deal more suffering if you

continue on your journey to Split Sky City. I don't trust these Chikosi. If you stayed here, however, you would be guaranteed the chance to discover this new man you have found yourself to be. You would have a home, here, with us—a chance to have family, children, and a respected place among us."

Trader took a deep breath. "You tempt me, High Chief."

"You have lived like a piece of driftwood. Forever carried on the currents of change. A man alone. Would it be so bad? To have a place for yourself?"

"No." Trader smiled at the thought. "I think, however, that I must see this thing through. I can do that now. For the first time in my life, I think I know where I am going. What I have to do."

"I still have time to persuade you to stay."

"I think, High Chief, that I must see this thing through." Trader paused. "Perhaps, however, when this is all over . . ."

". . . I will finally beat you at chunkey," Born-of-Sun finished with a smile.

Two Petals watched the moonlight as it lay over Rainbow City. Above, the stars glistened in crystalline clarity against the pale vault of sky. Where they slipped past thatch roofs, thin wreaths of smoke rose in the cold air, giving it a pungent aroma. The houses cast pointed shadows on the hard-packed earth. The people slept, but she could sense them: thousands of beating hearts, rising and falling lungs, the blood coursing through their bodies. Were she to let slip her control, their Dreams would overwhelm her. They swirled around her, rustling and murmuring, so many hopes, desires, hatreds, and longings.

I am a rock. She repeated the mantra to herself,

hardening her souls against the painful fantasies of so many souls.

One, in particular, drew her attention. This one, she could see, like a faint glow as it hovered over the old man. Two Petals carefully eased down the temple steps and followed, keeping her distance as Old White walked along the edge of the plaza. He stopped once, fingering the wood on one of the empty squares.

Two Petals watched, distantly aware of the curiosity and dread in the old man's souls. It took no Contrary's eyes to know that he imagined Trader hanging there, bleeding his life slowly away.

But that future is dead. Another was lining out for them.

When Old White resumed his pace, she followed, stopping at the square herself, allowing her fingers to run over the smooth wood. Old blood, pain, and death Sang from the wood. The despair and misery sent a shiver through her souls. As if burned, she jerked her fingers away.

"Life is part of Power," a familiar voice told her.

She turned, seeing Deer Man, his antlers gleaming in the moonlight. He stood no more than five paces away, his hoofed feet resting on the hard plaza clay. Dark eyes seemed to swim in his human face, while his deerlike ears stuck out from the side of his head.

He continued, *"Living things concentrate it, hold it, and then let it flow out and into the rest of the world. Those who die in the squares impregnate the wood with fear and horror; just as woodcarvers, potters, or stoneworkers impart hope and pride into their creations."*

"Do we ever lose it all? Is Power like water in a pot? Can it all be poured out?"

"Not all of it. Even when a person dies, there is enough left for the scavengers, insects, worms, and fungus." Deer Man smiled. *"It's all connected, you know. Power flows from the rocks, the soil, the rivers, and wind. What you impart to the weaving of a beautiful fabric is restored by marveling at a sunrise. Power is the breath of*

*Creation. What you draw into you must eventually be ex-
haled. Then, that same breath will be taken in by a tree, a
chipmunk, a deer, and a butterfly.*"

She walked slowly after Old White, aware that Deer
Man pranced gracefully beside her, his hoofed feet
silent on the clay as they crossed the chunkey court.

"*He is worried,*" Deer Man told her as she watched
Old White stare uneasily up at the high chief's palace.

"He wonders if Trader and I are still willing to accompany him to Split Sky City."

Deer Man paused beside her. "*You cannot tell him
what is coming. You know that, don't you?*"

Two Petals nodded. "The only way that a man can
move the world is if he doesn't know he's doing it."

"*Telling him the future would frighten him.*" A pause.
"*He wouldn't understand. It is in his nature to protect
you—even if it meant ruin for him and the destruction
of all he loves.*"

"The scarred man frightens me. He has midnight in
his eyes—a reflection of the rage in his souls. Just the
thought of him sends shivers down my skin. What he
will do to me . . ." She shook her head. "I tremble, even
knowing that I shall find my husband in the end."

"*He frightens the Spirit World. No one should possess
so much of the red Power. He is chaos, cunning, and hatred, with no balance. Left to his own, he will permanently upset the balance of Power. Only your husband
has the Power to destroy him.*"

"I understand." She shivered, her souls shaken.

"*Are you afraid of what you will have to do?*"

"I am only afraid of the past. Living it is like wading
in quicksand. With each step I worry about being
sucked down into the suffocating darkness."

"*And Trader? You know you must give him up to fate.
Is that a problem?*"

"We have shared Dreams, he and I." Her body tingled
with anticipation of his naked body against hers. "All of
life is sacrifice."

"But only when the time is right," Deer Man warned. *"Any sooner and he will not accept your sister when she is ready. Trader is still fragile, searching for his future. You must be very careful with him. He cannot know the role he is to play."*

"But I have so much to learn. Even knowing the future, a great deal is uncertain." She watched as Old White walked on, shoulders bent with the weight he had carried for so long.

"Soon," she whispered. "You need bear your burden for only a few more moons, Seeker. And then, on the equinox, at Split Sky City, all will come clear."

"Let us hope," Deer Man replied fervently.

Epilogue

A woman's cry disturbed Flying Hawk's Dream.

Disoriented, he blinked awake, glancing around his dark room. The Dream had been so real, the colors so vivid. The verdant green grass had smelled sweet; the feel of the air on his cheek had been so clear. Sunlight from a blue sky dotted with clouds had filled the clearing and danced on yellow, red, and blue flowers. The whir and clicking of insects mixed with birdsong from the surrounding forest of black oak, beech, and hickory.

In the darkness of his palace room, Flying Hawk rubbed a hand across his sweaty brow and gasped for breath. He'd been back there, beside his brother's dying body; an arrow-ridden buffalo lay dead to the side, its froth-bloody tongue lolled on the rich grass.

He had stared down with disbelief, watching scarlet ooze from his brother's head, heard the death rattle escaping his brother's lungs. But the worst thing had been his brother's eyes, fixed on his. They had pierced him with spears of betayal and disbelief.

Flying Hawk remembered panting, struggling to his feet in horror. Breaking his brother's gaze, he stared at the stone gripped so tightly in his hand. He barely remembered how it had come to him as he and his brother rolled around, kicking, striking, and scratching. But found it, he had. Memory of the smacking impact as he hammered it time after time into his brother's head was as much physical as auditory. The rock was crimson, strands of hair and brain matter stuck to its surface. It fell from his suddenly nerveless fingers to thump onto the grass and roll a couple of times.

Breath Maker, what have I done!

"Chosen your path," a voice had said from behind.

Flying Hawk had spun, startled by the dark man who stood, feet braced, and watched him with gleaming eyes. He had been young, the glow of Spirit Power surrounding him.

"It's the price of red Power. The choice you had to make to become high minko. It runs in the blood, Bear Tooth's blood. You remember what happened to him?"

Flying Hawk had swallowed dryly, nodding his head.

"Power is shifting," the stranger had said softly. "It will take strength and courage to maintain all that we've wrought over the years." The man pointed. "Do you think he has the cunning and will?"

Flying Hawk followed the pointing figure to the body sprawled on the grass.

Crying out, he'd jumped back, seeing not his brother, but Smoke Shield. His nephew was but a youth, a hideous wound in the side of his head, fresh blood oozing past his crushed cheek to pool in sleek black hair.

"No!" Flying Hawk cried. "I didn't do this!"

Smoke Shield's vacant eyes seemed to mock him.

"You have done everything," the stranger's voice intruded on the horror. "All that will be, you have wrought to obtain the high minko's chair. In the end, it is a struggle between brothers. It always comes down to brothers, doesn't it? You must pick one."

When Flying Hawk turned back, the stranger spread his arms wide; and from them, immense wings grew. The black iridescent feathers had a rainbow-like sheen in the sunlight. With a leap, the stranger sprang into the air. Flying Hawk ducked as the mighty wings pumped, and the backwash rolled over him. When he looked up, the stranger had vanished; only a midnight-black raven could be seen winging off over the trees.

That's when the woman had screamed.

"A Dream, only a Dream. But what did it mean?" He sucked air into his oddly starved lungs, then swung his feet over the side of his pole bed.

When had he grown so old and tired? Fragments of the Dream clung to his souls like colorful bits of light.

The woman's whimper carried in the silence.

Unable to sleep, Flying Hawk slipped a blanket over his shoulders and padded down the hallway. Across from Smoke Shield's room, he winced as he heard the familiar sound of carnal grunting. The woman was weeping softly, probably some slave that Smoke Shield had taken a fancy to.

By the Ancestors, what is it with him? Flying Hawk made a face as he passed into the great room. There the fire had burned low, illuminating the chamber in a soft red light.

He placed his hand on the familiar cougarhide covering of his stool. With the murder of his brother, the high minko's chair had become his by default. But at what price?

Murder?

"I would take that back, if I could, Brother."

In the Dream, his brother's body had become Smoke Shield's, the old pattern repeating itself. Except Smoke Shield had lived to become the man he now was.

"It always comes down to brothers," the Spirit being had said.

Flying Hawk stared up at the giant carving that hung on the rear wall. So many times he had gazed at the great hand, the fingers so perfectly rendered, the thumb tight to the side. Each of the knuckles was visible. The fingernails had been inlaid with white shell. The great eye in the palm had been sheathed in copper and stared out with a pupil fashioned from stained black walnut.

The symbol of his people, it seemed fixed on him; and the eerie gaze bored through his souls. Flying Hawk shivered. One day, soon, he would have to hand over authority to Smoke Shield. And after his death, Flying

Hawk's souls would make the journey westward. At the edge of the world, they would have to make the leap through the eye before proceeding to the land of the dead. He feared that day, feared he would be unable to make that terrifying leap—that his souls would fall, forever lost between the earth and the Sky World.

If that happens, it will be because I am unworthy.

"And what if I do make it?" he mused softly. "What will I find on the other side?"

The too-clear image of his dead brother's piercing stare lingered from both memory and Dream. The day would come when they faced each other again. What could he say in his defense?

"Smoke Shield and I," Flying Hawk whispered, "we have both dedicated our lives to the red Power. Did I make the right choices? When I am gone . . . what then for our people?"

Flying Hawk gasped. It had to be a trick of the light, for he swore he saw a single great tear form at the corner of the eye. It trickled down as he moved to the side, gleaming in the light, tracking down the polished wood as he stepped close.

Raising a trembling hand, he ran a finger over the wood, horrified to find it damp.

From the hallway, the unknown woman's weeping was the only sound.

Authors' Afterword

The story of Trader, Old White, Heron Wing, Smoke Shield, Two Petals, and Swimmer continues in *People of the Thunder.* When we began *People of the Weeping Eye* we didn't anticipate writing such a grand epic. Our job is to follow the characters where they take us, and to tell the story to the best of our ability. In the case of the late Mississippian world, the rich archaeological record, fascinating cultures, and vast landscape led us to delightful and complex characters. There are certain inescapable realities in publishing, and at our publisher's request, we have broken the story into two volumes. We hope that you will join us for the sequel, *People of the Thunder,* and travel back with us, once again, to the magic of America's past.

Bibliography

Adair, James
2005 *The History of the American Indians*. Reprint of the 1775 edition published by Edward and Charles Dilly. The University of Alabama Press, Tuscaloosa, Alabama.

Anderson, David G.
1994 *The Savannah River Chiefdoms*. The University Press of Alabama, Tuscaloosa, Alabama.
1997 The Role of Cahokia in the Evolution of Southeastern Mississippian Society. In *Cahokia: Domination and Ideology in the Mississippian World*, pp. 248–268. Bison Books, University of Nebraska Press, Lincoln, Nebraska.

Atkinson, James R.
2004 *Splendid Land, Splendid People: The Chickasaw Indians to Removal.* The University Press of Alabama, Tuscaloosa, Alabama.

Beck, Robin A., Jr.
2003 Consolidation and Hierarchy: Chiefdom Variability in the Mississippian Southeast. *American Antiquity* 68:641–664.

Bense, Judith A.
1994 *Archaeology of the Southeastern United States: PaleoIndian to World War I.* Academic Press, San Diego, California, New York, and London.

Blitz, John H.
1993 *Ancient Chiefdoms of the Tombigbee.* The University of Alabama Press, Tuscaloosa, Alabama.

Blitz, John H., and Patrick Livingood
    2004 Sociopolitical Implications of Mississippian Mound Volume. *American Antiquity* 69:291–303.

Brain, Jeffrey P., and Philip Phillips
    1996 *Shell Gorgets: Styles of the Late Prehistoric and Protohistoric Southeast.* Peabody Museum Press, Peabody Museum of Archaeology and Ethnology, Harvard University, Cambridge, Massachusetts.

Brown, Calvin S.
    1992 *Archaeology of Mississippi.* Reprint of 1926 edition. University Press of Mississippi, Jackson, Mississippi.

Brown, Ian W. (editor)
    2003 *Bottle Creek: A Pensacola Culture Site in South Alabama.* The University of Alabama Press, Tuscaloosa, Alabama.

Brown, James A.
    1996 *The Spiro Ceremonial Center.* Memoirs of the Museum of Anthropology University of Michigan No. 29. Ann Arbor, Michigan.

Carstens, Kenneth C., and Patty Jo Watson (editors)
    1996 *Of Caves and Shell Mounds.* The University of Alabama Press, Tuscaloosa, Alabama.

Cobb, Charles R.
    2000 *From Quarry to Cornfield: The Political Economy of Mississippian Hoe Production.* The University of Alabama Press, Tuscaloosa, Alabama.

Culin, Stewart
    1975 *Games of the North American Indians.* Reprint of the *Twenty-Fourth Annual Report of the Bureau of American Ethnology, 1902–1903.* Dover Publications, New York.

Davison, Gerald, John M. Neale, and Ann M. Kring
    2004 *Abnormal Psychology.* John Wiley & Sons, Hoboken, New Jersey.

DeJarnette, David L.
    1975 *Archaeological Salvage in the Walter F. George*

Basin of the Chattahoochee River in Alabama. The University of Alabama Press, Tuscaloosa, Alabama.

Diaz-Granados, Carol, and James R. Duncan
2004 *The Rock Art of Eastern North America: Capturing Images and Insight.* The University of Alabama Press, Tuscaloosa, Alabama.

Dickens, Roy S., Jr., and Trawick Ward (editors)
1985 *Structure and Process in Southeastern Archaeology.* The University of Alabama Press, Tuscaloosa, Alabama.

Dye, David H., and Cheryl Anne Cox
1990 *Towns and Temples Along the Mississippi.* The University Press of Alabama, Tuscaloosa, Alabama.

Emerson, Thomas E., Randall E. Hughes, Mary R. Hynes, and Sarah U. Wisseman
2003 The Sourcing and Interpretation of Cahokia-style Figurines in the Trans-Mississippi South and Southeast. *American Antiquity* 68:287–313.

Emerson, Thomas E., and R. Barry Lewis (editors)
1991 *Cahokia and the Hinterlands: Middle Mississippian Cultures of the Midwest.* University of Illinois Press, Urbana and Chicago.

Fairbanks, Charles H.
2003 *Archaeology of the Funeral Mound.* The University Press of Alabama, Tuscaloosa, Alabama.

Finger, Michael
2004 Shiloh: Emergency Archaeology. *American Archaeology* 8(2):30–38.

Fisher-Carroll, Rita
2001 *Mortuary Behavior at Upper Nodena.* Arkansas Archaeological Survey Research Series 59. Fayetteville, Arkansas.

Fundabrook, Emma L., and Mary Douglass Foreman
1957 *Sun Circles and Human Hands.* Southern Publications, Fairhope, Alabama.

Gibbons, Whit, Robert R. Haynes, and Joab L. Thomas
1990 *Poisonous Plants and Venomous Animals of*

Alabama. The University of Alabama Press, Tuscaloosa, Alabama.

Gibson, Arrell M.
1971 *The Chickasaws.* University of Oklahoma Press, Norman, Oklahoma.

Gibson, Jon L., and Philip J. Carr
2004 *Signs of Power: The Rise of Cultural Complexity in the Southeast.* The University of Alabama Press, Tuscaloosa, Alabama.

Granberry, Julian
1993 *A Grammar and Dictionary of the Timuca Language,* 3rd ed. The University of Alabama Press, Tuscaloosa, Alabama.
2005 *The Americas That Might Have Been: Native American Social Systems through Time.* The University of Alabama Press, Tuscaloosa, Alabama.

Grantham, Bill
2002 *Creation Myths and Legends of the Creek Indians.* University Press of Florida, Tallahassee, Florida.

Green, Michael Foster
2001 *Schizophrenia Revealed.* W. W. Norton, New York.

Hawkins, Benjamin
2003 *The Collected Works of Benjamin Hawkins, 1796–1810.* Edited by H. Thomas Foster II. The University Press of Alabama, Tuscaloosa, Alabama.

Howard, James H.
1968 *The Southeastern Ceremonial Complex and Its Interpretation.* Memoir Missouri Archaeological Society No. 6.

Hudson, Charles M.
1976 *The Southeastern Indians.* The University of Tennessee Press, Knoxville, Tennessee.
1979 *Black Drink: A Native American Tea.* The University of Georgia Press, Athens, Georgia.
2003 *Conversations with the High Priest of Coosa.* The University of North Carolina Press, Chapel Hill and London.

Jackson, H. Edwin, and Susan L. Scott
  2004 Patterns of Elite Faunal Utilization at Moundville, Alabama. *American Antiquity* 68:552–572.

Jenkins, Ned J., and Richard A. Krause
  1986 *The Tombigbee Watershed in Southeastern Prehistory.* The University of Alabama Press, Tuscaloosa, Alabama.

Jones, Charles C.
  1998 *Antiquities of the Southern Indians, Particularly the Georgia Tribes.* Reprint of the 1873 edition. The University Press of Alabama, Tuscaloosa, Alabama.

Keesing, Roger M.
  1975 *Kin Groups and Social Structure.* Holt, Rinehart and Winston, New York.

Kidder, Tristram R.
  2004 Plazas as Architecture: An Example from the Raffman Site, Northeastern Louisiana. *American Antiquity* 69:514–532.

King, Adam
  2003 *Etowah: The Political History of a Chiefdom Capital.* The University of Alabama Press, Tuscaloosa, Alabama.

Knight, Vernon James Jr.
  1986 The Institutional Organization of Mississippian Religion. *American Antiquity* 51:675–687.
  1990 Social Organization and the Evolution of Hierarchy in Southeastern Chiefdoms. *Journal of Anthropological Research* 46(1):1–23.
  1997 Some Developmental Parallels between Cahokia and Moundville. In *Cahokia: Domination and Ideology in the Mississippian World*, pp. 229–247. Bison Books, University of Nebraska Press, Lincoln, Nebraska.
  2005 Characterizing Elite Midden Deposits at Moundville. *American Antiquity* 69:304–321.

Knight, Vernon J., and Vincas Steponaitis
1998 *Archaeology and the Moundville Chiefdom.* Smithsonian Institution Press, Washington, D.C., and London.

Lacefield, Jim
2000 *Lost Worlds in Alabama Rocks: A Guide to the State's Ancient Life and Landscapes.* The Alabama Geological Society, Birmingham, Alabama.

Lambert, Patricia M.
1999 *Bioarchaeological Studies of Life in the Age of Agriculture.* The University Press of Alabama, Tuscaloosa, Alabama.

Lankford, George E.
1987 *Native American Legends. Southeastern Legends: Tales from the Natchez, Caddo Biloxi, Chicasaw, and Other Nations.* August House, Little Rock, Arkansas.
2004 World on a String: Some Cosmological Components of the Southeast Ceremonial Complex. In *Hero, Hawk, and Open Hand: American Indian Art in the Midwest and South.* The Art Institute of Chicago and Yale University Press.

Larson, Lewis H.
1980 *Aboriginal Subsistence Technology on the Southeastern Coastal Plain during the Late Prehistoric Period.* University Presses of Florida, Gainesville, Florida.

Lehman, Melissa, and Gerald Smith
1997 *Chucalissa: Excavations in Units 2 and 6, 1959–1967.* Occasional Papers No. 15. Memphis State University Anthropological Research Center.

Lewis, R. Barry, and Charles Stout (editors)
1998 *Mississippian Towns and Sacred Spaces.* The University of Alabama Press, Tuscaloosa, Alabama.

Lewis, Thomas M. N., and Madeline D. Kneburg Lewis
1995 *The Prehistory of the Chickamauga Basin, Tennessee.* Vols. I and II. Edited by Lynne P. Sullivan.

The University of Tennessee Press, Knoxville, Tennessee.

McEwan, Bonnie G.
2001 *Indians of the Greater Southeast*. University Press of Florida, Gainesville, Florida.

Martin, Joel W.
1991 *Sacred Revolt*. Beacon Press, Boston.

Martin, Susan R.
2000 *Wonderful Power: The Story of Ancient Copper Working in the Lake Superior Basin*. Wayne State University Press, Detroit, Michigan.

Mason, Carol L.
2005 *The Archaeology of Ocmulgee Old Fields, Macon, Georgia*. The University of Alabama Press, Tuscaloosa, Alabama.

Meyer, William Edward
1928 *Indian Trails of the Southeast. United States*. Bureau of American Ethnography Report No. 42. Smithsonian Institution, Washington, D.C.

Millspaugh, Charles F.
1974 *American Medicinal Plants*. Reprint of the 1892 edition. Dover Publications, New York.

Mirarchi, Robert E.
2004 *Alabama Wildlife*. Vol. I. The University of Alabama Press, Tuscaloosa, Alabama.

Mistovich, Tim S.
1994 Toward an Explanation of Variation in Moundville Phase Households in the Black Warrior Valley, Alabama. In *Mississippian Communities and Households,* edited by J. Daniel Rogers and Bruce D. Smith, pp. 156–180. Smithsonian Institution Press, Washington, D.C.

Moore, Clarence Bloomfield
1996 *The Moundville Expeditions of Clarence Bloomfield Moore*. Edited by Vernon James Knight Jr. Reprint of 1905 *Journal of the Academy of Natural Sciences in Philadelphia*. The University Press of Alabama, Tuscaloosa, Alabama.

Moore, David G.

2002 *Catawba Valley Mississippian: Ceramics, Chronology, and Catawba Indians*. The University of Alabama Press, Tuscaloosa, Alabama.

Moorehead, Warren K.

2002 *The Cahokia Mounds*. Edited by John E. Kelly. The University Press of Alabama, Tuscaloosa, Alabama.

Morgan, William N.

1999 *Precolumbian Architecture in Eastern North America*. The University Press of Florida, Gainesville, Florida.

Morse, Dan F., and Phyllis A. Morse (editors)

1983 *Archaeology of the Central Mississippi Valley*. Academic Press, New York.

1998 *The Lower Mississippi Valley Expeditions of Clarence Bloomfield Moore*. The University of Alabama Press, Tuscaloosa, Alabama.

Mould, Tom

2003 *Choctaw Prophecy: A Legacy of the Future*. The University of Alabama Press, Tuscaloosa, Alabama.

Mount, Robert H.

1975 *The Reptiles and Amphibians of Alabama*. The University of Alabama Press, Tuscaloosa, Alabama.

Muller, Jon

1997 *Mississippian Political Economy*. Plenum Press, New York and London.

Nairne, Thomas

1988 *Nairne's Muskogean Journals: The 1708 Expedition to the Mississippi River*. Edited by Alexander Moore. University of Mississippi Press, Jackson, Mississippi.

O'Brien, Michael J.

2003 *Mississippian Community Organization: The Powers Phase in Southeastern Missouri*. Kluwer Academic/Plenum Publishers, New York, Boston, London.

O'Brien, Michael J., and Robert C. Dunnell (editors)
1998 *Changing Perspectives on the Archaeology of the Central Mississippi Valley.* The University of Alabama Press, Tusacaloosa, Alabama.

Pauketat, Timothy R.
1993 *Temples for Cahokia Lords: Preston Holder's 1955–1956 Excavations of Kunnemann Mound.* Memoirs of the University of Michigan Museum of Anthropology No. 26. Ann Arbor, Michigan.
1994 *The Ascent of Chiefs: Cahokia and Mississippian Politics in Native North America.* The University Press of Alabama, Tuscaloosa, Alabama.
2004 Resettled Farmers and the Making of a Mississippian Polity. *American Antiquity* 68:39–66.

Pauketat, Timothy R., Lucretia S. Kelly, Gayle J. Fritz, Neal H. Lopinot, Scott Elias, and Eve Hargrave
2005 The Residues of Feasting and Public Ritual at Early Cahokia. *American Antiquity* 67:257–280.

Pauketat, Timothy R., and Thomas E. Emerson (editors)
1999 *Cahokia: Domination and Ideology in the Mississippian World.* Bison Books, University of Nebraska Press, Lincoln, Nebraska.

Pearson, James L.
2002 *Shamanism and the Ancient Mind: A Cognitive Approach to Archaeology.* Altamira Press, Walnut Creek, Lanham, New York, Oxford.

Petersen, James B.
1996 *A Most Indispensable Art: Native Fiber Industries from Eastern North America.* The University Press of Tennessee, Knoxville, Tennessee.

Phillips, Philip, and James A. Brown
1977 *Pre-Columbian Shell Engravings from the Craig Mound at Spiro, Oklahoma.* Part One. Peabody Museum of Archaeology and Ethnology, Peabody Museum Press, Cambridge, Massachusetts.
1984 *Pre-Columbian Shell Engravings from the Craig Mound at Spiro, Oklahoma.* Part Two. Peabody

Museum of Archaeology and Ethnology, Peabody Museum Press, Cambridge, Massachusetts.

Powell, Mary Lucas
1989 *Status and Health in Prehistory.* The University Press of Alabama, Tuscaloosa, Alabama.

Powell, Mary Lucas, Patricia S. Bridges, and Ann Marie Wagner Mires (editors)
1991 *What Mean These Bones.* The University Press of Alabama, Tuscaloosa, Alabama.

Power, Susan C.
2004 *Early Art of the Southeastern Indians: Feathered Serpents and Winged Beings.* The University of Georgia Press, Athens, Georgia.

Redmond, Elsa M.
1998 *Chiefdoms and Chieftaincy in the Americas.* University Press of Florida, Gainesville, Florida.

Rolingson, Martha Ann
2000 *Toltec Mounds and Plum Bayou Culture: Mound Excavations.* Arkansas Archaeological Research Series 54, Fayetteville, Arkansas.

Scarry, John F. (editor)
1995 *Political Structure and Change in the Prehistoric Southeastern United States.* University Press of Florida, Gainesville, Florida.

Scarry, Margaret, and Vincas P. Steponaitis
1996 Between Farmstead and Center: The Natural and Social Landscape of Moundville. In *People, Plants, and Landscapes: Studies in Paleobotany,* edited by Kristen J. Gremillion, pp. 107–122. The University Press of Alabama, Tuscaloosa, Alabama.

Schusky, Ernest L.
1983 *Manual for Kinship Analysis*, 2nd ed. University Press of America, New York.

Sheldon, Craig T. (editor)
2006 *The Southern and Central Alabama Expeditions of Clarence Bloomfield Moore.* The University Press of Alabama, Tuscaloosa, Alabama.

Shetrone, Henry Clyde
2004 *The Mound Builders.* Reprint of 1930 edition published by D. Appleton & Co. The University Press of Alabama, Tuscaloosa, Alabama.

Smith, Marvin T.
1990 *Archaeology of Aboriginal Change in the Interior Southeast.* Florida Museum of Natural History. University Press of Florida, Gainesville, Florida.

Speck, Frank G.
1909 *Ethnology of the Yuchi Indians.* Anthropological Publications of the University Museum, Vol.1, No.1. University of Pennsylvania, Philadelphia.

Squire, E. G., and E. H. Davis
1973 *Ancient Monuments of the Mississippi Valley Comprising the Results of Extensive Original Surveys and Explorations.* Reprint of the 1848 Vol. 1 of the Smithsonian Institution. AMS Press, New York.

Steponaitis, Vincas
1983 *Ceramics, Chronology, and Community Patterns: An Archaeological Study at Moundville.* Academic Press, New York.
1991 Contrasting Patterns of Mississippian Development. In *Chiefdoms, Power, Economy and Ideology*, edited by Timothy Earle. Cambridge University Press, Cambridge and New York.
1991 Excavations at 1Tu50, an Early Mississippian Center near Moundville. *Southeastern Archaeology* 11:1–13.

Stone, Linda
2000 *Kinship and Gender: An Introduction.* Westview Press, Boulder, Colorado.

Swanton, John R.
1928a *Aboriginal Culture of the Southeast.* United States Bureau of American Ethnography Report No. 42. Smithsonian Institution, Washington, D.C.
1928b *Religious Beliefs and Medicinal Practices of*

the Creek Indians. United States Bureau of American Ethnography Report No. 42. Smithsonian Institution, Washington, D.C.

1928c *Social Organization and Social Usages of the Indians of the Creek Confederacy.* United States Bureau of American Ethnography Report No. 42. Smithsonian Institution, Washington, D.C.

1929 *Myths and Tales of the Southeastern Indians.* Bureau of American Ethnology Bulletin No. 88. Smithsonian Institution, Washington, D.C.

1998a *Early History of the Creek Indians and Their Neighbors.* Reprint of 1922 Bureau of American Ethnography Bulletin No. 73. University Press of Florida, Gainesville, Florida.

1998b *Indian Tribes of the Lower Mississippi Valley and Adjacent Coast of the Gulf of Mexico.* Reprint of 1911 Bureau of Ethnography Bulletin No. 43. Dover Publications, Mineola, New York.

2000 *Creek Religion and Medicine.* Reprint of 1928 Bureau of American Ethnography Report No. 42. Bison Books, University of Nebraska Press, Lincoln, Nebraska.

2001 *Source Material for the Social and Ceremonial Life of the Choctaw Indians.* Reprint of the 1931 Bureau of American Ethnography Bulletin No. 103. The University Press of Alabama, Tuscaloosa, Alabama.

Sylestine, Cora, Heather K. Hardy, and Timothy Montler
1993 *The Dictionary of the Alabama Language.* The University of Texas Press, Austin, Texas.

Thomas, Cyrus
1985 *Report on the Mound Explorations of the Bureau of Ethnology.* Reprint of the 1894 12th Annual Report of the Bureau of American Ethnography. USGPO. Smithsonian Institution Press, Washington, D.C.

Townsend, Richard F., and Robert V. Sharpe (editors)
2004 *Hero, Hawk, and Open Hand: American Indian Art of the Ancient Midwest and South.* Yale University Press, New Haven and London.

Urban, Greg
1994 Social Organization in the Southeast. In *North American Indian Anthropology,* edited by Raymond J. Demallie and Alfonso Ortiz. University of Oklahoma Press, Norman, Oklahoma.

Walthall, John A.
1994 *Moundville: An Introduction to the Archaeology of a Mississippian Chiefdom.* Special Publication No. 1. Alabama Museum of Natural History. The University of Alabama, Tuscaloosa, Alabama
1980 *Prehistoric Indians of the Southeast: Archaeology of Alabama and the Middle South.* The University of Alabama Press, Tuscaloosa, Alabama.

Welch, Paul D.
2001 Political Economy in Late Prehistoric Southern Appalachia. In *Archaeology of the Appalachian Highlands*, edited by Lynne P. Sullivan and Susan C. Prezzano. The University of Tennessee Press, Knoxville, Tennessee.
1997 Control over Goods and the Political Stability of the Moundville Chiefdom. In *Political Structure and Change in the Prehistoric Southeastern United States*, edited by John F. Scarry, pp. 69–91. University Press of Florida, Gainesville.
1991 *Moundville's Economy.* The University Press of Alabama, Tuscaloosa, Alabama.

Williams, Mark, and Gary Shapiro (editors)
1991 *Lamar Archaeology: Chiefdoms in the Deep South.* The University of Alabama Press, Tuscaloosa, Alabama.

Winter, Joseph C.
2000 *Tobacco Use by Native Americans: Sacred Smoke and Silent Killer.* University of Oklahoma Press, Norman, Oklahoma

Yerkes, Richard W.
1986 *Prehistoric Life on the Mississippi Floodplain.* The University of Chicago Press, Chicago, Illinois.

Turn the page for a preview of

PEOPLE *of the*
THUNDER

W. MICHAEL GEAR
AND KATHLEEN O'NEAL GEAR

Available in January 2009

A FORGE HARDCOVER

ISBN-13: 978-0-7653-1439-0   ISBN-10: 0-7653-1439-8

One

The Contrary—the woman once known as Two Petals—walked through the quiet night. Her moccasin-clad feet scuffed the plaza's trampled surface, the sound of leather on clay like the whisper of distant ghosts. Her straight body moved purposefully, rounded hips swaying. Black flowing hair swung even with her buttocks, and she clutched a beaverhide blanket closely about her shoulders. With each exhalation, she watched her breath fog and rise toward the black, star-encrusted sky. Overhead, the constellations seemed to shimmer and wink against the winter night.

Around her, the great Yuchi capital known as Rainbow City slumbered. Even now the size of the city, with its tall, building-topped mounds, thousands of homes, temples, society houses, and granaries, amazed her. The city's sleeping soul surrounded her like the low hum of insect wings. She could feel the immensity of it: all those thousands of souls breathing, mired in Dreams, their passions muted by sleep.

This was the western capital of the Yuchi—called the Tsoyaha in their own language. The city had been built on a high bluff overlooking the Tenasee River. The location had been chosen not only because it was well above the worst of the great river's periodic floods, but it was strategically placed just below the river's bend. Sheer heights on the east and north provided a natural defense, while the western and southern approaches were protected by a tall palisade bolstered by archers' platforms every twenty paces. Rainbow City controlled passage up and down the Tenasee—the trade route carrying goods between the southeastern and northern river systems.

Though Two Petals had walked in the ghostly ruins of Cahokia and climbed its great mound, Rainbow City left her feeling humbled. Cahokia was a place of dried bones; Rainbow City flexed warm nerve and healthy muscle. It lived, thrived, and bristled with energy.

High temples, palaces, and society houses perched atop square earthen mounds capped by colored clays sacred to the Yuchi. The buildings reminded Two Petals of brooding guardians overlooking the empty plaza. The image was strengthened by steeply pitched thatch roofs that jutted arrogantly toward the heavens. Beyond them lay a packed maze of circular houses, their thickly plastered walls and roofs a uniquely Yuchi architectural form. The dark dwellings hunched in the night, as though weighted by the countless sleeping souls they sheltered.

The Contrary needed but close her eyes in order to sense the occupants. She experienced their Dreams the way an anchored rock knew the river's current. The weight of their loves, hatreds, lusts, hungers, triumphs, and fears flowed around her. Were she to surrender her control, all of those demanding souls would filter past her skin, slip through her ears, nostrils, and mouth. Like permeable soil her body and souls would absorb them. Then, in the manner of a saturated earthen dam, she would slowly give way, carried off in bits, pieces, and streamers by the flood.

"But I am not earth." *No, I am a great stone. I stand resolute, lapped only by the waves of their Dreams. Feel them, washing up against me, seeking a grasp, only to drain away before the next.* Two Petals clasped her arms around her chest, hugging herself for reassurance.

She had come from a small Oneota village in the north, rescued from a charge of witchcraft by Old

White. He was the legendary Seeker: the man who had traveled to the four corners of the world. Old White had chosen her to accompany him on this quest to the south. She'd heard of the great cities—places like Red Wing Town—and even seen the abandoned sprawl that had been Cahokia. Nothing had prepared her for this concentration of humanity. On the night of her arrival, the mass of Rainbow City's humanity had overwhelmed her. The impact had left her comatose, deafened, and paralyzed. Now, by dint of will alone, she barely kept panic at bay.

"You must learn to deal with what you have become," Two Petals told herself. "Trouble is coming."

She sighed, sensing the perpetual isolation of a person touched by Power. Forget the Dreams of others; her own were frightening enough. Not so many moons past, while in Cahokia, she had been carried away on Sister Datura's arms—borne off to the Spirit World. The Visions she had had of the future remained just behind her eyes, as clear as when she'd first seen them. Were she to beckon, they would come flowing forward. She would again see the terrible black-souled chief, his hand trembling as it reached out to caress her naked skin. Or know the guilt-stricken eyes of a woman whose bloody hands dripped red spatters onto hard ground while she trembled beneath the twists of fate. In other scenes an angry war chief led a thousand warriors through a deadly and silent forest. And finally, swirling water washed over a great scaled hide that shimmered with all the colors of the rainbow.

She fixed on that final image, staring into the serpent's great crystalline eye, as though looking through time and worlds into another reality. As she did, a faint Song began to fill her souls with a tremolo that echoed from her very bones. The melody rose and fell, lifting her spirits like a leaf on the breeze. Two Petals could feel herself rising, spinning, carried aloft on the vibrant notes. She began to Dance across the hard-packed plaza, arms undulating to the beat, souls swaying in time to her skipping feet. The Song played within her.

"Soon," she promised, her body spinning in time to the melody.

As quickly as it had come, the Song faded, leaving her to stand alone and motionless in Rainbow City's great plaza—but one more of the many shadows that mingled in the night. In that instant she felt utterly destitute.

"You are never truly alone," a familiar voice remarked. Over the years, she had grown used to the voices that spoke in her head. Sometimes they told convincingly of things she knew were untrue. Other times, they offered a startling insight into the confused reality around her.

This voice, though, she knew. Two Petals turned, seeing the eerie outline of Deer Man. He stood off to the side, watching her through large liquid-brown eyes. In the beginning, it had bothered her that only she could see him. That Deer Man could be so apparent to her, but not to Trader or Old White, had perplexed her. In the end, she simply accepted Deer Man's presence as a manifestation of her Contrary Power. Half-man, half-deer, he had a human face; deer antlers and ears sprouted from his head, and the sleek hair that covered his body could have graced a buck's winter hide.

Frowning, she studied him, wondering how he managed to balance on those slender deer legs that ended in delicately hoofed feet, or why he never left tracks in the soft dust or silty mud. Why the oddity of it continued to puzzle her was elusive. He was after all a Spirit being. She often had seen him standing on water, waves washing through his feet, and other times with his nether regions passing through some object like a pestle and mortar, cane wall, or fallen log. As with so many of the voices that spoke to her, or the Spirits, ghosts, and other oddities she saw, she had wondered if Deer Man were real.

"Real?" Deer Man asked, hearing her thoughts. *"Are*

any of them real? Old White? Trader? The Kala Hi'ki?" He paused. *"Are you real, Contrary?"*

She tightened her arms around her, feeling the warm beaverhide cape, aware of the soft swell of her breasts, of the skin, muscle, and ribs beneath. The rise and fall of her chest with each breath she took reassured her.

"I am. At least for this moment." She frowned. "Can't say for sure about tomorrow . . . or yesterday. Sometimes the world slips and shifts around me. It just up and moves, and I lose track of what's what. Who's whom. Things become muddled and rushed. Then, when it all stops, I'm not sure where I am, or how I got there."

"Come. Let me show you something." Deer Man turned, walking off toward the south.

Two Petals followed, head cocked as she watched his hoofed feet. Though Deer Man took long steps, his hooves never seemed to make actual contact with the earth; and though he moved at her speed, his feet seemed to be making faster progress than he was.

"How do you do that?"

"The same way every other creature does," he answered. *"It is no different than the way you move backward in time."*

Two Petals didn't answer. So many things were riddles. That the world ran backward around her was just one more.

"Still bothers you, doesn't it?"

"What?"

"That you're Contrary. That you can never be normal like Trader, Old White, or anyone else."

She nodded. "A part of me, way deep down inside, still wants to be like normal people. But it is growing smaller and smaller. Soon, as we get closer to the end, it will shrink away completely. All that will be left is the Contrary. Two Petals will have been like a raindrop in the sunlight."

"The Kala Hi'ki has helped. I can see it in you: a strength that you didn't know you possessed."

She remembered the night when she, Trader, and Old White had first landed at Rainbow City. She had been frightened, overwhelmed by the images of a future that soon would be her past. The flood of souls around her had washed over and through her, drowning and suffocating. She wasn't sure exactly what had happened, but Trader had told her later that she'd cried out and fallen over. He said that she'd turned as stiff as wood, her muscles and joints locked and immovable. He'd carried her to the Kala Hi'ki's temple like some sort of oddly shaped log. All she remembered was a thick blackness until she'd awakened in the Kala Hi'ki's room. The terror of it was still too close.

Power had brought her here. Well, Power and the Kala Hi'ki's not-too-friendly and well-armed warriors. During her long trip southward from her native Oneota lands, she'd caught glimpses of the Kala Hi'ki. Even as far away as Cahokia, she had seen him in her visions: a terrible man covered with burn scars, his nose slashed away to leave two gaping nostrils. He wore a cloth wrapped over the empty sockets of his eyes, and his maimed hand had reached out for her.

"He brought you here to destroy you," Deer Man reminded.

"Instead he Healed me."

"You were a mystery to him. Trader was merely a temptation. And Old White? Ah, in the end he would have been the Kala Hi'ki's destruction. Mystery, temptation, destruction. Such a curious combination Power weaves."

"Old White is dangerous?"

"The Seeker is the most dangerous man alive. Not even the Kala Hi'ki fully understands the Seeker's obsession . . . or the dark secret he carries hidden between his souls."

"Where are you taking me?" Two Petals asked as they passed the base of the Warrior Moiety's large temple. The structure had been built atop a square mound, the high building having a commanding view of the plaza. Protruding from the thatch roof's peak were carvings of Falcon, Ivory-billed Woodpecker, and Snapping Turtle, their dark eyes glaring down at her as though the very Spirit beasts themselves watched her.

"We're going there." Deer Man pointed past several houses to a large, square-sided structure that rose above a low mound. The walls beneath the overhanging thatch roof had been plastered black at the bottom with a red band just below the eaves. The Spirit poles standing outside the west-facing doorway had been carved into the shape of vultures.

At that moment a shift in the night breeze carried the pungent odor of decay. "It's a charnel house."

"Oh, yes." Deer Man inclined his antlered head, the pointed tines gleaming in the night. *"Come, let me show you something."*

Two Petals glanced warily around at the darkened houses, corn cribs, and ramadas as she followed Deer Man to the entrance. Nothing stirred, the silence oddly discomforting.

Deer Man ducked into the low doorway, his wide antlers passing through the thick-plastered wall as if it were smoke.

Two Petals placed her hand on the unforgiving plaster, feeling its dense resistance. She shook her head, ducked past the door hanging, and emerged into a large room. Benches lined each wall, and raised platforms had been placed in rows throughout the center of the room. Most of these supported corpses in varying states of decomposition. The intense odor hung at the back of her nose and cloyed in her throat. She couldn't help but make a face.

"Why do you wince?" Deer Man asked. *"You are a Contrary. The smell of death is just the odor of life turned backward."*

"I . . . I'm just not used to it." She stepped forward, staring down at the closest of the bodies. This one had been a young man. His flesh sagged loosely on the bones, dry eyes recessed into the orbits of his skull. White teeth were bared behind hardened lips frozen in a rictus. Each of the man's ribs pressed out through the skin. His belly was a hollow, and the bones of the young man's hips seemed to jut up uncomfortably. His penis looked like a dried tuber, testicles like stones in the stretched scrotum. Flesh sagged on his thin thighs, the knees like knotted roots.

"He was young," Deer Man told her. *"They called him 'Chigger.' Said he was a bit of a nuisance. He didn't pay attention to the curious black mold that was growing on old acorns. Anyone with sense would have thrown them out."*

Two Petals stared down at the wasted corpse. "Where are his souls?" She looked around, curious now as she cataloged the various bodies supine on the pole racks. Some were swollen with gas, others barely more than skeletons.

"That's what I brought you here to see. The souls are all around you, waiting. If you clear yourself of the noise made by the living, you will be able to recognize them."

She gestured to the bodies. "What will the Yuchi do with them?"

"When the time is right, the High Priest will slice what little flesh remains from the bones. He will pick away the loose tendons, strip off the scalp and any clinging tissue. Once the bones are cleaned, they will be Blessed, tied together, and given to the family for final burial in one of their mounds. Or maybe laid to rest in a place where the souls of the dead will remain close by and can help protect the living from the dangers in the Spirit world."

She tried to quiet her revulsion. As she did, she could make out the faintest yellow-orange objects, like dim lights glowing along the walls. Others hovered near the ceiling.

"Yes, you begin to see. Those are the souls of the dead."

"Why did you bring me here? I am not of these people. Why would my souls wish to lurk about watching my body rot? Who would I want to protect?"

"Exactly." Deer Man smiled. *"I wanted you to see how your body would end up should you fail to fulfill your Visions."*

"You mean if I don't find my husband?"

Deer Man smiled. *"He will find you when the time is right. It is, however, your decision whether to go to him, or not. People fear him for a reason, and it will take an extraordinary woman to go willingly into his lair. I wanted you to understand what would happen if you gave in to fear, temptation, or desire. You dare not love, Contrary. You can only surrender yourself to the future."*

She reached down, placing a finger on the sunken flesh inside the bowl of Chigger's hip. It gave, soft but leathery. When she withdrew her finger, the depression remained. She wondered what his souls thought of her poking him like that. Looking up, she saw two of the glowing lights drop, as though in concern. "Oh, I understand just fine, Deer Man."

"Are you sure?"

"I just have to take the most terrible man alive into my bed. And keep him from discovering what is happening right beneath his nose."

And if I fail, we will all die, and end up in a charnel house just like this one.

From Rainbow City, one could paddle up the Tenasee until it made its great eastern bend. By ascending one of the several tributaries that drained from the south, travelers could canoe their way up to the headwaters, then portage across the densely forested hills to the Origins of the Black Warrior River. Tumbling through the hills, the Black Warrior flowed south until it reached the fall line. There, after the last rapids, the river settled into a broad floodplain. The broken, forested uplands gave way to rolling country. The current grew lazy as the Black Warrior pursued its sinuous path toward the gulf. Back swamps, thick with bald cypress and tupelo, were dotted with canebrakes; and yellow lotus, cattails, and duckweed thrived. Hanging moss draped from low branches. Higher ground—on the terraces below the hills—with sandy, better-drained soils had long been home to the Albaamaha People.

It was said that the Albaamaha had come from deep in the earth, following the roots of the great World Tree to reach the earth's surface. There, half the people emerged from one side of the root to become the Albaamaha, the other half—separated from their brethren—called themselves the Koasati.

From the time of the emergence, the Albaamaha had farmed the Black Warrior terraces. In the dark forests of the surrounding uplands they hunted deer, wild turkey, and other forest game. The woodlands—rich in hickory, oak, and persimmons—had provided bountiful nut harvests from which the Albaamaha rendered food and oil. From the swamps they had taken roots, cane, waterfowl, and other game. The river provided fish, freshwater mussels, and clams. Up and down the river, the Albaamaha had built their bent-pole houses, thatched them with shocks of local grasses, and warred and squabbled among themselves for generations.

Then the Sky Hand had come—a Mos'kogean People from the great Father Water to the west. The Sky Hand had made their way down the Black Warrior River, following an advance of warriors. At a high bluff that dominated a bend in the river, they made their new home. Immediately they began the construction of Split Sky City. Many Albaamaha welcomed the Sky Hand, brokering alliances with the newcomers as a means of settling age-old vendettas against surrounding villages. Cunning, and skilled in political manipulations, the Sky Hand pitted one Albaamaha village against another. Too late, the Albaamaha realized that their new benefactors had come not to share the land, but to rule it. Some Albaamaha resisted. The poorly organized farmers and hunters were no match for trained and disciplined Sky Hand warriors. Within a generation, any Albaamaha resistance had been crushed, and the Sky Hand moved quickly to take advantage of Albaamaha labor in the construction of their great new city overlooking the Black Warrior River. Within twenty years land had been cleared, surveyed, earthworks erected, and the first palaces and temples built.

Nor did they stop there, but expanded up and down the river, building new settlements and installing chiefs to oversee the Albaamaha lands. The Albaamaha had nowhere to go. To the west lay the intimidating Chahta, another invading Mos'kogee nation. To the south, the Pensacola brooked no intrusion into their territory. Though cousins, the Koasati resisted the temptation to accept refugees, worried enough about holding their own lands. In the east, the Ockmulgee and Talapoosie peoples were just as dangerous as the Sky Hand. Going north into the Yuchi lands was unthinkable. The Yuchi had raided the Albaamaha for generations, taking spoils, scalps, and slaves.

Resigned but resentful, the Albaamaha had no choice but to accept their new overlords. The Sky Hand, for their part, provided protection from raids, enforced peace between the Albaamaha villages, and ensured order and security. In return the Albaamaha were required to expand their farms—the majority of the produce to be delivered as tribute to the high minko, or supreme ruler, of the Sky Hand. All the backbreaking work—building, logging, carrying, and earth moving—was done by Albaamaha labor.

The greatest accomplishment of Albaamaha sweat and tears was the construction of Split Sky City, a complex of high palaces, Council Houses, and Temples built atop large earthen mounds and laid out according to moiety and clan, each in its place. Hickory Moiety and its clans lay to the east, Old Camp Moiety to the west. A great central plaza was dominated by the tchkofa, or Council House. The entire city was surrounded on three sides by a defensive wall of pitch-pine logs, four times the height of a man. On the north, where Split Sky City overlooked the river, the slopes below the bluff were cut sheer to prohibit any kind of organized assault. Gangs of Albaamaha had logged the surrounding countryside, clearing forests for fields and delivering wood, cane, and thatch to teams who constructed Split Sky City's edifices.

Once built, a city consumes like a voracious beast. A steady stream of Albaamaha bore food, water, firewood, clay, stone, thatch, and wood into the city. Each fall, at harvest, lines of Albaamaha carried basket after basket of corn, beans, squash, sunflower seeds, lotus root, goosefoot, and forest nuts to the elevated granaries. So, too, came fish, clams, wildfowl, and meat. Any surplus such as tanned hides, matting, cordage, shell, feathers, or other things the Sky Hand might fancy were brought to Sky Hand City to be traded for brightly dyed fabrics, ceremonial ceramics, talismans, or special services such as Healing or divination that the Sky Hand had mastered.

The Sky Hand specialized in higher pursuits such as sculpting, ceramics, the arts of religion and Healing, politics, games, and most of all, war. Among all the peoples in the Southeast, Sky Hand warriors were the most highly trained, disciplined, and deadly. Neighboring peoples, even the irascible Yuchi, quickly came to the conclusion that maintaining peaceful relations with the Sky Hand tended to be the sanest course of action. At least most of the time. Power, after all, had to be kept in balance. Insults of any kind required immediate and violent response. Failure to do so affected the Spiritual health of the people. Any sign of weakness invited exploitation by the chaotic forces of the red Power.

The notion of Power preoccupied the Mos'kogee peoples. While Creation was separated into the Sky World, Earth, and Underworld, the Power that flowed through it consisted of the white Power of order, peace, serenity, contemplation, happiness, and security. Its equal and opposite was red: the Power of chaos, war, creativity, procreation, lust, ambition, and desire. While the great Priests—called *Hopaye* by the Sky Hand— taught that all Power had to be kept in balance, many utilized a specific Power for their own ends.

One such man was the Sky Hand war chief. His full name was Smoke Shield Mankiller, of the Chief Clan of the Hickory Moiety. As the high minko's nephew, War Chief Smoke Shield was next in line to assume the high minko's position. Smoke Shield needed two things: The first was for his uncle, High Minko Flying Hawk, to die, or step aside. That it would happen was but a matter of time. Second, but of even greater importance, Smoke Shield needed confirmation by the Sky Hand Council. That was key. The high minko might rule, but only with the assent of the Council. This was made up of the clan chiefs from both the Hickory and Old Camp moieties.

Nothing a man did was accomplished without the Blessing of Power, let alone being confirmed as high minko. Smoke Shield had long ago made his bargain with the red Power. In return for his devotion, it had granted him each and every one of his desires.

Smoke Shield had little use for the prattling teachings

of the *Hopaye*. The current one was a Panther Clan man called Pale Cat. Dedicated to tranquility, order, and reason, Pale Cat served the white Power. He and Smoke Shield had despised each other since they were boys. Things had grown worse in the years since Smoke Shield had married Heron Wing, Pale Cat's sister. Smoke Shield had used red Power to win the woman. Lies and manipulation had allowed him to prevail over his long-gone brother, Green Snake, but in the end, Smoke Shield emerged victorious, having caused his brother's exile, claimed the woman Green Snake loved, and secured succession to the high minko's panther-hide chair. Smoke Shield had an ugly scar that marred his head as proof that Power never gave its gifts freely.

As he considered that, Smoke Shield fingered the deep scar, remembering the blow his brother had given him. But for it, he would have been a handsome man. Then again, why did a man need beauty when he was muscular, and quick of mind and body? Smoke Shield was in the process of living through his twenty-sixth winter. Despite the ugly scar, his face was tattooed with a Chief Clan bar across his cheeks. Forked-eye designs had been tattooed around each eye—the one on the left a little distorted by his long-healed wound. This day he wore his hair in a tight bun at the back of his head. Three little white arrows, the highest honor bestowed upon a warrior, had been stuck through his hair. A single warrior's forelock hung down over his forehead and was decorated with three gleaming white beads. He wore an eagle-feather cape over his bare shoulders, and a white warrior's apron had been tied at his waist, its long tail hanging suggestively down between his knees.

Smoke Shield stood at the northeastern margin of Split Sky City's great plaza. Just to his left the high minko's mound rose up in a flat-topped pyramid of earth to support the mighty palace where he and Uncle Flying Hawk held sway. Off to his right, and slightly behind him, the tishu minko, a man called Seven Dead, chief of the Raccoon Clan, had his palace. The plaza itself was flat, dominated by the stickball grounds that ran east to west just behind the red-and-white-striped Tree of Life—a pole that represented the great tree at the Spiritual center of their world. To either side of that were clay chunkey courts where stone disks were rolled before men attempted to spear them with lances.

Despite the throngs of passing people, busy with their lives, Smoke Shield's attention was fixed on the line of wooden squares that stood empty along the plaza margin. He stood before one in particular. Made of hickory logs, the uprights set deeply into the earth, it was one of five. The square was composed of two uprights with crosspieces lashed across the top and bottom. It left a man-sized frame that would support a human body. Captives were tied inside the open square—wrists to each of the upper corners, ankles to the lower—so that their naked, spread-eagled bodies could be beaten, burned, mutilated, and otherwise abused.

On either side, Smoke Shield could see the other empty squares. Not so long ago, men had hung from them. He frowned, thinking of the captive who had died within the empty frame before him. His name had been Screaming Falcon. He'd once been the White Arrow Chahta's most promising young war chief.

Until I plucked him right out of his house, along with his high minko and the Chahta Priests, and took him prisoner. Smoke Shield had also burned White Arrow Town to the ground and stolen its matron: Screaming Falcon's young wife Morning Dew. Morning Dew had become the matron the instant Smoke Shield killed her mother during the raid. Her brother, Biloxi Mankiller— who had also hung from one of the squares—had been the Chahta high minko. In a stroke, Smoke Shield had decapitated the White Arrow leadership, and dealt the Chahta a stinging blow.

He smiled as he remembered the glorious procession his warriors had made as they arrived at Split Sky City, marching their captives up from the canoe landing, past the Old Camp Moiety Mounds, and around the sacred tchkofa, the Council House where the Sky Hand Mos'kogee deliberated and conducted their governmental business. Yes, that had been a *glorious* day.

And it would only be the beginning!

He reached out, fingering the wood, remembering Screaming Falcon's misery and horror as he had hung, right here, in this very wooden square. The young man's face had looked lopsided from his broken and swollen jaw, and his flesh had been mottled, blistered, brown, and cracked from where split-cane torches had been pressed against his skin.

"I should have paid better attention to you," Smoke Shield whispered to the empty wood. "Instead I was too preoccupied with your wife."

Pus and rot, what a disappointment. He'd planned the whole White Arrow Town raid around stealing Morning Dew. Once she'd looked at him with the same disdain she'd have given a worm in a fruit. After he'd taken her from Screaming Falcon, burned her town, captured her high minko brother, and wrought every other indignity upon her, she'd just surrendered herself to him without a fight.

What was the point of trying to break a woman who was already compliant?

"I expected more of you, Morning Dew." He cast a glance over his shoulder, across the corner of the plaza to where his first wife's house stood. These days Heron Wing owned Morning Dew. The thought of it rankled. Not so much the loss of his slave, but the way of it.

He turned back, peering closely at the heavy wood

square, seeing the dark patterns where blood had stained the wood.

Everything changed that night.

He remembered the fog: thick and clinging, so dense a man could hardly see his hand before his face. All of his irritation had been focused on Morning Dew, on the way she lay under him, as unresponsive to his thrusting manhood as a soggy cloth. And while he was wetting his shaft in Morning Dew, someone was out here in the foggy night, sneaking past the guard to drive a stone sword into Screaming Falcon's heart and then sever his genitals from his body.

"War Chief, I wanted to cut them off myself, just for the pleasure of watching your wife's horrified expression as I handed them to her." Perhaps that would have spurred some sort of violent reaction out of her. But someone had beaten him to it.

Who? That single act of murder had robbed the Sky Hand Mos'kogee of revenge on their victims. No claim had been made by any of the subservient Albaamaha. Not so much as a rumor floated among the Traders. What kind of miscreant would commit such a desperate act and then not utilize it as a means of belittling the Sky Hand?

Smoke Shield ran his finger over the deep pucker of his scar.

It had to be the Albaamaha. They still chafed under the humiliation of serving their Mos'kogee masters. He already knew they had tried to betray the White Arrow Town raid to the Chahta. They *had* to be behind the captives' murders. Anyone else would have bragged about it. Such a triumph would be shouted up and down the trails.

In an effort to discover the culprits, Smoke Shield had taken Councilor Red Awl and his wife, Lotus Root, captive. In a rude shelter, up above Clay Bank Crossing, he and the warrior Fast Legs had tortured the Albaamo mikko, and learned nothing.

Then it had all gone wrong. Red Awl and Lotus Root had escaped. He and Fast Legs had found the mikko later, dead of his wounds; but the woman . . . gods, where was she?

He reached out and placed his hand on the wood, feeling the polish of years. So many bodies had been tied here. "Screaming Falcon?" he asked softly. "Who killed you?"

If he could only figure that out, he could retaliate. It had to be the Albaamaha! They'd been stewing with revolt for years. He'd caught the Albaamo traitor, Crabapple, who had been sent to warn White Arrow Town. The man had confessed—implicating an old Albaamo named Paunch as the conspirator. So could the mysterious and missing Paunch be behind the ultimate outrage of killing the captives?

"Where are you, Paunch? Wherever it is, I *will* find you eventually."

He narrowed an eye, letting his finger chip some of the caked blood from the square. When he found Paunch, the man *would* talk. Perhaps he even had something to do with Smoke Shield's Hickory Moiety losing the winter solstice stickball game. He had bet everything on that game—and lost it all. His wealth, clothing, shell, and copper . . . even Morning Dew.

He shot a narrow glance back at his wife's house across the plaza. How had she known to bet against him? In collusion with the Albaamaha? No, that was ridiculous. Heron Wing was much too influential in Panther Clan politics. She'd just bet against him because she knew it would irritate him. Gods, why had he ever married that woman?

"Forget it," he told himself. "Taking her as a wife was your first great triumph. Your attention now must be on breaking the Albaamaha."

He took a deep breath, turning from the empty square. He would have his revenge. And somewhere, up in the north, his most trusted warrior, Fast Legs, was even now running the missing Lotus Root to ground. Fast Legs would already have disposed of Red Awl's body. When the woman was dead—and the stolen weapons she'd taken from Smoke Shield returned—then and only then would Smoke Shield begin to wreak havoc on the Albaamaha.

Fast Legs, what is taking you so long?